Mississippi
blues

Tor Books by Kathleen Ann Goonan

Queen City Jazz
The Bones of Time
Mississippi Blues

Kathleen Ann Goonan

◇◇◇◇◇◇◇◇◇◇◇◇◇◇◇◇◇◇◇◇◇◇◇◇◇◇◇◇◇◇◇◇

Mississippi
blues

TOR®

A TOM DOHERTY ASSOCIATES BOOK
NEW YORK

MISSISSIPPI BLUES

Quotes from *The Land Where the Blues Began* by Alan Lomax (copyright 1993, published by Dell Publishing) used by permission of the author. All rights reserved.

This book is printed on acid-free paper.

Edited by David G. Hartwell

A Tor Book
Published by Tom Doherty Associates, Inc.
175 Fifth Avenue
New York, NY 10010

Tor Books on the World Wide Web:
http://www.tor.com

Tor® is a registered trademark of Tom Doherty Associates, Inc.

Library of Congress Cataloging-in-Publication Data

Goonan, Kathleen Ann.
    Mississippi blues / Kathleen Ann Goonan.—1st ed.
        p.   cm.
    Sequel to: Queen city jazz.
    "A Tom Doherty Associates book."
    ISBN 0-312-85917-1
    I. Title.
PS3557.0628M5   1997
813'.54—dc21   97-21892
                                                CIP

First Edition: December 1997

Printed in the United States of America

0   9   8   7   6   5   4   3   2   1

*For my parents, Thomas Goonan and Irma Knott Goonan,
who made sure I had as many books as I wanted and all the
time in the world to read them, with love and gratitude for
all the joy.*

THANKS

The support and encouragement of my husband, Joseph Mansy, were essential to the completion of this book, and I thank him for this largesse and confidence with all my heart.

Thanks also to those who took the time to read and comment on the manuscript: Steve Brown, Tom Goonan, Pam Noles, Randy Simmons, Michaelene Pendleton, Kathleen Dalton-Woodbury, Tad Dembinski, and the Sycamore Hill workshop of 1995. As always, David Hartwell's shaping of the material was essential.

Minsky: We're going to make machines intelligent. We are going to make them conscious!

Englebart: You're going to do all that for the machines? What are you going to do for the people?

—Page 34, Out of Control, Kelly

Mississippi
blues

Prologue

◯◯◯◯◯◯◯◯◯◯◯◯⬡◯◯◯◯◯◯

Blaze

My name is Blaze. I am walking by the riverfront in Cincinnati. Cincinnati after the Third Nanotech Wave. I have to keep telling myself because I forget. There is something wrong with me. This is because I was dead, I guess.

It is twilight: chilly, with a slight mist rising from the dark river. It blurs the lights that flicker festively now and then from Roebling's ruined bridge, which extends bravely into the wild, earthquake-spawned confluence of the new and old Ohio Rivers. I know these things, can clap words to these qualities, and it is good for it means that language is returning. It is frightening for the connections between what you experience and the words, so infinitely rich, to vanish. The bottom falls out of the world.

A jostling, rowdy crowd fills the riverfront. They dance to no music I can focus on; it is all just bits and pieces of shouted song, arising seemingly at random from the melee, each fragment conflicting with a thousand others in the general roar. There is so much noise it's hard to think. But I have to keep going over what happened. Each time I remember a little more.

These are the main things: I was shot in the chest by John, my Shaker Brother, at Shaker Hill just outside deserted Dayton where we lived secluded from nan, near the little empty town of Miamisburg. I don't remember being shot, but that's what Verity tells me. Verity killed John by throwing her radio stone at his head before he could shoot anyone else. She always had a good strong pitch. Maybe this is partly what is making me so sick: it seems as if everything went crazy and I don't remember it.

Maybe I should feel like celebrating because of my resurrection but I don't. For a while I did, when I went into a bar with Sphere and played the piano while he played the saxophone. Then I was ecstatic—almost, truly, out of my body and out of my mind with joy. The language of music is lodged deep within me, and happily has not been lost. It is my core and always has been. But I can't find Sphere right now. My eyes are playing tricks on me anyway. Sometimes all I can see are brilliant, moving splashes of color that I can't visually parse, so I might not recognize him anyway.

I look uphill into the City, which flashes like lightning as parts of it reactivate briefly. The buildings, from historically varying times, stand row on row like silent stones in a spectacularly huge and strange grave-yard; then suddenly a vast splash of light illuminates a Tulip or a Rose on top of a building—terrifying, for these Flowers are out of scale, bigger than the deserted L. Steele Department Store just outside of Dayton. I am relieved when they darken again for I can forget that they exist when I don't see them.

Everyone I've ever known is dead, or gone, or, in the case of Verity, changed to some sort of inhuman being. Hot tears course down my cheeks. I collapse on a bench. I nod and take a beer some ecstatic soul presses into my hand before she reels away and swig it down, suddenly angry with everything. I clench my head between my trembling hands and a huge, single sob rips through me.

I leap from the bench and run, uphill, into the City, away from the wildness. Panting, drenched in sweat after three blocks of running, I stop, and sway.

Yes, this is a quiet street. Blessedly so, for I remember more of my story. I wasn't really aware of what was happening so it's just a story to me.

Okay. My chest was ripped open from John's rifle shot. Verity wrapped me in nan sheets that flashed with tiny lights. I was not conscious but my body did not deteriorate. Had John known that those sheets were there in the attic for so many years, he surely would have destroyed them. It would have made him supremely angry to be saved by them, as apparently he was, though he may still lie dead within them, somewhere. Verity braved the wilderness between Miamisburg and Cincinnati, stashed me (still alive but suspended) in Union Station, and dared to enter Cincinnati, this fortress surrounded by a nan-generated wall, enlivened within by nan.

There's that flickering again. It's unsettling. Verity said that's part of the rebooting process. Oh, God—a picture of Verity's face! But—now it's gone, leaving just a blank gray wall. It shone from the side of the building. For a moment it's hard to breathe.

But it really is like a dream here, so I'm not going to run screaming through the night, as seems appropriate. I can't get upset over every little thing. I keep walking.

Anyway, Verity did all this to find out how to revive me. But then, from what I can gather, she freed Cincinnati. I'm not sure what she freed it from. Something about how it was programmed, and how the people were filled with the thoughts and lives of others almost like slaves, year after year, and were stored somehow, suspended, between their brief flashes of lived time.

I'm about six blocks from the river and it's quiet. I remember—it's not too far from the library. Verity tried to get me to go in a little while ago but I refused. I see a lovely building on my right called the Netherlands Hotel and admire the beautiful phrasing of matter Verity says is Art Deco. But then it all twists and blurs before my eyes. I've never been sick in my life and it is just awful to be this way. Queasy, uneasy, and afflicted with visual processing problems, that's what Sphere called it.

Down the street, in the center of a sort of mall, a black man sits on the base of a fountain, playing a guitar.

He is a lone, dark figure, and his shadow-double looms large on the fountain behind him, bent where light causes it to climb the steps, and rippled where it rests against some ornate curves. His shadow moves in deliberate rhythm, and his hollering song rises above the soft splash of the fountain.

The music draws me down the darkened street. As I approach him the building next to him lightens for about ten seconds, revealing jewel-glowing lines of light, green and yellow and red, which race upward then vanish while light floods from all the windows so I get a good look at him though it's over fast and I'm still a long block away.

Guitar chords stutter from beneath his long, plucking fingers in a strange, halting rhythm. It's good and loud, and echoes down the empty street. The melodic quaver in his voice and the utterly new sound of this music sends a chill down my spine. He sings it harsh and straight and mournful, something about trouble in mind, which I certainly have.

I am dizzy. Sweat inches down my face. I might live the rest of my life, and it might be short, in this awful, kaleidoscopic half-world. Yet this music redeems me somehow, reaches through the sensory flotsam and organizes it, removes the sickness.

But he stops. I try to hurry forward but can't go fast enough. I shout but find to my horror that my plea is only in my mind; I can't make it emerge from my mouth. I try to run but my body won't obey and I fall, so slowly, it seems, onto the hard pavement, the breath knocked out of me. There's no point in trying to get up. The cool, rough pavement is at least dependable, cradles my aching body as an overwhelming despair washes through me. In this darkness, though I'm sure it's not full night yet but only another spell of the blindness I've been experiencing, I might almost be dead again.

Save for that distant music, beginning again, a bright, tenuous thread to which I cling.

1

Trouble in Mind

One

◇◇◇◇◇◇◇◇◇◇◇◇◇◇◇◇

Resurrection Blues

The first sunset after Cincinnati's awakening was fiery, flaring incandescent red and yellow sheets of light through transparent intense blue, coloring the coming night as the inhabitants stood on what was left of Roebling's suspension bridge cheering and weeping.

The roar of the Upper Falls on the New Ohio River was fierce. Flock after flock of dark starlings rose from the Kentucky forests expanding like the dissipation of darkness itself into the brilliant air, and rumor took its first steps toward legend as people began to talk about how it all happened, and to wonder what year it was—for even immortals, they discovered, like to know.

And several people jumped off the bridge, thinking that they could still fly.

Against the sunset a tremendous city shimmered, the last low rays of sun highlighting in gold and silver a perfectly melded vision of all the most wondrous manifestations of architectural thought in recent centuries. Art Deco and Beaux Arts, Chicago School and Postmodern, New Nan and even nineteenth-century stolid and gargoyled Victorian skyscrapers filled the skyline, perfectly placed so as to entrance the eye and fill the heart with wonder and awe.

Anyone not from the City might have felt more terror than awe at the huge Flowers blossoming from every high point, resembling roses, gladiolus, daisies, an entire spectrum of lilies, stretching to catch the last rays of sun.

Even more terrifying was the abrupt eruption of a swarm of human-sized Bees rising from the Cincinnati Zoo, at the heart of the City, as the Earth's turning intensified the burning, golden, disappearing sun.

The Bees swept over the City, and low over the bridge, with a sound like a thousand rushing engines, so close to the people on the bridge that the wind from the Bees' wings stirred their hair.

The swarm turned west, flew round the bend in the Ohio River, and vanished into the last gleaming fragment of light.

Around midnight, an old folktune rose from the City in unison, from the bridge, from parks, from rooftops, from bars where people spent hours on end sampling exotic brews gushing inexhaustibly from the heart of the City:

> Some rows up
> But we floats down
> Way down the Ohio to Shawneetown

And segued into:

> Oh the river is up and the channel is deep
> The wind is steady and strong
> Oh won't we have a jolly good time
> As we go sailing along
> Down the river, oh down the river, oh down the river we go
> Down the river, oh down the river, oh down the Ohio!

A great shout arose and then they cycled through the songs again. And again. And again.

The entire populace was jolted awake, torn free from decades of servitude to one woman's dreams, during which they had constantly re-created a living tapestry of novels, plays, music. They'd had no individual lives during this time.

But then Verity came, and changed the structure of the Cincinnati system.

From time to time people tried to access histories they did not remember by pressing their hands to glowing interstices running up the sides of the magnificent buildings. Their modified bodies framed queries translated into metapheromones by receptors in their hands. Those metapheromones were a precise language, and the questions were translated by the membrane of the interstice; that information met the DNA of the e. coli within. The DNA formed an unimaginably vast storage system.

But the buildings were not working correctly. SYSTEMWIDE CRASH was the disconcerting message given forth, and, even more alarming: 100 HOURS BEFORE CONVERSION—NEW INFORMATION AVAILABLE AT THAT TIME.

But the strangest message of all was much more simple and direct:
PLEASE DON'T LEAVE ME!
And sputtering through at odd times was a single word: VERITY.

The First Nanotech Wave occurred after a decade of nanotechnology's infancy, during which limited self-replication came into wide use, with applications ranging from manufacturing to medicine. During this period, self-replicating molecules entered the world via small secret labs and the vaults of prestigious international consortiums, promising heaven but often delivering hell. Some were legal. Most violated the international laws and treaties set up in haste.

Verity, who was absorbing this information from a learning cocoon, a clear membrane that surrounded her snugly as she lay within it on the third floor of the Cincinnati library, was jarred to awareness of the outside world by a faint vibration. It subsided quickly, though, and Verity sank back into the history she had never before known as into a rich, real dream.

Radio had failed. She knew this, of course. Go on, she prompted silently, her will translated into metapheromonal commands below the threshold of her consciousness.

The information flow resumed.

When radio failed, washed out more and more often by a puzzling source sometimes rumored to be a previously hidden quasar (this particular history had no further details concerning the matter, apparently), the Second Nanotech Wave emerged, and Flower Cities began to flourish. Radio waves and all magnetic mediums became completely undependable, sending civilization backward, but also forward into a new world where the human body itself could be modified to receive and transmit precise information. Nanotech terrorist acts constantly threatened the integrity of every link in the grid that maintained even fitful functioning. Work on nanotechnology took on new seriousness and intensity in industry, government, and at universities, then surged out of control in unforeseeable ways. Those who did not accept the changes were left behind in more primitive communities. Those who were *changed* experienced terror and wonder; enslavement, and release into utterly new ways of knowing.

As feared, international research came to an abrupt halt as communications ceased; terrorist destruction of wire and fiber optics proved far too easy in the post-nan world. But genetic engineering reached a state where it was not only possible but supremely sensible to integrate biology's speed, intensity, and precision into cities, making every Flower City almost a single biological entity. Nanotechnology was perfectly poised to inject the correct minuscule information into living matter and thus regulate its growth, its utility, any and all characteristics.

Pheromones, used by many living creatures for precise communication, were studied in great detail, isolated, and combined like an entirely new alphabet into metapheromones. People within the cities could choose to purchase biomodifications from developers. With these receptors, transformed humans could use metapheromones to communicate virtually any information swiftly, fully, and precisely.

Thus the Flower Cities were born.

New and magnificent, they studded North America. Each city that could afford to do so voted on whether or not to convert. Most did. Denver, New York, San Francisco, the eastern seaboard from Boston to Washington, Seattle, Houston, New Orleans all became part of a vast network of new, almost utopian cities. They were linked by the powerfully swift maglev train line known as NAMS, the North American Magline System, running on a switching amalgamation of solar power, steam, and electricity. Jets were unusable, since so many components of their operations were undependable, but NAMS was almost as swift, and much more convenient, delivering travelers within blocks of their destination. Small planes flown low, in daylight, were still used by some people, particularly those in the fiercely independent Aviators' Clubs.

Verity lost the flow as the building shuddered again. Again, the motion subsided quickly.

Verity struggled to subdue her rising panic and remain within the cocoon rather than rise in fear and flee. She believed that there were at least a few more hours until Cincinnati began its conversion in earnest, and information was quite precious. During her seventeen or so years as a Shaker, the history of the changes nanotechnology had wrought were scant. Now she was filled with a desire to *know*. She took a deep breath and returned to the lost history, a combination of images, voice, and simulated experiences.

During the heyday of the Flower Cities, pouches of business-imbued metapheromones flew back and forth on NAMS; literature hypertexed metapheromonally filled users with emotional intensity and immersion in authors' visions an infinity beyond clumsy old-fashioned virtual reality. Within the cities, information could be accessed or sent from any room. Glowing interstices filled with fluid transported information that converged in rooftop collectors. These evolved via nanotechnological breakthroughs into huge flowerlike entities. Taking advantage of the fascinating and precise communicative abilities of honeybees, nanotechnologists quickly realized that large genetically engineered Bees (tm) were far superior to the prototype cyborgs which originally collected information and disseminated it throughout the cities, particularly when implanted with human limbic tissue, which gave them an emotional imperative to deal in human information.

But the Information Wars, which raged worldwide, put an end to this brief magnificence.

Entire cities could be easily sabotaged, and nanotechnologists were put to work in top-secret laboratories and think tanks to find defenses. Some of these defenses turned out to be lethal. Airborne plagues could kill quickly, or change the neuronal patterns of the plagued to fill them with any thoughts the creator of the plague might desire. Plagues of thought—viruslike, airborne informational nan—released during the Information Wars were so compelling that those unwilling to be drawn into the strangeness could only isolate themselves and hope for favorable winds.

And when a series of long-predicted earthquakes shattered the northeast at the height of the Information Wars, a new phase began.

The Third Wave changed everything irrevocably, isolating the Flower Cities and turning North America into an unstable collection of independent, individual human frontiers. Cumulative tampering with ancient genetic programs governing aspects of human function and behavior, including the ability to survive famine resulted in a precipitous worldwide drop in population. Yet at the same time, for those so privileged, the old dream of human immortality took on a terrible reality.

"Terrible" was not a word most people would associate with immortality. But in Cincinnati, immortality had been terrible indeed.

The library trembled again, for over a minute. This time Verity could not ignore it.

As she sat up, the cocoon unfurled, freeing her. She tipped herself over the low clear edge and sat on the floor, trying to reorient herself after her suffusion in history. She realized, as she stared out the huge window at the Art Deco building across the street, that she had no idea if the history fed her by the library was reliable.

Verity stood slowly, battling dizziness. The clear, viscous fluid beneath the cocoon, held within a hard transparent oval, through which information flowed from the library and was transmitted to the cocoon, moved in a single slow wave which stilled quickly. She braced herself against another tremor, which lasted only a second, then stretched and began to pace the vast, smooth floor of the library, where there were no books, only cocoons. Anxious to leave, she felt that she was still not done with the library. How long did she have?

She had recently initiated drastic changes within the heart of Cincinnati, though she still wasn't sure how they would play out, or how long it would take to reset the deep, complex programs governing all aspects of the City, including the very shape of the buildings. The City trembled, literally, on the verge of a *conversion*—a nanotech surge that would sweep through the matter of Seam-enclosed Cincinnati and reconfigure everything, even the mental state and the very bodies of the inhabitants. The conversion would essentially reboot—*reprogram*—the City. Information would flow anew, readjusting the organization of the very matter of the place, filling those within it with whatever philosophy and goals were mastered into it.

Verity had penetrated to the very heart of that philosophy. Though she hoped that she had changed it, hoped that the conversion would instill Cincinnati with freedom and hope and the possibility for true growth, she had no idea at all if her changes would be successfully reflected in the conversion.

For that reason, she had thought it best that all leave Cincinnati, and allow it to mutate on its own—to generate new humans from the memory banks of the Hive, if it chose to do so; if it could. If the plans she had freed contained that capability.

To compel the inhabitants to flee, Verity had used that which she had grown up fearing as evil—the Territory Plague, or, as they called it here, the Norleans Plague—and infected the entire City.

The entire City. She stopped pacing and looked out the window, at the few people on the street below. Most were at the riverfront now. How many were there, in Cincinnati? It was a relatively small area, just the old downtown and several blocks outward. A fleeting figure named itself within her mind, information retrieved from her intimate connection with the City. Nine thousand seven hundred and forty-eight people. Of those, two thousand or more had already set off, plague-driven, to meet the awful risk of whatever lay beyond in the wilderness North America had become.

No one knew who had created the Norleans Plague, but those under its influence were overwhelmingly compelled down the Mississippi, beginning from remote tributaries if necessary, reliving the emotionally imperative journey of Jim and Huckleberry Finn, escaping the old, the abusive, the inebriated, the enslaving, at great personal peril.

Of course, Verity knew the more recent history of Cincinnati with every cell of her body: during the age of nanotechnology's birth, there lived a brilliant young nanoarchitect named Durancy, who was in love with his older cousin, Rose, a city planner. Durancy, crazed by guilt when his mother, India, died from a terrorist plague just before near-immortality became possible, preserved an emotionally warped India and replicated her within the depths of the Cincinnati system. Rose knew what he was doing, feared the worst, and created her own counterplan. Decades later, Verity had saved the City from perpetual replaying of India's twisted dream of American arts.

Just yesterday, in fact.

Or was it last week? Verity was further upset by the realization that time had blurred terribly for her. She turned away from the window and resumed her pacing. It felt good to move. How long had she been in the cocoon?

The responsibility, she thought, increasingly sick with fear. Norleans quite possibly did not even exist any longer.

But whether it did or not, she had to lead all the people she had released downriver to Norleans, or to whatever was in its place. Imprisoned by the City decades ago, their hearts, minds, and very beings pressed into service during which they relived the American arts—literature, music, painting—so the City could update its metapheromonal library, they were like innocent children now. They didn't remember what had befallen them and must now learn. Verity wasn't sure if they would be grateful. She had replaced one form of enslavement with another. Perhaps they would regain their identities; their individuality. But they still would be unable to exercise choice. They would be compelled to raft down the river, perhaps to their deaths. Or perhaps to true freedom, when they reached Norleans. That had been her hope.

But . . . did Norleans even exist? The only proof she had was the brief spurt of sound from her old radio stone, a woman proclaiming that she was broadcasting from a clear-channel station in Norleans. Verity had only heard this once in her entire life. Now she realized that she had bet all their lives on this tiny fragment of sound. She sighed and bowed her head. A small crack in the library floor mended itself as she watched.

She had no way of knowing what would really happen. It was a massive gamble. And the gamble was with the lives of others, who had not made this decision for themselves. They could not have done so, for they were trapped within the Cincinnati system. When she had given them all the Norleans Plague, she had thought that she was freeing them, tearing them from the City by inflicting upon them an even more powerful compulsion. Now they would all head out. Into the *Territory* . . .

This time, that word, "Territory," invoked a vision of a rough raft with a wigwam in the center, imbued with a tale which radically rearranged one young man's entire vision of the world from the inside out when he realized that all he had been taught was false, and that he had the power to form his own ideas and to act on them in the face of the opposition of his entire society.

Huckleberry Finn. The story at the heart of the Norleans Plague, which she too now had. It alone had the power to tear her from Cincinnati, from Abe Durancy's mad, replayed tale of guilt and power and pain. She remembered, dimly, reading it when much younger, curled in a chair in the small Shaker Hill library on a snowy day while a fire burned in the stove next to her.

The memory of Shaker Hill enveloped her like a beautiful dream.

Just outside of the old town of Miamisburg, near Dayton, the Shakers eschewed all nanotechnology—indeed, almost all technology—in a community created when the Flower Cities were going wild, and nanotech airborne plagues of thought drifted across the land. Some said even throughout the world. But no one at Shaker Hill seemed to know for sure.

Of one thing she was quite certain—at Shaker Hill, they had been terrified of the plague and its compulsions. The price they had paid for trying to avoid it was a loss of history.

Verity was beginning to think that perhaps no one—no one person— knew what had really happened during the Third Wave. She glanced over at the cocoon, gleaming in the low lights. It couldn't tell her something it did not know.

But what *had* happened? Not just to her, but to the world? There had once been a country, a government—the United States. Russ, an old man whose parents created Shaker Hill when he was a young man, always claimed they were better off without the goddamned government. But where had it gone?

The more she considered it, the worse her decision seemed. But it was done and there was no going back. If there was a cure for the Norleans Plague, no one she knew had ever heard of it. All that the Cincinnatians could possibly desire, now, was to go to Norleans. They *might* remember who they were and retrieve their personalities, buried under decades of reliving the stories of others. Norleans *might* still exist; but it was just a rumor. If it did, by some miracle, still exist, and if they did, by another miracle, get to Norleans, the plague *might* cease to matter once the victim reached the goal.

But the plague itself might kill them. The river might. Or any of the unforeseen perils of an unknown continent. Once it had been thickly peopled; now it was nearly deserted. Once there had been gasoline engines, dependable communication devices, governments, currencies, businesses. For the most part, these had vanished. But she didn't know much more than that. All her knowledge had come from the small library at Shaker Hill, from Russ, their only living link with the world before the Third Wave, and from the learning cocoons, which had agendas of their own and were not necessarily to be trusted.

The rafts, and the river . . . maybe that was a peril she could control.

A thought took hold. Maybe it would be better for everyone to go in one great boat. Or two. Safer, of course. Would the plague allow for that? Would the downriver impetus be enough to satisfy that craving for Norleans? Well, she had the plague, and she could consider going on a boat as well as on a raft. Of course, she was physiologically different from most of the Cincinnatians, though the exact parameters of the differences were something that she did not especially want to explore. That might explain her slight remove from the plague's effects so far.

She dropped into a chair and brooded. Boats sounded like a good idea. But where would she find a riverboat? Could the City perhaps make one? It was not exactly functioning at full capacity. And she no longer controlled the City. She no longer *wanted* to.

She'd solved one problem and created others, which now seemed equally serious.

The marble floor paled as the subtle lighting of the library awoke, triggered by the darkening sky. The sun was setting. The hours were ticking by. She could afford to lose no more time. She had to deal with the consequences of her actions, and quickly.

Verity went back to the learning cocoon she'd used, one of many scattered throughout the room, and paused next to it.

It was all she had, this glistening wrap of, quite possibly, seriously limited information; the only way to learn what they might face before setting out for the Territory. Maybe she could find out whether the City memories had stored somewhere the plans for boats.

She rolled back into it gently and felt its comforting membrane shrink to grip her lightly, silkily, ready to link deeply, to tailor whatever it had to impart to her specific learning style.

But this time the connection was different. More distant; more disorienting. Every few minutes, the floor of the library trembled, as if from an earthquake. Brief shrieks punctuated the celebratory songs Verity heard through holes in the windows that failed to self-heal as they shattered. She tried to readjust herself, for she was absorbing the history of the big earthquake that had changed the Ohio River above Cincinnati forty years earlier to an entirely new course. But it was no use. She was wrenched from the cocoon as the floor tilted, spilling her out roughly.

Dazed by the loss of connection, she staggered to her feet and rubbed her eyes. Colors ran together, blurring the outlines of all she saw. She felt ill, this time, and stumbled as the floor trembled again. The city was definitely changing. Or maybe the Norleans Plague was finally kicking in.

She hurried down stairs now still which had been designed to move, memory sharpening after her rough disconnection. It seemed that she'd found out nothing about the Territory into which they were heading . . . and she was crying . . .

But no wonder, when she thought of all that was lost—Shaker Hill, and her Shaker brothers and sisters—no wonder she dashed tears from her face as she searched for the exit, afraid that the library might collapse on her.

Yet the impetus of the plague, created by a mad designer of unknown intent, was powerful; overwhelming. After a moment song overrode everything else:

> Oh, the river is up and the channel is deep
> The wind is steady and strong
> Oh won't we have a jolly good time
> As we go sailing along.

Verity's clear voice sounded braver than she felt as she hurried across the large lobby.

The huge, arched doors stood open—*Lift up your heads, ye everlasting gates,* Verity's Shaker past sang. She added aloud, "And let me *out* of this place!" Out of Cincinnati, through the gates framed by the past, where all lay in ruins behind her, and onward, down the river, down the river, down the river we go. . . .

When she rushed out the door the chorus enveloped her. Everyone was singing it. Filled with joy, Verity hurried along with them, turning toward the riverfront, the part of her that was angry, even terrified, pushed aside for the moment.

How could she have been so worried? The unreasonably bright and happy waves of the Norleans Plague overwhelmed her. At least, she thought that must be what it was; the world had a golden sheen, though that might be from the setting sun. But even her hands looked golden when she passed through the shadow of a building.

Get away, the plague told her. Norleans means *freedom.* Freedom from slavery. To nan, to anything, to anyone. You'll miss the light at Cairo. But you'll be free in the end. From the inside out.

The plague-induced ecstasy was interrupted when she stumbled over the feet of a man sitting on the sidewalk a block from the library, his head in his hands. He looked up and she was completely startled.

The man was Blaze.

She dropped down next to him, stared into his eyes, and was deeply afraid. Something was dreadfully wrong.

Blaze, the Shaker Brother she had grown up with, the dear friend she had wrapped in nan sheets after he was shot in the chest, the almost-lover she had brought to Cincinnati in a desperate attempt to save his life, did not seem to recognize her.

At least, she thought, heart pounding, he was *alive.* But at what price? She pushed his red hair back from his sweaty forehead and it stood up in damp spikes. His head lolled back and he looked at her, his green eyes fearfully blank. His face was thin and pale, what she could see of it, for some of it was covered by a new, scraggly beard.

"Blaze, have you waited for me all this time?" He had refused to enter the library with her. But that had been quite some time ago.

She sat back on her heels, apprehensive, wondering what to do. The nanotech sheets that had kept him somewhere between life and death had evidently left him with neurological damage.

Hearing distant hammering, she looked over her shoulder and saw that the waterfront, a few blocks away, was mobbed with people. Stacks of lumber were piled in intervals on the concrete wharf, and it dawned on her that they were making *rafts*.

Yes, she remembered . . . some of them had left already, swirled downriver in swift ecstasy, singing; cheering. But how could they possibly make enough rafts to accommodate all of them in the time left before the conversion of Cincinnati, when it would, essentially, reboot and try to reabsorb them? They only had another day, at most. Boats, she had been thinking of boats . . .

Blaze moaned and rocked back and forth, interrupting her thoughts. She grabbed his shoulders and shook him.

"Blaze! It's me! Verity!" She could not succumb to fear, she told herself. He *had* remembered her since awakening in the train station. How long ago had that been? Days? More than a week?

He had forgotten who she was several times, too.

She pushed that thought away. He *would* get better, not worse.

Or would he? There was certainly nothing out in the Territory that could heal him. Helping Blaze stagger to his feet, she was surprised when just that simple thought—*the Territory*—put a smile on her face. She did not feel like smiling. Yet her face smiled in the service of the plague.

She put her arm around him and he leaned against her. Even though he was emaciated from his ordeal, she staggered beneath his weight. He was inches taller and probably three years older than she was, though neither knew their exact birthdays.

"What's *wrong?*" He spoke in a harsh whisper, his head bowed. "This keeps *happening.* I can't *see* . . . everything's dark. . . . There—it's lighter. But . . . it's so blurry." He squinted at her. "Verity, you're just like *particles* floating in the air . . . now it's all so *bright* . . ."

At least he remembers my name, she thought grimly.

"Take a step. Another. That's good."

"How far?" mumbled Blaze.

Then she heard singing.

"Where's that *music?*" asked Blaze, lifting his head. His eyes became more alert, his steps more sure.

"It's on the next block," she said.

They staggered toward an elongated ellipse of stone pedestals. Several fires in barrels illuminated a statue of a woman held aloft by one of the pedestals, stone children ranged around her, splashed by water. The spring air was chilly, now that the sun had set, and Verity edged close to a flame-mouthed barrel.

A black man sat on the steps below the statue. He was hunched over a guitar that she could barely hear over the hiss of the fountain. But Blaze stepped closer and she followed, until the singer's words were perfectly clear:

And I'm goin' to the river, take my boat and float,
And if my underworld mama quit me I'm gonna cut my throat
And it's, oh, I ain't gon do it no more
And it's, oh, I ain't gon do it no more
The last time I drank your whiskey, Mama, it made my belly sore.

The guitar music rose high above the notes the man sang, in an odd, catchy rhythm, short-long, short-long, two stringed notes fixed from each other in a strange interval that slid up and down as his finger did on the neck and quavered in a way that sent shivers down Verity's spine.

"What's that you're singing?" asked Blaze, as they stopped next to him. "Do it again. Please."

He squinted at Blaze in the dim light. "You all right, son?" he asked.

Blaze nodded desperately, his eyes pleading in the firelight. "Yes," he croaked.

As the player repeated the song, Blaze hummed along, eyes closed. His face relaxed, and then Verity saw a very slight smile.

"That's better," Blaze said when the music stopped. He sank down on a step. "What was that song?"

The guitar clunked hollowly as the player rested it on the concrete. "That's called 'Cincinnati Underworld Woman.' " His face was long and furrowed. A small scar slashed his cheek, and moved when he smiled. He lit a cigarette and took a deep drag.

"Is that who you're singing about?" Blaze asked, pointing at the statue above them.

The man shook his head. "She's another entity completely. More like a goddess, I guess. She's the Genius of Water. Been here since way past forever."

"What's your name?"

"Kid Cole, boy, Kid Cole. Glad to be in Cincinnati, my hometown. So glad. It's been a while." He finished his cigarette, tossed the butt on the ground, and picked up his guitar. "How about another?"

Verity bit her lip. He wasn't really Kid Cole, of course. He had been altered by the City to think he was. She was tremendously disappointed. He really should be more *himself* now. But maybe all she'd done was for nothing . . . maybe it hadn't worked. . . . "Blaze, there's something we have to—"

"What kind of music do you call that?" asked Blaze.

The man looked surprised. "Why, the blues," he said. He chorded up and down the neck of his guitar as he spoke, and soft music filled gaps in the fountain's splash. "I guess you could call it black folk music from the Delta. Made up of all different kinds of things—slave hollers, shouts, things from Africa, they say. The ring dance and drums. My father came up here on a riverboat. He was a free black. My mother was a runaway slave." His laugh was bitter. "Nasty place, really, for us, this city. For a while we were happy. I remember, from when I was little. Lincoln freed my mother. But so what? Nobody will give us a job, unless it's some job nobody else wants. My daddy had to go down South to work. I think he's a sharecropper but I don't know. We can't go to the schools and get educated. Used to be a fine Negro school here. But the whites were jealous of it—had it closed down, and they won't allow our children to go to their schools. It's hell. But boy, it's hell all over. I'm tellin' you, if I wasn't singin' I'd be cryin' about it all. It kind of helps, you know?"

Blaze glanced at him questioningly. "Are you talking about the Civil War? I read about that. I read about Lincoln. But the Civil War was a couple of hundred years ago, wasn't it?"

Kid Cole frowned. "Come to think of it . . ."

"Yes, it was," said Verity. "Thank you," she told the man. "Let's go."

Blaze stared up at the statue of the woman and passed his hand over his eyes. "Maybe I'd better. Listen, don't go away, all right? I'll be back soon."

"Aren't you going to Norleans?" asked Verity.

"Norleans!" he snorted. "I don't need Norleans. I've got the *blues.*" He plucked a series of high, defiant notes from the guitar. "But then again . . . maybe . . ."

As Verity hurried him away, Blaze said, "Where are we going?"

"Someplace where I can help you," she said.

They stopped a block away, at the Netherlands Hotel. Art Deco metal birds flanked the glass, flower-etched doors. An interstice glowed, pale and spooky in the darkness, not very wide, but rising in a thin stripe up the side of the building until it reached a ledge and vanished.

The door opened at her touch. She was relieved to find that this building worked; she had been prepared to try several since the City didn't seem to be functioning fully. Wall sconces lit as if in greeting as she and Blaze followed a lushly flowered runner through a glass-and-steel lobby. She held Blaze's hand, but was relieved that he was able to walk by himself now. She wanted to go up, close to the Flower at the top of the building, and so she went to the elevator, and of course it opened.

Blaze followed her inside, leaned against the wall, and closed his eyes.

"Hello, Rose," said a voice when the door closed. Verity jumped and her throat tightened.

"Who's talking?" asked Blaze, his eyes fluttering open. "I don't see anyone."

"To the top, please," she told the elevator. "It's . . . an old friend," said Verity to Blaze, swallowing hard. "And he's not really here."

"That's what I said, isn't it?" said Blaze. "Do we have to go up here?" He swayed a bit when the door opened, and glanced at the readout. "Are we really on the one hundred and twenty-third floor?"

Verity stepped cautiously out of the elevator, not knowing what she would find. On seeing that the room was empty, she took a deep breath and tried to relax.

"Is this floor marble?" asked Blaze, touching its smooth surface.

"It's exactly like marble," said Verity. "Of course it's marble. It was just grown, that's all. Nobody had to get it out of a quarry."

"Who grew it then?" asked Blaze.

I did, a part of her asserted. "Come over here," she said, leading Blaze to the window, a vast arch of glass set in iron girders that looked like a child's stylized rays of a rising sun.

They looked down on a sea of darkness studded by flickering bonfires people had lit on roofs. Cincinnatians, small with long shadows, danced round them. Most of the large Flowers were furled, though she saw one stubborn violet Iris many blocks away half-open, waving slowly and majestically in downriver wind.

"You used to talk about the Flowers when you were little," said Blaze. "You had nightmares about them. How did you know about them?"

"I came from Cincinnati," she said quietly. "I was—created here." She turned and said almost desperately, "I'm not *normal,* Blaze. I'm not like you. I was made for a special reason. But I didn't really know it until I came here—I didn't really know it entirely until just a few weeks ago. Or . . . well, I'm not that sure of the time. . . ." She stared out into the dark canyons.

"Tell me about it, Verity," said Blaze. He sighed and rubbed his face with both hands. "I'm feeling better now. I don't know what happened."

"I will," she said. "But there's no time now." I want to find a cocoon for you. Or create one, she thought, finding she was unwilling to speak it out loud, to tell Blaze all that she actually was capable of doing, for it was quite strange to her that she actually could, were the City working properly (and that was in doubt), do just about

Anything.

She felt intense and grave at the thought, which whispered through her, making her entire body tingle with something quite close to desire. To be hooked back into the heart of the City again, to *command* it!

"There's a holographic table behind us and I can have it manifest a cocoon for you, Blaze, and—"

"No!" shouted Blaze, stepping back from her, his face determined and horrified. "I'd rather die, Verity." His voice quieted. "I'm not exaggerating. I don't want to have anything to do with that. I've had enough of it. I had to push my way out of one in the train station. I didn't even know who I was, why I was there. Verity . . . there are times now when I can't even talk. It's like . . . all the meaning drops out of everything. There's nothing to connect to. And then . . . I'm even *better* than before. Sharper, somehow. I have even *more* words, more ways of saying things. I'm going through some sort of process. Some sort of healing. That music out there, *that's* what helps. Not some—*device."* He took a deep, shuddering breath. "I've been lucky. Very lucky. I'll never go back in one of those hellish . . . *cocoons,* or whatever you want to call them."

Tiny beads of sweat stood out on his pale face. Verity saw that he meant it. Yet she didn't know what else to do. He might just get worse and worse. The nan sheets he had been wrapped in put a lot of bodily functions on hold. Besides that, the sheets had been very old and probably hadn't functioned quite right. A cocoon could easily determine exactly what had happened and probably synthesize whatever was necessary to heal Blaze—a certain hormone, even genetic intervention.

What might it cost her to reach back into the City again? And if she did reconnect deeply enough to heal Blaze, she didn't even know, exactly, how to do so.

But that would come to her, once she entered it again. That was, in fact, what she feared. That was the part of herself that she had to leave behind. But she couldn't think of anything else to do at this point.

Biting her lip, she dropped onto a bench in front of the round, smooth table, and holographic icons appeared, ranged around its border. Flowers, all of them, and each with certain functions that could modify the others, a grammar of intricate immensity with which she could form any genetic possibility, any physical form, any thought or feeling. She could manipulate the entire City, on any level.

If she still dared.

She crossed her arms upon her chest and bowed her head for a moment.

Blaze stared at the table for a moment. Then he edged toward the elevator. "I think I should get out of here," he said, his voice shaking. He cleared his throat. "I'll meet you down at the square. By that singer. That *music.* It's wonderful. I felt better when I heard it, somehow. I'm sorry, Verity. It just scares me so *much* here. All those things that happened. I can barely remember them, but . . ."

He was about ten feet from the elevator when it opened. A tall man stepped out. The man brushed past Blaze, completely ignoring him.

Verity squinted, trying to see if the man was a holographic ghost or real. She glanced down to see if it might be possible that she had by accident activated some program. But just her *being* here, with her Queen-based metapheromonal capabilities, might be enough to affect things.

She sat very still, trying to think of what to do.

Abe Durancy's face looked blank at first, but he saw the huge window and strode over, pressed his face against it. "Good evening, Cincinnati," he said, his voice low and somewhat ironic. "What is it this time? What age? What lost glory?"

"Who is that?" whispered Blaze.

Abe turned from the window, tripped over a low table, stumbled, and cursed.

Unfortunately, he was not a ghost.

Transfixed by dread, Verity watched him. She put one finger to her lips to tell Blaze not to speak.

Durancy looked up and saw Verity. He glanced at Blaze, then back at Verity.

"Rose?" he said uncertainly, then advanced across the room.

"No," said Verity firmly. "I am not Rose. Rose is dead, Durancy, and so are you. Stay away from me."

"As I live and breathe," he laughed, "you *are* Rose."

Something clicked in Verity. Maybe she could somehow use this situation; turn Durancy's certainty to her advantage. She looked exactly like Rose, of course . . . and yes, she really was Rose. Not only was she Rose's physical clone, but she had been filled with Rose's memories, her personality and being. Rose always seemed ready to leap out and overwhelm her, a pressure hovering behind each thought. It seemed that the Rose part of her was particularly activated when she put pressure on the tiny nubs behind her ears, as if some sort of chemical was released thereby into her brain. She avoided touching those nubs. But Rose was too much a part of her to be entirely avoided in that way. She still didn't understand the barriers between herself and Rose, or indeed if there really were any.

Being Rose was what she was trying to leave behind.

"Of course, Abe," she said quietly, gently. "I am Rose. And I need your help." *I am not Rose,* she assured herself. *I am Verity. I am Verity. . . .*

"That's a switch, isn't it?" he asked, his voice sarcastic and yearning at once. "You know everything, don't you, Rose?"

"I wish I did," Verity replied. "But I'm—" She had been going to say that she was in a hurry, but changed her mind.

He lowered himself into a large comfortable chair a few feet from her. Blaze made some gestures behind Abe's back: should I bash him in the head? Verity stifled a near-hysterical giggle. She shook her head once at Blaze.

"Abe," she said, "I want a riverboat. You know, an old-fashioned one with a paddlewheel. Maybe boats. Yes, two would be better. And two thousand rafts. I want them all stocked with food and medical diagnostic equipment and all kinds of nan seeds." That's right, she thought, steeling herself. No telling what this world holds. Best be prepared for anything. Those who had left already had cobbled rafts together for themselves, but there wasn't time for that anymore.

"You're—you're leaving, Rose?" he asked, his voice sad and uncertain.

"I have to," she said. "You know that, Abe. Please help." If he helped, then she wouldn't have to surrender once again to the City in order to get this done. If she did, she might be forever submerged, captured.

Just the thought of it made her break out in a cold sweat.

"Maybe I'll go too," Abe said, his voice weary. As he turned toward the window his vision swept past Blaze again, but Abe still didn't seem to notice him. Of course not. Abe thought Blaze was just one of the pawns with which he'd filled the City in order to please India, his mother.

Abe stared out the window. "I feel . . . so tired. Disoriented. Every time—this happens—at every pause and change and *skip*—I have to come back and *fix* things . . . but I don't really remember why."

Verity felt great pity for him. She knew everything about him, his deepest memories, his most wrenching pain, his uncertainty and sadness.

And his insanity.

"Just show me how to do this," she said. "Surely your Cincinnati has riverboats, Abe! They're an integral part of its history. Cincinnati was born because of the Ohio River. Cincinnati was the goal of the great riverboat races from New Orleans."

"Yes!" he said. As he leaned over the bright light of the translucent table between them she saw that his face had not regrown just right; was mottled. One ear was just a nub.

Somehow she *had* changed things. Or maybe she had just damaged them enough so they would be skewed even worse when the conversion came.

Why should tears fill her eyes as she looked on his imperfection? She blinked them away angrily. This man—his *original,* anyway, still embedded in the programs of the City—had warped her entire life, had ruthlessly used her. Abe, his cousin Rose, and his mother India had battled for her very soul.

And lost, she reminded herself, and straightened her back. They all lost. Whoever she was, she was *herself.* And leaving, forever, soon.

"Please, Abe," she said. "Do this for me."

He took a deep breath and sat on the bench beside her, shoving her gently aside. "Anything, Rose," he said, his eyes sad and dark. "Now watch." He touched various bright icons in an entrancing rhythm and a slight smile turned up the corners of his mouth. All sadness left his eyes. "Yes. Yes, that's it. Cincinnati's two hundred fiftieth anniversary." He was eager now. "We had *many* riverboats here; it was glorious. I was a boy. India and I went for a ride on one. We had tea and she told me about *Life on the Mississippi.*"

This is all he is, Verity thought. All that's left.

He didn't seem to notice when Blaze rose and stood behind them, put one hand on Verity's shoulder, and gripped it so hard that it hurt.

She watched the center of the table, feeling more and more remote. Engineering plans rapidly fluttered across it, ephemeral, and Abe drew in his breath with a hiss as a bank of colors arose, each a bar, and the bars varied in height for a few minutes; then he fixed them with a nod and swept them into a holographic bin that appeared at the edge of the table.

"They are here. But what's this? What's happened? They've been tampered with. Never mind. It's always this way. Things go awry. I don't . . . know why . . . ah, my beautiful city. Yes, there we go. Now—details."

Verity was entranced in spite of herself at the sumptuous staterooms that flickered before her, small doll's rooms with furniture ornate and splendid. She forgot her exhaustion.

"Yes," he mused. "Let's see now. Where?" A map of the riverfront appeared and he said "This is a job for—yes, Sternmeyer's factory down at the wharf. It's large enough to make two at a time, plus the rafts, and the tanks will open into the river when they're done. Are you sure two are enough?"

"Two are enough," she said. Time was very short. She saw that each riverboat had beds for fifteen hundred people, at capacity, and were capable of carrying many tons of cargo. On the edge of the table she did some simple calculations and concluded that each boat could carry as many as five thousand people if, for instance, ten or fifteen people slept in each room, on the floor. There were also large halls and promenades that could be utilized. It would have to do.

The night passed for Verity in a blur of colorful schematics and brief episodes of dozing. The building did not tremble so much at night, and she assumed this was because the City drew so much of its energy from the sun.

When she noticed dawn coloring the buildings outside the enormous window, she was surprised. Her eyes burned. Blaze had sunk down next to the wall, his back propped against it. He was watching Abe.

As Verity glimpsed the river, shimmering pale blue beneath the broken bridges, a strange energy passed through her, like points of pixillation which, gathered together, filled her mind and heart.

She whispered a rafter song, encouraged by the bones of the lovely vessel, the *Robert E. Lee,* growing holographically on the table. Was it actually beginning to form even now, assembling in its tank on the river?

> Some rows up, but we floats down,
> Way down the Ohio to Shawneetown . . .

She stood, filled with Dance, lovely, floating *Dance,* her Shaker Gift. She took a halting step. She sang another few words, slowly, whispering. She wanted to stop . . . it was the plague, the wretched plague.

Abe looked up. He watched her, hands poised over the screen, and frowned.

Blaze stood warily, looking first at Abe, then Verity.

"Keep going," Verity told Abe, standing quite still with enormous effort.

Abe stood, tall and no longer so uncertain. "Verity!" he shouted. "You're not Rose! You're Verity! I'm beginning to remember now. Oh, yes, I remember it all! You think you're so clever, don't you? Well, I can't let you leave! Don't think for a minute that you can leave! You're a part of us now, forever and ever. You're inside the City, Verity, you were born here. Now that you know it you can't get away no matter how far you go. Don't be stupid. All this will be stopped . . . I'll stop it. . . ."

He raised his hand to sweep the embryonic boat from the table but Blaze tackled him, so that Durancy's hand cut the holographic boat in half instead, and that half went flying until it left the field and vanished. Blaze and Durancy both slid across the floor and slammed into the window. Blaze got to his feet unsteadily; Abe groaned and stirred, then slumped to the floor.

Fierceness surged through Verity then from a new and powerful place.

"No you won't!" she said. "I never needed you!" She felt enormously angry. Because she had to call on the part of herself she wanted to forget.

Rose.

Durancy's cousin, who knew as much or more than he did.

Knowledge came from the back of her mind, from her center, from all of her, from every cell, draining her, as she worked at the table, trying to restore what he had removed. "Don't let him get up, Blaze," she commanded. "I don't care what you do." She tried to ignore Blaze's expression: puzzled, as uncertain as Abe had recently been.

"He's out cold," she heard Blaze say, as if from far away. "I tied him up with his scarf. What a strange man. It's not cold. Why was he wearing a scarf? For decoration, I guess."

Her hands moved swiftly across the table as the sun came up full and bright, filling the City, shining the river to light, flooding the assembly table with renewed energy from the Flowers she was newly awakening with her imperative commands. Lost in a haze of thought, of memory, of command, Verity did not consciously have anything to do with what she had loosed; it was a part of her. It was the part of her that was Rose, old as nanotechnology's very birth, knowing the very core of nan's power and its limits.

Rose, the Rose part of Verity, built on what Abe had begun, commanding the riverboat, and rafts, to form, and to stock them with whatever was needed—*everything*—and hurry!—though the table said, "That is too fast, it cannot be completed in this timespan. Particularly since most systems are down."

"Then do the best you can," she whispered, wondering if she dared try and change the conversion schedule. No, no, just get away! If the rafters couldn't leave soon they just might jump into the river without rafts or riverboats.

A holographic raft appeared on the table. A deck of one by twelve boards lay across a frame supported by hollow flotation devices below each corner. Each raft would come with a wigwam, of canvas rather than boards, which could be raised on a platform in the middle of the deck. Other details such as mess kits and matches were listed for a few seconds, then vanished along with the raft.

A thrill of fear ran through Verity, watching Rose's hands fly, knowing that she, Verity, had lost control and that she, Verity, did not really know what Rose was setting up, unleashing. Pain blossomed on one side of her head and blackness spread across her vision and the floor was shaking and she was falling . . .

Blaze was dragging her to the elevator.

"No," she said, struggling. "Forget about the boats. I have to heal you. That's what I came for. I couldn't tell Durancy. Rose can do it. That's the most important thing. I—I'm sorry; I just got started with the boats. Go *back,* Blaze! Just go back and put your hand on the table—"

"No," said Blaze shortly, flatly, without compromise. He pulled her into the elevator. "How does this work? *Take us down to the ground! Now!*" he yelled, and lost his balance and stumbled against the side when the floor rushed suddenly downward.

"Blaze! No! It wasn't finished!" Verity wished that she was stronger than Blaze, so she could take him back there against his will, but she knew she was not.

"Enough of this nonsense!" he said roughly. "I'm going to be fine. At least I'm not dead which I probably will be if we stay here much longer. Couldn't you feel the floor shaking up there? We need to get *out* of here. I don't know what happened to you but I don't like it. And when that guy wakes up he's going to be pretty mad, don't you think? What if the roof collapses? I shouldn't have left him there."

The door opened and he pulled her through the lobby.

"Just touch that interstice," said Verity, desperate. "Something is terribly wrong with you, Blaze. Maybe it can diagnose you!"

"Touch the *what?*" He laughed shortly. "Not on your life. Look what's happened to *you.*" Then they were out the door and both of them were stumbling down to the waterfront.

Verity was completely drained. The rafters, hammering and sawing, were singing some song about "Blingo blango hammer with my hammer, Zingo zango sawin with my saw" that sounded distant, muted. They were simple patches of color moving in front of her eyes for no particular reason. She allowed Blaze to sit her down on a bench; he sat next to her and held her hand.

He took a deep breath. "As long as we're going to have a boat, can we make sure there's a piano on it?" he asked, somewhat meekly.

"I have no idea what will happen now," she said crossly. "Who do you think I am, Mother Ann?"

"I'm not sure, Verity," he said. "I'm just not sure." And he stared out at the river. Verity stretched out on the bench and fell asleep instantly.

She woke with a start and jumped to her feet. How could she have slept? How many hours did they have left? She looked around wildly and did not see Blaze. But about a quarter mile away she saw a huge crowd gathered at the riverfront, and some people were climbing onto warehouse roofs. She ran in that direction, down the tree-lined promenade. Judging from the position of the sun it was still before noon.

When she got closer she heard a woman shouting, "Get back, get back; no telling what might happen with this tank, this is a *huge* project."

By climbing on a low wall Verity managed to grab a branch of the tree next to her, and hoisted herself up.

The riverfront was a vast concrete wasteland, lined with huge, ugly buildings, some concrete, some corrugated aluminum, some seamless nan-stuff, which seemed the ugliest of all, their reds and greens and blues faded and mottled by design, not by nature.

Verity rested in the branches and gawked, as amazed as the rest of them though she had set it in motion.

Twin black smokestacks with fluted, flowerlike tops were supported by platforms of white, atop a small sea of viscous green fluid.

Each infinitely fine detail of the boat was precisely engineered to assemble in a complex orchestration of events no less amazing than the stages an embryo went through from zygote to viable being, events that depended upon one another as modifiers and checks.

As she watched, the green cleared, and the fluid was slowly infused with swirls of blue. Now the liquid seemed less thick; wind ruffled its surface. Verity blinked. The deep, crystalline blue, the blue of the sky . . . could a mere *color* make her dizzy, now?

She held tightly to the branches and visions seared the inside of her closed eyelids, flickering quickly, jumbled: a narrow cobblestone street; a black man playing a trumpet; a casket being pushed inside a small, strange house . . .

She opened her eyes and found that she had wrapped herself tightly around the branch. How long had the vision lasted?

The crowd was silent now. The boats were rising almost imperceptibly. Railings and gingerbread balustrades crept into the air with elephantine slowness.

Maybe, just maybe, this would work.

They looked smaller than she had imagined they would.

One-third smaller than the originals, whispered a part of her. *To hurry the process. You specified that you must leave before the conversion.*

By two in the afternoon the boats had almost completely risen, slowly pushed upward by platforms beneath to float on the liquid in the tanks. Pumps spewed water from the interior of the boats. Rafts, like an afterthought of the growing pool, gradually coalesced around the boats.

Excited, Verity finally climbed down and wormed her way through the crowd to the clear barrier around the tanks. The barrier was full of pictures and words which vanished and reappeared fitfully, eliciting groans and cheers from the crowd. 95% COMPLETED. DETAIL WORK REMAINING, she read in front of her. And then a list scrolled past. Some of the items were pictures; others were words: antibiotics, clarinets, cutlery, lamps, linens, sweaters, vases . . . She touched the picture of a lamp, and was treated to an invitation to learn the biochemistry that caused its illumination.

The boat in front of Verity did look finished—proud, intricately detailed. Metal cables distributed the structural forces of the tall black smokestacks and the wide, slightly concave decks. A pilothouse with sparkling windows perched up top just forward of the boat's midpoint. Huge wooden struts angled between the bottom and second decks. A vivid red paddlewheel gleamed in the sun.

The contents in drawers and cupboards had probably not come to rest in a very neat manner, and there were all kinds of loose things, if the list had been correct, that would probably have just settled on the floor as the fluid receded. Verity blinked. Was that the trophy head of an *elk* attached to the front of the pilothouse?

A woman next to her climbed over the barrier and plunged feet-first into the tank. She surfaced gasping and laughing. She was followed by two or three others, and then a plummeting rain of people splashed into the tank. They began to climb onto the rafts.

"No!" Verity shouted. "Leave them alone! They're not *ready!* Can't you read?" But the rafts were fairly simple, and did indeed look finished. It was probably the boats that weren't quite done.

People were bunched up at the gates that kept the replicator bath separate from the river. Of course, they wanted to release the rafts. Once the gates were opened, the replicators would quickly be rendered useless, she knew, for they contained a failsafe in case they came in contact with mediums they might contaminate. Such as people, and river water.

As she pushed her way through the crowd, Verity felt a slight tremor, and turned to see all the interstices flash, then darken again. She realized she was the only person who had noticed. Or who cared. She watched for a long jostled moment, but did not see the flash again. It may have just been the sun coming out from behind a passing cloud. But she did not think so. It meant that the conversion was going to happen quite soon.

Maybe the best thing was to liberate the boats. Even if they weren't finished. From her tree, they had looked almost finished. But there was a possibility that certain processes were still going on inside.

A cheer went up, and from its velocity she knew that the problem was moot. Giant gears long unused clanked slowly, and the gate slid open sideways, inch by inch. The river met the fluid inside in a flurry of whirlpools as the gap widened.

Soon the water in the tank was the color of the Ohio: a clear, sparkling green. The citizens of Cincinnati swam and laughed and shouted. Perhaps drawn by the beauty of the boats, or out of curiosity, some of the plaguers climbed onto the riverboats, using ladders that descended into the water. Verity saw them wander through the rooms like shadows, slowly, as if amazed. Some of them seemed to be righting furniture. They ascended the levels of the boat and ended up in the pilothouse, throwing open the windows. Verity could only hope that some of the rafters might understand, just as she did, the necessity of these boats. They would need all the support they could get in the wilderness downriver from Cincinnati. Rafts would not be enough. Perhaps the fact that riverboats were in *Huckleberry Finn* might be enough to lure them aboard. After all, she certainly didn't know the parameters of the plague.

Tired with relief, Verity let the plague overtake her. She slumped down, leaning her forehead against the clear cool barrier between her and the boats, letting her eyes run up and down the lines of them, taking in the details. The gingerbread, the tremendous paddlewheel at the rear, the curious blue tinge of the boats, somehow mingling with white. She realized the color must have something to do with collecting solar energy and sending it to some sort of storage. Probably the huge black smokestacks did the same.

The majesty of the journey filled her. The Territory! Surely there could be nothing so glorious as leaving the past behind, and entering the unknown. Just one of those rafts below, that was all a person needed; that and a fishing line.

What freedom.

What bitter irony, said a small voice within her, but the plague overrode it.

Some of the rafts swirled out onto the river, filled with exuberant rafters, shouting and waving as they commenced their journey. She felt their joy and waved back. Her worries seemed ridiculous. Some of the rafts remained in the tank or were pulled round with long lines to the wharf, and people started loading them with supplies from the warehouses and shops of Cincinnati, where the concept of money had not existed for decades.

She turned west to survey the situation.

The Seam of Cincinnati was a solid, self-healing wall. It marked the point at which the last Surge had stopped, when the replicators went wild and surged through the matter that was the City, changing it, and all within, swiftly and mercilessly. Twenty stories high, casting a shadow on the buildings within, the Seam extended smooth, impermeable, and unscalable into the Ohio River. Where it ended, a constant wave sprayed upward, spending itself in the air, for it was just above the Lower Falls, hidden by a bend in the river, which very few, if any, Cincinnatians now living had ever seen. They had been trapped within the Seam for decades. Verity knew, from information she'd learned in the library, that these falls were not like the Upper Falls—high, wide, and completely unnavigable. She was counting on them conforming to the map she'd glimpsed in the library, for a few seconds, where they were depicted as a long series of rapids. Of course, the map was very old, and might no longer be true.

She was immensely relieved to see that someone *had* chosen to attempt piloting. Maybe she was right about the *Huckleberry Finn* part. The *Robert E. Lee* was brought around to the wharf, after a fearful moment when it seemed as if it might be washed downriver. The current was probably quite strong here, and an inexperienced pilot could easily lose control. But once at the wharf it was moored by a gang of people. The *American Queen* followed. The gangplanks went down and streams of people began coming and going, adding various bundles taken from shops to the boat.

She rested her gaze on downtown Cincinnati, with Mount Adams rising behind it, all the beautiful Flower-Buildings of which Durancy had dreamed long ago, so long ago that no one could even remember when that had been, exactly.

What if it *didn't* go as she thought it would? What if she had failed?

Who then could fix her beloved City, the City where she had been created, the City of which she had dreamed as a child, thrust forth too young to be sure whether or not there was any reality to those haunting dreams?

This was her *home*. She *could* not leave. Maybe there was too much of Rose in her, and not enough Verity. Maybe the plague had not taken her strongly enough. Maybe Verity didn't really exist, was a ghost who would fade if she stayed. She would then be Rose, and she could help restore Abe Durancy. She remembered with pity how he had looked last night: ravaged, destroyed. Where was he? A part of her longed to help him.

The part of her that was Rose.

She moved to the stairs around the growing tank and hurried down. She turned and walked quickly toward the tall buildings of Cincinnati, which seemed to be calling her. . . .

Someone yelled her name and she turned. Blaze was behind her, his gait halting. She stopped and he caught up with her.

"Where are you going so fast?"

"Where have *you* been?" she asked.

Blaze's face lit up. "Sphere and I went into a little club and played for about an hour. After you left I had another one of my . . . spells, I guess you'd call them. But I feel *much* better, at least for now. And we found a store full of *wonderful* things—radio stones, things that Sphere calls records—"

Verity sighed. Sphere had been her lover, briefly, after they entered Cincinnati together, when Blaze had been dead, or nearly so. She would tell Blaze, soon, when there was time. She had met Sphere in the Cincinnati train station, where he had played the saxophone. Now, he was completely changed, tapped deep into the City's system. Or so he claimed.

She resumed walking. "I'm sorry. I mean, I'm glad that you're feeling better. Very glad. But I can't leave."

"Why not? What are you talking about?"

"It's too hard, Blaze. This is my home. My true home. I just can't *bear* to leave!" She started to run and he caught her arm and he was much stronger than she thought he'd be as he gripped it and whirled her around and held her tight.

His voice next to her ear was low and quiet and removed her from the din around her. "We're leaving, Verity. Sphere told me a lot about what happened, about Edgetown, and about who you are and what you did. Something about you being the Queen. I didn't really understand it. I *think* I remember waking you, finding you there, in the hive. . . ." He fell silent for a moment while he looked at her sharply, wonder and puzzlement in his eyes. Then he continued. "Sphere said you'd want to stay and that you couldn't, that you had to leave. He was afraid of what might happen to you if you stayed. Some kind of permanent cycle or freeze-up. Just like before. Whatever that was. He made me promise to make sure that you left."

"So where is he *now?*"

"He said he had some things to do. He said he'd come back and say good-bye. Let's go out on the bridge, all right? I think you need to get as far away from the City as possible."

If it had been anyone other than Blaze she would have wrenched free. His words made sense but something in her violently disagreed. Yet they made their way past the bevy of rafts moored on the long waterfront and eventually found their way to the stairs at the foot of the bridge and climbed, up and up, and Blaze was right; out here where the wind was blowing and the sky was so blue she felt better. Much better.

She watched the river for ten minutes, fifteen, studying the mesmerizing current below, slowly beginning to think in terms of what lay ahead, wishing she could predict the way the river twisted, wondering why her maps had suddenly stopped working, thinking that perhaps if she went to the top of the very tallest building she might get a glimpse, though the Seam was as high as that and in some places higher . . . wondering why she felt no fear and that did seem strange, surely this exodus was a fearful thing, not something that should ring this great joy through her cells like a low steady note of music. . . .

"I think we're almost ready," Blaze said finally, gently, startling her. He rested a hand on her shoulder and his touch calmed her even more. He said something about loading rafts.

The wind blew back her hair and the plague rose within her again, so it was almost as if she were floating above the river, instead of standing on a bridge and then turning, oriented by the sun, ready to take flight down the river like an arrow. Hurry! she thought. We must hurry! There is not a second to waste! A part of her looked at this from a distance, a part that seemed ready to vanish, swept away by the rising tide of the plague.

"Come on," whispered Blaze. "One of the riverboats left an hour ago. The other is waiting just beyond the stadium. It's time."

And then Sphere was walking out onto the bridge with his saxophone to say farewell.

A final wave of wild plagued rafters swarmed toward the river. Verity was among them, pushed and battered on the landing by a mob seized by a great roar of song. She did not remember coming down off the bridge. She stumbled and Blaze pulled her to her feet. His pale, frightened face spurred her to push onward until they came to the wharf's sudden edge.

The waterfront was lined six deep with rafts, bobbing about four feet below, several breaking away from the main mass every minute, as soon as eight or ten people filled them and cast off.

Verity turned back toward the city. Blaze grabbed her around the waist and they were both pushed to their knees by the crush of the crowd. Someone tripped over Verity and fell too; then Blaze was pulling them both up and carrying her . . . she was lost in a haze of color and scent; brilliant light flashed forth from the city and she must stay, she had to stay. . . .

Blaze pulled Verity down a ladder and she was too low to see the City. She felt herself being dragged across a rough surface; then a splash of cold water drenched her face.

She gasped and suddenly comprehended their situation. She grabbed Blaze's hand and staggered to her feet. Together they leaped across the stepping-stones of rafts until there were no more. That raft filled and someone pushed them away from the other rafts with a board. Their raft swirled out into the river, where a fast current seized it.

Verity braced her feet wide as the raft danced on the river's small waves, and looked back.

The conversion had begun.

Cincinnati flared with color. A dull glow suffused the buildings, then grew in color and intensity. The interstices began to flash in unison, thin lines of light rolling from ground level to the crowns of the buildings.

The City trembled.

It was as if the hard stones, the high sleek towers, the complex 1930s architecture, the canyons of lost commerce and life, melted; became more plastic; moved and changed according to directions issuing from deep within the City's heart: Rose's plan, taking form.

The roar of the river, loud as it was, could not drown out the screams of those still on the wharf. A wall of people jumped onto rafts and when the rafts were gone jumped into the river.

But a few others turned, paused, and walked back into town.

A slow wave of muted light moved across Cincinnati.

Verity saw one indigo Tulip slowly unfurl as golden streaks shot up each petal.

Then the Ohio's bend took them. The raft bounced on the rough water above the rapids. Verity had one final glimpse of golden, moving, surging matter. . . .

Good-bye, my lovely City.

Then they moved beyond that point, ever more swiftly.

Lighting out.

2

○○◇

Beautiful Ohio

Two

○○○○○○○○○○○○○○○○

Free-Fall Blues

Her own crazed laugh startled Verity. Torn from her, it blended with the whitecapped waves heaving round the raft. She raised her face to the sky; laughed. "We *did* it!" she shouted, then let go of the sweep and spun around, long wet hair swirling, arms stretched outward.

A sudden shift flung her to the heaving deck of the raft and someone grabbed her arm, jerked her to her feet. She staggered and regained her balance; turned and saw Blaze. She just missed stepping on a man holding tight to a rope as he lay on the deck.

Blaze's hair was plastered to his head; his face streamed with water. His eyes, concerned and angry, pulled her back to herself. "Steer!" he hollered, pointing to the stick at the rear of the raft, behind the collapsed wigwam—the sweep, Verity's plague told her, the simple steering oar that was all the control they had.

The turbulent water around her was crowded with rafts slipping and flowing down the mountainous furrows of the current, split everywhere with boulders. Screams mingled with the water's roar.

Something within her focussed when she grabbed the sweep. It was rough in her hands, and she felt the heart of the river through it; knew when to hang from it with all her weight and when to push against it. It was the plague at work. She shouted, her voice hoarse: "Heigh, ho, the boatmen row . . ."

Ahead, an island split the river. The left branch was smooth and compelling but she couldn't see where it led. The right branch was a wide maelstrom of foam surging between large rocks, then a slicksmooth tongue of green water—

She leaned on the sweep and took the right fork, terrified by the roar, the speed, the massive rocks they missed by inches. Yes! *Steer!*

In the river's grip, they swept down the chute. The raft swirled, almost knocking her off her feet, and as it turned she saw a terrible sight.

Behind and above them the *Robert E. Lee* teetered on the edge of the more extreme rapids they had just avoided, the left branch, where, she could now see, water fell from a rock ledge thirty feet high, thundering into a turbulent cauldron of boulders. She froze in fear. Whoever was piloting had made the wrong choice, simply by chance, the same reason she had made the right choice.

The *Robert E. Lee* ponderously tipped sideways. It slid down the white wall of water, and smashed onto the rocks sideways, splitting apart. People spilled from the decks into the foaming rapids.

Verity heard screams from those next to her on the heaving raft. The *Robert E. Lee*'s paddlewheel spun briefly in the air before the boat slowly completed its roll and was pinned to the rocks by the force of the water. Shattered remnants bobbed to the surface.

"STEER!" Verity heard again, and she looked forward and saw that they were on the edge of another drop.

The raft shot out over the edge and dropped back onto the water, only about a foot below. Verity staggered at the impact, holding tight to the oar. The current caught the corner of the raft and spun it so it faced backward; Verity leaned on the oar, caught the water's force, and completed the spin so the sweep was again at the rear. One side of the raft smashed against a rock and splintered with a rending crunch; then they were through the worst of it, for the moment.

Holding the sweep with one hand, Verity dropped to the deck facedown, reached into the river, and grasped the hand nearest her. A woman's face, twisted in fear and anguish, surfaced as Verity tried to hold on, but the hand slipped from hers and the woman vanished beneath a rush of foam.

"No," Verity breathed to herself.

"Verity!" Blaze shouted. "There's more rough water ahead!"

Luckily, these rapids were not as treacherous as the last, and they safely rode the gradual descent around the final rapids. The raft shot into a calm stretch of water.

The water was filled with bobbing heads and outstretched arms. Far ahead, she saw a flotilla of rafts and the *American Queen,* still afloat.

Verity and Blaze dragged people onto the raft, where they lay coughing in the sun. Soon a dozen rafters, bleeding from gashes on their heads, legs, and arms, sprawled on the wet wood, so that the raft rode low in the water.

The river was green and broad and smooth here. Heavy forest lined the Kentucky shore, and on the Ohio side the kudzu-covered detritus of quake-crazed suburbs formed low green hillocks where glints of shattered windows caught the sun.

"Where the hell are we?" demanded one woman after a coughing fit. A man quietly sobbed, and two boys stared at the scene around them with eyes deer-wide in stunned wonder.

A few more rafts swept through the rapids behind them and coasted into placid water.

Verity blinked, for they all glowed, faintly but unmistakably *golden,* as if very lightly brushed with phosphorescence. Those whose skin was darker were burnished by the plague as well.

The enormity of what she had done filled Verity anew. They were now her responsibility. They had never done a damned thing for themselves in all their lives—whatever "all their lives" meant to them. In Cincinnati, the life of an individual had not been worth much. They had spent decades helplessly immersed in India and Durancy's vision of the American arts—literature, music, drama, even comics.

And some of them had just died because of her, instead of living on for maybe hundreds of years as slaves of the city.

As the raft drifted into chilly shadows beneath overarching trees, she began to tremble violently. She remembered only in bits, in bright flashes, in dark valleys of helplessness, what had happened in Cincinnati before she freed it. The faces of people whose names she could not recall were superimposed on the river, transparent as dreams. She had better be right. She had chosen Norleans over home for all of them.

The raft was pulled by the current into sunlight once more and she was warmed. The sky was still brilliant blue overhead and another vision superseded the Cincinnati faces like a fine mist: an ancient street paved with stones; a dim-lit room filled with a million winking lights; a vast continent seen from the air for just a moment. She was filled with odd, imperative, overwhelming joy, a joy so strong she forgot where she was even in the midst of terrible danger, and let go of the sweep. She did not particularly like this joy, for she recognized it for what it was: the Norleans Plague. But maybe that recognition meant that she had a bit of control; some distance from it.

"Norleans!" a rafter shouted joyfully. "We're going to *Norleans!*"

The rafters broke into applause and two boys began to sing that froggie song with Cairo in the chorus, then began another rafter favorite, "The Erie Canal." Everyone joined in except Verity, who stared grimly forward and wondered what would become of them.

And Blaze, who seemed unable to sing.

He stared at Verity with panicked eyes, his mouth open, and she grabbed his hand and stared back, helpless. With gestures he indicated that he could not speak. Tears stood in his eyes. She could only hold his hand tightly. They had left behind anything that could seek out the source of his problem and heal him. They were on their own now, spurled out into the Territory like dry leaves in an autumn storm.

The songs, which soon began to wear on Verity, lasted until they all got hungry.

In late afternoon Blaze and Verity caught up with the *American Queen,* and along with several other rafts poled along the side until they found a ladder. The riverboat was anchored in a large, quiet cove out of the main current of the river.

As the air thrummed with the murmur of insects and the rustle of newly green leaves caught by the light breeze, Verity climbed the last steps of the ladder, hoisted herself onto the lower deck, and ran her hand over the railing in amazement. She had risked her identity—her newly won *life*—to make the city create this. She closed her eyes against the memory of Durancy, sadly monstrous, thinking her Rose—

Well, she did look like Rose. Exactly. There had been many Roses manifested by Cincinnati, apparently. And Rose was inside her, within her memory sponges, those nubs behind her ears. That was the plain, unpleasant truth. Rose's entire personality, memories, and being were there, ready to overwhelm her own if she was not strong enough to hold Rose back.

But she was out of that city. Forever. Yet she could not rejoice in her escape. Her heart ached for those on the wrecked boat. She was not even sure how this boat worked; what it could do. At least the *Queen* floated.

Debris from the wreck of the *Robert E. Lee* drifted past, and a pale, battered body fetched up on some weeds along the shore. Sadness washed through Verity. Already things had gone terribly wrong.

"Verity," said Blaze, and touched her shoulder. Relief washed through her as she turned.

"Your voice is back!"

He shrugged. "For now. Let's have a look around. Tell me how you did all this. Even though I was there, I don't know."

She shrugged, bone-tired. "The plans were in the City's memory. The *Queen* was a gambling boat, and went to New Orleans and back several times a year. Actually, there were several pre-nan *Queen*s—most of the famous riverboats went through several incarnations—different boat, same name. Anyway, these nanotech plans were developed in Cincinnati, with a few components from St. Louis and Pittsburgh. I think that the power plan came from Pittsburgh—I don't remember it that well, though. The—what was it?—*interior design* was done by a company from San Francisco!" Her laugh threatened to become hysterical.

"What is interior design?" asked Blaze, looking at the polished decks, the white railings, the long row of green louvered doors with gleaming brass doorknobs. He opened one of the doors.

"Oh," he said. "Wallpaper. With flowers. It's beautiful. It's against the Millennial Laws, that's for sure." He ran his hand across it and frowned. "No . . . it's not paper. It's just . . . the wall. I guess this is interior design, eh?" He drew back the curtains. "They're damp," he said. Light flooded a small, pretty couch, a four-poster bed draped with mosquito netting, and a marble-topped washtable. The washtable and a dresser were built in, of fine woods, but the bed had skidded across the floor, bunching up a rug beneath its legs. An overstuffed chair lay on its side. "Help me get this up," said Blaze, and together they set it upright. Water squished out beneath their hands. "I hope it doesn't mildew," said Blaze. "But it's pretty hot. I guess it will all dry out in a few days."

Verity said, "I told the program how long we had until the conversion. This boat is one-third smaller than the original so that it would be finished in time. The program made adjustments so that the rooms are still as large; there are just less of them." She went around the room touching things, quite amazed. Even *this* was like a chunk of the city, of Rose and Durancy and India. "It's still not completely finished, and now I guess it won't be, but I'm really not sure what was left out."

Well, if anything important was missing, they had rafts. And *rafts* were the main thing—Jim and Huck had used rafts. Verity understand that as deeply as the other rafters.

They went back outside. Blaze hailed rafts as they drifted around the last bend one after the other until there were over a hundred rafts crowding the cove.

"What about the ones already downstream?" asked Verity.

Blaze shrugged. "As far as I can tell, I'd say there must be thousands of people ahead of us. We left—well, we left at the last possible minute." Verity saw a shadow pass through his green eyes, and his face became grave. "There seems to be room for thousands on this riverboat. Must have been that many on the other boat—" He took a deep, shuddering breath. "Well, the rafters ahead of us are on their own, I guess. But really, so are we, right? I mean, we don't know much more than they do. And I don't think that everyone will stop with us anyway, just because I tell them to. Why should they?"

Blaze handed the megaphone to an old woman and showed her the tie-ups for the rafts, where rope ladders hung from the railings. "Come on," he said to Verity. "Let's look around."

Blaze picked up some lightsticks and Verity noticed that his hands shook. He looked pale, not golden.

"I thought you were feeling better."

"Sometimes."

"But you don't have the plague."

Blaze shook his head. "I don't think so."

"You did at Shaker Hill," said Verity.

Blaze paused in front of her. "I don't remember that," he said. "Why don't I still have it, then?"

Verity sighed. "I don't know. You've been through so much." She remembered, distantly, that she had taken the plague from him and infected everyone in the city with it. Maybe that had changed him somehow. And maybe if she were the Queen again, in full control of a healthy Cincinnati, she could figure out how she had done that, and replicate it. But she was as far from that state as an ant from the stars, and she wouldn't want to return to it even if she could. And maybe there was another reason—the other cocoon Blaze had been in, for instance.

"I guess you have too," said Blaze. "Come on, let's figure out what we've got here."

The rear of the main deck was filled with rooms of machinery—massive boilers, gears as big around as she was tall, pistons that vanished out a hole, linked, she supposed, to the paddlewheel. They moved toward the front of the boat; Blaze opened a door, smacked one of the light-sticks, and handed her the other. She saw a room of dark shapes. They stepped inside. Their lights cast a gentle glow over mountains of jumbled supplies. The room smelled of wood and damp canvas.

"It's a lot neater at the other end," he said, as she pushed around a huge canvas-covered lump. "The later it got the harder it was to keep everyone organized."

She said, "I guess I wasn't much help loading stuff—"

"You did great just getting on the raft. I was afraid you wouldn't come." He shook his head quickly, once, as if trying to shake away his memory of the conversion's beginning.

Verity remembered it, now, those initial moments when the buildings loosened their shape, subtly, coalescing to new form as she, next to Blaze, stretched her hands outward toward it, determined never, ever, to leave. . . .

"I—didn't you carry me?" The day shimmered behind her, a wild confusion of motion and light and aches where she had fallen.

Blaze was silent behind a large wooden crate. She passed around it and saw that he was right—things were more organized here. She saw countless barrels stamped FLOUR in large black letters. Bushel bags of OATS slumped to one side. There was DRIED MILK and DRIED BEAN CURD and, happily, COFFEE. Various other supplies were neatly stacked in rows.

"Look, Verity," said Blaze, relief in his voice. "Fishing line. A hundred yards a spool. Plenty of that." He rattled a box. "Thousands of hooks. Rifles and ammo. Good. We can't survive without them." He pushed aside some bags of flour and pulled out one of the rifles. "I was hoping they were on this boat. I found them in a store. Only about thirty or so. We'll pass them out later if some of them want to hunt." The air was absolutely still, though they could hear clumping on the deck above them.

"What's *this?*" asked Verity, pointing to a barrel that said CHICKEN MEDIUM. She wondered if there had not been, possibly, a better and more modern way to package and transport food, and was filled once again with dread and responsibility: a lot of the boat—substance and content—was the result of a personal symbiosis with the program. It had responded to something deep within her as she had given directions for the boat. It echoed her thoughts and experience except when there had been blank places, and then something else had filled in. Both facets troubled her.

Blaze turned suddenly. His eyes sought hers and she was caught by the pain she saw in them. They stared at each other barely breathing, seeing at the same time the same strange truth.

She was different. *He* was different. And that difference, wrought by the city and by who they had each become while apart, filled the light-stick glow between them like something solid, like glass, where they could see each other yet no longer touch. Still she raised one hand and *touched* his, just brushed his fingers—

"I feel so *lost,*" he whispered.

Before Verity could grasp his hand with a good, tight hold, a voice came from the direction of the stairs. "Anybody down there?"

Blaze gave Verity a troubled look. "Over here!" he yelled. "Get some help. We need to clear a path to the food and take it up to the galley." In a minute the hull was filled with people.

There were spoons and plastic cups but "chicken medium," enthusiastically mixed with water and doled out (won't matter if it's not heated, said the man who had appointed himself cook, or chemist) had little to do with chicken. Verity leaned back on a wooden bench and forced herself to swallow it. One spoonful in water rapidly expanded into a yellowish gelatinous mass. After a few bites she threw the rest in the river and rinsed the cup and spoon at a table with buckets of water someone had set up for that purpose.

Blaze worried about purifying the river water but was met with puzzled looks and a stampede to eat. His shoulders sloped downward and he was pale. He lifted a hand to brush back his hair, and it trembled slightly. He'd removed his shirt as he worked to help organize the food and she could see his ribs.

But, rather chillingly, there was no scar on his chest where he'd been shot point-blank at close range.

It was as if part of him had vanished. What else had vanished while he was within the sheets? She feared that it was something deep; essential.

She sighed. Blaze was alive, yes. But he was not at all well, it seemed. His state of being, whatever that was, the very *unsureness* of it, created within her an unshakable feeling of dread.

A few minutes later she glimpsed him on a higher deck, trying doors, until one opened and he went inside and closed it behind himself.

Oddly, she did not feel tired. As evening darkened to night the lemon glow of sunset gave way to deep velvet blue and stars. The light breeze brought the scent of the river and the forest, a scent free of coercion or thoughts of any kind. She stood on one of the lower decks and leaned against the railing. Fires flickered on the rafts, held in metal hemispheres someone had found in a warehouse down by the river—thousands of them, in boxes that declared "Grown from a program exclusively held by Wokmaster of San Francisco, all rights reserved, if tariff not paid product will disassemble in thirty days." Apparently, they had been properly paid for, long ago. She heard faint singing from some of the rafts, which ranged outward from the boat like stars in the night sky.

Restless, she paced the deck, her mind sharpening with each step. How could they stand to stay here? They must be getting on! They must not miss a moment in getting to Norleans! How far was it? How many nautical miles?

Norleans!

The very word ignited visions. For a moment she was surrounded by a mob of dancing, sparkling people, caught in their madness. She even glimpsed a street sign, BOURBON, and watched it swirl off behind her.

She moved from the plague-vision back to the present with a conscious effort, and grasped the railing. It was damp with dew. She listened to the slosh and swish of water hurrying beneath them, hurrying to . . .

"No," she said aloud. She would not let *Norleans,* whatever it might have been, or whatever it might be now, rule her. It would be her guide only.

Right. Her laugh was short and harsh. Why should *she* be the only one of all ever afflicted to shake free whenever she wished?

She heard voices above, found the stairs at the center of the boat, and climbed. The moon cast ornate shadows of gingerbread trim on the next deck. Here she saw only a row of closed cabin doors, people sleeping on the deck, a long white railing that curved with the curve of the boat so she could not see its end. The stairs to the upper deck were wide and the rise of each step slight.

She emerged on the top deck. It was open to the stars, and the twin smokestacks towered above. A circle of about twenty people sat in white wooden chairs. A lamp that cast a pale green glow stood on a table in the center. At least *that* lamp had been completed. Trees rustled in darkness, reminding Verity of moonlit nights on Bear Creek. Without thinking she reached to grasp Blaze's hand, then remembered that he wasn't there.

"My name is . . ." As Verity drew closer she heard the voice falter . . . "was . . ." It faltered again as she dropped into a chair on the outside of the circle, feeling dew penetrate the seat of her pants ". . . *is!*" The woman's voice continued, firmly, and with slight astonishment, "Higgins. My name *is* Higgins. Janet Elizabeth Higgins."

The woman-who-had-been-Janet was young and attractive. She wore her dark hair in a short cap which caught the light of the lantern. Dressed in jeans and a shirt, she pulled her long legs up onto the chair and clasped them as she spoke, staring into the lantern, rubbing her bare feet as the night cooled.

"After work . . . sometimes . . . yes, I remember now . . . I'd take the bus down to the Ohio . . . *this* very river . . . and walk out on the suspension bridge. I especially loved to be there on a summer's night when a storm was coming. There was the rush of traffic behind me and I'd face downriver and watch the dark heavy clouds come fast; then that hissing sheet of hard cold rain and wind. There was such a sense of release. And I'd think of what I was going to do, *someday,* maybe, when I had enough time to come up for air. They said that radio was going to go completely at any time, and anything broadcast, but it was just hard to believe, even though it was already spotty. When the Vote came, and the chance to get receptors, I knew I'd be in hock the rest of my life, but it seemed to me that life itself would be different and what did I care, anyway? I already *was* in hock, really, to meaningless work."

Janet's words rushed on, and Verity felt that it was a story she was telling *herself* as much as anyone else, caught in the keen poignant *remembering* of who she truly was beneath the layers imposed by the city. "Before that—for years before the Vote—I worked for Richardson in his nan factory in the Tenderloin district. Not a nice place, but I had two kids. I couldn't be too choosy. He let me know just about every day how goddamned lucky I was to even *have* a job." Verity saw heads nodding as she settled back into the chair and listened. Janet's voice, hushed at first, grew stronger.

"This was before the Infowars. We lived in two crummy rooms, all I could afford. I'm no genius but anyone with money got more with this nanotechnology stuff and the rest of us were worse off than ever no matter what they promised us would come eventually."

"Yeah," said an older man from the shadows. "Same here. Every once in a while we talked about a neighborhood co-op buying tanks and programs for clothes and little stuff like vid players and electronic things but there were always some kind of licensing hangups. Lawyer's fees— and who knows what kind of bribes . . ."

"Well," replied Janet, "a lot the people I knew were terrified of nan. Sometimes I thought they were scared because people wanted them to be scared, the people with money, to keep them from demanding things that at the beginning we all thought would be free." A look of bemusement crossed her face. "Right. People like me controlling our own lives. Yeah, sure."

Janet fell silent for a moment and Verity saw that the faces around her were thoughtful; somewhat puzzled. She wondered how many of them really remembered what their original lives were like. And how many of them *had* original lives, for that matter.

Janet continued, her dark eyes distant as if she were visualizing it as she spoke, dredging memories across a wide gulf.

"I was better off than most because I got some tech training. Richardson hired three workers. At first I wondered why he needed that many. What we did was pretty easy. And all he did was sit behind a window and hassle us, and smoke. Finally I realized he just liked being boss. Probably some kickback or tax bonus for hiring humans; who knows." Her voice filled with amazement. "I'm remembering. I'm really *remembering!*"

"He—" She paused.

"Go on," encouraged the woman next to her.

Janet frowned. "I'm thinking . . . yeah. That's it. The contract. He had a government contract but they didn't send him much work. Maybe one job every two weeks. It pissed him off. The jobs were always some kind of parts that went with something that was being made somewhere else. Maybe . . . they didn't want anybody to know what they were up to."

"Those were tests," threw in the old man.

Janet glanced at him. Nodded slowly. "Well . . . I did have the feeling that a lot of the things we made didn't really have any purpose except to see if their programs worked. Whenever something came in Richardson would follow us around raging that he'd lose his contract if we didn't step on it. But the job was made for idiots. The spheres—the plans were on crystal spheres—came like precious jewels in boxes filled with soft stuff. That was all for show. To impress us workers. They were wrapped with bands as hard to cut as steel but flexible as cloth. They'd done something to Richardson's body so that he could touch them and they would open but not just at his touch; the person who brought it had to be touching it, too. The boxes had two little indentations like the place you rest a cigarette on an ashtray, and Richardson would rest his finger in one and whoever brought the crystal would rest one finger in the one on the other side and when they did the fastenings came loose and he'd hand it to me. And then—" She closed her eyes, shook her head. "Then what?"

There was a tense silence, as if, Verity thought, everyone was afraid that Janet might lose her thread, subside back into dark unknowing . . . and a few sighs of relief when she continued.

"Yes," said Janet, firmly. "The tanks. After I popped the sphere into the computer . . . on a shelf above the main tank where things got assembled were a lot of tanks, each one a different color and with different numbers on them, and tubes that ran down to the main tank. The tanks and the laser were the only things that were clean in the whole place. One of the other people had to check out the tanks and keep them full of the right-numbered stuff, and run tests a couple times a day to make sure the mixtures were just right, not going bad or anything, and make sure the tubes were cleaned after each job."

"It was so old-fashioned, wasn't it?" whispered the woman next to Verity.

"Anyway, after I put the sphere in, there were specifications on the screen of whatever was being made, you know, like blueprints or mechanical drawings. There were layers and layers of specifications and views but I didn't know what they meant and didn't have to. All I had to do was make sure that each stage was executed correctly—the sensors checked that of course, and I just had to watch the screen and agree for the next step to occur if it all went okay. If it didn't we'd stop and clean out the tanks and tubes and start again. I remember that at first things would happen like we'd be making, say, a big batch of screws and they wouldn't have any threads, or the threads might not be at just the right angle, and then I'd have to save the mistake and send it back with the program.

"Anyway, first the tank filled with solution. The jets would kick in to keep the assemblers circulating. The jets had to go at just the right rate for the assemblers to attach to one another. The molecules in the tanks up top had to be piped into the solution at just the right time. I had to manually adjust things from time to time and whenever I did that adjustment got added to the sphere. Everything I did was recorded. Every once in a while Richardson would glare at me through the window and I'd wave at him and smile my cheeriest smile. It might have been in the back of his mind that since I knew more than him and could do more than him I could steal his pitiful little contracts."

"Yeah," muttered someone. "Just try and get in on the ground floor like they told us we could, the liars."

"Then what?" asked someone else.

"Well . . . yeah. About ten minutes after the finished product went through the dry cycle an armored truck would come. They'd check the sphere to make sure it was the same one and lock it up. Then they hauled off whatever we'd made that day. We never made anything too big for the truck. Our tank wasn't big enough."

She was silent for a moment. People shifted in their chairs.

Dark forest canopy arched above, rustling in the wind. The moon had vanished, and the sky was splashed with stars. As she looked at them, a memory touched Verity: walking up the back stairs from India's kitchen and seeing, on old brown papers, celestial maps.

Despite the hour, and the rigors of the day, Verity saw that only a few of them dozed. The rest were listening with hunger on their faces; with eagerness, she thought, to speak their tale.

These people, thought Verity, have been submerged in the City for . . . how many years? Decades before I was born, even. She was amazed at the clarity of Janet's recollection; wondered how real it was.

Yet, she realized, she had to reverence it and all the manifestations of these people. What else was there to do? Janet had a lot to be angry about. Verity wondered if they would remember what had happened to them in the City after the nan surge, the overlay of personality after personality, role after role, in the ecstatic dance that Durancy and India and even Rose had led them on.

Janet laughed wryly. She held her hands up in the dim light and looked at the back of them. "No wrinkles. I *know* I was older than *this* body. At least sixty. So long ago! I was so *happy* to be chosen! It was like the beginning of a whole new life. By then my boys had both gone west and my mother had died. Richardson had died too, though not in the way I'd so often fantasized. I wanted to push him into the big tank and watch him get made into some sort of machine part, hopefully with the memory that he was once human." She laughed again, and some of the others around the circle joined in.

When Verity was next aware of anything, it was of Blaze, shaking her awake, and it was morning. She squinted at the sun. Eight? Nine? How had she been able to sleep so long in this hard chair?

"Do I smell something baking?"

"I made biscuits. We have to feed them again, Verity," he said.

She groaned. Her thousand—or how many were there?—children. Like birds with open mouths. She got up, her stomach heaved, and she rushed to the railing and threw up.

"Ugh." She wiped her mouth with the back of her hand. "I hope we brought something besides chicken medium."

Three

○○○○○○○○○○○○○○○○○

Cincinnati Underworld Woman

Verity ran up the broad, shallow stairs at the center of the boat. The stairs were highly polished but her bare feet kept her from slipping. At each landing she saw the green surging river and across it scattered rafts like endless stepping-stones reaching from shore to shore.

She burst into the topmost room and halted suddenly.

In the flooding sunlight, a huge wooden wheel arched through the floor, reminding her of the lovely Art Deco arch of Union Station. She felt a pang, remembering that she had met Sphere in the Station.

At last there was time to tell Blaze she had slept with Sphere. It had been perplexing to find that although she had grown up with Blaze and was trying to rescue him from death, she might not necessarily be close only to him, forever. But it hadn't been as clear as that. Cincinnati had been unimaginably strange, and despite the pain and strangeness, she still had to live, and make choices, and she had done so. She did not regret it, though only a few months earlier she had believed that she would live her entire life as a celibate Shaker. How quickly the plague had changed everything.

She placed her hands on the wheel. The top was level with her eyes. Each spoke stuck out beyond the rim, but it was hard to turn. Maybe it would work better once they were moving.

Three walls of the pilothouse were double-hung windows pulled down from the top so a breeze blew through the room. The rear of the pilothouse was a wall of shelves and drawers made of various polished woods. Outside, almost like a vine that had attached itself to every straight edge, curling woodwork shaded the tops of the window. The oak floor was burnished honey-gold; the walls were knotty pine. The ceiling, of white beaded boards, was ten feet high. Several easy chairs upholstered in fine, flowered fabric were grouped around a large wooden table. A few books rested on the shelves. She walked over and looked at them. The covers were muted red, blue, and green. But they had no titles. She picked one up and leafed through it. The pages were blank.

One of the unfinished details.

Did I do this? she mused. Wonderingly, she touched the controls. She looked out over the hundreds of people on the rafts. Surely one of them— perhaps whoever had brought it these few miles below Cincinnati—would know better than she did how to pilot this thing. Yet she itched to master it.

Next to her shoulder, hanging from the ceiling, was the end of a black tube clearly meant for speaking. She picked it up and said into it, "Hello?" She jumped as her voice was broadcast over the river; people on the rafts stopped what they were doing and glanced at the boat before continuing.

Well, she thought, returning it to its hook, *that's* useful!

What powered the boat? Paint, she recalled, remembering at least one of the screens that had flashed before her eyes—or had it been *within* her, somehow?—when she had accessed the plans. Paint that gathered solar energy, transmitted it to fine tubes running throughout the boat's inner structure, and turned water into steam. It was something old— steam power—combined with something new, nan. Some energy was also stored in the part of the boat's structure which was a fine foam. But how much *did* she know about what she had wrought in Cincinnati? And how much had she forgotten?

For a moment, that forgetting was a vast blue space, nothing more, intense and absolutely, overpoweringly blue, a wave of color that filled her and the world and then vanished, leaving everything as it was before.

Below her, on the river, rafters dismantled the rope webwork that moored them. Verity touched a bare plate in front of her and a screen blinked to life, filled with options. She took a deep breath, then smiled and touched it once again, as the power of *information* surged through her and she sequed through screen after screen.

A schematic of the *Queen* showed that it had room for about two thousand passengers, and a lot more if they doubled up, though she figured only about five hundred were on board.

She watched rafts drift off down the river, passengers cheering and waving. At last the river was clear, and she touched another button. She heard the loud clank of their anchor being raised, pushed back panic at the thought of falls and rapids and touched the button which said *power.*

A quiet shudder ran through the boat. Elated, she moved a large, heavy lever forward, and the boat moved into the current.

What else was there to do but *move,* down the Ohio River. She touched and touched the screen and brought to view a chart of the Ohio, on which the *Queen* was a blinking light just below Cincinnati. Yes, move. Past Louisville. Past Old Shawneetown. To Cairo, where a light kept everlasting vigil, at the place where the Ohio merged with the Mississippi, where the water below became fierce and wild and beckoning.

But as she held to the wheel, she watched the chart re-form, and re-form, and re-form yet again, obviously uncertain. It was as she'd feared—all the information about the river was probably pre-earthquake, which was when Cincinnati had become absolutely isolated.

It been a horrible morning so far. After making breakfast, Blaze lost his composure again, became fuddled and tired. She had tried to organize matters but that was like trying to change the course of a flood and she had been completely unsuccessful though at last they had all gotten food.

Keeping an eye on the river, she tried to figure out what to do. With one hand she rummaged through the cupboard beneath the window, just to the right of the wheel, and found, to her relief, some paper and a pencil. The tablet was partly used, the pencil had a tooth mark in it, and the eraser was just a nub.

The memory of the City had apparently been vast and quite precise.

She was startled to hear from deep in her mind a sarcastic laugh, and the voice could almost have come from outside, somewhere: *Now, dear, do you understand the necessity for* control?

"Leave me alone!" Verity shouted. She propped the tablet on the wheel and scribbled "ORGANIZATION OF MEAL CHORES." Right. First, who exactly was there to organize? They had to have names, and a home raft, instead of shifting from raft to raft, and then—

A thin, middle-aged man peered in the door. The top of his head was bald and his eyes were pale blue.

"Was someone bothering you?" he asked hesitantly.

Verity was annoyed when he walked right in and plopped down in one of the chairs. She had to concentrate! And she felt so . . . so *restless!* Her hands tingled and she put down her pencil and rubbed them together.

"No," she said. "Sorry. I just have so much *work* to do and I have no idea how to go about it."

"What do you have to do?" he asked, clearly puzzled. "It's an absolutely beautiful day. That's the problem—don't you see? This is not a day to be under a roof, away from the sun! It's glorious! When the sun is out, it's your duty to let it into your eyes. Then everything will straighten out; you'll be the very picture of good cheer. Certain biochemical reactions take place, you know." He rose and took her arm gently. "Do come outside and see it all. While standing in the glorious bright summer sun. The river. It flows all the way to Norleans. And the trees. The fields. More beautiful than I could ever have imagined. Tremendous to be out in the world again, after all that time." He gave her a helpless look. "However long it was."

She pulled her arm away from him. The sun was yet another problem. Too much exposure to the sun was dangerous.

Or at least, it was for Shakers, who forswore any sort of genetic manipulation to deal with skin cancer. But these people were different, she reminded herself. It was possible that their skin was completely resistant to cancer because of restorative genetic engineering which kept cells normal. She looked at her golden arms. Without a doubt she was different now. Her body had changed in bizarre and wrenching ways. A life free of fear of the sun? Was that possible? Maybe that was the least of what was possible now. Or the most benign.

Some barrier within her vanished and opened her to a world of beautiful, welcome sunlight.

"I can see it all from here," she said, with a little less irritation. "What are we going to have for lunch? Who is going to fix it? Where will it come from? Who will distribute it and how?"

"Ah," he said. He looked at what Verity had written and picked up the pencil. "Don't you know? We've thought of that of course. It definitely occurred to us after that rampage this morning; I guess we were too tired to consider it last night."

He found a blank page and sketched lines and connecting circles onto the pad. He started writing things in the circles, like "dining rafts 1–6" and "kitchen duty" and "gathering crew" and "initiators." He frowned, set the pencil down, and rummaged through several drawers. "There's one," he said, finally, and pulled a small black scroll of some thin sleek material from a drawer.

He unrolled it, and it stayed flat, about three by five inches. He said "Wake up!" and the thing began to glow. He pulled on the edges and stretched it a bit larger. "There!" he said. "Look. It's all been taken care of. Didn't you know?" He looked at her quizzically and she felt very strange indeed. Not only was she not in control; she was not needed at all, it seemed.

For the wakened light on what was now a screen had become several colors and imitated what he had begun except the lines were straighter and all appeared instantly. "Look," he said. "We all coded in early on." He picked up the scroll and squeezed a corner and another screen appeared. "Yes," he said. "See? Tod L. Michmaster, that's me. That's *me!*"

His voice was tinged with awe. He looked at Verity again. "Yes," he said, "it's really *me!*"

He tossed the scroll back into the drawer and wandered out the door. He spread his arms wide as if to embrace all that he saw as he stood in the sunlight. Over the murmur of the boat, the rush of the river, she heard him laugh and then begin to sob. He hugged himself and bent over, sobbing and laughing, then held onto the railing, wiped his eyes, and stared at the river.

Verity took the scroll out of the drawer. It was extraordinarily smooth and pleasing to her touch. Below his name was a list of things he was apparently to do. He was to activate the bilge pumps. He was to run a rather complex water purity check and adjust for microbes. Impurities. And plagues.

She laughed, shortly. Yes, and plagues. That would be interesting, wouldn't it? Well, that was him and he had a job to do, but would he do it? Had he? Who—or what—had decided this? Had thought swept over them all somehow at the same time?

Or . . . had it somehow come from her?

No. She thought not. She had been a part of the hive only briefly, and then had only . . .

What had she done? What?

To avoid that darkness, she picked up the scroll and touched a green light at the top right, which was blinking.

R.D. #47, the scroll read, and she was chilled to the bone.

R.D.? Of course. The chill turned to anger. Rose Durancy. I was number forty-seven. That's me! And what, really, did it matter?

She'd have to figure out how to tell it her name was Verity, that was all. And what will your last name be? She laughed aloud. She'd never had one!

Fine then. What were the chores of R.D. #47? She read, scrolling, while trying to keep an eye on the river,

1. ACCESS AREA 72 BY PRESSING TOP RIGHT CORNER TWICE AND USE TUTORIAL.

2. DISTRIBUTE ANTIBACTERIAL FOR DISHWASHING TO TRENT SAMSON AND JONAH PINETTI AT 1:00 P.M. AB IS IN PLASTIC POUCHES STORED IN #38. GIVE THEM EACH A BOX OF FIFTY; ONE POUCH PER TEN GALLONS OF WATER. THEY WILL MEET YOU AT THE CABIN DOOR.

3. MEET LATER THIS EVENING WITH . . . *there was a blank, ha! thought Verity, not decided yet?* TO CONSIDER PROS AND CONS OF ACTIVATING RECYCLER. SEE PAGE 1425 FOR PROS AND CONS.

4. WALK FOR AT LEAST ONE HOUR AROUND DECK AS YOU ARE PREGNANT AND RENEW DAILY ANTI-NAUSEA AND VITAMIN PATCH #7 LABELED PRENATAL IN CUPBOARD #35 . . .

"What?" she shouted.

YOU ARE PREGNANT, repeated the scroll, then said, NORLEANS OR BUST! HAVE A LOVELY DAY.

It blanked, then lit again.

DO YOU WISH TO KNOW IF IT IS A BOY OR A GIRL?

"Not . . . just . . . yet," she muttered.

"Who are you talking to?"

She turned and saw Blaze. He wore a white T-shirt and tight black pants and was barefoot. His red hair, which Sare had usually cut, had grown shaggy almost to his shoulders, and curled and caught the sunlight. His beard was red-gold. A cut over his left cheekbone was healing. He looked much better than he had earlier this morning.

"This!" she said, and picked up the scroll from the table. It was not much thicker than a piece of paper. It lit again when she touched it. "It says I'm pregnant."

"Well," said Blaze calmly, after a short pause, "is that possible?"

She put her hands in her pockets. "Yes," she said, "it's *possible,* but it just seems unlikely."

"Oh," he said. He stepped in out of the sun and said again "Oh."

"Sphere," she said. "The father would be Sphere."

Blaze took a deep breath. "I always thought—" She saw tears glimmer in his eyes before he blinked them away.

"I know what you thought," she said. "I thought the same thing."

He sat on one of the chairs. "I guess—well it's strange." He frowned. "It's hard to say when I thought that it might even be possible. That we might—" He stopped and said nothing.

"Make love," she said. "That's one way to say it. And we couldn't. We weren't allowed. Remember how mad John was when we stayed in the Dayton Library? It was because he thought we *had."*

"Oh, Verity." He stood, walked over to her, and took her hand. He asked quietly, "Are you happy? Are you excited?"

"I don't know," she said. "I just found out. It's very strange."

For a while then they were silent, and the river enfolded them, entranced them, the green and winding corridor lined with forest from which large birds rose on wide dark wings, while small rafts slipped through patches of sunlight and shade downriver.

Four

◯◯◯◯◯◯◯◯◯◯◯◯◯◯◯◯◯

Lost World Blues

Indiana on the north shore (or more properly west, since the Ohio had taken a turn to the south) was a land of low, green hills. Innumerable tiny creeks fed the Ohio and glinted through the Kentucky forest in the distance. Sand and gravel bars ran alongside for stretches and after several hours of piloting Verity's back and shoulders were stiff from tension. She moved cautiously, as slowly as possible. There were no proper charts, apparently, and she knew from some of the older charts that there had been a lot of dams on the Ohio before the earthquake. Most had been low, locking dams. But she doubted if any were attended now. From time to time they passed channel markers—nuns, some were called, a reference screen told her, but they might be out in a vast wide wash and so far had meant nothing. She'd managed to thread the boat through the massive concrete pillars of a train bridge, barely breathing the entire time. When they anchored the second night, a green light blinked in the distance and she did not know what it meant, what place in the river it marked, though she had an old running chart called Character and Period of Light. It listed things like "People Moored Barge lights 2F.W 494.0 mi. from Pittsburgh. Gunpowder Light Gp Fl.W., 4 sec., 2 flashes."

On the evening of the third day, as the hubbub of dinner subsided, Verity searched for Blaze. She realized that she hadn't seen him in many hours. He was not in his room, and she was growing panicky when she heard the tones of a piano, so faint that they might be coming from another age. The age when showboats plied the Ohio, the Tennessee, the Green rivers, and all their tiny tributaries.

Drawn by the sound, she found herself in a short corridor which led to an arch of large, welcoming doors.

Next to them was a blank space, which she touched. As she expected, a poster appeared: BLOOMER GIRLS, GOOD FAMILY FUN—TUESDAY THROUGH THURSDAY NIGHTS, 8 P.M. After it vanished she touched it again, and this time saw a poster for TEN NIGHTS IN A BARROOM.

Next to the poster a sign hung over the corridor—FINE CHINA AND OTHER GIFTS.

Opening the double doors, she stood for a moment at the end of a long aisle that followed the curve of the hull, descending gently and rising toward the large stage at the other end.

An enormous room of empty velvet seats waited; a wine-colored curtain was drawn back on both sides and on the stage were the dark shapes of some set, behind the piano. On either side were balconies and several private booths rising above the stage.

Blaze was tiny on the faraway stage. Now that she could hear his music better, it was disturbing—halting and tortured. Mournful, like a cry. She hurried down the aisle but he did not seem to notice her; she climbed the steps at the side of the stage and stood next to him.

His face was as unearthly white as porcelain, but maybe that was because of the floodlight which bathed him. His shirt was patched with sweat, and sweat dripped from his forehead onto the keys, though it was cool in the auditorium. As his long fingers spanned the keys, he sang,

> And I'm goin' to the river, take my boat and float,
> And if my underworld mama quit me I'm gonna cut my throat
> And it's, oh, I ain't gon do it no more
> And it's, oh, I ain't gon do it no more
> The last time I drank your whiskey, Mama,
> It made my belly sore.

The song from Cincinnati.

He bent over the keys and pounded them in a frenzy, eliciting curious chords, and his fingers brushed the black keys or played two notes right next to each other, fleetingly. She was afraid to interrupt him.

When he finally turned his head and saw her, his eyes were blank for an awful long moment, as he continued to play and sing, and then his hands crashed down on the keys. The harsh sound echoed in the vast hall.

"Verity?" he whispered. He looked around. "Where am I? I was dreaming . . . dreaming . . . oh, Verity, you don't know what it's like to be dead. Where's Mother Ann? I kept looking for her, everywhere. . . ."

Still sitting, he grabbed her waist with both arms and held her tight, putting his head against her stomach. She stroked his head, wondering if this was what it would be like to have a child. He seemed so helpless, so lost. He shook for a few seconds with sobs.

"There was a man I met in Cincinnati," he said, his voice muffled against her shirt. "Kid Cole was his name. He was black, and thin. He was standing next to a big fountain of a woman and was playing a guitar and singing this song. I was looking all over for you, Verity, and couldn't find you, but then I kept forgetting what I was doing and everything was so . . . so *jumbled,* everything I saw and heard and felt, and then I heard this *music,* and I made him sing it *again* and *again* and *again* because when I listened, and sang with him, the awful sickness left me, I feel sick all over sometimes, and I remembered my name. You don't know how awful it is not to even be able to remember your *name."*

"I'm sorry, Blaze," she said, in a low voice, and hugged him, and rubbed his back, shocked to realize that he didn't even remember that she had been there with him. His trembling slowed, and his breathing became more normal. Finally he loosened his arms and looked up at her.

She sat next to him on the bench and their shoulders touched.

"Play it again, Blaze," she said, and he did, and his voice was stronger this time, and almost stilled the terror in her heart.

On the fourth morning they saw a town on a long straight stretch of river that was unlike those they had been passing.

This town had been partially drowned.

The water of the Ohio was fairly clear, and people knelt on the edge of their rafts and stared into it. A hush fell over the entourage, so that all was birdcalls in the forest, a steady insect buzz that rose and fell, the slip and slosh of water lapping the two-lane road that ran down the northwest bank and vanished into downtown.

Verity relinquished the piloting to Blaze. She stood on one of the high decks and glimpsed a cross caught in wavery parallax a moment before the *Queen* drifted over it with a hesitation—slight, yet Verity knew it was because the steeple was being torn from the waterlogged church.

An old woman came and stood next to Verity; gripped the rail with thin, withered hands. Her eyes were large and serene, delphinium blue; the skin on her face was translucent and networked with fine lines. Her hair was long, white, and rather stiff-looking.

"Now there's Rising Sun for you," she said, her voice a harsh whisper. "What a sight. They were a stubborn lot but it suited them. Worked out well, I guess, except for the earthquake that got them drowned."

"What worked out well?" asked Verity.

The woman continued gazing outward as they drifted across what looked like an industrial section of town, the peaked roofs of houses giving way to blunt flat roofs of warehouses and malls, all crumpled and un-even and often not there at all, revealing metal and concrete lineaments.

"The Preservation Federation," said the woman. "These folks out in the country were mad as hell. Said they wouldn't—now, how did my old man say it? 'We won't stand for none of this goddamned nanotechnol-ogy stuff being shoved down our throats!' Stood up there on Sunday in the pulpit and took the Name of the Lord in vain and what do you know—the whole congregation stood and cheered. I guess," she said, "that was a hell of a long time ago."

PF blinked in the upper right quadrant of Verity's vision, and a man's inflectionless voice began, *When Cincinnati voted to convert, the coun-tryside was already in disarray. Some looked upon conversion as a defen-sive gesture—*

"Stop!" yelled Verity, holding her head in her hands. Her shout rang out across the quiet river. The voice stopped. She took a deep breath and blinked.

"I assume you're not talking to me," said the old woman. "It's them voices buzzing like flies around dead meat. Well, I wouldn't listen to any of *them*"—she gestured downward with her thumb extended from her fist—"not my neighbors, not my dull, scared friends, and especially not my God-infested father. Look over there!"

Verity looked, and saw, mingled with the forest that was growing into the part of the town still on land, the very tip of a metal tower.

"W-G-O-D," said the woman, with wonder in her voice. "That's it. His tower. Yes—see the bones of that old shopping center? Westgate Mall, it was. Low, through the trees. His station was there; you could go and watch him rant through the plate glass. He was quite a terror in his day, you know. Soaked up money from all around. Bags of envelopes, all full of money—how he'd laugh with glee when the mail came! He was completely astonished I think. I sure was. He thought that mother would stop treating him like an old crackpot but she didn't, just said there were a lot more idiots in the world than she'd ever suspected. He bought him-self a big leather chair and put it in the station so he could froth at the mouth in comfort but I'm telling you he used just about every cent of that money for the Cause. It really hurt him when radio went. But dur-ing the years when it faded—the end of the world, you know; I guess he and that Bible were right, in a way—he gathered quite a different little town here. Why, if he told his disciples they were to walk around on their hands all day they'd do it and be glad. Strangest thing, I thought, then look what happened to me in Cincinnati. But you know, I can't really say as I'm sorry. No, I left the whole backward crew and went off to the big city. Now look! They're all dead, and I'm still alive! I might be a little daft, but then, I always was." Her raucous laugh shook her frail body.

"The only thing is," she said in a quieter voice, "I do wonder what year it is. Now. And how long they've been drowned. Probably all the people I knew were long dead by the time of the earthquake anyway. He is, I'm sure; more irony. I've got everlasting life, or something like it, and he's rotted away in the ground. Except maybe my sister's children. They might have made it. Maybe they got away. Look. It's the park. Nice library in the west corner, before he yanked most of the books."

Verity saw tears in the woman's brilliant blue eyes before she closed them and bowed her head.

Later in the afternoon Verity saw, a quarter mile away when they rounded a bend, Lock and Dam 33.

The words were painted in large white letters across the top, but it slanted at about a thirty-degree angle and was broken in places. The water ran fast and they were pulled to the west. Verity's mind watched as her hands pulled levers, so quickly she did not even notice a decision, but then she stopped, afraid that if she did manage to pull the boat to one side it might have worse consequences than if she did nothing. She stood helpless in the high pilothouse, clenching the wheel with both hands to hold it steady as the *Queen* slipped down a fast-moving incline. The dam was behind them before Verity could even think about it but afterward she took great gulps of air and held the wheel tight to stop her hands from trembling.

That evening, Verity stood on the texas deck and looked out over her kingdom. She knew it was the texas because she had studied a plan of the boat.

Above the main deck, supported by giant struts, was the boiler deck, with a wide ornate promenade down the center, carpeted and lit with chandeliers, with staterooms on both sides. The next layer was the hurricane deck, and, slightly above that, a smaller structure called the texas deck, upon which rested the texas. There was a story that staterooms were called staterooms because there was one for each state on one of the original riverboats—except they ran out of rooms before they got to texas. So the structure up top got that honor.

On top of the texas was the pilothouse, like a rectangular park gazebo. Verity was feeling more and more at home on the boat—even proprietary.

Over the course of the day everyone had responded to the directions on their little scrolls with an alacrity that troubled Verity. She had pecked in suggestions with the tiny keypads which became visible if one touched the upper left corner, about what they would make in the main galley to augment their meal, and what time they would stop. Even though that cooperativeness had been essential to decentralizing the food supply and distributing it among the rafts—now they all had their own chicken medium—she was troubled by it. She noticed some of them talking to their scrolls, and when she asked one man what he was doing he looked surprised. "Training it," he said.

The tang of water was in the air. Dusk deepened, and a thousand or so fires flickered around her—*one thousand three hundred and twenty-six*—

"Oh, what do I care!" she said impatiently and continued to gaze over her minions. Or dependents. Or companions. Or whatever they were. Half of them dead now, at least, of those who had so gaily boarded vessels on the Cincinnati wharfs. Dead for good. Except—

Of course their information was all stored in Cincinnati. And those were the kind of people who would populate the Earth now, apparently. And she was one of them, too.

And her child, in whose reality it was difficult to believe. Except that when she forgot to change her patch she had been so sick yesterday.

About six rafts over, eleven men and women sat in a circle, naked, and quiet as the raft bobbed on the smooth river. Verity thought their eyes were all closed but she couldn't be sure. It was a bit chilly for that sort of thing. Then one of them opened her mouth and spoke but Verity couldn't hear what she said. When she was finished, no one gave any sign that they had heard anything. Verity sighed.

They seemed to have settled into their routine easily enough, now that they had the scrolls. They gathered on the *Queen* for breakfast and dinner, though many preferred fishing and cooking for themselves on the rafts. Blaze fished for several hours a day from one of the rafts. They seemed to enjoy socializing among the rafts, and boarded the *Queen* freely whenever they pleased. Verity gave them a big head start in the mornings, and generally found them tied up in a cove somewhere around four in the afternoon, early enough to finish dinner by dark. At night they danced on their rafts, and sang. For the most part. Of course, it was to be expected that most of them were more addled than peahens.

On another raft, just below her, three girls played as a man washed dishes. "Stay away from that fire!" he warned.

"You be the Bee," said one girl and another replied "No, *you* be the Bee!" and they began shoving one another and the man jumped up from his dishes and said "Stop that now, how about a story?" and they quieted and sat. He did too. The girls stared at him. He didn't say anything for a long time.

"Tell us!" said the smallest one finally.

"I . . . don't know," he said, and his voice was troubled. "I was going to tell you some sort of story about the hole-in-the-rock pirates further down the river but . . ."

The oldest girl took his hand. "Tell us a different one then," she said. "We don't care."

After a moment, he began.

"Once upon a time three little girls and their mommy and daddy lived in a tall, tall tower in Cincinnati.

"Their mommy was a nanotechnologist who had moved to Cincinnati from Los Angeles during the First Wave. Their daddy was a carpenter who used to build houses and then went to one of their new strange colleges for a long time and now was in charge of maintenance in one of the towers. It was a tower called Wild Rose. The man and the woman saw each other for the first time during the monthly Wild Rose Homeowners' meeting. The homeowners liked to rake the man over the coals for any little thing that was not perfect with their unit. He was used to it but in the last month many had complained of contradictory news reports—they got these by touching their hands to the interstice, mind you—and that concerned him more than too few coffee cups in cupboard number twenty-two. Besides, they were blaming—

"—me. They were blaming me and saying I wasn't mixing the news packet properly—you kneaded the news up, inside its plastic bag, and the heat activated it, and then you broke the seal by touching a certain place and only certified people had the receptors to open the news and then you poured it into the news receptacle and it flowed up the interstice so you see that there wasn't much I could do wrong, but of course someone could possibly add misinformation if they knew how to get around the failsafes, or if they somehow copied my receptors. All kinds of strange crimes were possible, and without broadcasting we were all frantic for news. Anyway I had requested that one of the technologists attend the meeting mainly so that the blame could be shifted to where it belonged, the fact that the metapheromone packages were shipped all the way from Denver and I felt as if the quality assurance checks were not being performed correctly. At least that was my theory."

"You?" asked the middle girl. "You were the man? The daddy?"

"Yes," he said, a bit of a surprise in his voice. "I guess so. I mean, I didn't know that when the story started."

"Our daddy?" asked the youngest.

"Well . . ." He blinked and looked around at them. "That doesn't seem too possible does it? And what makes you think you're sisters?"

"We are," they said indignantly, all at the same time. "And furthermore," said the oldest, who had short red hair that seemed aflame in the firelight, "it would be easy enough to do a test, and . . ."

"All right, all right," said the man, and his voice sounded weary. "So then where's this woman in the story, your mother I suppose? I mean it sounds like a fairy tale to me. I might as well be telling a goddamned fairy tale! Where did you kids come from anyway?"

He stood up and looked around wildly. "Mary Ann! Mary *Ann!*" he shouted. "It's Dan! I'm here!"

"Daddy, sit down," said the little one. Her hair was pulled into braids, which were coming undone. They all wore shorts and T-shirts and no shoes.

"Well then where's your mother?" he asked, sobbing, and the redhead hugged him, and then the other two, and they stood on the gently bobbing raft until he was quiet.

"What will I do with all of you?" Verity wondered aloud as she watched. What stories were unfolding on the other rafts? Up on the top deck had the little story group gathered yet? Verity hadn't done much work all day, really; she'd only *felt,* but what she had felt, she now realized, had left her chest aching from muscles that had been constricted and tense since waking.

"Who put you in charge, anyway?" asked a quiet voice next to her.

"Where have you been all day, Blaze?"

He leaned on the railing, and his face was pale in the light of the rising moon, and his beard golden. "Oh, here and there. Everywhere. Fishing. Like that catfish you had for dinner?"

"Are you going to grow that very long?" asked Verity, and touched his beard. It was crinkly beneath her fingers. She gave it a slight yank and Blaze smiled though she couldn't really see his mouth. She was happy. He looked normal tonight, though tired, as if he had wrestled all day to just be Blaze.

"Maybe," he said. He pulled a white cylinder from his pocket and lit it with a match which he struck on the railing.

"A cigarette!" said Verity. "Where did you find that?"

"Cabinet number fourteen-B in Memphis stateroom. My room, in fact. Pretty nice." He took a puff.

"Let me try," said Verity.

"NO SMOKING PLEASE," said a voice in her pocket and she jumped. "YOU'RE PREGNANT AND WE ARE NOT CERTAIN THAT THE DETOX NAN IS FUNCTIONING. DO YOU WANT TO KNOW YET IF IT'S A BOY OR A GIRL?"

"How do you shut these things off?" asked Verity.

"Why don't you want to know?" asked Blaze.

"I just don't," she said, feeling cross.

"You seem awfully young to have a baby. You were only eighteen last January 31st."

"How do you know?" asked Verity, staring at him. She had never known her birthday. "I thought I was seventeen."

Blaze shrugged. "The scroll said so."

"How can *you* access information about *me?*" she asked. She pulled out the scroll and puzzled over it. "YOU DIDN'T PUT ON YOUR VITAMIN PATCH TODAY," it admonished. She stuffed it back in her pocket. "Besides, what does it matter? My name is Rose. Rose Durancy.

We're *all* Rose Durancy. For all I know I'll meet several of me on this trip. Little, big, old, young. I saw—I saw—in the hive—" She started to gasp, remembering small faces, smashed against a membrane—

Blaze's arm came around her and she leaned into him. "You were holding the scroll while you napped before supper. That's all. Remember? You fell asleep on the deck chair and I wheeled you into a spot that was still sunny and it came on."

"It's a girl," she said. "I think I can only have girls."

"Girls are nice," he said.

"You don't care?" she asked, staring out at the water. "I mean about Sphere . . ."

"I care about Sphere," said Blaze, his voice quiet. She looked at him, but he gazed out over the water. He took another puff from his cigarette and a brief look of astonishment passed over his face as the butt disintegrated. He said, "I guess it was finished."

He took a deep breath and turned to her. "What I mean to say, Verity, is that I care about Sphere, and I care about you. I know what I'm *supposed* to be feeling—all those things that people in books used to feel, right? Jealousy, anger, rage. Well. I don't. There seems to be—I don't know—lots of *space* around my feelings. They come from me. What there are of them. They don't come from outside me, like John's did, all those rules he had to make himself feel safe. I don't know. Maybe that means that I don't—don't love you?" His voice vanished into a whisper as he looked squarely into Verity's eyes.

"Maybe it means that you do," she said.

"Well I do," he said roughly, and stalked off down the deck. "I *do!*" he yelled back over his shoulder.

Verity took a few steps to follow him; then someone pulled on her shirt and she turned.

It was a boy, about six, thin, with light brown hair falling across his eyes. "Hurry," he said. "We need help."

As Verity jumped from raft to raft, following the young boy, she apologized to the people she encountered and sometimes stepped on. The boy ran right through the middle of the circle of naked people without batting an eye and neither, she noticed, did they. Once her foot slipped and she fell into the river but a woman reached down and pulled her out immediately, with surprising strength. Dripping and cold, Verity hurried on, across rafts where people spoke in low murmurs or slept, sprawled on the rough wood, oblivious.

"There!" shouted the boy, after pausing to take his bearings. Verity heard a man swearing, and when she stepped onto the raft where the boy was heading the man grabbed her roughly.

"Holy Queen, you're here at last!"

Well, Blaze, she thought, *someone* appointed me.

"I'm not the Queen anymore," she said. "I gave it up."

"Then we're alone," the man whispered under his breath, and Verity heard his tone as one of terror. Anger, or something deeper, swept over his face, making it beastlike; his eyes bulged and his mouth twisted. With a roar, he grabbed Verity's shoulders and began shaking her, hard; her head whipped back and forth dizzyingly. The boy set upon him like a small tornado of swirling fists, and then he let go and stepped back, panting.

Verity stumbled, and regained her balance. Anger surged through her. The man turned to the wigwam and grabbed one of the poles; it promptly collapsed, bringing two women and one man crawling out from under it.

"Then who is?" yelled the man. "Who is the Queen? Who brought us to this queenforsaken place?" He thrust his hands beneath Verity's eyes. She caught a glimmer of apology mixed with the desperation in his eyes. "I *need* it. I can't stay here! When do we get to the next City?"

Verity could see that his face was covered with sweat, though the night was chilly, and was frightened.

The pheromones.

His receptors were still active, of course, and he was addicted.

They all were.

What about the rest of them? She gazed out over the myriad rafts, to the *Queen,* with a few windows still alight.

How many? Thousands. Thousands of crazed addicts in withdrawal.

"Hey!" yelled one of the women, as the man kicked a bundle into the water as if it were a football. "Those were my clothes! I just got them this morning!"

"There's more where they came from, isn't that right, Miss Queen Bee?" His face was as ugly as his voice. "We can just make them, right, in a big clothes vat. Sure. I used to work in a clothing store. Yeah. Pissed me off. All those picky people—" His voice went mincing and high. " 'Oh, send it back. I *told* you no trim on the collar.' I didn't *want* these goddamned receptors. I just got *caught,* and then it was too late. But I've got 'em now, all right. Hey, how about a whole new *body* while you're at it? And don't forget the tattoo. It's the Mars ship. They said I didn't make the grade—who are *they* to say? *They* go around enhancing anyone they please—anyone willing to kiss their ass, which I wasn't—but I'm just not Mars material. Just because I refused the rehab nans in prison. Perfectly legal. Then they give me drone punishment by making me work in that stupid place—"

Verity's heart beat hard. She shoved her hands into her wet pockets, thinking. The Norleans Plague was no substitute for the pheromonal input these people were used to, though it had been strong enough to impel them to leave. Maybe this man hadn't had a full dose, or something. He certainly didn't have a full deck, she thought, but then who did, here? Certainly not her.

He grabbed Verity's arm, hard, and yanked her around. "Listen to me!" he yelled. "You're not paying attention!"

"Let go!" she yelled back and kicked him in the shin. He staggered backward.

"You—" he choked, bent over, then raised his arm to hit her.

The other four on the raft jumped on him and wrestled him down. His head hit the raft with a thump and he went limp.

One of the women sat next to him, looking dazed. The other woman stood and said, "What a jerk. Are you all right, honey?"

Verity shrugged her shoulders. "I guess. How do you feel?"

"Not like him, I guarandangtee it," she said. "But I don't know. Maybe I will. Hey, if you're the Queen, when are we going to get to Norleans? Will it take long?" Her dark eyes glowed in the firelight. She started to sing, "Some rows up, but we floats down—"

"We passed right over the top of Rising Sun this morning, in case you didn't notice," said the other man, rubbing his hands together nervously. "And I could use a little Burroughs at this point myself. I'd go back to Cincinnati if I didn't want to see Norleans so bad."

"Burroughs!" said the other woman, glancing up from the downed man. "You would."

The man laughed and crawled inside the wigwam. One side of it went up. "Help me straighten this out," he said, his voice muffled by canvas.

"Do you know him?" asked Verity, indicating the former criminal, who was stirring groggily.

"He's my brother," said the woman sitting next to him. "At least I think he is. I'm not sure why."

"Does he *look* like your brother?"

"Well, no," she said. "The last I remember of my brother he was about eighteen. He wasn't this old. He was a smart kid. And a smartass. Mom kicked him out about that time."

"I'm not old," the man protested, sitting up and rubbing his head. "And I'm not your brother. *My* sister always took my side. And *she's* not the Queen. I guess there's nothing anyone can do. I *am* going back."

Without another word he rolled into the river, surfaced, and swam for shore.

"Jake!" yelled the woman.

"Let him go," said the other man from the door of the wigwam, which he had resurrected. "I'm exhausted. Let's get some sleep. I've got a feeling it will take longer than you think to get to Norleans."

"Couldn't take more than a few weeks," said the woman.

The other woman stared after Jake. Verity wasn't sure what she should do if she dove into the river and tried to follow. Prevent her, she decided, but wasn't really sure why. The only real reason was that they were about sixty miles from Cincinnati. A pretty long walk. And Jake, if he got there, might not like what he found. If he could get inside at all.

Verity was shivering. "Sorry I couldn't help," she said, and turned to go back to the boat.

Verity climbed the ladder to the boiler deck with her last ounce of strength. Her entire body ached. She was deeply disoriented. So much had happened in the past few months. Her whole world had changed. And what had she done? Her conceit had been utterly ridiculous. She couldn't possibly help these people. The plague she had given them wasn't freedom, as she had believed, freedom from the tyranny of the City. It was confusion, dissolution, death. They would die on the river, from blundering like children into some hazard, by killing one another, or from lack of metapheromones. They were as much at a loss as she was, perhaps even more so.

She realized that she was gripping her scroll tightly as these feelings and thoughts swept through her. She wished she could squeeze it to splinters. She hated it and its ridiculous promise of control and order. Order could not come from one as helpless and ignorant as she. And she didn't want to control. She was utterly exhausted, her spirit as dark as the night between the stars.

Dew damped the railing on which she set the scroll. Night fires flickered and stories, she knew, were beginning, released from depths as distant as the secret to her own identity, but she did not want to hear them tonight.

As she turned to find a place to sleep, she shoved the scroll. It fell into the river without a sound.

Five

◯◯◯◇◯◇◯◇◯◇◯◇◯◇◯◯◯

Jack O' Diamonds and Lightnin' Lil

Around three in the afternoon of the next day the riverboat chugged along an Ohio River relaxed and broad.

For the moment.

Verity, doing her best to spot upcoming shoals, was frazzled and worn. She still didn't have much control over the huge boat. It was difficult to turn the big wheel, yet easy to overcorrect so the entire boat swung sideways in the river. Her arms ached. Blaze had tried to relieve her but she refused to leave so finally he told her that there was a lot to do and left.

She was finding more and more moments when she longed to be lying on her back on one of the rough rafts just seeing clouds drift past above, crawling into the wigwam for a lazy nap during the time of high sun, watching for that one particular light, which would be the freedom of Cairo . . .

She blinked. The vision thinned and instead she saw a split in the river ahead as it coursed around both sides of what looked like an island.

She hurriedly touched the cool chart screen, running her finger up and down it as she had found that the river map rushed along beneath her finger as she did so. But where were they? She ran her finger above the words atop the screen and touched FIX and a list of coordinates came onscreen, useless to her, and then she touched FIX again and there they were—the *Queen,* blinking in the river above the Falls of Louisville. Could that be true?

She felt terrific panic for a moment and then the map relented and said, "Shifted by earthquake, bear port around Gambler's Isle, more formally the Louisville Kentucky Gambling Annex Island." So what? Was this information any more current?

She took the right channel. A narrow spit of sand backed by thick green woods widened as they neared it. A bit to the south on the map was the legend LOUISVILLE DROWNED, written in a large curve over a five-mile circumference.

The island increased slightly in elevation. A few houses were scattered among the trees and then she saw a large stone landing rushing toward her—how fast? Fast enough!

Graceful mature trees shaded a hard-top road that led away from the landing. A large sign arched over the road: GAMBLING FOR LIFE STOP HERE!

"DO NOT, I REPEAT, DO NOT SET FOOT ON LAND UNTIL WE ASCERTAIN NONTOXICITY," hollered Verity into the mouthpiece of her speaking tube, then saw that she had got the one labeled ENGINE ROOM, not the one that would blare out over the speakers on top of the boat. She grabbed the other one and repeated her message, but no one heeded her. She wasn't sure what she meant by nontoxicity; just Danger, damn it! Do as I say! "I AM THE CAPTAIN. I COMMAND YOU TO BYPASS THIS ISLAND!"

But she watched with resignation the rafts sweep past the landing. Quite skillfully the pilots of the tiny crafts pulled on their sweeps and soon an entire flotilla was beached on a long sandy shore where the tattered remains of blue-striped cabanas hung still in the breezeless hot afternoon.

Blaze clomped up the stairs. "Are you going to stop, Verity?" he asked. There was excitement in his voice. "Look!"

Exasperated, Verity shaded her eyes and saw exactly what he wanted to stop for.

Amid small quaint shops, in a central park, grazed a herd of horses of ethereal beauty. Delicate yet strong, perfectly proportioned and a bit larger than the Shaker Hill horses, they stopped grazing and looked at the river, ears pricking forward, then took flight and seemed to vanish instantly though she could still hear the echo of their hooves clattering over ever-farther streets. She saw no people.

"Blaze," she said, but he was gone. Verity saw him emerge on the boiler deck below her. He turned and with broad emphatic swings of his arm motioned her closer to the landing. He lifted one heavy coil of rope to a shoulder and she saw that he was ready to jump. He seemed completely energized by the sight of the horses. That was a good sign.

"It's not as easy as you think," she muttered, and began pushing various levers experimentally, hoping she wouldn't smash the boat, then saw that the side of the landing was baffled.

By now the beach was covered with rafts. People were tearing off their clothes and diving into the river, whooping and laughing.

It *was* hot. Verity lifted her hair from her neck for an instant, then grabbed the wheel with both hands. Angling left, she was relieved to see Blaze complete his leap and land gracefully on the flat concrete landing, and quickly pull the rope through the metal rings bolted to it. He then ran to the back of the boat, yelling, and a rope come snaking across the widening slice of river as the end of the boat kept going, angling out into the river. Then she felt it catch. The gap lessened and the boat stilled as she cut the power.

She saw a small flood of people, an exodus from the riverboat in a happy laughing stream. Why was she not as carefree? Weren't they worried about who they might meet, what might happen to them here?

She didn't really want to go ashore. She enviously watched the rafters splashing in the river. They wouldn't be going anywhere soon.

She went to the lowest deck, back by the paddlewheel, and undressed.

Her dive was long and flat in case the water was shallow. The cold clear water was a welcome shock, tingling along her body as she swept beneath the surface of the river before emerging and taking a gulp of air. It cleared her head. She was just Verity, a young woman, possibly a month or so pregnant, swimming in a clear, cool river in early summer while big white clouds drifted in a clear blue sky. A fish jumped nearby, slapping the water. A flock of sparrows swooped through the sky, elongating and contracting as if one organism, then settled in a white-barked sycamore on the other shore. She remembered some information she had about flocking behavior and thought of the scrolls they all had. *Did* have; she didn't miss hers. But could there be some sort of connection?

Cool at last, she climbed back on the boat.

She dried herself with her shirt and dressed quickly, more relaxed, and curious about what might be happening in the town. She walked down the gangway onto the landing.

She passed through a block of warehouses with dirty windows, trying a door or two but they were locked, though it would be easy business to break into them. Needed supplies might be inside, and at Shaker Hill she had grown up used to scavenging from the deserted towns nearby. All of them had been deserted, and this island seemed to have no residents either. But what do we need? she wondered. They were moving so fast! They really needed to stop for a day, take stock, organize. Maybe this would be a good place to do so.

She walked farther and found herself on Main Street, which was the typical deserted avenue of so many small towns near Miamisburg— small, empty shops—and was dunned by a rain of whispers.

They stopped when she did, but resumed when she stepped forward:

eager voices, happy voices. "Win big at Jimmy's Fifth Street Arcade. Slot machines receptor-friendly. Megadose hard-to-find custom-designed Old Louisville and a thousand other megs to choose from. Permanent or temporary, your choice."

"Horses professionally handicapped by the finest nangineers at Churchill Downs all bets fair wins redeemable onboard or portable seconds left hurry races starting on the hour on three fast tracks real jockeys. Take Elm Street south."

She heard the blare of distant trumpets, and knew where Blaze had headed.

She continued to walk into the heart of town, though. Blaze was still disturbingly unable to speak at times. He would seem to not remember her. He wanted to know where Russ was, or, if he remembered Shaker Hill, he wondered who was taking care of the horses. Sometimes he babbled about Shaker Hill not being real, because there was no Heaven and there were no angels and no Mother Ann.

But he didn't have the plague. He was a lot more competent and able to look after himself than the plagues rafters, who were also dazed after their strange lives in Cincinnati.

It looked as if Jimmy's Arcade was already full of rafters. A large brilliantly lit arch proclaimed the address, and mechanical pings and whirrs issued forth along with smooth high tones constantly cut short. Verity felt as if they shouldn't go inside but wasn't really sure why; her faint panic might merely be the vestiges of John's blue voice gravely intoning the Shaker philosophy concerning gambling.

She stepped inside cautiously.

Every booth had a rafter leaning over it in intense concentration. The levers they kept pulling were iridescent, like rainbows; Verity suspected immediately that they meshed with the receptors in their hands, perhaps providing some sort of relief from the torment they'd been feeling.

At what cost? One young man reeled toward her, eyes vacant, a silly grin on his face, then saw and avoided her at the last instant, staggering to one side.

Alarmed, she took another step and someone grabbed her arm.

It was a goofy, leering clown, about seven feet tall, loose-jointed and wavery as if he were made of rubber.

His face was a narrow oval, stark white with bursts of blue and yellow lines around his eyes, which looked vacant and hungry beneath their grinning grimace. He yanked again and Verity yanked back but his grip was strong.

He wore a pointed yellow hat covered with large blue polka dots; it rested on wild orange hair fluffed out on both sides of his head. A wide white collar encircled his neck like a flower and his suit was black on one side and white on the other, filled with tiny designs which appeared and vanished like faintly shimmering electrical etchings.

"You have to pay, miss," he said, his voice deep and menacing.

"With what?" she asked, truly curious.

His laugh was not friendly. "What do you care, gambler woman? Ah, yes," he said, as he grabbed her hand and squeezed it. "Cincinnati! Most valuable!" His eyes widened as he looked at her and said, "Especially you! You have a lot to lose. And a lot to win! You came here of your own free will. You could win big. You could win untold riches in Gambler's World. We have everything here. All the power and glory anyone could want."

"How did you get it?" she asked.

"From our customers, of course." He laughed again, and the sound was cold and unpleasant. "What you win, others lose. What's gambling without an edge? If there's nothing to lose it's not a gamble is it? And that's why you're here, gambling woman."

"That's not why *I'm* here. What *are* you, anyway?"

He shoved her away, still laughing. "Your mother teach you to be rude, missy?" She saw that his teeth were sharp and yellow, and he chewed something, then turned his head for a second and spit into a metal pot next to him. "Come back in when your gambling head is on straight," he commanded—it had the tone of a command. "You won't be disappointed." He grabbed the man behind her and Verity headed toward the door. "Don't worry, the machines will take their toll," he yelled at her over his shoulder. "Nothing is free on Gambling Island. And that's why you came. That's why you came . . . for a taste of *real* life."

She passed machines which were inscribed with ornately lettered legends on the top which glowed: LUST, RELIGIOUS FERVOR, SEVENTH CIRCLE, VENUS VELOCITY, SIX MINUTES TO LIVE, EVERLASTING LIFE, ENDLESS TORMENT, THE VANISHMENT OF NORLEANS, THIRD SURGE IN ACAPULCO . . . the list went on and on, a dizzying array which attracted and repelled Verity. Each booth had a line in front of it.

Everyone had to pay.

How?

They had nothing but their bare lives, and all their brains held. They had strange blood and bizarre hope; they dreamed of freedom and of a place as strange as Heaven, where all their dreams would come true.

Did these machines steal the chemical by-products of hope, or hope itself? The titles looked menacing.

Whatever it was, she didn't like it. This place was enlivened to the hilt.

She rushed away from the building on the cobblestone street, wondering how to get everyone out and back on the rafts, wondering how to suck the power from those machines.

And where was Blaze? Well, that should be easy enough. She knew he'd follow those horses anywhere.

She hurried up the cobblestones, following the signs that read CHURCHILL DOWNS, and turned onto Elm Street, which was lined with deserted houses with broken windows. An empty gondola stopped next to her and asked "Churchill, miss?" She sighed, then got in. "Hurry," she said and it did, so that the wind swept her hair back and she had to hold on to the bar in front of her and was exhilarated by speed. "Stop!" she yelled as they approached neat whitewashed stables and what she thought was the entrance to the racetrack where fluttered and snapped a thousand bright triangular flags but the gondola did not stop and she thought she heard it laugh but was not sure. She stood and prepared to jump onto the intensely green lawn they trundled across and had to grab the back of the seat as it did stop, abruptly, then rushed off just as she stepped clear.

She looked around but did not see Blaze, and the stables appeared empty.

She walked into a corridor below the bleachers.

To her right she saw tall boards flashing with names. STARLIGHT EXPRESS 2:1; CRAZY FOR YOU 4:3; EASY WINNER 3:0.

The vast hall was empty and no clown tried to pull her in.

She climbed stairs and emerged into thousands of rows of seats, like Riverfront Stadium. They were all empty. "Place your bets for the third race, ladies and gentlemen," she heard a voice say over the loudspeaker and the voice was Blaze's.

She looked up and saw him, tiny, in an open-air booth, looking out over the racetrack.

"Hurry up here, Verity," he said, his voice booming out. "The view is wonderful."

She ran up the long shallow steps, breathing hard, vastly annoyed. "We have to get out of here," she yelled. "Come on!"

"After the race," Blaze returned over the loudspeaker. "I want the fastest horse. Look! They're going to the gate! It's amazing! A board down there asked me if I wanted to go to the races and I said sure, and trumpets blew and the horses all came up here!"

Verity turned and saw a prancing line of riderless horses parading over the green lawn and entering small booths. She hurried up the last few steps and ran into the grandstand. "This is a really bad place, Blaze," she said. "We need to get everybody back on the rafts," but Blaze pushed a button in front of him and the gates flew open all at once.

"And they're off!" he announced over his microphone, his voice choking with excitement. "It's Starlight Express in the lead, followed by Harvest Moon, then Stewball, Rambler Gambler, Ten Miles High, Fast and

Loose, and Speed Unlimited ladies and gentlemen it's Stewball coming up fast behind a two-year-old filly out of Green and Growing by Damn Straight the Triple Crown winner and odds-on favorite she's holding her own but now out front Rambler Gambler in the lead by a head but likely to burn out early in this three-mile race look it's Island Dreams on the inside rail . . ." He was reading words that appeared on a transparent screen in front of him.

Verity was caught in his unending patter and watched the amazing welter of golden, black, and brown horses, racing without jockeys, stretched out and flowing along the track as Blaze pushed another button and an invisible crowd cheered. The cheers seemed to spur the horses to greater speed, and Verity saw beads of sweat on Blaze's forehead, as if he were running himself.

She looked beyond the track. Over the tops of the trees she saw the end of the island and the channel they had not come down, which was white with boiling rapids. Between the island and the mainland what looked like a bridge of wires hung with tiny unmoving gondolas swayed in the wind. And beyond, a ghostly empty city choked with trees glittered golden where broken windows caught the waning sun.

"Blaze!" she said, but he was yelling, "And ladies and gentlemen, it's Stewball the winner!" He pushed another button and she heard a wild crowd cheer in deafening waves. She reached over and pushed the button that said OFF.

In the silence, after her ears adjusted, a wash of wind rustled the new green leaves on the trees.

"Are you ready to go now?" she asked.

He dropped the mike. "Come on."

She followed him down the steps but of course he ran much faster than she could and she was amazed when he ran right over to Stewball, a dark brown stallion who trotted toward him and stopped just in front of him. Blaze's head came up to Stewball's withers. Most of the horses were walking slowly back and forth, and nearby she saw oats emptying into a feeding trough through chutes from a large tank above the trough. A large digital sign above said 58:19, then 58:18.

"Aren't they wonderful, Verity? The trumpets call; they race—oh, they love to race, don't they!—and after they cool down the feeding trough will open. I bet that's what that time means." He patted Stewball and talked to him in a low voice.

Verity was not as excited about horses as Blaze, but then, his communion with horses had been one of his Shaker Gifts.

"You want one, Verity?" he asked. "Pick one. They're lonely. It would do them good to have some people."

Maybe a horse would help Blaze.

"*Pick* one?" she asked. "How?"

"Well, how about Mollie? She placed." Blaze whistled sharply and a gray mare cantered up. Verity didn't even wonder why; Blaze just had a way with horses and these were not ordinary ones.

"Pet her!" said Blaze. "Rub her nose."

"Blaze, we don't *need* horses. We can't take them on the boat. How will we feed them? How will they get exercise? And besides, don't they belong to somebody?" She knew when she said that, though, that these horses belonged to no one. They were just here, vestiges of when the island had functioned.

"We do need horses, Verity," he said. "In fact the *Queen* has stables. And plenty of oats. Just like the original, I bet. How do you think people used to take horses up and down the river? And in the evenings we can go out for a ride. Explore. It will be fun, don't you think?"

At least the horses cheer him up, she thought. That was something.

He ran over to a mounting block and Stewball followed obediently. He stepped up on the block and pulled himself over onto Stewball's back. "Come on, Verity."

"I can't ride her bareback," she said. She jumped when Mollie reached down and snorted against the back of her neck.

"We can get some bridles and saddles from the tack room." He clucked to Stewball and the horse trotted toward the tack room. "I can't believe how smooth his gait is!" Blaze yelled, his voice brimming with delight. He vanished through the tall dark doorway.

Verity followed, with Mollie behind her, taking care to stay well back from the heels of Stewball. As she stepped inside the stables the smell of horses, sweet hay, and sharp liniment made her blink with a sudden memory of Shaker Hill. Blaze slid from Stewball's back and landed with a soft thud in the sawdust. He selected two soft halters and handed one to Verity.

"They don't have bits," she objected.

"They don't *need* bits," said Blaze, his voice enthusiastic. He readied Mollie and boosted Verity up.

"You can't take them there horses," came a sharp voice from the shadows.

They turned. A man walked toward them slowly, holding a shotgun across his chest. His hair was long and grizzled, his clothes unkempt.

"Why not?" asked Blaze. "Who do they belong to? You?"

The old man looked puzzled and his grip on the rifle relaxed. He shook his head. "Nope. They're *old*. Some kind of fancy horses. Special-made by some highfalutin horse manufacturer in Louisville. They always been here. Ever since . . ."

He frowned and lowered his rifle. He squinted at Blaze. "Usta be more people . . . hired me . . . dressed-up folks . . . You one of them?" He looked at them with pleading in his eyes. He started breathing hard. "Haven't seen 'em in . . . *years?* Nor any other people. Just them god-damned *clowns.* Killed one last year. Think it was last . . . year . . ."

"Well, can we trade something for them?" Blaze asked. "I mean, you're the only one here, right?"

The look of fury returned to his face. "Shoot . . . to . . . *kill?* Yeah, that's right! Kill, they told me. Nobody calls me stupid! Yes, sir! I can follow directions. Shoot . . . to . . ." He raised his rifle.

Blaze leapt for his horse, grabbed his mane, and pulled himself up. "Let's go!" he said.

Mollie bolted. Verity grabbed her mane and ducked beneath the lintel. She heard shots.

They swept down a broad trail through the forest, Verity's face whipped by overhanging leaves as the path twisted beneath her. She caught glimpses of kudzu-covered houses off in the woods. "Hold on!" yelled Blaze, and she felt Mollie gather herself and leaned into the jump as Mollie leaped across a creek and scrambled up the opposite bank. They pounded through sun-dappled forest.

Ahead of her Blaze burst into the sunlit square. She kicked Mollie and surged ahead. She yelled "This way!" and veered left toward the arcade.

Mollie paused at the entrance, then stepped inside, but snorted and pranced to a halt when a clown leaped in front of them as the brilliant swirling lights of the interior and the clangs and chimes surrounded them. Verity heard Stewball's hooves behind her on the concrete floor.

"Ha!" yelled the clown. "You could not resist. Enter, enter!"

Verity blinked as seven more clowns joined him, swaying tall and menacing, advancing toward them. Beyond, she saw her hordes of rafters.

"Get out of here!" she yelled, as loud as she could, but her voice was but another component of the cacophony that filled the air.

She watched aghast as one booth dropped diaphanous sheetlike curtains around the man operating it. The sheet eddied inward around him; a lower corner caught his leg as he pulled the lever again and again. She could see his grin faintly through the sheets.

"Everybody has to leave!" she yelled, and slid down off Mollie's back, landing hard on the floor. She ran to the man as Blaze hollered, "Stay away from that, Verity!"

As she began tearing blindly at the sheets she heard the clowns laughing behind her. The stuff was stuck fast to the helpless man, and though he continued to pull the lever she saw panic on his face as he turned his head from side to side frantically. On the screen before him she saw only flashing numbers, green, which flew past for a second, stopped at a random number, then flashed rapidly again, halting at odd rhythmic intervals. One of the clowns grabbed her arm and she struggled with him, catching a glimpse of his eyes, which were grim and cold. "Get out of here, Bee-woman," he hissed, "before we keep you as well." Then he fell to the floor and she saw that Blaze had smacked him with a broom handle. "Come on, Verity," he panted. "He's right."

"No," she said, and began running from booth to booth, yelling and yanking and wishing she had time to figure out what to do really. She caught glimpses of Blaze near the entrance, trouncing the rubbery, weaving clowns; saw two run out the door and three downed and then the noise and fervor of the place gradually died, as if a balloon were deflating. The machines gave off slow halfhearted pings and finally the lights went off altogether.

In the dim light penetrating the dirty windows, Verity saw that everyone was moving toward the door with stunned slow steps. Not everyone moved; she saw two or three people lying tangled in sheets.

"Leave them, Verity." She heard Blaze's voice next to her, low between gasps for breath. "They're dead. I checked them. No pulse."

"But how?" she asked, stunned at the quickness of everything. "Why?" She thought wildly, Are there sheets on the boat to save them with? Maybe—maybe—

"We'll probably never know," he said. "But I don't know if there's anything left to save, after—" He gestured at the machines, bowed his head for an instant after she saw deep pity fill his eyes and pull his mouth downward. Then his arm went around her. "Want to go home?" he asked quietly.

"Where's that?" she asked. "Where in the world is home now?" She fought back brief discontinuous flashes of blue water that washed through her with a euphoria completely at odds with what was happening. She tried to stay grounded in what was happening and held tight to Blaze for an instant; that helped.

"Maybe it's the riverboat."

"All right," she said. "Let's go."

She stepped around the downed clowns, who lay in glorious still-shimmering suits on the floor at the entrance. She peered down at one; his eyelids flickered and a long fast arm reached out and grabbed her ankle. She yanked it away, staggering backward. "You'll be back," he whispered. "Everybody comes back."

Outside, thunderheads had gathered to the west and the wind was picking up. People were heading back to the rafts and boarding. Did they feel the blue pull, the euphoria? The clean air quickened gloriously and washed all fear and tiredness from her and she ran down to the *Queen,* but turned when she heard the clatter of hooves. Blaze was leading the horses.

"They really can't come with us," she said.

"Says who?" he asked without stopping, a grin on his face.

"They can't live on a boat."

He just continued, and the horses followed. The sun flashed beneath a dense dark tower of cloud, illuminating the river and the rafts and the boat in sharp clear outline as if they were etched on the river. The wind gusted.

Mollie halted at the gangplank but Blaze clucked and she followed. "This is a silly idea," Verity said in her firmest voice.

Blaze just continued and lead the horses to the right, toward the back of the boat. "These are really nice stalls, guys, I think you'll like it here," she heard him say. She sighed in exasperation.

But she had more pressing things to worry about. Where would they stop tonight? It was getting late. The river had lost its peacefulness; small waves smacked the hull and she saw the rafts, ahead of her, bobbing ever more rapidly. Some of them disappeared around a bend in the river and she wondered who would cast off. Blaze seemed to have forgotten. But he had been coherent. That was something. She climbed to the hurricane deck and turned, hearing shouts.

A tall, thin couple dressed in amazingly fancy clothing dashed toward the dock, along the cobblestone street beneath trees which now thrashed wildly in the rising wind. The woman held a hat on her head with one hand and a long white plume trailed out behind her. Verity did not understand how she could run in those high-heeled shoes but she did, with long strides, and both of them looked like they were laughing hard.

The woman ran to one of the ropes and crouched, a long slit in her dress revealing her thigh, and the man ran to the other mooring. Almost in unison they undid the ropes and tossed them with twin thumps upon the deck. The woman ran up the gangway first, followed by the man, and together they cranked it up.

"Who's the pilot of this tub?" yelled the man, looking around. He saw Verity and waved. "Start 'er up!"

Verity did not want to take these people with them. She didn't think they were from Cincinnati. But she saw some clowns staggering down the street toward the boat and she certainly didn't want to take any of them, so she ran up to the pilothouse two steps at a time and pushed the button that made the ship shudder, pushed forward the lever that made it go, and pulled the heavy wooden wheel with all her might.

As they swept past the beach it gleamed golden for one last instant before the rain swept down and pocked the river while wind buffeted the tall boat.

In a moment the door slammed open and Blaze came in, his hair darkened by rain. "What are we going to do about these rafters?" he asked. "They're like a bunch of kids."

Verity did not want to admit that she felt almost as they did. Perhaps it would be easier if she were entirely like them, but she was not. They heard footsteps and turned.

The two people burst in, soaking wet, and laughing.

They were both tall, taller than her by a good five or six inches. And thin. The woman's skin was ebony, sheened with rainwater. The man's face was several shades lighter, a golden dark brown.

The woman doubled over with laughter again, then sank into one of the big comfortable chairs to one side of Verity.

"Who are you?" asked Verity.

"I am so sorry there are no mutual acquaintances to introduce us properly," said the man, clearly trying to master himself, but started laughing again and the woman said, "I'm Lightnin' Lil, and he's Diamond Jack."

"Jack and Lil," said Verity, leaning on the wheel hard as a large rock came into view. She said nothing for over a minute, as the huge boat slowly responded. "You can't stay."

"Verity!" said Blaze. "What's gotten into you? First the horses and now—"

"Oh, yes, the horses," said Verity. "Maybe the horses belong to *them*. The man with the gun said the owners were well dressed."

"Why, thank you," said Lil.

"I saw horses," said Jack. "But they don't belong to us. Nothing on that island belongs to anybody, unless it's the clowns. It was declared a disaster area a while back. At first there was a warning sign, but the clowns tore it down."

"What are they?" asked Verity.

"They used to be part of the show, but then they took over the island. As to what they *are*, it's hard to say exactly."

"Well, you still can't stay," said Verity. "Blaze, here, hasn't been feeling well. He's in no position to issue invitations."

"What's wrong?" asked Lil.

Blaze shrugged. "I forget my name. Stuff like that. Something to do with some nan sheets I was wrapped in. I don't think I have the plague though. That's one good thing."

Lil didn't say anything. Her mouth trembled slightly.

"You'll likely survive," said Jack. "You're lucky, though."

"That's what I think," said Blaze. "Usually."

Lil's sigh was tremulous, but when Verity glanced at her she grinned back like she was trying to pretend she hadn't sounded that way. Jack pulled up a chair next to the small round table next to Lil. They had passed the island and were moving downriver at a fast clip.

Lil reached up and pulled large pins from her hat; swept it from her head and regarded the drenched feather with dismay.

"It'll dry," she said. "But it will never be the same." She tossed the hat on the floor, then loosened something else and thick hair fell halfway down her back, black and kinky. She wore an emerald-green dress with a high neckline and long sleeves—tight, but evidently of giving material. She kicked off her shoes and leaned back in the chair; Verity saw a shiver run through her. Blaze opened and closed cupboard doors and finally found a blanket, which he handed to her. She wrapped it around herself. "Thanks," she said. Her voice sounded as if she might have been crying not long ago, even though she'd been laughing so hard.

Jack reached into his vest pocket and pulled out a box of cards. "Good old Bee cards from the U.S. Playing Card Company in Cincinnati," he said, slitting it open and shaking out the deck. He glanced at Verity out of the corner of his eye as he said this and Verity was annoyed. "Dry as a bone." He shuffled them and pushed them toward Lil. "Cut," he said.

Blaze stood watching them, his hands in his pockets. Finally he asked, "What are you playing?"

"Five-card stud," said Jack. He fished in his pockets and pulled out a cigar; lit it.

Verity coughed and said, "Blaze, try and get these windows open." They had evidently closed themselves against the rain. She was irritated. They were careering down the wild river in a storm and all these people could do was smoke and play cards. "Are you gamblers?" she asked.

Lil's laugh was deep. "You could sure make a case for it," she said, then, "I'll stand."

"You need gamblers on a riverboat," said Jack, studying his cards. "Bet you don't have any."

"Don't listen to him," said Lil. "He'll bet on anything."

"We haven't been on the boat long enough to know," said Blaze. "I mean, if there's gamblers or not. I guess there could—"

"Are you from that island?" asked Verity. Blaze would tell them whatever he knew, which wasn't much, but it was more than they knew now. After those clowns, she did not feel very trustful.

"No. Just got there," Lil said, the same time Jack said, "Been waiting there."

"Waiting for what?" asked Verity.

"For the sky to fall," said Lil.

"For love-lee, *won*derful you," sang Jack, making it sound like a song and a joke at the same time. "I'm from Wheeling. Originally."

"Washington, D.C.," said Lil, "at one point. Well, I'm feeling better and better, Jack." She laid her cards on the table with a flourish.

"Shit," said Jack, and swept the cards up. As he riffled them together they made a soft, rapid sound which was quite companionable. It reminded Verity of something, yet she was sure it was a memory of Rose's. She set her lips grimly and tried to ignore it.

"Are you from Cincinnati?" asked Lil.

Verity shrugged. Blaze opened his mouth and she frowned at him. He closed it.

Jack set the cards on the table and stood next to Verity. Rain blurred the gray river. "You want to hug the Kentucky shore up here. The Louisville part of the river is nutsy cuckoo. Used to be a pretty fancy lock-and-dam setup. Got all twisted in the quake. Here, let me help—" He leaned into the wheel with Verity and they made the left channel through the surging, mud-yellow rush of storm-tossed water.

"You do this real well," he said.

"Don't try and flatter me," she said. "I don't want you on this boat. I don't know who you are." She bit her lip and steered hard to port and narrowly missed some rafters. "I don't even know if we should keep this big boat. It's a hazard."

"You do need us," said Jack. "Lil's an expert. And I'd advise you to keep the boat. Where are you going to get another one?" His cigar had gone out and he put it in a metal tube he took from his pocket.

"What is Lil an expert in?" Verity asked. "Having hysterical fits?"

"Verity, why are you being so rude?" asked Blaze.

"Statistics," said Jack, and both of them burst out laughing again. Can't get a straight answer out of these two, thought Verity.

Lil recovered from her laughter, gasped a few times, and said, "Don't listen to him. *He's* the statistician. Has a doctorate, even. Worked for the government."

Verity thought she saw Jack flash Lil a warning look. "She's very tired," he said gently.

"Where did you get a doctorate?" asked Blaze, and Verity could tell by the tone of his voice that he was swallowing everything these people said.

"What government?" asked Verity, but was ignored.

"Well," said Lil, "it was a"—she choked on laughter again—"a *correspondence course!"* and she and Jack broke up again. Lil found it so amusing that she pounded the table a few times with her fist and several cards fluttered to the floor. She leaned over and gathered them up. "Chances are, um"—she closed her eyes for an instant—"oh, eight to one, just to round things off, that you won't make it to Norleans. That's why—you need *us!"* She gasped a few times. She appeared to be almost hysterical. "Because we know so goddamned *much!"*

"That's *right,*" interjected Jack, and Verity was almost positive that he wanted to keep Lil from saying anything else. "We know everything there is about *entertainment.* Can't have a gambling boat without entertainment."

He leaned forward and set up a steady slow rhythm on the table with his hand. He began to sing, in a clear, low voice. Lil dashed tears from her face, took a deep, shuddering breath, and joined in after the first line. As rain sluiced down, Verity listened to their haunting mournful harmony:

> When I came to Georgie, money and clothes I had,
> Babe, all the money I had done gone
> My Sunday clothes in pawn, Sunday clothes in pawn,
> Sunday clothes in pawn.
> Dollar more, the deuce beats a nine,
> Dollar more, the deuce beats a nine, lovin babe
> Dollar more, the deuce beats a nine.

The song went on for several more verses. Verity was exasperated at the way Blaze hung on every line, nodding his head with their beat.

"What was *that?*" he asked, when they finished.

"Blues," said Jack. "Real old blues at that. Old guy name of Howell wrote it. Lil doesn't like the blues all that much. She likes classical music a lot better." He shrugged.

"Nothing but a lot of whiny black men complaining about how bad women are," she said. "Calmed *me* right down. And I was having *such* a good time." She pulled her blanket tighter around her shoulders.

"Yeah, well, everybody seems pretty ridiculous in those operas you like." Jack picked up the cards and shuffled them over and over.

Blaze said, "You know any more songs like that?"

"He knows thousands," said Lil, dryly.

After a few more shuffles Jack said to Verity, "There are all kinds of hazards ahead. You won't be sorry you took us."

"I already am," said Verity, and they headed down the river as fast as the current would carry them, and then a little faster, as Verity gunned the engine.

Six

○○○○○○○○○○○○○○○○○○

Mad Rafter Blues

Verity was absorbed in the shadow pattern of the gingerbread, repeated over the golden deck at her feet. It was quite lovely. A shout broke the spell. She looked up, startled; remembered. She was going somewhere— oh, yes. Blaze's room. Why had she slept so late? The boat was moving, but she had not had anything to do with it. She didn't care. Evidently this morning it was someone else's chore. She looked down at herself. At least I got dressed, she thought. She didn't remember doing so.

She passed the large hall that Lil and Jack had settled into, and heard wild laughter within. Jack was vague about how to use such oddities as a "roulette wheel" and a "craps table" but they were definitely there. She heard him curse and complain that one of the pool tables lacked a corner pocket and Lil of course laughed uproariously before Verity turned a corner. Lil seemed kind of unhinged. Verity hoped that she would calm down, but she had too much to think about to worry about that pair; enough trouble just staying on-balance and precariously centered in a vision of being Verity, no one else, just Verity from Shaker Hill staying in charge of her passel of refugees.

Blaze was hunched over a large wooden desk. The heavy, ornate wood was highly polished and shone warmly in the morning sun through the open French doors. She smelled something sweet and saw that he must have picked some lilacs from the bushes that flourished on the bank where they had stopped last night, for a gigantic bouquet of them filled a large widemouthed jar, their thick green stems distorted by water and glass. She vaguely remembered the tattoo of hooves on the deck early this morning, which she had woven into her dream.

Two unmade beds with iron head- and footboards were on one side of Blaze's large room, which also held two couches and three chairs, several lamps, and two enormous dressers.

Outside, the sleepy, periodic rise and fall of cicada whir paralleled the rise and fall of moans, punctuated by imprecations. It seemed that the rafters were getting worse. She certainly was.

"What are you doing?" she asked.

Blaze twisted in his chair, and Verity saw a large book open on the desk. He slammed it shut and put down his pen.

"Nothing," he said.

"Can I see it?" she asked, taking a step forward.

"No, you can *not* see it," he said, and she was surprised at his proprietary tone of voice.

"All right, all right," she said. "I won't look."

"Sorry," he said.

"It's all right." Her vision clouded, and she sat down hard on the chair next to her. Blaze hurried over to her. She felt his hand on her forehead.

"Are you all right?"

She was trembling. "No, damn it," she whispered, and then was gone.

She was flying over Cincinnati. *This* is life, she thought fiercely. She was vaguely aware of her body, sprawled in the chair, and that Blaze was putting a cool wet cloth on her forehead, but that reality became thin and insubstantial as she was jerked from the streets of Cincinnati to an entirely different vision.

The street was very narrow, and paved with cobblestones, which glistened dark and ruddy after the morning's shower. On both sides ancient buildings slanted inward above her, a hodgepodge of design and complexity. The sun touched only the tiny panes of the windows of the fifth floor. French doors opened onto tiny wrought-iron porches where droplets of water caught the sun, and pink and red geraniums glowed against rough brick. The air felt heavy on her arms, damp and hot, and she heard the cries of strange birds.

She turned into a narrow doorway with a heavy rough-hewn lintel and walked through a room that smelled of beer and was filled with pool tables, though it was empty of people. She climbed tiny stairs which turned sharply at a landing and emerged on the fifth floor, where a hallway opened into a large room with polished oak floors and many small tables. A few sleepy-looking people were sitting at tables sipping coffee and reading newspapers.

"Milk, please," she said to the tall, thin, woman behind the counter. Her hair was very short, and clung to her head in tight ringlets, showing the lovely shape of her skull. Her face was thin and strong, with high cheekbones and large brown eyes. Her skin was dark brown, with a dusting of darker freckles below her eyes. She wore a long yellow cotton sundress. She tamped coffee into a gleaming cup and inserted it into a machine. Steam hissed as she pulled down hard on a lever. Dark liquid streamed into a tiny white cup. Verity saw, in the light spilling through large double doors that opened onto a balcony, a tiny golden tattoo on her back, outlined in black, a few inches below her shoulder.

She leaned over to get a better look. "Is that a bee?"

The woman just smiled and put the cup on a small saucer and rested two cubes of sugar against it.

Verity took the cup and went out to the balcony. For a moment she remembered that she'd asked for milk, not coffee, and was confused. The balcony jutted out over a corner, so she had a 180-degree view. She sat on a white wooden chair and set her cup on the damp table. Below her was a jumble of rooftops, some peaked, some flat and filled with plants and furniture. The view beyond the rooftops took her breath away.

She saw nothing but blue, blue water and no other land anywhere, as if she were on the tip of a peninsula. She rose and leaned against the railing, dwelling for a long moment in utter and glad blueness.

Huge swells rose and fell as the sun glittered on a bright infinity of facets. The white sails of three boats were brilliant and tiny on the horizon. Something in her opened to the hugeness of the vista; something in her rejoiced. She longed to be here always; this was deep home; she must never, ever leave, or if she did, all her efforts must bring her back. The wind was strong against her and brought the scent of ocean. She turned and saw to her surprise a huge, open-grid structure, composed of what looked like beams of white steel.

"Verity, you've got to *help* them," she heard. Or had been hearing. Her eyes fluttered open. She sat up and took a deep breath, her being still full of a wide, blue, unfettered horizon and a tiny, ancient town that whispered mystery.

She became aware that Blaze was next to her, holding her hand, and that the air was filled with riotous shouts.

A picture on the wall across the room caught her eye: a painting of a woman in a blue dress.

As she stood to help them (help who she wondered) the blue of the dress expanded, a vibrant sheet of color, and

—she could not see where the waves broke; whether on a dock or on a shore. She had to see. She gulped her coffee, turned, and rushed back through the shop and into the street—

which turned into a flowered rug beneath her feet, and once more she could hear the shouts welling up all around, outside, and felt the boat lurch.

Blaze was out at the railing, his shoulders bowed. She went out and stood next to him.

"I'm sorry," she said. She felt as discouraged as he looked. She was in thrall to factors over which she had no control—and it was *she* who had done this, not just to herself, but to everyone. She had essentially kidnapped them from a life which, though bizarre, had been familiar to them, and put them at the mercy of the Norleans Plague.

The people on the rafts were in obvious agony.

Children wailed without end. Adults sat listlessly, moaning, though some paced back and forth on their rafts, and many were arguing. As they drifted downriver they roughly kept pace with one another on the slow current.

"What's wrong with everyone?" asked Blaze. "What are we going to do?"

"I'm not in charge," said Verity ruefully. She pulled a scroll from her pocket and saw that it was filled with unintelligible hieroglyphics. "See? Here's what we've decided today. The new plan of action. I don't even know who's running the boat right now. Look. It's not even telling me to take my vitamins anymore."

"It's not funny, Verity," said Blaze.

Then, with a start, she remembered that she had thrown her scroll away the other night.

Presumably no one was allowed to be without one. She digested that. Had someone crept in, furnished her with a new one, sticking it in the pocket of her jeans, thrown over a chair, while she slept? "What about you, Blaze. Do you have a scroll?"

"No. Do I need one?"

"Touch the screen." He shrugged his shoulders and touched it quickly. It went blank, but nothing else happened.

"Hmm," she said. "I guess it doesn't prove anything. It doesn't seem to be working anyway. . . ."

As she spoke, she saw a tall metal tower, standing alone, frighteningly huge, on a vast expanse of intensely blue water, beneath a cerulean sky. High waves swept through its open base. She shook her head, trying to clear her vision.

"What's wrong with them, Verity?" Blaze asked.

Blaze's voice helped. "These people all have receptors which received metapheromonal commands. Of course, the system wasn't designed to be one of command—quite the opposite. It was designed to facilitate information transfer. But it became the way the Queen was able to control everyone in the City—people *wanted* the information because they *needed* it. They can't live without it."

"Metapheromonal. I think you told me that before. I guess I'll have to study up on that kind of thing. But what do you mean—that they'll die?"

"I'm not sure," she said. "But it is a kind of food, to be sure." With a dark, sinking realization she understood that probably, somewhere within her was that information. The information of Rose and Durancy, the information she was trying to weave *herself* over, a fragile idea of one person, Verity. Not Durancy, Rose, the Queen. She wanted, so fiercely, to be *herself,* whoever that might be.

She made the idea of a separate self into one of those white-sailed boats far out on the blue, windy sea, and let that white sail vanish. And there was only blue left, infinite blue, wide and frightening, trackless. And free. She had to float on this, whatever it was, or drown in it. She had to let go of her old ideas of what was self and what was other in order to function fully.

Without her help, they probably would die. All of them were from Cincinnati, but only she had been to the center. Though she did not know how to access the information she had, she had to accept the fact that she could not push it aside. She had to allow it as part of her, however dark, however overwhelming. Freeing them from the City was only the initial part of the process that would truly free them. They would have to earn their freedom, she saw, for no matter how far she took them down that path, only their ability to make decisions could truly constitute freedom.

At first a sort of balance had welled up among them, making her think that everyone would adjust and move gladly down to Norleans. Now, in just a day, that had all fragmented horribly.

"Maybe there's nothing you *can* do," said Blaze gently. "You can't give them back their City. They're like children taken away from their parents. Like you were, like all of us at Shaker Hill. Orphans."

"They are like children," said Verity, "and they can't do anything for themselves. But I don't know if I can either. I can't seem to stay focussed. I get these damned *pictures*—I guess it's the Norleans Plague. But how did we get started this morning?"

"Oh, they all agreed on that necessity well enough, this morning. It doesn't take much to get moving. You just have to haul in the lines, after all, and the water does the rest."

"It frightens me," said Verity. "We need to know where we are on the river and where we're going and whether or not our information is any good. There are falls ahead, and rapids. I'm hoping that there will be locks around them. There used to be. I think we must be on the Old Ohio River again, since we passed over Rising Sun. Look. What's happening now?"

The rafts were squeezing closer together, as if those in the front had stopped.

They had, she saw, as they rounded the bend.

To their right, fertile fields spread out. Verity was soothed at the sight of knee-high corn, a white-blossomed orchard pacing over a low hill.

They drifted farther out around the bend's apogee and saw a small town.

She read the signs along the lowest street with something like wonder. HARRY'S BLACKSMITH—HORSES SHOED—TOOLS MENDED. FARMER'S MARKET. JANET RAY, DENTIST. DIARY CO-OP. The next tier of the town looked as if it comprised many small factories. BOONE NUT AND BOLT, read one deteriorated sign.

One particularly well lettered sign read ELIZA'S BREWERY, FINEST BEER FOR A HUNDRED MILES.

She saw a few people making their way across the rafts toward the landing.

"We can't let them get off," she said. She ran out to the railing and yelled as loud as she could, "Please stay on the rafts and continue downriver!"

No one paid any attention. "What's *wrong* with them?" she asked.

"Why should they listen to you?" asked Blaze.

"They can't just rush ashore any time they feel like it," she said.

"Why not?" asked Blaze.

"Because it's dangerous," she said.

"I guess they'll have to figure that out themselves," he said.

By now, a crowd was snaking its way up the street and disappearing into the brewery.

It was a yelling, rowdy crew, raising a cloud of dust, trooping across the rafts like lemmings. She heard faint choruses of "Caimaneero, down to Cairo," mixed like a round with "Fifteen years on the Erie Canal."

Verity's gut tightened as they made their way across the rafts, in the wake of the ragged exodus. A few people had stayed behind, lying in their wigwams; as she passed, some of them raised their arms and reached for her, or looked at her with pleading in their eyes, and she felt cruel and helpless as she passed them.

She climbed the ladder onto the wharf behind Blaze and they stepped into the town. The streets echoed with wild shouts.

"They'll kill us," she said. "We have to get these people back on the rafts and get out of here. And then tie them down." She remembered how Russ had hinted that even the Shakers had perhaps shot at Rafters from the bluffs above Miamisburg. This town had real inhabitants, unlike Gambling Island. That much was clear.

She and Blaze stopped at the first establishment on the street, a bakery. It was ransacked. Crumbs littered small round tables, chairs, the floor. Glass cases stood open and empty. "Coffee!" she said, spotting a large glass pot filled with brown liquid, but did not take any, though she wondered where it came from. This actually belonged to someone, unlike the things on Clown Island, and she was sick at this looting.

"Come on," said Blaze.

The next store, a grocery, was much the same. A hundred jars of put-up peaches, tomatoes, and ocra lay on the floor, as richly colored as a church window where the sun touched them, some smashed and drooling thick liquid. Burlap bags of flour sprawled in a corner like large sleeping animals where they had been pulled from shelves, slashed so that pale flour spilled across dark floorboards. Why? No reason. The rafters were completely out of control.

Apparently the brewery held their interest the best. The mob had halted there, and pressed with single, concentrated intent through the huge double doors at the front.

Blaze led Verity around to the side, and they peered in a window.

Near the back of the dim, barnlike building light caught rows of heavy mugs. Every few seconds someone grabbed a mug and filled it from a keg; a brigade passed them along, sipping as each mug passed.

The din was deafening, the laughing, singing, shouting.

Verity caught a movement on the next street up, which was lined with small factories and warehouses. "Come on," she said, and Blaze followed as she climbed one block away from the river.

"There!" she said, seeing this time a chubby blond toddler, a boy, vanish into a doorway.

They hurried down the street and went inside.

The vast building was filled with dark shapes except where light from high windows slanted in.

It was filled with ancient machinery. She walked beneath a gear as wide across as she was tall, like a huge rust flower with a filigreed edge and holes through which light streamed. Pale green lichen blossomed here and there, layering the grainy orange-umber roughness.

"It's all frozen up," said Blaze. He picked up a bent piece of metal from the clutter on the floor and hit the gear, which answered with a hollow clank. "Must not have been used for years. Wonder what they manufactured here?"

"Something that nan could do more cheaply, probably," said Verity. She smelled dry sweet sawdust, saw soft mounds of it piled around various saws in the back of the vast building. "Look," she said. They walked toward the saws.

The woodworking shop was dwarfed by the immensity of the old machinery around it, the separate pieces inexorably blending together in quiet oxidation.

Blaze examined the woodworking tools. "This one's a router," he said. "They must have electricity, somehow. They're plugged in. Maybe they have a dam on a creek somewhere, or something. But where *is* everybody?"

"Mommy?" they heard from a dark corner, a voice small and frightened.

Then behind her, from a side door, Verity heard the click of a rifle being cocked.

"Don't move."

A tall, thin woman wearing jeans sidled around into their field of vision. "Come on, Hunter," she said.

"Are you the only one who lives here?" asked Blaze.

"Now what kind of a damn fool question is that?" she asked. "Step back over to that wall. That's right. Come *on,* Hunter, before I warm your bottom!"

Instead, the little boy rushed over to Verity, and stopped several yards from her. She stepped back as far as she could. Up close, he looked older than she had first thought—maybe three and a half or four.

"No," whispered his mother, or at least Verity was pretty sure she *was* the mother—"Hunter, baby, please—don't *touch* her!"

"Go on back to your mother," said Verity. "Go on."

The boy looked at her doubtfully.

"Go on," said Verity. "She won't spank you. She's just kidding."

The boy pulled something from his pocket. "Listen," he said, and blew a chord on it.

"A harmonica!" said Blaze.

The boy threw it at him and ran over to the saws, laughing. "Yes, she will spank me, now," he said, and hid behind one of the big machines. He threw a screwdriver out from behind it and it clattered onto the floor. They heard a crash. Another howl of amusement. "Can't catch me!" he yelled.

"Why did you people stop, anyway?" said the woman. "Most people have the sense to just keep on going. And I've never seen so goddamned many rafters in my whole life. Usually we get up to the Granger barn and whoever it is, even if they stop, don't stay long. Where did you come from? Suddenly there are thousands of you. Solid, for days. We can't kill everybody who comes down the river—don't want to. Didn't you see the sign—Plaguers Keep Out? Of course, maybe you're too stupid or your brains are too frizzed to read. Hunter, if you don't get on up the hill, *now,* you won't be able to sit down for a week. And you've lost the harmonica Aunt Beth gave you. Now it's infected. I told her you were too little to take care of it." Her voice shook, though, and Verity knew she was terrified of the plague. She decided it was best to say nothing—the woman was so nervous that anything might set her off. But Blaze had apparently decided no such thing.

"I'm sorry," said Blaze. "We'll try to get them back on the rafts as soon as we can. If there's something you folks need that we have, maybe we can—"

"We've survived this long without getting tainted," she said. "No good reason to get crazed now." Her thin mouth twisted downward and she said, "I'm just trusting that Hunter's going to be all right. We don't need a damned thing that you have. We've got the R-net, and it comes from inland, not the river."

"The R-net?" asked Blaze.

"Rural Network. Goes almost to Michigan and as far west as the Mississippi. Maybe further for all I know." She turned at the sound of running footsteps. "Now where did he get to?"

"He went out the door," said Verity, and Blaze gave her an exasperated look.

"Good. I'd suggest that all of you get out of town as soon as possible," she said, "before somebody takes it into their mind to kill a few of you to hurry you along. I'd say that I'm just about the mildest person in town—lots of people would have shot you dead on the spot. And I'm pretty pissed about the beer. I'm Eliza." She turned and ran out the door.

"I wanted to ask her more questions," said Blaze, an annoyed tone in his voice.

"I'm afraid the gun made me a little nervous."

Blaze picked up the harmonica. "I guess they won't want this back," he said, and blew an experimental chord. "B flat," he said. "That's strange." He put it in his pocket.

Verity and Blaze tried to get the rafters back on the river, but it was difficult to keep them still; a certain percentage of them staggered to their feet and made their way back to land, careering dangerously over the gaps between rafts. Together they dragged about ten unconscious women and men out of town; then Verity found a wagon behind one of the buildings and it went a little easier after that. But eventually Verity sank down in a doorway, exhausted, and watched the legs of the revelers pass, listening to bits of drunken song and the shuffle of feet on dirt alleys and the old blacktop two-lane highway, reflecting that Cincinnati's record for beer consumption—the most gallons per year for decades, according to old statistics—probably remained unchallenged.

The sky filled with dark, heavy verges of clouds twisting in the chilling wind sweeping downriver. Verity wondered if there would be a storm every afternoon. She pushed back sweat-dampened hair, and let the wind cool her face.

Below, the flotilla of rafts spread out across the river, and the big boat shone white the last moments before the clouds covered the sun. The river was not very wide here. On the other side, she saw hints of old buildings—concrete pilings, and well back from the bank, just above the level of the treetops, a golden curve. But the forest had swallowed whatever had been there, and she watched the green mass moving in occasional gusts of breeze. The edge of the river was shallow and marshy, filled with grasses which bustled with tiny birds.

How nice it would be to gather a few supplies and just set out into the woods. Take those horses and head south. A map sputtered into her mind. Kentucky. Tennessee. Alabama. The ocean, blue . . .

Verity shook the overwhelming blueness from her mind and instead wondered how soon the impending cloudburst would startle them into near-sobriety, and wondered how to keep them from doing this again when she heard the crack of rifles from high above the two-street town.

The street erupted in screams. Verity jumped to her feet.

Up on the bluff stood three men and two women, holding shotguns. One of the men had a megaphone.

"Next time we'll shoot to kill," he yelled. "Get the hell out of town. You have ten minutes—"

The crack of thunder drowned out whatever he had to say next, and the sky let go.

Cold rain streamed down Verity's face, soaking her clothes, as she tried to herd the people onto the rafts. They seemed to understand the rifle, and began to trample down to the wharf and onto the rafts. Verity ran down the street and made a quick search of the buildings they had been in. She found one teenaged girl, passed out on the floor of the bingo hall, and Verity grabbed her beneath her arms and pulled her to the door. One of the women passing by took her without a word and continued dragging her to the river.

When Verity went back into the street she saw a knot of people on the next block. She ran to them and pushed her way into the middle.

A man of perhaps thirty, with light brown hair, had been shot in the shoulder. Verity's vision filled with Blaze, lying in the winter-bare orchard as snow began to fall, his chest red with blood. She turned away and took a deep breath, then turned back.

She yanked off her overshirt, laid it on top of his shoulder, leaned on it, hard, then yelled, "Tear me some strips to tie this down," and heard the sound of cloth ripping. Long pieces of green cloth were thrust into her face, and she grabbed them and bound the shirt tightly to the man's shoulder. He was breathing shallowly. "Let's go," said Verity. "Pick him up," she commanded, for she was bone tired, and she hoped they wouldn't drop him more than once or twice.

Some of the rafts were moving. The wind brought another sheet of rain sluicing over them. Behind her, the street was deserted, and she began to run down to the wharf.

Blaze glanced at Verity with concern every once in a while. Sometimes her eyes were open and she saw him do so, though she lay on the large bed in deep midnight shadow, and knew he couldn't see hers.

She'd groggily stripped off her wet clothes, sneezing, she remembered that; had pulled on a white cotton nightgown, then toppled into his bed, and he'd drawn a white lacy comforter over her. It had still been day, though rain lashed the boat. She'd used the last of her energy to get them all moved about two miles down the river, then collapsed.

Now it must be very late. She watched Blaze.

On Blaze's large desk a stained-glass lamp cast a glow, filled with the phosphate analog that made lightsticks shine.

On the wall next to the desk were large framed botanical prints, and just above it, a painting of a riverboat. She did not wish to look at it if it was floating on blue water, but whatever the color of the river it was grayed by night, only dimly illuminated by the lamp.

Next to Blaze's elbow was a small, hinged wooden box, which stood open. In the dark she could see that it was inlaid with some sort of gold lines that caught the light.

She watched him reach in and remove a green crystal and set it on the polished desk.

A radio stone.

She wondered how everyone was doing, then lost interest, caught in the glow of the radio stone. The rafters were either dead or alive; she really didn't care which, the idiots. The consensus power of their scrolls had apparently been lost in chaos, and perhaps it was up to her to insert the direction which would save them but not just now, particularly since she hadn't the faintest idea what that might be.

A cool breeze came in the open French doors, causing a wall hanging to flutter. She saw a few clear stars in the black square of night, and Blaze took out another radio stone, and then another. He stood over them, resting his weight on his arms.

Verity woke several times during the night, and either she was dreaming or Blaze had heaped his desk with wires and gizmos, and once she thought she heard tinny wild wails of sound which could not be music by any stretch of the imagination and saw, by the pale light of the stained-glass lamp, a look of reverence in Blaze's eyes as he tilted his head and listened.

Finally Verity could sleep no longer. It was still dark. Blaze was slumped over his desk, snoring, and the radio stones were dark.

Her hands had awakened her, she realized. They throbbed and itched. She rubbed them together and got out of bed, restless and alert. She wondered where Blaze had found his radio stones. Had they just grown in the drawers of his desk?

Well, she supposed, that was possible. There was much about the boat she didn't know. She had somehow given the commands for all this to grow. Layers and layers, shells of Durancy's exquisite metacommands.

Though it was surely possible that she had commanded these people to come forth and possibly die because their lives depended on the meta-pheromone jolt they'd received while in the City, she wondered if she had not known this would happen and provided for it. Their little scrolls had worked at first, she remembered, linking hivelike, brought to life by their shared information, and had then fallen to gibberish.

Opening the bottom drawer of a bureau she felt a sweater, pulled it out, and held it before her. It had a strange foreign smell and was very large but it would do. But when she pulled it on she pushed, puzzled, with her right hand, trying to find the arm of the sweater. Finally she pulled it back over her head and stepped around to the doorway where there was enough light for her to see on closer examination that it lacked an arm. She tossed it on the floor and found another, which had the correct number of arms.

Kicking around on the floor she found the clothes she had discarded, still wet. In the right pocket of her jeans she found the scroll and pulled it out, dried it on her nightgown, and slipped out barefoot onto the deck.

She could only see the rafts immediately below; the rest were obscured by fog. Her hands felt unpleasant, full of jitters; she shook and clenched them several times.

Strange clicking sounds stopped Verity as she passed a window. A light was on inside and the curtains were not fully drawn.

It was even more ornate than the other rooms. Tiffany lamps hung from the ceiling. Here and there were small tables covered with lace and things she thought of as gimcracks and geegaws, because the Gift Shop on the boiler deck sported a sign that described them as such.

Lil and Jack drifted into view, startling Verity. They were only about ten feet away. A cigarette dangled from Lil's mouth, and much to Verity's surprise she was carrying a long white stick. Verity was getting used to her dress—long tight sleeves, high in the back, with a low V-neck in the front. But this one was gold.

Lil perched on the edge of the pool table and leaned over, holding one end of the stick over her head.

"Lil," said Jack.

"Both my feet are on the floor," she said.

"Both your *shoes* are on the floor. Your dress isn't as long as you think."

"What are you going to do, shoot me?" asked Lil. "Five in the corner." She gave the stick a quick shove and Verity heard the clicking sound again.

"A day doesn't go by that you don't surprise me," said Jack. "But don't think that you can beat me at pool."

"Oh, heaven *forbid,*" said Lil. "Three in the side?" Again that sound.

"You make me nervous," said Jack.

"You should be."

"Not that you might beat me because I know you can't."

"Pretty puffed up, aren't you Jack Hamilton?"

"I'm nervous because our chance of success is pretty poor and I don't think you're helping things any. You're acting kind of—nutty."

"Oh, pooh," she said.

"Maybe you can't tell," he said, his voice worried.

Her voice turned steely. "Look, Jack, this was your idea and I think it was a good one. The only way. I'm staking everything on your faith— oh, sorry, on what you *know.* This is our last chance because nutty is what I've *been.* I'm trying to loosen up. That's the only way I'll make it. If I start thinking about what's at stake—and seeing all these plaguers is incredibly upsetting to me . . ."

"I know, Lil," he said in a low, apologetic voice. "Maybe this wasn't the best idea in the world. I'm worried about *you,"* he said, his voice tight, yet filled with emotion. "I don't really give a damn about anything else." He laughed and his voice cracked. "After all, Lil, if *you* don't make it . . . Look. Let's go back, think this over—"

"For another decade or two? Oh, stop it, Jack. You're only bringing me down. We've got to be committed. But we're only two people. All we can do is our best . . ." Her voice faltered. "Maybe you're right. Our best has been none too good in the past."

"You've always done as much as you could possibly do, Lil. And you've usually tried to do more than one person could do—that's the problem. I'm sorry I said anything. You aren't emotionally prepared for this. How could you be?"

"Bullshit, Jack." Her voice strengthened. "You're just a moosh. You think too much. You're stuck with me, babe. We're going down this river. To the bitter end. Face it. You want to get rid of me because you hate to lose and now—" There were two sharp cracks. "—you have."

"Shit. How did you *do* that?"

"I distracted you."

After that, Verity heard no more except soft clacks and the sound of them walking around, and Jack's occasional curse.

Part of her wanted to walk in and demand to know what they were talking about. Committed to what? She saw danger all around, but somehow she thought the danger Jack spoke of might be somewhat different.

But the nervousness seized her again. She clenched her hands, deprived now of metapheromonal input for many days. She had not counted on this. A transformation had occurred while she was in Cincinnati, a transformation she had feared and sought. Her body had changed, become capable of accessing and sending metapheromonal information. It was a hunger, keen and dark and completely unsettling.

She sat on a bench, then jumped up; it was wet. Using the sleeve of the overlarge sweater, she dried it as best she could, then sat again, propping her feet on the railing. She needed a map of the boat and what it contained. The river swished along in the dark.

She touched the scroll on, feeling urgent and invigorated, though her hands shook. Now, where was the tutorial she had been commanded to use? She closed her eyes and tried to remember, then opened them to see she didn't have to; the screen from the first morning had come back, telling her to take her vitamins, telling her that she was #47. She sighed, then went to the tutorial screen and was shortly amazed at the information she held in her hand, and at the power of it.

The sky had lightened just a shade when she looked up, over an hour later. She stood and hurried down two decks, glancing at her scroll as she turned left at the stairway and counted doorways. There. The fifth one. She held the scroll up to the number on the door and by its pale light read the cabin number: 32.

But it was locked. She could not turn the knob. Then a palmprint flashed and she put her hand to it and heard a click within, and then the knob turned freely.

She stepped inside the room and saw that it was windowless, but lit with a gentle glow. The walls were alive with tiny, dancing lights.

She sat in the only chair, which looked like a delicate graceful insect. In front of her was a narrow desklike down-slanted ledge, with an indentation that flashed. And as it flashed, the scroll in her hand flashed in unison, so she set it in the indentation and it appeared satisfied, for the urgent flashing stopped.

WHAT DO YOU WANT, #47? asked the scroll, the words floating within it. The colors the scroll used were never the same. This time she saw bright purple letters on a yellow field.

"The people from Cincinnati need metapheromones to survive," she said. "We can't function without them. Are there any on the boat?"

OF COURSE, said the scroll. IN RAW FORM. BOMBYKOL, DANAIDONE, IPSDIENOL, VERBENONE . . .

Tiny charts of straight lines and letters, the chemical shorthand for each, appeared next to every listed pheromone, of which there were thousands. As she watched they began to shift and link to one another like magnetized puzzles, and the information on the scroll overflowed onto the desk surface.

Verity felt both relieved and frightened. But she had no room for fear, and it was too soon to be relieved. She allowed those feelings to eddy away, and was left clear and focussed. What to ask? But you have more than three questions, she told herself. These are not the deadly questions of fairy tales, where what is in your own mind will weave you back into yourself only worse, showing you the awfulness of who you really are. This is a tool to unfold not only yourself but all of those around you, and you must believe that that is good. You have as many questions as you want.

Still she paused. She did not want to be in charge; she did not want those desperate hands yanking on her sleeve as she passed; she did not want to remain sober while everyone else drank; she did not want to be pregnant, even, and responsible for another life.

But no one else was able to be in charge; she was not free to do as whim dictated because innocent people would suffer, and unless the scroll was wrong she was most certainly pregnant.

She was able to remember the glowing bits of metapheromone Sphere had generated with music in the hive. He had become one with the City and claimed to be able to use it. She, on the other hand, was mostly used by it, and was only able to use its own energy to flip its momentum in a new direction. This room was small and primitive compared with the golden energy she had been filled with in the hive.

But she was pretty certain that it had what she needed, if she could only steel herself to use it.

"What do we need in order to function—to be able to think, and do our tasks, and survive—to be *human*—and what is the smallest dose of it, and how should it be administered?"

There. Too much at once? Many of the lights turned green, while others changed to a colored pattern rather than random winks, and it looked to her as if it was emerging into greater and greater order. Don't worry, she told herself, *it* can do the work; *it* can do the thinking.

She hoped. Her palms were sweating. She heard steps overhead, even heard dim shouts outside on the river, and knew that she didn't have a lot of time. They were waking up, no doubt in much worse shape than her. Yesterday's deterioration could only continue, and she feared the stories embedded within them—stories from American literature, the whole gamut, Raymond Chandler to Flannery O'Connor to Frank Baum to . . . well, just everything. Murder—she knew that. Pain, fear, love . . . the entire range of human emotion powerfully distilled by literature, but here with no outside stimulus, simply welling up from within and flowering in the brain like long-held poisons, manifesting in mad and inappropriate action; deadly action. They could not be so gripped; to survive they would have to be able to grasp their situation, to see their surroundings. She remembered that first morning, how the man had pulled her outside and commanded her to *see;* how they had all rejoiced in the beauty of their new freedom; how all had been harmonious. That was what they needed. Unless they could somehow get *through* this, and survive without the metapheromones. That was the best option; otherwise they were so limited. But she didn't know if that was possible.

She had been resting her hand in the palmprint and she was startled to see a message flash: MORE OF THAT #47 WE NEED TO KNOW WHAT WE ARE AIMING FOR.

Verity bit her lip. She did not want to program them any more; no. She wanted them to be able to survive on their own. She wanted their true individuality to emerge at last. For good *or* for ill, each to their own, for she had no right to make them into her own image of what a human should be; that would be as dangerous and lopsided an enterprise as Abe's mad Cincinnati.

The lights blinked all at once and the scroll said THANK YOU. WE NEED TIME FOR EVOLUTION TO OCCUR.

Fine, she thought; go ahead and program freedom. It seemed an absolute contradiction to her.

"How long do you need?"

Brief pause. VERY LONG. SEVEN MINUTES.

She smiled briefly. Such a worried sensibility. "Fine."

She rose and paced, feeling on the verge of Christmas. What wonderful pheromonal presents would emerge, and in what form? Would they splat forth, drinkable? Would a giant heap of wafers come spewing out?

She caught a glimpse of her scroll, and saw that it was composing odd pictures—chemical bonds, she recalled from her time in the Bee Library.

"What am I seeing?" she asked.

ARTIFICIAL METAPHEROMONES. WE HAVE MADE A MISCALCULATION. YOURS WILL BE READY SOON. THE REST WILL BE COMPLETED ASAP.

ASAP?

Then the lights went dark.

Verity stumbled and found the chair with one hand; sat, and discovered her scroll with the other; put her palm where the print had been but nothing happened.

Discouragement darkened her mind. Christmas indeed. Just another day of hell. "Wake up!" she yelled, but no lights occurred. "Function! Start! What's the answer? Too hard for you to figure out?"

She slumped in her chair. Well fine. It sensed your ambiguity and went one way instead of the other. It was probably for the best. She rose, grabbed her scroll (at least she could study the tutorial), and found the door, relieved to find that it would let her out. She walked slowly down the deck.

Her scroll beeped as she walked, and she took it out and looked at it.

The scroll said she was looking at a map of the boiler deck, and that the light that was blinking was in Stateroom 5.

She hurried down one flight of stairs and walked first one way, then the other, quickly. She came to a locked door but a palmplate flashed and it opened to her.

She went in, and closed the door behind her.

"Hello, number forty-seven," said the room.

"I am not number forty-seven, I am Verity," she said, and waited.

"We have thought the problem over and have decided that the best solution is gloves. Yours are in compartment number five thirty-eight." A tiny green light on the opposite wall came on and blinked.

"Gloves?"

"The gloves are made of a light, clear material infused with metapheromones individually tailored to your receptors. They will remind you of who you are, they will balance you, and they will do the same for everyone."

"Can they block the plague?" asked Verity, eagerly. "Yes! Make them so that we will also be freed of the Norleans Plague."

She waited an anxious moment before the voice came again. "The Norleans Plague, as you call it, cannot be hacked."

"Hacked?"

"Deciphered, decoded, disabled. It instantly re-forms when challenged. This is known."

"Known by who? I thought you were smart. Who are you?" asked Verity.

There was only silence.

"And how can they remind me of who I am when I'm only number forty-seven?"

There was no answer.

She heard the staggering footsteps of someone passing down the corridor. The person pounded on each door, once, as he passed. "For the love of God, help me, please," he moaned. "Somebody!"

Verity held her breath, hoping that the room wouldn't say anything as he passed. As the sound of the steps and the thumps grew more faint, the room said, "It is up to you."

"What will happen if they don't get these metapheromones?" she asked. There was silence for a minute. Then the room said, "We do not know."

Verity felt twitchy, unsettled, as if tiny bugs were crawling over her body, and her mind flashed blue again. *Norleans.*

All I have to do is put on those gloves, she thought, and I'll feel much better. I'll be able to think straight.

I'll know who I am.

You'll know who they tell who you are, she told herself, yet took a step toward the green, blinking light.

She stopped.

She wiped sweat from her forehead. Hadn't she freed them—and herself—from Cincinnati to get away from this sort of thing?

Angrily, she turned and left, slamming the door behind her.

Outside, all was chaos.

Seven

◯◯◯◯◯◯◯◯◯◯◯◯◯◯◯◯◯◯◯

Human Radio Blues

The scene before Verity reminded her of medieval etchings of purgatory from one of those musty books at the Shaker Hill library. One that John had not burned. But this had sound and motion.

The mass of humanity on the rafts writhed before her eyes. Cries of anguish rose and fell. Someone jumped from a deck above her and plummeted past; hit the water with a smack and did not resurface. Numb, Verity did not spring to action, though a part of her said, *Leap down and rescue him!*

The scene assumed dreamlike contours—softened; distant. A little girl wearing a bright blue shirt caught her eye, so far away that Verity could not see her face, only a mop of dark hair.

That particular shade . . . it was so lovely, so soothing. It was time to get under way. She wished these troublesome rafts would clear out soon or the riverboat would have to plow them under. Why was she not dressed yet? No matter. How many days did she have? There was something about needing to complete this trip . . . by . . . when? She hummed a few bars of "The Erie Canal."

"Verity!" It was Lil, towering over her, wearing, this fine morning, a dress covered with purple glitters. Verity blinked.

"Are you all right? Hell, you're as bad off as the rest of them." Lil's eyes were concerned. She frowned, jerked her head back to the door from which Verity had emerged. "What were you doing in there?"

Verity found she could barely remember. It was all rather muzzy. "Nothing," she said. "It's time to go. I've got to get the boat started."

Lil tried the door, but it was locked. Verity wasn't sure why, but was pleased at that fact. She walked away but turned when she heard a crunching sound. The door dangled from the hinges; Lil was braced against the railing.

She grinned at Verity. "I suppose you thought these fancy shoes were all show? Strong as steel, light as a feather, the ad said. And they last *forever.*"

Verity was impressed. She knew that she couldn't even walk in Lil's black heels, much less use them to kick down a door. Lil prowled inside, touched on a light. "My, my. What have we here?"

"None of your business," said Verity crossly. "Leave it alone."

"Oh," said Lil. "This is interesting." She stepped back outside, looked around. A ten-year-old boy was hurrying down the deck, eyes crazed, muttering, "They're not going to put me back in the trouble house, oh, no."

"Wait a minute," commanded Lil, and the boy shrank back.

"You're *not* going to put me in the trouble house!" he said and tried to run past Lil but she grabbed both wrists and he twisted vainly, panting. "Let go! I don't want to go to the trouble house." He started to sob as Lil adroitly avoided his kicks.

Lil pulled him inside the door and pushed him into the chair that Verity had been sitting in a few minutes earlier. "Sit still! I'm not sending you to the trouble house. But I might if you don't—here! That's right. Not an inch! Verity! I need your help."

Verity stood reluctantly in the doorway.

"Where's your scroll?" Lil asked the boy. Glaring at her, he pulled it from his shirt pocket. Lil took it.

"That's good. Hmmm. Nice little gizmos, eh?"

"Don't you have one?" asked Verity.

Lil ignored her. "Okay, good. Number three-fifty-six. Kind of slow and crude but—here—" Verity watched her give that number to the room using a keyboard she hadn't noticed. A sweet smell filled the air, just for an instant, so quickly that she thought maybe she had imagined it. A drawer glowed green briefly and Lil nodded to the boy. "Go ahead. Open it." She watched as he touched the circle on the door and it slid open soundlessly. Lil looked inside. "Well, I'll be. Gloves. That's novel. Go ahead." She nodded at the boy. "Put them on. Now!"

The boy shrugged and pulled them on. Verity watched them blend into his hands like a second skin. The only reason she could tell that he was wearing them was because a message glowed on the back of his left hand. He lifted it, looked at it. He blinked and took a deep breath. "My name is Jet?" he asked. The tremble in his voice vanished. He looked at Lil doubtfully. "Well, that's what the scroll said too. . . ."

"Okay," said Lil. "Great. Thanks, Jet. Run along now."

He looked at Lil and at Verity. "Who *are* you?"

"I said *move,*" commanded Lil. With a backward look, he continued down the deck, looking at the back of his hand as if reading a watch.

And no doubt, thought Verity, the correct time was in the gloves.

"Now for yours," said Lil.

"No," said Verity. "Jet was right. Who are you? What are you doing here? What do you know about me?"

"I can't answer any of those questions right now," she said, and Verity thought, At least she didn't say that she's Lightnin' Lil. "We need to get these gloves distributed."

"I don't think so," said Verity, able to focus at least on this conversation. "They're what we left the city to get away from."

"I won't quibble philosophy with you right at this moment," said Lil. "Though I will at some other time. But I don't need your permission."

Verity involuntarily glanced down at Lil's shoes.

"Don't you see," Verity argued, "they—we—need to get *through* this. Away from all this *control.*"

Lil shook her head briefly, impatiently. "You don't understand. Or maybe you don't want to. Or maybe you can't, right at this minute. It's not just a whim of theirs or a simple addiction like caffeine. These people have been mainlining information for so many cycles that they don't even know how long it's been. They've been doing this because of physical modifications made to their bodies—modifications they *paid* for. Dearly. And if you want to put it that way, they did have a choice in the beginning and they deserve to be able to live and sort it all out." Her voice was low and urgent. She began touching the flat panel like a pianist.

"How do you know all this?" asked Verity.

Lil looked up for a moment and her eyes looked ancient; weary. *She might be a hundred years old* flashed through Verity's mind.

Lil turned back to the keyboard. "Information wants to be free, Verity. It flows on, through us, around us, it doesn't matter. It doesn't need us but we need it. I can't say that I know much more than that, anymore. This is information. *They* are information. You and I are information." She frowned and continued on with a flurry of long fingers. A voice said, "Six thousand and thirty-two gloves being readied."

"How long?" asked Lil.

"Thirty-five minutes and seventeen seconds," said the voice. "You will find them in a bin to the right of the drawer."

Lil leaned back against the counter. Her purple sparkles flashed small rainbows around the tiny room. "Round up as many people as you can," she said. "We've got to distribute these as quickly as possible."

"What about . . . Lil, there are people ahead of us who won't have any gloves. What will happen to them?"

Lil bowed her head briefly, then looked back up at Verity. Verity had the fleeting impression that such a thought was nothing compared with what Lil might have had to consider before.

"That's life," she said bleakly; then, "They might get through it. It's possible. We can only think about here and now. That seems to be quite enough."

"But don't they have to come here, like Jet, with their scrolls?" asked Verity. "That will take forever."

Lil shook her head. "Their own bodies will individually initialize the gloves. That's what I just fixed."

Verity frowned. "But—does that mean that everyone's—"

"You're quick," said Lil. "It means that every last one of those people and more are in this system here; that's right. You've brought it all along with you. Each person will get the entire system and their specific metapheromone receptors will communicate with the gloves. Bionan is infinitesimally small, and infinitesimally powerful. At that point, the gloves will then respond with the proper mix for orientation and focus. And then—I'm not sure what will happen."

Dread filled Verity, weakening her knees. "The proper mix?" She felt so irrational, so disappointed, so *angry.* She tried again. "Lil, we all need to get *away* from that! We just need to be *normal."*

"Are you normal?" asked Lil gently, her eyes compassionate in the dim light. "Are you, Verity? Who, or what, are you? You're not like the rest of them."

Verity said nothing.

"Well, if you could be normal, would you want to be?"

Verity stood silently, her whole world turning on Lil's question. But she had heard it before. She would always, she realized, answer it in the same way.

"No," she whispered. She had to whisper, because the answer stuck in her throat. "I don't think I ever was normal. I don't think there's anything for me to go back to. But I don't think I would want to, either." Greed, she thought, greed for the new. For the ability to access information. Hunger for the visions.

"Give them the same freedom of choice," said Lil. "If they're dead, they've definitely lost that." Her mouth curved in a faint smile. She tilted her head and looked into Verity's eyes and stopped smiling. "You can talk to me, you know."

Then the wall beeped. Lil patted her on her shoulder and pulled a sheaf of gloves from a large bin and handed them to Verity. "Let's get to work," she said.

The morning sky deepened into a very satisfying blue as Verity passed out gloves. They were diaphanous, yet strong as spider silk, more like a web than a solid layer of material. A fresh breeze blew back her hair as she walked from raft to raft, passing out large quantities and instructing people to distribute them.

Lil was quite forceful with the gloves the first hour or so, cornering people and *making* them put on the gloves, then giving them a stack "fresh out of the oven," she said, and telling them to go forth and do like-wise. Once they were wearing them, they seemed to understand; now, three hours later, the scene before Verity was one of exhausted calm. At one point during the chaos everything had flipped from disorder to order. About twenty people had taken it upon themselves to initiate the breakfast chores, and while she watched some of the rafters carry their food back to their raft in a little basket, Verity wondered if food might not be a more efficient medium through which to calm them and sank down on a bench, horrified at the thought and feeling on the edge of sane. She learned forward, put her elbows on her knees, and locked her hands together.

"That would be good, Verity," she told herself, the words spinning out into the clear spring air like a song with which she could entertain herself. It was almost as if someone else were speaking. Perhaps there were many such selves waiting to have their say. "You could really look into this. You could figure out what you wanted them to think and do and feel and learn how to put it into their food. Something like, 'Ignore that city back there. Forget it all happened. Be happy!' Marvelous idea!" She pulled her legs close to her chest and bent her head down so that she was squeezed into one point and yelled, "I just want them to be *free!* I want them to be *free!* They need to be free!"

She couldn't seem to stop. It was satisfying just to yell while yet an-other part of her said this is silly, Verity, it's not doing any good at all and still she could hear the words over and over and over again—

Then someone was prying her hands apart.

"She's crying." That was Blaze. He wiped her face roughly with his shirt. "I don't know what to do." His voice was despairing.

It was Lil who grabbed her right hand, she saw when she squinted open her right eye just a bit.

"No!" she yelled.

"Hold her arm still," Lil said and Blaze's grip was like steel and then the glove was on.

She saw, as Lil pulled it on, pale green ovals in it which matched the receptor locations in her own hands and then they blended together. It felt warm, for a moment, and then tingly, and then she could not feel it at all.

"The other one for good measure," said Lil and it was easier for them to pry forth her other arm.

Then she was lying on her back on the bench listening to them.

"What's going on?" asked Blaze. "I just woke up. I can't believe I slept so long. I guess I was up pretty late."

Playing with the radio stones, thought Verity. Blaze could sleep through anything.

"Verity thought of a way to . . . orient everyone," said Lil.

I did not, thought Verity. Don't blame me. The boat did it.

"So how do you know all this?" Blaze asked Lil. "What's that you put on her hands? She didn't want it."

That's right, Blaze. Ask her! Ask her everything! I'd like to know too.

She wanted to know all these things. But she felt much too lazy to ask, as if she were floating in a warm, pleasant bath, with the blue sky overhead, which was a very strange thought because her baths had always been taken in a big white tub with white beaded boards overhead, using solar-heated water pumped with the red handle at the kitchen sink. Though she had from time to time floated on her back on Bear Creek; even in high summer the water was cold enough to turn her blue in ten minutes.

Blue . . .

She realized that Lil was not saying anything. Her head began to clear. She began to know things. These were not new things, but things that had existed in a haze, as if she had not been thinking straight and now she could.

She sat up on the bench. Blaze sat next to her and took her hand. "Are you feeling better?" He rubbed her hand a few times. "That thing just seems barely there."

She nodded and looked around. Lil's sparkly dress caught her eye as it disappeared around a corner.

"How did Lil know what to do?" asked Blaze.

Verity remembered the argument she'd overheard. "I think—maybe she's from the government," said Verity.

"The *goddamned* government?" asked Blaze, a faint smile on his face. That's what Russ had always called it.

"Must be," said Verity. "She knows something, that's for sure. There's a room down the deck with a—" She frowned, unsure what to call it. "—system node in it. It's a place where you can access the information in the boat." She laughed briefly. "I didn't put that information there. Rose did. Lil knew how to use it right off."

"That wouldn't be too hard, Verity," said Blaze. "I figured out how to use the Dayton Library pretty fast. It seems so natural. So—what's the word? Intuitive. That's it. The library told me that it was set up to work intuitively. Maybe that's the way this boat is."

Verity turned to Blaze and felt tears of helplessness well up again, though she blinked them back. "Oh, Blaze," she said, "I thought we were through with all that. I thought we could—" She stopped. She was no longer sure what she thought about the future, for now she had an entirely new past. She was not the person she had thought she was during all the years of her growing up on Shaker Hill. She touched the nub behind her right ear softly. A memory sponge; she had one behind each ear. Filled with thoughts others had put there . . .

Despite the new stability of the gloves, or maybe because of them allowing her to pause and take a breath in the onrush of biological buffeting, she began to sob deeply and harshly. Everything was gone. Everything. Nothing was the way she thought it was but what had replaced those certainties was like quicksand and in this world she was called on constantly to act, to make decisions that affected the lives of many others, with very little information.

Blaze caught her and held her tight against his chest. She felt his hands on her back and remembered for a moment the way he had looked at her, touched her that one time at Shaker Hill before he had been killed—

As if he could tell what she was thinking, he held her closer. "*Relax,* Verity," he whispered in her ear. "You're so *nervous.* Relax. Relax."

She did. It was a small miracle. She pushed back from Blaze, looked into his concerned eyes.

"This is all we have," he said. "There's nothing else. We're going to have to make the best of it."

"What do you mean, there's nothing else?" There was the whole world!

The look in his eyes did not change—steady, yet somehow bleak. "There is no heaven, Verity. I was dead. I didn't see angels, believe me."

There it was again. His despair at finding no heaven. "What did you see?" She tried to stop the images but they ran their course: her dear dog Cairo, spun round by the force of the bullet, John training the rifle on her, as she watched from her window above the yard. Blaze pulling on John and John turning faster than thought and shooting Blaze square in the chest.

And herself, flinging the radio stone, which struck John in the head and killed him.

"I'm not sure," he said. "But it wasn't angels."

"Maybe it's because you weren't really dead," she said, but she was pretty sure that he was right. She shrugged. "These people don't need heaven anyway. It seems as if they could live forever."

"They can live forever in a human world," said Blaze, standing and leaning on the railing. Miraculously, all was orderly now, almost subdued. They were probably exhausted. "They won't ever get to God's world. There is no God to get to." He turned and looked at Verity. "There is no point. And that's the strangest thing of all. It's very hard to get used to. I don't think you've tried, yet. But you'll have to."

Verity lay on her back on a bench on the very top deck. It was midafternoon. She was watching the polarization of the sun.

She sat up, and turned west. Her vision oriented her instantly, precisely.

Shall I fly? she thought. She took a deep breath, a breath of all the scents deep and revealing of what the others were thinking. Shall I speed to a City where the sheer joy of instantaneous communication is embedded in the very matter that surrounds me? Where I can communicate by simply thinking in a very particular practiced way that will then release precise metapheromones that the others of us can then *sense*...

Shall *we?*

She shifted to human vision just by wanting to and looked around.

Cumulus clouds drifted low over forest, and on the north shore the signs of an old partially submerged strip mall rippled the river's leisurely flow. ADRIANNE'S HAIR RAZORS. REPLICATORS BY HARRY FULLY LICENSED LIMITED NAN. WING-DING SUPERMART. The color had been leached from the bottom of the letters but their relief was still clear.

Rafters stood, as did she, on their various crafts, staring at the beauty of the day as if it had been suddenly revealed to them. It was so very beautiful. In color, in form, in sheer *being*. She looked at her hands, and found them beautiful too, their economy and grace. She had never really *looked* at her hands before. . . .

The sun gave it all a lovely clarity, this silent drifting, for a few minutes ago she had found even the wash of the paddlewheel intrusive on this early-summer crystalline beauty and then the sound had ceased. . . .

It had ceased with her *thought*. . . .

She brought her hand, a second ago so otherworldly, to her chest, as if it could still her rapidly beating heart.

No. Not my thought.

But yes. And yet . . . had it really been hers? Hers alone? Or had that thought been the echo of what the others were also thinking, feeling? Let us have silence so we can hear the beauty of the world around us. . . .

Could it be that they needed a Queen no longer?

She saw then that everyone was looking around like her. Puzzled. Tremulous. On the brink of some great Thought . . .

Drifting down the Great Ohio River, Beautiful Ohio, Most Blessed of Rivers, Most Glorious of Waterways . . .

Once the political demarcation between slave land and free.

The wonder of the land lay upon her. For a moment it was as if the very shores spoke. Beyond the strip mall was a tall, conical hill. An Indian Mound; they'd had one in Miamisburg. The burial sites of untold generations of people. And a pioneer town on a bluff, Clarksville, named after its founder, George Rogers Clark, Revolutionary War veteran. George's heart had been broken by Jefferson, who sent George's younger brother William off to explore the Louisiana Territory instead of him.

The *Territory.*

This had been the new land. The old inhabitants had been subdued, killed, like . . . like . . .

Verity shook her head, angry at the intrusive feelings that ran through her then, and the thought that surfaced from the tough yet gentle part of her that she was beginning to know as Rose. There was no mistaking her.

Like the people before nan. Soon there will be none of them left. I have seen them, in my travels, scattered in their reservation-like colonies, trying to preserve the old human ways, the old human mind, the separateness, the individuality. And I weep for them. I weep for them, for they are a vanishing species. And because I started out as one of them.

The spell, the clarity of the moment, or of the hour, however long it had been, was shattered. And it had been shattered by reality.

And yet . . .

It was not only Clarksville, she realized, drawing her legs close to her chest and letting the sun beat down on her head, happy to be out in its warmth without the fear of cancer which had kept her under broad-brimmed hats for most of her life. She knew that bionan now protected her, that mutations would be instantly repaired despite the greatly increased deadliness of the sun's rays.

There was more. Much more.

And she knew part of it. Everyone knew part of it. Their own part, what they had witnessed, what they had known. There was no real centrality to it. It was like a great mosaic. She only knew a few of the tiles of it, and could not even imagine where they fit within the entire history, which had many dimensions, so many that every new bit of information would change the whole picture.

They would not fly.

We shall not fly.

No matter that they could not, not now. For she realized, with more warmth than shock, that if they all so desired, they could create a new Flower City in the wilderness. Or even move into an existing, deserted town . . . Clarksville . . .

But they were looking outward now. And forward.

Forward, toward Norleans. And so there was no time to settle, no time to build. They were moving on, downriver, and it was all the Territory now, open and brilliant and filled with themselves.

What were the nexuses around which their story would coalesce?

Something on her glove caught her eye. Yes. There it was again, flickering, and then more solid, in bold black letters as if etched on the back of her hand:

THE INFORMATION WARS: ACT ONE.

And then to her delight phrases and images cascaded over her hands, one picture or word superseding the other swiftly, a babble of visions and razor-sharp tiny pagelike successions of text. When she stared at one line in which the word "Norwood" caught her eye it all slowed and she read an address, and then what appeared to be a genealogy tree, and then a similar one replied, on her other hand, and she was able to look up and realized that everyone she could see was staring at their hands, and that went on for at least an hour or maybe more, they were awash in a sea of information and memory. She saw a recipe for Ice Box Rolls, a favorite chair rocking on the porch in the breeze, a baby dressed in white eyelet, a jet streaking through blue sky.

And then a jolting, powerful melody broke forth, shattering the silence, and the pictures and print with them, but Verity laughed out loud as she recognized it: "The Erie Canal." But halting, hesitant, and coming from . . .

She ran down the stairs, and followed it to its source. It was not difficult. As those around her on the decks and on the rafts sang, and danced, some whirling partners, some alone, she ran. The auditorium door was open, and she leaned against the doorjamb, watching.

The calliope was rising from a hole in the stage! And Blaze, of course, was standing in front of it, pressing on the steam-powered keys with all his might. High windows slanted light onto the semicircle of steel gray pipes from which the music issued. The only thing she could think of to compare this music to was immensely loud flutes.

We are making our story as we go along, she thought, letting the sound wash over her, fill her, infuse her very bones. She settled on the threshold and listened as Blaze segued into some new song that she did not recognize.

A halting rhythm. Haunting. She saw his mouth open, but could not hear his voice at all for the instrument was so very loud.

Then someone stepped around her and she saw that it was Jack. And then Lil.

Tall, thin, and dark, formally dressed as always, they promenaded down to the stage and Jack mounted the small flight of stairs first, bowed to Lil, and assisted her up the stairs. She had never seen the like of the dance they did, holding hands, whirling back, clasping each other close, then parting and dancing alone.

And then there were more people behind her, and they poured past her so that she had to stand to see, and filled the seats, and stood in the seats, and danced on the seats, and danced in all the aisles, and on the stage, while Blaze played "Cincinnati Underworld Woman," and then other songs that she faintly recalled from what she had thought were dreams but that had probably been from the radio stones, blaring their music interruptus late at night when released from the quasar's sweep.

And her hands and lower arms, she saw, were filled with pulsing color, and they released sweet scent.

Remembering the City, remembering pasts she had not previously known, she found herself weeping, and did not know if it was from pain or joy, and did not care, and danced, first as Verity, then as Rose, and then as someone new whom she was just beginning to know. Her Shaker gift of dance expanded and searched out this new grammar of motion, past the dance-language of Bees, from whence it had come, and changed to something she could now only glimpse the edge of. She spun out into it, learning through motion its light.

And the Territory unfolded around them as faint, clear stars appeared in the blue sky of evening.

Ohio. Indiana. Kentucky. Illinois.

Mississippi. Arkansas. Louisiana. The Territory would be there, bold and free and new.

They would dance.

Eight

○○○○○○○○○○○○○○○○○○○

Ghostly Blues

Verity opened her eyes not knowing at first why, wrenched from a dream of heaven where she was able to float invisibly around Blaze's head and tell him that, yes, heaven did exist, had always existed, and always would exist. Like Mother Ann she was everywhere and could see his face brighten with the information and then that world was gone and she was in her dark cabin and Blaze's strange music sounded from very far away.

She blinked again and her heart froze. She could hear someone breathing, quite close to her in the darkness, in the small room she had taken as her own. She wished for a weapon but she had none and what if it was Blaze.

But Blaze would not hover over her, so spooky; he might kneel, he might kiss her; he would most definitely speak.

With one hand she quietly searched for the lightstick she kept handy for when she had to pee. Grasping it, she brought it round as hard as she could hoping to hit something.

The stick did hit something and lit. Verity gasped.

In the instant before he turned and fled she thought she recognized—but no. It couldn't be him.

Not Abe Durancy.

Her throat constricted. She had vanquished him and his plan, surely. In Cincinnati, the day she had ventured into the library to program the boats, that ruined, sorry version of him, incompletely manifested by the City, had wrung her heart with pain. If this prowler was Abe—and she could barely believe the possibility—why had he followed? To seek some sort of revenge?

She did the only thing she knew how to do in the face of fear.

She jumped out of bed and tried to run down the source.

All was dark on the river, save for a few fires that burned on rafts and painted orange winking flames on the face of the Ohio. She smelled faint woodsmoke and water. She heard nothing except the rush of the current. Her heart was beating hard, though. A stranger had been in her room.

She had no clue as to where he had gone. She had heard no splash. He could have ducked into any number of rooms, slipped round a dozen corners, climbed up or down stairways. Perhaps he was studying, even now, his ruined reflection in a gently lit mirror.

Could it have really been him? Could the outside world heal one as twisted as him, restore him to functioning health? Could he even survive? He was her blind spot, her nemesis, a dark side of her own self which she could never see. She had outmaneuvered him and the programs of his devising by only a hairbreadth. For a moment all her doubts and guilt about giving all of these people the Norleans Plague vanished. It had been right.

She knew his sickness intimately, a sickness composed in equal parts of twisted love and guilt and the need for total control. The Rose part of her had anticipated all that and had provided the tools for her to help release Cincinnati from his and India's bizarre rule.

Perhaps there was no place for him there, any longer.

It was impossible to predict what he might have in mind now. But maybe he'd been healed. If it really was him. Maybe he even had the plague himself.

She felt better out on the deck. The night was normal and quite beautiful. A breeze blew her white nightgown against her body, blew back her hair, and she leaned against the dew-beaded railing and wanted to gaze at the stars for a long time.

But she did not feel easy doing so. She turned and walked down the deck to Blaze's room.

But after a moment, she turned around. She would not cower in Blaze's room. If she did that tonight, why not tomorrow night? And the next night after that? Besides, Durancy had some explaining to do!

She thought of questions she would ask if she saw him again. *How can you survive out here? Tell me about Rose.* He couldn't hurt her, out here, away from the City. He couldn't.

Light lay in a wedge on the deck ahead. She quickened her step, realizing that it was the salon where she had seen Jack and Lil playing pool. She fully intended to walk right in the door, but stopped by the open window. Jack and Lil were shadows behind the curtain.

"This is useless, Lil. Utterly useless. And dangerous. For us and them too. It's really too late. I think my information was wrong."

Verity heard a sigh. "Oh, Jack, I hope not. It *can't* be wrong. It just *can't* be."

Verity stepped closer. Was Lil crying? That didn't seem like her.

"Well," said Jack. "Here. It'll be all right. Maybe I'm wrong. I mean right. To begin with. Oh, hell. I don't know what I mean anymore."

Lil gave a muffled, sobbing laugh.

"Anyway," continued Jack, "what better way to go, than riding down this glorious river on this wonderful boat?"

Lil said, "It's just that you're probably right, Jack. And it's so hard to bear."

Verity's nose itched and she sneezed.

"Who's that?" called Jack. His chair scraped back. "Could be that madman . . . I told him to leave us alone."

Verity heard him walk across the room. "It's me," she said.

Jack poked his head out the door and pushed it open a bit wider. "Come on in. How long you been out there?"

"Not long," she said. "I just got here. I can't sleep."

"You've come to the right place," said Jack. "Know how to play poker?"

Verity went inside. Lil's face looked puffy. "What's wrong?" She sat at the card table.

"Oh, I'm just a silly old lady," said Lil.

"How old are you?" asked Verity, as Jack rummaged around and muttered about how it was hard to keep a deck of cards in this place. "And what were you talking about just now?"

Jack and Lil looked at each other. Lil sighed and looked away. "Old enough to know better," she muttered. Verity was quite surprised when Lil reached over and patted her hand. "Later," she said. "Don't worry. You'll know everything when the time is right."

"But I want to know now," she said. "I *demand* that you tell me! I'm the captain."

Jack said "Aha!" and held up an unopened deck of cards. "We'll try not to be too hard on you, Verity. For the first half hour." He winked and opened the package.

Nine

○○○○○○○○○○○○○○○○○○

Information Blues

The grizzled old man stood up and pounded the table in the dining hall and proclaimed, "I was a general in the Information Wars and I could have told the whole lot of you to go to hell and you would have spent the rest of your lives hieing to the nearest volcano vent and jumping into it! But they trapped me inside Cincinnati, the enemy did! Helluva great strategy. Little did they know I'd escape someday!"

Homemade noodles, Blaze's latest attempt to use up the flour, went flying as he brandished a forkful. Verity was glad Blaze wasn't here; sometimes he played the piano while everyone ate. He would be pretty irritated. Verity was sitting at the general's table, and continued to calmly eat; she was famished, and Blaze made excellent noodles as Sare had taught him well. Hers were always tough. These were tender and swimming in butter or something quite *like* butter.

To Verity's surprise the woman sitting next to her stood; her chair fell backward with a clatter. "There were no generals in the Information Wars! I won't have you talking like that about what killed my father and my sisters! As if a little twerp like you had anything to do with it!" Her face was red and twisted. Verity decided that maybe she had better move if she wanted to finish her dinner; the woman picked up a glass and hurled it at the general and reached for a plate—*Verity's* plate—

"Hey!" said Verity.

And in another second the air was full of flying food and plates. Verity ducked beneath the table.

"Idiots," she heard hissed next to her. A familiar voice.

"Jack?"

He threw back the tablecloth so the light was better. In front of them was a lot of squished food and broken plates and moving legs. "I don't think I'm going to let them eat in the dining room again," said Verity, and Jack laughed heartily.

"I thought things would go more smoothly now," said Verity, complaint in her voice. "I thought they wouldn't act like . . ."

"Like children?" asked Jack. "They're finally *remembering,* I think. They've settled down enough for that. It's painful. There used to be something called therapy. Well, a lot of things called therapy. But *remembering,* and sometimes acting out the remembering, was a part of some therapies. Bringing what was lost back into the conscious mind so that it can be examined and learned from. Looks like this crowd runs along the acting-out theory."

"Well then, who *did* start the Information Wars?" shouted the general, whose quavery indignant voice was easy to recognize.

"France! Seattle! China! Ireland! The moon colony! Cuba!" Through the din Verity could pick out just about any country or place she could think of.

"The pity of it is," said Jack, "is that they're all correct."

"So tell me about it," said Verity. But Jack was gone, his long legs, clad in perfectly pressed pants, lost in the sea of legs.

"Russia! Anarchists! Fascists!"

Then the old general shouted again. "Hey, sit down. I think we might have something here."

Verity's glove blinked and a lit message appeared—TUNE IN NEXT TIME—it said. Then that fluttered and in its place, in stark letters, was a question.

TITLE?

Verity watched, fascinated, and many words fluttered on her glove, some overlapping, in various scripts, colors, and sizes, intermingled with images tiny but laser sharp. Then it slowed to a few repeated words—QUEEN CITY OF THE WEST, THE INFORMATION WARS, WHEN BEES PLAY STRIDE PIANO, HUMANITY LOST, THE RISING STORM, MATTER'S WHIRLWIND—and flashed among them for long minutes. Bees, thought Verity, wondering why, since she had no idea what was going on or what the title applied to.

Then it settled on SMALLER THAN SAND.

Hmph, thought Verity. An ugly title. WHO ASKED YOU? said the glove. Verity wished she had a glove for her glove and it went blank.

The room buzzed with conversation. Verity crept out from under the table, avoiding patches of squished food. She pounded on the table. Just like the general.

"Who's going to clean up this mess?" she yelled.

She was completely ignored. "I *said*—"

"We heard you," said a nearby woman. "We're busy."

So much for control, thought Verity. It did seem to come in handy at times. She climbed down from the table.

As she made her way through the small groups of people, she heard snatches of excited conversation—"Yes, I remember that. I was in Duluth—"

"But after that it was the worst. We didn't know anything for two months. Horrible!"

"My little girl—my little girl ran off and joined the Advance Squad. It was like the end of the world for me."

"Remember when China—"

Verity found a broom in a corner cupboard. She set it against the wall and started picking up the chairs and flipping them so their seats were resting on the table. They were very light. No one paid any attention to her, though when she got to work with the broom they moved out of her way. Her back began to ache. It was now dark outside. Their chatting hour, Verity supposed, though this had a different energy. A different feel. It was as if something had broken free.

They drifted out on deck as if by one accord, and Verity heard them clumping up the stairs. But someone was left.

It was Jack, working his way toward her from the other end of the dining room with a mop.

It felt good to be doing something simple, something with a result that was easily seen. The chandeliers, turned up bright so she could see everything, glittered above. She continued to work; after a while the floor was entirely swept and the dishes were piled in huge tubs, awaiting the dishwashers. Verity held up her hand and touched the first joint of her index finger. The night's schedule of chores appeared: blank.

Jack stood next to her, looking over her shoulder. "I'll do them," he said.

"But I don't understand," said Verity. "What happened? Everything was moving along so well; things finally seemed settled."

"It's what's known as a chaotic system, Verity," Jack said, grinning.

"Well, you can say that again."

"Chaos is actually an old theory which people at one time felt was the underlying commonality of dynamical systems. Which this is."

"Oh?" asked Verity. She pulled out a chair and sat down. "What do you mean by 'this'?"

Jack dimmed the chandeliers and sat in another chair. The river sloshed past outside the open windows, and Verity heard faint shouts now and then, presumably from the people upstairs.

"Good question," said Jack. "Well, weather is a good example of a dynamical system. The emerging awareness of the people heading downriver is another example. The initial spread of nanotechnology was an illustration of Chaos Theory, and the subsequent patterns that have emerged worldwide are another. A visual display of the various surges is quite fractal-like. Now we are awash in information, yet it is largely unusable. We are crippled."

Verity hoped he could not see on her face the thrill that ran through her body as she realized that Jack knew what he was talking about. She was suddenly dead sure that he had *been there*—

And that he did not really want her to know this. He must be kind of tired; punchy. She decided to bypass "fractal" for the moment.

"What did you do as a statistician, Jack?" she asked, covering a pretend yawn with her hand.

He gave her a sharp look. "I gambled," he said, and his voice sounded sad and defeated. "I gambled big. And I lost." He started to sing, his rich voice filling the room and echoing off the far walls and ceiling:

> A gamblin man he has no home
> A gamblin man he's bound to roam

Verity saw Blaze standing in the doorway, attracted to Jack's song, she knew, like a moth to a flame. He listened to a verse, then sat down on the piano stool. It was too low, so he got up, gave it a spin, sat down again, and started to play, running an alternating bass up the underside of Jack's lament, which Jack did not cease when joined. Instead he bent his head, nodding as Blaze played the break while he went silent, then picked up on the other side and repeated the first verse. He was silent for a moment after the music ended, and night noises suffused the cool, damp air.

Jack went over and leaned on the windowsill. "Did you know that the Ohio River was the boundary between the slave states and the free states? Why does that seem so recent to me? And all the years of growing up I never gave these things a thought. It was ancient history. We had important things to do. Yet whenever I'm here, I can't help but think of ancestors of mine who risked their lives trying to get to this river, and cross on over into freedom. It's like the river—and the land—are trying to make me remember. Like it's embedded in them, like they've been waiting for me. This river—there's something about this river." He sighed. "Ah, well. We are all flawed, all changed. None of us are pure anymore. There are no old humans left in the whole world. Oh, of course there are some. But they're statistically invisible. No longer a factor. The rising tide of change is lapping an inch beneath our noses. And the moon is full." His voice was low and musing.

After a minute he turned and walked through the dining room, past her and Blaze, and onto the deck, with a slow gait, his hands in his pockets, the expression on his face unreadable in the dim light.

Verity thought about what Jack had said. A chaotic system? Perhaps they had all been pushed into some new level, some critical imbalance, and there would later be a resolution. But all was now, actually, in flux. They were afloat and though they knew that they were heading west and when they got to Cairo they would head south, that was about all they knew. They didn't know who and what they really were anymore; they didn't know what the world was like though it seemed a bit more stable than Cincinnati. It was as if she had been to the future and now was back in a more familiar present but even that was not true. Had the Flower Cities risen briefly and then failed? Or had some become what they had been meant to be? Somewhere in the world, had nanotechnology delivered on its magnificent promises? Were humans capable of using it as it should be used? Who existed who could decide? The Durancys of the world?

She looked down at her gloves, which were swarming with words and tiny images. They had never told her who she was.

Because she was nobody. She was only #47, a person created for a particular reason. She looked like Rose. Rose was in her somehow, from when she had been an integral part of the City. Now she was faced with the task of creating herself. She had nothing in particular to remember. She knew all about Rose's life and death, had remembered them in Cincinnati, and her own creation too, and how a large Bee had dropped her outside Cincinnati, fifteen years ago. . . .

She reached up involuntarily with one hand, to touch the nub behind her right ear, but caught herself in time.

The memories in them were not her, either. She felt that, at all costs, she just wanted to keep Rose away. Build a barrier behind which to hide. No matter that Rose might have information that might come in handy. She'd been to the very bottom of that particular well; had sprung from the horrible suffocating depths with all the strength she could muster and barely made it to the top, gasping for her very life.

Let Rose sleep. Let whoever Verity might be learn to live.

Blaze put his hands back on the piano keys and began to play Jack's song again, with a slow solid rhythm. "Think you can dance to this, Verity?" he asked without turning around.

"It's strange—I don't feel much like dancing today." It was as if her gift had been too fragile for real life, had been overwhelmed. Or maybe it was hiding. Continuing the transmutation begun after she donned the gloves. She didn't really care. She was bone-tired.

She leaned back in the chair, closed her eyes, and listened to Blaze play, feeling deep joy in the pure fact of his aliveness.

It was enough for now.

* * *

She walked back to her cabin in the dark. Blaze would play all night and her heart was sore and her body tired. Fires flickered on the rafts and set tongues of gold dancing on the black river. The night was warm, touched by a slight breeze. Verity yawned and walked into her cabin; looked in a drawer and pulled out a nightgown.

"Rose."

It was a whisper from the door. She turned and saw Durancy standing there, shadowed.

"*Rose.* You must help me, my love. I'm sorry. Sorry about everything. Just—please listen. I'm starting to remember—damn memory! *Damn* memory! Memory is what I've tried to escape for so long."

His voice was harsh and ragged. The light in the bedroom was dim, just one small wall sconce. But his bleak look shook her to the core.

Somehow it called forth in her that whom he sought. Rose.

The heart of Rose awakened. It was Rose who allowed him to approach her, Rose who kept her steady, Rose who reached out to touch the side of his face, and the tears which crept silently down her face were those of the woman whose memories—the body memory that had grown her, and the memories she had found and absorbed while in Cincinnati, giving her the key to freeing it—composed a part of her she wanted and needed to leave behind.

It was no use. With Abe here, it was too damned hard to keep Rose sleeping.

"Abe," she whispered, and embraced him.

He wept aloud, in harsh, ragged sobs that shook him. He was skeleton-thin. "Thank you, Rose, thank you. Thank you."

It was the smell which brought her back to herself. Sweet and sickly, almost as if he were decaying. Verity, not Rose, pushed him back, though gently.

"Don't," he begged, clinging to her. "Just let me hold you. Come back to Cincinnati with me. I've . . . come to my senses. We can just—*live* there." A brief laugh shook his body slightly. "I don't even know what that means anymore. But we can try, you and I. I can't survive out here. The world has changed far beyond my imagining. Or maybe it was I who changed. Whatever. I need you to help me back. Oh, Rose, I'm so thankful that you're listening to me at last."

Verity stepped back then, and left him clinging to the bed rail with one hand, his eyes entreating, one hand reaching for her.

"Listen to me," she said gently, but very firmly, talking slowly and clearly as if to a child though her voice threatened to catch in her throat. "I am not Rose. I don't love you."

"I don't believe you," he said, and the voice was the sweet, entreating voice of a thousand cocoon dreams, all the memories of Rose and of

Cincinnati and of Abe Durancy himself, echoing within her, pulling her. His eyes held hers for a long time, and she could not look away. She looked into timeless agony, and felt Rose awakening even more fully—

She knew then that she had to be strong and even cruel to save all that she had gained, to make everything that she had been through mean anything at all.

"Go away and leave me alone," she said. "Please. As Rose and as Verity, I ask you to go. There can be nothing between us, ever again. I'm sorry. I'm sorry, Abe."

The look on his face made her long to fly to him and say that it wasn't so, that she lied, that she would help him back to whatever Cincinnati had become, and help restore him, help him become all that he might have been—

But he spoke. And saved her.

"I'm sorry too, Verity," he said, slowly, thoughtfully. "I love you, and I love Rose within you. Never before has one of you been so able, so . . . so like a bolt of *lightning*. So very *real*. I . . . I see that I must go."

But still, he lingered, and looked at her searchingly. She could not turn her eyes from his. Her heart beat hard.

"It's rather amazing," he said gently. "I think that even in this pitiful state I have the power to ruin you. That's something, isn't it? Funny! Funny what it's all come to." He reached for her with both arms. "A kiss, then?"

She almost took a step toward him, but he turned suddenly with a cry and rushed from the room, slamming the door behind him.

She forced herself to wait. She held on to the bed rail until her knuckles turned white. She did not think, tried not to remember or even to be. She wished that it were light, and that there were something blue to help her, but there was nothing, nothing but bleak darkness, the loss of all that had ever been for her and for him and for their long-ago Flower City.

Countless images flew through her mind, of shaded streets and old houses, of India and of those later heady days of planning what would be the pinnacle of humans, the Flower Cities, built on unavoidable catastrophe. How glorious, how golden it all was to have been. Her hand moved of its own accord. She could press the memory sponges, have more of this happiness, pure, sweet, intense. . . .

Then she heard the creak of the boat, and some rafters began to sing far off in the night.

Caimineero, down to Cairo . . .

As the plague had rescued them, so it rescued her.

She wiped her face roughly with her palms and took a deep breath and walked across the room and opened the door.

He was gone. The moon was out. She stood at the railing and gazed at it for a long, long time.

3

○ ◇ ○

Blaze Gets the Blues

Ten

○○○○○○○○○○○○○○○○○○○

Soul Change Blues

When Stewball and I got off the *Queen* that morning I wasn't too happy about leaving Verity for so long but it was the best thing to do in the circumstances. She was terribly concerned about the next stretch downriver.

We'd been lucky so far concerning dams. Way back when, it seems, there were numerous locking dams on the Ohio. The quakes had demolished quite a few of them, leaving dangerous breaches through which the current sped; we'd rushed through several with inches to spare, always a harrowing ride. Especially for Verity. She was getting pretty good, I thought—taking us between the massive piers of several abandoned railroad and highway bridges, metal filigree affairs like the one we used to cross to get to Miamisburg, but a whole lot longer. Dam Number Forty-two had been wrenched up from the riverbed so that all its metal innards were exposed. And I think that the river was in a whole new bed in some places. Jack, despite his brag, hadn't been a whole lot of help. But he too thought that between here and Cairo we needed caution. So I was the scout.

I did not know how much that day would change my life.

It seemed a normal early-summer morning, alive with scent and color. Stewball pranced eagerly down the gangplank. The wharf was so big it dwarfed the *Queen*; ten riverboats could have docked there. At one time, it seemed, the Ohio had been a major shipping highway.

Now, the blacktopped landing was pierced by a forest of spindly trees that shook with every gust of wind. The gangway was cranked up behind me; I'd advised Verity to anchor out in the river. There was no telling who might be in these parts, and the only people remotely capable of defending the boat were Jack and Lil. I didn't know about those two. Sometimes I thought they might throw us off and go on ahead with the boat. I regretted having agreed to take them on, but they probably would have managed to go with us anyway.

A huge metal warehouse filled one side of the wharf. It was pocked with rusted holes and the doors rested crumpled like huge pieces of stiff foil on the concrete. Inside were shadows—broken crates and the like— dotted by pinpoints of sunlight. The wind blew my big straw hat right off my head. I grabbed at it but it was gone, flying up above the trees where it lodged in a tall oak. That was unfortunate and I thought I'd better find another soon. I'd realized the previous day that the sun was really getting to me. Seemed as if it was something new every day. I'd described what had happened to me to Jack after we sang that night. He just shrugged and told me those sheets I'd been wrapped in were illegal, and we both laughed.

I was chilled, when I reached the end of the wharf, to see a long, low building emblazed with stylized flowers of concrete. It was in perfect repair. It was lovely, too, with a speedy train in relief beneath the flowers. I could not tell if the NAMS sign over the door was glowing on its own or because of the sunlight, but I certainly did not want to run into any passengers who may be debarking into this wasteland, having entered its depths who knows where. I saw no movement through its unshattered windows, though, and judged it long-unused, particularly considering the condition of the wharf. I saw no tracks, but most of the NAMS network was underground. Apparently the network had been extremely broad, and tendrils of it had reached into practically every block in the olden days. Despite my romantic love of trains and the lost world they represented to me, I felt apprehensive.

As I urged Stewball to a trot, I began to wonder what I was doing, where I thought I was going.

Not just this morning. In general. I was just following Verity, but my skin was not nan-golden, though my brain was somewhat warped. She had snatched me back from death, but what for? It is hard to think of a new life, I discovered, when the old one is gone. Very hard.

Still, I was determined to enjoy my day out. A huge solar road veered off to the north, and I was glad that it was going in the wrong direction for me. The larger the road and the better repair it was in, the more likely I would have to decide whether or not to use my rifle. Funny how quickly I'd been converted to the idea of using a gun as a weapon against other humans, rather than for killing food.

I took an EXIT that curved round and joined a small road winding along the river. The road looked very old, and trees arched over it, four lanes divided by a low railing of some smooth material.

I remembered dimly my brief sojourn in Cincinnati, but most of it had been agony and terror and now I had to confront the fact that I was out abroad, in the country. And that all the things the Shakers had tried to protect me from could be anywhere around me, taking any form. This was not a comforting thought. Miamisburg, Franklin, even Dayton—these had been known territories. But even a few miles could make a big difference now, with nan and all its workings abroad in the world.

I felt my thoughts scatter as they so often do, now. Only after singing, or playing, am I concentrated and able to think of myself as Blaze. It would sound outlandish to someone like Russ to try to imagine not being able to think of himself as Russ, but when I go too long without playing music it is as if the air is a hard outline around me, and everything is distant and meaningless, and I look into even Verity's eyes and feel nothing, nothing at all. Maybe this is change, or maybe it is nan, something I must fight, the aftereffects of death, or whatever happened to me while I was in the Cincinnati train station. Verity said that the cell I was in was activated, and that I was supposed to get some sort of information from it, some sort of briefing. But that process was interrupted, midway from death to life. I suppose I should be glad of that, somewhat, since had it finished its course I might not even have remembered my name or any of my past, but been filled with the personality of a completely different person.

I shuddered at that thought, and bid Stewball trot toward a rise, and sunlight, despite its power to scatter me, for it could also warm me. Take me from the ravaging thoughts of death.

There were buildings along the road now which spoke of a larger town than I had ever seen, barring Dayton and Cincinnati. My heart was beating harder, as I came to a rise, for all the buildings looked empty yet I felt I was being watched. I tried to think how it must have been, before plagues swept the country. It must have been like Cincinnati, teeming with people, everywhere. But that was hard to imagine.

I pulled my rifle from behind me and rested it on my saddle, and touched the gun inside my jacket, which Lil had slipped me. I realized that the buildings lining the road were all stores, of course, but from a more recent era, I supposed, than the old downtown of Dayton, or the small forgotten towns around Miamisburg, itself chiefly built in the early 1900s. A narrow track ran above the road and I saw elevators at regular intervals, small shafts for passengers to descend. They must have been lazy; the track was only about ten feet off the ground.

When we reached the crest of the hill I was glad to see that a large cobblestone square filled one side and we were able to get out to the end of it and see the river. The side of it was lined with small empty shops, in the old-fashioned style I was used to.

I got out my binoculars and followed the river along, closely, as best I was able though it was hidden here and there by hills. I was increasing the power with one finger and rather absorbed in my job when someone tapped me on the leg and I almost fell off the horse in fright.

My hand went to my gun but the voice of an old man said, "Wait, wait, son, no harm meant," and with the gun in my hand I looked down and saw him standing there, rather reminding me of Russ with his eyes, though he was tall and thin where Russ had been short and stocky. It was kind of strange though, because his voice was old and quavery, the way his eyes looked old, yet his face was no older than mine. He had long blond hair hanging curly down below his shoulders, and a long, curly blond beard.

"What are you doing here?" he asked, forcing his voice past the quaver. He smiled. "I surely wouldn't mind some company, if you have some time to spare. How about some breakfast?"

I was not about to get off my horse. "I don't know," I said. "I'm kind of in a hurry. I have to get moving." I blinked against the sunlight and longed to move into the shade. The river's glare, though half a mile away, scattered my thoughts like a mirror scatters light, and I guess my caution with it.

"Well, I don't blame you," he said. He gestured. "I live right over here, though, in that old bookstore."

"You live in it?" I asked, glancing around at all the deserted houses. "Why?"

"It's mine," he said. "That's why. Come on over."

The possibility of books drew me. I let Stewball amble behind him and briefly thought of all the information in the Dayton Library—the learning cocoons that I, by then plague-driven, had crawled into; the amazing ways in which information was stored and transmitted. I supposed, or hoped, that much of what I had learned was still with me, even though I couldn't remember it. Maybe it would come back someday. Maybe not.

We were in a square paved by cobblestones, about two hundred feet across, framed with many two- and three-story shops. I had seen several generations of merchandising in the area around Shaker Hill. Russ said that when he was young the rage was for all kinds of merchandise in one big spot, but that with nan a lot of that vanished, went back to small specialty stores or even shops that would grow anything you ordered with assemblers. I wasn't sure if what I was seeing was from times quite early or quite late. The cobblestones were an old touch but I had learned from Russ about nostalgia for old things and old ways. So it was hard to tell.

I saw a sign for a Pastry Shoppe and remembered Evangeline's pies. "Anything to eat in there?" I asked the old man.

"No," said the man. "But I have plenty to eat. Get down off that high horse and come on inside, young man. I just baked some bread this morning and I have some nice hot coffee to go with it."

The sunlight was scattering me and I said yes. I was not the best person to send on a scouting mission but I suppose I was better than any of the rafters. It looked to me as if they'd forget what they were supposed to do and never remember. I think that the only place that they could function at all was on the river, just like the only way I could function was through music. I hadn't forgotten what I was supposed to do. But I guess I was distracted.

I had one last thought of Verity waiting anxiously on the *Queen* and trying to hold back those idiotic rafters; then I drooped Stewball's reins over a metal post with a blank digital readout panel and a red arrow and the old man gestured toward the door of his shop, which stood open.

"My name's Moore," he said, pointing up at the sign above our heads, which said MOORE'S BOOKS and, below that in smaller letters, "Moore Books Than You'll Ever Have Time To Read."

He smiled briefly. "Unfortunately, or fortunately, depending on how you look at it, the second part is no longer necessarily true."

Through the open windows of the store a strange, exciting scent struck me as I stood there, equal parts fresh bread and dry old books. Thousands of them. I took one step, and then another, and soon I was inside, sitting at a small table with a red-checkered tablecloth, and craning my neck as I looked around at all the books. It looked as if this room, and those I glimpsed beyond, had a strange upward velocity because of all the vertical books. Moore walked through great stacks of them holding two steaming mugs of coffee. He pushed honey and cream at me and left, returning with a loaf of new bread cut raggedly, a plate of sliced sausage, and some sweet mustard. He beamed as I ate and I forgot my fear, though I did become much less scattered inside away from the sun and decided to eat quickly, remembering my mission.

"Are there any locks or falls below here?" I asked.

He looked puzzled. "Locks or falls?"

"Yes," I said, eating my third helping of sausage and bread. "We are heading downriver and—"

He jumped up so fast he knocked a great pile of books over. That raised some dust. "Your skin looks normal—" he said accusingly.

It was my turn to be puzzled. Then I understood. "Oh. I don't have the plague."

"I can't think of any other reason you would want to head down the Ohio River," he said.

"Sit down," I said. "Have some more coffee. Relax. I can think of a lot of reasons. Don't you want to find out—to know—"

He interrupted me as he sat again. "I do want to find out. And I can. In these books is everything I need to know. Everything."

"Oh," I said doubtfully. Although they were filled with many facts and stories, I did not think that if I had as much time as he thought now existed that I would be satisfied with just sitting here and reading them. They could not tell me what was going to happen to Verity and myself. They could not tell me the story of Jack and Lil, or what they were hiding. No matter what glorious tales or revelatory information those books held, they did not hold the story of my life, and if I sat reading them for a hundred years I would not have a life worth telling about.

"Do you have any books that can tell me about the blues?" I asked.

"Hmph," he said. "And what if I did. What would you use to pay me for them?"

"What is it you want and need?" I asked. "Do you want food? How do you get your food?" I had only chicken medium to offer, though, and I was pretty sure no sane person would consider it valuable.

"The rural network," he said. "They come about once a month and bring me what I need. Wheat and corn, ground. Corn oil. Fruits and vegetables, lots in the summer and I can and dry them to put by for the winter. I keep chickens and a cow in a field a few blocks over in what used to be a park. A woman lives over in Shumacker's Department Store makes sausage. I get along."

Apparently the rural network didn't reach as far as Miamisburg. Or maybe the earlier Shakers had not trusted their goods and drove them off.

"How do you pay for it?" I asked.

"I loan books," he said. "I don't sell them. I tried it, long ago, but it always made me unhappy to let them go forever. I hear tell that in Cairo there are as many books as a body could want, and sometimes I feel like going there to see. To bask in them. And that they have all the other things—the book environments and all, though I never took to them. But there are too many fearful things in Cairo."

"Like what?" I asked, aware that I had eaten close to half of his loaf of bread and almost all of the sausage, so I tried to stop, but he motioned me on.

"Eat," he said. "There's more where that come from. Well, for one thing, NAMS is still working in Cairo, you see. So they have a link with Los Angeles. Made Cairo grow, hear tell, for the town had dwindled to nothing more than a grease spot at the turn of the century. A long time ago they was sending doctors out from Los Angeles. Kind of like social workers. Supposed to inoculate us from the plague. One was killed here. I reckon they was just trying to do some good. But people felt as if they were part of the problem. I was just a boy, but I remember her. The doc.

She seemed like an old lady but she probably wasn't. I went to her house one day though my pa said I shouldn't ever speak to her—my ma was dead—and I had a plate of cookies. She watched me eat every one and said good boy. I was only about five. I think she was getting desperate at that point, because it was against the law to administer any sort of nanobiology without permission. I don't know exactly what she gave me, but I know I've never gotten a plague. And I'm well over eighty but I sure don't bear any resemblance to pa at this age. By then he'd had umpteen operations and then that last arthritis cure that I think did him in. It was experimental and not even licensed by the nan board but he had to go and do it. I guess this is as good as it's going to get for me. My voice has aged but the rest of me seems all right. It's a genetic thing and from what I've been able to read you can do things on a genetic level which are very discreet. But sometimes one thing leads to another and that other thing is something you don't want at all. So you see I would like to go to Cairo, someday, and get more books, after I've read all of these. But traders bring me books now and then—I'm known as the book man—so I haven't been forced into that quite yet."

My heart beat harder at his mention of the trains. NAMS—I feared NAMS because of one incident, all connected to my waking in the Cincinnati station that horrible day . . . not even able to remember my own name. But it hit me with a jolt why Verity had left me there. How often I'd talked about the beauty of the Cincinnati station, which I'd seen in books. I blinked back tears for just a second then. Imagine her doing that for me! Imagine her taking a dead young man and a dead dog on that journey to Cincinnati. . . .

And the glory of those trains! The fact that one was even running, connecting Cairo with Los Angeles. That must mean . . . that had to mean . . .

"So Los Angeles is still there?" I asked.

Moore shrugged. "Far as I know. The blues. The blues." He got up and wandered into another room while I polished off the rest of his food and coffee. I had to get going. I felt more focused now. I hummed a few bars of music, and hummed some more. I looked around, hoping he had a piano, but Moore appeared devoid of musical impulse. I pulled out my harmonica and started to play and walk through his rooms of books.

One caught my eye.

"Can I have this one?" I asked.

He gave a little scowl but nodded shortly. "It's not as if I haven't read it," he said gruffly. He had about four books in his arms. I looked around and saw a strange order to his books, but it was more like an order of subject than author. "And here," he said, shoving the other books at me.

I was overwhelmed. "Moore, I can't pay you. I'd like to, but I don't have anything. Nothing that you'd want."

"That's okay," he said shortly. "Just return them if you're ever back this way. And bring me more. Don't matter what. If you want to know about the blues, there's a woman who lives down on Front Street. Four-oh-eight. She knows a thing or two."

A thing or two! Holy Mother Ann.

The day was even more sunny when I stepped out the door, a brilliant, powerful day.

I stuffed the four books about the blues into my saddlebag without looking at them and thanked him profusely. I suspected that all the information I'd ever need about anything was right there in the riverboat, but I didn't know how to get to it and hadn't really had time to find out. I didn't have the "receptors" that the others were always talking about and didn't want them anyway, and it was the receptors that allowed them to access information. So I couldn't wait to get back and take a look at those books. But now I had to find out what lay downriver, and half the morning was gone. They were probably going nuts on the rafts. Much as I wanted to talk to the blues woman, I figured that would have to wait. Maybe I could double back after I'd given them the scout information.

I played some tunes on my harmonica as Stewball picked his way down the hill toward the river and as luck would have it we found ourselves on Front Street.

Front Street was about five miles long, or more. It seemed to stretch forever, broad and high on the edge of the bank. I could hear the river beyond the trees but not the roar of rapids or falls. I couldn't see it, though. I decided that it might be a good idea to get to higher ground. It looked as if there was a bluff up ahead, probably out of town, several miles away. I almost hoped that I could see some locks from there, and relieve Verity's tension. She'd showed me maps where the old Ohio had been tamed with a series of dams and locks. It was broken or age-ruined dams we had to fear, with no chance that we could portage around them. We'd have to abandon the riverboat and go ahead on rafts. So far we'd been lucky. But her maps showed the Loveland Dam somewhere not far from here, unless it had been ruined by the earthquake. It could be that some of the dams repaired themselves. Who knows?

I saw a few people, but they drew back into shadows when they saw me coming, which was fine with me. I hurried Stewball down the street, which eventually took a landward swing when most of the buildings had been passed. Far out in a hollow of land I saw the suburbs, thousands of identical houses so tiny in the distance I could not really see their disrepair, but only their creepy sameness as they marched up the low hills like rows of genetically engineered corn.

I had to negotiate a maze of curved ramps to get back down to the river but eventually we were down there on a small forgotten highway full of holes which rambled along the river and looked as if it might head out toward the bluff. I passed a huge sign which told of Alma's Jook House up ahead, showing a picture of dancing silhouettes, and at the bottom in smaller print which appeared and disappeared at regular intervals, "Where the Southern Cross the Dog."

We emerged from the trees and passed through some fields where corn and wheat grew, though I saw no one cultivating it. The sun was bright and in self-defense I pulled out my harmonica and we proceeded on toward a large stone building. Soon I saw that it was none other than the Jook House itself and what's more, the address on the front was the same as Moore had told me. Another small road crossed what used to be Front Street and headed north. I looked more closely at where the roads crossed and saw vestiges of an old railroad like the one that had run along the river in Miamisburg: worn rails, and a crumbled crosstie or two. I realized that Alma's had been a train station at one time.

I pulled Stewball to a halt and let him yank up grass and stared at the sign.

Alma May Johnson, it said, below where it said Jook House. Dr. of Philosophy. Musicologist. Transporter of Souls.

Next to that were a few notes of music and the worst part of it was that the thick wooden door swung open and the blues poured forth.

It wasn't just any blues. It was deep, sweet blues; painful blues; low-down blues that made me shiver, caused tears to well in my eyes.

"I been 'buked and I been scorned," sang a woman inside, in a husky, mournful voice.

I had never been 'buked and scorned, yet the music made me feel as if I had, as if all of history's injustices were heaped upon me, one single human who had to bear the weight of them all. And it was too much, just too much, except that the hairbreadth of the blues rescued me, kept my head above water, kept me from drowning in self-pity by helping me to laugh. The blues turned darkness to pure sound, sound that could cut listeners to slivers with its sharp honesty.

"Well don't waste time sittin' around out there," said the woman's voice. "Come on in, show's free. Leastwise, unless you got something I value. Which you may well have, young man. You may well have." Then I saw the woman standing in the door, just barely, because it was dark inside, but I did see her look me up and down and I did see her smile. "Bring that harp in here and let me hear you play. Put that horse in the back there, it's fenced."

I briefly checked the fence and slid the saddle off and hung it over the fence along with the bridle. Stewball trotted off, whinnying, and I stepped up on the broad cool porch of the Jook House with my harmonica in my hand.

"Leave your weapons at the door," said the woman and I hesitated for a moment but the music poured out almost drowning her command: that odd, syncopated guitar, a harmonica line that made my hand tremble with the desire to hold mine up to my mouth and imitate it, like a dog who wants to howl with the pack.

I set Lil's pistol next to the rifle and stepped inside.

A tall, thin black man sat on a beat-up stool on a low stage, playing the hell out of a piano. Another held a guitar, and a third stood at a microphone playing the harmonica, his hand wrapped around it and flapping outward once in a while and I watched carefully to try and see exactly what he did. I could tell right away that his harmonica was in a different key from mine or else I would have tried to play along.

The woman, with a mass of dark hair which hung down in long curls in a way I found quite enchanting, sat in a big yellow easy chair right next to the stage. She looked small and helpless in the large chair. I wondered about her being way out here in the country all alone and a stranger walking in the door but she didn't seem a bit worried.

"Want a beer?" she yelled out over the music. "Help yourself." She gestured toward a long high counter but I didn't see any beer. She watched me for a moment, said "Men!" and stood up. She pulled on a lever behind the bar and beer came out into a glass she'd grabbed from a shiny row; silly me. She handed it to me. "Hungry?"

I didn't think I'd be hungry for quite a while. I shook my head. I turned to stare at the men but suddenly they and the music vanished and the room was filled with quiet sunlight.

It took me a good long minute of gaping to realize that they had been ghosts. "How?" I croaked. "Who?"

Alma—I assumed her to be Alma—laughed. "Honey, that was Lightnin' Hopkins and Sunnyland Slim, back in 1986 in Chicago in some little club. Here, I can tell you the exact date and place—I can see you're interested. Not many people are."

She wasn't as tiny as she'd seemed in the chair, but she was not quite as tall as me and awful slim, and beautiful in her movements. She walked across the room and bent over a little white box and touched it a few times. "There," she said. "It was down on North State Street. Of course they didn't have holo recorders then, at least I don't think they did, not for every little thing. This was reconstructed, anyway, it says right here, from a television show."

"Play it again," I begged, utterly forgetting the boat, the dizzy rafters (but who was I to call someone else dizzy, eh?), and Mother Ann help me, even Verity, by now no doubt fuming and worrying in equal measure.

She just laughed. "Why you want to hear that one again? I've got thousands here. Memphis Minnie. How 'bout her?"

Memphis Minnie played the guitar and it was in B-flat and so I listened for a few bars then jumped in. Alma watched me from the bar, her face tilted, her eyes occasionally closed; then toward the end of the piece she started singing along, in a deep, rich voice that made me shiver. "You're not bad," she said, when Minnie vanished. "Not bad at all."

The Jook House erupted in sound and motion. It was filled, suddenly, with maybe forty black people, all dressed in strange clothing, all dancing, laughing, drinking, eating, having a time while a heavy woman stood on the stage this time and sang a steady, low, almost growling blues about some awful man she wanted to poison. A necklace of gold coins hung from her neck. She was majestic, powerful, like something out of a fable. There was no microphone, and a piano player accompanied her with a rough, tinkling tune. Her voice was so loud that it shook the whole Jook House; made the boards vibrate under my feet though I realized that Alma had control over the sound.

"Bessie, Bessie *Smith,*" yelled Alma into my ear, and pulled me out onto the floor. I finished my beer and set the glass down on that long shiny table and danced.

I'd never danced this way. Verity's precise and careful dances flashed through me for a second, high and golden then gone, replaced by this sweaty, bending, shouting movement that surged through me. Bessie Smith would shout and everybody on the floor would shout in return, including me. I grabbed Alma by the waist and swung her around and she laughed, her head thrown back, and came back and held me tight for a second before whirling out again.

We must have danced for almost an hour. Sometimes we stopped to drink a beer. Her eyes were eager and bright. Once she kissed me on the lips then swirled away like nothing had happened, just dancing like mad and holding on tight then letting loose only to grab me again as if she couldn't get enough of touching me. Finally, panting, she sprawled into the yellow chair and snapped her fingers a few times and the sound stopped and the stage was empty. I was dripping with sweat. "I've got to go," I gasped.

She caught her breath quickly and looked at me with her dark eyes. "I don't see why. I haven't had this much fun in ages."

"Where did you get all those ghosts?" I asked.

"Didn't you see the sign? I'm a music professor. I'm a Professor of the Blues at the Chicago Interactive University. Or at least I was," she said, standing up and putting her hands in her pockets and walking around the room with long, slow steps, like she was thinking hard. "At least I was," she said, sounding lost and alone. Her whole way of talking had changed, suddenly. She took another slow sip of beer. "I was born in Osaka. That's in Japan. My mother was working on some sort of molecular-engineering project that went haywire. I was an American citizen, but I grew up speaking Japanese too, at least until I was fifteen and the bottom fell out. Or *grew* out." She laughed, but I didn't understand why. "I first heard the blues in a club in Tokyo, when I was trying to escape. All the Americans were being impounded because they might be infected. I couldn't exactly blend in over there. But some friends took me to this club, and we fixed it up so that I was part of the act, and I got away. And after that I discovered my own culture. It felt like coming home.

"Look!" she said, whirling suddenly. "I can tell you like the blues. I've got a special treat for you."

And then a tall black man wearing a suit and tie was up there on stage, sitting in one of those beat-up chairs. He held a battered guitar. A cigarette dangled from one corner of his mouth. His voice was filled with strange clicks.

He sang something about hellhounds being on his trail. I watched, utterly spellbound, forgetting everything, then. "Who is that?"

"Robert Johnson," she said. "It's all made up, of course, extrapolated from just one photograph. Except the voice. That's real. I've kept the unenhanced version."

"What else do you have?"

And she played more.

And then the strangest thing happened. As I watched, he was joined by an older, heavy woman who belted out the blues in strange harmony, mixing with his voice as if she were his soul.

Her face was distorted as she sang, from low in her chest like Bessie had done. Her white and gray hair frizzed out around her head like a cloud of lightning. I felt like she and I would both explode from the power of her song. I was feeling more and more and more like myself, but different, like a new me was emerging like a moth from a chrysalis, and it hurt, it was like a dam bursting and I looked at Alma and saw she was crying and I looked again back and forth and I said, "She's . . . *you!*"

"I'm sorry," she said, wiping her tears and trying to smile. "I'm sorry. Yes, that *was* me. Alma May Johnson. I had a great show. First it was just me, myself. And it was good. I had fans all over the world, even in Europe and Asia. Before things got bad, I went on tours but live touring was pretty dangerous then so I went virtual. And then I had this idea of teaming up with all the people I loved. I think the blues was so big all over the world because it spoke to people, spoke to their hearts about what they were going through. It was like you were in or out of the Flower Cities, they were the citadels, the pinnacles, but most everyone was out, and it was a frightful time, a scary time, and the blues were something that everyone could feel. *Did* feel. I didn't need the money by then. I did it like a missionary might. I did it to help. And even after the

Surge, I landed on my feet, and I knew so much, I had several degrees in music, not just blues of course, and so I thought what better thing was there to do than teach? So all this music won't be lost. Disseminate it. *Give* it away. Give the heart and soul of my people away. Some would argue about that, sure. Some say the blues are too raw, too primitive. But it's folk music, the folk music of people who were slaves and after that when they were supposed to be free, things just got worse, and there was no law for them, only for whites, and there was no money for them, and families still couldn't afford to be together, and all this *music* came out of their suffering. The blues are the sublimed experience of our culture, a vital part of the history of the country this used to be. They're what's left of those people. That's what art really is—the sublimed truth. I love the blues. The blues bought me my freedom. And I *don't* want it to be lost. But oh, it *is,* it *is,* it *is!* Just like everything else!" Her voice was despairing.

I had to tell her. "It's not, Alma." And I went over to her and reached down and around her slender waist and hugged her, and she kissed me again but different, saying, "I think you understand, I think you really do," and the funny thing was I really did. She parted a curtain behind the bar and led me through it.

Her room, in the back of the Jook House, was filled with African things. Out the open window I could hear Stewball pounding around the paddock and whinnying like he knew I should be going but I didn't care.

Masks were on the walls of her room, with severe and distant features. A few small statutes, I guess you might call them, were arranged on a plain, almost Shaker-like table; they were abstract and beautiful but still I recognized them: a spider, a fox, a rabbit, a turtle. She saw me looking at them and started to talk, her voice low but precise, like she was teaching her class.

"Those are African Tricksters. They live to upset anything they possibly can. They like to cause chaos, create a whole new situation that lets in light and life. They are the enemies of the status quo. They seem tiny and powerless, but their power is the power of the mind. They help people survive in hard times by giving them a way to trick those in power without ever revealing themselves." She reached for a grinning wooden monkey which was on her bed table; handed him to me. "Meet Signifyin' Monkey. You can signify without revealing. The blues is all about signifying—and quoting, in a way. Showing; representing. Like all art, it's also about taking time and tearing it up—ragging time—re-forming it, repeating it, overlaying it, putting it back together in your own way. Taking from the world and making it new, giving it shape and form. That is what humans do—take raw information, nature, and make something else out of it. It is at the same time their gift and their curse. And the

African musical tradition is communal. What the musicians play is constantly modified by what the others play; modified by the dancers. We constantly incorporate the new, make it a part of what we are doing. Every moment is a new community synthesis."

I didn't care about all that, though; not really. "I'd like to be able to play the blues," I said, putting the monkey back on the table, and her eyes became very intense, so deep that I thought they had no bottom but reached back into serious time. She looked skeptical. "I've tried, but it's no good. I feel like . . . I'm only imitating."

"It's only for a few," she said. "You know the story of Robert Johnson, don't you?" she asked.

"No."

"They laughed him off the stage and he went away for a time. When he came back he could play like an angel. Or like the devil. He liked people to believe that he'd met the devil at the crossroads one moonlit night. The devil told him that he'd have to give up his soul, but in return he'd show him how to play the blues."

"Did he agree?" I asked. The Shakers had not talked about the devil much, and since I knew there was no heaven I wasn't afraid of the devil or hell. They weren't real either.

She laughed quietly. "Well, some people say he got a good start from other musicians, like Son House."

"That's what I need," I said. "Son House, or the devil." Maybe I smiled a little, I don't know, but I was suddenly desperate and she could tell. I needed the blues like I needed food and water, maybe more. To live. To pull together all the parts of myself that were in danger of dissipating forever—my memories, my very sense of self. To make something where there was now nothing; to create myself anew.

She sat at a low table on a cushion and opened a carved box. She took out a small ivory-colored vial and shut the box and stood up.

"Take this," she said.

"What will it do?" I asked.

"A musician named John Coltrane believed that the experience of certain organized tones leads to a particular state of mind. Brain scans of musicians show that they use their brains differently than nonmusicians. This will . . . remap your mind."

"I don't know," I said, suddenly remembering Verity and the boat and the rafters. The room seemed too small and my throat got dry when I tried to talk. It seemed like my mind had already been remapped, but maybe it had only been unmapped. Maybe I was just dissolving. I could hear my own heart beating. "It's nan, isn't it?"

"Everything is," she said, her voice going dreamy. "Here. Take it. Take it. Now."

I felt flushed despite the breeze blowing through the room. This was what I'd spent my entire life carefully avoiding. Maybe with good reason. "I've got to go," I said. "I don't have time. I've got to find out about the river and locks and dams. I was supposed to be back hours ago." I was talking fast and stammering and I felt kind of sick.

"So you really don't want to know the blues," she said. She turned away and walked back toward the table, still dreamlike and trancy. You're not the one, her hand said, as it opened the box. You don't deserve the blues, said the stern carved masks. You're white, laughed the Tricksters with wicked glee.

I watched her carefully seat the vial into the velvet. Her hand poised on the lid of the box.

I thought about how strange everything was now. Shaker Hill was gone, and John had shot me in the chest. Verity and I would never be—whatever I'd thought, lying there in my small white bedroom at Shaker Hill. Whatever I'd thought, we'd never be that. And I was somewhat ruined, imperfect, partially resurrected but undependable and strange even to myself. I did not know what the world held but I knew that when I heard the blues on the radio stone, when I tried in my dull way to play the blues, I felt focussed and as if things were right once again.

I knew then that I would sell my soul to be able to understand the blues. What did it matter? Did I even have a soul with which to barter? If ever I did it was sucked out of me by those sheets. I left it in the Cincinnati train station, in the yard at Shaker Hill, when my Shaker Brother John shot me. He shot it right out of me, and his own too. Verity didn't know what that was like. She never would. Afraid of nan! I was already up to my neck in nan. Might as well lift my feet and let the river take me; learn to swim.

Yes. I *did* want the blues! I wanted to swallow them, succumb to them, bathe in them, live them. What did I have to live for? Mother Ann? There is no Mother Ann. There is no God. There is no heaven. Verity, I thought, there is not even you, not anymore. But there is music. There is the blues.

And so I stepped next to Alma and put my hand on hers.

The blues had no taste, no flavor. They were heavy and silky on my tongue as she watched me with her dark eyes down them after she unscrewed the cap. The small holder was carved with tiny African symbols.

"Keep it," she said, and I felt then the irrevocableness of it all wash through me. Her eyes turned kind and she whispered, as she caught my hands and held them tight, "You won't regret it. I promise you. You have the history of your country inside you now. The true history. Even though you are not black. You are closer now to understanding. Maybe as close as a white person can be." She looked at me and her look went deep inside. "You are the horse. The blues is the rider." I didn't understand. Not then.

"Thank you," I remembered to say, and when I saw her face I knew it was the right thing.

"How—how long will it take?" I asked.

"I don't know," she said.

And then she said, "Watch," and snapped her fingers, and activated the strangest thing in her room.

It was a statue composed entirely of words, a ghost statue that glowed in one corner, taller than me. He was as dark as Alma, with forbidding features contradicted by a strange, sly smile. On his forehead was a red feather of light extending above his bald head. He was made of words, words glowing and floating in his blackness, defining his boundaries against the white wall.

"He's the African god Esu," she said. "He's had many names and incarnations. Legba, Eshu, Ellegua . . . sometimes he's the Devil, sometimes he's Jesus. He lives at the crossroads."

"Which crossroads?" I asked.

She smiled and her eyes gleamed. "Touch it," she said and so I did.

I touched the words that said "Stack O Lee," and heard the old tale. For I know not how long I touched words and heard prison blues; blues where chips flew and the jonnie wagon came and prisoners were whipped, beaten, and killed. I heard "Midnight Special"; I heard slave songs where the words meant one thing to the white overseer and another to the slaves. I heard levels and depths of music that took me to a world I couldn't have previously imagined, emotionally, harmonically, in form and complexity and beauty. Something happened deep in my mind and being; the hunger I'd felt since Cincinnati, the loss of heaven which nothing could fill, was satisfied, sated, and finally I hugged black light-filled Esu and my arms met and Alma pulled me back and she was within my arms instead, kissing me in a way that sent fire through my body; unbuttoning my shirt, unbuckling my belt. I tried to undress her gently but it was no use; I heard something rip and she laughed.

As she pulled me to her bed I saw her smile with Esu's smile, but she and I were both beyond angel and devil, dark and light, heaven and hell.

"Esu gives life," she said.

I know that it is true.

When she got out of bed, slim and beautiful and not at all like her old self in the holo though I saw the sameness in her face, her breasts were touched by the afternoon sun for an instant as she walked past the window. It was odd, I thought, how much I'd wondered what it would be like with a woman and this was what it was like and though I understood now, it was different from anything I'd ever read or imagined.

She pulled some sort of shift over her head and once she had it on she looked just like a girl. She could look various ways, I thought, somewhat confused. She pulled her hair back and fastened it with a silver clip and she looked like a woman again.

"It's time for you to go," she said. Her eyes were distant now, as if she didn't remember who I was or what we'd done.

I dressed, then walked out through the empty Jook room wanting to stay forever, seeing those long-dead men, learning what I did not know. About the blues. And about Alma, and her strange and beautiful life. And I might have, had not Verity been waiting, depending on me.

"Oh," Alma called, running out the door after I'd saddled Stewball, who I imagined eyed me coldly, and mounted up with my rifle and pistol secured. "You'll want this."

She was standing on the porch with a battered old guitar.

"I tuned it," she said.

I took it and my life began.

It must have been almost five in the afternoon but the spring days were getting longer. I kicked Stewball to a gallop and with the guitar bouncing gently against my back hurried toward the bluff. I might have asked Alma about the river but somehow I thought she knew and cared about the river as little as did Moore. And I'd had a kinder welcome here than any rafters would have had at Shaker Hill. It was best to count my many blessings and get on with it.

The warmth of the day, what there had been, was settling back down to the ground and the shadows of trees bridged the small country road. It was not self-healing and with all the holes I was afraid that Stewball might be injured but with the sun going down the urgency of my mission returned to memory and I cursed myself for dawdling.

But not too hard.

It took about half an hour for me to get to the head of the bluff. At one time the hill had been partially cleared and I passed the foundations of several homes with views that seemed to stretch all the way to Michigan. The small road switching up the hill must have been just for those homes. I hoped I would not be sidetracked by any more people on the way up, but these homes had not been built as sturdily as Moore's brick townhouse or Alma's stone Jook House, and most of the roofs had caved in and some had even been set afire.

I figured I had about forty-five minutes of daylight when we finally emerged from thick brush at the top of a cliff that plunged down to the river.

What I saw caused my blood to run cold.

Here came the *Queen,* heading downriver on a strong current.

She was still pretty far upriver. I figured that I hadn't come very far today, maybe six or seven miles, and surmised that the boat hadn't started off until just recently. I couldn't think of why Verity would decide to move so late in the day. Either some sort of commotion had taken place on the boat, or there had been a threat from the land.

Well, then I took the time to take the downriver look that I'd set out to do ages ago and saw the other half of the chilling sight.

What must be the dam Verity was thinking about was there, about half a mile beyond the bluff. With the binoculars I could clearly see that the upper gate to the locks were closed. The river was running high, and it looked as if the whole mess of them would just be washed over the top of the dam.

If all was as it should be, of course there would be a sign down below along the river, and the lock-people would be there to operate the lock and see them safely through to the level below.

The first rafts were already rounding the bend about level with Alma's place. I thought about trying to pry some huge boulders loose and letting them crash into the river to warn them but I didn't see any and besides with my luck they'd crash on top of a raft.

I could wait until they got closer and fire off my rifle. But with all the noise and commotion down there I figured they wouldn't hear that either, or take it for some sort of attack and try to go even faster.

I wheeled Stewball and we galloped like hell down that hill.

We left the road and tore through woods and backyards and I stuck to his back like a burr, hollering and kicking, and there was a crunching and cracking of branches as we smashed our way through. If he'd fallen I might have been killed. We detoured around a high-fenced woodlot where the trees were thick and random and caught the small road again at the bottom of the hill.

He remembered racing, then, and I swear he was moving faster than any of those NAMS trains could have gone. I scrunched myself up low and small on his back and let him out.

I figured that Verity had to stop before sunset but then why would she have gotten moving so late in the day? Something was wrong and I couldn't count on normal.

I was relieved to see that the area around the dam wasn't the usual gnarl of ramps and twisted concrete curlicues which might delay me by taking me to the wrong place.

No, the tower just sat out there pretty much in the middle of nowhere, with a red light blinking up top so I knew that something was working. As I urged Stewball down the final stretch with the sun starting to sink behind the flat fields of Indiana, that red-tinged tower looked like the end of the world to me. Surely everyone would see it, and try to stop. . . .

But the rafts had no way to stop. Much as the rafters annoyed me, the last thing I wanted was for them to die. Norleans was like heaven for them and I wanted them to get there if they possibly could. I hoped they would not be as disappointed with the whole damned idea of heaven-as-elsewhere as I was.

I pulled Stewball to a halt at the foot of the tower. I jumped off and I don't remember taking off the guitar and putting it down next to the tower but I must have because that's where I found it later. I almost cried with frustration when I saw how tall the tower was, and much as I hated elevators I was glad to see one but I shouted at it and punched buttons there for what seemed an hour but was probably only seconds and nothing happened so I took to the stairs.

They zigzagged up one side of the tower and my heart felt as if it was going to burst. Already I could see some rafters swirling around the bend and didn't bother to shout at them; they couldn't hear me over the roar of the water rushing over the top of the dam and over the upper part of the lock into the lower part. Once I looked down and it was a sheer drop of maybe sixty feet though foreshortened for me so I couldn't tell too closely. Might have been a hundred for all I knew. Then I saw what looked like bodies being swept over the dam, five or six together.

When I reached the top I saw a tiny room lit with the dim glow of a lot of lights. I felt like I was going to collapse. The door was locked and it wasn't glass in the big window but something a lot stronger. Then I saw that there was a window open just a crack. I stuck my fingers inside and pulled as hard as I could and with a wrenching sound the whole damned thing came off. I tossed it over the side of the tower and climbed inside.

There I saw all kinds of controls and various panels and knew with a sinking feeling that there was no way I could figure them out in the time I had. So when I saw a big EMERGENCY ALARM button I punched it hard and was enormously pleased when a powerful horn sounded every two seconds, interspersed with a message that said LOCK IS CLOSED! DANGER!, on a big arm that stretched out over the river with flashing lights although I was upset to see Stewball run off into the darkness when all the din began.

Powerful spotlights lit the falls and I saw one raft swept over.

I jumped back out the window and ran down the tower, down and down and down, and the side of the river was concrete here and filled with berths. I ran up the wharf waving and shouting and wishing I had a lightstick and first one rafter steered toward me and then another until they all pulled together as if magnetized and to my great relief I saw the

Queen steer toward the bank as well quite a bit upstream so as not to crush the rafts. It was getting cold now and I started to shiver with fatigue and desire for the blues.

I heard Verity yelling at me from the *Queen* and then the gangplank came down and she ran to the shore and hugged me tight.

"Blaze!" she said. "I thought they got you!"

They did, I thought. "Who?"

"Oh, it was terrible," she said. "Suddenly—at least it seemed sudden—the wharf was filled with people."

"There was a NAMS station there," I said.

"They all headed for the boat, yelling and saying they wanted us to take them downriver and waving some sort of tickets. I know they were tickets because I could hear them yelling 'I have a ticket good for Memphis! Or Cairo!' Or—Nawlins, they called Norleans. It couldn't have been more than an hour ago. We were anchored out in the river but that didn't seem to stop them; they jumped right in the water and started swimming. I guess it wasn't very nice of me but I didn't want them along and the rafters all had to hit them over the head with whatever they could."

Verity's face looked haggard and I could tell she was exhausted. I held her in my arms and smoothed back her hair and tried not to think of Alma.

"Where have you *been,* Blaze?" she asked. "What happened?"

"I'm afraid I got sidetracked," I said.

"Sidetracked! With everyone waiting . . . ?"

"I couldn't help it," I said. And even when I thought of those people washed over the dam I couldn't feel sorry about it. Was something wrong with me? Russ would never have allowed himself to feel this way, I was sure. It was like an important piece of myself was missing. I knew that it should be there but it was gone and I doubted whether I'd ever get it back. What was sliding in instead was new and strange, exciting and like something in the distance that I had to run to catch up to while it kept getting farther away.

Verity's face looked haunted and troubled then. She looked away. "I know what you mean," she muttered. "I know." There was more yelling and commotion and she said, "At least we got away from them, whoever they were." Over everything we could hear the din of the alarm. "I guess you found the dam?"

The night was actually quite cold. The quarter-moon shed a little light on rolling fields and through the windows of strange ugly houses as I searched and called for Stewball. I took out Mollie and began crisscrossing the area we'd come from, with the lightstick hung around her neck providing a pale green light. And the whole time with the moon and the night I felt songs welling up in me and realized anew how beautiful night was. A few dead satellites streaked by, catching the sun. They made me think of all that humans had lost when the quasar came and forced us all into Flower Cities, when it made us invent new ways to communicate and started the Information Wars. I wished I could remember all that Russ had told me about what he knew but for some reason all I could remember was him cursing the goddamned government. And his eyes. I knew that somewhere within me lay vast clusters of memories about Russ. But they were as distant and dead as those satellites, just giving off a glimmer of reflected light that was all the time before John killed me.

I came over a rise and saw below Alma's Jook Joint, emitting yellow light and distant music.

I could not resist. Mollie and I were picking our way gingerly through a field when I got close enough to see:

There were people, real people, milling around in the yard, shouting. I knew they were real; ghosts would not be so solid in the night with only the light from the house. It would have streamed right through them.

They were the NAMS people; I knew it in a minute. And I feared them. I feared them more than I craved the blues, right at that moment, though the stuff Alma had given me was working within me. A great wave of loneliness and exile hit me. I was not like the rafters, for somehow I was healed of the plague. Verity figured that most likely I'd developed some sort of immunity from having had it before. And I was not at all like Verity, with her nub-held memories, her Queenliness, her ability to lead.

And I was certainly not like the people below.

Wasn't I?

I shivered because, suddenly, I wasn't sure. If I went down there . . .

I heard twangs of music freed on the night air, loud singing, shouts; saw dancing. The searing core of the music glimmered in my mind like the night lights of Cincinnati, like the scales of a fish in deep water, and I wanted to dive down and catch it, hold it in my two hands, and then it was Alma I held there close to me, even closer than before, and for much, much longer. . . .

I would have flown to the blues like an arrow, then, had not I heard a glad whinny and then Stewball rushed up to Mollie nickering like mad and they rubbed noses and danced about.

I snagged Stewball's reins and we headed back toward the dam.

But the blues was inside me, you see, and I could not escape them so easily.

I didn't sleep very well and I was up before dawn.

I went off the boat, out into the chilly fog. There was a shadowy figure there, checking out the lock. I didn't recognize him, but I thought at first it was because of the fog and because of the multiplicity of rafters. He was not very tall, and slightly rotund. As I approached, I saw he was wearing gray work pants, a navy blue shirt unbuttoned at the top, and over it a zipper jacket made of some soft material. His shoes were sturdy, and covered with mud. He was examining the lock, looking down into the empty metallic cavern, hands on his hips.

"Who are you?" I asked, and he turned and jumped, as if I'd shocked him. The fog must have muffled my approach.

"Ah," he said, and held out his hand. "Jason Peabody. Engineer. At your service." His grasp was firm and his handshake businesslike. His face was round, and a very slight fringe of hair saved him from complete baldness. He had a mustache. Pale blue eyes peered from beneath bushy eyebrows as the sun broke forth from beneath a bank of low clouds, giving the air a bright silver quality. Peabody had an air of friendly competence; certainly, he was not afraid or furtive. I liked him immediately.

"Towers aren't working," he said, with a nod toward one. "Been in both of them." He pointed to another tower, black against the lightening sky, at the low end of the lock. "The alarm had a lot of backups, I guess. Beautiful boat you have there. Here's what we have to do." To my surprise, he pulled a small pad from his jacket pocket and with a pencil sketched a diagram of how the locks worked.

They were about a thousand feet long, hugging the concrete bank. A hundred feet wide and maybe eighty feet deep. As the sunlight grew stronger I gazed into the lower one, a big concrete box with all kinds of fascinatingly intricate metal webwork and various concrete formations. Big letters were written across the top of the dam: DAM NUMBER 48. "The lockmaster would have had a gondola to go between them," said Peabody. "Cables must have snapped. It's probably around here somewhere on the ground. Once he'd filled the lock and the boat was in it, he had to close the upper gates and let the water out until it was at the level of the lower river." I could see the gates, like barn doors that opened into the flow of the river.

Peabody's sketch showed how there were big valves that opened and allowed water to flow in and out of the locks through conduits embedded in the concrete under the lock chambers. The sun was up now, flooding the river valley with light. He tapped his diagram with his pencil. "Time to get to work."

"Oh," I said. "Right."

With Peabody directing, it still took a big crowd of us hours to loosen the manual valves, banging away at the wheels that stuck out of the concrete. After an hour we were all sweating and I was sure we'd have to leave the boat where it was and carry the rafts around. Peabody paced anxiously while we pounded with hammers and rocks, whatever we could find, and even hitched the horses to them. Finally the upper valve broke loose with a sudden wrench and the people who had been pulling with the horses stumbled and fell flat on the concrete and everybody cheered. Then Peabody muttered about how he hoped we hadn't broken the damned thing off, but water started swirling into the lock and his face relaxed.

It was just as hard to get the lever that opened the gates to work, once the water got as high as the upper river. "These things need more maintenance, damn it," said Peabody, as if there were city officials around who had deliberately neglected things. I figured that no big boats had been this way for a good long while, either up or down the river. Of course, once they got to Cincinnati that would have been the end of it anyway.

Verity got the boat into the lock all right. I knew she would. I could see her up there in the pilothouse, not her face, but I knew how she looked: jaw set, eyes staring straight ahead while she worked the controls by memory, like she was used to doing now in tight places. All the rafts got in too; the lock was made for huge long tows and it looked like there were acres of room.

We already had the lower valve loosened up, so it was kind of fun to close the upper gates and open the lower valve and let the water drain out. Jack watched the water level and gave us a wave and a shout when it was about right. Then we opened the lower gates, and they all left the lock.

As everyone boarded their vessels, I looked round to thank Peabody and saw that he was right next to me, holding a small, battered black valise.

"Do you mind," he said, "if I come along?"

I was startled. "Oh. I thought—I thought that you were the new lockmaster here, or something."

He shook his head. "No," he said, and I wondered if what I saw in his face was sadness. "No, I'm out of a job. I've come from Chicago. Rode as far as I could in a solar car, walked the last forty miles or so. To tell you the truth, I've been waiting for you. Heard tell of a large party making its way down the river. It's somewhat dangerous to try and make this trip alone. I've heard that there are pirates along the river."

The last of the stragglers were boarding. The late-spring sunlight was strong. Over a green rise a white steeple shone in the sun, but we'd had no curious townsfolk here at the lock.

"I don't know if you want to come with us," I felt obliged to tell him, though he seemed to be a handy enough fellow to have along. "Many of us are plagued."

His laugh boomed. "Well, now, I've spent all morning among you, haven't I?" His eyes looked oddly eager, rather than afraid.

"Why did you leave Chicago?"

Yes, the look I'd seen before was sadness, for it was back, and unmistakable. "Wife died. Couldn't stay. Couldn't stand it."

"Do you know anything about radio stones?" I asked.

"What is it you want to know?"

We walked up the gangway together.

It was only midafternoon by then but most of us were pretty tired. We only drifted for an hour, then decided to stay there for the evening. It was a pretty part of the river, not many factories or power plants like there had been closer to Cincinnati. We'd seen a lot of pretty little towns along the way, some of them on new-made islands, some of them partly drowned like Rising Sun, and sometimes a concrete wharf stranded a mile or so from the river. But all of them were curiously empty, like Miamisburg. It was like they were just waiting, kind of hopeful, for folks to move back in and use them, all the big-porched houses and high-ceilinged shops. It made me a little sad, to tell the truth. After supper I got out Alma's guitar and it wrote "Lost Town Blues" practically on its own. Still, it took hours to smooth things out, and work out all the words, and play it about a hundred times. But in the end I was satisfied, though I think I might have heard some rafters shouting at me to shut up so they could get some sleep.

I wasn't a bit tired, though. I remembered Peabody then. I'd forgotten about him, but that wasn't surprising. What was surprising was that I'd remembered him. Maybe I was starting to get better.

Peabody. Radio stones.

I opened my drawer and looked at them.

Sphere and I had taken them from a shop in Cincinnati where they lay scattered beneath a glass showcase looking for all the world like fancy jewelry.

I picked one up and held it. Cool, pinkish crystal, an inch long, a slight weight in my palm. I remembered Verity's radio stone, the one she had at Shaker Hill. It was forbidden to us, like all tech. It was our secret. She shared it rarely. I think she listened to it at night whenever it would work, which was sporadically, maybe once every two weeks and then only for minutes. She kept it under her pillow, but the sound was very faint, and apparently came from a place called Tokyo. She had heard someone say this in English once, but mostly it was some foreign language and strange music.

I'd asked Russ about broadcasting once, about why it didn't work. His answer was that he suspected that only a few people in the goddamned government knew for sure. "It all happened so quickly," he said. "Whole communication system crashed. Somebody knew it was coming.

And dollars to doughnuts somebody knew why, too. Oh, we had plenty of stories. Quasars, nanotech terrorists, aliens, cosmic rays, you name it. But when it came right down to it there wasn't a damned thing the little guy could do, as usual. Flower Cities came and went. People who invented the things that made Flower Cities possible made a bundle. Maybe they had something to do with it, the way I heard the old automobile industry put public transport out of business, or the way electric utility companies put alternative-energy companies and research out of business."

I'd asked him why those people who invented Flower Cities would even need money, since nanotechnology made everything so available. He just shrugged and said something about human nature being pretty hard to change no matter how you tried to dress it up.

I lined up my stones and the wires and mysterious gizmos Sphere had insisted that I take, even though he admitted that he didn't know what they did, either. They had a heavy, satisfying feel: soft, heavy copper wire wrapped around something made of glass; tubes that went in some kind of socket; a battery Sphere said he was sure must be dead, just a mishmash of stuff from that shop, where a sign said it had been established in 1948. Ancient stuff.

I was just going off to hunt up Peabody when he and Verity knocked on my open door.

Verity didn't mince words. "He says that you told him he could come along." She had that irritated look she had more and more often. Her mouth was a straight line, lips pressed together. Her voice was sharp.

"He's an engineer," I told her. "He already helped get us through the locks."

"We didn't need any help," she said.

Peabody was completely unruffled by all of this. His face lit up when he spied the radio paraphernalia. "Ah," he said, and crossed the room. He picked up a green crystal and held it beneath the lamp, tilting it thoughtfully.

"See? WLW. That's a station that an inventor named Powel Crosley, Jr., started in Cincinnati in 1922. That's because he manufactured radio sets. People had to have a reason to buy them and he gave them a reason. Clear channel, seventy kilocycles. Five hundred thousand watts at the end of the twenties—do you believe that? The nineteen-twenties, that is. Amazing! Crosley also manufactured small lightweight cars that nobody wanted, thirty years too soon, and refrigerators. He even built radios into his refrigerators. Later he manufactured television sets and started a television station as well."

"How do you know?" asked Verity. I relaxed. Maybe she'd see Peabody's value.

"Oh, I'm kind of a radio buff."

"I mean, what station it is?"

"Well," said Mr. Peabody, "one way is the color. Each frequency is picked up by a particular color, but actually it's not that easy because you've got a whole spectrum of colors and the differences can be quite subtle. So each crystal just grows the call letters deep inside. See? You've got to tilt it just right—they're very tiny—"

She took it and tilted it back and forth, then exclaimed, "Yes, I see it. Look, Blaze."

I tilted it back and forth and saw the letters, tiny as fleas but obviously magnified a bit by the material in which they were grown. I felt stupid. I'd spent many futile hours with them, but I'd never seen the letters. "What does the number mean?" I asked.

"That's the frequency," he said.

"Oh," I said, but didn't ask what that was. I rubbed it, but it did not come on. "Okay, Mr. Peabody, how do we make these work?"

"Well," he said, "it's easy," and then stopped. He looked bewildered. Then he said, heavily, "I don't remember. I don't . . . *remember.*"

He walked over to an easy chair next to the door and sank into it. "I—this has never happened to me before. Of course, it *has* been a shock to my system, leaving Chicago. I'll recover soon, I'm sure."

"Is Chicago a Flower City?" asked Verity.

"Oh, yes," he said eagerly, and a little wistfully. "But Anita died . . . yes, that's it, that's it." Now he looked very sad. He leaned back in the chair. "I'm sorry. I—I *am* an engineer, and a licensed, bonded nanotechnologist. And I do *not* have the plague. Not that it would matter to you. I chose to come here of my own free will after my wife died. I always wanted to see the country, but she wouldn't leave. She loved Chicago, she loved Lake Michigan."

"Why did she die?" asked Verity. "I thought people couldn't die in the Flower Cities."

Mr. Peabody looked at her sharply. "Oh, they can die, sure enough. Death is never vanquished finally. We can put it off for a good long while. She killed herself, you see." He bent over and began to sob, his face in his hands.

Verity rummaged through a small top drawer and found a handkerchief for him. Peabody blew his nose. I felt happy, despite his obvious pain. Verity had accepted him.

"At least take me to Cairo," he said, pronouncing it "kay-ro." "That's a free city."

"What do you mean?" asked Verity.

"The maglev still stops there. To the best of my knowledge. Which is old. Goes all the way to Los Angeles, when it can make it. The people who ride must be pretty brave. I've heard that terrorists regularly sabotage it along the way. Of course, it always regrows if damaged. Must really upset them. The saboteurs, I mean, not the passengers." He stood and brushed wrinkles from his suit. "Well, show me what you have there. Best medicine, I think. I'm sure it will come right back to me."

He rubbed his hands together and picked up one of the wire coils; nodded. He began to hum. I looked at Verity. She shrugged silently and left the room.

Peabody made pretty fast progress. He asked for a big sheet of paper and I tore one out of my log. He drew a map of the old United States complete with rivers and cities. Next to the cities he wrote call letters. He'd examine a stone, write the frequency on the map, and set the stone there.

"We don't have very many radio stones," he said presently. "It may be possible to get a full set in Cairo. Not many of these will work, I'm afraid—nothing to pick up at that particular frequency. Where did you get these?"

"A shop in Cincinnati," I told him, sick at all I'd had to leave behind. "It was full of . . . recorded music, and radio stones. I got a huge box of blues records too. That's what they're called, I think. But I don't have a machine to play them on."

"We can remedy that," said Peabody absently, and moved to the tangle of wire and membranes with which I'd vainly struggled for many nights.

"Ah, a battery," he said. "Simple and old-fashioned. But it will do." He bent over the mess and seemed to straighten everything magically in about fifteen minutes as I watched, fascinated. He took a very complicated knife from his pocket and began to cut plastic from the ends of wires and connect them to this and that.

And then—a miracle! Singing voices sputtered from another small box at Peabody's elbow.

*"Drinking Elbavox will cure
All that ails you that's for sure."*

Peabody laughed out loud. "Elbavox! Quaint!"

"What's Elbavox?" I asked.

"One of the earliest nan elixirs," said Peabody. "People really thought that ad was true. They went around sipping Elbavox or analogs of it morning noon and night. Supposed to cure colds, cancers, just about everything short of a broken bone."

"Did it work?"

"More or less," said Peabody. "It was crude, though. It wasn't a bit intelligent, so it might bypass what was ailing you, or it might make it worse. It was put out without FDA approval. The creators didn't care. El-bavox would have been sued out of existence but of course the developers had absconded with all the money by then. Made everyone more wary. And soon after that, money rather lost its importance. You've no idea what terrible uproars *that* caused."

"So—this is an advertisement, right?" I asked. "Why are we hearing it? Nobody is selling this anymore, right?"

Peabody looked at me with surprise. "Oh. I thought you knew. All these stations are completely unmanned. Running on automatic. The systems all know how to repair themselves."

The box had reverted to static after one round of the jingle. Peabody turned a knob and it quieted.

"That's funny," I said. "You'd think people would want to get hold of one of those stations and just . . . sit and talk."

"Well, for one thing," said Peabody, "most of them are heavily booby-trapped. Unless you knew exactly what had been done, you would probably die before you got into one."

"Why? Who would do that?"

"There's power there," said Peabody. "Kind of. You have to realize that the entire country became completely dependent on NAMS after the radio problem. And there were all sorts of failsafes involved in sending information. Let's say you're putting out one version of information and somebody is transmitting something entirely different. Even if you could only pick it up at erratic intervals, with gaps, say, of days or weeks, you could put out some pretty subversive messages."

"Such as?" asked Blaze.

"Such as . . . well, you tell people that a government had fallen or risen or that a plague was on its way."

"What's wrong with that?"

"Well," said Peabody, "what you heard would most likely be lies. It got down to that, eventually. You couldn't trust a damn thing outside." His smile was wistful beneath his bushy white mustache. He gazed with distant eyes at the neatly arranged glowing crystals on the table before him. His hands lay loose and relaxed on the table. He sighed. "And inside—"

"Inside the Flower Cities?" I asked.

"Of course. Inside it was like heaven. Everything was so perfect, so orderly. No physical need went unmet, and we were free to invent all kinds of other needs and just for the fun of satisfying them. Travel was so swift, so easy. My wife and I traveled a lot when we were young, to Seattle, Toronto, San Francisco. She was very . . . special." He sighed. "We were planning an Asian tour when it all—broke down." He sighed.

"After that, we were almost completely isolated. We lost the balance necessary to such a network, the . . . immunity to all sorts of problems for which diversity is the ideal inoculation."

I asked, "Did you have Bees?"

Peabody glanced at me. "My lands, yes, we had Bees. Still do. You have to have Bees to function. Bees are the juice, the glue."

"Did the Bees ever . . . take over?"

Peabody gravely shook his head. "We guarded well against that danger. I've heard rumors about other places where all kinds of things went wrong. But Chicago—I guess we were fortunate. Things went as planned. I was in paradise for—" He closed his eyes and massaged his eyelids with a thumb and two fingers as he frowned, then opened them wide. "You know, I don't like to think about it, but I am . . . well, older than I like to think about." He smiled sadly and flicked one of the stones. A sputtering sound came out of the box at his elbow. "Here we go. Think we have a live one."

Loud, twanging sounds burst from the box. "Your blues revolution," said a woman's voice, smooth and deep, over the music.

"The blues!" I exclaimed, terribly excited. "Get it back!" But the box remained silent despite Peabody's fiddling.

He smiled. "Like it? Anita didn't, not much. But we had a great lot of it in Chicago. Let's see—that's funny! Never saw call letters like this before. Definitely illegal . . . or . . . well, what does it matter."

"What are the letters?"

"STAX," said Peabody. "It should start with a K or a W." He rotated it a few times. "But that's what it says."

"Can we keep that hooked up somehow while we're trying the other stones out? What about this one? And this one?" I suddenly felt *connected,* connected to the world. Peabody would help me! Peabody actually *knew* something.

"Calm down," said Peabody, smiling. "We have all night."

Eleven

○○○○○○○○○○○○○○○○○

Dead Man Blues

Several evenings later I pulled back on the oars of my johnboat with all my might; leaned forward, then pulled back again, falling into a satisfying rhythm. A fishing pole, a frying pan, and a jar of crickets sat at my feet. A quiet evening out. An attempt to relax, to estrange myself from the inner turmoil I'd created in my quest for the blues.

Sweat broke out on my forehead and trickled down my face. The sun was a fireball low in the west and the thunderheads gathering promised a sultry evening, though I thought they might rumble off over the plains. I gritted my teeth and pulled again, again, again. The knottedness inside me did not relax so much as yield to the greater physical imperative and my thoughts of Verity stopped going round in my mind—*how strange she is how strange she is how strange she is*—for she was. She was strange. And she was a stranger. Not my friend, not my so-close Sister, not the girl I'd sometimes dreamed in wild moments of running off with, off into the wilderness of Ohio. That Verity was gone forever. And I missed her. Even the blues could not replace what Verity had meant to me. But they had to. A stubborn stranger had taken her place, taken over her body.

I would never see my friend again.

This was my life now. This was all I knew. All I would ever know. My life was not filled with angels and it was not filled with devils. Verity was not a demon, the Demon I affectionately named her when we were much younger, perhaps feeling even then her strangeness. But it was bewildering, compared with what went before: crazed, cracked, and unrepairable. It was up to me to let the light in through the cracks. It was up to me to follow the light wherever it went.

To me the light was music. Sound permeated my life. All the aural world fell into and out of patterns which I could not help hear, which I must imitate, regularize, lift to new intensity. Vision was music, when it fell to patterns again. It no longer sickened me when that happened, as it had after I woke from the dead in Cincinnati, for there was a rhythm to vision underlying the sense my mind had learned to make of it. The clink of the chain as the anchor was winched up was music. The voices of others when I did not hear the words but only the rhythms of the words, the rise and fall of distant conversation was music too. Everything was. The voice of the river, the voice of the forest, the voice of the birds. The voice of the radio stone, which pierced me at night, pulled me as if I were caught as surely as a fish on a hook, being reeled into some vast blues source more powerful and real in my mind than the idea of God ever was. I blessed the day Peabody had boarded the boat, and showed me that ever-opening world.

God! Where was God when John went insane? God did not keep him from committing an act that the real John, the true John, would have abhorred. John was stern, and strict, and sometimes afraid, but he was not a murderer. He trusted God. He followed all the rules that rightly, if God existed, would have protected him.

I could not help but hate the idea of God, the idea of Mother Ann, demanding obedience to all kinds of strictures and holding the reward behind their back with one hand, the reward that would never be. So much pain and delusion. All my life I wanted to know! To know what lay beyond that.

And now was my chance. I'd left the safety of the past, the safety of the orchard, which proved to be more dangerous than any of us could have possibly imagined. Oh, yes, I was remembering more and more now, but that was painful, for it just showed me how much I'd lost.

Row! Row! Row! Upriver, round the bend, away from the craziness, into the cooling evening where the rustle of leaves replaced the pressing shouts of the rafters, the endlessly recycled simple songs that grated on me so, where the breeze no longer carried the nauseating smell of chicken medium. Where I could think. I planned to pull over at a clearing, maybe start a fire, catch a fish, cook it, sleep under the stars, catch up with them again tomorrow sometime, letting the river carry me back down.

The setting sun fired the river and clouds with gold and red, then vanished behind green hills. The river was molten silver, shimmering outward from a heron's catch on the riverbank, from the splash of a fish, from the paddling of a duck family in the shallows. It was a calm, wide stretch. I rested my oars for a moment, and the johnboat turned in the current. A few faint stars appeared in the darkening sky, then were blotted out by clouds as the wind rose. Soon small waves smacked the side of my boat. Another evening storm. They were wild, but weatherable. If necessary, I could pull up on the shore and shelter beneath my boat.

I leaned forward and squinted. Was that a raft stuck on a sandbar? Was that a person, lying half out of the wigwam? Probably sick, I thought. So, what are you going to do? Heal him? I was surprised to find that my immediate instinct was to stay away. I'd just wanted some time alone.

But I sighed and grabbed the oars and rowed toward the raft. The current was stronger on the deep side of the sandbar and I struggled across the rush of water, pulling hard, coming in above and letting the current angle me toward the raft. Maybe the fellow was weak from hunger; perhaps he'd not eaten in a few days. I had my fishing pole and a jar of crickets; I could remedy that quickly enough if that was the problem. And perhaps I should just take him back to the *Queen* in my boat. A storm might dislodge his raft and he'd be completely at the mercy of the river.

The wind increased as I stepped on board the raft and tied up to it. It bobbed beneath me; my boat knocked against the raft once and was held there by the current. The man was behind the wigwam. The raft was unusually empty of the paraphernalia of rafting—fishing lines, pots, ropes. I stood over the man, but he didn't stir. A chill washed through me—could he be—?

I knelt and seized his shoulders, trying to think of the best way to turn him over, when the man jerked suddenly and with a moan turned on his side.

His long face was ravaged, and much too thin, what I could see of it beneath the wild beard. I had seen him before. I suddenly remembered where.

But I couldn't be sure, in the dimming light. I fumbled among the three or four knives I kept in my pockets and found my lightstick and smacked it on the raft.

You could have knocked me over with a feather. My knees were weak enough. Durancy! That guy from the tower in Cincinnati who kept calling Verity Rose. I had him by the shoulders when the wind blew his hat off and I got a good look. He looked like himself, all weird and sick like his face was melting off, except worse—thin and bony and he smelled real bad.

His eyes when he opened them and stared straight into mine were so dark, so painful. Something moved inside me then, he was so shattered and weak and alone.

Then thunder boomed and lightning flashed and rain swept across the river in a big white sheet.

I dragged him inside and laid him on the pallet. We were drenched.

He moaned a little and asked for water. That was easy enough; I stuck a cup out the door and caught the runoff from the wigwam. It was quite a cloudburst. I closed the flap against the wind. Then I saw there was some kindling and bigger wood laid by and I managed to get them lit. The wind helped the draw and soon it was nice and warm. The burning wood masked his smell or maybe I got used to it. He dropped his head back down after I gave him a drink and moaned some more. For some reason I thought of a line that I'd heard from Esu; all those songs were burned into me. Johnny Shines sang it: "I'll be glad to get to hell so I can lay down by the fire and rest." This guy looked like that line.

I tried to remember what Verity had told me about him, but my head was swimming what with all the strange things that had happened since. And with the blues, which was an old weary voice singing around me, just now, something about a long way from home. A long way from home.

I was starting to wonder what I should do, especially since if the night cleared off I suddenly wanted to go back and get Peabody and see if we could pull in some radio. I guess I wanted something familiar after seeing Durancy. The blues was about the only thing I cared about. I didn't like that feeling too much. It was too strange, when I compared it with what had been before; when I remembered how much I used to love everything about life, and how much I loved Verity, and Russ, and the horses, and everything about Shaker Hill no matter how much I wanted to leave, at times. But I could feel the blues gathering inside of me like it was going to blow the top of my head off. Peabody seemed to be help-ing, with the radio stones. Once, before Alma, I fired up the calliope in the middle of the night but people got pretty upset about that. I just wanted something good and loud, louder than the piano. Since Alma, I just got out the guitar and it almost seemed as if the guitar itself pulled the music out of me. I played and sang all night a few times. I thought I was making up the words but maybe I wasn't.

As the raft bobbed on the storm-lashed waves I pulled the harmon-ica out of my pocket and started to play something. I played a line and then I sang and made up words. I decided to call it "Dead Rafter Blues."

> A hundred miles from nowhere,
> A thousand miles from home
> A hundred miles from nowhere,
> A thousand miles from home,
> Afraid I'm going to die here,
> So cold and so alone.

I was just working out the harmonica part when Durancy started to mumble. It was so strange. He frowned and moaned from time to time, his eyes closed, and it was as if he was talking to somebody he knew very well and thought they could hear him. It was kind of pitiful, really. Kind of sad. He didn't even know I was there.

"I know that I sound rather normal. It's called flat affect. Really, I'm trying to tell you how I wish I had been. Reasonable. Sensible. Rational.

"But this is a fiction I'm feeding your cells. Despite myself. I am telling you, you see. Maybe. Or maybe I'm making up this level too. It's rather hard to tell anymore, myself.

"You see, it's hard to have killed your mother. It puts a strain on you. Did you ever see *The Wizard of Oz,* where the Wicked Witch of the West is melting, drifting away? I'm rather like that. Helpless. Very much afraid."

After he said those things about a witch melting, I knew that he was purely insane. He kept mumbling on, though.

"I am in the very center of something which I really don't understand. Despite my role in creating it. For instance, you have sex. You create a child. How? With your mind? No. On levels which are driving you. I'm like that now.

"The ways out . . . simply don't exist, I'm afraid. Already I've done too much controlling. Too much deciding. That's why I'm here in this tower making up the memories as I go along, creating fictions . . . but are they fictions, the way we wish we had been?

"Yes. Understand. I've thought about this a lot, quite a lot, enormously a lot. Rooms-At-The-End-Of-The-World a lot. The view from this room is just stunning.

"And you can talk all you like. Think, too. It's invisible. It's just an essence. Maybe in the new future thought itself will create matter, pheromonally. I've seen glimpses of that, to be sure, and laid down the gridwork. That's the future where some part of me will live again. Maybe. We can't see beyond this instant. As I well know. It's kind of like putting money in the bank. Worrying that you might outlive your money and then what? What horrific imagined reality? For your compulsive soul? Well. That may be a rather old-fashioned sort of thought for you, like heating with coal is for me, eh?

"I'm sorry. I wish that I could be more direct, much more direct, and helpful. Less emotional. But it hurts so much. You know, sometimes you just want to live again, to correct every mistake instead of like a rational adult letting it go. That's what Shakespeare is all about, though, isn't it Mom, at least the tragedies: the mistakes are so horrific, so final, that humans are shattered in the face of their ineptness, their greed, their so-powerful sins.

"So what's the alternative? To do nothing?

"I think not.

"We lurch on, we slouch on, as they say, we assimilate we plan we love the light and shun the dark. And light, light, my future one, is so various, so captivating, so powerful.

"Ah, thou of mystery, my mental offspring, you can't imagine the blessings I send forth to you."

Some kind of deranged prayer? He continued to intone.

"Do the right thing. But don't die trying. Live to think. And live to act another day. With better information."

Then he jerked up and opened his eyes. Rain drummed on the wigwam. He stared at me.

"Who are you?"

"I'm Blaze," I told him. "We met in Cincinnati."

His smile was kind of funny. "Cincinnati," he said. "What a coincidence."

"Well, I'm surprised to see you here," I told him. "I don't think Verity would be too happy to see you, though."

He really woke up then. He tried to sit but collapsed back onto the pallet. "Verity! You know Verity?" I think tears came to his eyes. They shone in the lantern light. "I—I need to see her. Take me to her. Please. I—I'm not as strong as I thought."

"You're right about that," I told him. "I don't think you're strong enough to go anywhere. How about some hot tea? Got anything to eat around here?" I don't know why I wanted to feed him. I didn't really like him very much. "Verity says you put those nubs behind her ears."

I just thought I'd try him on that. Verity wouldn't talk much about them. I knew that she wanted to tell me a lot of what happened to her in Cincinnati, but she just couldn't. It made me mad sometimes, because I wanted to know. I wanted to know everything about her. Everything. But she always ended up saying it was too confusing. And then I got mad because I thought she wasn't trying hard enough, or because it seemed like there were things she wanted to hide from me. Well why shouldn't she? We were two different people, right? That's what I told myself. That's what was reasonable.

But I never wanted to be a different person than Verity. I wanted us always to be together, sharing everything, becoming more and more strong together. Then it all went wrong.

Right in front of me was the man who had made Verity different from the start, so that the hopes I had were always futile. All the hope of years. All the hope I never even realized I had because it was so normal, as if there was never any doubt that it would be what happened. Here was the man who made it so that Verity went to the Dayton Library every year without telling anyone, and climbed into that cocoon, and learned things that I could never know.

He narrowed his eyes then like it was hard to see—it was, sort of, with the flickering shadows—and looked at me across the fire. "I know it's difficult for you to understand," he said. He talked real slow like it was hard for him. "You knew her when she was . . . out in the world, right? That's why you call her Verity. But she's really Rose."

I fed another stick to the fire. The rain was loud on the teepee and the river was roaring. "Who is Rose?"

"Rose is—Rose is—" He started to cry, then got hold of himself. It was hard to look at him when he was crying; it made me feel like crying too, so I just looked into the fire.

"Rose is my cousin. Very smart woman. Very smart indeed. Much more intelligent than I am. Much more kind, much more wise, much less selfish. I am everything corrupt and selfish. If there was a choice to make, I always took the wrong path."

"Why did you?" I asked.

"Well, of course I didn't know at the time. I thought that I was always doing the right thing, the good thing. I tried to save my mother, India, from one of the early terrorist plagues and I did; I had her read into the City's memory. But there was something wrong with the copy. During all the upheaval, later, she just . . . took over. And part of me . . . one of me . . . tried to remedy that situation. By allowing Rose to live again. The person you think of as Verity is one of those Roses. And it worked. It worked. But she's not Verity. She's Rose. And she needs to come back home with me. I promise that everything will be better now. Tell her that. I know she'll change her mind. This Verity person will disappear. Rose will come back. I know she'll come back. We have to go back. It's dangerous for us out here. It's too primitive. We need the City in order to survive."

The way he talked was still funny. He wasn't looking at me; he was just looking straight ahead. I saw that his cheeks were bright red and I reached over and felt that he was burning up with fever. Then I realized that he was delirious. And also that if he was sick maybe I shouldn't be there. I wondered why he couldn't heal himself, though. But maybe he couldn't. Maybe he needed the City to do that. A chill went through me, thinking that maybe Verity needed the City too.

His voice changed then, turned into John's voice when he was talking about Mother Ann. Kind of worshipful and filled with awe. "And it did work. It worked. Now we can start over again."

"Verity doesn't have to start over with anything," I said. "She's Verity."

He looked at me then and shook his head. "I'm sorry. I really am. But the best thing to do is to help her just be who she is. Rose. I suppose that she should remember who she thought she was, those few fleeting years she didn't understand who she really was, but I don't think that she can be happy or satisfied until she really comes to grips with who she is. I want to help her do that. I have ways of . . . reminding her." I saw that his hands were pressed together in front of his chest like he was praying. I didn't want him to remind her. I didn't know if he really could or if he was just touched, but I didn't want this lunatic around Verity any more. I didn't even want her to be reminded that he existed.

He bowed his head suddenly way down on his chest with a jerk. He coughed a few times. Then he lifted his head and looked at me with strange dark eyes that suddenly cleared.

"I'm sorry," he said. "I'm sorry," and his voice was different. "What have I been saying? I don't remember. I can imagine, though. If you see Verity, tell her I love her. And tell her . . . tell her that she is *right*. I finally realize that. I realize a lot of things. A lot of things. But it's hard. Very hard. You can't imagine how difficult it is. To be here. After all *that*." He could barely talk. He closed his eyes and slumped down. He looked about done in.

I knew that I wouldn't tell Verity any such thing. She was strange enough already. He could only make her worse.

To my shock and amazement, I realized that what I really wanted was for him to die.

I wished, as we sat out there on the river, on the raft, under a wigwam with the rain pouring down and lightning flashing and the river starting to run higher and higher, that he would die and then suddenly the raft was jolted hard and something, a stump maybe rushing down the river or the like, dislodged us and the raft began to move. Slowly at first then in a fast mad swirl, a quick up and down that made the fire fly up for just a second then settle again in the fire pan with a thump and a spray of sparks and we were off.

I went out on the deck and rushed to the back of the raft and grabbed the sweep. I saw my boat fly past; the rope had snapped. I was soaked and ice cold in about two minutes and hanging on to that oar though I soon realized it wouldn't do a whit of good, the river was so wild. I thought that maybe even a dam had broken upriver. I heard my teeth chattering, I was so cold. The wind was blowing hard.

It didn't take but a minute to fly past the *Queen,* all its beautiful filigrees lit, illuminating the sheets of rain that twisted around it. I thought I saw my window and Peabody's head bent over the radio stones wondering when I was going to come. Verity and Jack and Lil were there somewhere.

But there was nothing I could do. I shouted, but the wind swallowed my voice. We swept past them all in the night. I was hoping that we'd run into one of the other rafts, or get caught in their lines, but they were all tied up outside of the main current and then it was dark, dark, and we were alone on the huge raging river and I was afraid and then something happened inside me and I was wildly glad and didn't know why.

I started shouting and yelling into the night again, but it was different. This time it wasn't because I thought anybody would hear because I knew they couldn't but just because of the wildness the river brought out in me, because I had been dead and now I was alive, because I had always known where I was going and now I didn't.

"The hell with you, Mother Ann!" I heard myself yelling, and yelling, over and over and over again like something was broken inside of me. I stretched out my arms as wide as I could, I danced around like a madman even though a part of me realized that I could easily get tossed off the raft but I didn't care. I just didn't care. My main memory of that time, and I don't know how long it lasted, is one of ecstasy. A savage joy. We rushed on into the night, Durancy and I both mad and caught in the rush of the river. I remember feeling a strange kinship with him as I danced and yelled in the rain, and with Verity too. So this is how it feels to be mad, I thought. So loose and free! As if nothing matters! Like lightning! Which was flashing all around, while great booms of thunder shook the air. I was alone in the world, heading nowhere, my past gone, with people I didn't understand and who didn't, couldn't understand me.

When I went back inside I started wondering all over again if maybe there was a Mother Ann, and that maybe she cared about Verity and me and answered my shouted imprecations in her own way.

Because Durancy was dead.

4

◇◇◇

Down to Cairo

Twelve
○○○○○○○○○○○○○○○○○○

Winding Sheet Blues

Verity was concerned about Blaze, as he was nowhere to be found the next morning, but tried to ignore his absence. She had a lot to do, after all.

About noon they passed a raft that had gone aground on a long, narrow sand island. She would have thought it abandoned except that she saw someone walking around in the scrub trees and told one of the young women lounging on a bench in the pilothouse to take a johnboat and investigate.

"But I'll be left behind!" she objected.

"That's right," said Verity. "You can catch up with us tonight. Now go before it's too late. What's the matter? Afraid you'll get lost?"

The girl shrugged and Verity was purely disgusted at her cowardice. Well, that was all right—she'd welcome a change, herself. Slowing the boat with a reverse of the paddlewheel so that the girl slipped off her chair and fell with a thud on the floor and the sound of many small, distant crashes filled the air as other things fell from tables, she called for Peabody over the voice tube as the boat shuddered and groaned. "Hurry!" she added, and was relieved when he showed up within a minute. "Got a problem?" he asked.

"I want to take a johnboat and check on that raft we passed back there. Can you pilot the boat for a while?" Too bad Blaze wasn't around. This was the sort of thing he would enjoy.

In five minutes she had been lowered into the water via the davits. She unhooked the lines and swirled free of the wake of the *Queen*. She was alone, for the moment, on the river. The johnboat bobbed on small rough waves. The river had a pleasant, clean smell. The visor she had grabbed automatically darkened, protecting her eyes and face, and for an instant all flashed blue.

She tried to ignore the blue and the visions it invoked and pulled hard on the oars. She was almost at the southern tip of the island. Her tiny boat coasted over the chop as she labored upriver, but she was there, there, in that small room in New Orleans where she more and more often found herself.

The thin black woman was dressed plainly, the bee tattoo that nestled just below her neck covered by a brilliant yellow sweater. She rose and pulled the casement window closed and Verity was struck by the detail of the small panes divided by white-painted wood. As she closed it Verity caught the flash of intense blue outside which had to be water but which was much too blue for that. She sat at the table once more.

The table was covered with a tablecloth, but when the woman touched the tablecloth Verity realized that it was the same sort of material as their gloves. The woman frowned and sighed and leaned far back in her chair, dropping her chin to her chest as she crossed her arms tightly. Her face distorted and Verity realized that the woman felt some sort of anguish, some sort of loss, some terrible guilt or fatigue or both. She looked directly at Verity and said, "They are dying. I'm sorry. I'm so sorry."

The bottom of the boat grated on gravel, startling her. She rested the oars and jumped out, soaking her shoes and pants, and pulled the boat up onto the shore, heaving it out of the water as far as she could. She tied it up to a tiny sycamore and began to walk up the island, which was so long that she couldn't see the end. Above her on mounded dunes waved tall spring-green grasses scattered with daisies and red splashes of Indian paintbrush. She climbed the low hill to the island's top, covered with thick scrub and a line of adolescent oaks twisted by the constant wind.

She took a deep breath of the clean, lonely air. The Illinois shore had relaxed into flat plains, for the moment, but there were more bluffs ahead. Verity thought she could see a city glittering far off to the north, but she could be wrong about that. The Interstate was still there, though, and still empty. The noonday sun gave a peculiarly empty feel to the gold and green land. She walked briskly through low grasses.

After about ten minutes of walking, Verity looked for some sort of opening in the scrub. Then, through the screen of branches she saw Blaze, kneeling, with a board in his hand.

She opened her mouth to shout then closed it. Blaze tossed the board aside and picked up a crude cross. It was made of two sticks bound together with a vine, twisty and gnarled.

Blaze stood up with it in his hand and started to look around. Verity saw a big rock next to her and picked it up and pushed through the briars, ignoring their pull on her clothing and the brief scratches as they dug into her forearms. She broke through and yelled, "Need a hammer?" Blaze turned. "Verity?" He shielded his eyes with his free hand and saw her. As she approached him, Verity thought his face was very pale. "What happened?" she asked. "Who died?"

Blaze looked down at the mound of his makeshift grave. "Just . . . somebody," he said. "I went out last night with a johnboat and found him on a raft. Thought he should be buried." Without further comment he took the rock from Verity's hand and drove the cross into the sandy soil with a few sharp cracks. Then he tossed it onto the ground. It landed with a thud. "Won't last long. But it's better than nothing, don't you think?" His voice was shaky.

"Are you all right?" asked Verity. "I'm sorry you had to find him. How did he die?"

Blaze shrugged. "Who knows? Seemed like he had a fever."

"He was alive when you found him? Why didn't you come get us? Maybe somebody could have—"

"There's *nothing* you could have done!" said Blaze sharply, startling Verity. "I didn't realize that he was going to die. He just did."

"It's all right," said Verity hastily, raising her hand to touch his shoulder then dropping it as he pulled back. "Maybe we should have some kind of . . . prayer?"

"What for?" asked Blaze, his voice harsh. "To convey him safely to Mother Ann?" Then he sighed. "Sorry. Maybe we should do . . . something."

Sunlight washed the long, narrow island, and the weeds cast short waving shadows on the nearby dunes. Tennessee across the river was gathering herself into greening cliffs and rolling hills suggestive of mountains. Verity heard a whippoorwill from somewhere in the brush, maybe worried about her babies, and noticed a single set of rabbit tracks crossing the sandy clearing next to them. The sound of the river was hypnotic, a soothing, rushing sound, pulling at the gravel on the riverside shore.

Blaze pulled his harmonica from his pocket and began to play.

It was a mournful tune, piercing and slow, sad enough to squeeze tears from a stone. Verity felt the gone life of the person buried below her, lost after too-brief freedom, his whole life spent in thrall to the Bees in Cincinnati, barely remembering what it was like to be himself. What had it all been for? What?

Blaze stuck his harmonica back in his pocket and wiped her tears. "Come on," he said gruffly. "Let's go."

Thirteen

○○○○○○○○○○○○○○○○○○

Change Your Mind Blues

Verity whispered softly to Mollie as she slipped into the horse's stall, breathing the warm smell of horse and shredded marsh grasses which reflected the daily cleaning Blaze had assigned to a horse-smitten lad. Soft gray dawnlight washed in through the open casement window. "Stand still now," she said, and Mollie's ears flickered as Verity smoothed on the blanket and kicked the stool over close so she could stand up on it and drop the light saddle down and cinch it.

Mollie's slow hooves striking the deck made Verity wince; the echoes were magnified by the rocky bluff, which was crevassed with dark slashes of shadow. The bluffs downriver were translucent purple in the first rays of the rising sun.

When they'd crossed the gangplank Verity hoisted herself onto the saddle.

A cool rocky riprap trail led upward and she took it, brushed by still-wet overhanging branches, kicking Mollie gently so that she scrambled up the trail with a speed that might have frightened Verity had she not been so eager to get away, just *get away!* She glanced down and saw her gloves had quieted: it looked as if she were not wearing them at all. Good.

She was not sure she wanted to trade her autonomy for the contents of the minds of others, nor for their cumulative effect. But how long could she stay comfortable without their proximity?

Damn this conundrum!

Mollie surged over the rim of the bluff with one strong bound and Verity was almost breathless with the beauty before her.

She saw a land of low, rolling hills, newly green after spring rains. The hills were hazed with pink and white from stands of dogwood and, Verity surmised, old apple orchards. The path emerged in a field and continued onward.

She came to a sharp rise and there was the Interstate gleaming below, half a mile away, seeming sweetly undamaged yet silent and empty as the land. Verity shivered. Had she a solar car, how far could she go? What wild bands roamed these roads, flicking downroad, silver in a flash of sunspeed? Could they go to Denver, Arizona, Oregon? Could they go to the vast and legendary Country of Los Angeles, once domed against plagues and sunlight? The road looked clean and swift and beckoning and yet—

It was not blue.

She kicked and Mollie leaped forward. The path broadened to an old wagon road kept clear by someone, flanked by high grasses, and Verity felt those mooring lines which held her to her new community tighten and then snap as though she'd pushed through a binding membrane. She hunched down on Mollie's back and yelled and Mollie stretched out and took the land with speed, like the racehorse she was, almost out of Verity's control and she whooped again.

She had an instant's fear as Mollie went flying after topping a hill but it was a small creek and she kept her seat though Mollie braked sharply, suddenly in woods. She walked Mollie up the earth-smelling hill and then Mollie stopped short, to keep from falling off the cliff straight down into the river.

The shimmering ribbon twisted between the bluffs, almost turning back on itself. She heard leaves rustle behind her; jumped, and turned in the saddle.

It was Blaze, of course, on Stewball, coming up the hill behind her. "Why didn't you stop?" he asked. He brought Stewball up next to her, his eyes green as the Ohio but unlike the river tinged with anger. "I kept yelling at you to stop," he said. "You shouldn't be galloping around like that, should you? You're pregnant. Remember when Jewel lost her first foal—"

"I'm not a horse," she said. She knew he was right but of course couldn't say so. "You're the one who said we needed to get out."

"I didn't think you'd go riding like an idiot through unknown country at a speed like to break your neck! I thought we'd take rides together. And you need to take your rifle when you go out." He had his slung over his shoulder, as usual.

"You've been sleeping late in the mornings," she pointed out. "And I'm piloting the boat all day—I can't take off with you and get picked up downriver. But—I just can't stand it anymore! I had to get away."

"What can't you stand, Verity?" asked Blaze, his voice low. He looked at her steadily, and the anger went out of his eyes.

Below, there was movement on the rafts. The flow of people from raft to raft as they breakfasted ceased. Their distant, occasional shouts as they cast off and coiled mooring lines on their rafts echoed from the rocky bluff. Those at the forefront of the mass of rafts caught the Ohio's drift. In twos and threes they slipped through the silver shaft of sunlight at the river's curve and vanished from sight.

Their motion soothed Verity. Things could move without her; her effort was not needed to make the river flow or the wind blow.

"Verity—look!" said Blaze. He pointed toward the bluff.

"What?"

"Isn't that somebody . . . yes! There are people over there. It's a cave. They're coming out of a cave."

Verity shaded her eyes and studied the bluff. "I don't—oh. Yes. There they are."

She counted five people, tiny; they were at least a quarter mile away, walking down a path etched in the bluff. They were moving rather quickly, almost jogging downhill.

"I don't know who they are or what they want but they seem hellbent on getting to the boat." Most of the rafts had swirled downstream by now, and the *Queen* was just waiting for Verity and Blaze. "We'd better get back," Blaze said, and gathered Stewball's reins.

But before they could turn, the tranquility of the morning was broken by a powerful explosion from the bluff. An arc of smoke hung in the air as a huge splash geysered from the center of the river, just off the bow of the *Queen.* Mollie reared and Verity grabbed the reins tightly, frightened at the narrowness of the promontory. Rocks and dirt from Mollie's frantic hooves tumbled down the bluff.

"Get back!" yelled Blaze. "Come on."

She managed to get Mollie turned and followed Blaze down the trail for a few hundred feet, feeling completely disoriented. They stopped at an opening in the trees.

"Look," said Blaze.

From a black cave, another shot erupted. "It's a *cannon,"* said Blaze. It took off a chunk of the boat's railing, which splintered high and white in the morning sun before falling into the river like hail.

The cannon boomed again.

A few people ran around on the decks. It looked as though they were preparing to cast off. Blaze unslung his rifle and raised it, pointing it toward the cliff.

"What are you *doing?"* yelled Verity.

Then the people from the trail burst from the canopy of trees and ran across the gangway onto the boat, hitting those who tried to fight them off. One person fell in the river.

Blaze put his rifle across his back as they wheeled their horses and crashed down the trail.

It only took them a few minutes to descend the hill but it seemed an eternity to Verity. Then they were free of the forest and galloping across the field, low on the backs of their horses, Blaze yelling at Stewball to go faster, faster . . .

Blaze's horse disappeared beneath the trees fringing the river. Verity gained the brush as a shot rang out. Mollie, spooked by the sound, veered wildly off the trail and Verity thought she'd be thrown over Mollie's head but the horse skidded straight down to the river on her haunches amid snapping branches which stung as they drew blood from Verity's bare arms.

They landed in the river with a loud splash. Verity gasped at the frigid grip of the water and Mollie made a beeline straight for the shore. Verity loosed her feet from the stirrups and floated free; struck out for the aft ladder, just a few yards away.

She swam to the boat and peered cautiously around the side.

Stewball stood on the gangplank, and in a moment Mollie joined him, her hooves loud and slow. But Blaze was nowhere in sight.

Verity cautiously climbed the ladder, wincing at each small creak, shivering in the cool morning air. She stuck her head slowly over the railing of the deck.

She saw no one.

She scrambled over the railing and dropped down behind a huge coil of rope. She heard voices that seemed to be coming from the next deck.

"We know it's here. Hand it over—everything you've got."

"I don't know what you're talking about." Jack's rich, gravelly voice was unmistakable. "I'd advise you to get the hell out of here."

"We can kill every last one of you dingbats and look for ourselves, if that's the way you want it." A woman's voice.

Verity's teeth were chattering. Her shoes squished with water as she crept forward. Her rifle was in her room. She pried off her shoes and left them behind. Someone had left a stout walking stick leaning against the engine-room door, and she grabbed it.

"Who are you, anyway?"

"We're the Cave in the Rock Pirates," the woman said.

"Shut up, Nancy."

"We're a network, see? The Cave in the Rock Confederacy. CRC. All for one and one for all. Up and down the river."

"*Nancy!* It's none of their business—"

"Who cares? We're going to kill the plagued lot of them anyway. Do our little bit. It's an ill wind that blows *no* good, eh? Norleans!" An unintelligible sound. "Full of the rats of whatever's left of the sick nation.

Them that put us in this position. Not that I mind it so much. It's a fine, fine life. So come on, I want to hear some tongues wag. You, black man. Never saw such a fancy boat in all my life. Where you from, anyway? Pittsburgh?"

Another cannonball whistled through the air, and shook the boat with a rending crunch.

"Not very well organized, are you?" asked Lil. "I guess it's just a kick to fire the damned thing off. They don't seem to care much if you're on the boat. Do they?"

"Shut up," said Nancy.

Verity leaned against the side of the cabin, wondering. Was there some sort of weapon, some nanotech aspect of the boat, that she could use against these pirates? What did they want, anyway? The boat? Why not let them have the boat? Rafts were the thing, anyway. Everyone else agreed on that; they only came onto the boat in the evenings. Just a raft, drifting, while fish hung on the line behind and the sun shone overhead . . .

The stick was wrenched in her grip and someone grabbed her around the waist. She managed to twist the stick and give it some force as she was bent double and she heard a *whuff* behind her and a heavy thump as she was released. She turned and raised the stick and struck her assailant sharply on the head with the butt end and he lay still. But it was too late. A skinny blond kid, maybe seventeen, emerged from the door, holding Blaze's rifle.

The fallen man groaned, pushed long brown hair away from his blood-streaked face, and glared up at Verity.

The blond kid said to Verity, "Well, cone on in and join the party." He motioned with Blaze's rifle.

Blaze looked at her miserably as she entered the room.

The self-proclaimed pirate gang was ranged throughout the room. One of the women had long, straight black hair. She too held a rifle and wore a glowing purple headband that flashed NANCY off and on, in white letters, which was rather distracting. Another teenaged girl wore a black jumpsuit beneath a short rabbit-fur vest. Verity stared, for from the bottom of it dangled the plastic heads of dolls, each attached to the jacket by their hair.

The teenager, seeing Verity's scrutiny, puffed up her chest. "Bet you've never seen anything like this," she declared solemnly. Verity thought that maybe she was fifteen. In fact, they all looked pretty young. Nancy was the oldest. But of course they had no real need to look any particular age. And she was only eighteen herself. Except for all those years stuffed inside her . . . She fought an urge to burst out laughing at the grotesque jacket.

"No," said Verity gravely. "Never."

"Come on, Trish," said Nancy.

"Genuine Barbie heads," Trish said, ignoring her fellow pirate. "Got it off some rafters from Pittsburgh. It's a real antique. Watch this!"

She shook them with a sharp twist of her torso so that they swayed, and all the heads said at once, in a small, squeaking chorus, "Ken is an asshole."

Lil's laugh began with a long, low whoop; she drew in her breath and then the laugh began again, a bit higher. She gasped for breath again and Verity saw tears on her cheeks before she doubled over, clutching her stomach.

When she straightened she had a gun in her hand.

She aimed it at Nancy.

"Drop the rifle," Lil said.

"You," said Nancy, and fired once through the wall.

Jack took two huge steps across the room and wrenched the rifle from Nancy's hands. Verity grabbed a chair and whacked the brown-haired man, who had wandered in the door and was looking at all of this dazed; it didn't seem to faze him but Blaze punched him and he staggered back. The blond kid raised his rifle. Verity yelled "Lil!" and Lil whirled and fired; the kid fell to the carpet with a spatter of blood.

In the melee Verity thought she saw a look pass between Nancy and the blond kid; thought he gave a quick nod, and that Nancy returned it. Then she ran with the rest of them, out the door and down the gangway.

Lil dropped down next to the fallen man. "Damn," she said. "Don't be dead." She absently reached through the slit at the side of her dress and stuck her gun back into a black holster around her thigh; Verity suddenly understood the utility of her strange mode of dressing.

"Lil," said Verity, and put her hand on the woman's thin shoulder. "Don't feel bad. I—"

"Hell," said Lil, standing up. "I don't feel bad. I feel alive. It wouldn't upset me if he was stone-cold dead. The only reason I'd feel bad is because I want to ask him some questions." She grinned and poked him with the pointed toe of her shoe. "He's breathing. Let's take him to the pool room, Jack. We can lay him on the table and circle him menacingly—" She took a few long slow stalking steps and made her eyes narrow and mean.

"You've got to be kidding," Jack replied with a vehemence that surprised Verity. "I'm not going to let him bleed all over my table. I've been waiting *years* to have enough time to play pool."

"Poor baby," said Lil. "I wanted him to suffer. I wanted a little drama—"

"Haven't had your morning's dose yet?" interjected Jack.

Lil flashed him a look. "But I see you are against me. All right. Wrap the evil one in satin and give him some nice, hot tea."

The boy groaned.

"They've deserted you, kid," said Lil. "Nice lot of friends you've chosen." She knelt and lifted his head. "How much nan you got stockpiled up there? How many different assemblers? Know what any of them do?"

"Leave me alone, bitch," said the kid.

Lil spat, but directed it to the floor, and let his head drop back with a thud. She stood and straightened her dress. "Whatever you say, O mighty King of the Pirates. I guess we'll just have to head up there and root them out to get some answers. How old are you anyway? Sixteen? Sure you're ready for the consequences of a life of crime?"

The boy avoided Lil's stare. He tried to raise himself up on his elbows but groaned and fell back. He looked at his abdomen, felt his bloody clothes. "It hurts," he said.

"I can fix it," Lil said. "For a price. You're a pirate, aren't you? A nan pirate, right? Get my drift?"

"Just . . . don't . . . hurt . . . them," he said, and fell back.

"Post a guard," Lil told Verity. Then she smiled. "I guess that means you and Jack. You too, Peabody, if you can muster the gall. Or maybe you can get this tub moving."

Another cannonball shook the ship. Peabody ran from the room, his face pale and serious. Verity was surprised that he could move so fast.

Lil motioned to Blaze. "Help me carry this deluded kid to a nice down bed." She lifted his shoulders and Blaze took his feet. "Careful now, be gentle to the poor angel," she said, and dropped his shoulders. He screamed in pain. "Whoops. This is too awkward. Blaze, can you just . . . thanks." Blaze scooped up the wounded pirate with some effort and carried him sideways through the door. Lil followed.

Verity and Jack picked up rifles and stepped cautiously out on deck. The boat vibrated and chains clanked as the anchor rose, but before it was fully in, the boat began to move faster than Verity had thought possible.

One last cannonball came sailing out of the dark mouth of the cave, and landed behind them. Then they rounded the bend.

Safe!

All the rafts were long gone, swept downriver for their morning's tour. Verity felt the familiar anxiety in the pit of her stomach: they were heading with little control into unknown territory. Waterfalls, rapids . . .

"Hey!" said Jack. "You okay? I think the kid will be all right. Lil might seem tough, but she's got healing ways."

"I'm fine," said Verity, realizing with surprise that she was. The morning's gore had not upset her as much as she expected, but maybe that was because the kid would be all right. "What does Lil want to find out?"

Jack gestured with his rifle toward the cave, a black gash in the cliff face. "You didn't hear the whole thing. They burst inside, demanding that we hand over any sort of nan we had on board."

Any sort of nan. The fact of the patent enlivenment of the boat overwhelmed Verity for a moment, taking her breath away. She managed to push it out of her mind most of the time. But there it was—every bit of the boat had been grown by nanotechnology, powerful molecular engineering, directed by a part of her she was trying desperately to avoid knowing, as if it were some sort of diamond-hard tumor she might someday excise.

Absently, she rubbed one of her nubs. *Don't touch!* warned a whisper in her mind and she jerked her hand back to the familiar stock of the rifle. She had grown up thinking of a rifle as a helpful tool, with which she'd shot rabbits, and sometimes deer, though always reluctantly, for her Shaker community back on Bear Creek. She looked at it doubtfully, now, as its gray barrel caught the spring sun. She had never dreamed that a gun might be turned against other humans, as John had used his, to kill Blaze; as Lil had so swiftly pulled out her pearl-handled pistol and shot the boy . . .

"I think you might need to rest a bit," said Jack, his voice concerned. "You look awful pale. Those kids aren't going to storm back down here. Right now they're cowering up in their cave, worried about their friend. But not worried enough to die trying to save him."

Verity breathed deeply. "No, really, I'm okay." She ignored the way her stomach felt. It had nothing to do with the events of the day. "Why do they want nan?"

Jack shrugged. "All sorts of possible reasons. I'd say that they don't have the infrastructure to use it. They don't have the background, either. They're probably descended from the Pure People. There are enclaves of them in these parts."

"The Pure People?"

Jack grinned. "A long time ago . . . oh, a very long time ago, the country manifested a last gasp of white supremacists . . ."

"White what?"

"People who believed that the white race was born to rule the earth, was the best sort of human, chosen by God to prevail, and, of course, that all other races were evil and had to be wiped out . . ."

"Really?" asked Verity, a bit stunned. She remembered Tai Tai—her dark African skin, the beautiful slant of her eyes which added some sort of Asian background, exotic-seeming next to Verity's humdrum whiteness. Tai Tai had been, as far as Verity could tell, a mathematical genius of some sort. That was one thing Verity had longed for as a child—*difference* . . .

Well, she certainly had *that*.

"Really," said Jack gently. "You are a naive child, I can see that. Racism is a very fundamental human trait. Not limited to Caucasians by any means. One of the things nan could do with ease was change racial markers like skin color which had for so long kept us all separate and at war. Of course new markers of thought arose quite rapidly. But nan made it possible to actually change one's race. The Pures naturally believed that all Africans, all Asians, everyone that didn't fit their template might disguise themselves in this way. Of course, hardly anyone aspired to such nefarious ends!" Jack laughed hugely for a moment, quite tickled, apparently, at the very thought of turning white.

"They waged a war against all nan. For this reason. Lots of groups did. They all had their own reasons. Looks like they might have been right. Nanotech has certainly changed things. But what can you do? There are some 'antidotes,' I suppose you might call them. But it was like trying to stop a flood with a teacup. I'd say that bunch up there has made a living for some time by selling captured nan to a network which assures them that it's being destroyed. But actually, they then use it themselves."

"For what?" asked Verity.

Jack's eyebrows rose. "Just about anything, my dear. That's the fun of it all. And that's the terror of it all too."

"How do you know all this?" asked Verity.

"Well," said Jack, "I've obviously been around longer than you. I can take care of this end of things." Blaze was coming down the deck. "Give Blaze your rifle and go sit in with Lil."

Instead, Verity made her way to the pilothouse. She was worried about the boat.

One corner of the roof had been ripped off by a cannonball. Splintered debris was scattered across the floor, and the gaping hole was ragged. Peabody stood in a flood of sunlight. He had stuffed a cushion between the wall and a lever so that the console was shaded and readable. Glancing at the river every other second, he spent the other seconds staring at the console with a frown on his face. "Damndest thing I've ever seen," he muttered, then looked up. "Oh. Verity. Good. Can you keep an eye on the river while I fool with this?"

Verity stepped up to the wheel and saw that her customary charts were not on the screen.

Instead, Peabody had invoked some icons she had not seen before.

"What's that?" she asked.

"Damned if I know. I need some sort of translation. This boat's from Cincinnati, right?"

"Yes," she said.

"It's amazing how much the systems seem to have diverged after NAMS was destroyed." He frowned again. "The pumps are on but I think we're taking on water. Look, maybe you can help. I need a schematic of the entire *Queen*. Give me back the wheel."

They traded places. She touched the screen and invoked a boat icon, about a foot long. It hovered in front of the cushion. She wasn't sure how she knew how to do this. The motions came from a place she did not know. *This is Rose's boat, that's how I know these things.* And it was somewhat of an emergency. She'd found that Rose—or at least information Rose would know—had a tendency to break into her mind at those times.

Rose, the ever-helpful, she thought sarcastically.

Her fingers danced on very particular parts of the screen. She touched it once, and saw a network of pipes; again; and the boat was a fine web through which coursed three colors of fluid. As she watched, the colors blended to make every color imaginable and then fixed on a particular spectrum, which changed slightly every second.

"That's the replicator network," said Peabody. "But it's not reflecting the boat as it is. For instance . . ." He touched the portion of the icon that corresponded to the pilothouse, but nothing happened. "See, it's a very specialized system, and I'm just not part of it, my dear. I'm not of much help. But can you try and show this pilothouse as it is now?"

Minutes passed while Verity fooled with the system. Having a particular goal helped. Before, not knowing its capabilities, she had been lost in the very multiplicity of information available.

She finally flattened the boat onto the screen and by touching the pilothouse replicated it, but still intact, not showing the morning's damage.

"Is there a date function?" asked Peabody, pulling back on the throttle as they approached a raw new island on the right, where the river ran muddy. "Maybe you can get to it that way."

Verity suddenly realized that she didn't really know what year it was. Russ had kept the dates, of course, but she'd never paid much attention to them. It had never really mattered, adrift in time as they were.

And now?

She found a chart of the river and made it very small. With a tiny pointer she followed the course of the boat down the river and the screen ran down the minutes and then the hours and then the days, hours, minutes, and seconds they were from Cincinnati.

"That will do," said Peabody. "Keep going till the clock stops."

When she got to the present—she was surprised to see that this was their twenty-eighth day out—she again manifested the pilothouse and there it was, or rather, there it was *not,* the roof missing.

"Good," said Peabody. "Now the whole boat. Good. Well. Big bash on the right bow but just above the waterline. Now, if I could just get into the subprogram and . . . well, you can do it . . . let's see . . ."

"How about this?" asked Verity. She put the smashed boat and the

perfect boat side by side. Then she pushed them together so they were superimposed.

"Well," said Peabody doubtfully. "I don't know . . ."

"Look," said Verity.

A crack in the window in front of them was slowly vanishing. So
slowly that it almost seemed not to be happening, like the setting of
the sun.

Then it was gone.

"You've done it," said Peabody. "Congratulations. I guess I'm all but
useless out here. Funny!" He turned back to the river, an odd look on his
face.

"But where is the *matter* coming from?" she asked. "I mean, the window can probably rearrange slightly, and knit, but the top of the pilothouse went into the river. The boat grew from special fluid in
Cincinnati."

"Water," said Peabody. "It will take a hell of a lot of water. But there's
particulate matter in the water, and I'm sure if we knew more we could
access its composition. It looks as if there's a furnace that uses other fuels
too, if necessary. If I were designing a boat like this I'd have the whole
hull be a processing membrane. In fact, I'd have the whole damned thing
be unsinkable." He glanced at her. "You look tired, child. I think we've
got it now. Go have a rest."

"But—" she said, suddenly noticing that his hand, in the shadow of
the cushion, had that slight, golden sheen . . .

He followed her look and smiled slightly, though his eyes had a sad,
distant look. "Oh. Yes. I was hoping for that, actually."

"Why?"

"Because, don't you see, my dear?"

"See what?"

"It will give me something to live for."

Verity slipped inside the bright stateroom where the very young man lay
in the center of a huge bed. His bloody shirt was a crumpled heap on a
green rug next to the bed, and he wore a white bandage across his chest.
He appeared awake and alert and Lil turned her head and nodded to
Verity.

"His name's Eliot," said Lil. "He might have some internal injuries.
But of course he'd rather die than be healed by nan."

The kid just glanced wearily at Lil.

"And I told him that we certainly have some good old-fashioned non-
nan painkillers somewhere. But he'll have to cooperate. Of course, there's
really nothing to keep me from using nan on him, is there? Not just healing nan, but all kinds of plagued stuff—"

Eliot twisted on the bed as if to spring away but Lil leaned over and grabbed his wrists. He thrashed and started to kick. Lil raised her fist and held it squarely above his face and he quieted.

"His orders are just to *steal* nan," Lil told Verity. "He's not supposed to actually benefit from it himself. That's for his boss. He's been trained to think of actually using it himself as the worst sort of heresy." She turned to Eliot. "How many are there?"

"Fifty," he said. "And they'll kill you. Cut you off downriver. With nets."

"If there are ten of you I'd be surprised," said Lil. "I guess you usually get what you want?"

"Why didn't you come last night?" asked Verity.

"We were planning our strategy," said Eliot.

"They were shaking in their boots," said Lil. "They were waiting until the rafts left. But my guess—no, more than a guess, truth be told—is that there's some despotic old bum up there—"

"He's *not* a bum!" said Eliot.

"—Eliot's father, maybe." Lil grinned while Eliot glowered. "Been there since kingdom come. Takes young ones off rafts and raises them up."

"We don't take any plaguers from rafts. I'm from—"

"From where?" asked Lil sharply, but Eliot shut up.

"Well, he's a kind old man," Lil continued. "Loving as the day is long. Never hits. Never yells." She leaned over Eliot. "He's been leading you on, kid. He's well preserved. He's about a hundred and fifty years old. Because of nan. Because of the things he has you steal—"

"He is *not!*" yelled Eliot. This time he did make it off the bed but only staggered a foot before grabbing the dresser. He clutched his side, gasping. "It hurts," he said, and tears filled his eyes. He did not blink, but stood and walked slowly and carefully to the window, supporting himself on the sill.

"It's the only life you've ever known, isn't it?" asked Lil gently. "Robbing and killing. How many people have you killed?"

He shrugged, his shoulders thin and pale from behind.

"You don't have to," said Lil. "I know you're planning to slip off as soon as possible. But you can come with us, and welcome. You can be free of that tyrant."

"He's *not* welcome," said Verity.

"Stay and get the *plague*," he whispered, wheeling and sagging against the window. "That's why we have to kill them. Like vermin, he says. It spreads everywhere."

It was why Shaker Hill was created, Verity thought, remembering Russ's brief mentions of guards with guns posted down at the New Ohio River bluffs during the early years.

Eliot continued. "We're helping the world. We're bound by an oath. A blood oath, like in the books. All the nan—he gives it to people who deactivate it. It's horrible stuff. Horrible. The work of the—"

"Devil," finished Lil, dryly. "Like the blues itself—the devil's music. The devil's technology. Unfortunately, it was all made by humans. With a little help from AI."

"Ae-I?" asked Verity. "What's that?"

Lil turned her head. It was clear that she'd almost forgotten that Verity was there.

"Artificial intelligence," said Lil.

"How do you know all this?"

"It's not a secret," she said.

"I mean about the pirates—this group—"

Lil sighed. "Just guessing," she said, but Verity did not believe her. She decided to say nothing about it, though, in front of Eliot, who was bound by a terrible pirate blood oath to kill them all. Why keep him around? The first chance he got he'd kill them.

"Let him go," she told Lil.

"Why?" asked Lil. "So he can kill more people? We need to go back there and clean out the lot of them, with or without his help."

"What do you mean, clean them out?"

"Oh," Lil laughed. "I don't mean kill them. I mean convert them."

"How?" asked Verity.

"With information," said Lil. *"This."*

And before she or Eliot could move Lil pulled a small vial from her pocket, reached around Eliot, and squirted it beneath his nose. Eliot sneezed and looked at her in terror. "What have you *done?"*

He began sobbing, then rushed her. Lil handily grabbed him around the waist and flung him down on the bed, where he lay panting. He started to rise again, then fell back and passed out.

"What *did* you do?" asked Verity. "Where did you get that?"

"I think you know quite well what I did," said Lil, breathing hard. "He's quite a handful. I guess I've had my exercise for the week—"

"Lil?"

Verity and Lil turned. Jack was standing in the doorway. The look on his face was sad; almost wistful.

"Well?" said Lil. "He *irritated* me."

Jack said quietly, "Are you all right? I was afraid this would be too much. It's been a long time since you were . . . around so many people. It's stressful. You can't save the world, remember? You didn't ask his permission. You didn't give him any information. You didn't give him any *choice—"*

He took a step toward her.

"Nobody gave *me* a choice," yelled Lil. "And I'm happy as a clam, see? See?" She shrugged elaborately and dropped into a chair.

Jack just sighed and looked worried. "Everything you've ever done has been your choice and you know it. Don't you? Or are you forgetting what you are, what we're supposed to be doing. Lil, has there been any sort of . . . I mean . . ."

"I'm intact," said Lil. "No wolves or tigers yet." She looked defiant.

"What are you talking about? When are you going to use that on us? Or have you already?" asked Verity.

Lil burst out laughing. Wildly. Hysterically. Tears rolled down her cheeks. "You? You're all on such strong stuff that this wouldn't make a dent in it. The Norleans Plague is the strongest there is, Verity. Oh, it certainly *is!"*

Then Jack was hugging her, shushing her. She continued talking after a minute, more subdued, looking at Verity over Jack's shoulder. "No, this is just a mild pacifier. It's working on his limbic system. Replacing this and that."

"Replacing this and that," said Jack, dropping his arms, his voice heavy with sarcastic mimic. "So easy," said Jack. "Take away his life, his *community.* The people who love him and care about him."

"Community? Love? Excuse me, but I don't think those words apply. You think I should go on letting him kill people?" asked Lil. "When I have the power to stop it?"

"Yeah and all because information wants to be free," said Jack. "Well you can stuff your old information."

"We'll let him go now," said Lil. "He'll infect them all."

"They'll kill him straight off," said Jack, "and you know it. Pick him off on the way up the cliff. He's contaminated. He's yours, Lil. Your little pet."

Lil smiled. But—were her eyes glimmering with tears? Her sudden laugh seemed to belie them. "So hard to save the world."

Verity looked back and forth between them. She didn't know what to say.

"I think you're wrong," she finally told Lil, and started to leave.

"What? After keeping them from killing all of you? Like I said," replied Lil with a heavy mock sigh. "Like I said." She sat in a swatch of sunlight, gazing thoughtfully at Eliot, as he slowly blinked his eyes and a slight smile lit his face.

"We're going to Cairo, aren't we?" he said. He sounded strangely satisfied. He turned and looked straight into Verity's eyes. "If you can't beat 'em, join 'em, right?"

Lil frowned. "It never worked *that* fast before."

Fourteen

○○○○○○○○○○○○○○○○

Revelation Blues

The breakfast table where Lil and Verity helped themselves to yellow mounds of scrambled eggs and the never-ending biscuits was splashed with sunlight. One of the children had discovered a great store of dried eggs, much to everyone's relief. Verity decided she preferred the red-checked tablecloths she had found in an upper cabinet to the white linen that somehow cleaned itself after every meal, stains gradually fading.

"I don't recommend you stopping in Cairo," said Lil. She poured a dollop of honey into her coffee and stirred. There was plenty of honey. "I hear everyone talking about it and it's just not a good idea."

"Why not?" asked Verity, feeling her usual irritation with Lil, which had to do with how much Lil seemed to know and how little she said about anything. She was a bit thinner, lately, if such a thing was possible. Every day she wore one of those dresses which seemed like they might get pretty warm and confining, since they had those long sleeves and were so tight and covered her so completely. Her cheekbones had not been quite so visible a few weeks ago, had they?

"It's not a nice place," said Lil.

"Why not? What's wrong with it? Are there pirates there?"

Eliot looked up from the next table. "Pirates?" he asked with his empty, angelic smile, then went back to eating. He spent a lot of time in his room with the door shut, or else he was poking around the ship, wandering in his demented way into storage rooms and even, once, the pilothouse, always smiling.

Lil sighed and leaned back in her chair. She bowed her head briefly, then raised it and spoke. "Of course. But not only pirates. Cairo is a strange town. Your whole trip could fall apart there."

Not mine, thought Verity, as a flash of a bluebird flying past the window caught her eye. *Nothing* could stop my trip. "So what?" she asked. "I'm getting tired of all these people, if you want to know the truth. If they want to go to Norleans—*Nawlins,* they're calling it now—by themselves, fine! Let them! All they do is whine and complain about how they're not in Cincinnati anymore, and about how it's all my fault. I thought I was *helping* them."

Lil nodded thoughtfully, and took another bite of toast. "It is hard to help people, certainly. But now that they've left Cincinnati, their womb, so to speak, it's really your responsibility to get them to their goal."

"It seems to me that the plague will get them to their goal regardless," said Verity.

"That's the problem," said Lil, leaning forward suddenly. "Time. They *have* to get there in a certain amount of time."

"Why?" asked Verity. "How do you know?" She suddenly wished that there was a whole history that she could open, somewhere, hook into, and curl up, absorbing it all, knowing it all at last, the good and the bad and why this and why that. Why humans were different now, how it had all happened, where it was leading. "Why is this all a goddamned *secret?*"

She pushed her chair over backward and stood up. *Why are you getting so excited?* a part of her asked. *Just calm down—*

"I will *not* calm down! I will not!" she heard herself yelling.

"You're pregnant, aren't you?" asked Lil, looking Verity up and down suddenly. "That's it! Why did it take me so long to figure it out? Oh, honey, that's wonderful!" She got up and hugged Verity and Verity pushed her away.

"It's none of your business," she yelled, feeling worse than ever.

"That's okay, Verity," said Jack, from the doorway. She stood there shaking as he grabbed a plate, went to the table, sat down, and started filling it up with breakfast stuff. "Hey. Rave on. Lil has the same effect on me. You're pregnant? That's wonderful!"

"Oh, *stop* it!" she said. But she sat down again, rather worn out. She could hardly keep her pregnancy a secret, but Jack and Lil already knew too much about her. "I'm just tired of not knowing anything. Lil said something about how we have to get to Norleans in a certain amount of time, that's all."

"Oh?" asked Jack, glancing at Lil. Her lips set in a line and she didn't look back at him.

"And what will happen if we don't?" asked Verity.

Lil sighed, then said, "The Nawlins Plague is degenerative. It gives a big push to all sorts of areas of brain growth. But those chemicals cease to be secreted after a certain amount of time. I'm really not sure how long. But once they are no longer secreted, people die. That's one reason the plague is so strong. It's a tradeoff. I've heard that the last stretch of the Mississippi is filled with dead bodies. Or was, at one point." She stood suddenly and left the room.

"She seemed kind of angry," said Jack, as he peppered his eggs and sighed.

"She doesn't think we should stop at Cairo," said Verity. "But I don't see how I can stop anybody from doing whatever they want." She felt a sudden stab of fear. What would this mean for the baby? Too late to worry about that now.

"I think you could, if you really wanted to," said Jack. He piled eggs on a piece of toast and took a bite.

"What do you know about Cairo?" asked Verity.

Jack ate in silence for a minute, but Verity could tell he was just thinking.

"They voted to convert, back at the beginning," he said. "But then they voted to stop it. Got scared. It was half-finished. I'm not sure how they stopped it at that point, but there are vestiges of the conversion all around. It's a lot larger than it used to be, back around 2000. Once the trains came back, it grew fast. All kinds of people show up there. All *kinds*. People heading west. People heading south."

"People heading east?" asked Verity.

"Nobody heads east," said Jack. He folded the rest of his toast and stuffed it in his mouth.

"Why not?"

"They just don't."

"Right. Have you ever been to Cairo?"

"Oh yes," said Jack, his face sad. "I've been there."

"What for? How did you get there?"

"I had to do a report," he said. "And I got there via NAMS."

Blaze came in and picked up a plate. He turned when Jack said NAMS. "What?" he asked, his face pale so that his freckles stood out.

"You're up early this morning," Verity said.

Blaze ignored her. "What about NAMS?"

Jack shrugged. "What about it? I was telling Verity about using NAMS."

Blaze set his plate back on the pile and sank into a chair. "NAMS," he whispered. "I thought I'd forgotten. But I haven't. I wish I had. It was so horrible."

"What was?" asked Verity, alarmed.

"Riding NAMS into Cincinnati. I . . . Cairo had just woken me. It's like I felt a jolt, somehow, and opened my eyes all of a sudden and instead of being at Shaker Hill I didn't know where I was and Cairo was pulling those sheets off of me, just gripping a little bit with her teeth and pulling, and growling, and licking me."

"Poor Cairo," said Verity. A black wave of sadness suffused her. "She was a good dog."

Blaze raised his eyes to hers. "I didn't know who I was, Verity. I didn't know where I was. I didn't know how I got there. I felt sick, so sick. It was like I was dreaming." He started breathing harder, as if breathing was difficult.

"Calm down," said Jack, reaching over and rubbing Blaze's back.

"I remember the worst thing," Blaze said dully. "The worst thing was that there was no heaven. It was just all kind of blank and awful and hurting . . . faces . . . pain . . ."

"Because you weren't *dead,* Blaze," Verity said, trying not to scream at him. "I never believed you were dead! Not for one minute!" She was trembling. "But you don't care, do you? All you care about is that—that *music!* And the *radio stones.* You're just like all the rest of them. You don't care how hard it was for me to save you!" She jumped up and rushed out the door, ignoring Blaze's "Wait!" She ran very fast so that he couldn't catch her if he was following her and ducked around a corner and sat there curled up, shaking with anger.

But after a few minutes, she began to laugh, and wiped her tears away as she stood up. "Why should they care?" she asked herself. "What do you want? A medal?"

It was time to get under way. She walked up the stairs to the pilot-house and stepped into her domain, where the flashing blue-green of the river pulled her on, and on, and on.

Later on in the day, she relinquished a bit of piloting to Mr. Peabody, after he insisted that she take a rest. He was, as Blaze had said, a competent fellow. She felt more comfortable with him on the boat. Not quite as alone and nervous.

As she passed the auditorium, she heard the faint strains of a blues song coming faintly from the auditorium. She stopped still and the words came clear.

> I got nineteen men and I want one more
> I got nineteen men and I want one more
> If I get one more I'll let those nineteen go.

There were two female voices, one singing the first line, the other responding with the second. As she listened, the song ended, and dialogue began.

Curious, she descended the stairs, opened the tall doors to the auditorium, and slipped inside. She sat on one of the velvet chairs at the very
back. No one onstage paid her any attention.

She saw three black girls. Verity thought they were probably twelve.
One of them had her hair cut very close to her head, so close she looked
almost bald. Another had very long hair which curled in strands so that,
with her golden-brown skin, she looked almost lionlike in the warm
lights of the stage. The third wore a large jeweled headdress.

The short-haired girl reached for the headdress. "It's my turn to be
Bessie," she said.

The first one kept the headdress firmly on her head with both hands.
Her dress glittered and she wore a necklace of gold coins around her
neck. "No! I get to be Bessie the whole time today. That's what we
agreed."

"That's right, Sarah," the other one pointed out. "Quit making trouble. Jesse's right. We have two more acts to go. Now where were we?"

"New York," said Sarah. "I was getting ready to make my first
record. Hey," she yelled, "don't we get some props, people?"

"We're still working on them," came a yell from a console where a boy
and a girl were sitting with a look of concentration on their faces. A
background depicting a small room with a ghost engineer manipulating
dials and wearing headphones wavered around the girls for a moment,
then faded away.

"Forget it," said one of the girls. "How about a microphone, at least?"

"We made this for real," said the boy, and dragged on a large placard
with an advertisement for race records.

"Well," said the other girl doubtfully. "Better than nothing I guess.
Now are we in Harlem or what?"

The play moved along. Bessie got a check for $125.00, all she would
ever make for a record side though a record might sell hundreds of thousands of copies. She never got any royalties. They went to a man who
coopted them without telling her. Apparently this was the way many
blues singers were treated well into the thirties.

"I can't *believe* this," said Jesse.

"That's not what you're supposed to say," said Sarah.

"Well, I don't know much about money . . ."

"I'll say you don't."

"Well, who does? But this doesn't seem fair."

"So what? She was happy."

"Maybe she didn't know any better."

"She fired a few managers because of it."

"It's kind of like . . . what's fair? My mother signed up for me to have
receptors. She got them too. But all the good stuff was withheld until

they were paid off. Even after the original conversion. She used to come home screaming mad after meetings with the class-action lawyers. Not at me but at CintiBeez, Inc. They were the original company. I'll tell you who made a killing—the lawyers. My mom was the curator of the Museum of African-American Arts." In the spotlight, she lowered her head and closed her eyes. "I can still remember what was inscribed over the door . . . 'Only the art, the distilled culture of the subjugated people, survives.' In our case, I guess that was music and dance.

"Anyway, we couldn't really use all the services the city offered until it was all paid off. So, like, the richies were having all these loony fantasies and living in those flower towers, and we were had to live in houses at various stages of enlivenment. I mean, you couldn't even get into a tower without the right receptors." She opened her eyes and looked at her hands. "I don't know. I guess I was . . . sleeping . . . for a while." She grinned. "But then the True Queen came, and gave access to *all* of us!"

"And now here we are," said Jesse sourly, "floating down the river like a bunch of low-grade idiots."

"But Jesse," said Sarah, her smile broadening, "remember where we're *going.*"

"I know," said Jesse. "I remember all that history. Right into the heart of the land of slavery. Ugh."

"No," said Sarah in a gentle voice. "That was long ago. We're going there *now.*" And Sarah began to sing, some sort of blues song about going to Nawlins.

At first, Jesse had her back turned. But by the chorus, the others had joined in, even the crew in the back, the members of which wandered onstage. Their voices were haunting; the harmonies were strange to Verity's ears and the rhythms within the music changed constantly. Suddenly Verity didn't know if their dialogue was real, or was just part of the play.

Verity was drawn into the strange music as she never had been before, the bits she'd heard on the radio stones, Blaze's fumbling guitar attempts to imitate what he was hearing. Which, she had to admit, had improved quite a bit lately. Her heart was torn by the simple tales of woe, hard times, and the broken relationships of people whose families had been wrenched apart by force for generations and now that slavery was officially over found themselves in an economic reality that duplicated many of the same conditions: constant indebtedness to sharecroppers, inability to attend good schools, vote, or have recourse to the legal system. She heard, woven into the music, a history of it; how the coded messages conveyed in field hollers evolved into the music played at night, at family parties on weekends, in jook joints in out-of-the-way places, worn shacks that had no value to the whites.

Then she was startled from that stream by a new voice.

Rich and deep, it came from a tiny black woman onstage. She was accompanied by a guitar, but she was not playing it. She was standing alone in a spotlight. Behind her, sitting on a stool, was Blaze, with his guitar. She wondered again where he had found it.

The woman sang a song about jealousy and loss. Blaze's guitar work held the woman's voice perfectly in a musical web which constantly changed, in tenor, in rhythm, in intensity. It keened in flattened intervals above her voice, swooped from below and touched it in brief unison. With a pang, Verity remembered the way he used to play to her dancing: like this. But this music was more intense, and so much more personal. When the woman stopped singing, he played on, but without her voice he made the guitar sing like a woman, and misery and pain exploded in Verity's heart.

Was it his, she wondered, or hers?

Maybe it came from both of them. How distant he had been lately. She missed him . . . but it was the old Blaze she missed. This new Blaze was more and more a stranger.

At least he's alive, she thought, I saved him from death but this is what the cure did to him and to us, and her mind went round and round in that same circle while his blues played on and on.

There was some commotion and she went up on deck. She was surprised to see that they were locking through a dam. For an instant she felt panic; then it subsided—Peabody could handle this as well as or better than she. And this time there was a lockmaster, a woman.

Verity saw her as she rode the gondola between the two towers; stared up at her shadowy, impersonal profile as she opened the lower gates and let them through. There was no town visible. Just the dam, the lock, and the woman. Verity waved at her as they rounded the bend, but she did not wave back.

When Verity next went to the auditorium, on a rainy evening, she was surprised to see Jack and Lil.

Lil's long legs were draped over the chair in front of her and Jack's extended into the aisle. Lil wore a green dress tonight, as glittery as all the others. Or maybe, thought Verity, narrowing her eyes in the glow of the footlights, it was the same dress every time. Self-cleaning, changing color with Lil's whim.

Of course. Why had it taken her so long to realize this?

Jack turned and waved her down the aisle. Verity dropped into a seat behind them and leaned forward. "How do you—" she began, but Jack shushed her with a wave of his hand.

Three people were arguing onstage, but not projecting. Finally the word PARIS dissolved on a screen set on an easel on one side of the stage and was replaced by washington, d.c. A muscle in Jack's cheek began to tic; then the lights went down and rehearsal began.

The sign changed again, this time to blues alley. A couple came on-stage and sat at a small table.

Tiny lines of dialogue had appeared on Verity's hands quite often during the days as the play evolved. The words changed almost con-stantly as the concepts were smoothed by the group mind of the awak-ening rafters, sifted for importance and tested against what others might know. She ignored the words, though, for the most part, completely fo-cussed on the river by the unseen dangers it held, and held somewhat apart from that emerging mind by her difference, by her very Roseness. Now the words came back to her like echoes.

Woman: What time does the show start?
Man: What do you care? I thought you only came because I in-sisted.
Woman: I just want to get it over with. I've got a lot of work to do.
Man: I know. But you always liked Alberta Hunter. I thought you'd like to see her in person. Kind of.
Woman: Oh, I don't know. I just don't know anymore. All this . . . id-iotic nonsense. Re-creating long-dead singers. Visiting the "real" Henry Ford. It's just—toys for children.
Man: But why does it upset you so? Your hands are shaking!
Woman: You're supposed to reach across and hold them.
Man: Oh. Sorry.
Woman: Um . . . It's kind of chilly in here, isn't it? I may have to go to Salt Lake City tomorrow. I just got the message on the way here to meet you.
Man: Salt Lake City!

Jack sat up straight and said "Salt Lake City!"
Lil yanked him back down and said "Shhh."

Man: What for? I've heard rumors . . .
Woman: Nothing important. Putting out fires, that's all.

Jack's bitter laugh filled the theater and the actors looked up, squint-ing in the footlights.
"Fires," muttered Jack. "A nice way to put it."
Lil said, "Want to leave?"
Jack stayed put and Lil shrugged.

Man: An awful lot of these fires lately, aren't there? Look, I'm no molecular-engineering expert like you, but . . . well, I guess

WOMAN: you can't tell *me* anything anyway, can you. I'm just a commoner . . . a mere ordinary human caught up in all this . . .
WOMAN: Aren't you supposed to laugh bitterly right here?
MAN: Oh, yeah. Sorry. (Laugh) How's that?

A woman stepped up behind them and began to sing in a spot while the rest of the stage darkened.

WOMAN: It's okay, don't worry—shhh—Alberta! It . . . no, *she* . . . really *is* amazing. She sounds—just like those old recordings. Thanks for asking me.

Jack said, "But it didn't happen in Salt Lake City, did it, Miss Molecular Biologist? We did a good job there. At least, *that* time. No, it happened right at home. Right in Washington, D.C." He took a flagon from his jacket pocket, unscrewed the lid with his thumb, and took a big swig.

"What happened, Jack?" asked Verity.

"Oh," said Jack. "Forgot you were there."

Lil snorted. "I think you forgot anyone was here. But that's kind of the plan, isn't it?" She pushed past Jack roughly and strode up the aisle. The door slammed behind her.

"What's wrong with her?" asked Verity.

"Too close to home," said Jack. "Guess I'd better go talk to her."

"I'll go with you," said Verity. She hurried to keep up with Jack; with his long legs he took only one stride to Verity's two. "What were they talking about there? It's just a play, isn't it?"

"I'm not sure," said Jack, and pushed open the door. "You first."

They found Lil right outside, leaning against the railing, her head in her hands.

"Kind of chilly out here, isn't it?" asked Jack. He pulled off his jacket and flung it around Lil's shoulders. "Of course if you dressed sensibly—just kidding, just kidding," he finished as she gave him a withering look.

"I don't know why you have to go swigging that stuff all the time," said Lil.

"Why not?" asked Jack. "It can't hurt me."

"It hurts *me*," said Lil. "It hurts all of us. It makes you careless." She looked at him again and then saw Verity. "What are *you* doing here?"

"What you don't seem to understand, Lil, is that it doesn't make a hell of a lot of difference that she's here. Or what she may or may not know."

"I disagree," said Lil. "I haven't given up. I guess I did, for a long time. You're the one who kept me going, Jack. What's come over you?" She sighed. "I don't know why I stay with you." Her long black hair cascaded down her back, catching the moonlight with uncountable kinky strands.

"I wonder the same thing. Is it because I owe you money?" Jack took another deep drink. "But I'm going to win it back. Have no fear. Besides, I think I've advised you to go back. More than once, if I recall. I still do. I made the wrong decision. It's too late."

"Oh, you're impossible!" Lil frowned and turned away.

"So what happened in Washington?" asked Verity. "It seems as if we're all going to piece it together pretty soon. Why not tell me now?"

"They're just making it up," said Jack.

"Why not ask them?" said Lil.

"Why not just get off the boat?" said Verity.

"Now, now," said Jack.

"Maybe we will," said Lil, her voice cool. "And maybe we won't."

"I'm not getting off the boat," said Jack. "Easiest stretch I've done in quite a while. Enormously pleasant. Wine, women, and song. Craps and poker, music and pool, from morning till night." He leaned back against the railing. "I've become a virtual millionaire."

Lil raised her voice. "You're an idiot, Jack Hamilton."

Jack nodded. "I'm sure of it. You are most astute, my dear."

"Don't condescend to me."

Jack widened his eyes. "Me? Why, I always treat you with the utmost respect—"

"Fuck you!" said Lil, and walked off into the night.

"Guess I made her mad," said Jack.

Verity sat next to him on the bench. "She doesn't want to talk about it."

"About what?"

Verity could see why Lil would be reduced to screaming, but she persevered. "About what happened in Washington, D.C. When did it happen? What was it? Was it like Cincinnati?"

"You've been through a bit of it yourself, haven't you?"

"Hasn't everyone?"

Jack nodded. He looked completely sober to her. His face fell into its usual serious lines. "We lost control, to put it simply. We just lost control."

"What do you mean, we?"

Jack bowed his head. "Really," he said quietly, "that's all I want to say right now. It's just very painful. Lil is more . . . positive than me. She sees a light at the end of the tunnel. It was the other way around for a long time. I stayed part of the network. Did my job. Followed orders. When there *were* orders. Sometimes I just had to make them up. Sometimes I issued them.

"But she's grasping at straws. We're all going down fast. I couldn't quite realize it until I was here, on the boat—among *normal* people!" He laughed shortly. "Humans are a vanishing species. What's coming is . . . well, different. Maybe that's as it should be. There's nothing so special about us, no reason for us to last forever. We brought it all on ourselves, but we thought it was all for the best. And for a while, it was. It really was magnificent, Verity."

He rose and patted her on the shoulder. "Enjoy it while you can, child. Enjoy it while you can." He pulled out the flask and looked at it. "Wish this stuff worked better. Too bad it has no effect on me. It seemed like a good idea at the time. Just like everything else." He stuck it back in his pocket. "It's kind of fun to tease Lil, though. She doesn't know." He sighed. "Simple pleasures."

His steps were slow and somber as he followed Lil.

Maybe I should have left them all to their little games in Cincinnati, thought Verity. She curled up on the bench and listened to the river rush below. What had she done?

What had happened in the world, to make it such a dangerous place? Where would it end?

Norleans, washed a whispery voice through her mind, and she did not know if it was the rush of the river, something she'd made up, or a voice that came from her nubs.

And she didn't really care.

Fifteen

○○○○○○○○○○○○○○○○○○○

Midnight Special

The chill rain of early spring deluged them today, rather than the warm greening rains of early summer. Icy wind pushed spray and waves against the hull of the *Queen,* and Verity feared for the rafters in this roughness as she surveyed the darkening day from the pilothouse.

She pulled down the voicetube and held the cold coil in her hand to speak into it, then remembered that it was obsolete. Smiling, she saw the back of her hand blink the message SHELTER IN THE NEXT COVE. As the *Queen* rounded the bend, new white apple blossoms filled the air like snow and a hundred strands of wigwam smoke were pulled sideways by the powerful wind. The dark green water was lake-calm in the protected cove.

Verity felt exceptionally irritable toward everything and everyone. Particularly the rafters. Let them sink or swim. Let them argue or dance to their own crazed chemicals. Let Lil loose infinite nan upon the world. Let the world perish, madly or quietly, in revelry or regret. What did it matter to her?

Her hand went to her stomach, barely swollen. She should care. She had to. She carried the new world within her. She wondered if all parents believed that their child might be the turning fulcrum of something powerful as the light of stars.

At least, unlike herself, her child would have a mother.

Verity put down the binoculars and stared out at the gray sheets of sleety rain sweeping across the river. Absently she touched the brass compass, thinking about that strange compass in her heart which pointed so unerringly toward Norleans, and lifted the binoculars in a swift angry motion and brought them down hard on the compass. The binoculars bounced off the clear surface of the compass cover and crashed onto the floor.

She closed her eyes and saw a gray street, and in that gray street, in morning mist, thin men with drooping shoulders walked toward the end of the street, away from her, in drifting, aimless cadence, weaving a pattern of which they were an unknowing part. The vision was haunting. The muffling silence of fog, the gray men flitting like leaves caught in a slow whirl of wind as they receded from her; their floating aspect.

But the vision was not hers.

Where was the street? Whose memory was this? So many shards within her, battling for their moment in consciousness, the few seconds when she might review them, give them life. But they were not her memories. She still was not free. And what had happened to Durancy? He could come round at any moment, and she might just follow him back to Cincinnati. No. Despite her battle, she was not free, nor were any of those rafters. What made her think that Norleans would free her? The golden burnish of her skin, the deeper glow of those with African blood, bespoke enslavement.

Yet, she was more free; *they* were more free than they had been in Cincinnati. There were glimmers of hope. The blue she saw was sharp as a flavor she'd never actually tasted, which lay out of reach of her ability to describe it, like a sweet, alien fruit from a foreign land. Though she had wondered about Mother Ann and heaven, she did not wonder about the reality of this. That in itself was rather disquieting.

Perhaps there were only degrees of freedom, nothing more. She looked down at her hand. ACT IV, it said. A fine drizzle drifted across the river, swathing the hills in a gray mist. What else was there to do? She turned and started back toward the auditorium.

A thin black woman with wild hair stood in the aisle yelling at the people onstage "No, that's *not* it!" just about every time someone spoke a line, and Verity could tell that the actors were getting irritated. Finally one of the older men yelled, "The hell with you, you're not the boss," and she stomped past her row with clenched fists, frowning, and slammed the door as she left. The sound reverberated in the high-ceilinged auditorium.

"Okay," said the man, looking around at the rest of them. "This is the Berlin segment, right?"

"This is taking way too long," complained a boy Verity recognized as Fred. "This play is about a week long."

"So what?" asked a young woman next to him. They were about fifty feet away, but the stage was designed to carry voices. "If that's what it takes, then that's what it takes."

"Berlin," muttered Jack, whom she had settled next to. Lil was in the row in front of them, and Eliot was right down at the stage, most likely with that vacant grin on his face. She knew that Lil felt bad about Eliot. When she tried to talk to him he just smiled and said nothing.

"They're missing all the good parts," said Jack, in a curiously ironic voice. "Nothing happened in Berlin."

"Shut up," said Lil over her shoulder. "I'm trying to hear."

"Skip Berlin," said the old man up on the stage impatiently. "We did Berlin okay. It only takes one run-through. The general's son is demonstrating against nan when he gets a whiff of terrorist nan. The general decides that she can't take it anymore. Starts to organize against the government. Knows too much. She's kidnapped and when she gets back all she can do is knit."

"Fine," said another man. "I want to go back a little further." He walked over to an easel on the stage and touched the top of it a few times. "How do I stop these pictures—oh, right, I have it now." He bent over it, frowning. "The timeline. Here we go. More of that hypertext stuff . . . fine . . . rivers . . . Columbia, Colorado, Mississippi, Tennessee, shit, at last, Potomac. Okay, map, Alexandria . . . that's right . . . Angela, you be the GS-eighteen, Carl, you be the triple agent. What's his name? Triage. Huh. That's a *name?* Okay, the storefront scene. In . . . Alexandria, Virginia. Pasta. *Generous George's Cosmically Advanced Cuisine.* Bring it up. That's right. Fred, you're not old enough . . . Janet, you be the . . ."

"Shit," said Jack softly, and sat up straight, staring at the scene evoked by the holo projectors. "Shit. Lil, we have to *stop* them."

Lil lounged farther back in her seat, and hooked her legs over the seat back in front of her. "Right, Jack. Isn't that what I've been saying? And you've been saying, here we are in the middle of nowhere, who cares."

"We are *heading* toward Cairo, Lil. Haven't—"

"Shut up, Jack," said Lil, and Verity saw her glare at Jack in the bright reflection of the stage lights. Then she removed her legs from the chair in front of her and leaned forward.

"Do you have it?" asked the woman onstage.

The man nodded.

"Say yes," directed the old man. "Don't just shake your head."

"Yes, I have it," said the man. "How much will you pay?"

"I need verification," said the woman. "Proof."

The man laughed. "You ought to be afraid to have proof," he said. "You ought to be terrified."

"More of that," said the director. "You know. *Terrified.*"

Verity saw that Jack's hands were shaking as he held on tight to his bottle. Sweat stood out on his forehead. He threw the silver flask down and it went spinning across the aisle. He erupted from his chair like a waterspout and ran down the aisle toward the stage.

"Yo! Jack!" yelled Lil.

Jack bounded up on stage and pulled the easel down, bending it back and forth. He threw it on the floor and stomped it flat while the actors watched, stunned.

"How do you kill this fucking thing? This is idiotic!" Jack yelled. He picked up a chair and started whacking the easel. "This is dangerous. Terribly dangerous. You have no idea . . ."

Lil ran up next to him and pulled him away, grabbing his arms and leading him firmly offstage. "Sorry," she yelled over her shoulder. "He's had way too much to . . . to drink."

Verity sat and watched the players complain for a few minutes and try to straighten things up, then got up and left too. What had come over Jack? It was that odd word. Triage.

The deck was wet from a steady rain. It seemed for all the world like a normal night at Shaker Hill. She welcomed the cool, damp air on her face. Any minute now Sare would call her in, yell from the kitchen window and tell her that she'd catch her death of cold standing around outside in the damp . . .

The river rushed past and she could see brief white flickers out in the middle. The rafters were snug in their wigwams though she thought she could hear a round of the new song that was sweeping through, just now; Blaze called it a blues song and it was about the river too, but it wasn't jolly and happy as "Down the Ohio" or "The Erie Canal." It was about knowing what it meant to miss New Orleans.

She looked for Jack and Lil in the poolroom, but did not find them. She hurried on to their next choice, the ornate bar, but they were nowhere to be found.

She figured it was a short-day run to Cairo, now. Maybe less. It was hard to be precise. Why was she so worried? The boat was running fine; they had all the routines down. They'd take a breather there. It had not converted, Peabody said, so she was not worried about it. And once past Cairo, how long would it take to get to Norleans . . . Nawlins?

Shivering, she decided to go try and figure it out, if she could. She climbed the stairs to the texas, and let herself into her pilot room, and saw a shadowy figure standing by the navigation table.

"Who are you?" she asked, and the person turned around, surprising her. "What are you doing here?" she asked Lil.

The table glowed, lighting Lil's face from beneath. For the first time she was not wearing a glittery dress. She was wearing a tight-fitting black sweater and black pants that looked fluffy and warm. She wore boots that came up above her ankles, like Verity, instead of her high heels.

"I'm just looking at the charts. Is that all right?"

"I guess," said Verity. What could she say about it? She was once again irritated with Lil, who obviously knew more than she did but who volunteered nothing. "Who are you, Lil?" she asked. "I mean, really. What are you doing here?"

"You don't want to know," said Lil.

"I wouldn't have asked if I didn't want to know," Verity said, trying to keep her voice level.

Lil flounced onto the couch and crossed her arms and legs and looked levelly at Verity across the glow of the screen. "What do you think is going on?" she asked.

Verity felt an instant's vertigo and gripped the map table. She averted her eyes from the blue of the river on the screen and touched it off. She sat in a straight chair next to the stove, welcoming the warmth.

"All I know is that I'm responsible for all these people and that I don't think I'm doing a very good job."

Lil leaned forward, her eyes on Verity's face. "Why are you responsible for them?" she asked.

Verity said nothing. "You see?" said Lil. "It's not as easy to trust someone else as you think. You've really told us nothing about yourself."

"Why should I?" asked Verity. "Surely you can talk to anyone else and figure it out. You're the ones hitching a ride on my boat. I'm the captain. I think I'll put you and Jack off at Cairo." Even as she said it she realized that putting Jack and Lil off would be difficult.

And she also realized that she did not want to put them off, not really.

She had a great hunger to know about the world. They were the first people she'd ever met who might be able to tell her something about what lay beyond the rim of the horizon.

But they would not do so voluntarily. Not unless they had to. There was some great secret, something they could not or would not talk about. And that was what she wanted to know.

"Lil," she said, "I feel very much alone here. I'm trying to hold things together but it's hard. I don't know where we're going, and I don't really know why. We're just caught in the flow of the river and we have to follow it to the end."

Lil stood and in a swift surprising motion reached up and gently touched the nub behind one of Verity's ears. "Fine. When you want to tell me more, let me know. I'll be around."

Lil let herself out the door.

Jack was sitting alone in the poolroom.

Rain slashed at the windows, and light from a flickering candle Jack had on the table limned the drops that danced on the window.

Verity stood in the doorway and watched him. He moved his arm languorously, every moment or so, taking sips from a small clear glass of amber liquid that she was sure was whiskey. She shivered a bit in the chill air and hugged her sweater around her more closely. "I thought that didn't have any effect on you," she said.

Jack's smile was slight and lasted only a second. "That was yesterday. Anything encoded can be decoded, Verity. I decided that a little decoding was in order. It's best to enjoy the finer things in life. Like Tennessee whiskey."

"So you carry a little decoder around with you?" she asked.

He took another sip, then refilled his glass from the bottle sitting at his elbow. "Do I detect an edge of hostility? Do you think Lil is the only one with any brains? I wouldn't be surprised. Come, sit down. What are you doing up so late?" He pulled out a chair next to him.

"I don't know. I'm kind of nervous, I guess. But I'm not sure why. What time is it?"

"Oh," he said, and shrugged. "One, one-thirty. Here. Let me get you a glass of whiskey. It's soothing. Good for what ails you."

"No thanks," she said. "Why were you so upset in the auditorium?"

"Was I upset?"

"You ran down the aisle and tried to destroy their information screen. And you told Lil that you had to stop this." She leaned forward so she could see his eyes better. "Jack, stop *what?*"

"I just don't like plays," he said. "Never have. They put me in a bad mood."

"No, you said things. Like . . . like, 'Nothing happened in Berlin.' How do *you* know what happened in Berlin? They're just making it all up, anyway, right? And when did nothing happen in Berlin?"

"A long time ago, Verity," he said. "It was a very, very long time ago that nothing happened in Berlin. Ages ago, so to speak. I'm just a little sensitive, that's all."

"So how do you know about all this?" she asked. "Did you work for the government?"

"I told you that I did, didn't I?"

"But what did you do? Why did you get so upset about that—that word, 'Triage.' "

"Damn it, Verity, can't you just leave me alone?"

"No, Jack, I can't. You and Lil are on my boat and I find both of you very strange. You're secretive. I don't know where you come from or what you're doing or why you want to be here. Is someone following you? Someone who might endanger us?"

Jack took another drink and stared at her.

"Tell me!" she shouted, and banged her fist on the table.

"What's the first thing you destroy if you're trying to cripple your enemy?" he asked.

"What?"

"You heard me. What do you destroy?"

"I . . . I don't know. I've never really thought that way . . ."

"Well, plenty of us have, Verity. We just can't seem to help it. I don't know. Maybe that's what needed to be changed, really. But you can bet that it's been tried. And you can bet that someone, somewhere, succeeded."

"What are you talking about?"

"Thinking like us and them. We are good. They are bad. Get it?"

"Yes, of course," she said slowly. She'd learned us-and-them. Us, the pure Shakers. Them, the poor crazed Rafters. She laughed. She was one of *them* now. What's so funny? she wondered, seized by intense laughter. John had killed Blaze because of us-and-them. Yet she laughed until she choked and tears were coming from her eyes and Jack was thumping her on the back.

"Yeah, it is pretty funny," he said, when her hiccoughing stopped. "Gotta admit, I find it hilarious." He poured another small glass of whiskey. His speech was slightly slurred. "Hee-*lar*ious!" But he did not laugh. "To get back to my original question."

He looked at her for a long moment and the shadows on his face danced in the candlelight. He said slowly, softly, and clearly, "Okay, lesson number one. In a war, when you want to destroy the enemy's capability, *what is the first thing you think of?*"

The look in his eyes was strange and deep and helpless. The intensity of his question almost frightened Verity. And yet there was a hard edge in that look, a sort of defiance; maybe even pride.

"Communication," he said after a long pause, during which Verity wondered if he'd forgotten his question. "You destroy their ability to communicate."

Something deep stirred in Verity then, like a glimmer of light, like something she really ought to know but which still lurked too far beneath the day's tiredness to summon up.

"I guess that makes sense," she said, beginning to feel her way through the web of inferences that suddenly filled her mind.

Then a faint shudder ran through the boat. "What was that?" She jumped out of her chair.

"That would be Lil," said Jack, pouring the remainder of the bottle into the glass.

"What do you mean, 'that would be Lil'? You mean she's starting the boat? We can't go anywhere this time of night. It's too dangerous." Now the jolt of the paddlewheel biting the river vibrated beneath her feet. "Come *on!*" she yelled, but Jack just sat there as she ran out the door and rushed back up to the texas.

The lights of the boat were on and they illuminated storm-tossed waves and hapless rafts caught in their wake. Anger boiled up in Verity as she ran and when she got to the door she saw Lil inside, her face illuminated by the faint green light of the readouts and dials. She tried to open the door but it was locked. The palmprint panel was dark. All the windows were shut tight. She pounded on the door, pounded on the windows, yelled at Lil, but Lil did not even glance at her.

"Stop the boat!" she screamed. "You're going to hurt people. You're swamping the rafts! Lil, are you nuts?"

Lil did not even glance at her. Her chin was set defiantly and she stared straight ahead, a frown of concentration on her face. Loud blues music pulsed within the pilothouse, drowning out Verity's yells.

"Shit!" said Verity and looked around to try and find something with which to break the glass. In the next cabin she grabbed the poker for the stove and returned, and began to wildly bash at the window. But it resisted all her efforts and she found that she was beginning to shake.

What was it? What was Lil trying to do? She *had* to be insane. Either that, or . . .

The rush of the river quickened. The fog parted for a moment and she saw a light.

It was tiny in the distance. She might have taken it for a low star had it not pulsed. Regularly. Every two seconds. And then it was obscured by the fog once more.

"The Cairo light," she breathed.

Lil was trying to bypass Cairo.

The decks were filled with dazed people. They were muttering and wandering around; some were shouting, and from the river came back shouts which echoed strangely within the fog, as if they were all in a large room.

She had to stop this headlong rush. They needed to stop in Cairo. They needed supplies. They needed to be on dry land, if only briefly.

And, she realized, the thought seeming to come from nowhere, they had to get to Cairo because they had to put on their play.

Their play.

She looked at Lil and then she understood. It all came together.

Somewhere in that play were things that Jack and Lil did not want other people to know. The information was buried within the minds of the Cincinnatians, and was now flowing forth: the history of the Information Wars, and nanotechnology.

The reasons the world had fallen into a brilliant darkness, illuminated now only by the insane, the enslaved, the nan-possessed survivors rushing downriver to Nawlins, in the grip of the plague.

She still did not know what the rest of the world was like. And Jack and Lil would not tell her.

Perhaps there were some answers there in Cairo.

Gritting her teeth, Verity picked up the poker and began smashing at the window once more, reeling backward and forward as the boat tossed on the wild river. She thought she saw Jack out ahead, standing at the railing, staring at the Cairo light through the darkness, while some of the sleepy players joined him. "Help me!" she yelled, but no one did and she had the fleeting thought that at times control really did come in handy.

Then Blaze was there behind her, bless him, and he had . . . a baseball bat? "Get back, Verity," he commanded, and broke through the glass in the window with a few quick blows. Still Lil did not look at them, but struggled with the wheel. The water was rougher now, and even this huge riverboat was tossed in the new turbulence. The confluence, thought Verity, with a thrill, despite the desperation of the moment, holding tight to the railing. Soon they would come to it, just past Cairo, a tad past the light, which was just beyond the landing according to her old charts. The confluence of the Ohio and the Mississippi, two great rivers, where the muddy Mississippi did not mingle with the clear green Ohio for over a mile, where the two rivers flowed shoulder to shoulder in a line that was clear and unmistakable.

I'm leaving the Ohio River, thought Verity. All my past, I'm leaving behind. My history. Russ and Sare and Evangeline, Shaker Hill, my childhood; even Cincinnati, the Queen City. I'll never be back again. It's over. And I don't know what's ahead.

She took a deep breath and observed the passing instant.

Then Blaze reached inside the broken window and pulled the door open and together they rushed in. "Stay back," said Blaze and lunged at Lil, but she swatted him aside with hardly any trouble. She was fighting the wheel now, and the clouds parted and Cairo was a line of brilliant lights against the dark water. Verity gave a cry just upon seeing it. It was not a Flower City. Why was Lil so afraid?

She rushed at the wheel as Blaze grabbed Lil from behind once more, pinning her arms and dragging her away. Lil struggled and Verity took care to stay out of range of her legs.

"Damn it," Lil said, and her voice was full of anguish as Mr. Peabody, of all people, joined Blaze in helping pull her away from the wheel.

"Watch out for her gun," said Verity, as she put all her weight on the wheel, angry at being forced to navigate this rough stretch by night, which might be filled with snags and whirlpools. She thought she saw Jack still standing there, about ten feet ahead, on the starboard bow, a dark figure with rain dripping off his hat, as rain began sheeting down once more.

"You don't know what you're doing," said Lil, her voice harsh. "Verity, it's not too late. Stay away from Cairo."

"Why?" asked Verity.

But Lil said grimly, "I guess it *is* too late," and slipped out of the pilothouse.

Verity heard faint singing. And then, to her surprise, she joined in, the song coursing through her like lightning, like enlivenment, like the greatest joy that she could have ever imagined:

> Caimeneero, down to Cairo
> Caimaneero, Cairo
> Straddleaddleaddle baba ladababa linktum
> Linktum body mitchie cambo.

Why am I crying? she wondered. She was crying and singing at once, deliriously happy, moved by some deep joy to these strange tears. Cairo. The word kicked up plague-induced memories of a hundred thousand pioneers, heading for Cairo, thence to cross the Mississippi, and enter the Territory.

They were almost there.

Lightning flashed, and Verity saw Jack and Lil standing like figureheads at the prow of the boat. Lil's hair streamed out behind, and when the roiling clouds parted for a moment, caught the moonlight and glowed as if electric. One arm clasped Jack's waist tightly.

Cairo looked glorious to Verity: first a low smudge of light on the horizon, glowing through heavy fog and spitting rain, like nothing she had ever seen from the outskirts of the dead towns and cities they had scavenged back in Ohio. Maybe Dayton had once looked as exciting from afar of a summer's night. As they careered closer, Cairo's lights were like stars, scintillating through the storm's veil. So this was what a city, a live city, was like! She dashed away her tears of joy but still felt just as glad.

Running lights came on, suddenly. Peabody, of course. In their glow she saw rafts swept downriver, into the darkness beyond. Rain blew through the hole Blaze had bashed in the window.

Blaze, next to her, gripped the brass railing and he certainly wasn't talking to her—his remarks were to the darkness, to the storm, to the space where Mother Ann once waited with outspread arms and the listening mien of those who take note of prayers: "It's so beautiful. I'm so *hungry* for all this. It doesn't *matter* that there's no heaven. This is *enough.* Driving rain, cold wind, the boat plowing through turbulent night toward a foreign shore of lights." Blaze waxing poetic. This was new.

But she forgot it as a bridge loomed seemingly out of nowhere, black and shining wet in their lights. She only had a second to be afraid; the boat rushed between vast concrete footings with inches to spare as she was paralyzed with fear that the current would smash them against the piers.

The *Queen* rocked across the wild currents and Verity's arms and shoulders seized with pain as she struggled with the huge wheel.

"Want some help?" Blaze asked. His eyes were clear as he looked at her, as if he'd just awakened from a trance.

" 'M okay," she managed, panting. "I wonder if there's a clear channel to those lights or if there's sandbars in the way. *Damn* that Lil!"

"Maybe we should let down the anchor here tonight—if the current slows—"

She shook her head. "I thought of that. But look—see that snag? There's another. Some of those stumps and logs are heavy as houses. I'm not sure how quickly the boat could heal itself if one of them hit it."

"But if we run aground . . ."

"We might *not* run aground," she snapped, leaning on the wheel with all her weight. Suddenly it spun around the other way, sending her sprawling across the floor. Sharp pain lanced the arm on which she landed.

Blaze grabbed the wheel. Whatever had caused the momentary recalcitrance was gone. The pitch of the boat threw Verity to the deck the first time she tried to stand. She grabbed a railing and pulled herself up, and saw that Blaze had the boat under control.

The lights of Cairo welcomed them, splashing light onto the high concrete landing. A mass of people waved and pointed.

"Are you all right?" Blaze asked. "Is that blood?"

She pushed up her sweater sleeve and looked at her arm, where a long dark gash oozed. She didn't feel anything. "A cut. I'll live. Look *out!*" she yelled. She grabbed the wheel and pulled, along with Blaze, but wasn't sure that the boat responded. She saw a raft, two pairs of wild eyes, and then the dark river again.

"You've got to pay attention!" she said, her voice sharp.

They were closing in fast. People in rain-shined coats waited on the wharf, holding ropes as big around as their legs. Verity pushed Blaze aside and slammed a lever down which put them into reverse. The rear of the boat swung round. With Blaze's help she brought the boat parallel to the wharf with only a few rough smashes against the old tires roped to the concrete.

Jack and Lil didn't budge from their post, only turned a bit to look out into the dark night instead of at the city. The wharf teemed with people, though it must have been two in the morning.

As the Cincinnatians lined the rails in deep, silent curiosity, Verity realized that for many of them this was their first real contact with outsiders in . . . how many years?

A few rowdies on the wharf broke into a chorus of "Froggie Went A-Courtin'," and when they got to the bit about Cairo the people on the boat joined in with a great roar.

They got the gangplank situated and poured out of the boat, mingling with the good Caironians, who were apparently as eager to share their drink as the Cincinnatians were to sample it.

Verity leaned back against a tall chair, drained. She watched Jack and Lil out the window and mopped blood from her arm with her sweater.

Without another word, not even to his muse, Blaze walked out the door and a few moments later she saw him on the wharf, his red hair lit in the glare of the tall lights before he turned a corner. Strange. Jack and Lil just stood there, arms around each other, also puzzling: they'd been so at odds with each other.

She even saw Eliot on the gangplank, unmistakable with his blond hair aglow in the lights of the wharf, stuffing something into a large bag slung over his shoulder. She thought about calling him back, but he looked around then hurried off up a narrow street. Verity hoped he'd be all right. Whatever Lil had done had left him quite empty-headed.

She glanced down at the back of her hands, where images often played. They were fractured into a kaleidoscope of color. But it wasn't even that organized—more like wild flashes, and long stretches of simple white, as if the chaos of all their impressions canceled all of it into static. She let her hand drop. Her organizational impulse, at this point, was utterly nil.

She stepped out onto the small balcony and was lost in a flood of sound, jarring after weeks of the soothing rush of the river and the sound of the wind through the trees. Three men danced down the wharf, arm in arm, their legs engaged in intricate kicks, and one of them glanced up at Verity and waved. Startled, she began to wave back, but a twinge of pain stopped her. She noticed someone approaching the door and went back through the cabin to open it.

A tall woman with long blond hair stood there. Her attire was odd: a short, tight beige skirt, a matching jacket, both of linen. A startling blue silk shirt that matched her eyes. Around her neck was a black ribbon from which hung a large, round brass pendant engraved with the word CAIRO and tiny buildings and symbols too small for Verity to make out. She stuck out her hand. "Hello. I'm Mayor Lyle. Linda."

"Um—hello," said Verity, and realized that she was to shake this woman's hand, which she did, grimacing. "Verity."

"What's wrong?" asked Linda. "Can I come in?" Without waiting for a reply she stepped over the threshold and Verity was again surprised, at her shoes: pointed toes and higher heels than Lil's.

"Is it like this every night?" asked Verity, gesturing out the window.

"More or less," Linda said, sitting in one of the chairs and crossing her long legs. She linked her arms over the low back of the chair. "Oh, you're bleeding. What happened?"

"It's a cut. It'll be all right."

"No, you need to wrap it up, or something," said Linda, springing up and prowling round the cabin.

"Ah, here!" said Linda, pushing a button that said FIRST AID, at which a door in the wall slid open. She pulled out scissors, bottles, tubes, and finally a tight white roll of cloth. "Let's clean it up and get it bandaged." She ripped open packages of gauze, squirted something from the kit on it, and mopped at Verity's arm. Verity was too tired and bemused to object.

"This is a very deep cut." Linda unfurled something and wrapped it around Verity's arm. Verity smelled a light, pleasant scent as the woman's hair spilled onto her arm when she bent over and reached around Verity's neck. "There, now," she said. She briskly straightened up the first-aid kit.

Then she paced round the pilothouse as if looking for something—even peering into cupboards. Verity was too tired to object. She wondered how Linda Lyle could be so lively, and so beautifully dressed, at this hour of the night.

"Where are you from?" Linda asked after another moment of poking around. She seemed awfully nosy. "You came from upriver. That's rather unusual. No one goes east. We get a fair amount of traffic from St. Louis. But no one comes from the east except rafters."

"Why not?" asked Verity, resting against the stool, dazed and tired. She noticed that Lil and Jack were gone, and the emptiness of the *American Queen* rose up from all its lovely, intricate rooms, enticing her for one wild moment to think she could fill each one with its own long and unique life. It was a thought that India might have, and she did not like it much. But there it was. Perhaps the madwoman would always be with her, an inner, diaphanous skein of being and intent, waiting to overwhelm her.

She steeled herself against such gloomy thoughts and tried to pay attention to Mayor Lyle, whose voice was unfortunately far too soothing and beautifully modulated to keep her awake.

". . . plague," Linda finished, crossed her arms, looked at the floor, and continued. "Of course, it doesn't seem to be a whole lot better in the west, but it's particularly wild and lawless to the east and south. It's harder for people to live out on their own in the west, and I think that cities are such a civilizing influence, don't you?"

"Maybe too much so," blurted Verity without thinking. "I mean, Cincinnati was *really* civilized . . ."

"Cincinnati!" Linda jumped up, her eyes wide, and assumed a stance which looked as if she thought Verity might attack her. "You didn't tell me that you were from Cincinnati! I thought maybe from Wheeling. Except I've heard there are falls . . . Well. Hmmm. Um, plaguers don't bother us here," she said proudly, drawing herself up a bit. "No! After all, this is a *cosmopolitan* place, not like those backwoods towns, those places that can't accept change. And there've been a hell of a lot of rafts passing by lately. Not many of them could make it over this way. Current's too strong. The ones who *did* make it here were stark raving mad."

No gloves, thought Verity sadly.

"But—" said Linda, and she started to back away now—"are *all* of you . . . plagued?"

Verity crossed her own arms and nodded. "Yup." She yawned hugely. "I'm sorry," she said, "but I really need to sleep now."

Linda looked around. Even exhausted, Verity could see that this examination held a new quality of assessment. "Hmmm. We—um, we require a Docking Inspection and Docking Permit, here in Cairo. That's right—we simply must inspect this boat from top to bottom and inside out. Consider it impounded."

"Impounded?"

"You can't leave Cairo."

"That's ridiculous," said Verity, more amused than angry. "We'll leave whenever we feel like it."

"It's the law," intoned Linda, as if that settled it. "I'll send our inspector by first thing in the morning."

"I don't think we need an inspection," said Verity.

"Well, then, you'll have to leave. Right now," said Linda, evidently trying to put somewhat of an edge in her voice and failing.

"I thought we were impounded," said Verity. "Make up your mind."

"You are trying to put words in my mouth, young lady. I might have to fine you for impertinence."

"Right this minute, I have other plans," said Verity, walking out the door past Linda.

Linda followed her down the deck, her trip-trapping shoes reminding Verity of hoofed animals in odd promenade. She yammered the entire way, something about danger and riots. Verity stopped at her cabin and put her hand on the knob and was about to turn it when a lanky man with brown muttonchop whiskers, a top hat, and old-fashioned black tails rushed up and practically pushed Linda over. Linda grabbed the railing and sprawled back against it. It was clear from her face and gestures that she was trying to say something, but the barrage of welcome that flowed from the man's genial, smiling face was booming and constant and completely obliterated whatever it was.

"Sorry my dear Linda and hello, hello, hell*o* young lady, that is, Captain Young Lady! I am *so* happy to make your acquaintance." He bowed low but did not stop talking for a second. He helped Linda up and kissed her on the cheek and she frowned. "Mayor Thistlewood at your service, madam, we are always delighted when vessels of commerce choose to dock at our fair city. We are at your service. Many fine eating establishments await the pleasure of your crew and passengers, for I am sure that your chef deserves a rest. Tomorrow morning Mr. and Mrs. Ogleby await your call at ten A.M.; they own the mill which mills the finest flour between here and Memphis. It might be to your advantage to allow us to bid on whatever commerce you are carrying on your own behalf, sir . . . I mean, madam . . . and just what *are* you carrying?" He peered round with sharp eyes, and touched the doorframe over Verity's shoulder lightly several times with his fingertips.

"Get *out* of here, Thistlewood!" exclaimed Linda, giving him a rude shove, which he completely ignored. "There's something you don't *know!* Don't pay any attention to him," Linda told Verity, stepping in front of Thistlewood. "He's not really the mayor. *I* am. There was a Mayor Thistlewood right after the Civil War—oh, I try to run a decent town but look what happens!" She whirled and yelled at Thistlewood, "Why don't you go back to your mansion? I mean it! I hate it when you're like this! You're such a—a *mountebank!*"

Verity was about to pat her on the back and say, There, there, but Linda burst into tears and stomped away as best she could in those strange shoes, grabbing Thistlewood by the arm as he spouted invitations and pulling him along too.

Verity opened her door, slipped inside, firmly shut it, and fell onto her bed, sick of all of them.

5

○◇○

Mattie

Sixteen

○○○○○○○○○○○○○○○○○

Big Bee Blues

The wind was hot and dry. It was always hot and dry.

The curtains in Mattie's window had been white when she made them, but were now gray from constant dust. It was no use washing them. She watched them snap in the wind for a minute after she woke. Her skin was covered with fine grit.

She rolled out of her narrow bed. The sun was a low, hot ball, barely breaking the horizon, but white. Mattie didn't know what was worse—bone chilling winter or blazing summer. And it was only June.

"June, June, June. Just because it's June, June, June!" she muttered, knowing that she couldn't carry a tune and not caring. It was just a joke anyway, lines left over from some play one of her aunts, the schoolteacher one, had organized many years ago. That aunt had broken down crying, backstage, in the middle of the play because the entire community was jeering at the play, at the sentiments, the absurdity, the silliness of going to all that trouble. But the words and music still stuck in Mattie's mind.

Mattie ran a quart of murky water into the plugged sink, splashed herself, and let the wind dry her. Next to the sink fluttered her latest collection of self-painted mandalas, tacked to the wall, filled with suns, arrows, and trains. She pulled on her plaid dress and the purple stretch shoes with hard soles she'd found in the abandoned solar car the week before, and poked her fingers through her frizzy hair to take out the flat parts she saw in the mirror.

" 'Bout time you got up," said her father, when she walked into the kitchen. He was sitting at the table, eating bread and drinking soymilk. "You ought to get an early start hoeing the soybeans. It's gonna be a hot one."

Mattie nodded and sliced some bread and got some cheese from the refrigerator. "It's puddling again," she noted, pointing a toe at the water stain.

"I talked to Hebrita about finding a new one last week. Think this one's about shot."

"Her gang's no good," said Mattie, sitting down at the table. "Jason says they don't have the balls to blow up the train. If we could just get whatever's on that train—"

"Jason doesn't know what balls are," said her father. "I'd like to see *him* blow up the train. You're too young to remember, but it's not like people haven't tried. And they didn't want the stuff on it. They were trying to blow the damned thing to hell. I'd like to see Jason get within half a mile of it, the chickenshit. If he'd just get the energy to go to that appliance warehouse that's supposed to be in Tyler I'd be satisfied. Before everything in it's gone for good. I think we just need a new part. Maybe I can rustle one up in the shop next week. They got a small army guarding that warehouse, anyway—those folks from Prairie Rose. I guess they killed off most everybody in Tyler. At least they won't come round here—there's nothing here worth killing for."

"Jason *has* been—" Then she stopped. No point in telling her dad that she and her cousin Jason had stood within ten feet of the magtrain many times, both arms wrapped around one of the metal posts which used to generate the force field out west of town, talking about what they'd do in LA when they got there. But the train never stopped. Week after week, month after month, year after year, it never stopped. It had been running before she'd been born; it would be running after she died. Mattie was sure she'd seen the same pale face pressed to the glass more than once, and that the woman had even waved to her in that one flash vouchsafed by the fast train as it replaced the distant brown mountains with iridescence for a long streaking moment.

Her father didn't notice that she'd stopped talking, but clapped his hat on his head and left the room without another word. Her mother was out hunting. She usually was gone for a week at a time, with a band of other hunters. Sometimes they brought back buffalo. The last time, less fortunate, they brought back large white-meat lizards. Inside the right thigh of each one grew a stamp they'd never seen before. "Maybe it's Mexican," her mother had said. "Eat it."

Alexa, her friend, twelve years old like her, burst in the door. "Listen," she said, shifting back and forth like she did when she was nervous. "I have something I want to show you."

"Gold?" asked Mattie, tying on her sun hat. They'd been down in several mines and that was their dream. They weren't sure what they'd do with gold. They weren't even sure that they had been gold mines, or some other kind of mine. But the many dangers of the ancient shafts lent its pursuit great excitement.

"Better," whispered Alexa, her face a pale spot as she stood inside the dark doorway. "Come on."

"Come on, what? I have to weed the soybeans."

"It's a—a *Flower* thing. But we have to hurry. I think it's going to die. Bring a jug of water, okay?" She wheeled and set off at a fast trot before Mattie could further object.

Not that she would have. She scooped up the plastic jug she'd been intending to carry to the fields, making sure the cap was tight, and hurried after Alexa.

Her father was already out of sight. The fields were to the east of Elysia and they were heading west. The Orgummy Mountains were purple-shaded to the north, between the old frame houses. That wasn't their real name, she called them that because when she was little her uncle used to fold orgummy things for her, and in the mountain's sharp shadows she often saw the same figures—the Crane, the Butterfly— mornings when the shadows were deep. Their real name was the Deso- lates.

The blacktop was already hot beneath her new soles as she passed the soy dairy where floated the lovely bean-curd squares, and there was Mrs. Cook's battered blue solar car creeping townward on Route 10 as usual, and her breath began to burn in her throat. The rays, a bank of about fifty solar panels, charging batteries that townsfolk took and replaced for recharging as needed, glinted behind Main Street. "Wait up," she yelled, but Alexa just turned and walked a few steps going backward then took off again faster.

She took the fork to the abandoned Tolliver place, where the big sycamore still grew next to the spring. The Tollivers' place was nice, with green plants filling up the dip in the land by the tree, bearing small white flowers. No one would move into the empty white frame house, though, where the paint remained eerily intact through the harsh seasons. "Time's aren't so bad yet that we have to steal what isn't ours," her father said. "I look for Lenny Tolliver to come back someday." But parts of the barn roof, over a hundred years old, had fallen in, and that's where Alexa's mystery was, on the concrete slab beneath a crazed section of sagging beams.

Mattie rounded the corner of the barn and smashed into Alexa. "Why—"

"Shhh. I think it's asleep. The storm last night must have blown it in. Must've hidden in here."

"Jesusjumpinjehosophat!" breathed Mattie. "A Bee."

Sweat poured down Mattie's face and stung her eyes. She pushed her hat off her head so that it hung from her neck, absently reached into her pocket, and looped the soft sweatband she found there around her head.

The Bee's legs scrabbled weakly on the floor, making scritching sounds. The girls jumped back.

"See what I mean?" said Alexa. "It must be thirsty, and hungry. Maybe we should have brought it some sugar."

"It's not a real bee, silly," said Mattie. They spoke in nervous whispers. "I don't even know if they get thirsty."

As if in answer to their whispers, a long thin tongue unfurled from the Bee's mouth.

"Go on," said Alexa. "Give it the water."

"You," said Mattie, but felt the Bee's strange eye fix on her and moved forward one slow step at a time.

"Hand me a bucket or something," she said without looking away. She held her hand back to grab whatever Alexa might find but couldn't tear her eyes from the Bee. She heard Alexa's footsteps recede and things rattling elsewhere in the barn. In that moment sunlight angled through the holes in the side of the barn and the Bee glowed just like gold.

She could see that it wasn't really that much like a real bee. It was gold all over, and the ends of the tiny hairs that covered its body sparkled like splayed fiber-optic cable. On the end of its legs were pads covered with moist stuff that looked sticky. It was bent up in a funny way, kind of crumpled. Clear viscous fluid leaked from a gash in its side.

She'd seen Bees before, but they were always dead, dried out and hollow, and when you poked them with a stick they crunched nicely and the dried stuff blew away on the wind, harmless, they said, though adults avoided them and told children to keep away too. They got blown away from their cities by storms. Most of the ones she'd seen, few enough to remember each incident, had been from Denver. Everybody in these parts knew what the Denver Bees looked like. This one looked kind of different, or maybe that was because it was still alive.

She knew that different cities had different Bees and she took a step closer and peered around to see if she could read anything. Maybe on the flat place between its eyes . . .

"Mattie!"

Alexa's sharp voice made her jump and in that instant the Bee reached out one of her legs, perhaps in entreaty, and smeared Mattie's arm with goo.

Mattie wiped at it frantically while Alexa stared. "Well, don't just *stand* there!" she said. "Pour that jug of water over me."

But Alexa ran out the door and down the road screaming, a flash of green shirt and yellow hair, her feet raising small puffs of dust.

"Well, now, that's a fine thing, isn't it?" Mattie asked after Alexa rounded the bend. The silence had a new quality, more profound, and Mattie felt all around her the pressure of something—*something*—which now just had to happen. She knew she should fear it but the sun was too bright for that, the sky too blue.

She'd heard that Bees had once been people. It didn't make much sense but then stuff from the cities didn't, generally.

For a moment she watched golden dust motes dance in the shaft of sunlight. "They're small things," she said, looking at her arm, thinking of how the bad stuff traveled. "Very small." Some metal thing clanged in the wind out by the house. The Desolates, seen through a wide chink in the wall, assumed the flat unvarying blue of midmorning. The air smelled of dust and dried weeds. It all was much more beautiful to Mattie than it ever had been before. It also seemed to her that she was too young to die but that she probably would, maybe in the next five minutes.

Moving slowly because she knew it probably wouldn't make much difference, she took the bucket Alexa had dropped and poured the water from her jug over her arms and hands into the bucket, rubbing violently, preserving the water without even thinking about it. Her hands tingled. "Here," she said and shoved the bucket toward the Bee. "Oh, what does it matter now?" She tipped the bucket and was thrilled to see the Bee suck water into its mouth.

She knew that she had to leave now. Not leave the Bee. Leave Elysia. In case the goo didn't kill her.

She walked closer to the Bee, staring at it. "So strange," she whispered, walking around the staring dark eye, big as a dinner plate but an arched, raised surface of interconnecting flat triangles like a buckydome. There it was, marching across what might be the cheek. The copyright and city of origin. Twainbee IV (tm) St. Louis, Missouri. Back East.

She sat cross-legged and watched the Bee while she waited.

After half an hour a shadow fell across the door, but it was not that of the raging crowd she'd expected.

"Mattie," her father said, and she had never heard him say her name like that before, kind of choking and sad. "Why?"

"It was an accident." She stood and faced him. Neither of them had any idea what would happen to her. Maybe nothing.

"How do you feel?"

"Hot," she said. "Too hot." She staggered toward him and fell.

She woke on the Tollivers' fancy couch, soft and covered with pretty pink fabric, smooth and cool. Her father sat across from her in a rocking chair, staring at her. It was getting dark.

"How did I get here?" she asked. She didn't feel like sitting up. She was rather light-headed. Everything looked kind of glimmery, like it was all made of particles glowing in the dusk, like itsy bitsy suns encased in a billion transparent colors. She was terribly thirsty.

"I carried you," he said. "I rolled you in the blanket from the couch. Found some gloves in the barn."

"No sense taking chances," said Mattie. She sat up and was dizzy. He rose and put a package on the table that sat between them on the carpet, then stepped back. "Food's in there," he said. "Jerky, roasted soy nuts, stuff like that. And your mother's old forty-four that belonged to her dad. Ammo. It's heavy but you've practiced with it enough."

"She won't like that much," said Mattie.

"She won't mind," he said. "She'd want you to have it."

Mattie stood shakily and pulled the table toward her, taking care not to spill the glass of water, strangely lucid compared with the particulate stuff in town. "They really do have good water here, don't they?" She drank the sweet water down at once and set the glass back on the table. "How's the Bee."

"Dead," he said, and Mattie thought he had probably smashed it to smithereens. She reached into the pack and pulled out a familiar smooth container. "Your raisins? Pa—"

"Mattie, I'll never see you again," he said, and his voice was cracked and desperate. He stood and paced across the darkening room, his boots striking the floorboards sharply. "I don't know where to tell you to go. If only your mother was here. She could tell you plenty of places I'm sure. But I don't think Alexa can keep her trap shut for long. You'll have to leave as soon as you can. I think there's a little cabin in the Desolates, if you follow Route Ten and turn . . ."

She shook her head. "I know where I want to go."

Where the Bee was from.

St. Louis.

The food revived her. Her hands were really tingling now, and the sight of her father in the doorway, waving, brought tears to her eyes. That surprised her. She never thought she'd be sad to leave this place or anyone in it. In the twilight, she looked at her palms, always lighter than the back of her hands, but now almost glowing with splotches of deep pink and blue arranged in some pattern, the way a lizard or a snake might be patterned.

She knew she was burning with fever and her vision was playing tricks since the Tolliver house seemed to sparkle in the dusk. She turned right onto Route 10 and the moon threw a strong light as the sky darkened, luckily, since her dad had forgotten to pack a lightstick. The shadows shifted with the wind. She felt light and free. And then hot and sick.

The train came through eastbound every Tuesday night but she'd never thought about the time, though if people had clocks instead of infinite timepieces they set them by the train. She'd strained to see an engineer countless times, peering up at that high sleek mountain of steel since she was a little girl; looking at it from a far rooftop with binoculars, climbing some abandoned steel pole near the track by using the metal things that must have been put there just for climbing. But the glass was always blank. She'd stopped waving when she was seven.

The road was cooling but she kept an eye out for snakes. She forced herself to hurry even though she felt so sick, and felt stirrings of irritation with everything. Everything! Everyone in town, the fools. God, especially, someone she'd never given much thought to, despite the urging of some of her more militant Bible-thumping relatives, who were constantly insisting that the end of the world was quite obviously nigh. The night opened up like some new vast thing she'd never seen before and something in it was coming to get her, swooping toward her from an unimaginable distance . . .

There! The kind of thoughts they were all so afraid of. Clear eccentricity, to think of anything besides crops and hunting. So what! Let them live and die there in Elysia. She was going somewhere. She was going to do something. She would have to tell them all . . . the truth. The unkind, urgent truth. Just for the telling. Tell them what they already knew but were afraid to say out loud.

She started to run, heart pounding, when ever so far away she saw the great burning headlight, tiny as a pinprick in the night sky from here, but it would grow fast. She turned off the road toward the blue light of the box, pushing through scratchy scrub, stumbling on the uneven ground. Only a quarter mile to the switchbox. Only a hundred yards. Only . . .

Panting, her breath burning in her throat, she staggered to the switchbox. She and Jason had opened it many times, stared at the strange flat panels, tried unsuccessfully to inflict various kinds of damage on it, tried to confound the tiny blinking lights, or coax from it a new pattern somehow. Nothing had ever changed.

The train was a vast roar now, and the wind whipped her hat away. She pried at the box, crying in frustration. "Stick now, will you?" she hollered and smashed at the clasp with a rock. It popped open.

She knew what to do now.

As the engine flashed past she grabbed the pole with one hand and pressed her other against the flat screen.

"Stop, damn you!" she screamed. "I'm *here!* I'm *here!*"

She saw individual windows fly past, and then she could catch details inside, and then it was . . . yes . . . with a change so gradual she could not gauge it, it slowed . . . it slowed . . . it . . .

Stopped.

It stood stock-still, like a well-trained horse waiting to be mounted.

"Well, I'll be goddamned," she whispered as a door slid open and some steps unfolded down to the ground half a car away. She picked up her bundle and ran toward them.

Elysia had few lights, and they grew small quite swiftly and then were swallowed by night.

6

○○○

Cairo

Seventeen
⬡⬡⬡⬡⬡⬡⬡⬡⬡⬡⬡⬡⬡⬡⬡⬡⬡
Big Town Blues

Verity woke late, judging by the light. A quick check revealed that the boat was deserted. No wonder. She had a dim memory of Blaze trying to wake her earlier, but he'd not succeeded.

She washed, pulled on some pants and a shirt with a bee on the front, and walked out onto the wharf.

Oh, what a day!

She recalled that Cairo was farther south than Washington, D.C., that forgotten capital of the forgotten Goddamned Government. The day would be hot, and already it was muggy. She could feel that the fluffy white cumulus afloat in the clear blue sky of early summer would by evening gather into a luminous silver tower of water and unsatisfied electricity.

The river was broad as a lake. She'd never seen water like this, so big and wild: currents swirled through it, raising continuous waves. White-caps flirted with wind and with the floating debris of wood that rushed along on the surface, except when caught in whirlpools. The opposite shore was just a distant brown line with low scrub islands between here and there. Verity marveled that they had made it through this mess. And the sky was so blue . . .

She paused, looking around, to fix it all in her memory. Despite their troubles, she had grown used to the slow beauty of the Ohio, and the seemingly timeless spring days spent upon it. She had a feeling that their pace would quicken now.

This was the first real city she had seen. Cincinnati—how could that have been real? This was real, real like in the olden days, before nan, before the Flower Cities! An American town, with a mayor and everything. Two of them, in fact. Maybe more. One of them clearly living in the past.

Yeah. Pretty real, all right.

She shielded her eyes against the sun and took in the regular streets, which ran perpendicular to the wharf; the low, brightly painted shops and houses on streets that rose only a bit above the river. The town ended rather abruptly a mile or two to the northeast, but sprawled northwest perhaps all the way to the Mississippi, which must be at that far point to her left. She saw no buildings over six stories high.

The streets teemed with people, horses, and bicycles. She was startled as a small cart fixed with a sail bumped down the street, a woman at the till and a box of green melons in the back.

No one took any particular notice of her, which pleased Verity. At a market shaded by a trellis she saw bushels of apples, green and red and yellow shot with pink stripes, and she felt like making pies of them. Rows of river trout lay on ice, eyes staring. The smell of fresh bread wafted through the air.

She climbed up Twenty-eighth Street for a block, then stepped into the Blue Café. A nice name.

It was hot inside. The booths were of some sort of soft blue plastic and Verity stuck to hers as she slid in. The café was crowded with people who paid no attention to her, and their many conversations wove together into a pleasing patchwork of unconnected words drifting into the air of summer. Yes, summer—or almost; it was early June. They had taken six weeks to gingerly navigate the Lower Ohio River.

She pushed her hair back from her face and lifted it off her neck for a moment, then took a menu from a metal holder and ordered apple pie and ice cream from a girl who looked about fifteen. The girl raised her eyebrows and said, "For breakfast?"

Sunlight streamed through the large plate-glass windows, and huge fans mounted on the ceilings stirred the white paper napkin beneath Verity's fork. Electricity. Hmmm.

She soon finished her pie and coffee and was about to leave when the waitress returned and gave her a piece of paper that said $4.31. "You're asking me for money?" asked Verity.

"Durn tootin'," said the girl. "Four crisp Cairo City bills and change, lady. Some for me, some for the Blue Café, and some for George. And I don't got all day."

"And I don't have any money," Verity said, irritated with herself for forgetting about money. Never in her life had she been asked for money. She'd have to get some, she supposed, and wondered how. "Who's George?"

"You from out of town? He owns Cairo. You shoulda stopped at the Customs House first. Didn't you see the sign at the wharf? You can trade for money at the Custom House or at the Rural Network building or at any of the three branches of the Cairo Bank. All owned by George, of course, and the network too, I know he skims off the top of that. Where you trade is just a matter of your convenience. What you get for your goods is according to the list the committee makes and they work on the list all the time to keep everything fair. Nobody comes here without something to trade." She paused and shifted back and forth impatiently. "You didn't, did you?"

"Evidently so," said Verity.

The waitress tapped her pencil against her pad and sighed. "I hate it when this happens. Look, I'll take that shirt then, and pay the bill myself. My mom will kill me when she sees it." Her eyes lit, apparently in anticipation of irritating her mother. "Where'd it come from?"

"Cincinnati," said Verity, suddenly loath to give up her shirt. "What will I wear?"

"Cincinnati!" the waitress said, her mouth falling open for a moment. "No shit! You can have mine," she said, indicating her plain white shirt. She looked around furtively. "I wouldn't tell anyone else if I were you."

"Why not?" asked Verity, sliding out of the booth.

"I don't know. It's just—people are funny, that's all."

"Who is—are—those men?" asked Verity, passing a booth where four identical white-bearded men sat in white suits, smoking cigars.

"Mark Twains," said the girl, sounding bored. "Old ones. They come in all ages, y'know, along with Huck Finns and Tom Sawyers. We had a river-pilot-aged one in here about an hour ago. Younger guy. The Mississippi River is right around the point. They come down from Hannibal a lot. Then they don't know what to do. Nobody wants to pay for Mark Twains anymore. They're all the same. They say the originals were Historical Attractions, or something. And went around giving performances. Way, way back when there were lots of tourists. My mom says."

"There aren't many tourists now?" asked Verity.

The girl said, "You really are from out of town, aren't you?"

They changed in the bathroom and she chattered questions without giving Verity a chance to reply. "Oooh, you're pregnant. Boy or girl? I never seen anybody from Cincinnati. What's it like? You a plaguer? I'm immune, don'cha know. They have Bees there, don't they? And all kinds of nan? Any kind of nan in this shirt?" She smoothed it over her breasts and poked the bee experimentally.

Only all of it, thought Verity, amused. "I have no idea," she said. "Why are you immune?"

"I dunno. Because I was born here, I think," she said. "George says we owe it all to him. I get sick and tired of George sometimes. We have to listen to him give a speech in the park once a month. I mean, every-body *has* to go. He always wears that silly hat. Hoo-ray for Cairo, and we must keep the enemy at bay! Same old stuff. How did you get here?" she asked as they left the bathroom.

"On a riverboat."

"A *riverboat?*" The girl grabbed her by the shoulders. "Oh! I saw it this morning. So big! I thought it was from St. Louis. Take me with you. Please! Wherever you're going! I really want to go to LA except . . . that's too scary. Every time I stand there next to the lev I chicken out. The lev is so big and strange and you can't see in the windows and it goes *straight into* a Flower City, at least they think it does and I'm not even allowed to talk about them and I'm not even supposed to *go* to the train station. It's spooky there. And people die on the way, the lev doesn't always make it, sometimes they get blown up and stuff. Then they heal themselves. That's what my mom said but maybe she's lying. Just to scare me. But every time I don't go I feel really bad. Sometimes it just stops across the river and we can see it way out there. It should get here any time and it will leave tonight. There's never anyone on it. If there is they don't stick around. I've heard there's a train up on the line north of town that has zombies on it. I mean, I wouldn't want to get on a train with a bunch of zombies would you? But the river—*that's* not scary. I've seen it every day of my life. I've seen every bit of this town inside out and I need to get away. Please! Please!"

By now she was pulling on the sleeve of the shirt Verity was wearing, and Verity noticed three small stains splattered across the front.

She gently removed the girl's hands. "We'll see," she said. "I have to go now." She wasn't sure where she was going, except to see as much as she could of the town this girl was so tired of.

She stepped into the street, into steamy summer air filled with the scents and sounds of a functioning city. A real city, just like they used to be, before people like her existed. Money. Private property. Bees a distant legend. Immunity to the plague. Wouldn't *that* have been handy at Shaker Hill! But of course they hadn't even known that it was possible. The price they paid for their isolation. All that was here.

All that and a NAMS maglev to Los Angeles.

She shivered, thinking of Blaze. He loved trains. Had always talked about riding on one. Where was he, anyway?

A good chance that he was at that train station.

She wished for maps, but none came. She was different now. What had changed her? Cincinnati itself? Her ordeal? Her pregnancy? She'd left something behind. She felt oddly lonely as she walked past the many small shops of Cairo—clothiers, restaurants, market stalls, and the Rural Network building, two brick stories. In the plate-glass window next to the sidewalk she saw a map, apparently of the Rural Network, and studied it with interest. It spread like a tree through Indiana, Michigan, and Illinois, the only states visible. Without thinking she pressed her hands against it but of course her hands couldn't access anything here. There was nothing to access.

As she walked away, a man rushed out of the building and rubbed the window with a cloth, glaring at Verity.

A group of five people hurried past her and she recognized rafters by their somewhat shabby river clothing. One of them climbed up the side of a wrought-iron arch that led into a green, cool-looking park and after a few minutes succeeded in unfurling a banner that said:

FABULOUS ENTERTAINMENT ON THE AMERICAN QUEEN!
"WHEN BEES PLAYED STRIDE PIANO"
A Revelatory Drama
TONIGHT AT SEVEN
Come One, Come All!

After they secured it, they hurried off, carrying what looked like several more banners beneath their arms. Passersby stopped to take note and walked on.

The play that Jack and Lil had been so worried about. The play that sprang from their long-suppressed minds, from who they were and what they knew before Cincinnati enslaved them. A mosaic of history, a play that almost composed itself, an order that emerged from the chaos of their memories. A revelatory drama. Revelatory of their own hidden history. Well, thought Verity, this should be interesting. At least they'd changed the name from *Smaller than Sand.* In a way, she wished she'd been part of it, but there was still, and always was, something unique about her. Rose, of course. There would always be Rose. And Rose's history had not been suppressed. It had lived within Cincinnati, waiting to unfurl within Verity's being.

Verity frowned and turned from the banner. It was too bright a day to get irritated.

But she was. She was now on Washington Street, quite a few blocks from the river. She headed back toward downtown, wet with sweat that didn't seem to cool her, wondering where the train station might be. It was already afternoon—maybe one o'clock, judging from the sun. Blaze was gone, Jack and Lil were too; the rafters were running around advertising their play, and she was pregnant and discouraged. All the weight of tiredness that the patches had remedied seemed to descend on her at once. It looked as if a cool park with a crown of trees was just a block away, up on a hill. She headed toward it.

A few minutes later she trudged through the gate of a tall, stately mansion—MAGNOLIA MANOR, said the sign, and indeed, the grounds were filled with huge magnolia trees, the sweet smell of the white blossoms permeating the heavy air. Not a park, but a private estate. She counted three stories, and the many arched windows were crowned with metal hoods like eyelids. The house was brick, with several porches and verandas. There were the ruins of Victorian mansions in Miamisburg, including a particularly well preserved one at Fifth and Linden, with stained glass and a lovely fireplace. But none this grand, and none that seemed as living. A green bike was lying on the lawn next to the porch.

"Some lemonade?" she heard, and looked up to see where the voice was coming from.

The man dwarfed by the enormous porch looked familiar. "Thistle-wood?" she asked.

He nodded vigorously. "Yes, thank you for remembering my invitation. Please come on up." He hurried her along with a welcoming gesture of his arm. "That's right, quite a few steps, eh? You should have seen the Grant entourage descending the morning I gave my speech. They stayed here with the Galligers, you know. Grant burnt a hole in one of Mrs. Galliger's linen sheets with his cigar." His voice boomed out as she climbed the stairs to the porch, which was about twenty feet above the ground.

Verity was glad of the coolness beneath the roof. She felt rather at home with Mr. Thistlewood's delusion. He was still dressed in his outlandish manner, though lacking a top hat.

"Welcome to my veranda," said Thistlewood.

She turned to survey the green, lush grounds. The spray of a small fountain glinted in a shaft of sun, which pierced the canopy of trees. White wrought-iron benches were scattered here and there on the lawn. She saw only a glimpse of the city bustle just outside the gate, and its sounds were muted. She might still be on the boat, surrounded as she was by gingerbread. A gust of air issued from the wide-open front door.

"It's cool!" she said, holding out her arms so she could have the full advantage, discovering the reason Thistlewood did not have to descend to uncouth dress simply because of the heat.

"Yes, it's my secret," he said, "or rather, the secret of Magnolia Manor. The house stores the cool of the night, and the walls are a double thickness of brick with an air space between. The cool air sits in the house, though I probably shouldn't squander it like this. Sit down and I'll bring out the lemonade."

Verity wondered if he lived here alone but said nothing. She was grateful to sit on the chintz cushion of a huge white wicker rocking chair and rest her feet on the stool in front of it as Thistlewood entered the overwhelmingly tall front door and vanished into the cool dim foyer.

She felt disconnected from everything here. It was quite pleasant. Everything was green, and there were no voices in her head, no blue visions of otherwhere, no troublesome rafters, no worry about what the next turn in the river might bring. Now that she was sitting, she was much cooler anyway, never mind the special properties of the house. A breeze rustled the huge, waxy leaves all around her and white petals drifted down and settled on the lush lawn. Her eyes closed but then she heard footsteps on the concrete steps.

"Hello," said a man wearing navy-blue shorts and a white shirt with an embroidered badge that read CAIRO POSTAL SERVICE. He handed her a white envelope. "Letter for George, from Linda."

"George?"

"Nobody else here, lady," he replied. She looked at the envelope, which just read, George Mills, Magnolia Manor, written in a rather stern, square hand.

Thistlewood emerged carrying an ornate silver tray and a sweating cut-glass pitcher of lemonade with quartered lemons floating in it. He glanced at her anxiously from beneath bushy eyebrows as he set it on a low table next to her. "After I went in I thought you might have rather had iced tea."

"Lemonade is wonderful," she said. "I've never had it before. Here's a letter for George."

Thistlewood fished a pocketknife from his pocket and slit open the envelope. As he read the letter, he frowned, then glanced quickly at Verity before looking back at the letter.

"Are you George Mills?" she asked.

"Oh, sorry," he said, and folded the letter and stuffed it in his breast pocket. "Well, actually, I am." He dropped into a chair across from her and poured them both tall glasses of lemonade. It was sweet and sour and invigorating and Verity drank the entire glass in one long gulp.

"Thank you," she said, as he poured another. "I thought you were Mayor Thistlewood."

"Well, I am he as well," said the man. He looked down and cleared his throat. He appeared to be thinking. Then he grinned at Verity and suddenly looked a lot younger. "To tell you the truth, I have been in love with Linda for lo these many years and she paid me not a whit of attention. I went away for a while, then came back and found she was the mayor. Since I was living here, in the home of the most famous mayor of Cairo, it seemed quite natural to offer her a bit of competition. Show her what a real mayor is like. At least now she's annoyed with me." He threw back his head and his three short laughs reminded Verity of a barking dog. "Well, there's no law against it! I wouldn't be surprised if she tried to make one, though, she and her shyster lawyer friend, Alexander Pittentot. The Pit, I call him. She almost married me, once. Before I went away. She should still. The Pit hasn't a breath of humor in him. Dull, dull, dull! Well, how would you like to see the house?"

"I'd love to," said Verity, refreshed. "Mind if I call you George, then?"

"Delighted."

In the foyer, where the ceiling towered far overhead, was a spiral staircase. She looked upward through its snail-like curve and saw a round light. "The skylight," he said. "But let's start at the bottom and work our way up."

He chattered his way through a kitchen as big as the barn at Shaker Hill. On the marble table she saw a heap of squeezed lemons. A large ceiling fan turned lazily above.

"You have electricity?" she asked. She wondered how much technology they used here. And how much nan. There was obviously some—look at the Mark Twains. And NAMS came here as well. Unease lapped at her sense of well-being. Lil had gone to a lot of trouble to try and avoid Cairo—but why? She had her own agenda, linked to some wider reality which she had not shared. Cairo was oddly insulated. Alive and functioning, but certainly not a Flower City. More like a small, healthy hub, a center of trade.

"Oh, of course," he said. "We have all manner of energy—wind, solar, and of course, water velocity. We use solar energy to produce steam which in turn produces electricity. Of course, it doesn't always work, as the magnetic fluctuations in the atmosphere have an effect on the turbines."

"Does the solar road come here?"

He gave her a strange look, pausing before leading her into the dining room, their footsteps echoing in the huge old house with its lovely wallpaper and high embossed plaster ceilings.

"No, of course not," he said. "It passed many miles north of here. Cairo was just a forgotten spit of land during the road's heyday in the early twenty-first century—river commerce was no longer as important as it once had been, nor were railroads, so the town almost vanished. The one solar road that came down to Cairo is completely cut off. Now the river is the main thing again—full circle, eh? The old Interstate system is a conduit for all manner of outlaws. Which you well know, don't you?" He looked at her with keen, suspicious eyes.

"I'm not a solar road outlaw," she laughed. The dining-room table, its surface shining and dark, looked to be as long as the entire house at Shaker Hill. An immense number of places were set, old silverware glowing dimly in the muted light, the various goblets, wineglasses, and coffee cups at each place turned upside down.

"Is your boat on the way upriver then, to Hannibal? We can always use new Rural Network links. See, I *do* have an official function in that regard—"

"No," she said.

"Not going up the Ohio, are you?" he asked, his voice more guarded. There were several doors to the room, Verity noticed, and the windows all stood open. "No," she said, just as guardedly. "Thank you for the tour, but I should be going now."

"Going back downriver?" he persisted, as she turned and walked back to the kitchen. She said nothing, but kept walking.

"Then you *are* from the Ohio," he said, and she thought she detected awe in his statement, so low that he had really been talking to himself. "Linda said so—but I can hardly believe it. Please wait," he said, rushing to catch up with her. "Please accept my sincere apology." He caught up her hand and closed his eyes for just a second, then blinked. She pulled her hand away. "I didn't want to offend you by saying it right off—most people would consider it an insult."

She walked out onto the porch, feeling relieved and much safer. She turned, holding on to the railing. "Why?"

His eyes filled with tears. He blinked and they overflowed and he pulled a white handkerchief from his pocket and wiped his face. To her amazement he collapsed onto the wicker couch and bent over, sobbing outright, his head in his hands. "I'm sorry," he managed, looking up at her with eyes washed and brilliant blue. He blew his nose. "I thought all these feelings were long gone. Long gone. Funny. They're not.

"My mother voted for conversion here in Cairo," he continued. "I was just a boy. I remember the times. So exciting. She was a wild woman, at least my father always said so, and even after she left he sounded proud when he did. He loved her to his death. Even though she left us, after our conversion was interrrupted."

"It was interrupted?" asked Verity.

He nodded. He continued to talk, and after a while, she relaxed enough to sit on the top step as she listened.

"She voted for it, my father voted against. They argued a lot those days. I was ten. She'd already taken my sister and I to Denver once. In those days you could travel to all the Flower Cities on NAMS. Ah, it was lovely, so lovely. We took the night train there and the top of the train was clear and my sister and mother and I lay in our bunk and watched the stars, one of her arms around each of us as she pointed out the constellations, and we talked about the moon colony where her father worked—"

"The moon colony!" said Verity, sitting up straight.

"Yes," he said, looking at her curiously. "Did you know someone there too? I never met my grandfather."

Verity shook her head. "Go on. Please."

"Denver is like a dream to me now. You had to take on a temporary initialization pack that allowed you to function while you were there.

Well, you didn't have to, but my mother thought we should, to enhance our enjoyment of the city, that's why she went, of course, to try it out. My father didn't go. He was against it. Said nan was going to ruin the world. I guess he was right."

"But didn't they have to do something?" asked Verity. "I mean, because of the quasar?"

He was silent for a moment, studying her. "Quasar. Hmm." He cleared his throat. "Yes, I guess they thought they had to," he said. "Certainly a lot of people were all for it, starry-eyed, like her. I can't blame them. Denver was a wonderland. We could only take in so much of it, of course, not only because of time but because we weren't fully converted. I still remember the Bees." His eyes were wistful. "I remember wanting to go for a ride on one of them. They didn't look like the Bees in Cincinnati. They were called Bees because they did carry information between the buildings, which did have the interstices, which meant nothing to our hands." Verity involuntarily clenched her own, glad that her receptors were covered by the now-invisible gloves, which were thankfully free of pictures right now, as if some sort of pact had been reached among them not to communicate in that way right now. Or maybe she was just too far from the rest of them.

". . . those Bees were much more machinelike," continued George, his eyes shut, as if he saw it all inside his head, that long-ago trip. "We went to see them, of course. We got to touch the sensors they used. They felt funny, kind of soft and a little bit rough, and looked like a rainbow because each of those—oh, how many artificial pheromones did they end up creating?—metapheromones adhered to a different-colored receptor, all so very tiny of course but the result was kind of a rippling colored surface. Everyone was talking about how people would have new senses now, how people themselves would be all new, so different! Heady times! And when Cairo changed its mind after the conversion began it was so very strange! So many of us have vestiges of the conversion within us. My mother took my sister and went to Cincinnati.

"After Cincinnati surged, and you couldn't get in or out, my dad took me up there and we flew as close as we could. He had a friend who was in the Aviator's Club and had a small plane. I was terrified at first and then it was exciting. I was about fifteen by then and I knew it was silly to think that I could see Mom and Melinda. The Bees of Cincinnati kept us from getting very close. The whole City, the Seam and everything, scintillated. Sparkled. I'm not boring you, am I?"

"No," said Verity, her voice low. "Not at all."

He sighed deeply. His hands were clasped between his knees, and his back was bowed as he gazed at the floor. "My dad felt guilty the rest of his life. It was almost like he had a fever, a fever of guilt, and these sort of guilt waves came off of him. I had to get away from him, I couldn't stand it, and then of course I felt guilty about that. I had wanted to go with her. But it was some kind of deal they made, him and her. They didn't ask us. I bet Melinda would have been just as happy to stay behind. Sometimes dad thought he should have gone with her, other times he was yelling that he should have stopped her, she was too wild for her own good. I wanted to reach out and touch those Bees, when I saw them, one of them came so close to us I could see right into her eyes . . . I couldn't call her 'it.' The eyes were so *aware*. The Surge made some kind of *difference*. It wasn't like Denver. They were all different, the Cities, when they started surging. And then, that's when I knew I had to do *something—*"

"So what did you do?"

George started and looked at her as if he'd forgotten that she was there.

"If you're here," he said, his eyes hungry, "so many of you, that means that something has happened in Cincinnati . . ."

She felt great pity for George, suddenly. He seemed to have so little to take up the time of his life. "Something has happened," she said. "Cincinnati has been freed. Kind of." Freedom! The word was like ashes in her mouth.

George leaned over and grabbed her hands and held them tightly. "Don't make fun of me! Don't! I couldn't stand it! Can it be true?"

Verity tried to take back her hands but he wouldn't let go. His eyes were very blue, very piercing.

"It's true," she said.

George sprang up, and looked across the green grounds. "This is the happiest news of my life. And if you have come from there . . . where are you going?"

"Norleans," she said.

"Ah," he said, thoughtfully. He looked at her for a moment. Then he said, "Come to the most beautiful part of the house. The roof. You can see the confluence from there. It's tricky. You must study it. A lot of boats run aground on Bird Island. Cincinnati! What a change! Like a dream come true! My life's work!"

It seemed important to view the confluence. They had been lucky to make it to Cairo last night. She followed him into the house.

"Your life's work?" asked Verity, but he didn't appear to hear her. He kept talking, and she could barely catch his words as they walked past a partially open door. George turned a corner, but something had caught Verity's eye. Glancing in, she saw strange equipment, several flat screens embedded in the high wainscoting, library shelves holding rows of jars . . .

She dropped to one knee and pretended to tie a loose shoestring.

She must have a longer look. But George stuck his head out from round the corner as she finished her double knot.

"Come on," he said, frowning and glancing at the open door. "What's taking you?"

Strange symbols flickered briefly in the back of Verity's mind, then vanished as a breeze blew down the hallway from a tall window at the end. He helped her up and she did not like his hand on her arm but he let go right away. He hurried onward, resuming his questions.

"Would she have come with you? My mother? How can I find out? Will you help me? Maybe I can go on the boat and look around. Would that be all right with you? Yes, I'll come down and make a thorough inspection."

Verity didn't have the heart to tell him, as he rushed her up the spiral stairs, one flight, then another, and another, twisting round so she was getting dizzy, that if his mother still existed she might not remember, or that she might have been one of the rafters who by now had died, or that she might die if she didn't get to Norleans in time, according to the blue vision of the woman with the bee tattoo . . .

They emerged on the roof, which was furnished with wrought-iron chairs. The Ohio, almost hidden beneath a canopy of trees before it burst forth to the east, glinted blue in the late-afternoon sun, reflecting the sky. She struggled to keep the plague visions at bay. *Keep thinking. Keep your eyes moving.* The massive, ruined bridge was crumpled, rust-red, stranded in the middle of the river. The Ohio passed Cairo and carried her eye west and she had her first glimpse of the Mississippi.

A muddy, roiling brown snake. She was amazed that the two rivers kept their own identity for such a long way, blending only very far downriver, perhaps farther than she could really see very clearly. The Ohio, a wide green jewel-ribbon, was gradually soiled by the Mississippi. Verity felt a bit affronted that the Ohio lost its name here, rather than the Mississippi.

George said, "You could probably get some help from some of the other pilots, but nobody else is in town right now. How many people are on your boat, anyway?"

"I'm not sure. So there are a lot of boats on the river?" she asked, settling in a chair beneath a large green umbrella and taking in the magnificent view.

"A few. Do you have the plague?" asked George suddenly, staring at her.

"I—" she said, rising.

"No, no, sit, I'm not worried. I'm supposed to be immune. We all are. That's what makes Cairo so accessible. It was a special thing I—"

He stopped suddenly.

"A special thing you *what?*" Verity asked, absorbed in the view.

"Something that makes Cairo special. We don't have to be afraid."
Verity was suddenly irrationally afraid that she would become immune. Why not? she asked. Everyone is free now. *Everyone* could become immune. . . .

Why did she hate the thought that something might save them all?
Lil was right. The plague was *tough.* "How did this special thing happen?" she asked.

George pulled up a chair next to her, scraping it loudly on the rough
roof, which was surrounded by an ornate metal rail, and smiled broadly.
She wondered why she thought the smile was somewhat false.

"I can almost see the wheels turn," he said, taking her hand gently. He
patted it with his other hand and she pulled it away. She stuck her hands
in her pockets and resolved not to take them out. "Once you have the
plague, my dear, you can't turn back. That's not why these people would
fear you. But there's a lot of sentiment here about when the conversion
was halted. Feelings are still quite bitter. The beginnings of conversion
left vestiges everywhere. But no need for someone like you to think about
such horrible things. Look over there. Would you like me to take you for
a ride in my glider?"

Not really, she thought. But he clearly wasn't going to answer her
question. "What's a glider?"

"There," he said, and pointed north.

She saw an area the size of about five acres on the outskirts of town,
not far away. Lined up on the edge were—airplanes? Two were white
and two were black.

"But are they all gliders? The black ones have propellers."

"You are a sharp young woman."

It did not seem as if sharpness was required to notice this, only good
vision.

"The white ones are gliders," he said. "The black ones are airplanes.
Biplanes, actually. For the double wings. I was doing some work on them
earlier in the day. They should have been put up by now. Ah—good.
Here comes my boy."

Verity saw a young man bump down the dirt road toward the small
airport on a bike. He got off and walked round to the wheels of one of
the gliders and did something; then he hooked a rope to the nose and
started pulling it toward a large, metal barnlike building.

"But who's that?" George asked. He pointed to a man riding away on
a bike. Apparently he had been behind the glider.

It was really too far away to tell, but Verity thought it might be
Peabody, for some reason she couldn't put her finger on.

"Why do you need so many?" she asked. "Are you the only one who
flies them?"

"Ah . . . you never know when one might break."

"What do they run on?" she asked.

"The gliders run on thermals," he said. "The wind." His voice grew more excited. "I tried a method of launching them from a steam launcher for a while. But their lightness renders them too fragile. My latest method works pretty well—a friend of mine pilots a hot-air balloon which lifts them high enough to be released. Ah, the view! Magnificent! I cruised almost all the way to Memphis one day and back. But you have to know the weather." The young man came out of the building and started to pull the other glider in.

"What about the biplanes?" she asked. "How do you power them?" Now the boy was pulling the first one toward the building. It did not look as if it was very heavy. Verity knew that there were ways of making materials which were very light and also very strong. "Don't they have to go very fast to get off the ground?"

He pursed his lips and his eyes did not look at all merry. They looked as if he were measuring her. "You are certainly full of questions," he said after a pause. "It is a very complicated matter and I don't think you'd understand it."

"Do any of them use nanotechnology?" she asked, irritated. There were any number of approaches, Rose was telling her—several quite dependable nanotech methods of utilizing the solar power collected by the black wings. And many small ways to make the planes smart. It was a bit of a surprise how unobtrusively the information became available.

Rose *did* come in handy.

"My dear," he said gravely. His voice became more chiding, a bit pompous. "You have no idea of the deep evils of nanotechnology. I've been preaching that—yes, preaching, I don't know a better word for it—to the people of Cairo for many years now. It is a sin. That's all. A crime against nature. It's the devil's work. Coming from Cincinnati, you should know this."

The devil's work. The Shakers had never believed in the devil. Would he think nanotechnology so bad if his mother really *was* alive?

But if she was alive, she might not be for long. She might have already died on the Ohio; she might die on the Mississippi. Verity remembered the bee woman in her blue visions of Norleans, and her warning about dying, and her eyes filling with tears.

Verity held on to the railing tightly and stared at the blue. What had she done? Taken eternal life from them all, from *herself!* If sin really did exist, this probably was sin. She'd given them this horrible plague from which they could only be released by death or by some unknown being in Norleans who might not even exist! How foolhardy! Feelings roiled up in her and she just could not help it. You're pregnant, a part of her said. That's why.

"Why are you crying?" asked George, and put his arm around her. "Surely it's not all that bad."

She stepped away from him. "It *is*," she shouted, surprising herself. "It's all my fault. I don't know if your mother is here! She may have died. Because of me, because of what I did!"

"I don't understand," murmured George. "How can it be all your fault?"

"Because I was the Queen!" she shouted. She took great gulping breaths of clean water-laden air. She was drenched with sweat. Having a baby was an odd business. It seemed to make her prone to shouting. A sort of pressure seemed to build up. People could be so irritating. Everything was irritating. She noticed with one part of her that was still noticing such things that the golden plains to the north, past the distant, glimmering solar Interstate which appeared just once between low hills and a gap in some trees, were darkened by a lowering, intense black cloud which grew as she watched it.

"Oh, don't get so upset," George said, looking at her in a curious way, in a way that Verity really didn't quite understand. Part fear and part eagerness? "Such delusions can be terribly strong. The Queen never would have left her city. Come, sit. Relax."

Walking in what she hoped was a casual manner back toward the open doorway, Verity looked back at the riverfront and saw the boats at rest there. A crowd thronged the boat, as if all of Cairo was trying to crowd onto it, and she was filled with misgiving. What if Linda, last night, was right about riots?

"Do you think they might hurt the boat?" she asked.

"Didn't I hear something about a play earlier today?" he asked. Verity saw lightning flash across the vast distance of the plains, out beyond the Mississippi. "I'm sure that's what they're there for. Don't worry. That storm won't be here for hours, if it gets here at all. And there's nothing we like more than a good play. It will be like olden times on the river, you know, and Cairo honors its past quite deeply. We hope you will stay for weeks. Yes, weeks. Really settle in. Don't be in a hurry. What is the play about?"

"I don't know," said Verity, then decided she might as well tell him. He'd know soon enough. She leaned against the doorframe. "The Information Wars."

He stared at her in stark amazement. "I'll be," he said finally.

Verity pointed toward the one quadrant she'd missed. She saw a low, sleek building glimmering in the low sun's rays.

"What's that?" she asked, though in her heart she knew.

"The NAMS station," he said. "The train is there, though we can't see it. It's underground. It should leave in about an hour—wait!"

But Verity whirled and ran headlong down the stairs, getting dizzy on the roundabouts.

"Hey, what's your name?" yelled George over the balcony a flight or two above her. "Slow down! I like you!"

Judging from his continued shouts and heavy breathing, she was at least a minute ahead of him when she got to the bottom of the stairs. She dashed past some newly opened French doors, then *had* to back up and take a closer look.

Yes. It *was* Eliot.

He was sitting at a large table that was covered with all manner of strange devices. He looked up at her and his eyes were no longer empty.

But then they were again and he smiled.

George was down the stairs now and reaching for her.

She ran out onto the porch, down the steps, grabbed up the bike, and jumped on it while running.

"Don't hurry off like this! We can help each other! You are quite extraordinary . . ."

She sped off down the winding walkway and shot out into the street. George's shouts faded.

She whipped down the street, cooled by the wind, headed in the general direction of the station. Why did she think Blaze would be there?

Always, always, he had longed to see the mighty trains. To ride them.

She pedaled faster and the bike leaped forward. If Eliot was normal, he certainly could have answered all of George's questions about the boat. Had he recovered? His eyes had looked so . . . odd, in that moment. And George knew they were from Cincinnati all along. What was he up to, anyway? Worming information out of her—but why?

Well, she'd think about Eliot and George later. She had to catch Blaze.

She wove in and out of pedestrians and saw to her surprise a sign shaped like a flower that said NAMS and she followed it around a long curve to the left and coasted to a stop beneath a small, glowing flower, where before her was an arched gap in a plain gray wall.

A girl of about twelve emerged from it, a look of determination on her face. She did not even glance at Verity as she passed.

This station had none of the beauty of the Cincinnati station. Verity wondered why they allowed it here, if they hated nan so. Maybe it was impossible to destroy.

Though the outer wall of the train station was low and plain, the inside was more impressive.

She coasted down a long ramp which gradually widened in a grand curve and she realized that it was a spiral. After she descended about fifty feet, she judged, though on the ramp it took a while, she was in a grand hall lit by golden light.

She braked, wondering where to go. The place was completely deserted. Maybe Blaze wasn't here after all.

The floor was a complex tile-mosaic map of the old United States, big as a city block, for she was standing in the middle of Florida (which she believed was now submerged by the rising ocean), and Georgia was ten feet away.

She looked to her left. Norleans! There it was, a star on the map but with the old spelling, New Orleans. And toward it twisted the blue-tile Mississippi, and on the river was even a small, tiled, fanciful riverboat.

She did not really understand why the station was enlivened, for it was. The people of Cairo had evidently found some way to control the station, to live with it. Yet they did not use it. They preferred to face the past—not the recent past, but the distant past, existing in the river-based world of the nineteenth century. Someone had bequeathed them immunity from the plague. Someone had sown some sort of strictures round the station. The trains led to the great Flower civilization of North America, what was left of it.

Perhaps not much was left of it.

Around the high, golden arch of the interior was the familiar frieze of flowers, indented into the wall and lit from the interior so that it glowed quietly.

She told herself that she must not succumb to the power of the place, to the wonder of nan, a world that she could *control*—or could have, in Cincinnati. . . .

As she slowly walked across the map of the United States, voices filled her head.

In a few steps her shoes touched New Orleans and she was surrounded by utterly familiar brick buildings, with wrought-iron balconies, and ghosts swept through her, a bit taller than her as if all were magnified in New Orleans, and a cool female voice said, "The City of New Orleans leaves each afternoon at four forty-seven P.M., with stops in New Madrid, Memphis, and Natchez." Verity watched transfixed as images of the trip unreeled around her: long vistas of river, a grand city, presumably Memphis; swamps and bayous, which flashed past flat; hammocks of palms and mangroves supplanted by a table covered with white linen. She saw a half-submerged champagne bottle, a vase holding a pink rose, a plate of opened oysters and some fresh bread . . . she could even *smell* the bread . . .

"Verity. *Verity!*"

Startled, Verity looked up as the images faded and Blaze stood there, his face sunburnt, his red beard gold at the edges. He looked relieved. His guitar was slung over his back. They stared at each other for a moment.

"Please don't go!" she said, surprised when it burst out of her.

"Come and see the lev, Verity," he said, and from the tone of his voice she knew it was no use.

She didn't move and he took her hand and led her across the map where one voice blended to another as she walked through the NAMS trains schedule of . . . how long ago? From what lost age? Crowds of people appeared and vanished and she said, "It must have been pretty confusing when a lot of people were here."

"Maybe," said Blaze, as they walked into a tunnel at the far end which said TRAINS. "But I think that somebody's probably just been playing with this. There are so many functions!" His voice was filled with awe. His steps hastened and she had to hurry to keep up with him.

"Doesn't this frighten you?" she asked.

"Of course," he said, but his voice was calm and deep and did not sound frightened. Her heart was beating hard and fast, thinking him gone and when would they meet again, if ever, yet it did not seem to bother him in the least. The walls of the tunnel flashed with constant advertisements, though thankfully they were soundless, and then they came to the end of the tunnel and she saw it.

"The Western Zephyr, nonstop service to Los Angeles, departs from track three in fifteen minutes," said the stern voice. Blaze hurried forward toward the shining, monstrous train.

But, she realized, as the coolness of the tunnel made her shiver, it was tremendously beautiful! Low and sleek, the engine shaped like . . . a fish, perhaps, pointed and low and rising gradually. The air was filled with a deep, pervading sound of immense energy, and she had the feeling for a moment that Blaze was going to run up and embrace the train, but suddenly the platform was boiling with people running toward the track. They were caught in a mass of ghosts wearing strange clothing, carrying parcels, their coats flashing with messages, talking to one another, all hurrying to their cars, some embracing others for an instant.

She saw that the passenger car was lit inside and appeared to be full of passengers. Then they all vanished suddenly.

"Blaze, there's no one on it!" she said in despair, as if this would make any difference. "How do you know that it will get there? How do you know what LA is like? How can you *leave* me?"

"I'm not sure," he said, but caught and held her tightly. "Verity, you don't need me! But I need *this!* Don't you see? It's what I've always dreamed of. It's been going between Cairo and LA for years. I found the horses a good home in town, so you don't have to worry about exercising them. I talked to a lot of people today, about the train. But it's true . . ." His voice caught for a moment. ". . . it's true that I couldn't find anyone who had ever *been* to LA . . ."

She pulled back and looked into his eyes. "Maybe they're killed as soon as they get off the train. Did you ever think of that?" She felt him sigh. They had never embraced for this long. Her arms tightened around him. "I can't bear for you to leave." She tried to blink back tears, but they overflowed.

To her surprise, he kissed her then.

It was their first kiss, their first kiss not as celibate Shakers, Brother and Sister. She grabbed the back of his head almost in a panic, felt his rough hair, and when the kiss ended pressed the side of her face to his. He was crying, too, she could feel it, all those emotions squeezed into his center with no place to go except another kiss—longer this time, and even more hungry—

"I *have* to go, Verity. I just *have* to. Don't try and stop me!" And he whirled and jumped on the train and the door slid shut behind him as if it had just been waiting for him and the ghosts flickered but it was just her standing alone on the cold platform.

Blaze appeared in the window and tried to open it, then just pressed his face against it as the train filled the station with harsh echoes. In seconds his window was gone and they all slid past in a blur of light and the tunnel was dark and empty.

It was all so sudden. This was all that she could think. So sudden, sudden as death. Like death.

No plague was strong enough to keep her from following. She would wait for the next train. Let them go to Norleans without her!

Someone touched her shoulder and she took off running.

"Verity!" She turned. It was Lil.

"We need you, Verity," and in Lil's voice she heard deep compassion.

"What business is it of yours what I do?" Lil wasn't going to stop her! "How did you know I was here?"

"A little bird told me."

Verity stared down the vanishing track at the empty black space which led everywhere. That tunnel led into her country's past, the past hidden from them. It led into Blaze's future, which would go on without her.

Lil had made her dress blue, and it shimmered, iridescent, as if lit from within, and this made Verity even more angry, for she was sure that Lil knew what the color did to her. She looked away, back into the blackness. She imagined Blaze riding, alone, the stars brilliant overhead.

Riding to nowhere.

Well, what was she doing? She didn't even know if Norleans even existed anymore. New Orleans, Los Angeles, Denver, Washington, D.C. . . . if they still lived, if people inhabited them, why were they all so silent? Why was the country so still?

What was the point of anything?

Just to live, like George Mills, pretending to be someone else, drinking lemonade alone in a great mansion?

"Oh, Lil," she said, wiping tears from her face, "what's the use?"

To her surprise Lil hugged her gently, and stroked her hair back from her forehead. "I know, honey. Sometimes I feel the same damned way. Let's go."

They walked back out through the station, through the enlivenment, which Verity ignored, her heart dead. She hated Cairo. "You were right about Cairo. I wish we'd never come here."

They came to the map. She picked George's bike up from where it lay on the Gulf of Mexico and walked it up the ramp into the sultry air of Cairo, where thunder rumbled and great gusts of wind pushed on them then suddenly ceased, as if the gods of storm were only testing the air, and finding it not quite ready.

A last deepening verge of blue glowed on the horizon, where Venus shone.

Excitement stirred in Verity as the wind gusted again and the dark clouds drew closer.

Let him go, then!

She jumped on the bike and Lil gave her a push. "See you later," Lil yelled, and Verity waved without looking back and coasted down through the streets of Cairo, in the direction everyone was going.

Toward the *Queen,* and the evening's Fabulous Entertainment.

Verity leaned the bike against the gate of Magnolia Manor, which loomed dark and forbidding against the gathering clouds, and remembered Eliot. She should have told Lil. But then, Lil didn't tell her much.

She turned and ran down toward the wharf, falling in with a crowd of people dressed in all manner of styles.

"Are you excited about the play?" asked a woman walking next to her, wearing a pink sunbonnet and a long calico dress. "What do you think it will be about?"

"I have no idea," said Verity. She pushed on ahead, and saw a great mob roiling about on the wharf, trying to jam their way onto the boat. Floodlights came on suddenly, illuminating the scene in sharp relief. A banner with hasty, crooked lettering was being unrolled and fastened onto the lower deck of the *Queen.* It advertised the play for the next five days.

Nice of them to ask the captain how long we'd be here, she thought. She looked west, wondered how far past the river Blaze's train went before it surfaced, imagined the lights streaking across the dark, empty countryside west of the Mississippi.

The Territory.

And he hadn't even asked her to go.

The crowd inched forward and the back of Verity's hand lit. STAGE CREW PLEASE REPORT NOW! THIS MEANS YOU!

Not me, thought Verity, but her hand insisted. YES, YOU.

She sighed. Well, it would definitely distract her. She shoved her way through the crowd, angry for a moment about the horses—hadn't he thought that she might want to keep them?—then forgetting it all in the hubbub and excitement.

Every seat was filled, creating a dark mass behind the bright footlights. Programs rustled in the quiet, after the calliope ceased playing "Miss the Mississippi" in deafening off-key tones. Apparently Blaze was the only one who had mastered the recalcitrant instrument.

Murmurs in the audience grew during the second act. A family was arguing about what was happening, each of four members crying out their version: China has conquered Russia! Unity, the moon colony, has died. A nanotech lab in Japan has surged, and the entire country is quarantined. The entire world has become Buddhist! No, Muslim! No—! They sat in their small kitchen and argued. For there was no longer a reliable source of news.

There was shouting from the audience between the second and third acts, but the players ignored it. Verity's small spate of directions subsided, having mostly to do with carrying on the props that had to be real and not holo, such as the kitchen chairs around the table.

Jack and Lil came backstage then, rippling along behind the velvet curtain and bursting out. "Verity," whispered Lil.

"I meant to tell you," Verity interrupted, also whispering so as not to disturb the beginning third act, "I saw Eliot today. In that big mansion. He looked as if he got better."

"Why, that—" said Lil, quite loudly.

"Shhh," said Jack. "There's going to be trouble. People might get hurt."

Lil said, "I was hoping till yesterday that we could bypass all this— I was going to tell you more but I didn't know we were so close—"

Verity had never seen Lil look worried before. "You had plenty of time beforehand," said Verity. "I don't know why you had to wait until the last minute."

"I was really hoping to avoid the entire issue," said Lil. "But I'm sure that Eliot has made it worse. We just didn't realize that George's network was so sophisticated. I can't *believe* I was so stupid!" Her mouth twisted in utter disgust. "What I did to Eliot didn't do anything to him. Ever hear of Bre'r Rabbit, the Trickster?"

"Yes . . . but Lil, George . . . George is just worried about his mother.

Isn't he? He told me the whole story—" She stopped as Lil let out a loud guffaw.

The curtain parted behind them then, and a man burst through the opening, hiding Lil behind velvet folds. "You!" he said, pointing at Jack.

"George!" said Verity.

"I remember you," said George, still staring at Jack. He was wearing his Thistlewood clothes. But his face, twisted with an almost manic hatred, seemed that of a different man. "I thought you might be among this crew, bringing your ratty philosophy with you. All that bullshit about information wanting to be free. After meeting *her*—" He pointed at Verity. "—I hope you haven't corrupted her. She's so sweet and innocent."

Verity thought she heard a muffled snort behind the curtain but George didn't notice it.

"And once the play started," George continued, "I *knew* you had to be here. You told the people on the *Queen* all kinds of scurrilous lies about me, didn't you? And now the people of Cairo—*my* people—are hearing this nonsense. Those lies will ruin me. I was hoping that I'd killed you when we had that little encounter in St. Louis. Such a long time ago. No such luck."

He turned to Verity. His face assumed yet another visage—kind; imploring. It was such an extreme change that Verity stepped back, startled by it.

"You didn't let me finish what I was going to say earlier today," George said. "I want you to stay." He jerked his head sideways at Jack. "Surely you'd never believe anything a person of his race said. I've been trying to *help* the good people of Cairo, improve their lives. With a Queen—someone who knows about Flower Cities—don't you see, there's no limit to what we could do together! We could create *splendor!* I've been working for decades, amassing what I need to create a Flower City right here in Cairo. My *own* Flower City. Not like that aborted early attempt. I only need someone who knows how to put it together. You! Like a gift from heaven! Oh, can't you see that it was meant to be, you and I, together? Some lucky twist of your fate brought you here. You of course would be equal to me in all respects. I'm a rich, powerful man. I could make you wealthy beyond your dreams. Stay. Please. Please say yes!"

"No," said Verity, decisively.

George's expression became quite ugly. He reached into his jacket pocket and pulled out a clear gel pack the size of an onion. "Remember," he said in a low, threatening voice, "I was *fair!* I'm a fair man! I offered you more than I've offered any woman in my entire life! But you have the gall—the *stupidity*—to turn me down. Well, I have another deal to propose." His voice had risen to a shout. "Come with me, *now,* or I'll destroy this boat and you along with it!" He raised his arm high above his head. He was breathing hard.

Lil stepped out from behind the curtain and smacked George over the head with a wooden chair, breaking the seat. He crumbled to the floor, blood from a deep cut in his forehead spreading across his slack face.

"You took your damned time," complained Jack, as Verity let out a cry.

"What is going on?" she demanded of Jack and Lil. "What was he talking about?"

"The Information Wars aren't over yet," said Jack heavily. "I guess they never can be." He stared at a puddle on the floor which issued from the clear membrane, which apparently had ruptured when George fell. "It's leaking," he whispered.

The curtain billowed again as someone fumbled on the other side. "I know you're in there somewhere," a voice said, and out burst Linda Lyle. Today her outfit was red, and matched her lipstick. "George!" she shrieked. "Darling! What have they done?" She dropped down beside him for a moment and touched the blood on his face. "Help! Murder!" she shouted, and ran out onto the stage. They could see her from the side, brilliant in the footlights. "Mobilize!" she screamed. "People of Cairo, it is time for us to fight!"

Lil bent and felt his neck. "It's only a scalp wound, idiot!" she yelled, but Jack yanked her arm and said, "Let's go."

Jack, Lil, and Verity slipped out the door next to the dressing rooms. Behind her, Verity heard rising voices and stampeding feet.

"Get the boat ready to go!" Jack yelled. He grabbed a passing woman and Verity heard him say something about the gel pack. The woman turned pale and ran toward the auditorium. Jack and Lil ran out onto the wharf.

Lightning raced through the sky. Thunder boomed. Jack bent over, the wind catching his tie and jacket, and began to unwind the heavy rope from the massive cleat embedded in the wharf. Lil hiked up her dress and ran to the back of the boat, and worked on the other rope.

Verity noticed the back of her hand glowing, and the words DEPART IMMEDIATELY appeared and then vanished. No kidding, she thought.

She ran up the gangplank as a sheet of cold rain swept across the river and whipped the lines to a clanking fury. In the light from the wharf, she saw a swarm of rafts whirl into the night and vanish. Another flash of lightning showed them several hundred yards away, tiny, the rafters leaning on sweeps and lashing their wigwams against the wind.

Huge splats of rain began to fall. A flood of people stampeded down the gangplank as Verity headed toward the pilothouse. Others ran wildly around the boat in preparation for leaving, and a mob from the auditorium prevented her from climbing the main stairs to the pilothouse. The rain was now a surging downpour hammering the boat. Standing at the railing, completely soaked and shivering in the cold wind, she could barely see Lil as she struggled with one of the ropes. They were not loose yet.

Verity pushed her way up another flight of stairs and paused at the railing. Fighting erupted on the gangplank. Rafters were throwing barrels onto the wharf in an attempt to deter attackers who were now swarming down from the town. Two men ran up behind Lil, and Verity yelled as loud as she could and Lil turned and began kicking them with high kicks that punched one of them in the chest and knocked him flat. The other one turned and ran and then Jack was there, dragging Lil toward the gangplank. Someone was cranking it up but they jumped for it and landed on their hands and knees.

The boat was free! Verity dashed up the stairs. Lightning flashed, and her heart was beating hard. The *American Queen* was moving, at last, out onto the great Mississippi River.

She fought her way through the crowd, screaming, "Let me through! I'm the pilot!," and the great boat bucked and rolled in the storm's fury as it left the lights of Cairo behind.

7

Fast Train Blues

Eighteen

○○○○○○○○○○○○○○○○

New World Blues

Terror. What I felt was pure terror. I couldn't get out of the train!

Verity was on the platform, on the other side of glass too thick to break, running alongside the train, tear streaks on her face shining in subterranean light, and the doors wouldn't open for me, and I could not, could not leave her behind. I would tell her everything that was happening to me—the blues, Alma, everything—and that would heal us, bring us through all these changes so that we could connect with each other again, just as if she might be Mother Ann, the Being I always told everything to, a new sort of Mother Ann—

Mother Ann, made from nan, Mother Ann, made from nan, ran through my mind as Verity vanished backward into the absurdity of it all, the way I had run into this trap, the goddamned newness of me, the way the train rushed into a tunnel of streaming lights and a woman's voice filled the air with "We are now beneath the Mississippi River"—*beneath! beneath!*—called forth laughter and tears until I was little better than a maniac, screaming "Verity!" as the voice said, "Please take your seat until we reach cruising speed, sir."

Acceleration rather than volition pushed me into the seat. It was soft and covered with silver leather and as I was pressed back into it a more intimate voice in my ear said, "Welcome to first-class service to Los Angeles aboard the Western Zephyr."

Well, now I'd done it. I'd severed myself from all that was even remotely familiar. I was moving like an arrow of light into unknown territory so fast it almost took my breath away. Not only that, the train was eerily empty. Everyone in Cairo, apparently, thought this a bad idea.

I jumped up though speed pressed me against the back of the seat and looked around. My guitar!

I was looking backward thinking I may have put it on the floor between the seats and it slid that way when someone tapped me on my shoulder and my heart nearly jumped out of my chest.

I whipped around ready to kill and saw my guitar, held by a man in a suit so white it almost gleamed. I looked up into eyes blue and strangely blank. "Sorry to startle you, sir. My sensors are not working properly and to get a strong enough sample I had to touch you. You left this on one of the seats up front."

I grabbed it from him and barely refrained from hugging it. "What sensors?" I asked.

He tapped his nose. "My met processor. At one time I could get a more than sufficient sample from the air. I only needed one part per million. And I could sort *very* quickly! Now . . ." He shrugged and looked at his hands.

"Met processor?"

"Yes, sir." He dropped into the seat next to me and his eyes were now earnest as well as blank, if that is possible. I realized that the eyes of most people are framed by a constantly shifting musculatory landscape, which he lacked. I swallowed hard as my throat was suddenly quite dry.

"Metapheromones." He brushed the guitar with his fingertips and then showed them to me. They glimmered with a complex pattern of color, mostly purple and gold. He touched me with his other hand and displayed both of them. The pattern on the fingertips of both hands looked identical. "I'm sorry. It's roundabout, I know."

"I'm the only person in here anyway, aren't I? I mean, besides—you." I didn't mean to be rude. But I couldn't really think of him as a person. I didn't know what other category to put him in though.

"Oh, no, sir, not at all."

I wasn't sure how to take that. "Where are they?"

He held up one finger and smiled. "Five cars back. I must go see to her." He patted my shoulder lightly. "Don't be sad."

"Sad?" I asked, startled.

He glanced at his hands, and added, "Or melancholy, or bereft." He stood. "Why not order your dinner?" He strode off behind me.

"When can I get off?" I shouted over my shoulder, but the door at the back of the car was sliding shut and I was alone.

Numbers of light at the front of the car, just above the door, hovered around 74 MPH. Although this was faster than I had ever moved, I thought that it must be slow for this kind of train. We had long ago emerged from beneath the river and I was sorry that I had let the attendant distract me from the moment. I was on the train now, I might as well experience it fully. Exhilaration washed in and lapped loneliness until I was suffused with an odd mixture of both. As I leaned toward the window the interior light above me dimmed so that I could see out.

Twilight deepened the sky, and the landscape was one of green rolling hills, low and clothed in young pines with long needles that caught the sun's last rays. Indeed, we moved past them so swiftly that it was more of a panorama than I had expected, and when I glimpsed a white house down a lane I wondered if I had only imagined it, so short was that instant.

Behind us the sky was black and lightning played through the clouds every few seconds, connecting with Cairo, now just a small low prickle of lights. Then I could not even see that and instead stared into the final orange glare of the sun beneath lowering clouds and then that too was swallowed by a V in the low hills and a spectacular greenish twilight gave way to indigo gleaming with stars. It was strange to be separated from the weather.

"Would you like a drink?" the voice asked, interrupting my thoughts. I looked around, but it seemed to be coming from the air.

"I'm not thirsty."

"Dinner is served in the dining car in fifteen minutes," said the voice. "Do you wish to order?"

That was choose. I knew that. "How?"

"Do you wish to have an appetizer?"

"An appetizer?"

"Oysters on the half shell, crayfish chowder, fois gras."

I was starting to get tired of asking questions. "Oysters?"

"Blue-point or Olympia. I apologize for the limited selection but we have experienced a minute disintegration in our program for Point Reyes Thirty-three and do not feel as if they are up to our high standards."

"Crayfish chowder?"

"Real crayfish fresh from Cairo, sir. Loaded less than three hours ago. Highly recommended."

"What was that other thing?"

"Goose liver."

I'd eaten plenty of goose livers in my life and didn't especially see the need to have any more. "Crayfish," I said.

"Excellent choice, sir. You may order the rest of your dinner when you arrive in the dining car."

"How do I get there?" I asked, but there was no reply.

I pulled my guitar strap over my shoulder and headed toward the back of the car.

Some of the seat backs had little colored pictures playing across them. One caught my eye—some Flower City. But as I watched, the colors flowed swiftly upward and changed into a pattern wild and entrancing, dancing flames of yellow and violet shifting gradually through the spectrum. I felt as though I could watch that cycle for hours and for that reason walked on swiftly and did not allow my eyes to rest on any of the other screens.

A door slid open as I approached the end of the car and I crossed an interface containing the noise of wind but otherwise silent and walked into the next car.

This was arranged differently. I was in a narrow corridor punctuated every few steps by doors. I wondered what was inside them but continued on until I heard a voice say, "Sir, this is your compartment. Would you care to freshen up before dinner?"

I stopped. A picture of myself hovered on the door and I found myself studying it as if it were the image of a stranger.

As it was. But not completely. We had no mirrors at Shaker Hill, and, eerily, this was not one. But I'd seen myself on plenty of occasions. Verity and I often cavorted in Kaleen's Elegant Dresses in downtown Miamisburg, in clothes we belted around ourselves with gleeful derision. The selection in the small shop was limited, but we dared brave the mall only once, with lightsticks, as it was huge and always dark. The *Queen* had mirrors aplenty but I had been too busy to pay much attention to myself.

My eyes were staring, green and wide and ingenuous. My skin had darkened somewhat but was still rather pale and there were freckles all over my cheekbones, which stood out. My red hair was shot with gold, from the sun I presumed, and swirled outward like a lion's mane. A curly thick beard covered my lower face completely and I was pleased about this: vanity. Seeing my mouth reminded me of Verity's kiss, so desperate and intense. I wanted another.

"Well, open up then," I growled, and when the door didn't open I kicked it a few times and then looked down to see an indentation glowing and touched it. The door slid open.

A small neat bunk to my right had been made up. Below it was a low, comfortable-looking couch.

"Would you like us to prepare any reading material for this evening?"

I didn't like the voice coming from everywhere. "Like what?"

"Your choice, sir."

How does one choose from infinity? I remembered one of the books I had left behind on the boat. I kept wanting to read it again. *"Huckleberry Finn,"* I said.

"Very good, sir. It is now receptor-ready."

"I have no receptors."

A short silence. "We will need to remedy that before arrival, sir. The cost will be seven thousand four hundred ninety-two dollars and fifteen cents if you lock in now."

"No thanks." I pushed my guitar back and put my hands beneath the faucet and splashed my face with the cool water that flowed into them. "Please get me a real book," I commanded as I left the room, determined to avoid awe if possible.

My determination evaporated as I came to the end of the car and was suddenly surrounded by open country.

The horizon still glowed orange from sunset but the sky overhead was fiercely black and the whiteness of the stars was just as fierce. The moon was low and huge and golden. Trapped inside that clear tube as I was, I'm not sure why something I had seen since childhood newly moved me but it was so. Perhaps it was the small green numbers glowing above the door membrane which read 200 MPH.

We were moving fast, and dark shapes close rose and fell in a kind of rhythm, jerky, like some blues.

I was moving. I was going. I was heading out.

Out into the Territory.

I wished it were not night, or that the train would stop and resume at dawn so that I would not miss a mile.

"Stop the train!" I said.

"Is it an emergency?"

"Yes."

"Describe the nature of the emergency."

"I need to see everything slowly."

"That is not an emergency."

"It seems like one to me."

The voice was silent. The train barreled on.

I passed through two more cars of empty seats and finally arrived in the dining car.

About twenty small tables were lit by soft membranes that glowed on the wall in the shapes of various flowers. I did not appreciate the additional decorative touch of small glowing bees, one about every foot in a straight line between the flowers. Each table had a white tablecloth and was set in anticipation of a full train of hungry passengers. To my surprise, a woman sat at a table midway in the car and raised one hand in a languid wave.

"Join me," she said, as I approached.

The chairs were green wicker with white cushions. I settled my guitar in the chair next to me as I sat.

Her hair was cut very straight, just below her ears. Her eyes were black and her face quite pale. She smiled faintly. "Hello. My name is Masa. What's yours?"

"Blaze," I managed. She wore a simple turquoise scarf of sheer fabric around her neck, and her white dress showed her collarbones angling down below her pointed chin. Her lips were red and so were her cheeks. She looked exquisite.

I must have been staring, for she laughed. "You look pretty strange yourself," she said and I said, "It's not that—"

She patted my hand and said, "Look, here come our appetizers. I was rather disappointed with the selection tonight, weren't you?"

"What did you want?"

"This is your first time on the train, isn't it?"

I nodded. "Not yours?" Her clothing was not all that strange, but its very simplicity was not Midwestern.

She shook her head, a slight smile playing around her lips.

Excitement was an explosion in my chest. "Where are you from then?" In my eagerness I think I stuttered. "Where have you been?"

She displayed an open hand halfway across the table and looked at me expectantly. After a few long seconds, she withdrew it and slipped it into her lap, hunched her shoulders, and looked down at the table. "Sorry," she muttered. "We *have* just met." Her words were clipped and short.

"What are you sorry for?" I asked. "I only asked where you'd been."

The same attendant brought our food. Well, I actually didn't know if it was the same one or not, really, but he looked identical. "I guess those are oysters," I said, as her plate was set in front of her. Small gray blobs on iridescent crescents. Fragrant steam rose from my soup; it was rich and delicious and filled with small meaty chunks. Something in it made my mouth burn in a pleasant way. Masa took a small bottle from the side of the table and sprinkled something over her oysters. Then she picked up one shell and let the oyster slide into her mouth. I don't think she chewed. She did that six times, jerking her head so that her hair fell back, revealing ears oddly small.

The man returned and said to me, "Have you decided yet?"

"Decided on what?"

"Dinner," said Masa.

"I want dinner. The soup was good. It was all edible."

Her laugh fluttered upward. "Of *course*. And though I'm terribly bored by the vat-grown beef, if this is your first trip you might like it." She nodded expectantly. "Go ahead, try it."

"All right," I said.

The attendant still stood there.

"And wine," said Masa. She was cheering up. "Shall I choose?"

"Go ahead," I told her.

She pressed one finger on one of the bees next to her and nodded. "Wild River 2031. Quite lovely. I'm sure you'll like it."

The man turned and left with our dishes. Masa looked at me for some reason much more friendly now. "You don't have any seps, do you?"

"Seps?"

"Receptors."

"No," I said. "And I don't want them."

Her eyes become darker and more intense. "I've never met a naked person before."

"Is that what you call people without receptors?"

"What's it like?"

"What do you think?" I retorted sharply, aware that she found me incredibly primitive. "Absolutely normal." I buttered a feather-light roll and ate it slowly, determined to enjoy myself despite her. The butter had none of the pungency of our own butter, made from the milk of our own cows, but was light and bland. For a second the thought that I was probably eating nanotech crossed my mind and I snorted.

"What?"

"Nothing." I buttered another roll, even more lavishly. The man brought a salad and I recognized at least six varieties of lettuce, leaves red and spiky, or spring-green and innocently smooth.

"Where are you going?" I asked.

"Oh, look!" she said, and pointed out the window. It was dark, and I saw only our reflection, and that of the table.

"Where can I get off? The train won't answer me."

"Los Angeles," she said, and hunched her shoulders a bit more.

"But the train goes back to Cairo?"

She brightened. "Oh, yes. It turns right around. Actually, it doesn't really turn around. There's an engine on both ends. My, what an interesting few days I've had. First the girl, and now you. If I were superstitious I'd say that something's going to change. I haven't seen so many passengers since—"

The waiter arrived and showed her a bottle of wine. I anticipated it eagerly. I'd never had any wine, much less fine wine. She nodded and he extracted the cork and poured us each a swirling red glass. "Of course it's just right," she said, sipping. "We'll have a different one with dessert. I apologize for being so remiss. I ought to have ordered for each course. And this will be your only dinner."

"It will?"

She nodded as the waiter set our dinners before us. My beef was quite red and tremendously aromatic.

"We'll be in Los Angeles just after lunch tomorrow." She began to shovel her food down like—well, like a farmer. She glanced up and smiled. "I'm hungry," she said.

"Have you ever been in Los Angeles?"

Her fork paused midway to her mouth. Her eyes became bleak. "Of course," she said. She resumed eating, but now she was frowning. I was sorry I'd asked, but I had to ask more questions as well. I supposed that I could ask the train all that I wanted, but the train struck me as being somewhat prejudiced, unreliable, and out of touch.

And I was positive that she hadn't gotten on the train in Cairo.

"When was the last time the oyster program worked?"

She threw her fork down on her plate and it bounced off onto the floor. The waiter appeared immediately and proffered a new one but she ignored it. She stood, flung her crumpled napkin on top of her food, and stormed up the aisle. Her white dress was cut low in the back. I wondered what Verity would look like in it. For a brief instant I saw her again, capering around the clothing store in something quite similar, but much more baggy on her fourteen-year-old body, as we collapsed in gales of laughter.

"I'm sorry!" I said, leaving my fine dinner. I suspected I could get another whenever I pleased. I hurried up the aisle behind her. She turned and her face was contorted. She was crying and her fists were clenched.

"Why do you have to ruin everything? Why can't you just enjoy—(hiccup)—this lovely—(hiccup)—TRAIN!!" Then to my amazement she flung herself at me and there was nothing for me to do but embrace her while she sobbed in my arms and I thought, of course, of Verity.

If this happened every time I asked a question, I'd need every minute between here and Los Angeles to get any answers.

"The oyster program has *never* worked," she said, sniffling.

"Why are you on the train?"

"I don't have to answer all your questions! Just leave me alone."

"No, of course you don't," I said. "I'm just curious, that's all."

"Well, then, what are *you* doing on the train?"

I told her everything. During the next hour we drifted back to a car with soft, luxurious seats that folded down almost flat. She touched something that made the top and sides of the car transparent—she wanted the floor clear too but I begged her to leave it alone—and I told her everything. All about Russ, and John, and Shaker Hill, and Verity. I told her about Alma and the blues and the radio stones and the plague. Whenever I talked about the plague she'd close her eyes and scrunch up her face like it hurt. After a while I realized that she'd fallen asleep while stars burned all around us. She had succeeded in telling me nothing.

I rose and wandered back to the dining car. All the tables were empty, and the silver glowed in the moonlight. I sat down next to a window and turned the chair toward it and watched.

The waiter came and poured me some wine. It was different wine from the one Masa had ordered. The train had begun to climb. "If you would like a guide, press that bee," the waiter said quietly as he poured another glass.

"You have chosen to take NAMS' deluxe over-the-Rockies route," said the voice, infusing the words with a strangely artificial enthusiasm. "We know that you will appreciate the fact that it takes a bit longer than going under the mountains, as you will be rewarded with rich vistas."

"Why don't you schedule it so that it goes this way during the day?" I asked.

"This NAMS route is serviced every four hours from Cairo. For a complete schedule press twice."

"Never mind," I said.

Silent moonlight drenched a panorama of jumbled cliffs, huge jutting pines. My heart was in my throat as we crossed a black gorge; we were suspended on a thin thread of steel I could not even see. I'd never been so high in my life. And we climbed higher. I prowled from one end of the car to the other. I shouldered my guitar, picked up my glass, pulled the bottle from its ice bath, and made my way to the back of the train. I came to Masa, still sleeping, her face silvered by moonlight. I pulled the blanket the attendant had covered her with up to her chin and she stirred sleepily. I wondered what sad story she held within. Were there no normal people anywhere?

I was beginning to realize that there might not be. Everyone I'd ever know, everyone I met, was troubled and disturbed by the great changes wrought by nan. I wondered how quickly these changes had come about. I realized how very little I knew.

I dropped into the seat across from Masa and watched the stars some more. They and the wine pulled thoughts from deep inside me, thoughts that jumped the black chasm of death and melded my Shaker past to this strange, new present, which had existed all around us when we were young, as if Shaker Hill had been the still, unchanging center round which whirled unimaginable terror and wonder. I felt the blues grow inside me, clamoring to burst forth. I grabbed the bottle and headed for the rear of the train.

There, as I had hoped, was a clear bubble with some chairs, though beyond was a door that was stuck fast. I was even able to open windows and expected a great roar from the wind but there were some sorts of funnels or bumps that channeled the rushing air and tempered it to a quiet hiss. I could see that it was quite windy outside; the tall pines swayed and tossed, black silhouettes, and the moon made a path across three small lakes tiered away below me in the distance like three great teardrops. I asked the train for strong coffee and the tireless attendant brought it to me in a silver pot and another bottle of wine as well and a roast-beef sandwich.

The guitar was still tuned. I plucked the strings in wonder; it had been through so much. I could untune it. But after a few minutes the strings regained their former tension. Alma had tuned it indeed. . . .

I plucked one exploratory note; then another. I ran my fingers down the strings and distorted them and they cried out lonely as the moonlight. I saw a satellite flash across the sky and then another and then another and it occurred to me to wonder if they really were dead, or if they could somehow be enlivened again. Even death had changed its nature. Humans had begun something, and then that change had expanded and grown on its own, reinfusing the humans. . . .

As I thought, my hands moved. My fingers chorded up and down the neck of the blues guitar (I did not think that it would deign to play a cakewalk or rag with me but later found I had badly underestimated it) and a song grew through me, growling and low and aching—

> I followed her to the station
> With a suitcase in my hand
> Well it's hard to tell it's hard to tell
> When all your love's in vain
>
> When the train rolled up to the station
> I looked her in the eye
> Well I was lonesome I felt so lonesome
> I could not help but cry
> All my love's in vain

It was the song of that Robert Hellhound Johnson, I knew, and his blues fell down on me like hail. My hands did not dance on the neck, on the strings, as they did on the keys of a piano. They moved deliberately, with strength and calculation, chorded to something deep within me, rising and falling in odd stuttering cadences, singing of distance and of loss and of pain. I drank but I did not eat. The swift troubled life of Robert Johnson flashed through me relentless and raw. I saw the long straight black dirt roads of the Delta fringed by endless fields of cotton superimposed on the Territory as I flashed past, a place I'd longed to be all my life, a place distant from Shaker Hill as heaven, and now I was crossing it, singing and playing my guts out, smelling the whiskey-soaked floors of the countless jook houses as I ducked into them from the hot afternoon sun; playing for the laborers whose fathers had been promised freedom by Lincoln, then had it taken away from them by reconstruction, and I remembered then with complete clarity the last chapter of *Huckleberry Finn,* read as a child, when I wondered at the charade of Jim being repeatedly freed and imprisoned and finally understood it. The men and women surrounding me, drinking and dancing and whooping, were feeling the only freedom they could in a world that had cruelly canceled their participation and left them with ashes and grits. And music.

I sang as the train tilted downward and I sang as we rushed through dawn onto an amazing flat dry distance, brown and purple brushed here and there with green, and my fingers were raw and bleeding and I fell fighting into sleep staring straight into the sun so that the darkness would not take me ever again.

I woke with a start. My head was aching. My hands were puffy. It was horrifically early, as the sun was just inching above the horizon, but it was strong enough to hurt my eyes. Masa, still in her white dress, stood over me grinning but it looked like a leer to me.

"Poor dear," she said. "I can help."

She immersed my hands in water brought by the attendant in an ornate crystal bowl. Only there was something in the water, because besides being cooling it healed my fingers. I felt the tips of the fingers of my left hand with my thumb. They were thickened somewhat. So were the ends of my right-hand fingers.

I was in the future and I had to accept it.

Hey, it wasn't all bad!

Masa ordered breakfast and I ate it. Hard-boiled eggs, white toasted bread, that same bland butter, and little black fish eggs, caviar, crunchy and salty. My headache vanished as I drank champagne, bubbles exploding on my tongue and effervescing through the glass of the stuff. I felt tremendous.

"Where are we?"

"Near Salt Lake City."

"Salt Lake City! Oh! Will we stop?"

I was seized with great excitement. Los Angeles was a distant, abstract blur. I knew nothing about it. But I'd grown up with Russ's tales of Denver, and Salt Lake City, during the early days of the Flower Cities.

"We stop for five minutes," she said, and her eyes were strange. "But the doors never open."

"I find that very surprising," I said. "Can't you make them open? We—at least I—could get off."

"Then you'd be left behind!" Her eyes went wide and I saw fear.

I shrugged. "So what? And there's another train. I can just get on that one."

"There is no other train," she said flatly. She got up and left. I'd made her mad again.

I went back to my compartment, took a shower, put on the new clean clothes waiting for me. I could get used to this.

W, proclaimed small green emblems in the windows, on my mirror. *W*! *W* for West! The Territory! This land is my land! This land is your land! Oh, the music that bubbled through me. I ride an old paint. I lead an old dan. I've gone to Montana to throw the hoolihan. What's a dan? What's a hoolihan? And where the hell was Montana? I didn't care.

I heard a piercing scream down the corridor. I rushed out into it and hurried toward its source. When I got to the dining car, I saw that it was, of course, Masa. The attendant had his arms around her. He was stroking her back and saying Shhh, it's all right, it's all right.

Over her shoulders he looked at me and said, "It's all right, sir, she's always like this when we get to Salt Lake City." He turned and led her away. She looked frail and pathetic. I was a little afraid, but not much.

But then I saw Salt Lake City, out the window. That had to be it, at the foot of the mountain we were skirting, and I too was seized with terror. I fought it as best I could. It was not reasonable.

But there were those Flowers, those awful Flowers.

They were not, I realized, as we rapidly approached the city through a flotsam of abandoned communities where I saw absolutely no one on empty streets flooded with sunlight, like the Flowers of Cincinnati. They were stiff, unmoving. As we moved closer, I saw glints, and colors did not grow as I had expected.

Instead, these Flowers resembled nothing so much as the ancient abandoned machinery we had seen in the little town on the Ohio, but on a much more massive scale. The buildings were all metallic, and their interstices clear as water, giving it all a monochromal look. The Flowers were not at all flowerlike but were instead spiked or curved nodes surrounding a central indentation. The buildings were copper, brass, stainless-steel, aluminum. Or so it seemed.

Every once in a while I thought I saw a golden glittery thing arise above the buildings, but couldn't be sure, and we descended then into a dark tunnel.

We were going very fast, and after a few seconds the interior of the train glowed with light and apologized for the delay. It announced our arrival in two minutes and told those debarking to gather their things.

I grabbed my guitar and hurried toward a door. But as we emerged into the station and stopped I saw an awful thing.

On the platform was a line of people. They all had guns. Their clothing was a ludicrous mix of pioneer garb, late-twentieth-century business suits, women wearing high heels or huge puffy colorful boots or long evening gowns. They all had weapons. Guns and big tubes bigger than guns. They raised them, pointed them at the train. I hit the floor. I heard loud explosions, muffled shouts outside, scuffling. A panel on the door blinked green. I raised my head to the window and stared down the barrel of a gun. I dropped back down. The train began to move. We were in the tunnel again. The attendant came through. He looked surprised to see me.

"Oh, sir, I apologize. I suppose you wished to debark?"

"Not really," I muttered.

"They are always there," he said. "Not all of them are real. I think that only a few of them are real. But Masa's brother thought none of them were real. She watched him die."

"How long ago was that?"

"Sir, I . . ." He blinked. "I am sorry. But I really shouldn't tell you that."

I grabbed his shoulders and shook him. He remained completely passive. His head whipped back and forth. Horrified at what I was doing I stopped and said, "I'm sorry. I'm so sorry!"

"Years, sir," he whispered, staring at me. "Years."

I blinked and let him go. I stormed down the aisle, looking into compartments and yelling her name until I found her. She was lying on a bed. Her eyes were red. She sat up. "I'll be better soon," she said.

"Why do you do this?" I asked.

"My brother and I were moving to Salt Lake City," she said, and her voice shocked me: rather dreamy, calm, and distant. "Or Denver. Or anywhere viable. This was just the first place we got to. We were so excited. We'd been wanting to leave the dome for so long."

"The dome?"

"Los Angeles. Don't interrupt," she said petulantly. "We planned it for a long time. It was the first step in getting out. An intermediate place."

Out? I wondered, but did not say anything.

"We first had to condense," she said, and there she lost me completely. "That was the hardest part, we thought. Because no one seemed to remember how. We worked really hard to figure it all out. There's really no time there, or it's very different—more speedy, more jerky, but disconnected and not linear, just linked. And it never ends. So that's not really time, is it? But we worked our way back to DNA from binary code. We knew, of course, what we were. We were just so curious, so hungry. Our parents had done it to us. We were little kids when they did it. I could still remember everything. I really could. James said that I couldn't, but I did. Our living room in that house in the Hollywood Hills. We could go there any time, of course I remembered it, but I *really* remembered it, from before. He said that they must have put that curiosity in us for some reason, that there was some mission for us, that we had to work our way back. Not everyone had made it. Not everyone was translated after the loading. We didn't think that our parents had been. Sometimes glitches occurred. Read errors and such. We looked for them everywhere, with every search engine there was. He said that they could very well be in an identical living room somewhere, waiting for us, waiting and waiting. Or that our copies were there, and they didn't realize that we had divided."

I sat down. I listened.

"I wanted to see the real ocean, you know? I wanted to touch it. To have it all over my body. Not just a *program* of it. Not just an *algorithm.* But real." Her voice was low and intense now. I certainly believed her. I just wasn't sure what she meant.

"We thought the Flower Cities would welcome us. We'd learned so much about them. We'd evolved from them, in a way. We knew every aspect about how they functioned, of course. In there. Out here there isn't enough memory for that. I wish I'd known that before. I don't know why we didn't. We were so blind, so foolish. But we were young. We'd never known anything else. We thought we were so smart—passing through all the failsafes. Recondensing. Waking in those cocoons. With bodies! Real bodies! Oh, it was heavenly, really it was. Almost worth it."

"But Salt Lake City is frozen and those people killed James when he stepped off the train." She started to choke. Her eyes got wild and darting and I took her hand. She breathed in great gulping sighs. "That's all," she said. She closed her eyes. She curled up and pressed her fists beneath her chin. She began to breathe deeply.

"Come, sir," said the attendant. "I gave her something to help her relax. She always needs a sedative here. She'll sleep for a while."

I felt like sleeping myself but didn't dare. Out the window I saw only a vast, white, glittering plain and an old, empty solar road next to our track. Behind us—well, I glanced at Salt Lake City, but quickly looked away. The brown-and-blue mountains were much smaller now. It appeared that we'd taken a southward turn.

I went back to my guitar and hugged it. Music flared through me, distant at first, then nagging, then insistent. I had no choice but to play it—

> I went to the crossroad, fell down on my knee
> Asked the Lord above, Have mercy, save poor . . . Masa
> If you please

It was Bob's plea, Robert Johnson's, but it fit Masa and there was nothing I could do except sing for her, sing for her . . . to a Lord no longer there, unable to dispense a shred of mercy.

Just after lunch, she said. Just after lunch. Just after lunch.

As I stared out the window, there were mesas, strange red rock towers, broken and dry-looking mountains in the distance, and an occasional majestic peak. I was told that it was lunchtime by some voices, but I ignored them. My stomach was knotted tight. We flashed through a great, flat desert. Distance. Shimmering places that looked like water but that I thought were not. Another rush up brown mountains, again the scattered pines, the lakes, round and unworldly green. Down, down, and then I saw it.

The dome.

Beyond, the Pacific Ocean. The dome itself was not on flat land, but climbed the side of wrinkled brown mountains. I saw the tips of sunken buildings beyond it, beautifully filigreed, with strong, arresting crowns, glass unbroken and shining. The ocean was so clear that I could follow their forms down into it for a ways with my eyes. White, frothing waves crashed around them; at least I imagined them crashing, like in books. From this distance the waves were just white lines etched on blue. The day was bright and fine; sunny and beautiful. I pressed my face to the window.

"Enlargement, sir?" He touched the window and everything was magnified.

White birds circled the tops of the buildings, settling and rising every few minutes in great clouds. The waves were indeed massive, licking up the seaward sides of the buildings for a story or two. On the upper balconies, palm trees waved in the wind and viny growths cascaded down the sides. I swear I thought I saw a person sitting on one of the balconies but it must have been my imagination, as was the small boat I might have seen bobbing in an enclosed pond that had once been a huge terrace.

Just south of this was the dome: curved, glowing, crisscrossed with interstices that hopscotched across one another in the sunlight. Small concave dishes spouted from it here and there; Peabody had taught me enough so that I knew that they were satellite dishes. What were they doing with them, I wondered, if the satellites were dead? What was the diameter of the dome? Thirty miles? Fifty? It was frightfully massive.

Masa joined me. She appeared rested, her simple, beautiful white dress as clean and fresh as if she had not worn it since I got on the train. Her face was serene.

"Are you going to stay?" she asked.

"How could I?" I asked.

"You could," she said. She pressed a pad next to us and a voice said, "The present cost of initiation is thirty thousand four hundred sixty-eight dollars and twenty-two cents if you lock in *now*. Now. Now. Now," it repeated, and then she pushed the pad again and it stopped.

"That really doesn't mean anything once you're in," she said.

"Would you do it?" I asked.

Her eyes were troubled. "Every time, I think that I will. I do it, almost. I could see James again. But then—I don't know. I'm afraid. It's like jumping off a high building."

"Why don't you ever get off in Cairo?" Years, the attendant had said. Years.

"James isn't there. He's here. I don't have to decide yet. I really don't. There's always another trip."

"Of course you don't," I said gently.

"Then why are you forcing me to?" she screamed and the attendant rushed in and gave me a disapproving look. The dome was much larger now and it had no openings at all. They couldn't see out. I couldn't see in.

"We'll get out again? Out of the dome?" I asked. "We won't get stuck in there, will we?"

"Why are you bothering me?" she asked crossly. She stood and started pacing back and forth across the small space. Her agitation grew until she was muttering in a small, fretful voice. We were approaching the dome at a tremendous speed.

"Look," I said desperately, suddenly terribly afraid, "if you stop the train we can go down to the ocean. The real ocean. I think I saw people—"

She gave me a single wry look. And then we were in.

"Oh" was all she said, her face and hands pressed against the glass as we rushed into a corridor of light. She began muttering. "Home. I'm home. James. I know you're here. I need you. But I'm afraid. So afraid." The same phrases, over and over again. I noticed the attendant hovering behind her.

It was pure light. The inside of the dome. There was nothing else there. The entire train became transparent, even the track, and we floated through light. It glowed all around us. Like heaven. And like heaven, there were high, singing voices.

"James! I'm home! I'm really home. This time I will! I promise!"

"Come on, Masa," said the attendant, stepping forward.

"Leave her alone," I said, suddenly remembering the sedative.

I heard a tearing sound and glanced toward it. Masa was pulling the left side of her dress apart; apparently that's how it came off. She stepped out of it, completely naked, and kicked off her shoes. How beautiful she was! Her pale skin caught the light through the windows and she was utterly unself-conscious as I stared. She pressed her body against the glass again, her arms wide as if embracing the light.

She turned to the side, toward me, pressing against the glass with all her might, pushing with her legs, her face scrunched and frowning mightily. "Yes," she breathed, as if in answer to what the voices sang. "Yes, yes, yes."

And then I saw a face outside the window. It coalesced there and followed the train along, re-forming constantly in the luminous field of twisting colors. Her face charged with wonder, eyes wide open, Masa placed both hands at the sides of the face, her eyes grave. She nodded again. "Yes. Yes. Yes," she whispered, in intervals, as if in answer to questions I could not hear. Then, "Upload. *Now.*"

I had already seen many strange things in my life. But I was not prepared for this.

She splayed herself out on the concave curve of the window, pressing the entire front of her body against it. An interface between her skin and the glass began to glow, and then her body began to glow as well, like that of a plague victim, golden. The glass seemed to melt and form around her and from the side I could see her face, lit with ecstasy, though her eyes were closed. This seemed to last an eternity, but was probably only minutes. I was in agony. Did I need to do something? Was she going to die? At one point I must have jumped up but felt the attendant's warning hand on my arm, his whispered "It's too late, sir. You would damage her now." His hand was like steel and held me much too tightly.

Without warning, the membrane around her withdrew and there was no tension at all in her body. Her head jerked back and she slumped to the floor.

And, I swear, I saw her outside the train for an instant, waving at me. Then she was gone.

The attendant was sobbing. It took me a minute to realize it since the sounds were wooden, harsh; almost like an imitation of someone crying. But I could tell that his feelings were real enough. He stood over her body and glared murderously at me through his tears, which coursed down his oddly unaffected face. I was afraid.

Then the hate left his eyes. He said resignedly, "I knew it would happen someday."

He gathered up her body tenderly and carried it away.

I was glad of the rush of the train on the return trip. I still fell deeply into the distant buffs and purples of the mountains, the scrub of the desert, the majesty of distant red spires rising straight out of the flat plains at sunset. During it all I could feel the blues coming on as if this strange voyage had washed me clean of the past and left room for them to burn into my soul. I was in a damned hurry to get back. Back to the Mississippi, which flowed down to the Delta. When I got to the Delta, I would really *understand.*

It seemed to me that all of us were trapped somehow, slaves to something. Masa, trapped on the train, for how many years? Why hadn't she just gotten off somewhere other than Salt Lake City—Cairo, I suppose— and tried to see what else there was to see? Trapped by a memory. Returning to that which she'd escaped. The luminous place was awful to me, but I suppose that's because I didn't really understand it. And I didn't want to. Some things are best left alone. But the division between myself and that place was not very deep. I had only to agree to pay them whatever they demanded and I could have melted into it like her.

Or died trying.

I asked the attendant why he hadn't done so, for he was disconsolate at his loss. I came upon him standing at an open doorway, seeming to contemplate the rush of the ground next to him in a thoughtful manner. I touched the panel that closed the door and he shrugged. "What's to keep me here now?"

"Why don't you go to Los Angeles, then, like Masa?" I asked him.

"You have to be human," he said.

"It doesn't look that way to me," I said.

"The train won't even tell me how much it would cost," he said, with an air of finality.

"Then get off in Cairo with me. I'm going to go down the Mississippi River."

He was silent.

"Think about it," I told him. Not that I wanted to be around his moping, but I was worried about him, whatever he was. He did have feelings. I didn't know what about him was not human. What exactly was human, anyway? I remembered Russ talking about DNA and wondered if the attendant had DNA. Russ said that everything living had DNA except for viruses, which were different somehow.

I wondered if the man was a virus.

Salt Lake City was the same. I watched the performance on the platform with great curiosity. One of the women stepped forward and raised some sort of barrel and a blast of flame licked the window just inches from my face. I drew back in shock and when the flame ceased the woman stared into my eyes with grim satisfaction and gave one quick nod. She mouthed something and shook her fist as the train pulled away. Well, I got the message. The early Shakers had been no different. Apparently one of the blessings of nan had been to completely isolate everyone.

I felt isolated enough. I began to worry about whether or not I would be able to get off the train. It would be the worst sort of horror to be slung back and forth across the country like Masa. With no company except that strange moping thing. I was amazed that she had done it for so long. She must have had every little hill and gully memorized.

I sang the last verse of "Love in Vain" for her:

> When the train, it left the station,
> With two lights on behind
> Well the blue light was my baby
> And the red light was my mind
> All my love's in vain.

But it wasn't anymore. She'd felt that way every time she went through Salt Lake City. But her love wasn't in vain anymore.

Was mine?

Verity was pregnant, and the father of her child was Sphere. Did she miss him? I did. I still did. I could understand what she felt for him.

But it still upset me. There was an ache inside me, a hollowness that refused healing. Even though I understood, a bit more, since Alma, what had happened, I could not let my illusions about Verity go. In a way, I understood Mother Ann even better. Sex had not been a sin for Shakers. But it stood in the way of true relationships between Sisters and Brothers, and was therefore put aside in order for a deeper union to be achieved.

The hell with that. The blues urged me to scream in a jealous rage.

So I did, with music. Or at least I tried. "Evil Woman Blues"—ah, but I couldn't think of Verity as evil. Well, then, "Heartbreak Blues"! Better . . . closer . . . "Angry-Hearted Me."

Hmmm. As I ran through the lyrics of so many blues I realized that the problem that I was having was that I never felt as if I *owned* Verity, the way these songwriters seemed to feel as if they owned others and all their actions and decisions too. Russ had brought us up differently. Even with the blues inside me, I couldn't believe that there was anything bad about Verity, the way all those blues songs wanted me to think. She had been a young woman in the midst of a strange new life, finding things out about it and about herself, the way I was. She had brought me back to life.

It was unutterably surly to be angry with someone who had risked so much for me. It was my own hopes and dreams that were changed, in a way, as if I had dreamed of a certain kind of heaven which was now out of my reach. But was it? Without talking to Verity about it, I had no way of knowing whether it was or it wasn't. She had certainly kissed me eagerly enough. . . .

I wondered what it must have been like for Masa—to have heaven so near yet denied her by something inside her very self, I didn't really know what. To be ferried right into the middle of it twice a week yet not being able to touch it without dying first.

It must have been something like that for the men and women who wrote the blues. They were supposed to be free, but in the South they were denied schooling, the vote, and property—dignity, really. And when they went north to the land of milk and honey it was the same. Better jobs, sometimes, but homesickness and in the end the denial of entry into society.

I was amazed at this unknown history, like a dark thread winding round the bright one I'd absorbed from the few American History books at Shaker Hill. I interrupted the attendant from his new pastime of standing on an open platform and watching the ground rush past and asked him about the informational capabilities of the train and of course he was happy as a puppy to help out. He showed me how to access the Harlem Renaissance, to begin with, all those fierce, happy young women and men unleashing their stories at last, the stories of their people, their stories of suffering and joy. A deep voice read me passages from Sojourner Truth's *Narrative* and I wept. I experienced the majesty of Scott Joplin's black opera, *Treemonisha*.

And after that, ah, was Ma Rainey, Bessie Smith, those independent divas of the road and of early black recordings on what the industry called race records. Memphis Minnie, Blind Blake, as if all the stuff Alma had put into me was reflected back in a mirror. I was like a wire with the current of the blues running through me; I was like a radio stone finally receiving a station; I looked at my ghostly skin and wondered at this gift and wondered if I could ever fully understand it without being black myself.

The South blossomed into rhythm-and-blues as the train rushed through the night and I was beginning to regret that I would soon debark. The attendant did something that made the train one huge pulse of sound that I imagined flared for miles around, startling animals and any of the meager towns we flashed past, lights glaring, a party they could never attend. I shoved aside tables and danced in the dining car like a madman, wishing for Verity, or Masa. I grabbed the attendant and he smiled and closed his eyes and added flourishes of his own as I spun him round in clumsy approximation of the dances the music and Alma's potion awakened in my cells.

The next morning the land had scrunched in on itself. It was all cramped and crowded together. Old forgotten towns straggled out of sight, rural and empty. They were cupped in land hilly and green and I saw whole hillsides covered with flaming pink-blossomed trees like a fairyland. I had but one thought in my mind:

Memphis.

The Cairo station was like a strange dream of a life long past, though it had been less than a week since I'd been there before. In a way I thought Verity might be waiting there for me but of course she was not and brief bitterness flashed through me.

I kidnapped the attendant from the train. I set my guitar carefully on the platform then grabbed him from the steps and held him with sheer strength while he screamed and kicked and punched out at me. When the train slid down the track he slumped to the floor.

"Why?" he whispered. "I cannot live out here. Can I?"

"We'll find out, won't we?" I said somewhat callously I suppose. "I didn't think you'd last long alone anyway."

"I was going to try to join Masa," he said reproachfully.

"Like hell," I replied. "You don't have the nerve. What's your name, anyway?" I asked, ashamed of my unkindness to this thing.

"James," he said, somewhat sullenly. "I named myself. I never told her." He paused. "She never asked, either." He laughed unexpectedly, startling me.

Perhaps there was hope for him. I picked up my guitar.

As he staggered through the empty station he kept talking. "It feels funny not to be moving. I think I'm going to fall down." He stretched out his arms. "There's so much *room.*"

I felt as if my lifelong passion for trains had been cured quite definitively. I'd been on the train ride of a lifetime, on a train from the deluxe future, which was really my past. What I'd seen was so far in the future that I couldn't imagine what it might be like there. And I didn't want to. The scents of Cairo—asphalt cooking in the summer sun, the shouts of someone hawking watermelon ("Red! Sweet! Cold!") out on the street, the hot blast of pure sunlight unfiltered by tinted windows, the babble of voices—reached down into the cool station of the future with its ghosts and advertisements for a long-dead world, and pulled me out. I emerged into the sunlight and wept, briefly, and wiped my eyes, so damned glad to be back.

"What is it?" asked James, staring around in something that approximated wonder. "What's going on?"

"Life," I said. "That's what's going on. Come on."

James started wheezing, and then couldn't seem to catch his breath. He gasped for air and I didn't know what to do. He staggered forward and sprawled on the pavement. "There's too *much,"* he said breathlessly. "Too *much!"* I reached down for his hand and saw that it danced with colors and patterns, and he clenched them as if in pain. His eyes were shut tightly.

"Come on," I said, helping him stand. "A little bit at a time, all right?"

"The sun is so *bright,"* he complained, stumbling alongside me. I remembered that on the boat we had dark glasses, though I'd done without them all my life and didn't seem to need them. The street was lined with little shops and we went into several and finally one man said, "There's a junk shop around the corner, think I saw a pair last week."

The girl in the shop found them, on a table surrounded with all manner of strange things of metal and plastic, switches and whatnot, apparently scavenged from machines that no longer worked. I was surprised when James, blinking, pulled a coin from his pocket and gave it to the girl behind the counter. She looked at it suspiciously.

"It's good," said James. "It's from Cairo." He had regained his composure. "I got it from a passenger as a tip. Carried it with me ever since. It's the only tip I ever got."

"Yes," she said, "but it's thirty years old."

We left with her still staring at it. On the sunny street, he slipped on the glasses and nodded. "These are nice," he said. "They have a music chip and an encyclopedia too. Awfully outdated, though."

I thought I felt someone watching me from that creepy big house surrounded by magnolia trees as we went down Washington Street but we hurried onward, toward the landing. I thought I passed several people I recognized, rafters who must have shaken the plague, or perhaps it was just lying in wait deep in their cells awaiting the next chemical instruction. It was revelatory to be in a living city, and myself truly alive. There seemed to be a lot less people here than there had been just a few days before, but maybe that was my imagination.

James walked next to me, exclaiming about something every minute or so. "I can't touch everyone," he said in anguish. "I'll never be able to tell them apart."

I vaguely remembered Cincinnati but it was the way a ghost might remember his past life while haunting dusty corridors and trying desperately to make himself known. I remembered fleeting images, like the Bee sweeping down upon me, like the baseball game with all those inept players, and, mostly, running, and horrible pain.

But now I was alive, fully alive, doubly alive, because of the blues! I ducked into a small café that proffered a tempting array of breads and cheeses. James had no more coins, so I sat and played for the few customers for half an hour; soon their heads were nodding and they were deep in a current of blues and reverie, and I got a big bag full of bread and cheese with apples thrown in. I asked where the rest of the people were and they were surprised that I didn't know that the plague had come to Cairo, after all these years, a strain from Cincinnati to which most were not immune, sweeping half the population down the river.

I continued down hill to the wharf; of course, the riverboat was gone. I felt a brief pang, and a somewhat deeper chagrin at having made Verity travel on without me.

But James and I boarded a raft tied up there and I surveyed with satisfaction the line and hooks, the wigwam, the firebox with dirt in it and the little tin of matches. I unwound the line and pushed off as several angry people rushed toward me from one of the riverfront cafés, yelling and shaking their fists but turning back shrugging after a few minutes of the sport. I knew that I was heading toward the blues as much as toward Verity.

James just stood around looking helpless until I told him to sit down, then he sat, like a puppet, putting his arms around his white-clad legs, the ridiculous blue-and-yellow braids on his shoulders bright and crisp in the midday sun.

"What should I do?" he asked.

I shrugged. "Rest. Enjoy the view. You're on vacation now."

"I have to have something to do," he said, with desperation in his voice all out of proportion to what was happening. "This is all so *big.*"

He looked at the increasing distance between ourselves and Cairo.

"You'll have your wish in just a minute," I said, for the current was increasing dramatically and we were approaching an eerie division of waters—the green-blue of the Ohio appeared to be running right alongside the brown Mississippi, flowing fast from the other side of Cairo Point, and then we crossed that line and were in the Mississippi River.

It was a magnificent moment.

Without planning on it in the least, I tore off my clothes, grabbed the thick rope used to tie up the raft, and dove into the river.

The water was full of grit and when I opened my eyes I couldn't see my hand. I swept to the surface and whooped for pure joy, throwing my hair back and sluicing water from my face with my free hand. I let the rope pull me along for a couple hundred yards, cutting through the water that fed the blues. The fact that James was standing on the raft scream-ing bloody murder only added to the fun. But the current was picking up and I pulled myself in, hand over hand. "You ought to try it," I told him, as I climbed dripping and naked onto the raft.

"You scared me," he said reproachfully. "I didn't know what to do. I thought you were—" He closed his eyes for a minute. "—drowning."

"Look ahead," I said. "We just might drown."

And then we were into some rapids, which we probably could have avoided had I not indulged in my little prank. Water swept across the deck as we tilted crazily and scraped along some rocks. I grabbed a pole and pushed and amazingly so did James, getting the idea quick enough, and we ran from side to side bouncing the raft off rocks until a smooth, powerful swirl caught us and shot us out into the calm river below. On the other side of the narrow island we'd just passed I saw that the river dropped gradually.

I studied this new place, hoping that I, like the plaguers, was now im-mune to skin cancer, because the hot sun felt so good on my bare, pale skin. I felt like making some music. I looked around. "Where's the gui-tar?" I asked.

A quick search of the raft revealed that it was gone, probably swept off somewhere in the rapids. "Why didn't you watch it?" I yelled at James.

He just hung his head in an irritating way.

I rummaged around and found some binoculars, but couldn't see it anywhere. The river was full of flotsam but I thought I'd recognize the guitar. I considered going back, for an instant, jumping off, walking up-river, and trying to spot it, but that was silly. It might be anywhere. There was no way to find it.

"What are you doing?" I asked. James had removed his jacket and shirt and had his arm stuck in the water to his elbow.

"Sampling," he said.

He sampled for about thirty seconds and stood up. "Can you get around to the other side of that big rock?" he asked, pointing to a gray boulder ahead just off the shore.

"What for?"

"Your guitar should be there."

"Right."

I think he looked wounded. "I am good for something, you know."

"Can't hurt," I said.

It was actually remarkably easy to catch a swirl of current with the oar. We might have gone there on our own.

The guitar had. The rock was actually about thirty feet long, and hooked around at the end like the tail of a lizard. Alma's guitar bobbed there in the quiet pool formed by the curve of the rock.

"How did you do that?" I asked.

I swear he looked smug. "I simply analyzed the currents and plugged them into a fractal analysis program. There was really a huge chance that it wouldn't be here, but, averaging everything together including the factors that it was impossible for me to know, this was the most likely place. I couldn't predict much further than that, but . . . well, it worked, didn't it?" He had a pleading look in his eyes. I wondered how I could have thought them blank on the train. But maybe they had been. Maybe he was just a fast learner.

"Thank you, James," I said. We poled close to the rock. Some sticks and leaves were trapped in the still water with the guitar. I lifted it out and as I examined it he pushed us around the rock and we were off again. As we swirled down the river I dried the guitar reverently with my abandoned clothes. There were no nicks. It was in tune. I sighed. It was an evil thing, made for the devil's music. It was nan, something created by humans that had doubled back and enslaved its makers. It had certainly enslaved me.

I smiled and hugged it.

I settled back on the raft, leaning against a box filled with whatnot the previous owners must have scavenged from the river, sitting on a folded blanket on the east side of the wigwam, in the shade.

The guitar insisted on a slow, steady rhythm. The disconsolate tune came from somewhere deep inside me:

Out by the levee
Early in the morn
I lost my honey babe
Where the Cairo bridge come down

I was so tickled to have the guitar back. I just played and watched as we were swept along.

This was a different river. I could see it right away. Soon the ruined bridges of Cairo were far behind us. I really have no idea how fast we were going but we were moving. The Mississippi did not stick to its banks like the Ohio; it spread out wherever it could take its leave, and so the shore was not a single demarcation but often a zone where land and water mingled.

The low land had no defense against the water. On the eastern side were blue, undulating hills, not very high. It was a living, breathing river, constantly on the lookout for more ways to enlarge its boundaries, taking a swipe at this bank over here, overrunning an island there.

James could not sit still; he was constantly asking what he could do to help. He'd finally removed his shirt and his chest was sculptured like one of those old plastic dolls we found hundreds of in a store one time. I wondered if he had bones and blood inside, he looked so perfect. But he did eat and I saw him pee off the side before too long, so . . . So at least there's that, I told myself, unable to infer more.

Soon I was having the time of my life, rushing to and fro, taking in the sights, feeling so alive, after being closed in the train. I showed James how to bait the hook with some jerky that was on the raft; didn't know what it would bring but it was all that we had that would stick on. I told him to toss it in and leave it. I'd had a lovely light fly-fishing rod at Shaker Hill and a fine set of flies I'd tied myself. Of course we'd admired any number of complicated rigs in the forbidden stores, because at some time in the past it had been easy to drive up north to the vast, sparkling lakes described by Russ, and the Big Lake, which was more like an ocean where one could not see the other side. But this was just a springy green pole, half-inch in diameter, a nylon line tied through a hole someone had pierced in the end, to keep it from slipping off, some weights, and a rusty hook. The *Queen* had all kinds of gear to choose from and we'd tried to distribute them at first. But they'd gone into the drink, because the Norleans Plague dictated this sort of primitive fishing rod. At least, so we surmised.

It didn't matter, because after about five minutes James whooped and the pole bent. By the time he pulled the fish in, he was panting; it took him about ten minutes. It was a catfish, ten pounds at least, flopping all over the raft, and I pulled it to the middle so it would not get away. He stared at it, clearly puzzled, and I dispatched it by hitting it on the head several times with a heavy pot I found among the cooking gear. James gasped when I did this and stepped back and stared at me.

"You had beef on the train," I reminded him. "Someone had to kill those cows. Um . . . I guess . . ." But no. There were no cows on the train and it never stopped.

"That was grown," he said flatly. "It was grown in the shapes that we told it to grow in."

And then he told me how that worked. In great detail. And how his metapheromonal processors worked. I never did really understand how he knew where the guitar was. This took up most of the afternoon.

I didn't have a whole lot to give him in return. I showed him how to gut the catfish. I showed him how to build a fire. He knew how to cook the thing, once all those particulars were taken care of.

We ate in the light of a gorgeous sunset, and decided to drift down the river for the night.

Nineteen

○○○○○○○○○○○○○○○○○

Mississippi Blues

I wasn't sure how far it was to Memphis but I figured that it would take a few days. I also hoped we would overtake the riverboat at some point, but that was more chancy. They had power, and possibly a few days' head start. I longed to see Verity, yet was willing to keep that yearning in abeyance. Somehow her presence shut down the world for me, narrowed it in to one point. The wideness of everything without her was strange, even a bit scary, but most of all exhilarating.

And Memphis *was* the blues.

It was so much quieter on the river without that blasted paddlewheel churning away. There was a bleakness in this wilderness through which we drifted; or perhaps it wasn't bleakness but just a feeling of the place being unpopulated and difficult to traverse.

Heavy forest lined the shores we drifted past. I say shores because of the innumerable coves and islands, because of the sheer irregularity of the river. Headlong we floated, with little control, sometimes fast and sometimes slow. From time to time we saw another raft in the distance and hailed each other, but that was it. No boats, no barges, nothing. Well, that's not entirely true. Before dawn the churn of a steam engine woke us and its wake almost capsized us. In the heavy mist, as it slid past us, heading upriver, a sheath of rust-streaked black metal lumpy with rivets, I thought I saw a faded RN on the side, for Rural Network, I presumed. But that was all.

I was awake then, and sat waiting for the mist to burn off. The ephemeral blues and grays of the river gave way to gold-shot green along the banks. The air was fresh with only a hint of the heat the coming day would bring. We were full into summer now.

I relished the wilderness. I saw deer leaping along the bank of an island and figured that the land harbored any number of edible critters. But the raft held no rifle, which made me feel a bit helpless and kept us dependent on fish. They were quite plentiful, though—just throw in the hook and find one on it when one thought to check. James was thus occupied at the back of the raft just now, crouched and staring into the muddy water as if he might actually be able to see the fish. The raft made a kind of swishing, burbling sound now and again as it was slapped by a wavelet or rose a bit and fell over a patch of current-braided water. I stood and watched in fascination and fear as we passed a kind of boiling place in the water where the surface was disturbed from below in a circular, upchurning pattern, wondering what caused it. Then it was gone, but we were to pass more of them as the day went on.

We got caught in a large whirlpool shortly before noon. At first it was amusing—we were swept round in a long, slow circle about fifty yards in diameter. James squatted on the side of the boat and stared at the water, apparently deep in thought, if that was possible. Some long sticks, a board, and an old shoe kept pace with us, at exactly the same distance from us.

"It's like us," he said, about the third time around. I was getting a little bit edgy at that point. How would we break free?

"What are you talking about?"

"It's like everything. How everything came about. We're a part of the pattern here, like those sticks. We're not the energy itself. We're just held in this position by these forces. That's how everything came about. The universe. Matter. Time. Evolution. Consciousness."

He was certainly hitting on all the big ones. "Yeah," I said. "But how do we get out?"

"It doesn't matter," he said. "Something else will come into the pattern."

"It matters to *us*," I said. "Here. I'll paddle while you steer."

After about ten minutes he hit on the idea of snagging the board and holding it in front of us to slow us down. While he broke the water I hung on the sweep and we gradually moved out of the whirl and spurled out into the main current. I was exhausted. He looked back on the whirlpool as if he would miss it.

"That was pretty interesting, James," I said, as I lay panting on the raft. "How did you think that up?"

"I could tell you eventually," he said, "but we'd have to start from scratch."

"What do you mean, from scratch?"

"Well, there are these things called amino acids."

"Oh," I said. "Well, go on. It's not like we have anything else to do." But James had a kind of stiff, droning voice which began to blend with the mechanical keening of the cicadas. It dropped into the background as I watched the shore roll past.

Despite all this beauty a strange darkness was growing in my being, a mournfulness, a dread I could not shake. I tried to think what it might come from.

Beyond the wild shore I could see glimpses now and then of a high green wall. The levee. Must be broken in places for sure, after the quake. But it made a kind of double barrier. The levee—the thought of it troubled me. What a lot of work it must have been to pile up all that dirt! As an hour passed, and another, and it became more imposing, I began to think of how long the river might be, and to wonder if the levee ran down both sides complete to the sea. Between the levees I was helpless, at the mercy of the river, a *prisoner* of the river. . . .

Prisoner.

With that word my mind began to dance with horrific images.

I was hallucinating in the broad daylight. I think that I retched over the side of the raft but I'm not certain. Because my mind and my body were not my own. They were possessed by the ghosts of the bluesmen and blueswomen who had once roamed this part of the country.

I felt James's hands on my shoulder and his face swam into view. "Are you all right? What's wrong? What can I do?"

"Nothing," I gasped. "Nothing." And all I could do was sing while the images flashed through me, more than a memory, flowing from my own brain's rearrangements of chemicals now that the blues had seeped deeply into me and blossomed into a reality too intense to avoid, too awful to bear. My only release was to sing.

And so I sang, that long day, while the raft shot through a jungle-bound chute between two islands.

> Long-chain Charlie
> He's got me in his claw

I was starving. No, I was *being* starved. No point in feeding me much. I was convict labor, leased from the State of Mississippi in 1876 by one Mr. Hamilton for $1.10 a month. Then he charged the railroads $9 a month for my labor, with barely any food and no medical care provided. When I died, I would be tossed in a shallow grave and replaced.

I was walking down the road one fine spring day when Sheriff Connally come along. Arrest me. When I ask what I'd done he said I'd broke the law and had to pay. Seems I'd stole a pig from Mr. Tam. When I told him I'd done no such thing he said he had witnesses and that the judge would hear the case. That was a joke but the joke was on me. The judge didn't hear nothin I said and fined me extra for disagreein. If I could of run then I would of because I seed which way the wind was a-blowin. But Long-chain Cholly clapped me in his grip, give me the round stripes to wear, tell me to build this levee. Wheelbarrow after wheelbarrow. More dirt. More dirt. More dirt. More dirt.

Dey fetch us up before daylight and fling us back on the ground after dark. Two men drop dead yestidday and dey roll em out da way and bury em in da night. Got guns and dogs on us all through the hot sun day. A man right next to me shot dead for sassin the trusty. Give me nothing to eat. Got a rash all over from sleepin on de groun. I tell shotgun I need more to eat. Now I ache in a dozen places and burn in a dozen other. Big leather strap with holes in it he keep at his side just to beat people with. Name of Mollie. "What you say?" It go on long past forever, till I stagger bleedin an screamin to pick up the filthy rags they call clothes then lay moanin in the cool dirt for a long time before I even try to move.

I shook James's hand from my shoulder and gasped for a minute after that, but Alma's blues didn't give me much time to rest.

Then I was an sick old man working away the last life in me. I wrote a letter to my old master: I werked for you for fifty yeers an now I need ten doller fo the doctor for a oprashun. Cud you pleas help yur old Eliza. But there was never an answer and

> You shoulda been on the river, nineteen and nine,
> Number one was runnin, number two was flyin,
> Number three was hollerin, number four was cryin,
> Number five was draggin, and the pull-do's dyin.
> Why don't you wake up, dead man, help me drive my row?
> My row is so grassy, I can't hardly go.
> They have murdered my partner, plan on killin me.
> If I get my chance, buddy, I'm gonna try to run free.

I was on the number-two hoe squad, there on that Texas prison farm, and my whole body burned with the way I had to move, and keep moving, without a rest, no matter how my muscles and lungs cried out. James told me that I was writhing around naked, begging for mercy, and that he could not wake me from this nightmare though he tried.

COAHOMA COUNTY, that was the place, the bad place, hell on earth, with the long roads heading nowhere down the infinite rows of cotton. I was born in one of them little shacks you see over there and grew up rough as my daddy before me. My momma, she had to work hard too, and I was out there when I was four doing what I could to help. I learned to gamble young and when I was twelve I won enough money to buy my own guitar at the five-and-dime. One day I's sent to take a package to the foreman. His daughter Miss Ellie May meet me at the side door, take the package, close the door, that's all. Next thing I hear her daddy's accusin me of rape and I'm off and runnin'. Beat the hounds and the mob laying for me. Saw a man soaked with gasoline last year, hoisted up under his arms and burned near an hour. Course they cut off his fingers and ears for souvenirs first fore he was damaged by the fire. Everyone in the country came round and drank lemonade and watched and said they wished they could kill him ten times over he was that bad. With that in the back of my mind I run like a rabbit and don't stop till I hit Texas.

Fall in with a blind man who plays for pennies on the street holdin out a tin cup. All he could do to make a livin but he damned good at it. Took to carryin him round where he want to go, he tell me and we get there somehow and I learn all the jook joints for fifty miles and learn how he play too, with a broken filed bottleneck to run up an down coaxin sweet or mournful deep-down blue curves of sound from the strings. His songs mostly bout pickin cotton and muleskinners and bein in prison and bein lonesome and how mean the wimmens treat him. Don know about that last, they seems to fawn all over him. In a jook joint one night we're rollin the dice and the man they call Mouse cuse me of cheatin. I know what's comin and draw faster. His shot goes wild but mine flies true and he lays bleedin and dyin. His friends eye me mad and afraid. I run out of there leavin behind a price on my head and a bad-looking picture of me pasted round two counties; I see it in the train station an rip it down. Last time I see the blind man. But I gots him in my fingers now.

I ride the train back up home and it's been a few years and the ruckus has died down I think.

I must have lived fifty of these histories. They assumed an awful sameness. Alma's blues was filled with statistics; after all, she was a scholar too.

Then it was Bessie Smith in the big city, and a voice so big that it could fill a concert hall. Try and get a handle on *that*. Her songs were so dreadfully and unvaryingly mournful, like dirges, that before long I was ready to jump in the river and drown, too. There were happy blues too, running like a shining thread through the darkness. But they were mostly awful sad.

I sang until my voice was just a raw whisper. I cried the blues from the pit where I was buried, with all the others, from that endless row where the shooter called out "ten minutes" so I could step out of line because the guy next to me was in a bad mood and I had to try and kill him before he killed me. I sang the happy blues of a gentle country sharecropper who lived and died on the Delta, who worked hard and taught his children how to read and write and told them to get out of there and not look back, head on up to Chicago.

I finally came to late in the afternoon, with "Midnight Special" falling from my lips. I'd lived a hundred lives as a slave, then as a convict laborer, building the plantations, the railroads, the levees of the South, denied my rights as a human, spat upon, treated like dirt, a member of the "inferior race." I'd been raped by white men and our children—his own children!—sold for slaves.

I sobbed, incredulous at the history of this country. It was a bad joke. It was a tragic joke. The laws were not for me. The land was not for me. The riches or even what meager profit I might make was not for me. Education was not for me. I was to labor and thank them for the opportunity and be quiet and die before I was a burden.

I couldn't believe it. It was unspeakable.

If that country was gone—good riddance! Land of the free! Home of the brave! More like home of the slaves, land of the cowards who mobbed together to kill innocent men just because their skin was black. Then congratulated one another on doing "justice."

I was cold. Shivering, my teeth clacking, despite the blanket James had thrown over me. I felt my body all over, amazed to find it unbroken. I felt my face, my nose—whole and straight. No scars from knives or whips. Dazed, I looked around, gradually remembered who I was and where I was and why, and that that time I'd dreamed was long past, long, long past. James was napping. It was dusk. I thought then of *Huckleberry Finn*. It had just been a story for me back there at Shaker Hill. I'd read the Constitution, the Declaration of Independence. The jury of peers, to which John said, "A jury of my peers would be twelve Shakers with black beards and overalls, then."

I poked at the coals of the fire and it blazed up, crackling part of a fish James must have put on hours ago. I pulled it off the fire and it burned my fingers; I let it cool on the raft and then ate it, crunching the thin burned bones between my teeth as if I could chew up that burnt history I'd drunk, chew it up and change it with anger, even though it was long past. James had carefully stacked a pile of sticks snagged from the river on one corner of the raft. I wondered if they were too wet to burn. They weren't. I settled down to watch the wavering flames, hoping that they would not somehow trigger the blues because I was so very, very tired. I did not deserve to have the blues, I realized. Though bad things had happened to me, I had never been mistreated. I had grown up loved, with an abundance of food, with the underpinnings of religion; fake as it turned out to be, it sustained us for so long.

I longed for the information that I knew the air was full of: radio waves. We were coming closer to Memphis, and STAX. I had no idea whether or not anything was there besides a radio tower. Memphis could be drowned; it could be deserted. It could be terribly dangerous.

It could be heaven on earth.

Blues Boy had turned to B.B. in Memphis. Beale Street jumped with the blues. The devil's music found fertile ground and flourished there.

Esu the Trickster was still alive. I could tell. He was inside me now, transforming me from the inside out.

I fell asleep to dreams, dreams that were simply dreams and nothing more, a dream of walking into a dark Chicago bar one rainy Saturday afternoon. Four people were sitting at the bar, and Sunnyland Slim and a side man were blasting the place out, Sunnyland at a tall, square piano, the other man playing bass. I got cigarettes from a machine and ordered a beer. I lit a cigarette and sat at a scarred table. Sunnyland played the blues for the sake of the blues, because he couldn't do anything else, and the wide floorboards vibrated with them as I smoked the pack down and drank beers which I did not count and wondered why the place was empty.

Well, maybe it wasn't a dream.

I woke to James's shout and to the vast wheel rending the raft and me flying through the air and plunging deep into the cold and the shocked pain in my head as I breathed water, this was all at once for me, then only darkness.

8

◇◇◇

Bright Mississippi

Twenty

◯◯◯◯◯◯◯◯◯◯◯◯◯◯◯◯◯◯

Doppelgänger Blues

As the *American Queen* careened away from the wharf, pulled by the current, Verity finally pushed through the mob and reached the texas. She flung open the pilothouse door and stopped in astonishment. A man about as tall as herself, dressed in a finely cut black formal suit with a gold chain hanging from his vest pocket, stood at the wheel with a look of anticipation on his face.

"Who are you?"

The man turned, and, in the glow of the chart screen, Verity recognized him, except this one looked younger than those in the Blue Café. Fierce eyebrows overshadowed even fiercer eyes. His reddish hair, wild and curly, was streaked dramatically with gray, and she could not see his mouth for a huge mustache.

"Mark Twain, at your service. We have departed, then? An emergency situation, it seems." He frowned, then accurately touched the start button, and the boat rumbled to life as the paddlewheel began to churn, slowly at first, then more rapidly as they continued into the confluence through silvery sheets of rain.

"I don't care who you are," said Verity. "Get out of my way. This is my boat."

"Begging your pardon, Captain, ma'am, but—"

"I *mean* it!" she yelled.

He replied, "Then you must be slightly insane. But, as you wish." He nodded, stepped back, and offered her the wheel.

The current immediately seized the boat. The *Queen* had never felt so large and, at the same time, so fragile. She struggled with the wheel; she could not see where she was going; her arms ached with effort. When lightning flashed she saw a wilderness of frothing white water filled with debris and whirlpools.

"Excuse me, please," said the Mark Twain, "but I *must!*"

He pushed her away and grabbed the wheel. He turned it so sharply that everything not nailed down slid to the floor in a loud crash. Lightning flashed once more and Verity saw, directly in front of the boat, the island George had pointed out earlier.

Waves pounded a dark shore. Looming trees reached outward as if to seize the *Queen* with vigorously shaking limbs that stretched yearningly over the waves. She was astounded that they were so close; the island had looked such a long way off when she had seen it from the roof of Magnolia Manor.

Twain pushed the large lever that gave more power to the paddle-wheel as they veered sideways. The *Queen* leaped forward as the tree began to slowly topple forward. Verity heard a loud, chilling crunch. She ran out the door onto the deck and saw that the tree had indeed caught on the railing of the top deck. The railing ripped from the deck, and the wind sent splinters of wood flying.

She went back inside and closed the door, soaked.

Twain kept his steady eyes on the river, seemingly unruffled. He hummed and chewed on his cigar.

For the next fifteen minutes they rode out the storm until it subsided with low mutters of thunder. The rain turned sweet and slow and warm. After another ten minutes of cautious travel Twain said, "We'll anchor here," and she said, "Fine."

Verity busied herself with the controls to let down the anchor, thinking how lucky it was that Mark Twain, or whoever he was, had come on board. The clouds moved rapidly, revealing the moon.

Then a girl stood in the doorway, illuminated by the moonlight. Verity recognized her as the girl who had wandered out of the train station.

Her plaid cotton dress was plastered to her thin body, and dripped, darkening the floor. Beneath one arm was firmly anchored a wooden box. She pointed imperiously at Mark Twain.

"You, sir, are an impostor!" Her voice throbbed with fury. She whirled and said to Verity, her brown eyes full of deep rage, "He is! I tell you, he is!"

She slammed her box—a cigar box, Verity noted—down on the table and turned back to Twain, her hands on her hips. She stood straight as a young maple; Verity thought of a good sturdy fencepost, rooted in the ground. Her face twitched and her nostrils were pinched. "You!" she fairly spat. "Stealing another writer's name! Writing that wretched, laughable stuff! Thinking you were so funny when you were only pathetic!"

"How was I to know that I'd become famous?" rejoined Twain, astonishing Verity. "Way out there on the West Coast." He straightened, and jerked on the bottom of his vest with both hands. "How was I to know?"

"You were an idiot," the girl agreed. "Truly. And you're still an imposter, you're *always* and *forever* an impostor. *I* am Samuel Clemens. Afraid of who you really were. That's what I think. Clemens! A fine name! Connotations of mercy, of kindness! When did you ever show mercy? You laughed at the Indians, laughed at the Hawaiians, laughed at anyone poor and not white—"

"Not *so!*" hollered Twain, his face growing red. "You wretched pipsqueak! Who do you think you are, you little rat of a girl!" He stepped forward and grabbed her by her shoulders. Verity moved to help but the girl flashed her a look of scorn and twisted free with an easy shake of her shoulders.

"I laughed at *everyone,* I'll have you know," he said. "Rich Europeans, stuffy old religious ladies, the lot of them, yes. And myself most of all."

"And yourself most of all," said the girl more quietly.

Verity could see that her lips were blue; waves of violent shivers shook her. "Let me tell you," she began, but then Twain opened the box of cigars and reached inside.

"Mine!" the girl yelled, and leaped forward, smashing the lid on Twain's hand with her fist. The thin wood cracked. Twain pulled his hand free and looked at the bleeding scrape in amazement. "Why, you little—" Then he began to laugh. "Have it your way, my dear," he said. He turned and walked down the stairs.

Tears stood in the girl's eyes, but Verity could tell that they were tears of anger. "He's an *asshole,*" she whispered through trembling lips. "To think—"

"Quiet," said Verity, and held her close to still her trembling.

"They were after me," she said, her voice muffled by Verity's clothing. "I stole the very best cigars." Verity felt her laugh, a single brief shake. She felt the girl's knobby spine, thought that it was possible she could span her small waist with her hands. She knelt and looked into the girl's face.

It was a plain face. Her skin was the color of coffee with rich cream in it. Her hair was light brown streaked with gold and stood out around her face in kinky splendor. Her nose was straight and imperious. She looked almost homely, but something in the way her face was put together—the slightly slanted set of her eyes? her high cheekbones?—saved her from that. She stared at Verity and blinked.

"What's your name?" asked Verity.

"I told you! Samuel—"

"Your real name," she said as gently as possible, and looked long into the girl's eyes. Something stubborn melted.

"Mattie," she said. "My name's Mattie." She swayed slightly.

"Well, Mattie," she said, "how about a hot bath?"

She led Mattie to the doorway, then the girl broke loose, ran back, and grabbed the box of cigars.

"I hope you don't actually smoke them," said Verity, as they descended the stairs.

"I most certainly do," said Mattie. "I hope that son of a bitch didn't crush any."

Verity woke to a sensation of movement and loss. She jumped out of bed—yes, they were under way! Without even her say-so! Who did this Twain person think he was, anyway? She dressed in a fury, which helped push back the memory of Blaze, his face pressed to the train window. Where would he be now? Denver? Did the train go to Denver? Russ had been there. Denver would have been interesting. Perhaps . . .

A bluebird lit on her open windowsill and just that patch was enough. She zipped her jeans with difficulty—she needed to get some larger clothes—tied her shoes, and marched onto the deck, invigorated. They had passed Cairo! This was the Mississippi River!

And the shore, she noted as she climbed the stairs to the pilothouse, was so distant that the trees were a green and brown blur. The land was wild and flat and she thought, as she went higher, that she saw marshes shimmer to the west.

Leaning against the railing of the hurricane deck, she looked up and down the river. There were possibly twenty rafts in sight. Had any rafters perished in the Cairo melee? Or perhaps a lot of them had gone on ahead in the night. . . .

Lil had been right. Cairo had been a disaster.

Her heart heavy, she walked in the door to the pilothouse, in no mood for the Twains.

Mark Twain stood at the wheel, puffing on a cigar, wearing the same river pilot's suit she had seen the Twains wearing in the restaurant. An ash fell onto his lapel and he brushed it away with a scowl. At any rate the dark smudge vanished rather quickly. "You have no idea how many microbes and diseases cloth harbors," he growled.

"You have no idea," Mattie mimicked. She stood on an upended wooden box, both hands gripping the brass rail below the front window. "You *really* have no idea—about anything. I can't *believe* how primitive you are. You have the mind of an amusement-park attraction."

"You are disturbing my concentration, brat," returned Twain. "I am normally kind to children. I love all children as I love my own children. But you are not a normal child."

Mattie stared ahead. "Assuredly, I am not. I advise you to bear port around that island—"

"Keep out of this. This is a man's work."

"Actually," said Verity, "it is *my* work. Please step aside."

"This is not the correct time for a cub to take the wheel," said Twain. The river *did* seem to be running a bit more swiftly now, but Verity was irritated. "Move, I said. I *command* you to move."

Twain and Mattie each snorted, with an identical snort, identically timed. Twain stepped back, his face amused. "Be my guest."

Verity stepped up to the wheel and touched the map.

THE MISSISSIPPI SEGMENTS OF THESE MAPS HAVE NOT BEEN UPDATED SINCE 2050.

"Hmm," said Verity, wondering if that was the last time information from downriver got into Cincinnati. "Well . . ."

"*Watch out!*" Twain and Mattie yelled in tandem, and Mattie grabbed the wheel and wrenched it to the right. Verity heard the ominous scrape of a snag along the side of the boat.

"As I said," Twain remarked, and stepped forward, but Mattie shoved her box over in front of the wheel, jumped onto it, and grabbed two of the polished spokes. Twain merely lifted her up beneath her arms and set her on the floor after prying her hands loose.

"You!" Mattie said, eyes blazing, fists clenched. "We'll see about this!" She marched out of the cabin.

Twain chuckled and chewed his cigar. "Spirited imp, isn't she?"

Jack came in the door and crossed his arms. "Well, well. That's a relief."

"What's a relief?" asked Verity.

"We've got a real pilot at last," said Jack.

Verity demanded, "What do you mean by *that?*"

"Just what I said. He may be limited, but one thing he does have is lots of piloting reflexes." Jack smiled.

Twain turned, scowling. "What do you mean, 'limited'? You'd best get below. Back to your work."

"Yes sir," said Jack. "Come on, Verity."

She stood hesitant.

"It's all right," said Jack softly. He took her arm and led her outside. "Breakfast?"

"Oh, I guess," she said.

"You have to eat," said Lil, showing up beside her and patting Verity's stomach.

"You are both making me very cross," she said.

"I'm not sure if we're entirely to blame," said Lil. "Peabody was looking for Blaze. He seems rather downhearted."

"I hope Blaze is having a grand time," said Verity, with a savage twist that surprised her.

Twenty-one

○○○○○○○○○○○○○○○○

New Mind Blues

Mattie watched Mark Twain from a chair in the pilothouse as she took languid puffs from her cigar. They no longer made her dizzy; instead, they sharpened her thoughts. She had guarded them jealously at first, but this morning that nice Peabody fellow had showed her how the boat could replicate them, after Twain threw a fit and called her a greedy pig. Well, he had been more clever and elegant than that. But that's what he had meant.

Twain was bigger than she, so he prevailed when it came to deciding who would do the piloting. For now. She kept a steady eye on him but had to admit that he was doing an adequate job. Twain's red hair, only lightly streaked with gray, gleamed in the sunlight flooding through the windows. He was in high spirits, especially since she had agreed to share her cigars with him. Well, now she could afford to be generous.

The river had changed since "he"—the Mark Twain inside *her*—had been here. She could see the difference, superimposed on his memories. Of course, all those memories were just taken from books of his. So they weren't that precise anyway. But some of the little towns were far inland, others had been swallowed by the river. Apparently there had been an earthquake even worse than the one in 1812, when Reelfoot Lake had been formed. The Mississippi River had run backward for several hours way back then, and the first steamboat to try to go to Cincinnati and return to New Orleans had the bad luck to try the maiden journey at just that time. They had succeeded, though, despite the terrifying conditions.

Livy. Livy and the children and the great debt they had to pay off. Sunlight coaxed the trees on the far shore to unimaginable greenness. Beyond that rose the levee. Mattie took another puff of the cigar and the bluish bluffs ahead and the smell of the water and the view from the pilothouse washed the girl Mattie away for a few seconds.

He'd been such a damned fool to keep pouring money into that Paige Typesetting Machine. Now he was up against it—years of grueling lecture tours; Livy, his conscience, quite rightly would not let him get out of his debts so easily with a simple bankruptcy. No, everyone had to be paid back. A great void opened within him. Out of it roared bitter words. He closed his eyes and thought about how best to arrange them. He took another puff of his cigar.

Suddenly she choked and tossed the cigar in the ashcan.

Suddenly she was Mattie.

But she knew that she was also Twain. And when she was Twain, she realized, usually, that she was Mattie. That last time, though . . . Twain seemed more intense. It all came from books and critical papers—in fact, her Twain was the proud scholarly creation of Missouri State University, copyright 2053, a message that had flashed swiftly through her mind at one point on the train. But it was a Twain intensely refined by research, a Twain who had obviously lived uncountable times within students and professors, who had added all that *they* knew, a Twain created to be sharp and whole and complete, all-encompassing, overwhelming and powerful, to react to situations, to think. But she could not help but know the truth, being in this body. She was still Mattie. Really she was.

She glanced up at the Mark Twain competently piloting the boat. His entire body was a model of Twain's. He didn't seem to have any other identity. She didn't know if he'd had a childhood or if he had somehow been created to be this particular age. In Elysia, they'd known that things like this were going on elsewhere. That's why most of them kept to Elysia.

They were ignorant, she now realized. Fear had kept them in the dark. Mattie could not believe her own good fortune. There was a price to pay—she had to suffer Twain. He was a pain in the ass—but he was also fascinating. Through him she had access to all kinds of information. History, and how it felt to go through all the things he'd been through. Piloting expertise, which was very real, since it didn't depend on just him. It might have been assembled from a real, living pilot. Certainly the river was alive with meaning for her. And, even more remarkable, at least in her eyes, she was beginning to realize that he'd been round the world several times. Several times! She'd barely dreamed of leaving Elysia, and then it was always on the train, with the destination a great blank. She'd barely known anything of the world. Of course the world was different now than it had been for Twain.

But he seemed to have had some sort of . . . prescience, now that was a word that came straight out of his head . . . that things were on a downhill slide. A dark and bitter vision that seemed true, but was sometimes hard to bear. Joy had completely fled his life, and he realized what a lot of people in Elysia still had not realized—there was no God. He had pretty much preached No-God for the last decade of his life, howling with the truth, trying to get the world to face the facts.

She knew that the Twain next to her was younger, and not as dark, as the latter-day Twain, who emerged after debt and death and heartbreak. This Twain was at the height of his bloom and of his happiness.

"But I'm dark," she said aloud. "I'm the dark side of Twain."

"Your skin is dark," he agreed, glancing at her. "But you're no Twain."

"We are both Twain, the two of us, and that's the problem," she said. "It's death that divided us—death and pain and guilt. I read Darwin. I began to see too clearly what you always suspected. And then while I was touring the world to pay off the debts you made, Susy was blinded by meningitis and died alone and insane, while just a young woman. It took over a week. No one could reach us in time. We didn't even know how horribly she was suffering." Mattie gasped a few times at the pain of Twain's grief.

"Don't you *ever* say *anything* so *foolish* again!" said Twain, turning a deeply horrified face toward her. "Why, it's like walking on someone's *grave*. My little Susy—the smartest, the liveliest—why, I wouldn't leave her alone like that, to die—that's the worst blasphemy—"

Mattie kept talking as if she hadn't heard him. "Though you're at his piloting age, when he was still Sam Clemens, you seem to have knowledge from his married life. I suppose they made you into this historical and humorous mishmash for the pleasure of sentimental spectators who preferred to ignore the *real* Twain, the *dark* Twain—"

"What *is* all that blather about?" he demanded, staring at her with stern, intense eyes.

"Nothing," she said. "Enjoy yourself. I can at least try to do so. My parents brought me up to be sensible."

Yes, there was every reason for her to rejoice. Here was more water than they dreamed of, back in Elysia. Here, they didn't have to jealously hoard everything—they could make new stuff just as good as the old stuff. Why were they all hiding, out there in the dry dusty wasteland? She had been released to a land of milk and honey as surely as if she had died and gone to heaven. As far as they were concerned, she had died. Maybe that was what death was really like. Just like Aunt Evvie always said. You left your body behind, but your spirit went to heaven.

She pinched herself. So far, her body, if not her mind, was intact.

But with the thoughts of death and heaven anger swept through her, causing her to open her mouth and shout, " 'I bring you the stately matron named Christendom, returning bedraggled, besmirched, and dishonored from pirate-raids in Kiao-chow, Manchuria, South Africa, and the Philippines, with her soul full of meanness, her pocket full of boodle, and her mouth full of pious hypocrisies. Give her soap and a towel, but *hide the looking-glass.*' " *A Pen Warmed Up in Hell,* noted something inside her, along with some numbers, for an instant.

Twain sighed. "What's gotten into you now? I'm telling you, life is tremendously grand, there isn't a drawback to it. Times like these I could almost believe in a God—a beneficent God, that is. Not the God who goes round punishing and torturing for no good reason. Not the God who set us up to fail, that intolerable blaggart. But you wouldn't believe that grand house I have in Hartford, girlie, fit for a king, and no end of friends and neighbors—all *artists,* I'll have you know, the cream of the crop, like Harriet Beecher Stowe and Charles Warner—to entertain and to be entertained by—simply no *end.* It's absolutely topnotch. Why, we're so booked to the hilt with parties and entertainments that Livy and the girls are hard-pressed to keep up, and I have to go away for several months of each year just to get any work done."

" 'What an ass you are!' " Mattie replied. " 'Are you so unobservant as not to have found out that sanity and happiness are an impossible combination? No sane man can be happy, for to him life is real, and he sees what a fearful thing it is.' "

"I assure you, it's real to me," said Twain, spinning the wheel. "Though I can't claim much on the sanity issue. It's so real and perfect I'm beginning to believe in angels and all manner of pious nonsense. Why, if God Almighty came along and told me that Livy was sent straight from heaven I might believe the Great Mountebank himself and take out a lifetime subscription."

"I'm just trying to tell you that you'd do better to work than spend all your money on ice sculptures," said Mattie sourly, limp and suddenly exhausted. "You'll soon be singing a different tune." They tickled the back of her mind, these words, and sometimes pictures came with them and then she was him, full-blown, this puffing fool. She felt pretty sick then, but figured it must be the cigars. She did hate how things could change from good to bad in the wink of an eye. But there—it passed quickly.

"Looks like there's a sandbar ahead," she offered. "Those ripples—"

"Don't worry, whippersnapper," Twain said. "Already accounted for."

"If only we could read life as clearly as we can read the river. It looks so smooth, so beautiful. It's marvelously accommodating, taking us along for a ride. But underneath—"

"Your cheap philosophizing needs a bit of polish," remarked Twain. "Come back when you're older than twelve and we might have a nice chew over the matter."

Mattie sighed, suddenly more sorry for than irritated with the man. "I've had too damned many years. That's the problem." Waves of deep sadness washed through her. She struggled to keep from bursting into tears. Everyone gone! Everything changed! Hannibal full of old men and what's more those misshapen old men were his childhood friends! The very shape of the river had changed. And the life itself was gone. Railroads had taken it. After the time out West, where he learned to entertain, to *write;* he eventually began to earn money, good money. Yes, he'd had wealth, a family on which to lavish it, health and happiness, fame and solvency, for a few short years.

But that was all gone now. Vanished behind the churning paddlewheel. Susy, Livy, Jean, dead. And not dead to rise again. Even Livy— pious, accepting Livy—had lost her faith once he got hold of her. He'd reasoned it out of her. The century had turned, the country had gone to hell, the world not far behind, and all humanity, when you thought of the science end of things, of planets and space and time, was clearly just a momentary flash of light and dust. . . .

Mattie gasped as *she* came back into focus.

But it made little difference. She was not so different from this cantankerous old man, this dandy who went round wearing suits so white they almost gleamed. With every minute more of him bubbled forth.

But *she* knew there was no heaven, no matter how that woman on the train had babbled about it, the white light, an infinity of time, some sort of *change* you went through when you left your body behind.

It was all scientific, what was happening to her. She knew that. If she repeated one word over and over and over again, which she used to do a lot when she was little because it made everything seem strange and new like "gate, gate, gate, gate," her mind would let go of the word and she would be faced with a *thing* there, just *existing.* She had tried to teach Alexa but Alexa thought it was stupid. Well, she had been doing it on the train, her disengaging exercises, and a cascade of images was released and she could see how her brain was changing, like a mote would get in your eye except this was a flood of transparent stuff washing quick through your vision. The nice lady on the train had been awfully worried about her and actually she'd had to rip away from her grasping hands and had felt so relieved when the doors opened at Cairo, about the closest she could get to St. Louis apparently and that man was standing there on the platform with the guitar although he had not seen her when she debarked, since he was looking the other way.

But it had all worked out perfectly. Perfectly! Here she was on the

Mississippi. The center of the country. If such things were possible maybe there was a heaven. If she could just shove that troublesome, dumbed-down Twain out of the way and take the wheel, she would be in heaven. Absolutely. She glared at him and he hummed a wretched little tune. Just to irritate her, no doubt.

The tall black woman, Lil, stuck her head in the door. "Hi, honey." She had a nice smile. She reminded Mattie of her aunt Zelda, who had died three years ago. "Come out and sit with me awhile. You must be getting tired standing there so long."

"I don't know about *her,* but it would afford *me* a welcome respite," remarked Twain.

I suppose I am tired, thought Mattie, as she allowed Lil to help her down and lead her out the door into the sunlight. They went round to the prow of the boat, on the broad promenade lined with white wicker chairs, and sat on a cushioned couch that creaked, and stretched out their legs on an ottoman. Mattie admired Lil's shoes. They looked very strange. Mattie liked Lil. Jack was pretty nice too. Verity was in a bad mood, and too busy to talk.

The boat was on a serene stretch of river, overhung by delicate green willows on the west bank, and there would probably not be any piloting emergencies for a while.

"You look like you have some African blood in you," said Lil.

"My grandfather was black," said Mattie. "And one of my grandmothers on the other side of my family was a Hopi. The United States were a big mixing . . . basket. Or something like that. My aunt used to tell me."

Lil nodded. "Absolutely. So what brought you here, anyway?"

"A Bee," said Mattie. "A St. Louis Bee. But I was born in Elysia. That's where I came from. Or was it Florida? Yes—Florida, Missouri. I remember . . ."

"Elysia," said Lil firmly and squeezed her hand hard.

"You don't know where that is," said Mattie.

"But I do," said Lil. "It's on the NAMS line. Tell me about it."

"Well, Elysia has been there since the eighteen-eighties. They thought there was gold there at first but if there ever was they got it out fast and left. My dad's family's been there all along, even during the times when hardly anyone lived there. Bunch of farmers. He says the reason that Elysia's survived is that Elysians are mean by nature. My mother calls it strong and self-sufficient. My grandma, the one that was a Hopi, moved to Denver and became a lawyer. My mother liked the reservation in Arizona better, and spent a lot of time there when she was little. My grandma argued that the Flower Cities were unconstitutional before the Supreme Court."

"There were some famous cases," said Lil. "She lost, I guess."

Mattie said, "My mom said that she won, but that it didn't really make any difference. She'd taken my mom with her to Washington. My mom was only ten. Some terrorists blew up the train track near Elysia and my grandma died. My dad's family took my mom in."

As Mattie described her childhood Lil took her hand, looked at it. "Germ-line receptors," she said.

"What?" asked Mattie.

"Your receptors are inherited. Those ovals."

"Yes," she said. "My grandmother had them. Whatever they are. My mother says they don't do anything anymore." She kept talking, and Lil continued to hold her hand as she gazed out over the river. After a few minutes Mattie's hand began to tingle and she withdrew it. Lil appeared not to notice, and prompted her to continue her tale.

But Mattie's eyelids were fluttering shut. "Time," Mattie heard herself saying, in a strange drawl. "Time is the worst sort of fooler. If we could but fix ourselves in that one special time, that perfect season of joy and happiness, who would dare to look outside it, who would dare pierce its membrane and be drawn into the darkness which lies on the other side?" She was thinking of several things at once as she spoke. Those few years at Nook Farm, in the beautiful mansion he built, when Susy and Clara and Jean were small, the money was rolling in, and the world was at his feet.

And then something that woman on the train had talked about, so earnestly, wondering if it was wrong, dishonest, or a betrayal of her brother to want to return to the place of timelessness, where she could choose always to forget that which made her unhappy. Where she would lose a part of herself.

The two streams came together and flowed into the words. When she remembered who she was—Mattie from Elysia—and where she was—on the hurricane deck of a Mississippi riverboat—Lil was looking at her with concern, and putting a hand to her forehead, feeling for fever. But that was silly. She wasn't hot. She was very, very cold.

Lil insisted that she take a nap, as if she were a baby.

Later, when she woke up, she had to admit that it had been refreshing. After splashing her face with water, she took the dressing-table stool from her stateroom and carried it up to the pilothouse. She'd give that limited Twain a run for his money. Stupidity could be dangerous. She'd have to keep a close eye on him.

She spared one last thought for Elysia, set the stool on the texas deck, and opened the door to the pilothouse.

* * *

Verity couldn't seem to stay away from the pilothouse. After all, it was *her* boat! But Twain seemed to be doing all right as he piloted—jaunty as a king, though Peabody, at her elbow, seemed nervous as well.

Mattie flung open the door. "Afternoon." She shoved a velvet-covered stool through the door in front of her.

Twain looked at her and frowned. Mattie set the stool next to Twain and climbed up on it. "Nice," she said, wiggling around. "No wobble."

"Don't crowd me, girl," Twain said.

"It's my watch soon," she replied.

"How do you figure that?" asked Twain.

"Four hours on, four hours off, that's the watch schedule."

"Who says I need to sleep?" asked Twain.

"It's only fair," Mattie replied.

Twain shrugged. "Life isn't fair. I thought that's what you spent a good half-hour trying to convey to me earlier this morning."

"The current is picking up. I think we're coming to a chute."

"I don't think so. I'm going to take the outer bend," said Twain.

"I suppose we're in no hurry. It's just that everyone's going nuts, that's all." As far as Mattie could tell, the people on the boat *did* seem rather agitated.

"You, especially," rejoined Twain.

Verity leaned around Mattie and touched the screen. It obligingly featured a map which was Engineering Authority Map 67.5, accurate in 1934. It was swiftly superseded by another, a Satellite Enlargement with about fifteen rows of letters and numbers beneath the latitudinal and longitudinal description of the area. She put them next to each other. "They're so different," she said. The course of the river had apparently moved west by more than half a mile, and could very well have moved back since then. "I don't understand. The Ohio is pretty much the same as it's been for at least a few centuries, even with the earthquake."

Peabody said, "There's no shortage of faults in this area. And the bed of the river itself isn't moraine, like that of the Ohio. This river bottom is nothing but mud."

Twain gestured toward the riverbank on the right. A portion of the bank had collapsed almost straight down into the river, so that the tree-tops still stood straight though their trunks were submerged. Another several hundred yards were in the process of crumbling, and as they watched, a tree at least a hundred feet high crashed into the river. Just beyond, another bobbed up and down, apparently still rooted, but grabbed by the force of the river so that the crown and trunk regularly surfaced, then were pulled underneath, again and again.

"That's a sawyer," said Twain. "Wreaks all kinds of havoc if you come across a sawyer while you're going through a chute. It's a trickster.

You might come around a bend and not see it because it's underwater. Then—wham! Knock the brains out of your boat."

"That's why you called your trickster Tom Sawyer?" asked Peabody, a smile of understanding slowly spreading across his face.

"Now that would be the sort of highfalutin thing somebody like Bret Harte might try, someone with pretensions and the will to put all kinds of double meanings into what they're writing. It's purely enough work just to tell a good story, that's the way I look at it." Despite his tone, a smile crept onto Twain's face.

"Liar!" said Mattie. "You never wrote anything pure and simple in your life."

"You're calling me a liar? You're saying I wrought works of complexity and deviousness? Why, now I've had the pleasure of two compliments in a very short time. If you're not careful you'll make my head swell up and explode." Twain grinned broadly.

"Stop it, you two," said Verity. "The current's picking up and we seem to be heading straight toward this island."

"What are the leads?" Twain bellowed into the speaking tube so that it boomed all over the boat. "Wake up down there."

"The leads are right here," said Mattie, pointing at the information displayed on the screen. "I told you before but you seem too stupid to learn anything. Right now it says mark six."

"You are ceasing to amuse me," said Twain, as he pulled on the wheel.

"There's a sandbar!" screamed Mattie, and everyone on the boat appeared to be out at the railings now, following the proceedings with great attention.

Twain pulled on a lever and reversed the paddlewheel, causing things to fly off tables onto the floor. Just as quickly, he stopped its turning completely. As they drifted, silence filled the boat. Even Mattie didn't breathe a word as they brushed the trees hanging over the water.

In that instant Twain sprang into action, pulling levers and spouting orders to which no one attended. But the paddlewheel erupted with a great roar, and the boat backed smartly and the front swung round and slid through a narrow channel suddenly revealed in the island's heart.

They were in a swift-running chute, completely enclosed on two sides by junglelike forest laced with vines. Birds fled in confusion as the *Queen* smashed through the branches and Twain's booming laugh filled the pilothouse. The chute widened to a pleasant little waterway, still with plenty of current.

"High water, in early summer," he remarked. "The river is up."

"And the channel is deep," offered Peabody.

"Exactly," agreed Twain.

Mattie was frowning.

"Jealousy doesn't become a lovely young lady such as yourself," said Twain.

"I'm not jealous, I'm not a young lady, and I'm not lovely. I'm older than you and a good deal wiser." Her voice was steady and assured. "I am just wondering about the mouth of the chute, that's all. It may be silted over."

"Not to my reckoning," said Twain. "Not unless it . . . turns." And the chute took a sharp turn west.

He glanced down at Mattie, new respect in his eyes.

"Full throttle!" he yelled, but followed his own command with the lever. "Stoke the fire down there! Pour on speed!" Their velocity increased; the boat sped recklessly through the green, light-dappled corridor.

Suddenly they saw the end, a silver arch, and Twain chomped down hard on his cigar. "This is it," he said, and leaned into the wheel.

There was a grating sound and a loud gravelly hiss, and the front of the boat rose—only slightly, but being several tons its descent caused a very respectable splash, and a wave that set out across the river, and loose objects and even furniture went flying through the air amid the screams of the passengers.

Twain and Mattie both laughed to beat the band. Tears rolled down Mattie's face and she wiped them away with the back of her hand. "Good ride!" she said. "Excellent work!"

Verity was stunned. "You had no right to take such chances! We *must* get to Norleans," she said, her voice shaking.

"The Mississippi River is nothing but one great chance," said Twain. "You'll see wrecked boats all along the river. Piloting is an art on which I've staked my life more than one time."

"It's a more honorable profession than telling lies," said Mattie.

"Amen to that, pipsqueak," agreed Twain. He turned to Verity. "Madam Captain, you are no longer on the tame Ohio. You are on the river of the frontier. The great Mississippi. It drains a watershed of thousands of square miles. It changes according to whether the water is high or low. Channels are lost and gained with each passing day. It has been thus since DeSoto came up the river claiming it for Spain and was stuffed into a hollow log for his trouble. It has wiped out entire cities overnight, and stranded others miles from its former banks so that they may as well have been submerged. It has created and lost fortunes for men. I suggest that you pass the time as captains usually do. Avail yourself of the bar and the dining room. You might try checkers or a hand of faro. Or a good book." He chuckled.

Verity looked at him and then at the girl, Mattie. They shared a language and a consensus about the river that she lacked. Verity didn't know how much of Twain this person possessed, but he'd obviously reached the piloting stage.

She was surprised at the relief that washed through her. It would be wonderful not to have to worry so much about trying to pilot the boat herself. The Ohio had been nerve-racking at times, and it looked as if the Mississippi would be far worse.

"Thank you Mr. Twain," she said. "I'll take your advice."

Twenty-two
○○○○○○○○○○○○○○○○○
Bomber Blues

Their second day out from Cairo, the boat was once again surrounded by a bobbing carpet of rafts. Many rafters had pulled into coves to recover from their terrible night journey, when they had been swept past Cairo. Verity insisted, over the clamor of Twain and Mattie and most of the passengers, not to mention her own Norleans-yearning compass, on waiting for those who might have been delayed by the riots when they left Cairo.

Late in the afternoon, rafts of people, some injured, began drifting into view; these were hauled onto the riverboat and tended to.

One woman had jumped from the wharf onto a raft. She had a broken ankle; her face was dirty and streaked with tears beneath short-cropped black hair.

"It was awful," she hollered at them as she was pulled up in a sling with a winch. "Why did you desert us? How were we supposed to get away? Get Adelaide out of the wigwam; she was burned. They tried to tar and feather her. They claimed that we were all criminals and deserved to be lynched. They said we gave them the plague. They were coming after us with ropes. *Ropes!*" She covered her face with her hands and burst into sobs; the people waiting on the deck for her gently lifted her from the sling and a large man picked her up.

Lil said, "We'll have to set up an infirmary."

"I'm—er, I was, a doctor," said one man, looking confused. "It's been a long time."

"Come on," said Lil.

Before long about fifty injured people occupied a long row of previously unused staterooms. Moans issued from doors that stood open in the steamy heat of the afternoon. Several of the men and women made themselves useful by cleaning wounds inflicted by the angry citizens of Cairo. Apparently there had been more than one death. Verity digested this information and wondered again why she had disregarded Lil's advice.

"You'll always feel guilty about them if you don't watch out," said Jack, who fell in next to her as she walked from room to room.

"I *am* responsible for them," she said, battling a sinking feeling as she watched a young man gently wash a large abrasion on a little girl's abdomen. Apparently she had fallen and was then pushed across the concrete wharf by the feet of the surging mob. Luckily, she had found shelter behind a fishmonger's stall.

"In a way, I suppose," said Jack. "But you can't control the world, and you can't control them. It's all out of your control now. Whatever you did in Cincinnati, and I'm not entirely sure what that was, it was something that you had to do. I know that much about you. It was not a frivolous decision. Was it?"

"No," said Verity.

"Could you have made a different decision?"

"Not really," she admitted, surprised that in spite of the truth of this she was loath to give up the deep certainty that this was all her fault.

"Come on," he said. "Maybe Lil is cooking up something."

Jack led Verity back to the small room where the gloves had been made. Lil sat in the small swivel chair surrounded by softly blinking lights, and with her was the doctor.

"We need a painkiller—an opiate," the doctor was saying.

Lil called up an array of capital letters connected to one another by lines. "An opiate," she said, biting her lip.

"Wait! I'm remembering now. When I studied nanicine, we used Opinan for pain. That was the brand name. Why not just try that word and see what happens?"

Lil typed in the word, impatiently wiping sweat from her eyes. "I think it's more important to worry about infection, isn't it?"

"Bactronan," said the doctor. "That's easy. In a salve. And Indonan for internal use."

Lil glanced at him.

"Really," he said.

"Well, now I consider my medical training to be complete," said Lil, with sarcasm in her voice.

He didn't seem to notice, and leaned over eagerly as figures popped up on the screen. Then the screen went dark.

Lil frowned and touched the pads in a swift, sure cadence. There was a slight flicker and she leaned forward and touched a few more pads. She leaned back in the chair and stared at the screen.

"Start up the boat," she said.

"But there are rafts—" said Verity.

"Clear them out and *start up the boat!*"

In ten minutes the paddlewheel was churning and Verity was hurrying back toward Lil's room. They were progressing at the slowest possible speed downriver. Verity thought about having Twain turn the boat upriver so as not to further outdistance any other rafts still to catch up with them, but she wasn't sure exactly why Lil wanted them moving.

She burst into the room, where people were crowded around Lil so that she had to push her way through. "Okay?"

"Not okay," said Lil. "Something is very wrong. Even with the energy generated by the boat, everything is crashing. I'm trying to isolate . . . I'm trying to see if I can figure out exactly what the problem is before I lose the diagnostics."

There were more cries outside and Verity ran out to see what was going on.

Below, from the boiler deck, a rope snaked out and those on a raft about twenty feet away managed to catch it after a few tries. As they drew closer, Verity recognized the girl holding on to the rope, mainly because of the bee shirt that she'd traded for her apple pie.

She hurried down to help them onto the boat.

First, there were two young men. Their clothes were torn and bloody. They had a look of dim exhaustion about them, and it was difficult for them to ascend the rope ladder. They did not look at Verity as they staggered onto the deck.

Then only the girl was left.

She looked up. Her blond hair, bloodied from a gash on her forehead, fell back. As she recognized Verity, her eyes widened and her face lit with a smile. Verity leaned down and grasped her hand as she climbed the ladder. In the shadow of the boat, it was golden.

"Welcome aboard," said Verity, thinking that soon enough they'd want to be back on the rafts, to drift free down the Mississippi, toward blue, blue Norleans. But maybe now they were hungry. "I thought you were immune to the plague," she said.

"We did too," said the girl, slowly. "But thank God we were wrong!" She smiled again, angelically. "Oh, I'm *so* happy," she sighed, and Verity's heart sank.

Then she heard a sound she'd never heard before, insistent and growing, a harsh buzz. Not the melodious buzz of Bees, but impersonal. Terrifying, as it grew and surrounded them.

"A plane!" people were crying out, and indeed it was.

"George," said the girl, shading her eyes. "Look. It's his plane. They're all his planes, of course. Like everything *else* in Cairo. *Come on, George,*" she yelled. *"Just try and squeeze money out of us now, you bastard!"*

The black biplane floated in the blue sky of afternoon.

Towering just behind the plane was a black thunderhead that had come up quite suddenly, pushing before it a breeze that kicked up small waves. The rafts on the river bobbed as the waves grew larger.

The plane was much closer now; Verity could distinguish the propellers. Another came up from behind and joined it, the identical black plane from Cairo.

They seemed to pause motionless for a terribly long time before one swooped in a sudden dive straight toward the boat.

A gust of wind blew it sideways and she saw the wings wobble as it bore down upon them. A white fog spewed from beneath the plane but it was blown away as fast as it was released in the wind from the upcoming storm.

The plane veered upward just after passing over the top of the boat, barely clearing the smokestacks, with a deafening roar that shook the boat.

Peabody rushed past Verity, up the stairs, pale and intent, as the second plane began a swift, relentless descent.

There was nothing to do but watch helplessly. This time a series of missiles plummeted from the sides of the plane; as the first two fell Verity could see that two others were attached to the side of the plane. They were both released in the same instant.

Transfixed by fear, Verity watched as the missiles sent up an irregular row of towering geysers. One hit a rock only a few yards from the paddlewheel.

Fiery fragments of bomb and rock smashed into the *Queen* with unexpected force. The boat bucked like a horse in the wake of the explosions and the huge waves sweeping downriver, flinging people to the deck. Planks from a raft rained down upon the boat and splashed into the river.

General panic erupted. People plunged into the river from even the higher decks. Verity turned and ran against the surge of the crowd toward the pilothouse, intending to give directions, but wondered, *What?* She looked down at her hands but saw nothing coherent. The plane rose high and circled for another run. This time he would surely hit them.

Instead he streaked by only twenty feet above the pilothouse, narrowly missing a smokestack. Verity glimpsed George in the open cockpit, though his face was covered by goggles and he wore a ridiculous scarf that swept out behind him in the wind. He appeared to be struggling with something—perhaps he was trying to release the missile that Verity saw attached to the other side of the plane. His plane took an abrupt upward turn.

The other plane, crossing the river not far behind them, unfurled a huge banner, catching the sun's last brilliant flash before it was eclipsed by the black cloud.

SURRENDER, VERITY
AND JACK!

A deep gasp arose from those watching, almost in unison. Some people screamed, "We surrender! We surrender!" Others tore off white shirts, if they were wearing them, and waved them off the side of the boat.

Then a great *boom* shook the boat and the screams doubled in volume.

A whistling sound accompanied a streak of light that flew straight toward the plane and exploded, shimmering in the air and shredding the banner. The missile clearly missed the plane, but the plane nonetheless spiraled earthward as a white parachute blossomed against the thunderhead. Verity heard cheers.

She ran up the stairs, panting. Another long, drawn-out whistle; she emerged on the texas deck just in time to see another explosion as the plane falling out of the sky burst into flames.

Peabody was out there on the deck, next to a small black cannon, screaming maniacally, jumping up and down and waving his fist in the air. "You wasted it!" he screamed to Jack, who apparently had aimed the weapon. "Go for George!"

Verity was astounded. Peabody enraged surprised her almost as much as the attack and the counterattack combined.

As Peabody leaped and yelled, Jack poured gunpowder into the cannon and tamped it with a large wooden tool. The second Jack pulled out the tamper Peabody staggered over with a cannonball and let it roll down the barrel. He jumped aside and Jack sat on a small stool and followed the remaining plane through the air with the barrel, which was apparently not difficult to maneuver. He struck a match, lit a fuse, and rolled across the deck all in one motion. The cannonball whistled through the sky, and the cannon rolled back several feet with the explosion.

"You missed!" yelled Peabody. The remaining plane banked high, then began laboring upriver against the wind as lightning forked through the sky.

Lil, Twain, and Mattie had joined them on the deck.

"He'll be back," said Lil. "What should we do, Jack?"

"You're asking *me?*" said Jack. "This is a first!"

"This is no time for jokes," said Lil, her face grim. "We can't be responsible for this."

"What are you talking about?" asked Verity.

"He wants us," said Jack. "Lil and me. That's all. We'll make a bargain. He won't get Verity."

"Well, he's not going to get you either," said Peabody. His face was streaked with black grease and his white hair was in disarray. "He wants a mechanical war? He wants to fight fair? He wants to return to the good old days? He hates the insecurity of the Information Wars? I know his kind! Blow 'em up, the honest way. Chicago was swarming with them in my youth. I'll give him a mechanical war—an *honest* war!—right up the wazoo." He clapped his hands together once and clenched them, smiling broadly. "I wasn't just gaggling around in Cairo stirring up a hornet's nest like some of you."

"I don't think he wants an honest war, as you call it," said Jack. "His first offense got blown away."

"No," said Lil. "His first offense worked."

"What do you mean?" asked Peabody.

"He dropped something on the stage," said Lil. "We got rid of it right away, but some of the molecules must have invaded the *Queen*. Just a small amount, so things are deteriorating quite slowly."

"Well, it must have been hit-or-miss. He wouldn't have had time or any way to create a very precise offense," replied Peabody. "We were in Cairo for less than twenty-four hours."

"Eliot," said Verity. "Eliot took something from the boat. I saw him take something in a bag when he left."

"With the right equipment, it wouldn't take long for something to evolve," said Lil.

Peabody frowned. "Eliot?"

"I saw Eliot in George's house," said Verity.

"Nobody told *me,*" said Peabody.

Jack stared at Peabody and looked as if he was going to say something but then just walked away. "Come on, Lil," he said. "Let's see if we can figure something out." They hurried away.

"Where did we get this cannon, or whatever it is?" asked Verity.

"*We* didn't get it," said Peabody. "*I* did. While you fools were gadding about I checked out a few things and decided to be prepared. Picked it up in Cairo on Washington Street. Great little shop there. Full of all kinds of stuff. It's a stockpiling center for the Rural Network. Fantastic bargains. I got a bazooka too, but I'm not sure if it will work."

Verity was not at all pleased by the gunpowder aboard. "That could blow us all up," she said. "Look. There's a fire down on that railing right now." Some people below were splashing the railing with pans of water and soon it was doused.

"As you can see, it saved everyone's life," said Peabody in a maddeningly equitable voice she was sure he reserved for small children. He bent over the cannon and a breeze teased his sparse hair into a little dance. "Nice and dependable." He looked as if he might even pat the thing.

Twain arrived on the deck. "Will the captain give me the pleasure of her orders?" he demanded. "I thought at first the boiler had blown." His craggy face saddened. "Reminded me of when my brother Henry died after the *Missouri* exploded. What's this?" He looked at the cannon with interest. "Perhaps I can lend some expertise. I fought in the Civil War."

"And deserted, you coward," said Mattie, who was always at his side.

"Understandably!" roared Twain, rounding suddenly. Mattie just glared at him and Twain lowered his head, deflated. "It was a horrible war," he said sadly. "All wars are. And I was on the wrong side. Why did you remind me? What branch of hell sent you? I'm beginning to believe in Satan. Truth to tell it would be quite a relief to have something to believe in besides the evil of the human race. Blame it on a higher power. How could we, helpless motes, ever contend against God or the Devil?"

"Now you're getting the picture," said Mattie dourly.

"I guess you don't want to help with the cannon," interrupted Peabody, just to keep them from yammering, guessed Verity.

Twain turned round. "What made the cannonballs blow up in midair, anyway?" he asked. "That's a useful invention. Is it yours? Is it too late to get in on the ground floor?"

"Well, I just put them on a straight timer for that. I wasn't sure the remote that guy sold me would work," said Peabody. "Depends on the atmosphere."

"I thought you had the plague," said Verity. "You seem a lot more alert than most of the rafters."

Peabody grinned. "As you well know yourself, the plague doesn't make one dim-witted. Obviously, I'm devoting all my mental energies toward getting us to Naw-*leens*. We just took out half of the Cairo Air Force. Probably by the time they regroup we'll be out of their range. But we need to stay prepared. Later on tonight I'll run more tests."

"I wonder who was flying the other plane," said Verity.

"Oh, come now," said Peabody. "Who do you think?"

"Eliot?"

Peabody snorted. "Lovely Linda Lyle."

"But they don't get along at all," said Verity.

"They certainly make a good case for that in public, don't they? I had a glimpse of them myself, while I was poking round. Early in the morning. They make a great team. Ought to take their act on the road."

"On the road?" asked Verity.

"Never mind," said Peabody. "Get inside!"

The storm swept over them, peppering the boat with pellets of hail which slashed into the river; the rattling surge was so loud that speech was impossible. Verity did not seek cover but helped two rafts full of shivering people aboard and left one dead person in a wigwam. He had a hideous injury that she did not want to fully examine.

In moments the hail had passed. The air was filled with the stink of smoldering wood mixed with the freshness of chilled air. Steam rose from a dozen small fires as they sputtered out.

Verity looked out across the river, white-pocked by hard rain that fell with a strange, hushed sizzle on the water's brown surface. She spotted some people waving on the far bank, downriver. Probably some of those who had abandoned ship during the attack.

She put some matches in a small waterproof box and slid it into her pocket. Then, soaked to the skin and shivering, she lowered a boat and pulled hard for the shore. They'd probably have to launch from upriver a ways in order to get back. While the storm passed they could shelter under one of the towering live oaks, and maybe start a fire, if anything was dry. She'd have a talk with Jack and Lil later, she promised herself, though they were slippery as snakes when it came to imparting useful information.

Or maybe it wouldn't be useful, she mused, slowly crossing the muddy, leaping current. She wished she'd at least brought a hat to keep the rain from dripping into her eyes.

But it would be pretty damned interesting, whatever they had to say. As Russ would say. Pretty goddamned interesting.

She hit mud and the stranded rafters were waiting to pull the boat ashore.

Twenty-three
◯◯◯◯◯◯◯◯◯◯◯◯◯◯◯◯◯◯

Nan in the Moon Blues

Two hours later it was evening. The storm had passed and the sky was a delicate, washed blue. Verity paced the deck, impatient to be off.

The debris had been cleaned up, as best as it could be, and those who knew how were trying to repair the damage. Peabody and Lil were working on trying to stem the progress of whatever sort of molecular-level havoc George had inflicted on the boat in Cairo. It could be that his hastily composed weapon would not be able to generate enough change, quickly enough, to overpower whatever defenses might have been built into the *Queen*. But there would be tiny, constant breakdowns as each new phase of replicators was produced.

Peabody seemed surprisingly well prepared for the task of getting the *Queen* to Norleans. He appeared to work on the same level as George. Verity wondered seriously about Chicago and Peabody's story. But she was sure that he did have the plague, and she trusted him to look out for their interests. That would have to do.

But the sky was so blue. The stop was driving her nuts.

The surrounding countryside was wild and forbidding, and swampy as well. An island lay between them and the river's eastern shore, a wave of white sand over a mile long, wind-washed and rising stark above the muddy, roiling water. Cottonwoods fringed the shore and reeds gave way to high grasses that shimmered in the wind below the brilliant white-gold peak.

There was still at least an hour before sunset.

In five minutes she was in the johnboat, pulling hard on the oars. It swirled once, caught in a faster stream of water, then sped to a crashing halt against a submerged stump ten feet from land.

She tied up the boat and slid cautiously into the water, knee-high and curiously warm, and struggled against the slippery bottom onto more solid footing. A flock of birds flashed past, white wings reflecting the pink of the lowering sun.

She picked up a stout dry stick and broke it over her knee so that it was only as tall as she, and used it to beat the grass in front of her to scare off snakes. A heron she had not noticed startled her by erupting out of a nearby treetop and flapping awkwardly downriver.

Soon she was above the grass and into the sand, still warm, and climbed till she reached the top of the dune. She sank down to rest, sand sticking to her wet legs. The river widened below the island, assuming a most probably deceitful smoothness, a shimmering silver southward curve. She absently shredded some sweet, aromatic leaves between her fingers.

After a moment she thought she heard music, piano music.

Of course, it was more of that blues stuff in her head and before long she'd be filled with the willies about taking so long to get to Norleans.

What was there? What would they find? She had images aplenty by now: wrought iron, narrow cobblestone streets, more like a European city glimpsed in a dry lithograph than a sensible foursquare Midwestern town.

But who was that woman she kept seeing, the one with the Bee tattoo on her shoulder? The one who had wept?

The one who had told her to hurry?

How long ago had that imploring look been recorded and sent aloft?

How many people, over the years, had been infected with the Norleans Plague? How many had made it all the way downriver? Not only that, but one old satellite map, and she had no idea of its age, showed Norleans as drowned. Where were they heading? Someplace dead, following a signal that was by now meaningless?

The music grew louder, chords building to a crescendo, then softened into some sweet old-fashioned tune, the kind Blaze used to play before that awful blues stuff filled his head.

Well, he was gone now. She'd never see him again.

To ease the tightness in her chest, she stood and brushed dried sand off her legs and her shoes. This music . . . this music was different . . . maybe it was *not* in her head.

She slogged higher on the sandy ridge, and some rabbits feeding on the grasses fled before her. She thought she saw a deer melt into the shadows of a small forest that was revealed when she got to the top and could see the other side of the island.

The other side was much larger than she expected, with a small stand of sycamores and live oaks. She looked more carefully, and then she saw it—a white frame house in the small hollow within the trees. Two stories, but still not large, with a porch on which sat wicker furniture. The house was sparkling white, and so were the chairs. She walked closer and the music got louder. A woman sang, in a low voice oddly rough and soothing at the same time:

"Miss the Mississippi and you, dear . . ."

A woman with long white hair pulled into a ponytail that cascaded down her straight back looked up from her piano and saw Verity, who by now was peering in the window.

"I'm sorry," said Verity. "Keep playing."

"You near scared me to death," said the old woman. She was wearing a neat white shirt and pressed khaki shorts and brown boots sturdy and clean. She was thin and tan and looked strong and healthy. Despite her white hair, her face had few wrinkles. "Who are you? What are you doing on Widder's Island?"

"We're just passing by on a boat," Verity said. "I needed to go for a walk."

"Oh. Well come and sit a spell then. I'm the widder. Widder Jones, they call me. Or they would if there was anyone else here. I'm not sure if I'm really a widder or not, but Frank ain't been home now in quite a few years and I'm way past crying about it—least in the broad daylight. Nights, now, that's the hardest, specially considering what happened to him. But I'm too old and smart to feel sorry for myself. You shouldn't go tramping around by yourself, young lady. You never know what sort of roughnecks you might meet round the river." She reached down next to the piano bench and pulled up a rifle, which she brandished. "Lucky I didn't blow your head off. Come in, come in, I don't have to beg, do I?"

Verity walked past some peony bushes with fat white flowers to the front porch and realized that the house was really a raft, sitting on a foundation of pilings. Ready to float free in high water. A hundred questions crowded her mind as she climbed the porch stairs and opened the screen door.

The woman had shrewd blue eyes that looked Verity up and down. Quick as a wink she grabbed Verity's hand and turned it palm upward. "Well, I'll be," she said. "Cincinnati, eh? And stranger than that to boot. You been washed a far piece from home, my girl."

"I'm not really from Cincinnati," said Verity.

"Plain as day, you are. Lemonade?"

"You have lemons?" asked Verity. Lemonade was quite the drink in these parts.

"You sit right there"—she pointed to a wing chair upholstered with blue fabric on which floated a repeated white mansion—"and I'll show you who has lemons." She left Verity alone while she went into the kitchen.

Verity took in the polished wood, the lace-covered tables crammed with knickknacks, the pale, worn Oriental rug on wide boards, and spied a curious, black cube on a table across the room.

"Dammit, you stupid thing, I said *lemons,* not *limes!"* Verity heard from the kitchen, and stepped closer to the cube.

Something about her presence activated it, for out from its sides blossomed pictures. A man pulled a hefty fish out of the river, waved, squinted in the sun, held it up for inspection. The same man smiled beneath a huge steel arch that spanned a city block. Jones was standing next to him.

"St. Louis," said the dry voice behind her, and Verity heard sounds of pouring and the clatter of ice. "He'd retired and they called him back. Bastards. After all those years in Texas they called him back. We thought we'd escaped good and proper too. Back to our home on the old river shore, as the song says. Try it."

Verity took a sip. "Good!" she said.

"It came out limes, but it's okay," the lady said. "Now watch this." She tapped the top of the cube. "Come on now, you contrary thing."

Verity was amazed to see a huge sleek white thing gradually separate from the earth, then turn to a cone of light above blue ocean. The close-up heads of a few people, seen from behind, bobbed across the bottom of the picture. "Not many of us there. They weren't going to let me see it but Frank insisted. And he told me to take pictures too, which was forbidden but how would they know anyway? The photopanel was in my hat, hidden in the bottom loop of the S. Last I saw anything of him. Well, drink up, don't let it go to waste. It's not every day I have company."

"He went into . . . space?" asked Verity.

The old woman grinned. "That's right, dear. Don't let anyone tell you different, either. That was only about forty years ago. Hardly a blink of time, if things went the way they planned."

"And what did they plan?" asked Verity, gulping down her limeade.

"Well—" Jones sighed. "He wouldn't tell me. Not exactly. I only know that it was big, a long project. Something to do with the signal."

"The signal?" asked Verity.

"Land sakes, girl. Where have you been? The reason why radio's such a pisser, for starters."

"I thought it was because of a quasar."

She laughed. "Well, rumors were running hot for a long, long time, I suppose. No, it was pretty clear that it was a signal, a deliberate signal. And he was heading toward the source. I guess they really didn't want anyone to know but he told me and I wasn't even supposed to know of course. A long trip. They didn't know how long. I'm all set up here, this was our retirement place, we come back to the river where we grew up. I'm thinking that Frank had just this kind of thing in mind when he planned it all out. He insisted that I have some kind of treatments in St. Louis. I guess I don't look all that wonderful but I can recognize myself, despite that young technician lady who was sure everybody in creation wanted to look just like her, big eyes, high cheekbones, blond hair. No reason I shouldn't last as long as Frank if the rabbits hold out. Plenty of fish in the river again. The main question is, will I still want him and will he still want me?"

She sighed. "Well, I'm babbling on I see. I wouldn't mind some company. You're in a hurry though, I bet. I saw your boat out there. It's a beauty. And lands, all that commotion today! I was hoping that idiot in the plane wouldn't spot my place, I'm under the trees but my panels have to be out in the sun. I've seen him before, and some other planes, but sometimes it's a year between times. Those aviators like to follow the river, makes it easy for them. He sure had a bee in his bonnet."

"Why don't you come with us?" Verity said. "We're going to Norleans."

"Course you are," said the woman gently. She patted Verity on the shoulder and took her empty glass. "You take care. It'll get dark fast now that the sun's gone down. I'll see you to the top of the hill. I bet that boat's lit up prettier than St. Louis at night. I might sit up there and watch it awhile, if the bugs aren't too bad."

She grabbed a lightstick hanging from the door and led the way to a path made soft by pine needles, and Verity followed her through the cooling night as the stars came out between the boughs of huge trees.

Jones was walking in front of her and Verity asked, "What makes you think I'm from Cincinnati?"

Jones stopped and turned around. "Hold out your hand." She held the lightstick over it. "See this display below the right index finger?"

"That greenish circle?" asked Verity. When it was displayed, which was fairly often, it contained an unvarying pattern of red blips that were meaningless to her.

"I wasn't always an old nut living alone playing the piano," Jones said, her head bent over Verity's hand. "I was an epidemiologist."

"A what?"

"I studied the distribution of diseases. Plagues were my specialty. Now, one thing that the First Wave did was put everybody's DNA on a display for medical reasons. For one thing, it made it easy to tell whether or not there was a problem, or if a particular therapy worked. Not everyone was happy about it, of course. But all kinds of other markers are on there too—city of origin, of course, right there—see? Cincinnati was ten. I remember all the biggies."

"I don't see a ten," said Verity.

"That red doohickey there. And no black dots. Add a black dot and you'd have eleven, Dayton. I could get a lot more depth out of the display if I touched it with a light pen—the sugars rearrange themselves." She folded Verity's hand up, patted it, and continued briskly up the needle-softened path. Verity followed, pondering how little she knew of what had happened in the past fifty years or so. Although *Rose* probably knew . . . if she only had the strength to let Rose into her—to become whole, to acknowledge the being hidden within her—

But no. She shivered, remembering Durancy. She'd been too busy to think of him. No doubt he'd show up again when she had the least strength to resist him . . . and maybe remembering Rose caused certain metapheromones to be produced, which might possibly rouse him, were he living on the boat, in some room he rarely left.

No. She could not allow Rose into her conscious mind. Even though she was only half a person without her.

As they paused at the top of the dune, admiring the way the boat's lights lay on the water in delicate stripes of color, an explosion rang out.

Light and a whistling sound erupted from an upper deck, and then far off in the sky there was a brilliant explosion. They heard a few distinct, distant cheers, a smattering of applause.

"Good for you!" said the woman, and clapped Verity on the back. "Teach them to come round here dropping bombs."

Verity found Jack and Lil in the poolroom. "Seven in the corner," said Jack, and Lil laughed in derision but Jack pulled back sharply on his cue after striking the ball just left of bottom center and set an utterly precise sequence of events into play which indeed ended as he claimed it would.

"Pay up," he said, strolling around to the other side of the table.

Lil said, "I'm going to do something to you but that's not exactly it. I'm afraid it may involve some pain."

"I'm sorry to interrupt your fun," said Verity, "but I'm really pretty curious."

"No more than we," said Jack. "We're pretty much in the dark."

"Well, I'm a lot more in the dark than you," said Verity. "Who is George? I know why he wants me. Why is he after you? And what did you mean, the Information Wars aren't over yet." There hadn't been a quiet minute since Cairo. Or when there had been, she had been fuming about Blaze.

"The straight answer is we're not going to tell you," said Lil. "Jack shouldn't have said anything."

"Then you can just get the hell off this boat," said Verity hotly. "You owe us an explanation."

"Okay," said Lil. "Come on, Jack. Let's go."

Jack nodded absently, studying the table. "Wait a minute. What a setup! That three goes in the corner, six in the side . . ."

Peabody came in the door, wiping his hands on a rag. "Ah, there you are. Been looking all over for you, Verity. I thought maybe we should discuss our strategy for tomorrow."

"Yes," said Jack. "Good idea." The balls cracked together and Jack nodded with satisfaction.

"Showoff," said Lil.

"It passes the time," said Jack agreeably. "It just gets kind of boring, not having anyone to play against." He winked at Verity.

"Now it really *is* time to leave," said Lil. "Verity, it's been great to know you—"

"Where are you going?" asked Peabody.

"I told them to leave," said Verity. "They won't even tell me why we're being dive-bombed."

"Oh, that," said Peabody. "I thought you knew. Jack and Lil—or whatever their names are—are secret agents. Or whatever you want to call them. They probably have some more fancy title for themselves that some hierarchy gave them in—where *is* the seat of government now? New York? Front Royal? Hard to keep up, isn't it? Even when you're *in* the government. Or want to imagine that it still exists. But if I had to lay odds I'd say that they're nanarchists. When it comes round to government and antigovernment, though, there's sometimes little distinction."

Jack and Lil stared at Peabody. "What do you know about it?" asked Jack.

"Oh," said Peabody vaguely, "I was on some committees, in Chicago. We tried to keep up, but you see, it really didn't interest us much. In fact, Chicago is pretty stable, unlike most of the Cities. I'd like to think that I had a hand in that. Kind of medieval, in a way, but it seems to work. I had you two pegged soon as I got on the boat. Well, I admire your spunk. But I think it's a lost cause. We're all going to go down. Just like that poor George if he's brainless enough to return at dawn and avenge Linda Lyle—who is most likely fine, except that she has to get home the hard way. But you have to go through the motions, I guess. Even Chicago has its weaknesses, as I know only too well. We've been damned lucky. It's as simple as the prevailing winds. If the climate changes much more that city could go down in a week, blood and chaos and death. Big-time." He gave them his stern look again. "We've got to get to Norleans, that's all. That's all that matters. Simplicity is always the best approach. I've always said that. Solid and dependable and everything that really works shakes down to what's simple. At least it does in my world."

He took a deep, satisfied breath. "Lovely, this plague. Absolutely heavenly. I've got to hand it to whoever designed it. I mean, without it, what would there be to believe in? Humans are meaning machines, that's all. We can manufacture meaning out of thin air. Sometimes, though, it seems the more you know, the less there is to believe in. And that can be a very unhappy place. But now I believe in Norleans."

"We're just going through a period of chaos," said Lil uncertainly, as if Peabody had started an argument to which she had to respond. "But it's starting to draw together again. It's starting to organize. It's *predictable.* Jack says—tell them, Jack—there's a fifty-eight-percent chance that—"

"Come on, Lil," said Jack, in a surprisingly gentle voice. "If Verity doesn't want us here there are other ways to get down the river."

"But I wanted to help them—" said Lil. She had an oddly concerned look on her face. Odd for Lil, anyway.

"You can see that we're not. We're only drawing fire."

"George and Linda won't have any idea that you're gone," said Peabody. "They're hell-bent on blowing us to kingdom come. George thinks that nan can be stamped out completely."

"He doesn't," said Verity. "He had some in his house."

"George is not as simple as he seems," said Jack. "He's part of a small group of people who want to re-amass nan for their own exclusive use, fantastic as that sounds. I had a run-in with him in St. Louis, years ago. They want to stamp out all practical knowledge of how it works— not that there's much of that left anyway. Their goal is to return the world to complete ignorance so they can lord it over everyone. George, for instance, wanted Verity because he thought she could help him connect all the ragtags of nanotechnology he's collected through his pirate ring and turn Cairo into his very own Flower City. These groups, collectively, have pretty much succeeded in suppressing information. All those treaties the nations had, back in the early days of nanotechnology—they were all for the protection of the owners, not for the protection of the world from nan. We didn't need to be protected from nan. We needed to be protected from the humans who wanted to use it in certain ways."

"As usual," said Mattie, standing in the doorway, exuding the smell of stale tobacco. "But it's the growth of the military and their industry that caused the bad in humans to get so magnified out of proportion. Sounds like that's what you're getting at. You ought to read *Following the Equator.* In it I discussed the matter in great detail. By 1900 we'd ruined any number of foreign countries. Any whiskey around here?" She stepped inside and started to rattle through the cupboards.

Twain came in behind her. "There you are, Peabody. Been looking high and low for you. Thought you fell overboard. You said you'd be right back. Any whiskey around here?"

"So we can stay?" asked Lil, surprisingly humble.

"Please?" Jack added. His eyes were unusually serious. "Cast a vote, Verity. Be on our side."

Verity looked round at everyone and shrugged. "I still don't know what I'm voting for. But go ahead. Stay. I guess it really doesn't matter either way."

"It does," said Jack. "It matters more than anything."

"Oh, come now," said Twain, having poured himself a glass of whiskey. "What could matter more than a game of pool? Except, perhaps, billiards. You any good?" he asked Jack.

"He thinks so," said Lil, handing Twain her cue stick. "I hope you beat the crap out of him."

9

○ ◇ ○

Memphis

Twenty-four

○○○○○○○○○○○○○○○○○○○

Revolution Blues

"Here come some more of those infernal engines of war," growled Twain around the cigar clamped between his teeth.

Verity turned to look behind them, upriver, but Twain said, "No, straight ahead," and pointed. He lifted the speaking tube, held it to his mouth, and bellowed "Peabody!"

Verity whisked the binoculars from their hook and focussed them with a touch. She was chilled by what she saw, and had to clear her throat twice before she was able to speak.

"Those aren't planes," she managed.

"Let me see." He took off his glasses and held the binoculars up to his eyes. He snorted. "They look like nothing more than bees."

"That's what they are," said Verity.

"Then why are they so large?"

"Because they're more than bees," she said.

Peabody entered the cabin, huffing from having run up the steps. "What is it this time?"

Twain pointed. "Thought they were a fleet of those aeroplanes. But they're only bees."

Peabody took a look through the binoculars. "I thought so, but of course you can't be sure of much these days."

"Thought what?" asked Verity.

"Thought that perhaps Memphis was still viable. We picked up a radio signal but that means nothing. Not a signifier in itself. I wonder . . ." He raised the binoculars again and stared. "Too far to see a trademark of course. At one time Memphis contracted with Midwest Information Systems for their Bees. The MIS Bees were not fully tested and approved but they were cheap."

"Tested and approved by whom?" asked Verity.

Peabody continued to stare through the binoculars as he spoke. "There was a Federal Agency—a United States Government Agency called the Federal Communication Commission—responsible for thoroughly testing the Bees. They and the Food and Drug Administration fought over jurisdiction, but the FCC won. Had a whole battery of tests they put any Bee proposal through. Parity had to be statistically impeccable, that is, with as little distortion as possible from message to message. Of course when you get into this bionan stuff you have evolution pure and simple and there had to be all sorts of guards and failsafes against the evolution of information into something other than what it started out as. Legally, only a one-Bee link—called a BL, bell, of course—was allowed, when sending any sort of business or legal or technical information. One bell meant the highest standard of reliability. For anything where precision was required, you had to take the information from one source and deliver it directly to the receiver. If you stored it at an interim point then it became two bells or more. Four or five bells was deemed acceptable for certain types of information—advertisements, for example. That cost a lot less, and was still pretty reliable. It was just not guaranteed. Storage temperature was another important factor. There's a certain range in which the *e. coli* is happy and the DNA does not deteriorate."

Twain was steering and ringing bells and occupied with sandbars and snags. He glanced over at them every once in a while and made contributions such as, "Unbelievable," and "The devil's work," and, "If only I'd had an opportunity to invest in these creatures." The rest of the time he turned the air blue with curses which were magnitudes beyond any that Russ had favored them with at his most creative. He seemed to be enjoying himself immensely.

"So there's something not right about these Bees?" asked Verity.

"Probably a lot of things, by this time. Once they take over a city, it's doomed. Of course, they all evolve in different ways, but in the end it just means a ruined, sick place. If you know how you can slip any kind of message into their directions."

"But they could be put on the right track again, too, couldn't they?" asked Verity.

"My, you are young," said Peabody. "Who's to decide what that might be? It would take a formidable AI to see that far ahead, anyway."

"But if the basis is well thought out," said Lil, behind them, "you can restore a City to health. Let me look."

Peabody handed over the binoculars.

"Toxic," she said.

"How can you tell?" asked Verity.

"It's my job."

"Oh, really?" asked Peabody with undisguised sarcasm.

"Really," said Lil calmly. "Closest I can tell you is that it's as intuitive as reading a thousand slides to find one diseased cell. When you see it you know it. Okay. Look. Every physical characteristic is meaningful. See the set of the antenna? See how the forelegs have one extra joint?"

"Bad juju?" asked Peabody.

"Exactly."

Peabody snorted.

"But how are they bad?" asked Verity. "What do they do? Are there any people in there?"

"Sure there are," said Lil. "Poor things."

"They probably don't feel that way," said Peabody.

"Probably not," Lil agreed.

"So can we help them?" asked Verity.

Lil looked at her with a trace of pity in her eyes. "No, we can't. That's not our job."

"That's not *your* job," said Verity.

"There's nothing to be done. It's self-limiting. What do you want to do—raze the place? Our information sources tell us that they release no plagues to the atmosphere."

Jack was standing next to her. "Those sources are pretty old, Lil. And they have a lot of . . . negativity . . . to release."

Lil frowned. "As I recall, the reports were rather ambiguous. But we do know that something unsavory is going on there. It's a Class-Six City. That's not too good."

"What is Cincinnati?" asked Verity. "Class Six?"

"No," said Lil. "Cincinnati was a Class-Three City. It was very different from Memphis. Much more sophisticated, in a variety of ways."

"Chicago is Class-One," said Peabody. "A-one."

"True," said Lil. "And completely neutral in the Information Wars."

"With defenses as good as can be devised," said Peabody.

"Yeah," said Lil. "Just put that feel-good stuff in the water . . ."

"We do nothing of the sort," said Peabody. "Human contentment is actually possible, believe it or not. You'd do well to study Chicago."

"We sent some people to do just that," said Lil.

"They didn't want to leave once they got there."

"That's right," said Lil. "They were rendered completely useless. Some of our best people. Disabled."

Peabody smiled. "They became content."

Lil frowned. "They became selfish."

Peabody countered, "They learned what happiness is."

"Their minds turned to shit!" Lil shouted.

"It's all in how you look at it," said Peabody, unruffled.

"What I'd like to know is, are we going to stop in Memphis and take on supplies?" asked Twain.

"No!" said Peabody and Lil at the same time.

"Absolutely not," added Peabody.

"Under no circumstances do we stop," said Lil.

"Memphis used to be a pretty hot town," said Twain rather wistfully.

"It's a pretty hot town now," said Peabody. "It would fry you in a city minute."

Late that afternoon the river turned shimmering silver and then varying shades of pink, orange, and gold. Twilight lingered long.

Twain grumbled about not being able to stop in Memphis, but showed no signs of possible mutiny.

After dinner Verity went for a stroll on the deck. If only Blaze were here, things would be as near-perfect as they could be, considering everything.

The air was pure and sweet as the sky darkened. And as they came around a broad curve her eyes met a felicity of lights, pale and high in the gray dusk. Verity was glad that Twain was piloting. She raised binoculars to her eyes and scanned the river for the island the latest charts showed across a narrow channel from the city. But it was not there. Mud Island had apparently been swept away, washed down to the gulf.

Memphis itself was on the Fourth Chicasaw Bluff and that, apparently, had survived. But at the expense of much of Memphis, for the channel broadened like a lake and parted, drifting round to the east. It looked as if it had flooded and cut away the foundation of most of the great skyscrapers. They appeared to have fallen slowly, and a few were still leaning into the river, ready to fall, tomorrow or in fifty years, onto the glinting mountain of debris that Verity had to climb to the top deck to see.

She picked out four bridges, rising one after another but vanishing midway into thick forest on the Arkansas side, finishing half their journey above land. The riverbank had silted in on that side.

The current freshened. The first bridge lit against twilight, throwing intersecting lines of gold, blue, and red across the river. The lights showed that the bridge had sustained a great deal of damage, for it was comprised of disconnected angles that pedestrians would have had trouble ascending, not to mention vehicles. Its bed shot almost straight toward the sky in one or two places. But a portion had been cleared from the river and perhaps the channel kept dredged—by the Rural Network? Green lights began blinking atop black buoys just below the bridge, showing the channel.

A glint of silver on shore caught Verity's eyes and she swung the binoculars round, focussed, then focussed again, to make sure that she was seeing clearly.

It was bizarre. A gargantuan silver pyramid rose from the shore, hundreds of feet high. A huge, calm eye stared out from the very point. Curiouser and curiouser. Memphis, she recalled, was an Egyptian name, as was Cairo. But . . . a pyramid? She would have laughed out loud if it were not for the fear she had at traversing so close to what Lil insisted was an unsavory place. She swallowed hard. What could be worse than Cincinnati? She picked out a Bee settling down among the streets before it became too dark to see. It was tiny but she could tell that was what it was by the way it moved.

She dropped her binoculars, took deep breaths, tried to loosen her chest from the tight feeling of being trapped, trapped with her sisters in the great, golden hive. It was over. It could not happen again. She was free, out on the river, more free than she had ever been in her life! The hateful Bell was gone, no longer compelling her. No matter that she had the plague. The plague called her to glorious Nawlins, where life would begin anew, where she would have her child. . . . She closed her eyes to bask in those visions with which she had become so familiar, as if she were returning home instead of going somewhere she'd never been.

A blast of sound scared the bejesus out of her. "THIS IS S-T-A-X, YOUR MEMPHIS BLUES SOURCE," a soft, rich female voice said. "For the revo*lu*tion!" Then followed the usual sounds of whining static. "Drat!" she heard, and realized that she was outside Peabody's window. Then a steady bass and drumbeat overcame the static, and a man sang, "I'm gonna put a spell on you. . . ."

The lights of the city were breathtaking; stars against the starry night. The river was narrowing; they had no choice but to go through the cut in the bridge and trust there were more beyond, and as well lit, for Lil had insisted on shooting past and getting downriver despite the hour, and anchoring below. "We're just a target if we stop here for the night," she said grimly.

Verity opened her eyes and took another look.

The bridge loomed almost overhead, breathtakingly huge. The wharf bustled with activity, even more so than Cairo's. It appeared that people were dancing. Yes, that must be a band up on that low stage. A woman and two men played guitars, and another woman sang. There seemed to be horns. The powerful thrash of the paddlewheel precluded hearing any of it. People jostled Verity on both sides as the crowd at the railings swelled. A single red light blinked high atop a fragile-looking metal tower.

"TURN OFF THE LIGHTS," hollered Twain urgently. "I CAN'T SEE A DAMNED THING WITH THE LIGHTS ON!"

Verity hurried toward the pilothouse; evidently Twain didn't know that he could control all the lights from there.

Then there was horrible rending sound and the paddlewheel mechanism groaned to a halt. The boat shook. A jangle of bells and curses rang out from the pilothouse. The *Queen* swung sideways in the current. They had collided with something.

A raft! Fragments of it flew up over the boat and crashed onto the upper deck, and planks littered the water. A ragged portion of wet taupe-colored wigwam was plastered to one of the hurricane deck staterooms. Horrified, Verity rushed to the back to see if anyone could be rescued.

In the light that still shone from the windows, she saw below on the river a man holding to a scrap of wood, which was rushing away in the current. He held another man fast, faceup, one strong arm flung across his chest, and there was his face—Blaze's face! unmistakable and chillingly without awareness as the two were swept through the patch of light and then into the darkness of the surging river.

"Help me!" she yelled, ran down to the boiler deck and struggled to let down the johnboat. As she climbed down into it Lil leaned over the railing.

"Don't you go into Memphis, Verity!"

"It was Blaze!" she shouted over her shoulder.

"I don't care if it was God Almighty, you stay out of that city. Do you hear me, Verity?"

Lil's voice grew faint. Verity caught the oars and pulled in the direction of the current, hoping to overtake them before it was too late.

Though she was still a hundred yards out, she spotted the man who had Blaze in his grip. His head bobbed up right next to the high concrete wharf which rose from the water, a massive, seamless balustrade, blotched with great pale green and red stains which were illuminated by overhanging lights. She hoped that the man still held Blaze. His tiny head moved at a fast clip downriver. Verity was afraid he would smash into the wharf but then she saw his arm rise from the water and grab at something and then she saw the narrow flight of steps cut into the wall.

Yes! He rolled a limp body onto the steps, pulled himself up, flung Blaze over his shoulder like a sack of grain and hurried up the stairs, at an amazing speed considering his burden and his swim.

"Hey," she yelled constantly as she rowed closer, struggling against an eddy which kept pushing her back toward the middle of the river.

"STOP! I'M BLAZE'S FRIEND! I'LL TAKE YOU TO THE BOAT!" Her shouts echoed back to her from the wall, but apparently he did not hear, or did not want to. He gained the top and vanished; she couldn't see beyond the edge and she was still about fifty feet out.

Verity pulled hard on her oars. She had to get to the wharf upriver from the steps. If she was swept past she couldn't go round again; she'd just have to watch sharp for her next chance. She pulled closer—closer—finding that the current slowed helpfully at this point—and stood to grab the rusted bar embedded in the wall next to the steps. As she reached, a log rammed her boat and she fell backward onto the seat, smashing her leg and arm. The river grabbed the boat again and sent it racing away.

Cursing as fiercely as Twain, she scrambled back onto the seat and took up the oars again. Tears of frustration coursed down her face. There *had* to be another way to get in! There *had* to be!

And finally, there it was. Only a few blocks past the first place, but better, a concrete arm reaching out into the river like a broad scoop, forming a harbor place large enough for eight or ten small boats. A few were tied up, and the place even had lights. She let the current push her into the tiny harbor, delicately using her oars to maneuver herself into a slip. In the boats she saw fishing rods and nets. These people couldn't be too bad, could they?

It was quieter in this part of the City. She heard no sounds of revelry. She wished she knew what Lil knew about it. To darkly warn against something without explaining it was not much of a deterrent. Lil had warned against Cairo, and Lil had been right, though she suspected that if Jack and Lil, or whatever their names were, had not been on the boat the debacle would not have occurred.

She feared Bees. She feared them past all reason. If they wanted to, they could probably latch hold of her somehow and imprison her here forever.

Who was that man who was carrying Blaze? Why wasn't Blaze on the train? Why had he returned?

No matter. Joy leaped in her heart. He had come back, and that was all that mattered.

Now she had to go in and find him.

The shadowed concrete steps were moss-covered and Verity slipped on them in her haste. Their dank smell enveloped and followed her onto the landing above and she realized that it was the smell of Memphis, entire. Victim of the river but still surviving as best it could, hazed with evening mist. The gold and blue lights of the bridge glowed through the mist like dense close stars.

Around her were unlit alleys and a street down which she glimpsed old, sagging mansions. She saw someone on one of the porches, saw a dark figure rise and say, "Miss, don't go that way, it's dangerous, hear?" But she ran from him, toward the lights of the dancing wharf, where Blaze's music blared like a new way of being.

The concrete of the landing was cracked; lined with great gouts of weeds over which she tripped; littered with broken glass. The verge of the crowd was sudden, as if there was some invisible line, presumably that of the overhead lights, which delineated its border. She drew closer, wondering if they would be hostile or friendly, these dancers to the strong, harsh rhythm of powerful guitars and horns. She slowed as a cramp stitched her side, took a deep breath of the odd-scented air of evening, glanced out at the river where the *Queen* had anchored, in Lil's danger zone. She gasped more of the dank river air, in it intertwined other smells—beer, tobacco smoke, the sweat of the dance, and another scent unknown to her.

Before her, the crowd ceased to be dancing people, but merely moving shapes of color which lacked intent, and then even their colors faded. A part of her noticed this and thought it strange, and another part was deeply frightened as her vision transmuted. But most of her simply watched as she stood unmoving, and then it passed. An energetic burst of horns, backed by a powerful drumbeat, pulled her in as she caught the rhythm of the dancers and slipped into the crowd.

This was the place where the man had carried Blaze. He had to be in there somewhere. She was enveloped by dancing, smiling people. Their eyes were filled with joy and odd purpose, and a few looked at her as if trying to pass important information to her through the air, with their eyes, but she did not understand what that might be. Warnings mingled with looks of alarm and oddly serious faces.

Most of the people were black, brown, golden, a tremendous variety of dark, burnished hues. She was swept into their grace but resisted their dance, which took on sudden changes that passed through the crowd like wind flattening a field of grass. They moved their arms in cadence, shook their hips, danced forward and then back. She passed through a circle of dancers as they shouted, raised their arms as one, danced back, and then she passed out the other side. The music, which invaded the air as thoroughly as wind or rain, had a deep, full texture of pain and longing and redemption that she'd never heard before when Blaze was playing the blues.

Where was he?

She began to feel frantic. She would never find him in this melee. She broke into a run, shouting his name, pushing between people who didn't even seem to notice her, until one man said, "The dance is all," grabbed her waist, and caught her in their rhythm. She stepped lightly with him without thinking, as if born to it. "Dance! Yes! Do it with us. Join us. Help us." And he kissed her, full on the mouth.

His hands on hers, his mouth, his presence . . . part of her awoke and realize that this was joy, but a desperate joy, coupled with the fierceness of warriors. She stopped and stared at him. "What is it?" she whispered. "What's wrong?" But he did not hear, and was absorbed by the crowd in an instant.

Verity felt tremendous despair. More of what Blaze wanted. Everything here. Had he not found what he wanted on the train? If not, it was here, then, the essence of what he was looking for: life with a mission, blues so deep he'd fall into them and if she wanted him to leave she'd be the traitor, the enemy.

She stood still for a moment, trying to will information out of the dancers, out of their shouts, their wild yet informed motion. Dance was a message, and always a message, she knew this deep in her being. What was the message, here? She turned to look behind her. The texture of the crowd thinned for a moment, and she saw it, with a jolt.

The huge unearthly pyramid.

It glowed silver against the dark river. No one was near it, not within a hundred yards. She'd made her way through the crowd and was out the other side.

The pyramid was hypnotic. It almost . . . pulsed. Could she hear another music coming from it, one of high voices? Or was a it a low, brooding tone, almost beneath hearing, but vibrating in her bones? Dirgelike. It brought to mind pictures of Dante's Purgatory she'd seen in one of the books John approved of.

She thought a whispery voice laughed in her ear but there was no one near. She tilted her head. Nothing. Nothing but the blues. She stepped closer, in order to hear better. Maybe here was information about Memphis. Maybe she could access the city, the way she'd been able to access Cincinnati, and everyone in it if she wished, just by touching an interstice. Interstices, filled with the fluid that translated metapheromones, must be here.

The air smelled sweet, not of the river, not the overwhelming smell of liquor, behind her, but a pleasant one, like flowers. Flowers . . .

Her vision blurred, and she blinked, and a gust of wind blew the smell of flowers from her. Ahead of her, from behind one corner of the pyramid, a man stepped out.

In the faint silvery light emitted by the pyramid, she saw his bald head shine. He was dressed completely in black. His shoulders sloped downward. She seemed unable to move, as if she was in a dream.

She expected him to approach, but instead he turned and walked toward the river. He arrived at a bench not far from her, sat, and stared out at the water.

In the shadow of the pyramid, as Verity's eyes adjusted to the darkness beyond, she saw Bees.

They were resting, having apparently sunk to the ground at sundown. Without the sun they could not see.

The surface of the pyramid appeared to be in motion. She heard a warning shout behind her, from one of the dancers, but took another step closer.

She saw a face, and then another. Faces, like silvery holographic images, flowed upward in lines toward the great eye at the top. It was fascinating and frightful. The faces were all different, and all distressed.

"Don't worry," she heard clearly from the man on the bench, who spoke without turning his head. His voice was harsh, low, whispery. "You'll be a part of this eventually. Everything will. In the last instant, you'll thank me. You rowed in from the boat. Not many visitors here. Not like before. Used to have half the air force under me." He nodded toward the pyramid, then turned on the bench and looked at Verity, his eyes like two dark pits. He waved one hand toward the dancers. "Even them. They'll thank me too. Brave souls. I can't help but admire them. But . . ." He shrugged, and turned back to watch the water. "Takes all my will to stay and finish things."

Verity was able, then, to back away, and to run. She thought she saw him rise and follow her, slowly, as if speed didn't matter.

She plunged back into the crowd. She'd never felt so terrified in her life, not even within the depths of the hive at Cincinnati. And she was not even sure what she was afraid of. Just darkness. Just . . . nothing. She could feel it all around, like a hand wanting to choke the life out of her.

And then it was swept away, that nothing, by the joy of the dancers.

But she soon realized that she couldn't stay hidden within them, where it seemed safe. She'd have to venture into the streets that edged the wharf. She pushed through and through the crowd and never saw Blaze. He might be there. She might have missed him.

Or he could have gone into town.

A steady night breeze washed the cloying humid air from the wharf. She made it to the edge of the crowd and was relieved to see that the crowd didn't actually end.

In front of her was a narrow, brick-paved street. Neon signs vied with one another above dark doorways. The mass of dancers flowed down the streets, drinking and hollering and having a good time. The air was filled with the clash of many bands. Apparently each club had their own.

She pushed her way down the street.

These buildings did indeed have interstices, like Cincinnati. One pulsed next to the doorway, neon green.

If she were in Cincinnati, she could touch an interstice and receive a wide variety of information. Such as where to find a man of a certain description. She could send him a message, had he receptors with which to access the interstices. Blaze had no receptors.

Hers were covered by gloves. Were the gloves permeable? She could feel through them; they were weightless; so thin that she completely forgot they were there most of the time. Metapheromones were manufactured by them, but did that mean that her receptors would not work here? She didn't think so.

However, Memphis was a different system than Cincinnati. Each Flower City was individual. But maybe it was learnable. Maybe she would be automatically initiated . . .

But maybe not.

As she stood there, a dancer smashed into her from behind, pushing her toward the interstice. Without thinking, she held up one hand to break her fall, and it met the interstice.

As when she had been exposed to the strange scent on the border of the crowd, her vision altered.

She could not make sense of what she was seeing. All was shapes and colors, like in the visions of Modern Art she'd had when in the Dayton Library. She leaned against the brick wall breathing deeply, hoping that this would pass.

Slowly, her vision resolved. But she felt a deep inner tremor, as if she'd just wakened without having slept enough.

Well, now she knew that the interstices didn't work!

She was dizzy. She had to concentrate to walk down the street. Next to her she heard a soft voice say, "Wait."

She turned toward the voice and was startled to see a face on a door. It was a living face, the face of a black woman with many braids falling across her face. Next to her face was a picture of a radio tower, emanating lightning bolts. Below the picture of the tower the door said STAX, Radio Energy for the Revolution!

Verity stepped closer, soothed, reminded of how Sphere had mastered Cincinnati and appeared in this way to her.

"Who are you?" she managed to ask.

"I'm the Shadow Woman. I play the blues. For the revolution. For the world. For life. Stay away from Clean Mind. He'd love a tasty tidbit like you. He's following you. Go back to your boat."

"How did you—I can't," said Verity. "I have to find—" But the face vanished.

Verity stood there for a minute. She tried to open the door but it was locked. She didn't have time to fool with the Shadow Woman or Clean Mind or anyone. An open door next to her blared music. Blaze's kind of place.

She pushed her way inside the bar. It was uncomfortably hot. The overwhelmingly loud music was almost physical, like a wall. The room was tiny, but as stuffed with people as the wharf.

She climbed onto a table to get a better view, standing carefully as it was not well-balanced, trying not to step on plates and ashtrays. No one seemed to notice or care, not even those using the table.

She studied every corner of the dimly lit room, noting uncomfortably the ever-present bee motif repeated and glowing on the walls, a kind of wallpaper. The small table tipped a bit as she stepped back toward the chair she'd used as a stepstool. The two men sitting at the table grabbed their beers simultaneously without turning away from the stage, where a heavy black man hollered indecipherable words. A hand grabbed Verity's own and steadied her as she crouched down.

"The truth will set you free," the man holding her hand said, close to her ear. Her hand flared with unpleasant sensation. Darkness flowed into her from his touch, dimming her vision and her heart.

She looked down into black, fathomless eyes. She wondered how his voice could be so clear in all this blaring noise.

"Your receptors have been initiated now. Every little bit helps spread the truth. But you don't have to stay out here. Please join the others; join *us;* our cause. Come with me to the pyramid—"

She jerked her hand away in horror, slipped on the wet table, and fell. The table toppled sideways. The man pushed backward through the crowd.

The two men sitting at the table jumped up and grabbed her in an instant, before she even reached the floor, and set her on her feet as smoothly as if it were all part of an act. The man holding Verity's arm said, "Shit, how did *he* get in here?" and Verity followed the man's gaze and saw the bald-headed man disappearing out the doorway.

A great shout erupted, and the bar rapidly emptied. She heard cries of "Get him! Kill the bastard!" But they all seemed rather distant. Even the musicians jumped off the stage to give chase, so that soon the place was empty, though it still vibrated with sounds from the other sides of both walls.

Verity sat down slowly in a chair. The room spun around her. She felt dizzy, as if she were falling. And sick, very sick. She vomited onto the floor. She couldn't help it. Couldn't be the pregnancy, she thought dimly. That was all adjusted for. It was the lights, their brightness, their garish colors. Their awful, invading colors were giving her a headache. She took a sip of beer to clear her mouth. Maybe someone would come along to clean things up. She really didn't care.

She looked at her right hand, which he'd held. His touch had been a jolt of utterly sickening feelings which rushed through her. Horrific images, of war and death and pain. The accumulated horror of what being human had meant to millions caught in the countless wars that plagued the planet. She knew this, clearly, and knew she was meant to know this. This was a vast, painful, truth, impossible for any one person to fully bear. This man indeed thought of himself as a truth-giver. A hero.

There was a little spotlight above her table and she set her hand, palm up, in the center of the spot on the table.

It was turning blue. But maybe that was just the light. It had to be the light. Living flesh didn't get so blue.

She put her left hand next to it.

It was pale, her own color. But then it slowly started to turn blue as well.

She clenched both hands tightly. Where were all the people? The room spun away from her. It was really a very big room. The walls were so far away.

People started trudging back in, quiet, their faces grim. One woman dropped into the seat next to her. "I'm sorry, honey," she said. "I've never seen him so bold. Have you, Circle?"

A man with a spiral tattooed on his cheekbone below his eye shook his head. "Snuck right in here. Took a big chance. He must have thought you were really something," he said to Verity. "He always hangs out with his Bees. Stays away from us at night. We rule the night. The blues rule the night. The Bees can't see at night. We take it all back, then. Where are you from? Not from Memphis."

"From the boat," suggested the woman.

Their conversation seemed more and more distant to Verity. The woman's eyes looked upside down. Her long braids twisted like snakes. Verity looked down at her hands again and they were gray. "I'm . . . looking . . . for . . . someone," she said. Her voice sounded funny to her. The band started up again.

The woman shouted in her ear. "We have to get you back to your boat," she said. "He won't dare come back here tonight. But you should leave—the sooner the better."

"No!" shouted Verity and much more quickly than she thought she could she rose and ran through the bar, slipping between the dancers, then was out the door, onto the street, hiding around a corner, then continuing down an alley. She staggered and the dimly shining bricks of the pavement reeled up to meet her. She slowly got to her feet and knew that her palms were torn and bleeding but it didn't seem to matter.

She stood stock-still in the alley. She became aware of a large eye in her field of vision.

Yes. It was the All-Seeing Eye. Like at the top of the pyramid.

Then a new band struck up, in the street at the end of the alley. The music retrieved her, somehow, struck clear through her and focussed her thoughts. She was sheeted with dampness; mist from the river; sweat from the hot summer night.

"Blaze," she whispered. "Got to find you." She walked unevenly, for there was something wrong with her legs. Or maybe her balance. She had to concentrate. She couldn't forget. She seemed to be forgetting, and the neon signs on the street she found at the end of the alley weren't brilliantly colored, like those on the other street. This street was in tones of gray, white, and black. It was strange. But the music was loud, and for a moment, the Eye vanished.

Twenty-five

○○○○○○○○○○○○○○○○○○○

Memphis Blues

I woke to a paroxysm of coughing and dreadful, burning pain in my throat and nose and pounding on my chest and then I was thrashing round and black water just then water was black the color of death poured from my mouth and I was sick, sick, sick.

There were brilliant lights and colors and pulsing music all round me and I lay on hard wet concrete, soaked, shivering, and buck naked. Faces pressed round me and I thought, second time dead and no angels this time but perhaps there was one, before, and there was one this time too, and his name was James.

"Are you all right?" he asked anxiously. I noticed incongruously that his hair was much longer than on the train—it grows, I thought. . . .

To stop those strangers staring at me I nodded and forced my voice past the burning and it set me to coughing again. "Yes," I whispered, and vigorously nodded as water and drool spewed from me. Drowning is an awful mess.

Music pounded in the air. The feet around me resumed dancing. We were in a circle of rhythm. I began to breathe easier, though it still hurt. James helped me sit up. "Wait here," he said, "I'll try and find you some clothes." He looked around fearfully. "There are too many people," he muttered, "it's a hundred times worse than Cairo," then set his jaw and wove through the dancers and was gone and I hoped he could find his way back. No one paid much attention to me, naked as I was. Maybe they were just being polite. The smell of whiskey was heavy in the air and it dawned on me. I was in *Memphis*.

Not the home of the blues, no. The home of the blues was down on the Delta, the hottest, meanest place this side of hell.

But the blues had come to live here, and made themselves quite comfortable indeed.

Alma's potion tossed out more facts for me, as if my mind was a river shore just aching to snag whatever floated downstream.

W. C. Handy had written "Memphis Blues" here, and earned himself the somewhat exaggerated moniker "Father of the Blues." Robert Church, a onetime slave, bought up all the real estate he could grab after Memphis lost its city charter because most of the city had died of cholera and malaria. He brought the city back to life and became a millionaire. Riley King from Itta Benna, Mississippi, metamorphosed into Blues Boy and sold the mildly inebriating Pepticon over WDIA and played the blues between commercials. Sam Phillips started Stax Records, which helped the crossover to white audiences, and got a lot of black performers started. The inclusion of a white boy named Elvis puzzled me, but Alma's potion told me he was one of the bridges taking the blues from a black audience to white, and that he was deep into the blues, imitating the very best nuance for nuance.

The river night was hot, steamy, and loud. And this was the blues, playing now.

I stood up, forgetting my nakedness. No one cared so why should I? They were stark raving mad so I could walk around stark naked. The night was hot, and sweat replaced river water. I dimly remembered the wreck, when the boat plowed into us, waking me, the crunch of wood, the flight through the air and the hardness of the water, which stunned me. I remembered hearing James's frantic shouts at the same time I was tossed. I wondered if it had been the *Queen;* we'd seen only one other boat, a shadow the previous night, heading upriver.

If it was, then Verity would still be downriver whenever we left.

If we left . . .

For Alma's blues history flowered deliciously in my brain even more fully as I listened with a faculty that was deeper than mere listening. There was nothing but the sweaty night, and that massive sound that cut me to ribbons. I even recognized the style of how he pulled the notes out low and throbbing—the voice—

"Muddy Waters!" I shouted. I was overwhelmed.

I imagined his guitar in my hands, long smooth neck held low, trying to fathom the mastery with which he pulled sound and emotion from the guitar, echoing what he felt inside. So *alive;* so raw and powerful.

James broke through the crowd and thrust some clothes at me. "Here. Get dressed," he shouted over the blare of the music. "Hurry. Then let's get out of here. I don't think we should stay." Over his shoulder, above the bobbing heads of the crowd, I saw something bizarre: the glittering point of a huge pyramid. Well, I'd seen stranger things in Cincinnati.

"You've got to be kidding," I shouted back, overriding the pain in my chest. "Didn't I tell you that this is where I wanted to go? Why didn't you wake me up when you saw it? This has got to be Memphis, unless I died and heaven is real. And I know it's not. Let's go find some cigarettes."

I'm sure he felt horrified and he diligently tried to express this with a frown. Since he'd been off the train he'd been practicing applicable facial expressions.

"Come on," I said. "They can't hurt us." While I spoke I was pulling on some black leather pants a little too tight for me and struggling to zip them up. I pulled on a black T-shirt and pushed barefoot through the crowd. "Thanks for the clothes."

"You don't understand," he said breathlessly as we reached the fringe of the wharf where the music wasn't quite as loud. "I—I think there's something very strange about this place." He took a deep breath. He frowned harder. "There's too much isopentyl acetate for State 18946 and yet that's the one we must be in since I find no closer parity . . ." He muttered on in this fashion at my side as I walked on, peered down a street of colored jewels, flashing in various rhythms, proclaiming performers and other services. "Beale Street," I breathed, as excited as if I'd stumbled into heaven. NEURON PAWN/SEX MAGIC/SEVEN SWINGING ELVI/MEMPHIS MINNIE, I managed to pick out as the signs vied with one another, a fantastic, glittery overlay in continuous flux.

"Oh, glory," I muttered. Where to begin?

I pushed past James and I admit that I did feel a twinge of trepidation when I noticed that intermingled with all the big signs were innumerable tiny Bees—not real flying ones but Bee signifiers, as if to remind everyone constantly. . . . Closeup, I could see that even the letters of one of the signs were composed of pixel-like Bees.

I continued regardless. I'd made it out of Cincinnati, hadn't I? Not through your own efforts, a little voice reminded me, but I told it to shut up.

The streets were brick and the buildings were only a few stories high. Music issued from every door. I soaked it up. It exploded in my mind. Who needed heaven? This was enough! The night reeled around me. I ignored the dazed looks in the eyes of the people around me.

I paused at a door with a picture of a metal tower on it. Lightning bolts, or radio waves, or something, issued from the top. Below the picture a sign said,

STAX
BLUES FOR LIFE

I pounded on the door, which was locked. "Let me in!" I yelled. I set up quite a din. James tried to pull me away but I wouldn't budge. Finally someone tapped me on the shoulder.

"You can't get in there," a man told me. "Only the Shadow Woman gets in there. I only heard of her. Never seen her. She plays old blues records for broadcast. For the *revolution.* I hear tell sometimes the broadcast works."

"It *does!* I want to see her!" I said.

He smiled. "You're not the only one." He vanished into the crowd.

I imagined the Shadow Woman with reverence. I pounded some more, to no avail. And finally I couldn't resist. I succumbed to my immediate surroundings and entered the next open door.

A wave of sound almost floored me.

The entire audience was black, as were the performers. The air was filled with a sweet, maddening scent and oh, the ecstasy it induced. *Bees,* whispered something from the back of my mind which I easily ignored. I floated into blues heaven and slow-dragged and clapped and yelled and drank the innumerable cold and delicious beers pressed into my waiting hand. There was that powerful blues feeling of suffering in the air, a feeling that only the music was holding back the chaos of utter despair and endless night. Blues was the life raft, the only positive energy, the only light. And that dichotomy gave it overwhelming power. It was *religious,* just as religious as anything Mother Ann thought up. It was pure and holy, like light, on the side of good. On the side of *life.*

After a while James pulled me out of the crowd. He was very strong. Out in the street, which still held heat, but where my ears rang in the sudden cessation of blaring sound, he looked at me sternly and I marveled in my drunkenness at how quickly he was *changing . . . growing . . .*

"Had enough?" he asked. "You've been in there for hours. The metas here seem to be held in abeyance, somehow. They're all around, in the air. But—I touched a few of these people—actually, I couldn't *help* it; it's so crowded. And it's very curious. Their . . . how can I put this? Their state of *being* doesn't reflect what they should, given these metas."

"What are you *talking* about?" I asked.

"Extremely precise states of mind are endemic to Flower Cities. It's something that we bypassed in the domes. We took a different route. The states of mind are precise and repeatable because of metapheromones. These people should be in an entirely different state of mind, given the metapheromones being pumped into this place . . . best I can figure, it's some kind of war. They're the resistance."

"That's ridiculous!" I said. "This isn't a war. It's a party! Besides, I don't have anything to worry about. Those things don't affect me. I'm just a hundred-per-cent-normal human being. It does have its advantages." *Except for Alma's blues . . .*

He stared at me with his bland blue eyes and I could tell he was trying to summon something from his memory banks, or whatever he had inside. Finally he just looked resigned. "Maybe some exercise would help," he said. He took my arm and walked me down Beale Street. I wanted to go more slowly but he kept pulling me along when I stopped to peer into doorways.

"I'm fine," I protested. "Right as rain." But he kept on walking and I said, "Where are we going?"

"Where I can think," he said, and I found that funny and began to laugh and he just pulled me on more quickly, yanking me to my feet when I stumbled.

"I always gave Masa coffee when she got like this," he muttered. "Where's the coffee?"

The streets quickly gave way to a stretch of chain fences and warehouses and concrete for a few blocks. James stopped and turned around. "There seems to be someone following us," he said.

I turned and saw a shadowy figure about five blocks behind us, very far, on the edge of the music district. He was stumbling and weaving about. Then he keeled over. "He's not following us," I said. "He's just drunk." Then I saw a sign up ahead. "Maybe there's coffee there," I said, though I hoped it was another blues bar. But as we got closer I saw that it said instead NATIONAL CIVIL RIGHTS MUSEUM.

Something flicked into my mind. The Lorraine Motel. A man had been killed here. What did that have to do with the blues? Why was it in Alma's curriculum? "Let's look in here," I said.

"At least it's quiet," said James. He followed me in.

It was cold inside and there was no one there. No one alive. But it was full of ghosts. James took a deep breath. "This is better," he said. "Much better."

Once again, this time in front of me instead of inside of me: the history of black slavery in the United States. The Declaration of Independence and the Constitution, documents from the old United States of America. I read the highlighted words again, marveling at how my ancestors had deliberately chosen to not apply those fine ideas to black people. The South grew rich on their misery. I saw on a map the flowering of huge plantations, the very bricks of their mansions made and stacked by humans who had no choice but to labor at whatever task was set for them. I saw the University of Virginia being built by slave labor. I stood in a circle on the floor and found myself in a line of slaves, with the overseer cracking his whip, the rough feel of the hoe in my hand. I even felt exhausted and utterly hopeless and wondered how the museum accomplished *that*. Then it changed from the year 1820 to 1920 and I was a prisoner, hefting a great ax straight overhead as did my immediate neighbors and we brought them straight down on a great log that was in front of us and as the chips flew our holler seemed to shake the ground, the lead man singing first, the rest of us overlapping on the downstroke:

> Well, it's early in the morn
>> In the mornin
> Baby, when I rise,
>> Lordy, Mama
> It's I have a misery,
>> Berta
> Well-ah, in my right side . . .

Bottle Eye, Little Red, Tangle Eye, and Hard Hair sang this with me and when we were through the huge live oak crashed over. I stepped out of the circle and the hallucination vanished. It was just a simulation of a Parchman Farm worksong, but even that was frightening for it contained the awful aura of that infamous prison plantation, run at a profit by the State of Mississippi for so many years, providing so much fodder for blues songs, filled with people unfairly imprisoned. And if they had committed crimes, the sentences far outweighed what a white man would get for the same offense.

The pleasant beer buzz receded and soon I was painfully stone cold sober. I saw Clyde Kennard, a black Army Paratrooper who served in Germany and Korea, apply to Mississippi Southern. He'd already completed two years of college at the University of Chicago, but returned to Mississippi to care for his sick stepfather. His application was turned down, but although he refused legal aid from the NAACP, to which he belonged, he wrote reasoned letters to the newspapers about the situation. Within a month, an all-white jury took ten minutes to convict him of a frame-up accusation of stealing $25 worth of chicken feed from a warehouse, a felony that would deny him entry to any state university, and which carried a seven-year hard labor sentence to Parchman Farm. Even after he had a cancerous growth removed and lost forty pounds, he was sent back to the fields and denied further medical care by Parchman officials. In spring of 1963 he was pardoned by a new governor to avoid further bad publicity, but died two months later. His was just one story out of thousands. Generations of blacks kept poor and uneducated, brutalized without recourse to law, lynched and raped and scorned, twisted up inside me as disbelief grew. These were Americans? The callousness of these people shook me.

I probably watched ten times the schoolgirls walking brave and scared down the gauntlet of soldiers with full-grown white men jeering at them. All they wanted to do was go to school! I don't know how many times I would have watched the terrified, innocent faces of those girls and contrasted them with the twisted evil surrounding them but James pulled me away and wiped my tears as I imagined he had wiped Masa's countless times.

"Maybe this is worse than the blues," he whispered. "Let's go back."

"This is why there is the blues," I whispered back. I saw how unworthy I was of Alma's gift.

The music of these people, the music graciously granted life by their captors because it helped keep the slaves plowing the fields, picking the cotton, building the levees, laying the tracks, doing the laundry, had risen up and conquered the nation. It washed away the remnants of strict-metered well-mannered European songs in a great flood of syncopation, blue notes, bent notes, and irrepressible life, leaving the world awash in its spawn—the blues, jazz, and rock and roll. I saw that too, colorful streams of music surrounding a holographic globe. I could touch one part of it and see a Coltrane concert in Japan, after a mob of cheering fans engulfed his plane on the runway, causing him to wonder what celebrity was on the plane. I touched another and saw Louis Armstrong at Versailles, treated like royalty.

I saw how they had claimed their civil rights—boldly, at last, with loss of life, fighting hard for every bloody inch. I saw how even the white Freedom Riders had been murdered, as was Martin Luther King, Jr., in this very building, a holy spot for that. A shrine, where I stood, undeserving, in America's burning center, at the heart of the rift which divided the country with untruth and bad faith and the infliction of generations of hell upon an entire people.

I stumbled from it at last, hours after entering, dazed and numb. I headed back toward Beale Street, and James did not try and stop me. Fog eddied knee-deep in the streets and I hurried back toward the lights and noise and liquor. They met my anguish with open arms and hugged me tightly to them, and it was back into a café where I ate barbecue and hush puppies and cole slaw and drank beer and felt the low, hot pulse of blues louder than thunder in my very bones. I got to dancing and carrying on again as a huge black woman stood up on the stage and belted out:

Once I led the life of a millionaire—

There was a break in the music, after her. The band left the stage unguarded from me, as it were.

I took one step and then another and the third and fourth steps had me standing on the stage. Alone, and a shining red guitar stood waiting next to me on a stand. I felt right at home. There were drums, and another guitar, which I ignored in the face of this glory. So *lovely*. FENDER STRATOCASTER flowed across the red guitar in gold script and the knobs looked gold too.

It was like water in the desert. How had this wonderful juxtaposition

of events, this apex of all my desires, occurred? Something in the club
sensed the yearning within me? I don't know; it was a magical night.

"What yo' name?" someone yelled out.

"Blaze," I yelled back, slightly startled at the way my voice was magnified and echoed.

"For his hair," I translated to myself as one woman said to the man
next to her, "Foh his hay-ah." They all talked that way, the blacks and the
few whites, softening every word that crossed their lips. It occurred to me
that of course, my whole life had been leading up to this moment, even
my being named for a physical characteristic, my bright red hair, by
long-dead Sister Serena. Half Ear, Whining Boy, their names whispered
through me and I felt privileged and pushed back the louder whisper that
said white boy what do you know of those blues. Unlike the old bluesmen, though, I had no idea what my given name was, and I never would.

I reverently plucked the guitar from the stand and looped the strap
over my neck. I brought one hand toward the shining steel strings and
was rewarded by an ear-piercing whine; some instinct made me reach for
the knobs and that fixed it. There was a pedal at my foot and I knew what
that was for too.

I didn't need my calluses with this magical instrument. I tore into
"Drowning Man Blues" with fierce intensity and the audience whooped
and clapped:

> Rollin and tumblin
> River's got me in her grip
> Rollin and tumblin
> River's got me in her grip
> Like to wash me down to New Orleans
> If I take a slip

They yelled back, go white boy, go. My fingers went wild. The bass
player and drummer returned from their break and took up their
places again, sliding in naturally behind me without missing a beat,
grounding me. The fellow whose guitar I assumed I played sat at a table
and drank, unperturbed. A blues came into my head and it was "Big Bee
Blues":

> Now you big Bees of Memphis
> You think that you're the king
> Well fly on down to New Orleans
> And burn your evil wings

Then James was pulling me off the stage. "You're really stupid," he
said, and I kept hold of the guitar as the leads popped out and that hor-

rible screaming whine commenced again. I heard a commotion behind me. "I need more whiskey," I said. "Let go of me." I yanked away too stoned to pay much attention to the fact that the old plaster crown molding running around the ceiling flashed with menacing red-light bees. "Fucking parasites!" I yelled, infused with a powerful new vocabulary. I had no choice but to stumble after James; he was stronger than me anyway and stone-cold sober. I kept a grip on the guitar. It was mine, meant for me, made for me. It had met its destiny. I caught a glimpse of the owner sitting in a whirlwind of commotion, sipping whiskey, as I flew past, and he just raised his glass and gave me a nod. I figured it wasn't too hard to come across such things in Memphis. It sure as hell would be anywhere else. I clutched it to my chest.

We tumbled onto the street where mist was flowing downhill like a river and the sky was graying with dawn. "They're going to be up soon," he said. "We have to get out of here."

"I'm not afraid of no fucking Bees," I said belligerently, marvelously empowered by beer, whiskey, and God knows what else.

"I am," he said. "You're just too stupid to be afraid."

I mulled that over for about a second, and cut down a back alley to the right, carrying my lovely trophy, angry at James for spoiling my fun. And it was more than fun. It was some vast fulfillment, a tremendous awakening. I felt like *worshiping* the damned Bees! They'd kept the Blues alive!

Then I stumbled right into one.

I was surprised. I always thought they spent their time cruising above, flying menacingly overhead. Not that I knew a whole lot about them, I realized, my mouth fuzzy and my head beginning to ache.

It was about as tall as I, but longer. It danced back, startled, I guess, and appraised me. It reached out a shiny black leg and I jumped back.

I guess my foreignness, or something, startled it. It backed off. I did not like its looks. There was nothing felicitous about it, nothing fuzzy and round like your normal bumblebee. It was thin, more like a wasp, and parts of it were metallic, or something like, because it had to be pretty light in order to fly. I took in the strange insignia tattooed between its eyes—a snake. Now why would a bee want a picture of a snake on its head I wondered crazily. Beneath it was some writing too small to read and as soon as I thought this it enlarged and it said Nan Is All, Surrender. Then it reached for me again and I smelled that smell and held my breath and ran.

All sorts of thoughts bubbled through my mind as I flew back down that alley. For one, I decided that the Bees had nothing to do with keeping the blues alive. For another, how big, really, was Memphis? Just a few blocks of blues mayhem? I could see more buildings at the end of the dank, shadowy alley and glancing up I could see what I'd missed the night before, towering, dreadfully high buildings, all with their interstices glowing dully, without color, as the night turned to day, and behind them was the massive tumbled carcass of another and I thought I saw water lapping the building as it lay at that extreme angle but wasn't sure for the mist.

My footsteps echoed in the empty alley, and I thought I could hear the scritch of that monster behind me. I don't know what I thought, nothing rational, it was just big and alien and frightening. I did not know what it wanted of me. I suddenly knew that I didn't want the blues forever, not if I had to stay in Memphis to have them. Above me, I saw a few Bees in the gray sky.

Oh, the dawn was sweet as I burst out onto the wharf, its cover of fog silver and rose. Within the fog, coming from the wilderness around Memphis, was a tone too deep to hear, though I could feel it whirring in my bones. The river was swift and to my joy I saw, through rifts in the fog, the *Queen,* waiting above the ruined bridge. A breeze shredded the fog.

The Bees appeared to be massing above me. And a big circle of them were dancing on the wharf. Yes, dancing, their circle tight and probably about forty feet in diameter.

The wharf was littered with bottles, which were being gathered by some sort of low round things like turtles that scuttled about; I had to take care not to trip over them. People lay on the concrete as if dead and the turtles went carefully around them, feeding the bottles into holes on their backs. The Bees were between me and the boat; I'd have to make a large detour and hope that I didn't attract their attention.

Just at that moment, something in their dance dictated a backward move. Their circle enlarged and I could see through to the middle.

Verity was there.

I called out her name and she turned, slowly. But she didn't seem to recognize me. I hurried toward her; the Bees did not pause in their steps. I was apparently nothing to them.

I stopped outside the circle, about fifteen feet from her. She looked at me blankly, then looked back at one of the Bees.

The guitar was slowing me down. I stooped and laid it on the concrete. Then something caught my eye, something that had been invisible in the gray fog, but that assumed looming form as the sun gained strength.

The pyramid, massive and overwhelming. It was constructed of panels, and in the panels were faces, ever-changing faces, rushing upward toward that terrible eye, each filled with anguish. I knew that they were the faces of people trapped inside, without even thinking about it.

I glanced at it for only a second before looking back at the Bees. Now that it was lighter, I could see that they were covered with all sorts of words and runes, some of them skulls and crossbones and some of them less easy to understand. Verity cast a long shadow across the concrete, as did the Bees, as the sun suddenly flooded the wharf.

They resumed their dance.

I was mesmerized for a moment. Their movements were graceful, fantastically so. Their rear ends moved in a syncopated waggle. They would back up and then go forward and each time they were a bit closer to Verity.

She cried out and ran for a gap between two of them but they just danced closer and closed it and reached out to touch her. She stumbled back, clearly exhausted.

"How did you get here?" I yelled. The Bees bowed on their knees as if one and it gave me the creeps.

She gazed dully at me but did not speak. She moaned and rubbed her hands together as if they were in pain.

I took a step back, grabbed that Fender Stratocaster by the neck and ran toward that circle holding it straight up over my head. Screaming.

I bashed one of the Bees on its tail and it began to ponderously turn and I ran round its other side, smashing the Bee next to it. "Run," I yelled at Verity and she ran out through the gap. The circle moved, capturing me within.

I was terrified. I laid into one of them with the guitar, just whacked him straight on the head, distantly surprised that the guitar did not break. The Bee staggered back and I was happy to see that they could be hurt. But I wasn't fast enough to make it through.

They were no longer surprised. Their eyes fixed on me, they began emitting some sort of sweet smell. I tried not to breathe. The Bees approached to claim me, I knew not what for. Beyond them the pyramid flashed with faces, faster and faster, a blur, streaming upward toward that apex, that ghastly eye. In my daze I noticed that one of the tall buildings beyond had those symbols all over them, the skull and crossbones, the snake. I knew them for blues signs, and wondered if their very presence fought this eye.

The blues started running through my head, a musing, deep voice singing, and I sang along, loud as I could, taking deep breaths of that tainted air, and saw the Bees pause.

Then Jack was there, somehow, brandishing a gun, shooting at them and hollering to beat the band. He dropped one, then another while I stared, completely amazed.

"Well, come *on,*" he shouted. "We don't have all day." I heard Lil yelling from somewhere I couldn't see, "Jack, get back to the boat! Don't you know what will happen if they get hold of you?"

I ran around the downed Bees and I knew that the others were pursuing me. I didn't know how fast they could run. I heard the scritch of their legs, the whirr and buzz of their wings as they took flight, their ominous shadows chasing my own. Jack had hold of Verity and they dashed south along the wharf as if they knew where they were going. I looked back and hollered, "James! James!," but there was no sign of him. I stopped. "I have to go back," I yelled, surprised at myself. The Bees hovered over me. I stood up straighter, despite my deep fear. What could they do? A deep, dim memory awoke . . . plenty.

Relief washed through me as James shot out of an alley, sprinting like lightning, and woke me from that dream. He'd be good on a baseball team. If we ever got out of this mess . . .

We dashed down a long flight of steps and into a waiting boat. The five of us almost capsized it. Jack told Lil to cast off and kept his gun trained upward. One Bee swooped close and Jack fired. The Bee crashed onto the steps and bumped toward us and splashed into the water where our boat had been as Lil pushed us off with a mighty heave.

As the boat swept into the river, the sky over Memphis was black with Bees. Lil said tersely, "Jack, if they had gotten you, it would have been all over. *All* over."

"I know," he said calmly.

"I can't believe you risked it all like that."

"Believe it," said Jack, still holding his gun while Lil pulled on the oars.

I shivered and held my Stratocaster tighter, and James, panting, looked at me with what was surely disgust.

Twenty-six

○○○○○○○○○○○○○○○○○

Evil Eye Blues

A sharp tattoo of shots stuttered from the general direction of the *Queen* as Lil pulled out onto the river, and several Bees plummeted into the water, swirling to the surface downstream.

"Peabody sure was busy in Cairo," said Jack. "He collected a regular arsenal. Isn't that some kind of antique machine gun?"

"Wouldn't know," said Lil through gritted teeth as she pulled back on the oars with her entire weight. "Kind of convenient how you have to keep watch with that gun while I row, isn't it, Jack?"

"Here, take it and I'll switch with you," he said, instantly contrite.

"You'll swamp us," she said, pulling again.

"You make a terrific martyr," said Jack. "I mean it, Lil. The best. I never would have suspected. It's good enough to synthesize . . ." He picked off two Bees which were swooping down on them.

"Shut *up*, Jack. I'm warning you."

The *Queen* let out a deep, mighty tone that shook the air and the paddlewheel began to turn.

Verity saw all this as if from a great distance. It did not really matter. The day seemed kind of pretty but really there was blackness inside of it. The river, the trees, the boat, the people—everything she saw was just a disguise for a whole lot of nothing. Inside all of the particles which made it up. Before, she had thought that there was light inside those particles but she knew now that it was not true. Inside everything was so much nothingness that it could not be comprehended. There was no reason for these people to be trying to protect them from the Bees. Or from anything else. But there was no reason to try and stop them from doing it, either.

The young man squeezed next to her on the seat put his arm around her and kept hugging her tighter and tighter while he said things like are you all right, I'm sorry, don't worry, I won't leave again, but it was kind of a nuisance to be jarred around like that.

The only thing was her hands hurt and she turned them palm up. They were covered with something and she tried to pry it off but it was stuck.

Verity, what are you doing? asked the man who was hugging her and she stopped tugging and just watched pale pink lines streak crookedly up her arms and then turn red.

The small boat lurched in heavy waves. The riverboat was coming toward them fast. On the shore was that enormous, bright pyramid, catching the sun's light, so bright but she knew it was filled with a horrible kind of blackness that could spew out into the air through the All-Seeing Eye, once it had distilled enough energy from human misery. The All-Seeing Eye was part of what used to be on the dollar bill. The All-Seeing Eye had looked around a long time ago and thought to itself, We need to have these slaves to do our work for free so we can have big, fat dollar bills. So thought the All-Seeing Eye. It thought these things in the name of Freedom and Democracy and, even better, in the Name of Jesus Christ. They could tell the slaves about Jesus and that would be a good thing. It would help the slaves, because before that they didn't know about Jesus and heaven. It could even remember that that's what the Spanish did, teach the Indians Spanish so that they would know about Jesus Christ before they were slaughtered. Life on earth was short and brutal, but that was all right for they'd have their reward in heaven. The All-Seeing Eye saw, like the Popes had, how this type of thinking helped everything move along better. People were much more content with wretchedness, and you didn't have to share things with them. You could take it all for yourself. Later, the All-Seeing Eye created all sorts of tools of death and destruction, like bombs and chemicals which poisoned, slowly or quickly; diseases incredibly deadly; and even later all kinds of wonderfully complex nan weapons of an unprecedented variety and cunning deadliness. These weapons would help the pure and noble philosophy of democracy, which the All-Seeing Eye pretended to believe in, to be foisted on people who did not much care for it because they had their own way of thinking. It was hard for the All-Seeing Eye when people thought differently, and tried to take control of their own lives, but there were all sorts of remedies for that. The nice thing about it was that all the remedies—the guns, the drugs, the diseases, the nan, all so cunningly conceived and so vigorously pushed upon the world—

helped fatten the All-Seeing Eye with more of the energy of nothingness.

She could help that nothingness spew out of the All-Seeing Eye. It would be released into the atmosphere and she could even see how long it would take to swirl everywhere: to fall as soft rain over Paris; to freeze solid on the edge of a glacier in Nepal and rush that summer into the rivers of China, to work itself into the water table of droughted Western North America.

The beauty of it was that once this happened no one would ever care about anything again. In the face of the blackness, the nothingness, the destructive power amassed and invented by humans and all of the emotions that went into it (which, when you took into account that the way the All-Seeing Eye got so big and fat was from people paying for all this black nothingness, was quite a lot, more than just about anything else there ever was), there was no way to care about anything at all. Humans would finally disappear, leaving room for what would come next, whatever that might be. Giant brains that knew better. Intelligent gases now confined to vacuum tubes. Creatures without DNA. There were forces against the All-Seeing Eye, but they could not stand against this, the awesome power within the pyramid.

Why are you crying? asked the man next to her. His beard was red. Look the boat is coming and I won't leave again. We're going to be all right. I can't believe you went in there. I just can't believe it.

Three Bees swooped all at once toward them, in the shadow of the great boat. Verity shook off the man's arm and stood to meet them and held up her hands which were burning burning. In them was information which could help release the nothingness. If she did that everything would stop hurting. TAKE ME she heard someone shout and it was her.

The boat capsized as Jack leaped for her and they were all in the drink.

Nobody ever listens to me, complained the black woman swimming next to her as they surfaced.

Verity lay sick with the sickness of the All-Seeing Eye in one of the staterooms. She told them about it and about what the Eye could do and how she wanted to help and people stood around her bed looking grim. The woman Lil brought her all kinds of nothing stuff to eat and she woke up once to Lil poking a needle into her but she still kept telling them about the Eye and all that it was made out of and all that it could do.

Her mind was filled with images of the wonderfully subtle weaponry of nan. It was so beautiful because people had spent a lot of time thinking about every little detail. These weapons were among the most clever things ever thought up by human beings. Tiny, tiny gears that could be just about anywhere. Molecular interfaces which changed shape easily when the right interlocking atom clump came along. Things which could lie in wait until awakened with the message from a tiny collection of precisely oriented molecules.

Mark Twain and the girl who Verity recognized as embodying the older Twain, who had long ago recognized the essence of the All-Seeing Eye and had tried, too late in life, to become a force against it, now came and sat at the side of her bed and argued about it. They were always arguing. Verity knew that at one time this would have irritated her but now it was part of the nothing and it was quite all right. It went in one ear and out the other. She knew it did because Lil came in and said stop it now, it doesn't matter to her, it just goes in one ear and out the other but the Twains paid no attention to Lil. This was no surprise, because she said no one ever did.

The bright nothing sun glowed golden. Verity lay there bathed in it. Some of that music was playing from very far away and she once would have disliked it but now its tunes were not mournful or depressing or insulting, not even the Evil Woman Blues. They all made sense, it was all true. They should all jump off of tall buildings on Stormy Monday but why bother?

Sam Clemens sat in a straight-backed chair on one side of her bed and Mark Twain sat in an identical chair on the opposite side. It was easy to see why they talked across her as if she weren't there, because of course it didn't matter whether she was or wasn't there. Lil kept talking about her baby who she had to live for but it was a shame to bring a baby into all this nothingness.

"You travel around the world as much as I have and you'll see that imperialism is what's ruining the country. It's going to ruin the world, mark my words. Countries taking over other countries all in the name of some fine ideal but at the bottom of it all is greed, the greed of countries," said Mark Twain. "I've written lots about it but Livy's afraid for me to publish it or say it in lectures, at least not flat-out."

"You're coming along," said Mattie. "Making some progress. But after a few more whirls you'll realize that humanity is destroying itself. It can't help it. And good riddance." She sat up straighter and cleared her throat, and her voice became more gruff. " 'Two or three centuries from now it will be recognized that all the competent killers are Christians; then the pagan world will go to school with the Christian—not to acquire his religion, but his guns.' I said that in *The Mysterious Stranger.*"

That's right, thought Verity. I'm with her. The sun touched the riot of Mattie's tight brown curls to a blazing, tawny lion's aureole. Her face had thinned out and her eyes looked much larger above her high cheekbones. They had fire in them. She had taken to wearing white clothing so bright that it hurt Verity's eyes to see the dress she had on today, lit as it was by the sun.

"Well, all that plays fine in lectures, I'll grant you," said Twain. "I've been having great success with lectures. I've mastered the form. I've mastered the *audience*. Sometimes it seems to me as if I'm the happiest man alive. My house is the loveliest, the richest, the swankest house in the swankest, most air-putting-on neighborhood in Concord. Olivia Langdon believed my pledge to stop drinking but I've won *her* over now and she has a beer and bitters before bed and allows me whiskey before breakfast. The boy died"—his face grew sad—"but I have three of the loveliest, smartest little girls you'd ever want to see—they're *miles* more clever than any of the girls they play with."

Mattie's face hardened. "And you tried to keep them little girls forever. You made Clara suffer—*I* made Clara suffer, because I didn't think it ladylike to be a concert singer."

Twain roared with laughter. "No daughter of *mine* would even *consider* singing on the stage! Next thing you know she'd be dancing the cancan."

"I'm trying to help you, you idiot!" returned Mattie. "You have another chance. You can wake up. You can reform."

"Reform? I've been reforming my entire life, I'll have you know. I don't know how many times I've taken the pledge."

"You're misunderstanding me."

"It's easy enough to do."

Verity understood that they were both a lot of nothing. Neither of them was real. But they thought they were real and that was all that mattered to them. She herself was not real, either. All her thoughts and memories of herself were simply fortuitous constructions. "Fortuitous" meant "accidental" and they were, just a grand accident. Beneath them all was nothing. Why worry?

She noticed for a moment that the room was sky-blue and she felt sorry for Lil, who had insisted on this particular room. It didn't make any difference to her, color. Not like it had before. She was completely reborn into blackness. For moments at a time it even seemed to her as if she wasn't seeing colors anymore, but that they were gradually fading. Then they would return again. It was an interesting effect.

Mattie slumped in her chair and a funny look crossed her face. She sighed deeply and said to Twain, "Hadn't you better go back and see to the boat? I'm not sure if Peabody is the best pilot."

"Good Lord, no! I only meant to pay my respects and you enticed me into this absurd argument." Twain jumped out of his chair and strode from the room. He could stride very well for a man only about as tall as herself, Verity thought.

Lil came back and bent over Verity. Her eyes were troubled.

"What's wrong with her?" asked Mattie, and Verity heard a young girl's voice, not the harsh, acerbic tones she affected when she was Clemens. "What's wrong with *me?*"

Verity, propped up on a pillow, saw and heard everything. Not that it made any difference.

Lil slid back into a large, soft chaise. The floral pattern was green for a moment then faded to shades of gray. Verity would have been frightened except for the lack of meaning in everything. The cherry trim, polished like glass, was a graceful furl of dark roses and leaves, and still caught the light as before.

Lil patted the cushion next to her. "Come sit next to me, Mattie," and Mattie looked almost as if she might cry as she slipped in next to Lil and Lil put one arm around Mattie's shoulders as she nestled close, like a little girl.

"I miss my mom and dad," she whispered.

"I know," said Lil. "Do you want to go back?"

"I can't," said Mattie. "They'll kill me. Not them, but the people in Elysia. I've seen them kill before. They like to do it in public. It's like a big party. It's all a dream, anyway, isn't it?"

"What do you mean?" asked Lil, looking at the side of Mattie's face.

"This Mark Twain dream. It's kind of like—kind of like a dream the whole country used to have, isn't it? When it used to be a country? Almost like he dreamed thoughts into them and made them laugh but I'm not sure they understood how angry he really was. There was that—" Her smooth forehead wrinkled a bit. "—that Darwin, and Twain believed him and thought religion was absurd, and God, and all that. But in Elysia they're still like the people he made fun of. And that was so long ago. I guess it's hard for people to understand. How little they matter. That there's no one big to help them. There's no one to help *me.*" Her eyes flashed for a moment. "And that's fine with *me*. But I'm not sure if it's a dream to the person who just left, the Mark Twain. I feel so sorry for him. I'm not sure if he ever wakes up, like I do. Does he?"

"I don't know," mused Lil. The look on her face was thoughtful. "It's against the law to create people like that. The process started out as a black-market enhancement for actors. But a lot of people thought it would be *nice* to have a different body, a different *mind-set,* for a limited time. So for a while, *that* was all the rage. Unfortunately, these Twains are essentially slaves. It's quite tragic. The creators booked them on tours and made money off of them. Quite a to-do, at one point, about bringing people like them to justice. But that the creators are long gone, so the Twains have no legal recourse. Not that there's any legal network anymore . . . it's all local rule now."

"So he's stuck in his dream," said Mattie, sadly. "I feel sorry for him. Even though it seems like such a *complete* kind of dream. No matter what happens, he makes it all a part of his dream. I wish I could help him wake up. There's nothing wrong with dreams, if you wake up. My mother dreams. She goes out and has visions. Sometimes she tells me about them. Sometimes she doesn't. She has visions of the country, she says. But she wakes up. She knows who she is. I'm afraid that I won't, one of these times."

"What kind of visions?" asked Lil, a slight smile playing over her lips.

"Oh, all the people living in harmony, that kind of thing," said Mattie. "About how there's going to be a big change, and a person who helps bring it all to pass. A person who sacrifices herself. My dad says we all just have to work hard and do what we can to help the other fellow along. He thinks it's a waste of good time and energy for her to go out and have these visions. He likes planning things out, like the crops. He doesn't think visions about harmony are very useful."

"They're the most useful thing there is," said Lil. "Nothing gets done without some sort of vision. But if you try and see them through it can get kind of complicated."

"Is that the kind of dream you have?" asked Mattie.

"It is," said Lil.

"Is it complicated?" asked Mattie.

"Very," said Lil.

Mattie nestled closer. "Lil?"

"Mmm?"

"Why is it that sometimes when I touch you I see . . . oh, a big whirlwind of animals and plants and bugs and stuff?"

Verity saw how Lil's face went still, but Mattie didn't because her eyes were closed.

"Oh," said Lil lightly, "I don't know, sweetie."

"Don't lie to me," mumbled Mattie. "I hate lies. If you can't tell me, that's okay. Lil?"

"What?" asked Lil, letting out her breath.

"Sometimes I'm afraid of what's happening to me," said Mattie. She curled a bit closer to Lil. Lil hugged her tighter and frowned. She glanced over and met Verity's eyes and Verity thought she saw tears in Lil's eyes.

"I know," Lil said. "I know."

"Tell me a story," said Mattie drowsily. "My mother always did."

Lil looked afraid for a second. Then she took a deep breath.

"Once upon a time there was a little girl. She lived in West Virginia . . ."

Verity closed her eyes.

"Is the little girl you, Lil?" asked Mattie.

Lil was silent for a moment.

"Don't *lie* to me, Lil," said Mattie. Her voice was sleepy and sharp at the same time.

"It was me," said Lil.

"Tell me," said Mattie, her voice hungry.

Lil's voice was soothing and low. Verity knew somehow that Lil meant for her to hear this and that it was some kind of strange apology but it didn't really matter to Verity. Her eyes were closed but her ears listened anyway.

"I was born in the middle of the Second Wave. My parents were actually pretty old. My father was sixty-five and my mother was fifty-five. They lived in Knoxville, Tennessee. My mother was a maintenance engineer for the university there, and my father was a professor of African-American literature. I think that they were very happy for many years and my father had made a name for himself with his spontaneous lectures, deliberately so, to avoid being replaced by a simulacrum. People were very creative around that time in trying to make themselves unique. He loved teaching and thought he couldn't live without it. My mother's job was quite secure. And she made it her business to keep up with the latest in everything. She realized that a lot of information was censored but she had ways of getting around it.

"They'd never had children because of the zero-population-growth laws. People could live longer and there was kind of a lottery, or waiting list. When someone did die, one couple was awarded the right to have a child. This situation encouraged the growth of young, murderous vigilante bands roaming the country, furious because the State blocked fertility at birth, or when your parents brought you in for inoculations, or whenever you had to have some sort of interaction with the world at large. A lot of those blocks are still in effect, one way or another. It's easy to keep the rebels down if they die out after a generation.

"My parents had always been law-abiding, and then something happened to change them. I'm not sure exactly what it was. Something my mother saw, or learned, about the hypocrisy of the system. It really shook her up. Anyway, I think she kind of bullied my father into having me, since he loved his job, but she stole something at the medical school that restored her fertility—it was even possible at her age, if you won the lottery, to have a baby—and they resigned and left. They weren't sure where to go, so they ended up in a pretty remote place, the mountains of West Virginia near the Virginia state line. My father contented himself with the thought that a huge technical university was only about forty miles away, and with the fact that they were experimenting with a prototype Flower Village. Sometimes he'd go down and talk to people there but I'm not sure what he told them about himself. The town we lived in was practically deserted. At one time it was a coal town but that was all gone, that era. My parents were friendly, nice folk, and they made friends with the few people around and were welcomed. There was a history of independence and privacy there which suited them. Nobody pried too hard; they all had their own secrets. There was a library full of bookman programs, though a lot of them were deteriorated. It was really irritating to get halfway through a book and have it turn to garbage on the screen. There were thousands of real books there, and I started to read them instead. The pages were brittle and a lot of them were eaten by bugs, but there were more than I could ever read anyway. My parents taught me everything they knew, which was quite a lot.

"Then my mother got sick. It was something that was easily curable, some melanoma that could have been wiped out in a week with the right bionan. They weren't sure what it was at first, but finally they exhausted the local medical network. One of the doctors told them what he thought and my father loaded us into the car one night and we drove all the way to the University of Virginia Medical School. Eighty-one was still a decent solar road back then and it only took about five hours, since we were lucky enough not to run into any anti-tech vigilantes or pirates.

"But when we got there my mother was refused treatment. She was not a Person any longer, they said; she was not in the system. Neither were my father and I. My father stashed me in a little motel and came back to give me reports. I was fourteen at the time and no dummy. A little older than you, I guess. One night he didn't come back. I woke up early. It was still dark. I was really worried. I got dressed and went out for a walk on a little hill above the motel where my father and I usually went each day and watched the sun rise. When I was walking back through the woods I looked down at the motel and saw a police car parking in front of my room. A man got out. He knocked for a minute, then he kicked the door in.

"I didn't know what to do. I knew from listening to my parents' stories that these people, the enforcer class, were cruel but I didn't know then that a lot of workers had been infected with cruelty, or at least a lack of empathy. I was sick with fear for my parents.

"I heard a noise behind me and jumped and turned but it was my father. He hugged me tight. He was crying. 'You have to get out of here,' he said. 'Your mother is dead. They refused to treat her. They could tell that she'd had a child. They got her records from Knoxville. They could have helped. I'm sure they could have. But they wouldn't.' I'd never seen him look that way.

" 'You're coming with me?' I asked. Somehow his news did not surprise me. I had felt it, I think, her passing, the night before. I didn't really know what to make of it. Death was new to me. I guess I was in shock.

"He shook his head. He gave me the address of his brother in Alexandria and told me that it was only a few hours to the north. He wasn't sure if his brother was still there or even if I would be welcome, but it was all he could do, he said. He said that it wasn't safe for me to be with him. I cried and clung to him. He told me to remember him and my mother. He said that they didn't have any information about me other than that I existed and that I had to try and keep it that way. 'Maybe you can change things' were the last words he said to me. A form of money was still in circulation then, and he gave me all he had. It was all coded of course, the government had ways to know who spent money and on what and who got money and what for.

"He'd left the car a few blocks away in anticipation of this sort of development. I took it and drove out of town and found some back roads. Roads in the mountains are tricky; they twist and wind and get you going in circles, but the compass helped and there were some old maps in the system. It was still a lot like West Virginia out of town, off the main roads, but it was only a few hours before I realized that I'd have to risk taking one of the big highways. I studied the maps and got on Two-fifty. I was amazed at all the cars there were! I was glad that the automatic steering worked because I would have been too nervous to steer, I think. There was a kind of franticness in the city which worked to my advantage. So I was blessedly anonymous. My uncle welcomed me with open arms, though he wasn't easy to find. He's the one who put me in touch with the underground. And they gave me an identity and sent me to school."

Lil paused. "I guess I put you both to sleep," she said.

Verity was not asleep but she did not say so. She heard Lil get up and shut the door quietly.

After a while, Verity heard Mattie stir.

"It's evil," she said. "It's evil to do this to people."

The door creaked as it was opened. Mattie slammed it behind her.

Twenty-seven

○○○○○○○○○○○○○○○○○○

Reunion Blues

Blaze sat with his head in his hands on a chair outside Verity's door and waited for Lil to relent and let him in. She had told him sharply that Verity shouldn't be bothered when he stuck his head in the door. He figured Lil was just mad because he'd left, though he wasn't quite sure why it was any of her business.

It was only ten in the morning, but the air was thick with heat. They were moving along at a good clip—some sort of Mark Twain being was the pilot now. Every time Blaze thought nothing new would surprise him, something did.

The steady churn of the paddlewheel was lulling, despite his concern for Verity. The *Queen* looked the same. But being back on it felt completely different, starting with the way they all huddled around Verity after they fished her out of the drink and hustled her to her room while pushing him aside as if he weren't even there.

Masa's transformation, the luminous dome of LA, the overwhelming torrent of ravaging images that informed him of the roots of the blues formed an unclear, yet powerful, juxtaposition within him, a new lens through which he saw everything. But as yet there was no clear focus.

And no, the *Queen* wasn't *really* the same. His room was definitely smaller.

And the worst thing was, he'd lost Alma's guitar. He wondered if he could still play the blues, or if they'd be lost to him. But the blues were in him, Alma had said. He was the horse, the blues was the rider. . . .

The girl Mattie was shaking his shoulder. He must have dozed off. "Go on in," she whispered. "Lil's gone. Verity's the same." Mattie gave him a sad look and left.

His eyes burned and his head throbbed. Last night in Memphis, he certainly hadn't worried about sleep.

At first glance, he was frightened. Verity looked like a corpse, pale and still. She lay in the middle of a big iron bed. They'd put her in a white shift and covered her with a flowered sheet. Her arms were stiff at her sides, on top of the sheet. Next to her bed was a large, open window.

She stared at the ceiling. She didn't even notice when he came in.

"Verity?"

When she didn't respond, he sat next to her on the bed, wondering if he should be careful or if it would be better to startle her in some way.

"Verity! It's me! I *know* you can hear me!"

It was too strange.

He bent and kissed her cheek, her forehead, even her mouth. Twice. The lack of response deepened his anxiety.

He stroked her hair back from her forehead. She was so beautiful, and so young. She had twice risked everything for him. She'd apparently been in Memphis all night, looking for him. He guiltily remembered the supposed drunk who had been following him from several blocks away. Had it been Verity?

Of course, he told himself, if I had known she was there, I would have found her and taken her out to the boat.

Would you have? asked something inside him. Or would you have just stayed there with the blues?

Well, I didn't, did I? he shot back and the thing slunk away.

"I have some things to tell you, Verity," he said. He might have been talking to a tree for all the response she made. He picked up her hand, which was limp and unresisting and lay in his like a dead weight.

First he told Verity about Alma and the blues and how he understood now about Sphere and her. He told her about the potion he'd drunk and as best he could how searing the blues really were.

"I was really afraid of nan. I only drank the blues because . . . well, why not? I had nothing to lose, I thought. Before that, I was trying to pretend that I wasn't a part of the world. Maybe I was trying to stay a Shaker. Maybe I hoped I'd believe in all that again. Everything was so dark without God, without heaven, or Mother Ann, all those made-up ideas. I couldn't see that I still had *you.*"

She blinked a few times, but not in conjunction with anything he said. He decided that although it made him feel better to tell her these things maybe he'd have to tell her again later when she could talk back.

Then he tried the train trip. Surely she'd be interested. She'd always cared about the things he cared about. He was sure that what happened to Masa would get some kind of reaction out of her.

No—but maybe she just flat-out didn't believe him. Then he told her about how Cairo was plagued now and she kind of stirred under the sheet.

"What's been happening since I left, Verity?" he asked, his chest tight with fear. "How's Peabody? I missed him. I missed you, too. You know that, don't you?" Maybe she could tell how free he'd felt on the raft, how the world seemed so wide. Maybe she was angry about that.

Or maybe not. They were both tremendously different than they had been just a few months ago. Their whole world had changed, so quickly, and was still changing. It looked like this new world might kill her. Blaze wondered if she would ever care about him again. He realized that was a little selfish, so he wondered if she would ever care about anything again. Not that either kind of wondering would help her.

He slumped back into the chair, overwhelmed with melancholy.

A blues began to tickle the edge of his mind, a blues by Big Bill Broonzy. He sang it to her in a low, quiet voice, a strange song; poetic and pointed. It was called "Just a Dream."

He sang about how he dreamed he had a million dollars, and had a mermaid for his wife, about how he won the Brooklyn Bridge on his knees shooting dice; about how he won so much money that he didn't know what to do. But it was just a dream that he had on his mind and when he woke up in the morning not a penny did he find.

The next verse that came to him made him choke as he sang it. He dreamed that he was in the White House and the president shook his hand and said he was glad that he was there. But when he woke up from *that* dream, Jim Crow was all that he could find. It was all a dream, man. Acceptance of black men by their country was just a dream.

Just a dream. Money, a happy family, political parity, the thought of heaven—just a dream to those who lived and wrote the blues.

That was the way everything was beginning to seem to Blaze. And maybe Verity.

But they would never wake from this dream and find it all put back the way it had been.

Her eyes were closed the whole time but he thought he saw her smile a little. Maybe it was just his imagination. He squeezed her hand and maybe she squeezed back, just a tiny little bit.

Lil came in and told him to get some rest. He didn't want to leave but she said she'd stay there. He was tired and hungry so he left.

After a few hours' sleep he found Jack playing pool. A glass of whiskey sat on the bar and Jack took a sip between each shot as he walked in a slow calculating way around the table. Just looking at the whiskey made Blaze's headache worse.

"You look like hell," said Jack.

"I feel like hell," he said. "Isn't there something I can take to feel better?"

"Boat's broke," Jack said. "Game?"

"Tell me the rules again."

Blaze played very badly but Jack didn't seem to mind. "So where have you been?" Jack asked.

"Los Angeles."

Jack hit the cue ball funny and it jumped the rail and rolled across the floor.

"So . . . what's it like?" Jack asked after a very long pause, during which he just stared at Blaze. He chased down the ball and retrieved it. He set the ball down behind the mark and said, "Your shot."

Blaze lined up his shot deliberately and to his surprise it went in the pocket he'd predicted. He casually walked around the table and chalked up the cue stick while he thought the situation over.

He knew that it irritated Verity that Jack and Lil wouldn't talk about themselves. He realized that up to now he hadn't really cared that much. He hadn't cared about much of anything except the blues and being angry.

But now he knew that he wasn't alone. Radical changes had happened to everybody. Everything. Every place. Even glowing beings like Masa, even made-up creatures like James. The whole world was haywire and strange. Why?

"You and Lil know a lot more about what's going on than we do," he said to Jack. "So far Verity's put up with you, but it seems a lot more important now that we know more. Verity's pretty sick. I'll tell you about the train, and Los Angeles—what I can figure out about it, anyway. But you need to tell me what you know too. For instance, what's wrong with Memphis?" It made him tremendously sad that the blues was juxtaposed with whatever awful thing was happening there.

Jack took a big swig of whiskey.

"I don't know if you know this," Blaze said, starting to get mad, "but I've known Verity all my life. *All* my life. She's like a sister to me. I care about her more than anyone."

"Then why did you leave?" Jack asked. He started cleaning up the table, one ball after another, click-thump, as they fell into the pockets.

It was Blaze's turn to shrug. "I had to. But I'm back, aren't I?"

"Run across a man calls himself Clean Mind in Memphis?" asked Jack. "I was kind of on the lookout for him."

"I met a Clean Head," Blaze said, trying to cast back through the whirling blur of the previous night. "Great bluesman. Is he the same?"

Jack shook his head. "I doubt it. This guy is really a creep. You'd remember him." A creep? wondered Blaze, but didn't interrupt. "Clean Mind got hold of a nan augmentation device a long time ago. Best we can tell, he paid someone to make exactly what he wanted. Then he tested it on the guy to make sure it worked. His name then was Ken Simmons."

The hairs on the back of Blaze's neck rose but he just racked up the balls. "So then he went to Memphis?"

"He was stationed in Memphis at the Air Force Base," said Jack. "After the Second Wave we lost touch with him. We lost touch with just about everybody. Rumors came back to us that he'd set up his own little empire there. And after a while a kind of blackmail request came. Make him a general or he'd release a plague so bad that it would decimate the world in two years. He sent us a little sample. One of our volunteers took it—"

"A *volunteer?*" Blaze asked. "Who would volunteer for something like that?"

"We're at war," said Jack.

He was just stating what was to him a simple fact, the world he lived in every day. Blaze could see that. But it shook him to the core. This was an *organized* thing? People were taking *sides?*

Oh.

Jack looked at Blaze. "This is a new kind of war. It's a war being fought all over the world in a very new way. The problem is that no one seems to know what the stakes are, what they want. There is the potential for lots of profiteering. There's also the opportunity for people to sit down for the first time and try and decide the direction humanity should take. Before it's too late. It's almost too late, in my opinion. But I guess it's never too late to try. That's what Lil and I are doing. Trying. Maybe humans can evolve to the point where each of us can control nan. All of us, not just the rich, not just governments. Information for the people. Or," Jack laughed, "whatever we might *be,* at that point.

"But to get back to what happened. Brave people sacrifice themselves during wartime," Jack continued. "Taking it was the only way to really see what would happen so we could try to hack it. How to disarm it. We couldn't find a way. The volunteer tried to kill herself several times and finally succeeded. It's pretty difficult to keep someone from killing themselves if they really want to." He sighed deeply. "I wish I could remember some of the particulars of the stuff, but I wasn't really in on that end of things." He perched on the stool and poured himself more whiskey. "Clean Mind just got to thinking too hard about humans and decided that we'd all be better off dead. But he was an economical, free-choice sort of fellow. Thought we should all know the score and then take care of the details ourselves. Not a lot of overhead that way."

"So what about the pyramid?"

"I don't know," said Jack. "We don't know. Maybe it's better not to know. We've lost a few people trying to find out. We wouldn't have stopped at all if it weren't for Verity. I looked for her all night. Memphis is bigger than it seems."

"Did *you* see Clean Mind?" Blaze asked.

Jack shook his head. "I saw a lot of happy people," he said. "Who knows—maybe they hide in the day. The blues rule the night, the Bees rule the day. One woman even told me that." He was quiet for a minute. "I don't know if I'd recognize him anyway—or if he'd recognize me. It's a long way from K Street."

"K Street?"

Jack nodded. "We shared an office on K Street in Washington, D.C. Statue of an old general on a horse there, right below my window, in a beautiful green park. D.C. was lovely back in those days. At least, that part of town was. Other parts weren't." He smiled. Blaze thought his smile always looked like he was using it to make fun of something. "Everything was pretty up-to-date there. You couldn't even ride on the Metro without being scanned for poison, any sort of open-ended un-locked nan, chemical weapons, you name it. If they could have scanned you for having a bad hair day they would have."

"Bad hair day?"

"Something that got stuck in the language," he said.

"What would you have done if you had seen him?" asked Blaze.

"I would have killed him," said Jack. "He's definitely on the roster." He looked at Blaze.

Blaze looked back.

"Well, you asked," said Jack. "Anything else you want to know about the world?"

"Well . . . did you have that horrible kind of life like they did in the blues?"

"What?"

"You know," Blaze said. "They made people work on the levees and the railroads without paying them and put them in prison and wouldn't let them vote. . . ."

"Oh!" He laughed. "It isn't funny, actually. It's just interesting that you might think that all blacks had it so hard. But no, of course not. I, and millions of other blacks, and our parents and their parents before them, had perfectly normal middle-class lives. Or became perfectly nor-mal millionaires, or scientists, or artists."

Blaze was relieved. "So all that stuff" (all that stuff from Alma, he was thinking), "all that stuff isn't true."

"Well," said Jack, "it *is* true, and it was *horribly* true for a whole lot of people. The reason that it wasn't true for me is that a lot of people made it their life's work to change things. If a lot of people work together for a long time on something that's right, it helps. Of course, a lot of people can work together on something that's wrong for a long time too, either on purpose or because they're misinformed or because they're fooling themselves. And that can certainly have an effect on things. But discrimination was a fact, even for my parents. I don't really think I experienced any, at least not because of the color of my skin. But I was always pretty preoccupied with one thing or another. I might not have noticed unless it smacked me in the face."

"So things are better now."

"In some ways," he said, but he sounded doubtful. "Maybe there's just a certain balance of human misery that has to stay constant. A certain number of conflicts simmering. A certain number of people dying. Maybe it's for reasons we are not even aware of. Like that Gaian Meme Plague that got loose a few years back."

"Gaian? Meme?" It was interesting when Jack got to talking.

"Yeah. Bunch of people who believed that humans were killing the Earth. Well, of course they are. Or at least they were. It was supposed to make people aware that we all live in an interdependent web. They claimed that the Earth is a living organism. Makes sense to me. It's a cold, hard fact that after the rain forests were gone, a lot of species vanished that were kind of contributing to the overall effect of things. There were worldwide famines that wiped out whole peoples. There were climate changes. It didn't help that a lot of people had bought a germ-line genetic modification that kept not only you but your children from being able to store a lot of fat. You got a discount on your insurance and you could eat like a pig without gaining weight. So a storage system that had worked pretty good was gone. And on the other hand people were deciding not to have children, and a lot of other people had been sterilized by their governments. I don't know if the Gaian Meme really works, but the thinking behind it was to help humans become aware of the deep self-regulating systems of the Earth and tune themselves to them. There are a whole lot of factors in the decline of the human population, and those are a few of them. I think we're down to a few billion now. Maybe less."

Blaze wasn't really sure how many that was. It still sounded like a lot.

"Now it's your turn," said Jack, settling on a stool.

Blaze told him about the train. Told him about Masa, and Salt Lake City. Jack got kind of a grim look in his eyes at that point and shook his head. "We lost it there," he said softly. "Really lost it. Go on."

"Who lost it?"

Jack laughed shortly. "The forces of good. I thought. It doesn't really matter anymore. At least that's what it seems like sometimes. So, is there a dome at LA?"

"You know all this?"

"Rumors and suppositions," Jack said. "I used to know some of the people who were into that artificial-intelligence stuff, a long time ago. LA was the target for their own particular kind of conversion, their own kind of immortality. I'm not sure I understand it myself. But I think that there are quite a few domes worldwide. Well, maybe ten, fifteen. So this James was on the train?"

Blaze suddenly felt unaccountably protective of James. He just nodded.

"Interesting," said Jack. "I guess he's just kind of a pinched-off piece of intelligence."

"I'm not sure I follow you," said Blaze.

"Well, I suppose the entire dome experiences some form of consciousness that we really couldn't possibly understand. But James is like a tiny piece of it. Like an entire hologram is in every portion of itself."

"Oh." Another thing Blaze would have to learn about. "Do you have any children, Jack?" He wasn't sure where the question came from.

Jack looked kind of amused.

"What?" Blaze asked.

"Would you believe that I haven't had time?" He shook his head and there was that smile again, that slight nod. "Yep. Been pretty booked up."

The blues stirred in Blaze's hands again. They flared up, needed to get out. He closed his eyes for a minute, making sure, thanking Alma . . . *Sorry, Alma, so sorry I lost your guitar.*

"Have you seen that guitar I brought from Memphis?" he asked Jack.

"Seen it?" asked Jack. "I was hoping you might just forget about it." He opened a closet, pulled it out, and handed it to Blaze. "Damn, it's a nice one."

Blaze pulled the strap of the beautiful, gleaming Stratocaster over his head, and played a good, hard, B fifth diminished.

It emitted a faint, tired *twang.*

He was aghast. "What's wrong? It was so nice and *loud* last night."

Jack about fell off his stool laughing. "Come on," he said. "Maybe Peabody can help, if he has time."

Verity was dreaming, or something like it. The All-Seeing Eye was spewing out magic carpets of dollars that could fly. There was a person on every dollar and they flew all around the world heaving things overboard—bombs, nan weapons that would propagate themselves to the end of time, leaflets of lies. Every person on every flying dollar was Verity. She just touched the icon of the All-Seeing Eye and death spewed out and the blue of the sky changed a little bit more toward twilight. When she was finished, it would be night, more than night, a night with no dawn. It was very important that this work be done. There was nothing more important than this. Nothing. Nothing. Nada . . .

A loud twang jolted her awake and then two crazed voices joined in a strong, blued interval:

> The devil went to Memphis
> And you know what he found?
> The blues alive an' kickin
> And he was awful proud.

10

◯◇◯

Alice and the Mysterious Stranger

Twenty-eight

○○○○○○○○○○○○○○○○○○

Alice Blue Gown

The boards of the old warped dock were cool, damp, and splintery beneath Alice's bare feet.

Her frail blue shift touched her lightly as dawn breeze brushed the surface of the Mississippi, and the dull ovate leaves of the live oak next to her rustled then were still. Ropes of Spanish moss festooned the branches.

She started, hearing the smash and tinkle of glass behind her, but did not even turn to look at the white mansion on the hill. She grinned as she settled on the end of the dock, keeping her coffee cup level as she lowered herself down. Her bones protested with snapping sounds, and she dangled her feet over the edge, sipping her hot, sweet drink. She could hear him: he called himself the Professor, for reasons unknown to her. But perhaps the genesis of his name was as distant as that of her title: Doc.

"You can't keep me locked up like this! Aren't there any law-enforcement officers in this godforsaken back-assward shithole?" Frantic rattling of the wooden sash, but the young, strong Inue brothers, her handymen-on-call, had done a good job of nailing it shut from the outside for her.

The Mississippi shimmered, ephemeral as dream in this light. The heat of the coming day was tamped down, a beast preparing to rise, lazily, and expand into muggy sensuality, hugging the trees at noon and later turning the live-oak leaves brightly upward if that heat-beast compressed into a thunderstorm.

But now it was cool. The other side of the river was a blue-green haze a mile away and the river itself was olive-green snaked with silvery lines as the sun began to burn away the fog. A wood stork floated down on wide white wings, folded them, and stood next to her on the dock, impassive.

"No fish yet this morning, bud," Alice said, and squinted upriver against the silver shimmer. Sometimes Norleaners stopped on the island halfway across the river for the night. They had gradually become less common than five years ago, when she'd arrived from Montana after almost a year's journey, realizing that the Mississippi satisfied her eastward, homeward urge. And that she was simply too tired to go any farther, and was afraid of what she might find if she did. Reports were bad; had been for years. The whole Southeast a patchwork of nanotech zones, humans transformed into zombies; strange and unimaginable effects left over from the Information Wars and general self-inflicted mismanagement. But lately, great clots of rafts had passed the Landing.

She wasn't sure what else she could do with the Professor. He'd been going round with some sort of cure-all kit for a week, with resulting chaos in the close-knit town of four hundred souls. Already Sal Hendricks had run off, after the Professor did something to him, leaving his wife hysterical and the kids without a father. Then Talulah Smith proclaimed to her astonished elderly children that she'd been an internationally wanted nanotech terrorist way back when, which was how she'd paid to have all her life-prolonging treatments. Apparently she'd not been a kindergarten teacher, as she'd told them all along, and used her hard-earned pension money. Talulah said that she was plenty relieved and that her secret had caused her an overlong lifetime of debilitating stress, but the revelation engendered no end of caustic debate among her relatives; already one of her daughters had decided on a divorce rather than listen to further invective about her dear old mother.

When confronted, the Professor just shrugged and said that his job was to restore the balance of the universe and that he would continue to do so.

Alice had decided that he could do his restoration work away from Madge's Landing, particularly since restoring the balance of young Alfonso Traynor had caused him to chase his mother around the kitchen with a sharp knife. When Alice asked him to explain *that,* the Professor nodded quietly, looked rather pleased, and said that the Lord moved in mysterious ways, and that sometimes balancing took place in several stages, over time.

The little girl who had been apparently cured of seizures nagged at Alice. Nothing she had tried had worked. But the rest of this uproar was more than tiny Madge's Landing could endure.

Even after Alice asked him to leave, the Professor had insisted on hanging around. She'd found it necessary to lock him in her spare bedroom, with the help of the Inue brothers, who were quite able to resist the Professor's increasingly hysterical suggestion, as they carried him upstairs, that they too needed to become more balanced.

Then he'd ripped up her good peony drapes last night and tried to use them to climb down from the roof. When she saw him fall past her window and land with a thump on the front lawn she threw down the book she'd been reading while eating dinner, deeply exasperated.

She found the old roly-poly lying on his back, looking like a stunned penguin in the stained tuxedo he affected. She ran to the shed and got a rope, rolled him over, tied his hands and feet, then went off for the Inue brothers. She ignored the swarm of colorful, complex schematics that blinded her when she touched him. She walked the path as firmly as if she could see just fine for the minute or two they took to subside, for she knew her grounds by heart. This was the last straw. She absolutely *hated* to touch anyone.

Now, she sipped her chicory-tinged coffee and enjoyed the sun's first heat on her dark brown arms. When the next bunch of Norleaners came down the river, she intended to toss him on board and wash her hands of him. They'd be happy to have him, no doubt, and it would get him out of town. She shivered despite the growing heat. She'd come a far piece to stay out of the way of noodleheads, and to do what she could to protect her adopted town from them. She did have a certain amount of responsibility, damn it. Well she'd been the one who insisted on going to medical school so many years ago, in Charlottesville. She wanted to Help People, she'd told her father, her chin in the air, and had been so angry when he laughed! That was *my* plan too, he told her, but there's no help for any of us now, he told her more soberly. Nothing a *physician* can do. As I've found. You really want to be a government technician? Can't you see what I've been reduced to? But he patted her on the shoulder and said well then let 'er rip. Dead years ago, when a nan surge caught D.C. and all the surrounding suburbs unaware. Maybe his body lived, still, but he was dead.

The Professor hollered again and she blessed him for interrupting her memories. She rose and poured the rest of her coffee into the river. Josh the giant catfish swirled near the dock to see if there was anything good coming down. Once she'd caught from him chilly visions of sun-pierced depths as he brushed her hand with his long fat length after snatching a piece of food from her. They were blurry and vague, but she didn't think she was imagining it. She suspected that he was the spawn of some genetic-engineering experiments in interspecies communication. She imagined that could make even a fish lonely. But she avoided touching him again. Her cat was quite enough responsibility for her.

"Hungry?" she yelled, as she strolled up the walk. The Professor glared at her through the small rectangles that still held shards of glass around the edges. Two jays squabbled in the tree next to her, and her cat darted halfway up the trunk, claws scrabbling. "Do you like grits?"

"Not fit for man nor beast!" he retorted, and turned away from the window, a look of utter disgust on his face.

The first dozen or so rafts that hove into view that day were filled with suspicious, jeering folk. Something was going on upriver but Alice didn't care. That's what she loved about Madge's Landing. Nothing shook their quiet world here. Except that interloper.

Alice tried to wave them down from her landing, shouting and cajoling and offering food, but they drifted past, making no effort to come ashore, and treating her to various obscene gestures in reply and faint bursts of those tired old rafter songs. Hands on hips, she watched them float past. It was getting to be late afternoon. She'd have to keep old Roly another day. And maybe another. But sooner or later, he'd go.

She stopped in the garden on her way back up to the house, kneeling in rich black-dirt rows amid vegetable bounty. The lettuce would bolt soon and she pulled it all, light green and ruby red both, snaking white roots holding dirt she'd hose off at the house. Zucchinis, tomatoes, baby red potatoes and fingerling carrots. She'd give old Roly a feast tonight, that was for sure. Not that he'd appreciate it. Here she was, willing to arrange a free river trip for him, and he was acting so ungrateful. She rose, tried to rub the dirt from her bare knees, raised the basket, and picked a few delphiniums and zinnias on the way to the house.

She about jumped out of her skin when out of the air next to her on the porch she heard, "Alice, go back down to the river."

Her heart beating hard, she dropped the basket and whirled around. "Who's there?"

Another, more distant voice sounded, this time riverward.

"Al-ice! Oh, Al-ice! Hur-ry!"

To her surprise, she heard a faint, discordant blare that was indeed coming from the river.

From her porch she searched the tranquil water. From bend to bend, she saw nothing. "Who the hell?" she asked. She thought she heard a chuckle coming from somewhere, and then the boat rounded the bend.

A riverboat! She'd hit the jackpot.

She ran down to the river, shouting and waving.

To her delight, the boat began to turn.

"Why are we stopping?" asked Mattie.

"For that woman," said Twain. "She either wants to put something on or embark as a passenger. That's what we're here for, isn't it?"

Lil burst in the door. "Why are we stopping? It won't be dark for another few hours."

"Unless I get an order to the contrary from the captain, it's my duty to stop when someone signals me. As is that woman."

On a small dock below a low green hill where perched a ragged-looking white mansion, a woman shouted and waved frantically.

"I'm the captain now," said Lil.

"I don't *think* so," said Twain equably, and steered the boat toward the landing. "Pretty deep here. Current's scoured it out well. I'd say she'd best move her house well back before the river takes it. Won't be long."

Jack and Blaze were really cooking when the *Queen* rounded the bend, Jack on the piano and Blaze with his guitar.

Jack stopped in midsong. "Why are we slowing down? Is it getting dark?"

Blaze pulled the curtain aside. "No." He took another sip of whiskey.

Lil came to the door, agitated, as usual.

"Jack, I need you."

He sighed, rose from the piano bench, and followed her. So did Blaze. It was a lovely place, Madge's Landing. Blaze feasted his eyes on it. It was almost like Ohio—green and farmlike. It lacked the desolation they'd seen along the river so far; the loneliness.

He went to Verity's room. She was still lying there on the bed, under the sheet. She opened her eyes and looked at him. Her look made him uneasy. But at least she was looking at him.

"Verity, I'm sorry. I'm sorry about everything."

She didn't move, she didn't blink, she gave no indication that she heard anything. Blaze bent down and hugged her. Just a little at first and then more tightly and then he was just squeezing her and crying because she was like a rag doll.

Mattie came in behind him and touched him on the shoulder.

"Are you all right?"

Funny, he thought, her asking me. She was nuts, herself. But at least she was lively. He put Verity down gently, smoothed back her hair, and stood up.

"I guess so," he said.

"You were on the train, weren't you?" she asked.

He nodded.

"You met the weird lady?"

He nodded again.

"How is she?"

He opened his mouth to tell her. Why not. But he found that he just couldn't describe what had happened. "She's . . . all right," he said, and Mattie looked at him suspiciously. "Come on, let's see what's going on."

He left Verity's door open because the sunset was streaming in and it was so pretty. "I'll be back with some dinner," he told her.

Alice looked around her dinner table with shrewd eyes as she passed around zucchini pancakes, new potato salad, and fried chicken. She'd rinsed dust off some bottles of wine from the cellar and they sparkled green in the last rays of sunlight as she swirled golden wine into long-stemmed, and long-unused, crystal. The dining room was like the prow of a boat, with windows all round. She had unfolded a white lace tablecloth over the mahogany claw-footed table, with Jack's help, while Blaze and Lil worked in the kitchen. They all acted starved for real food. She wondered what they had to eat on that boat. She wondered about the boat, too. But it didn't matter to her. She had a deal to close. Take the roly man and be gone. Take him for free. Nice meeting you, guys. No, hey, I'm just fine. Enjoy your trip. A wave, and back to her books and her garden.

Jack, some sort of flimflam river man. The river spawned them like fry. Lil, his sparkly lady friend, kept removing the wine bottle from his hand. Blaze looked just plain hungover, but underneath strong and fit, a good kid. Mark Twain, a young one this time; she'd not seen many lately but then she made a pretty respectable effort to see no one at all. Mattie, the girl, had a determined sort of face, but kind of lost-looking. She had some sort of sickness but Alice wasn't sure what. When she looked at Mattie, though, something struck at her heart—the innocence of her face contrasted with the fierce, proud despair in her eyes. Her color was high and Alice thought she might have a fever. Not your business, she told herself sternly, but of course it was. You asked them here, she told herself, as she lowered the chandelier with a pulley and let them help light the candles. It *was* pretty, the light glinting off the old silver she had Blaze take out of the buffet that they used for the baked apples with fresh whipped cream.

While carrying plates back to the kitchen, Blaze stopped in the short hallway to study something on the wall. Alice's heart sank.

"You're a doctor?" Blaze called from the hallway.

" 'Fraid so," she said. "But I haven't practiced in years." Lie. But what she did around here really didn't count.

"We need help," he said.

"Of course you do," she said, with resignation. Nothing was free in this world.

"It says the University of Virginia," continued the intrusive lad. Lil looked at her sharply and Alice upgraded her opinion of her. More than meets the eye. That was for sure.

"Quite a long time ago, you'll see," said Alice. "I have a pretty poor memory." That's why I carry all this horrible nondeletable inforam. She clenched her hands under the table. Tools of the trade. Gone awry, like just about everything else.

"I'm sure you do," said Peabody, helping himself to more potato salad.

She was pretty sure that whatever was going on on that boat, it was far beyond her. As long as she kept her hands to herself.

The Professor pounded on the floor and then she heard, as if it were coming from right next to her, "This lady is a criminal! She's keeping me prisoner upstairs! She has not even offered me dinner."

They all looked at Alice with indignation and surprise.

"Who's that?" asked Mattie.

"I guess it's the Professor," she said. "Excuse me while I take him some dinner."

"Who's he?" asked Lil.

"Oh, just . . . a highly cultured guest of mine. He prefers to take his dinner in his room. He needs to get downriver. I thought you all might be able to take him."

"Liar," said Mattie.

"No," said Lil.

"Of course," said Blaze.

"Thank you," said Alice to Blaze, smiling. "I'm sure he'll appreciate your hospitality."

"Please, sir, I want some more," said a high boy's voice in a British accent. Alice heaped some food on a plate and fled. They heard her running up the stairs, and they also heard a normal male voice at the table: "Thank you for your gracious invitation. I'd rather go through ten medium-sized hells than stay here another day. Grits for breakfast, gruel for . . . Oh, hello, dear doctor."

"Tolerable good voice-thrower," remarked Peabody. Mattie just stared at the place where the voice had been coming from. Then, as if with one impulse, they pushed back their chairs and began cleaning up.

The long solstice sunset burnished the river as Alice and the Professor walked down through the garden and the grassy field to the *Queen,* surrounded by the entourage.

Alice was thoughtful, as she walked. She would have to diagnose this person Verity without touching her, of course. Perhaps it was some new strain of malaria, or appendicitis.

"I feel as if I'm being hustled, I do," complained the Professor, clutching his little black bag of cure-alls. His old suit was shiny in the setting sun; the repair nans standard in almost all cloth for the last few decades must have given out, for Alice saw a frayed place on the elbow.

"I could do a lot of good in your little town. Why, my reputation has followed me far and wide—"

"You'll just love life on the river," said Alice. "You can build up a whole new clientele."

"What's in that bag?" asked Lil.

"The finest medicines money can buy, my good woman. Elixirs which can work veritable miracles."

"We'll have to have a look at them before we can allow them on the boat," said Lil.

"Why?" asked Jack. "I mean, doesn't information want to be free?"

"Shut up, Jack," said Lil, flashing him a frown. "We've got enough problems with whatever George dumped in the auditorium. Verity's been swamped. Maybe we don't need any more factors here. Maybe I'm just nervous. Whose side are you on, anyway?"

"Why, I'm on the side of information, of course," Jack said, with mock surprise in his voice. "I thought you were too. You're the one who convinced me how important it is. But I understand. The results of freedom can sometimes be inconvenient. This is very interesting, Lil. Could it be that you're undergoing a philosophical conversion?"

"Jack, I'm warning you!"

"Maybe I'll just stay here," said the Professor.

"Oh, no," said Alice. "Look, I don't care what you do with his bag. That's between you and him. But if he doesn't go downriver with you, I'm not going to be able to help you." She knew that she would no matter what, but she made her voice as firm as possible.

Lil stopped walking. "So can we look in the bag, Professor?"

"Anything for a price, madam," he said, with a slight bow.

"What's your price?" asked Jack, sounding amused. "How about a fifth of Tennessee Whiskey?"

"Didn't you lay on any Mark Twain Whiskey?" asked Twain, sounding aggrieved. "It's quite easy to procure in Cairo, and I get a percentage."

"If it's Twain, you'll have to make it two fifths," remarked the Professor, as they trooped onto the landing. "No, three. That's terrible harsh stuff."

"It's so hot," complained Mattie. "When is it going to cool off?"

"In another five months or so," said Alice. "Why not go for a swim?"

"A swim?" asked Mattie. The thought seemed to astonish her. "I do know how to swim. There's a lake in the Desolates. Like ice." She looked at the water doubtfully, a muddy calm pool sheltered by the landing.

"You'll be quite safe if you stick close to shore," said Alice. "I swim almost every day. It's not cold."

"You all get on the boat so you can't see me," said Mattie. She started to unbutton her white dress.

"I'll keep an eye on you while I look through this stuff," said Lil, reaching for the bag.

"Ah—" said the Professor, pulling it back.

"Get him his whiskey, please, Jack," said Lil, as Mattie stripped down to her underwear and dove off the landing.

The floor of the boat echoed beneath their feet as they trooped aboard. Alice admired the graceful beauty of the boat, the wealth of detail, the way it spoke of the short but opulent steamboat era of the Mississippi, when the river carried most of the trade of the young United States.

Blaze led Alice up a flight of stairs and along the railing.

Verity was bathed in the light of the sunset as Blaze said, "Verity, I've brought a doctor for you," and pushed the door fully open.

Alice stood on the threshold and her heart sank.

The young woman was lying on her back on a big white bed, propped up on two pillows and wearing a light shift. She had long, shining black hair. The sun shone straight into her eyes but she didn't blink.

Alice put the woman's body-age at somewhere between seventeen and twenty, whether natural or chosen. Her hands, palms down, rested as still at her sides as if she were a doll. They were red and puffy. And she was pregnant. Just barely, but unmistakably, showing.

"Close the door and pull the curtain, please," said Alice. "Do you have candles?"

Blaze did as she asked and the room lit with a soft glow from some sort of line around the ceiling and Alice's heart beat faster for a moment. Nan. Well, she'd be off the boat soon. She wasn't a superstitious ninny. She'd had the finest nanicine training available when she had gone to medical school. She'd taken her training to areas of need. Africa and Montana. But she'd had her fill of it, all those technical fixes, one after another, that whirled out of control. She could heal without them. After what happened to her father—

But she wouldn't get started on that again.

She walked over to Verity and Verity's eyes did not track her.

"Hello," she said. "I'm Alice Winford. I'm a doctor. Your friends brought me to examine you. They're a little concerned. What happened?"

Verity did not speak. Alice looked at Blaze and he looked uncomfortable. "I'm not sure—" he began.

"If no one will talk to me I can't help at all," she said. "It's somewhat of a handicap."

"There were Bees," he began.

"Bees. Yes. Well, that narrows things down. Where?"

"Memphis."

"Oh." Alice pulled up a chair and sat down, rested her elbows on her knees, and clenched her hands together. She wished for the thousandth time that some sort of glove could shield her from the effects of her inforam, but she'd never found anything completely impermeable. The effects only took a bit longer to manifest.

"You *are* a doctor, aren't you?" asked Blaze anxiously. "A real doctor?"

Alice nodded.

"We never had one at Shaker Hill."

"Is that where you're from? Where's that?"

"In Ohio. Near Dayton. But—"

"But what?"

"It's gone now. Verity—" His voice cracked. "Verity took me to Cincinnati to save my life. She was—she was the Queen."

Shit, thought Alice. It would have been better just to keep the Professor.

"What do you think is wrong with her hands?" She leaned over and looked at one closer. She ached to pick it up. She didn't dare. "What's that *on* her hands? Some kind of transparent cover?"

"Gloves," said Blaze. "They get messages on them. Or at least they used to. The people here on the boat. I'm not sure if they're working anymore."

"Can you take them off?"

"I'm not sure—" said Blaze.

"Try it. Please," said Alice.

Blaze shot her a look with eyes amazingly green. Then he sat down on the bed and tried to peel off the left one, the one next to Alice.

The covering was melded to her skin. "I'm afraid I'm going to hurt her," he said.

"She's been like this since Memphis?" asked Alice.

"Yes. It was on the wharf. She was in Memphis all night. Looking for me. I didn't know she was there—" His voice was rising.

"It's all right," said Alice, and patted his back.

"I just can't—I just can't—" He began to cry, quietly and desperately. His fingers picked at the gloves, explored her hand, again and again, until he began to shake. "Verity! Wake up!" he yelled, and Alice stood and pulled him away. After a few seconds Blaze's schematics died down.

"It's all my fault," he said. "It's all my fault. If I hadn't gotten on the train—"

"Yes, well," said Alice. "Whatever."

Verity had not shown any sign of noticing his touch.

"Is she using the bathroom?" asked Alice.

"She gets up every once in a while," said Blaze.

"Hmm," said Alice. "Who's in charge here, anyway?"

"Verity used to be," said Blaze. "When we left Cincinnati. Then it seemed like they all were, for a while."

"They?"

"The people from Cincinnati."

"Really," murmured Alice. "Most extraordinary. Were there many of them?"

"Thousands," said Blaze, and Alice thought, something is changing. "They used those gloves to communicate. It helped them. Before they had them they were going nuts."

"You don't have them," said Alice.

"I don't have seps," said Blaze, and showed her his hands.

"Seps?"

"Receptors."

"Turn her hand over for me again, please," said Alice.

"Why can't you do it?"

"Please do as I ask."

Blaze turned Verity's palm up. Alice looked at it with her magnifying glass and sighed, but didn't comment. The woman was definitely from Cincinnati. But Alice couldn't get much more information this way. She sat in the chair again.

"You don't have the plague," she said.

"No."

"Does anyone else on the boat?"

"I think there are still some rafters aboard, and most of them are plagued," said Blaze. "A lot of them were injured in the attack. They're on the boat. And some people from Cairo too. I don't know much about it, I wasn't here."

"You were on the train."

"Yes. I'm not sure about Jack and Lil. I don't think they do. James is from the train and I'm not sure if he's even a person."

Worse and worse, thought Alice.

"Mattie's crazy, and Twain is some sort of actor creation from St. Louis. I've only known Mattie for a day or two, but it seems as if she thinks she's Mark Twain too—"

"Don't ever call me that!" The door slammed open and they squinted in the last brilliant flare of sunlight before the hills swallowed it. Mattie stood there. She had put her dress on again and was dripping wet. "My name is Samuel Clemens. That old fake destroyed himself by denying his real name and his real self. He made my life—*our* life—into a living hell!" She marched to the bureau and yanked open a drawer. "I thought I left some cigars in here this morning. Who took them? You have a really strange fish here. He's *big*."

"He's a catfish. His name is Josh."

"That's not his name," said Mattie.

Alice leaned back in her chair thoughtfully.

Everyone was gone. It was dark.

Verity got out of bed. She walked over to the door and opened it. She walked out onto the deck and stood at the railing. There was a thin new moon low in the sky. She thought she felt a stirring within her but it didn't matter.

The water below was dark, very dark.

Verity climbed to the aft deck where the cannon still sat, blunt and black. There was a box there and it was full of cannonballs. She slid the lid over, knelt, and picked one up.

She could barely stand. It was very heavy. She walked over to the railing.

If she jumped off and held this cannonball she would go right to the bottom.

But maybe she would accidentally let go of it. Maybe it wasn't very deep here and her feet would just get stuck in the mud.

She slowly lowered the cannonball back into the box so that it wouldn't make a sound. She slid the lid back on. No rush. There would always be time until there was no more. Either way was all right. It was chilly. She walked back to her room and got back into bed. She wished the Eye would come back. At least it was something. Anything was better than this. Was she crying? It didn't matter. But she was. Yes. She was.

The paddlewheel jumped to motion late the next morning.

Alice's cat vanished once on board. They had spent several hours this morning loading not only Alice's larder but a good supply of all manner of foods from the Madge's Landing General Store, where the proprietor had been pleased to get several hundred yards of silk in trade. Or, "nano–silk," as Alice took great pains to point out to him, not that he cared. Karen Jackson had profited as well when they bought out her entire woodlot. Apparently some of the nanotech features of their boat were failing, or they anticipated failure soon.

Alice stood holding the railing of the boat and thought, what a beautiful house! I wonder who lives there? She must have a wonderful life. Bucolic and carefree. Isolated and independent. Boy, she must have it made.

Too bad she has this problem of feeling responsible for other people.

She watched her house until the boat went round the wide bend below the landing.

Then she sighed, turned, and entered Verity's room.

Twenty-nine

○○○○○○○○○○○○○○○○○○

Them Old Kozmic Blues

Verity was the same as she had been the previous day.

Alice paced the floor back and forth. "You have to eat," she said. "You have a baby. I think you're about fourteen weeks pregnant. Am I right?"

That did get a blink out of her. That or the sun.

Alice put her hands on her hips. "There are a lot of injured people on board that need care." She was particularly anxious to examine Mattie. "There are a lot of time-consuming problems. Burns, broken bones. I need to get back to them."

Nothing. But she had known that cajoling wouldn't work. There was deep, serious, neurochemical trouble here.

Alice rubbed her hands on her jeans nervously. She pulled up a chair, sat next to Verity, and picked up her hand.

A rush of schematics of chemical bonds flowed across her vision. All sorts of unpleasant clenchings and joltings took place throughout her body. She dropped the hand, took a deep breath, and picked it up again. Feeling what the other people felt was a malfunction of the inform she carried. I'm just here to help, she reminded herself, and tried to get to that place she'd found where it would not affect her, where she could instead concentrate on the information at hand, so to speak.

What she saw was the neurochemistry of severe depression. That certainly fit the woman's demeanor. There appeared to be a few extra bonds, though, that she would think about later. Her handheld recorder, which would store this information so that she could retrieve it at a touch without disturbing the patient (or herself, once the initial contact had been made), was missing from her hastily grabbed bag. That little Treadwell boy had rummaged all through her bag while she tended to his daddy's burn a few weeks ago. That was probably where it had gone. She was sure that she'd miss all kinds of things in the next days and weeks. Well, there was no going back.

She pulled up Verity's shift and palpated her abdomen, which was normal. She put on her stethoscope and listened to her breathe; listened to her heartbeat. No problems there.

"Could you please sit up?" she asked. No answer.

"Look, I just saw you get up and go to the bathroom." At least she'd been able to get a urine sample, though it hadn't been easy. Gritting her teeth, she reached under Verity's back and began yanking her hips toward the pillow, boosting her upright with one hand around her neck. Verity suddenly sat up very straight and crossed her legs but the expression on her face didn't change.

"Thank you," said Alice, and pulled Verity's long hair back so she could get a good look at the bump she'd felt behind the woman's ear. Sitting on the bed and looking straight at Verity, she brought her own hands forward and touched both of the nubs at the same time.

Verity jerked her head away and glared at her.

"Ah," said Alice. "Sensitive, are we? Memory matrices are quite unusual. Old-fashioned but overwhelmingly powerful." She raised her hand and Verity jerked away from it.

"If you'd deign to talk to me, you could tell me what happens when I do that," said Alice. "As it is, I think that I might as well try it again."

Verity's lips moved but nothing came out.

"Try *again,*" said Alice, grabbing Verity's shoulders and giving the matrix a good hard push. Verity screamed.

Alice heard running feet and the door burst open. "What are you doing to her?" demanded Blaze. His face was flushed.

"Examining her," said Alice. "Maybe you can help. How long have you known her?"

"All my life," said Blaze.

"How long has she had the matrices?"

"The what?"

"The bumps behind her ears."

"Always," said Blaze. "We were afraid to touch them."

"I think the first steps here would be to remove the gloves and to remove the matrices. However, the gloves have apparently become incorporated into her body like a graft. Her veins and nerves have grown into this layer. I've never seen anything like it, but then I've been retired for quite a while too. And really, there's no limit . . ." She paused thoughtfully.

"I don't know anything about the nubs," said Blaze. "What do you think will happen?"

"Do you care about Verity?" asked Alice.

"I love her," said Blaze, his voice catching a bit.

"Then sit here and hold her hand. In the absence of more precise information, that might help a bit right now. I need to think about it. I really hesitate to remove the matrices without her permission."

Blaze sat next to Verity on the bed and took one of her hands in both of his. "It's hot."

Alice nodded. "There's an information flow there and it's causing the heat. You say that you were in Memphis and that's when this started? She was all right before then?"

"Pretty much," said Blaze. "I mean, considering."

"Right. You said she was the Queen? What do you mean by that?"

"She was the Queen of Cincinnati," said Blaze.

Alice was pretty sure that Blaze was sane. "Tell me about it," she said.

It took about half an hour. Blaze had kind of a limited perspective, but it was an extraordinary tale. Alice was sure he didn't know the half of it. "She's been through quite a lot."

"Yeah, and then I left her," said Blaze. "She begged me not to go."

"Blaze, I don't want to denigrate your self-image or anything, but I think she would have gotten over it in time. People do. So stop kicking yourself. Apparently she saw you go into Memphis and followed you, correct?"

"Yes, but I didn't know—"

"Right. So she was in there all night, wandering around. These Cities are very powerful systems. Generally one has to be initiated in some way or other before using a City. Now, you weren't, but since you have no receptors I guess it didn't matter—the City's system didn't really interact with you a lot. It didn't make you sick or disable you in any way. Correct?"

"Well—I played a lot of blues and drank a lot of beer—" Alice could see that there was something he wasn't telling her.

"And?"

"Well, I have the blues inside me. I mean, it's something I—I'll tell you about later." He glanced at Verity.

"All right," said Alice. "But Verity is exquisitely sensitive to such things. What else can you tell me about Memphis? I've heard unpleasant rumors."

Blaze told her what Jack had told him.

"Oh," said Alice, irritated. "Why didn't someone tell me sooner? Apparently she has the capability to transmit this information, this depression, to all of the people from Cincinnati metapheromonally, right?"

"I guess," said Blaze. "But, like I said, since I've been back, everything is different. Maybe something happened in Cairo. All the Cincinnatians seem to have splintered apart. Maybe that's good. There haven't been any messages on her gloves and I haven't seen them on anyone else's."

Alice sighed. This was a bit beyond her.

Lil opened the door. "Can I come in?"

"Please," said Alice. "What can you tell me about these gloves?" She saw Lil hesitate. "Look, we're talking life and death here. If you know something I suggest you tell me. Now. Please."

Lil's eyes darted to Verity. "You can't help her?"

"I'm considering a few alternatives. But I need more information. All right? Now, last night I thought you were just one of the gang. Until you ran through the Professor's bag. You knew what you were doing."

"All right," said Lil. "Follow me."

"Watch her," said Alice to Blaze.

It was just a numbered stateroom but inside Alice saw a world she had hoped to put behind her forever. "Things have been moving right along, haven't they?" she mused. She sat down and ran through a few screens. "Damn. This is from Cincinnati?"

"Mmm-hmmm," said Lil. "And it's not exactly up-to-date. And neither is it dependable. We've been having problems since Cairo."

"It'll do," said Alice. "What kind of person is Verity?"

"Determined," said Lil. "Confused. She feels guilty about Cincinnati."

"What have you told her? Anything she didn't already know?"

"Like what?" asked Lil.

"I lived in Washington, D.C., just before the Third Wave, Lil. Or whatever your name is. I know your type. My father was a doctor too. Just trying to help. He laughed at me at first when I said that's what I was going to do. And then he tried to stop me. He's probably still there, you know. Or something quite like him." She sighed.

"I'm . . . sorry," said Lil, in a low voice.

Alice looked at her sharply. "It was long time ago. Anyway . . . memory matrices really aren't happy things. They're an early technology that proved much too overpowering for the architecture of the brain. She would be better off without them. I think. I think that whatever she picked up in Memphis has been augmented by the matrices. She's not an ordinary person by any stretch of the imagination."

"No," said Lil. "She's not."

"But maybe she'd like to be. Or maybe not. I don't know. She probably doesn't either. I wonder what was originally in the matrices?"

"I don't know," said Lil. Alice looked at her for a long minute. "I really don't," she said. "She doesn't talk about it. We know about her, of course, because of the other Cincinnatians. But she keeps pretty quiet."

"Well," said Alice. She sighed. "I think that it may be possible to neutralize the gloves. It will take a while to figure out how to do it."

"But—" said Lil.

"What's your objection."

"It could be . . . dangerous."

"Why do you think it could be dangerous? What do you know about it? Anything specific? What's your background?"

"I was a bionan behavioral scientist," Lil said after a minute. "That was my training."

"And where did you do your training?" asked Alice.

"Howard," said Lil, tossing her head back a little and looking Alice in the eye. "And Johns Hopkins."

"I'm kind of tempted to asked what—or who—you did your training *on,* but I suppose that would be rude."

"You got some kind of burr under your saddle?" asked Lil.

"I'd just like to know what your stake is in keeping this woman nutted out."

"It's a new sort of mind here," said Lil, quite earnestly for such fluff, Alice thought, considering how no-nonsense she looked. "An emergent mind. It may be important. Not just to them but to the whole world."

"Oh," said Alice. "Kind of an experiment, eh?"

"No," said Lil. "That's not what I said—"

"New mind, *hell,*" said Alice, in a low, tough, voice. She favored Lil with her best patient-advocate glare. "I've got one sick young woman here. So just take your emergent bullshit and stuff it. I've got work to do. And I may not have much time."

To her surprise, Lil said, "I guess you're right," and left.

"Do you want me to help you?"

Verity heard a voice in her restless dreams, as she lay tossing on her bed. She dimly realized that there was no one near—Jack was sitting at least twenty feet away, outside her open door, eating dinner. It was early evening.

Alert, now, she looked around. But there was no one in the room. It could not be Mother Ann; the voice was a man's voice.

"Do you?"

"Yes," she said.

"Who's there?" asked Jack. He jumped up and came into the room, holding a chicken leg. He looked around. "Must have been hearing things," he said.

Thirty

○○○○○○○○○○○○○○○○○○

Free Will Blues

It was dark but that did not frighten Mattie. Insects made a wall of sound around her as she lay on the pilothouse roof on her back, and the fresh clean smell of the river was sublime: water. So much water. She loved the night. She had always felt at home at night in Elysia, where she liked to sneak out on the roof after everybody was asleep and lie there and watch the stars. Some of them came round and round and round again, and those were the satellites.

The stars were the same here, and so were the satellites, but the sky seemed smaller somehow. Probably all those trees and the damp, which misted the night sky over sometimes. And now, that comet was coming after her, but she didn't even mind that. It would transform her, somehow. Maybe it could take her outward, outward from this planet, into that brilliant, diamond-studded infinity. Why not? She had left Elysia. She would not mind leaving the whole planet. She could not imagine anything finer.

She heard a sound below and turned over on her stomach, inched toward the side of the pilothouse, and looked over the edge.

Below on the texas deck sat the Professor, on a bench. There was a wrought-iron table next to him. On it sat a lightstick. He lifted up his black bag, set it on the table, dialed a combination, and opened it. The colored vials inside winked in the light like jewels.

He picked up one vial and held it up to the light, nodded in a satisfied way, and picked up the next one.

"I thought Lil got rid of all that," whispered Mattie.

She grinned as the Professor slammed the lid shut and glared up at her. "What are you doing up there?" he hissed.

"Watching the stars." She turned, found the ladder with her feet, and climbed down.

He opened his bag once more.

"The bottles are all full again," said Mattie. When she first swam with Josh the other night at Madge's landing, she had watched Lil carefully pour the contents of all the vials into a metal container and then dump some powder into it before sliding the case back to the Professor.

"Don't tell her," he said. "They're getting there. I just had to re-replicate everything, that's all. It has secret compartments for just that contingency. It is almost impossible to travel around this country doing good without small-minded people becoming agitated from time to time. It isn't the first time this has happened. Want some?"

His question was eager. His eyes and his slight smile were both sincere. "It will cure what ails you. Even things you don't know about. I won't charge anything. All my needs are being taken care of here. And I like you."

"No," said Mattie. "What's that sign say?" A brass plate was screwed onto the velvet backing of the interior of the case.

"That's where I got it from," he said. "I ordered it many years ago when I was living in Texas. It was expensive, but well worth it. I had it shipped to me on NAMS. I left to roam the country then, to do good, yes ma'am. In fact, the very hour I picked it up in the train station, I made a snap decision and took the next train out. Once I opened the kit I knew it was my calling. I haven't seen my wife since. I don't believe she missed me though. She often expressed a hearty desire to see me gone. And I was sure that after she discovered I'd cleaned out our bank account to buy my kit she would lean even more strongly in that direction."

"Hold the light closer," said Mattie. The plate said,

BAY REPLICATORS INC.
COMPLETE UNIVERSAL RESTORATION KIT
POSITIVE RESULTS GUARANTEED
Patent Pending

"They fix everything," said the Professor. "They really do. The directions said that everything is a pattern. Patterns of memory, patterns of mind and thought and being. Patterns of flesh and bone and gene. We're all just a temporary pattern. This finds the main pattern and restores it. That's what it said on page five, section c, though I lost the booklet long ago. It didn't matter, though. The ad said 'all-purpose, easy to use,' and it was correct. So reassuring, don't you think, in this world of hyperbole and lies? And I am a religious man. Every time I use the kit, I pray."

"I don't believe in God," said Mattie.

"I can fix that," said the Professor.

"No, thanks," said Mattie. "Why didn't everyone in the world get one of these bags?"

"Well, my dear," said the Professor, "this bag broke any number of laws. It was not easy to procure. I became a criminal the minute I ordered it. Can you imagine all the people it would have put out of work? Psychiatrists, physicians, pharmaceutical companies, hospitals . . . it was simply unthinkable. The very right of something like this to exist had been litigated into oblivion. It was created by some sort of radical do-gooder cult of doctors. Only a limited number were made and shipped before the FDA found these people and forced them out of business."

Mattie said, "I asked Alice what was wrong with your bag and she said that it was a technofix and that she was tired of technofixes. She said that it's what's caused all the problems in the first place. It just all got out of control." She raised her voice a bit. "You can come out now, whatever you are."

"My name is James." He stepped out from behind the corner.

"You're always following me around," said Mattie.

"Yes," said James. "That's true."

"Humans and technology are like the double helix of DNA," continued the Professor. "Humans *are* technology. There is no other face to technology. There is no way to separate technology from humans, or humans from technology. Those who remain apart become extinct—those too poor to have access to medicine, or electricity, or those who for philosophical reasons isolate themselves from all technology. Every attempt to use technology is simply evolution. Humans have never been without technology, from a simple tool like a planting stick or spear on to here, where we are now. And beyond. There is a beyond, you know. Probably when the first person made a spear, all the others declared the world was going to hell in a handbasket. Alice is silly. But I think she's unhappy about something."

"It seems like just about everybody is," said Mattie. "Everybody except me. And Clemens *loved* technology. Went round claiming that *Huckleberry Finn* was the first novel written on a typewriter. Had the first phone in town." She leaned against the pilothouse and crossed her arms.

"Alice poses an interesting point, though," said the Professor, settling into his chair. "Let's look at this from the point of view of an old technology. At one time weavers of cloth were in demand. They mastered a skill and could be independent. Then people who could afford to build cloth mills. Not only did this technology put the weavers out of business, but the people who labored in the mills worked long hours in unhealthy conditions for very little money. They did not receive a proportionate return for their labor. After the expense of building the mill and the ongoing expense of raw material and labor, the owner generally made enough money to live in a much finer and healthier manner than the workers which made it possible. In fact, the workers lived miserable lives. Was the technology to create beautiful cloth quickly and relatively cheaply a bad thing? No. People need cloth. What was wrong was the exploitation. That was the human element, the exploitation. The motive for exploitation is what has to be gotten rid of, not the technology. You could say that the free will of the workers was taken away by technology, but that would be a false conclusion. The free will of the workers was taken away by the *owners* of the technology. That was the problem."

"Are you really a professor?" asked Mattie.

"I was merely a humble high school teacher," said the Professor. "My lectures appeared virtually via a private high-school consortium. They kept very poor records about how often I appeared, and how much they ought to pay me. I claimed they were cheating me. I think they were going to fire me. I decided a career change was in order."

"*I* think you're the Mysterious Stranger," said Mattie.

The Professor nodded. "Apropos," he said. "If I remember correctly, Twain's Mysterious Stranger gave humans autonomy."

"He healed them of their faith in God," said Mattie. "He made them realize they had to make up their own minds about things. It was pretty scary."

"I'm not sure I like being compared to the Devil," mused the Professor. "Seeing as how I'm about the Lord's work. Though it's been suggested before. Loudly, by people chasing me."

"I suppose you could think of the Devil as bad," said Mattie, "but he's the main proponent of free will." She frowned and scrunched up her face. "Wait a minute . . . there's a dissenting paper here . . . but that student got a pretty bad grade."

"You don't have free will," said James to Mattie. "You think you're Mark Twain."

Mattie glared at him. "Don't worry, James. My will is free as a bird. Not that it's any of your business."

He shook his head. "It doesn't look like it to me. I don't think that you know when you're going to be Twain and when you're going to be Mattie. I don't think you chose this. Did you?"

"I'm choosing to *stay* this way," said Mattie. "You're a fine one to talk about free will. You don't even have a brain."

"On the contrary," he said. "That's all I am."

"You're a fake man," she said.

"I've been thinking about that lately, and I disagree with you," said James. "I evolved from the LA dome. I was manifested by it. I . . . I condensed—I was *caused* to be condensed—out of the same material as all of them, the same stuff as Masa. I don't have a past as a human, certainly, like the people on the train; no memories to return to; no one to miss. I was manifested for the convenience of the people on the train. But I am as human as they were."

"Which is to say, not much," said Mattie, with a sniff. "That lady was *weird.*"

"It was her humanity that made her seem that way, not the part from the dome," said James, with an odd look on his face.

"You are *not* human," said Mattie.

"Let me tell you why you have that sense of me," said James. A breeze brushed his light brown hair from his brow and a fish jumped, slapping the water. His put his hands in his pockets and bowed his head. "While I was on the train, I didn't think that I was as human as them," James said. "They didn't treat me as if I was, and I never really minded—all I cared about was *her.* . . ." He was silent for a moment. "But since I've been off the boat, all that has changed. Thanks to Blaze."

"You still haven't convinced me," said Mattie. "You just don't *seem* like it. It's your face. The way you act. They just made you, right? Thought you up?"

"Well . . ." James looked at Mattie. "The closest I can come to it in English is they *needed* me. They *wanted* me. I just conformed to their vision, that's all. And I guess the train wasn't as stimulating as all this out here. Brains need stimulation, variety, to grow, to make connections."

"Well," said Mattie indignantly, "That's not fair! If they made you, and you need all that in order to be . . . to be *real,* it was cruel of them not to help you! They should be shot!"

"One of them was," said James, and his mouth turned down at the corners. "I probably seem different because I'm actually more than human. Kind of on a sideways track. My DNA is artificial. It's possible that the entire idea of being human evolved far past where you are now, in the dome. I don't particularly *want* to be human, mind you. But it seems important to you." He gestured at the Professor's open bag. "May I please sample some of that?"

"What do you mean?" the Professor asked. "I'd be happy to treat you—"

"I just want to see what's in those vials. Touch it. That's one way I learn."

"You understand that it might change you? Touch is how it works."

James nodded. "DMSO," he said. "Transdermal."

"I don't know about all that," said the Professor. "How about the diagnostic first." He selected the vial that had a label of DIAGNOSE.

"That looks pretty easy," said Mattie.

"I told you that it is. But there is another step." He quickly pushed a small white oval onto James's palm and took it off.

"Interesting," said James, holding his palm in the light. "I see nothing, and feel no pain, but you've created a thousand tiny breaches in my skin."

"Hold out your hand," the Professor said to James.

The Professor put a bean-sized drop on James's palm, and it flattened out. "Hold it under the light," he said. He stared at it for a minute. He looked at James's face. "It's not working," he said. "Something's wrong. It's supposed to turn colors. It's just staying clear." He sighed. "Maybe something's happened to the kit."

"Don't worry. I'm sure it's fine. Try one of those other vials," suggested James.

The Professor said, "I don't think that would be very responsible. I've never seen this before."

"I don't think it will hurt me," said James. He glanced at Mattie and the corners of his mouth turned up. "Not if Mattie is right about me."

"He can joke!" said Mattie, with a sarcastic twist that might have been Twain's.

"Can that heal the Norleans Plague?" asked Mattie. "Somehow I think Twain would be pretty proud of that plague—the rafts and all."

The Professor said, "The Norleans Plague, best I understand it, *is* a balance, of sorts. At any rate, no, I've had no success with it."

A dot of the red goo sat on James's palm. He said, "This contains retroviruses that carry genetic repair information. A cocktail of megavitamins. All kinds of antibiotics. Hormones. Some are absorbed through the skin. The retroviruses are too large for that, but they slip easily into the bloodstream via the breaches you created."

"I've never gotten that technical," said the Professor. "It's the Lord's work. No matter what Mattie says about the Mysterious Stranger. The way I think about it is this: Human hopes and dreams have a certain configuration in the brain. There's a baseline of normalcy in what's happening in the human body, in the communication between all its different systems. But each whole being is unique. Used to be, in old-style medicine, that they'd fix one thing and that fix would push something else out of whack, create a new problem. To me, that's what a technofix is. That's the way things used to be. The brochure said the kit was created to resolve physical, philosophical, and psychological pressures. And that such pressures are caused by imbalances in the body." He looked at Mattie. "Which is what you have, young lady."

Mattie said gravely, "I like my philosophical and psychological pressures, thank you. I feel alive. I feel useful. Sam Clemens felt useful. Even his darkest writings were an attempt to make himself useful by trying to tell everyone how deluded they were. He disguised his darkness with that jolly Mark Twain stuff, but that all fell away at the end. He was trying to save them. And he was trying to save his whole country from the evils that came from people benefiting from the death of others by selling weapons and by starting wars abroad. Trying to save people gives you a real purpose in life."

"Mattie," said James, hesitantly, "you've been changed by some sort of technology gone awry. I heard you telling Masa what happened to you on the train. Maybe what the Professor has here could rebalance you. It could make you human again. Twain has taken you over. You don't have any free will of your own anymore."

Mattie flared instantly. "*I* don't want my balance restored. I like being who I am, what I am, *now.* If I weren't Twain, I couldn't even *say* these things, not this well. I *choose* to be who I am. If balance means going back, I don't want it." Beneath the stars, she could feel Twain's facility with words shaping her thoughts, thoughts that had their seed in hardscrabble Elysia but that had taken root on the unimaginable train and begun to put forth shoots on the riverboat. What the flower would be, she did not know, but she could feel its beauty and majesty within her, as potential that would soon be realized in some powerful way. Maybe it was all these stars that made her feel this way. Or maybe it was that comet, sweeping closer. . . .

"I'm a new sort of person. It may be strange, but that's what I am, now. And that's what I'll be." Invisible trees rustled in the wind, and Mattie stared at them across the dark river. "In Elysia, you play the hand you're dealt. You do the work you're given, for the good of everybody. You don't shirk or whine. This is an opportunity, not a curse, and I won't have it taken away from me. I never could have imagined such thoughts before. *This* is my glory. *This* is my dream. *This* is my vision. It's who and what I am, right now. It's what I'll do because of who I am. You think you're human, James. Do you have a vision? Do you have a dream?"

James tilted his head and looked at Mattie. "No," he said. He frowned. "In the dome, we . . . it . . . or whatever I used to be . . . it's different than out here. In the dome, every thought/place leads to another thought/place. It's all already there. Closed. Finished. The *idea* of glory, of vision, is there, I guess. You can *experience* it. It's already done, accomplished, finished. There's nothing new. You just move to that space."

"That's not human," said Mattie, triumphantly. "There wasn't even a real *you* there. And you didn't *decide* anything. You just splashed around like water in a pond."

"No," said James to Mattie. "There was more to it than that. Things . . . I can't talk about."

"Why not?" asked Mattie. "Why can't you talk about it?"

"I've never really tried," said James. "I know I'll be able to eventually. This is just all so *new*. If you're a new kind of person, then so am I."

"Post-human," suggested the Professor, closing his kit.

"I like the sound of that," said James.

"Sounds a lot more high-class than fake man, doesn't it?" said Mattie.

Thirty-one

○○○○○○○○○○○○○○○○○○

Past Blues

Blaze and James went up to the pilothouse to see the lay of the river. There was a fine view and Blaze thought it might help take his mind off whatever Doc was doing to Verity. She'd had knives. They were small and shaped funny but they were still knives and very sharp ones at that which she pulled from her bag. She smiled at the knives almost fondly and said something about knives being a fallback that never went out of style in medicine. When Blaze started to argue with her she threw him out of the room.

As Blaze walked toward the pilothouse Lil rushed by him. Her eyes were red from crying. She wouldn't stop to talk to him. Half a minute later Jack came running by and asked Blaze if he'd seen her.

"What's got her so upset?" he asked.

"Two people killed themselves last night—one hanged herself, the other one cut his wrists," said Jack. "And another one injured in the Cairo riot died."

Blaze sighed. People had been dying regularly, about one a day, from injuries too devastating for the boat to handle, especially now that it was crippled. And sometimes they died even if they weren't injured, but nobody knew why. Alice probably hadn't slept since coming on the boat. Before he could ask Jack anything else, Jack ran off again.

Blaze felt helpless. It didn't seem as if anything could help these people. He'd stayed up half the night playing the blues for Verity, but it was hard to tell whether or not she liked it.

Mattie was in the pilothouse, on her stool, as usual. Today she wore a cool-looking white dress, part of the white wardrobe she'd asked Peabody to have the boat make her way upriver. The boat had done a pretty good job with that. It had a mind of its own now. Sometimes it worked, sometimes it didn't. Which made it good that they'd picked up food at Madge's Landing.

But, Blaze thought, Norleans couldn't be far away. Only a few more days. If it wasn't drowned, like Verity had said. It seemed like they could hold out for a few days. Just a few more days.

Mattie was taking a stronger line with Twain than she had the day before regarding navigation. "We're coming to a dead channel," she said, about three times.

"Just leave the hard lifting to me, cub," he said. "And nip me off another cigar."

"It's your turn to do the nipping and my turn to take the wheel," she replied.

"Here, ma'am, I'll fix the cigar for you," said James. He really seemed to like Mattie. Blaze knew he missed Masa. He was capable of that.

James whipped a cigar out of the box and had it cut and lit before anyone could say boo, and practically stuck it in her mouth and smoked it for her too. "Some whiskey, perhaps? Or some lemonade? How about some iced tea. Refreshing in this weather. Or maybe whiskey with water and lemon or . . .

"I'm fine," she said, and her little face was anxious as she studied the river. But he kept badgering her and finally she snarled, "Leave me *alone,* man! I'm trying to think!"

James stepped back and Blaze expected to see his usual hurt look cross his face. It was just about his only expression.

Instead, he smiled a little, seemed surprised at his smile, then smiled again, this time indulgently. "That's all right," he said. "You're just a little girl. You probably shouldn't be smoking or drinking whiskey."

"That's all right," she said in a mimicking tone, clearly irritated by this obvious condescension. She turned an imperious stare on him. "Call me 'just a little girl' if you like. You don't know much. Only what's been put into you. We had a word for you in Elysia. Simulacrum. We'd just never seen one. You and that woman on the train. Both cracked. But I think she was real. Post-human, my eye." She seemed to have snapped back to being Mattie, for a moment, though that was getting more and more rare.

"Simulacarum," James said thoughtfully. "A . . . representation . . . an *image* of something . . . an imitation or sham . . . Hmmm. Well, although I am supposed to be, in a way, an imitation in that I look as if I'm human, I was created to be something more. Something different."

"Pretty fancy stuff for a fake man," Mattie replied.

"What if *I* were rude to you, James?" Blaze asked. "Would you be hurt? Would you smile?" He was aware that it was a rude question, in and of itself, but he tried to frame it in a curious, rather than rude, tone.

"You're always rude to me," James said. His smile was broader. Apparently he was developing a sense of sarcasm. Probably absorbing it directly from Mattie somehow. Blaze wasn't sure he liked it.

"But you know," Mattie said musingly, taking another puff before Twain borrowed her cigar, "A simulacrum might not be half-bad. They'd be better humans. Better *than* humans. They could leave humanity in their wake. They would make more sense of things than humans. Wouldn't they, James? You had no name on the train," she said. "And you couldn't smile."

"I had a name. I just didn't tell anyone."

"The smile?"

"You're right. I couldn't."

"That's because . . ." Her voice changed; then she continued in a lower, rougher voice. " '. . . you are not *you*—you have no body, no blood, no bones, you are but a *thought*. I myself have no existence; I am but a dream—your dream, a creature of your imagination.' "

"That's pretty good," remarked Twain. "I'll have to remember that."

"You will," said Mattie, in her own voice. "You will. But when you do, you'll believe it, and it won't be a joke to you either."

"By God, you're really starting to wear me down," said Twain.

"Somebody has to do it before it's too late and you've made too many mistakes that you can't take back, wasted all your money on the Machine, spoken harshly to your poor daughter Susy to whom you can never apologize after she's dead—"

"ENOUGH!" thundered Twain. "Remove this flea from the pilot-house."

"Take the left channel," said Mattie, with quiet authority. "The right has filled in."

"You are wrong, pipsqueak," said Twain, turning the wheel to the right. They had about a quarter mile to make the choice and the distance was closing fast. An island divided the river, a sight they'd seen a hundred times by now. Both sides looked equally mysterious.

"Damn you!" shouted Mattie. "You'll kill us all yet!" She yanked on the wheel and Twain picked her up, set her outside the door, locked it, and returned to his post.

Outside the window, she looked shocked for an instant, then set up a screaming that shook Blaze's very teeth, climbed through the open window, and rushed Twain. James grabbed her and carried her from the room, slamming the door behind them. It seemed appropriate. Blaze could hear her screams diminish as he took her to the back of the boat.

"What if she's right?" Blaze asked Twain.

"I know this river like I know my own face," Twain replied in an irritated voice. "Have you any idea how long, how tedious the training—"

"But it might have changed, mightn't it?"

"Get out!" he shouted. "A man has to concentrate."

He took the right channel.

Blaze sighed, then went back down to see if Alice would let him back in to see Verity.

She was sitting in a chair with her head in her hands. She looked up when he came in.

"What's wrong?" Blaze asked. The gleaming knives were laid out on a piece of cloth that said STERILIZING on it, like it was something that kept happening. Maybe it did. But the knives weren't making her smile anymore.

She sighed and leaned back in the chair. She looked at Verity sadly. "It seems that the boat's not working," she said. "Of course it's been years—*decades,* I suppose—since I've tried anything like this, but I used to be pretty good at it. You can't imagine all the bizarre things I've seen."

Blaze thought he could probably could get a good running start at it, but an answer didn't seem to be required.

"Well, it seems as if it's spreading. Whatever was in Memphis. I thought that I could separate it out. But it's really intertwined too deeply. It affects all the neuronal pathways." She stood up, suddenly decisive. "I'm glad you're back. You can sit with her while I anesthetize her hand."

Verity looked the same, and it gave Blaze a chill to see her just staring into space like that, with no expression on her face.

"What?"

"Numb her hand," she said. "Probably not necessary, just polite. I'm trying another approach. I'm going to cut a very tiny patch out and analyze the interface. This will take very little energy from the boat. If we're lucky, the synthesizer can—"

"The what?"

"The room that made the gloves," she said. "I used it to show Verity what was happening inside her body, but of course she didn't care. I don't blame her. It's actually pretty depressing in and of itself. Anyway, I want the synthesizer to create an enzyme that can slide along the interface between the glove and her skin and divide them."

She looked up. The Professor was standing outside the window, gazing in at Verity with a curious, wistful look on his face. It struck Blaze that the fellow wore the strangest costume—some kind of formal black suit with ruffles on the white shirt, long tails on the jacket that did not fit round him, and a top hat. His white shirt was stained and his black hat was faded.

Alice stared at him, eye to eye. "Shoo!" she said.

He sidled away.

"I know you're a doctor," Blaze said, "and I know you're trying to help. But why do you want to fool with the gloves? They were all insane when they didn't have the gloves. They needed Cincinnati, whatever was in Cincinnati. They needed it more than Twain needs whiskey. It was awful. Is that going to happen again?"

"I don't know," said Alice. "But she's insane now. Which is better?"

Blaze said, "I think the question should be, Which is worse."

The low, silky blue of Jack insinuated itself through the open window. His blues were quiet and sedate, at least now, so early in the morning. He had taken the music up with a vengeance. Blaze thought Jack was kind of depressed too. He was singing something about Memphis.

"Ropes and knives and bridges," said Verity, startling us both. She stared straight ahead, though, and didn't move. Her mouth barely moved. "Ropes and knives and bridges."

"What are they for?" asked Alice.

"Nothing," she said.

"You could kill yourself with those things," Alice said.

Blaze said, "Now just wait a minute!"

Verity said, dreamily, "Yes."

"You want to kill yourself?" Blaze asked incredulously. Such a thought was beyond him. It was absurd and horrible both at the same time. "She'd never do that. She couldn't."

"She could, and more easily than you might think," Alice told him. "I talked to Jack about Memphis too. Look at it this way. If she doesn't kill herself, and whatever was in Memphis can somehow use her as a conduit, then that would be a pretty bad thing. She might realize this."

Verity blinked.

"Couple this with the depression that this philosophy causes and I don't think it's so far-fetched," said Doc.

"Well, I guess you could try the glove thing," Blaze said.

"I'm also going to remove the matrices," she said.

Jack's music got a little louder.

Verity's eyes filled with tears. "Rose," she said. "I am Rose." She touched one matrix, pushed it, pushed it again. And again.

"Why don't you stop her?" Blaze asked, panic in his voice.

Alice just looked at Verity shrewdly. In the silence, Jack's voice rang out, the steady cadence of his blues.

"Are you Rose yet?" Alice asked.

"Always Rose," she said, her voice dull.

"Are you ever Verity?"

"I've never been Verity. Always Rose. Always."

Blaze was astonished at the tears which began to flow.

Sobs shook Verity's thin body. He had never seen her face so anguished, not in all their life together, through all their seasons of being Shakers. She pulled her legs tightly against her body and rocked back and forth. Her voice was muffled when she spoke. "No one else. Nothing else. There's nothing else to me. There can't be."

"That's not *true,*" Blaze said. He dropped down next to her and gently pushed his arm between her legs and her chest and held her close. Her breasts pressed against him; he felt her backbone beneath his splayed hands and she was so very thin and frail, which startled him. "You've always been Verity to me! Always! Please come back, Verity! Don't . . . don't do any of those terrible things. I love you!"

"Verity, please let me remove the matrix," said Alice. Her voice was quiet but insistent.

"But without them—"

"There will be *you,*" said Alice.

Verity's shoulders stiffened. "No," she said.

Just then the boat let loose with a huge roar—the reversal of the paddlewheel.

Verity and Blaze were thrown from the bed and everything on the dresser and table crashed to the floor.

Alice and Blaze ran out the door and saw the sign that said WELCOME TO ANGELVILLE where the river ended. DOLLARS ALL TYPES WELCOME.

Thirty-two

◯◯◯◯◯◯◯◯◯◯◯◯◯◯◯◯◯◯

Heavenly Blues

Verity hid in one of the rooms until they got the gangplank down and while she was hiding she pulled on some too-large clothes she found in the bureau and bunched up her hair and stuck it under a straw hat. They were trying to kill her and she had to get away. She knew that did not make sense because after all she had just tried to kill herself the other night so what difference did it make, but there it was. They were trying to kill her and she had to get away. That doctor would take away Cincinnati and take away the messages and everyone in her mind in one fell swoop and there would be nothing left of her except . . .

All that nothing.

Her hands ached though and she ripped off the shirt she was trying to button but could not because her fingers were too puffy and instead threw clothes out of the drawer until she found a T-shirt.

Blaze ran down the deck yelling for her and when his voice got close she crouched behind the bureau and when he stuck his head in and yelled he didn't even see her, and ran on, his shouts receding. How simple it was.

Scores of people flooded down the gangplank. Abandoned rafts littered the rocky beach and more rafters drifted around the river's bend in the *Queen*'s wake. Verity heard the Twains arguing up above as she crossed over to the shore. She saw Peabody back at the mud-jammed paddlewheel yelling and gesticulating.

Up ahead she saw a smiling man directing everyone up the path. "*Wel*-come to the *ho*-ly city of *An*-gelville," he said or rather yelled not at her but at anyone, everyone, as if they were all going to the circus. "For the glory of *God* and to praise his *ho*-ly name *mor*ning *noon* and *night* and as a refuge for sinners. Donations *wel*-come!"

Verity was completely indifferent to his message but hurried along so she could get over the rise and away from the boat. Another sign said that there was a Revival every night. "We're back in America," said the woman next to her, in a happy, swooning sort of voice, and ran on ahead.

Verity wondered what had happened to the plague in all these folks, but probably not all of them were from Cincinnati. Maybe some of them were from Cairo and others of them appeared to have been here for a good long time. There was a big building down by the river that said TRADING POST. She noticed that the next hill over was covered with white crosses, rows and rows and rows of them, shining in the sun. How many? Five hundred? A thousand? Was that but the local harvest of the Norleans Plague?

She stopped on the rise and looked back at the boat. Blaze was there. Looking for her. The doctor wanted to take away her memory sponges and the receptors and everything. So she had to leave.

"I can tell them no," she said, and sat down on the rise. People walked past her.

The strange darkness had lifted.

She did not know why. And she was afraid when she thought of it for it could come back at any time. That was the scariest thing of all. Maybe just thinking about it could bring it back. But how could she not think about it? Trying not to think about it would remind her of it. Maybe it would be better if she just killed herself. The world would be better without her. That was a fact. There was a huge live oak not a hundred feet away, with pale green Spanish moss stirring in the breeze. She could climb up on it and jump. That would not take very long. She would have to try and get as high as possible. Once she was dead could the nan creep out of her, that dark stuff from Memphis? Could it go on without her? She did not know. It was something to think about. Maybe she could set herself on fire somehow and it would all burn up. That might be better.

The doctor had another alternative. Knives and enzymes. But why would changing *her* so much take away the darkness?

Because the nan from Memphis had apparently lodged within the vortices of the nan she already bore and used it to grow faster and to intensify itself. The doctor had shown her pictures of it, she remembered now, though she hadn't paid much attention at the time. The doctor had taken Verity down to the glove room and Verity had seen it moving through her body, and growing. If she understood the doctor correctly, the memory sponges . . . "matrices" was the proper name . . . were an augmentation device.

An augmentation device that she'd had almost all of her life. Would she remember *anything* without them? She had recalled, once, the scene and the circumstances of their insertion. They were inserted solely to rescue Cincinnati. Which she had done. And that had been her goal in life, but not one that she had chosen herself.

Maybe it was time to choose one instead of being driven willy-nilly by all of this. One good thing was that without color vision, the plague was not invoked so often! So the darkness was a respite, of sorts.

And her hands! She looked down at them.

Silent for so long, perhaps it meant that the mind which had been borning was now fractured. The gloves had served their purpose. Maybe it was time to just be *herself.*

Whoever that might be.

She held up her hands and examined them. To her surprise she could find few vestiges of the gloves. They had been a thin, clear, light covering, skintight. She could not see where they ended at her wrists. They had completely melded with her hands. The marking were still there—for instance, the green circle that had said Cincinnati to Jones. Her hands were still kind of puffy, kind of warm, but the swelling was going down. Some sort of process had been completed, perhaps.

But she wished she did not feel so woozy. So dull.

"You are tarred with the blackness of sin," said a sweet-looking middle-aged woman, bending over and looking into Verity's eyes. "Come with me and we will save you." She reached down and took Verity's hand but when she did so she pulled away after only a second of futile tugging. She stared into Verity's eyes for a long moment, then walked off without saying anything.

And she will give it to someone else and she will give it to someone else and what do I care? thought Verity. What does it matter?

Then the thought struck her: What is it doing to my baby?

What do you care, that dark part of her said. It is better off not being born. You could save it a lot of trouble. You could get a sharp knife and cut your wrists, isn't that how it's done?

"Shut up," she said. She sat there for another few minutes. Everything was in shades of white and black and gray. Down at the dark gray river a huge crowd of people were pushing the boat backward, slipping and splashing into the river, using long boards as levers. They must be the ones who still had the plague, or maybe they just didn't like Angelville. Peabody was yelling and so was Twain, over the voicetube, his voice booming out over the river.

It was amazing. She looked again. They were actually moving the boat! Just a little at first. Then more, and then a bit more, until at last it slid smoothly backward as if down an underwater hill. A wave, a cheer.

The All-Seeing Eye was beginning to stir.

She could feel it. Its tendrils were cold and snaked through her brain. It whispered messages about how nothing meant anything. Personality, the organization of matter, the hopes and dreams of humans. They all meant nothing. The messages were true. It was the truth.

And then Rose was there.

Was it Rose? Sitting next to her? Or was it just someone she imagined?

Rose's voice was gentle, not threatening. Comforting, not imperative. *We will pull through, you and I. We've done so much, against tremendous odds. You are a very brave person. Without you I would be nothing. Without you I could have done nothing. Now you need to heal. Rest, and accept help. Don't push everything away. You need the world to live.*

Verity squinted into the sun, which was glaring down on the *Queen.* "How do you know?" she asked. "You don't know about this blackness. You don't know about the All-Seeing Eye."

What do you think it was like for me in Cincinnati? An eon of darkness. An eon of pain. Until you came. Until you came with your energy and your truth and your anger. I could not be angry with Abe. I loved him too much. I failed my city. It was you *who saved it. With your hope and with your being.*

Rose's face was full of lines and pain and love. Then she vanished.

That's what comes of playing with those memory sponges, Verity thought. Alice had been poking at them for days.

But what did it matter whether or not Rose had been sitting there? Rose *had* been real, and Rose *had* been within her.

And Rose was very strong. It could not have been herself who was strong. She was tired, and weak, and small.

Peabody and Jack and Blaze were scurrying around on the hurricane deck. That was of mild interest. She watched as kegs of something or other were rolled onto the boat. Water? Food? She must have been sitting here longer than she thought. What about all those cords of wood being carted up the gangplank? That was strange. They didn't use wood for fuel. Did they? She hadn't really been keeping up with things. She should be. It was her *job!* Her *responsibility!*

But she was so tired.

Rest. You've earned it. You need it. Rest. And think.

Then the veil of the All-Seeing Eye quieted Rose's voice, divorced it from the part of her that could acknowledge Rose, acknowledge her own being and her own past. The All-Seeing Eye sucked color and meaning from the scene until it was once again something happening in the distance. Those men on the deck, one of them sitting at the piano, another with a guitar, a third fiddling with some sort of box . . . what were they up to? She kept forgetting their names.

The guitar man eased into a sad, sharp tune in which he picked out individual notes, then struck the same chord four times and paused. Another powerful chord ripped through the air and by now everyone on shore had turned in amazement.

He began to sing, in a voice filled with pathos:

> Mississippi blues, rollin through my mind
> I'm lost on you big river, and there's no end in sight
> I'm rollin,
> I'm Norleans bound
> But without my baby,
> Lord, I'm goin down.

> Mississippi blues, oh I've lost my mind to you
> Oh, river, big river, you're so long and so blue
> I'm rollin
> Yes, I'm Norleans bound
> But without my sweet baby,
> I just may as well drown.

As each new verse of "Mississippi Blues" filled the air, vibrant and mournful at the same time, Verity watched the black cold tendrils of the All-Seeing Eye pause. It was very interesting. It was like they were superimposed on what she saw—the hill, the people, the boat, the sky, the island beyond which had turned out not to be an island but a peninsula. She could see from her hill where the river started back up, a glimmering ribbon across a narrow isthmus.

Their names were back. Blaze was playing the blues notes in a fluid, fast riff, while Jack kept the solid beat going underneath. It reminded her of Shaker Hill, a little, but most of all Cincinnati when she'd been so bold and where it had been so necessary to fight to the death to release those who were imprisoned.

She stood uncertainly and started to dust off her hands but stopped because that hurt. She did not know what she would do. She looked over at the graveyard. If Blaze was right and there was no heaven, she could really rest there. But if Blaze really thought that was true, why didn't he feel this same nothing? It was a mystery worth considering, how he could still go on like that. She stood looking at the boat.

A man who had been preaching all kinds of things about damnation and hell from several tents over amid a babble of other preachers ran over to her and grabbed her wrist. "It's the Devil's music," he said. "Don't be tempted. You must resist it. God is waiting for you. Perfect love. Come."

Something kicked in, then. "It's not the Devil's music," she said. "I know the Devil and Devil doesn't have any music at all. The Devil just has an All-Seeing Eye."

The man dropped her wrist as if it had burned him. He walked round to face Verity and his voice was harsh. "You say you know the Devil?" he said.

She looked at him in utter amazement. "John?"

His beard was much longer now, and filled with bits of food. He smelled awful. His voice was much more rough, as if he used it mostly for shouting. His eyes were no longer kind and stern. They were fixed, staring, angry.

Well, what do you think your eyes look like, Verity? Sane as rainwater?

"My name is John," he said. "But I don't know you." He looked at her doubtfully, as if he didn't believe his own words.

"I'm *Verity.*"

"Verity," he whispered. He raised a hand to his forehead, to the place where the radio stone had hit him. She saw that like Blaze he retained no scar after being wrapped in the sheets.

He started to back away from her. "You're a sinner. You said you know the Devil—"

"John," she said gently, the part of her that was Verity surfacing strongly, somehow driving back the darkness. It seemed so important that John remember. The light of the past arose, a past beautiful and complete, drowning out the darkness.

That was what was so important about Shaker Hill, she suddenly realized. Not that the Shakers had been made up. But that such a refuge of harmony and joy had even existed at all.

"John. Shakers don't believe in the Devil. Not like this. You're a Shaker. Remember? Remember Russ, Tai Tai, Shaker Hill . . ."

His eyes held horror and pain, then. He nodded. "Yes. Yes. But it was so long ago. Before I knew the *truth.* Verity, I . . ." He buried his face in his hands and began to sob. His shoulders shook. "Oh, Blaze."

"He's all right," she told him. She embraced him.

At first he pushed away from her; then he allowed her to hold him close. "Really?" he whispered.

"He's alive."

"Oh, my God," he said, brightness stealing across his face, restoring his eyes, his *being.* "It's a miracle."

"It *is* a miracle," she said, yet something in her disagreed. It *seemed* a miracle—but she had almost given her life to bring it about. And *she* had decided to do it . . . but John would have it be a miracle no matter what. That was all right. Maybe it was.

"Where is he?" John asked.

"He's on the boat."

John whirled. *"That* boat? The boat that's playing the Devil's music?"

She had not known how deep pity could be. "John, it's just music. There is no Devil." She decided not to tell him that Blaze was playing that music.

"You blaspheme," John said, looking at her with his stranger's eyes. "The Devil is real. Very real. The Devil was in you at Shaker Hill. He was in me. We didn't know it. But events revealed it to be so. I have renounced the Devil. You must renounce him too."

Verity struggled to be calm. But it was hard. And what did it matter. And what could *she* do, anyway? Nothing.

But the music beat into her like a live flame. It mattered.

"John. You had the plague. It wasn't the—" She stopped herself from saying Devil. "It was the Norleans Plague. You didn't know what you were doing. And Russ—Russ loved you so, even then. Russ saved your life. We still love you, Blaze and I. You don't have to be this way. We forgive you."

"I don't need *your* forgiveness," he said coldly. He was so very thin. Verity was sure he was sick.

"You're not well—"

"I am as God wishes me to be."

Despair and darkness were returning. Maybe he was right. What did it matter. It was as it was.

"Where are Sare and Evangeline?" she asked, grabbing on to the eagerness she felt when she realized they must be here too. The loving, gentle twins, the only mothers Verity had ever had. They had taken John, wrapped in the sheets, and left for Norleans. Surely they wouldn't be this way. Guilt and pain had changed John. Whatever was happening to him, it was wretchedly sad. A tragedy. A waste of a truly good person.

John's eyes grew even more distant. He did not reply.

Dread struck Verity.

She looked around wildly, while the blues played in a rising crescendo. "Where are they? They went down the river with you on the raft Russ gave them. What happened to them?"

Tears filled John's eyes once again, and overflowed. He nodded toward the graveyard.

"They're—*dead?* No, it can't be true. It *can't* be!"

"It's your fault!" said John, his voice filled with grief. "Because of your sin! I remember now! You went to the Library—it was forbidden! Forbidden to go there, to use tech, to use *nan . . .*" John's voice rose, became hysterical. "They died—because of *you!* You *are* a consort of the Devil!"

Verity grabbed his shoulders. "John, come with us. Please. It's all right.

I'm so sorry about Sare. Evangeline. My dear Sisters. I can't believe—"
She choked on her sobs.

Then she continued. "But it's *not your fault.* Come to Norleans. Blaze
and I love you. You can get better—"

He shook her hands away. A look of revulsion crossed his face. "Norleans! Believe me, you are going to hell!" he whispered.

Suddenly, she was angry. "I'm going no such place," she retorted.

"You will burn," he said sternly, and all she had ever known of John
was gone from his eyes, from his face. And his face was the face of the
world—distant, implacable, unbending in its uncaringness, while the
fragile brightness woven over time by human hope and love dissolved, revealing the infinite dark.

The All-Seeing Eye rose like a specter in front of her. She thought she
heard laughter; evil, dark laughter.

Then the music became louder, overwhelmingly loud. She backed
away from John, turned, and began to run downhill.

"She's a consort of the Devil!" the man who had been John screamed.
"Kill her!"

A stone hit her shoulder and made her stumble and shots rang out
behind her. A bullet pocked the dust at her feet. Why are you running?
a part of her said and she slowed a bit.

"Verity RUN!" screamed Blaze and she heard the rat-a-tat-tat of
Peabody's gun returning fire.

At the sound of Blaze's voice her feet flew; she was almost floating,
she would fly above them on her new wings, she would kill them all,
with bombs and drugs and mostly with thoughts, mostly with thoughts,
mostly with thoughts—

Blaze grabbed her and there were more shouting orders over the
voicetube and the paddlewheel began to turn, slowly at first and then
faster, spewing up great clots of mud. They ran onto the gangplank and
as they jumped on the boat it was ripped from the side as the steamboat
ponderously but surely backed out of the channel, away from Angelville,
and the last thing she heard was a chant they took up—"RE-PENT!
RE-PENT! RE-PENT!"

"That was a close one," said Blaze, and hugged her tightly to him. "I
looked all over for you. We didn't know where you were. Then Jack had
this idea about the music. If the music hadn't worked, we would have had
quite a battle on our hands."

"Aren't you afraid of me?" she asked.

He laughed out loud and pulled her close and kissed her. His beard
was rough. "Oh, you're *talking!* Never," he whispered. "Never."

"Well, you should be," she said, and he laughed again. Then he
sobered.

"There's something I've been meaning to tell you. I was afraid it would make you worse. But who knows." He paused. "Durancy's dead," he said gently. "I buried him on that island there, off the Illinois shore—"

Rose was back instantly and strongly and overwhelmingly and she sobbed; deeply and wrenchingly, as if her heart was broken.

It was gone, all of it, all of the past, glorious and painful and dreadful and bright. Bright with the promise of the unknown day—

And then Verity was laughing, laughing hysterically through tears, and dancing, whirling round the deck, shouting, I'm free! I'm free at last!, and Blaze's face was so puzzled, so worried, so astounded, and then she calmed, gradually, as if a great storm had passed.

Sitting next to him on a bench, exhausted but clearheaded for the first time in a long time, nestled in his arm, she remembered what had just happened. In a slow, halting voice, she told him about John, and Sare, and Evangeline.

And as she did, the blackness returned. There was no escape.

There never could be.

So he took her back to her room and put her to bed and played for her because he said it made *him* feel better and because it was music against the darkness, there in Memphis, and he thought it kept those people alive and kept the darkness at bay and she said fine, and listened, and fell asleep listening.

Verity's room was bathed in silvery moonlight. She opened her eyes at the creak of the door and saw the man in the strange suit and funny hat shut the door behind himself, tiptoe across the room, and sit on the chair. She had fallen asleep a while ago. Blaze had been there, playing the guitar quietly. In fact, he was still here, she saw—asleep with all his clothes on, sprawled across the other bed.

The man watched her for a long time. She watched him too.

Finally he reached out and took her hand where it lay outside the sheet. He held it for a moment. Then he put it down so that it remained palm upward.

He leaned over and opened his black bag. Glass vials gleamed with colored liquids, held in neat rows by some sort of foam. They looked quite pretty in the moonlight.

"This won't hurt," he said. He placed a white eye-sized patch on Verity's palm and it adhered. He quickly pulled it off and set it aside.

Then he selected a vial. He held it up and it was clear. The top of the bottle was an eyedropper. He unscrewed it and put some drops on Verity's palm where the patch had been. He carefully closed the bottle and put it back in its place.

He held her hand up to the moonlight and studied it for a moment. "Green. Definitely green."

Blaze stirred but didn't wake.

The man reached down and picked up the green vial. He set it on the table and got a clear bag from a little compartment next to the vials. He opened the bag, removed the sponge that was inside, and set the sponge and the bag on the table next to the green vial. He pulled out some rubber gloves and snapped them on.

He opened the green vial and the sponge fit exactly onto the top. "Your hand again, please," he said.

Verity held her hand out for him. He upended the vial and soaked the sponge with the green stuff. He started brushing it onto Verity's hand.

"I heal thee in the Meme of the Most Holy Lord," he said.

"Thank you," said Verity.

The green stuff was a cool gel. It was quickly absorbed by her skin.

When he was finished, he opened yet another vial, again clear, but much larger. He filled the green vial, now half-empty, back to the top. With a small white cloth, he wiped the mouth of the clear vial and put the lid back on, then did the same to the green one. He sealed the cloth, the used sponge, and the inside-out gloves in the bag where the sponge had been, after tipping in a few grains of a white powder from yet another vial. He put this in a drawer on the other side of his valise and secured it with a little hook. Then he closed the valise, twisted the combination lock, nodded at Verity, and left, closing the door quietly behind himself.

Thirty-three

○○○○○○○○○○○○○○○○○

Big Fish Blues

Mattie watched the Professor from the railing at the back of the boat. He had only been in Verity's room about twenty minutes. He sensed her gaze, turned, and raised his hand in salute, and she did the same. He seemed to need as little sleep as she did. He walked the other way and disappeared into the shadows.

She shrugged off her robe. She'd found it in the closet of her room, and it was way too long for her. She had to take care not to trip over it. Beneath she was wearing her lovely white bathing suit. Blaze had told her that it would turn brown if she kept wearing it in the river, but he was wrong. In the moonlight it was gleaming, powerful white. Quite beautiful, in fact. And absolutely microbe-free. She'd specified that to Peabody, and he'd laughed, then looked at her sadly, then nodded his head.

Now she would have to take care. The bucket of food scraps was heavy and liable to spill. She picked up a handful of bread and tossed it into the river. It floated on the surface. Nothing. How about some fish scraps, cannibal . . .

There! A ripple, and the cooked fish was snatched away.

Using all her strength, she lowered the heavy bucket down to the water on the rope, which was tied to the ladder, making sure the bucket bobbed upright. Then she climbed down next to it and sat on the small wooden seat just below the water's surface.

She gave Josh one or two more tidbits. His whiskers brushed her legs. He was as big as a cow. Or at least a hog. She closed her eyes, then slid into the river.

It was cool, but not shockingly so. Holding on to the ladder with one hand, she touched his side.

Within her closed eyes a schematic lit, as it had that first time she touched him at Madge's Landing. He'd nudged her and instead of being afraid she had patted him, all over, as the pictures became stronger and stronger.

It had taken her a day's travel to realize that it was a map of the river. A present-time map of the river, which the boat lacked. She thought Josh might have been invented to be some sort of spy.

She saw blue lines on a white background. Red lines arrowed off the blue lines—they were dead ends, filled-in channels. Distance was fairly precise, she had found. The vision burned into her mind. Boils were tiny stars. But they were not constant. Rapids were also red. Whirlpools were yellow. A wide branch went off to the west in half a mile, then ended, as had the one at Angelville. And there was a cut through an island which was too narrow as yet for a boat.

This would take them about seven miles.

Good.

Josh nudged her, hard. She dumped the entire contents of the bucket into the water and scrambled up the ladder as the water boiled. She hoped he would stay hungry. It was a dangerous journey. Most of these people, including Twain, did not know how dangerous. Without Josh they would have been crushed in some rapids today. Luckily, Twain had agreed with her suggestion on that matter. But he did not always agree. He was a fool.

She pulled up the empty bucket by the rope, pulled on the robe, and, holding the robe up so she wouldn't trip over it, hurried back to her room. She would add this to her latest mandala, so she wouldn't forget.

Sam Clemens was quieter at night. She figured he needed his sleep.

Thirty-four

○○○○○○○○○○○○○○○○○

Healing Blues

Alice did not like Verity's suggestion. "You can't just heal yourself," she said, standing next to Verity's bed with crossed arms. Lil leaned against a dresser.

"I'm not," said Verity. "The blues is healing me. I feel much better."

"Not for long," Alice pointed out. "After an hour of normality the symptoms return. You can't see colors. You have suicidal ideation. I can't let you. And even though we've isolated you, the symptoms are spreading among the other Cincinnatians. We can't keep a close eye on everyone unless we tie them all down."

"But you have no guarantee that removing the matrices is going to help," Lil said.

"It's radical," said Alice. "But I think that it's our best bet. Sorry to interrupt your experiment."

Lil's lips tightened, but she didn't say anything.

Verity liked to touch the matrices now. Her mind filled with vivid images when she did so. They were not as vivid as when she had been in Cincinnati, though, when the entire City had entered into their orchestration. They were not overwhelming. They did not pull at the core of her being. They were merely informative. They were a memory, not the present.

At least, not right now. But Rose was much more present, and she liked living a lot. Rose liked the blues.

"Where's Blaze?" she asked. "I feel a lot better when he plays music." When he wasn't playing music, she felt more and more childish and irritable and unable to cope with anything.

"I bet music helps," said Lil. "Really."

"Balderdash," said Alice. "But I suppose it's somewhat distracting."

"It's more than that," said Lil. "Blaze told Jack that he thought that the blues was keeping Clean Mind at bay in Memphis. He said that the Civil Rights Museum and the blues and everything that's going on there *had* to have a powerful effect. . . ."

"That's a lovely theory," said Alice. "It sounds ever so plausible. If you're wrong, will you let me remove the matrices? It's not just Verity. I'm concerned about everyone on the boat. It's too late to do anything about the gloves. I don't know if you've noticed, but those snakes and eyes and all have been showing up on the gloves. The augmentation in the matrices is real. I saw it, Verity saw it, and I'll show it to you again just for good measure. Is the boat working? I was in the synthesizer room early this morning and it finally just shut down."

Lil looked sad and uncertain. "I don't know."

"Well," said Alice. "Do you even *care* about all those people?"

Lil's eyes burned with something but Alice wasn't sure what it was.

"Okay," Lil said. "Come on. Let's get Peabody and *make* the damned thing work."

"Where are we going?" asked Verity as she stumbled along next to Alice an hour or so later. She felt as if she should remember but she didn't. "I'm tired. I want to lie down."

"You will," said Alice. "In just a minute."

Verity did not understand why she had to move around so much. Her stomach was so full. She felt like throwing up. Alice had made her eat this morning, eat a lot of nothing tasteless food. It had not been nothing and tasteless at the time but had colors and taste and she had wolfed it all down like an idiot. Crunchy toast with butter, scrambled eggs with cheese, applesauce, coffee with cream. It would take a long time to starve to death if she kept backsliding like this. She stopped and leaned over the railing and Alice grabbed her arm.

"Oh, no, you don't. Come on, we're almost there."

Jack and Blaze were sitting out on the deck next to the room where Alice stopped. She realized where she was. The glove room. She hung back. How silly to put a piano out there on the deck. There wasn't room for anyone to get around it. Blaze's red guitar was there too. She only remembered that it was red. Right now it was black as night.

Alice pulled her inside the little room and slid open a door and there was a cocoon.

"No," she said, fear bubbling up in her.

It was clear, as were all the cocoons Verity had ever seen—the one in the Dayton Library, the many she had seen in Cincinnati. They all put things into her mind when what needed to happen was for everything to drain out of her mind.

Before she knew what was happening Alice had done some sort of little flip on her knees and back and she was lying in the cocoon and it enfolded her with sleek, cool softness, something she could barely feel. It was like she was floating in space. She struggled but she couldn't get out.

"Let me go," she said, but not very loud, not as loudly as she wanted to, because it really didn't matter all that much. Let the doctor play her silly games. "I wanted to get away from this" burst out of her mouth, from someplace she had forgotten, some other part of her mind, a foolish part that still cared about things.

"It's hard to get away from it," said Alice. "I tried. And here I am." All the while Alice was frowning, pushing pads and making lights flicker and sounds ping at the console.

Verity closed her eyes. The better to see the All-Seeing Eye. It was kind of faint today. That was strange. She scrunched her eyes tighter.

Alice ran the initial diagnostics. She'd been up all night trying to get them right, in the stutter of the system that was off now more than on. She was not entirely familiar with this particular manifestation of the technology. But—yes, it was working, about as well as it had when she'd shown Verity a glimpse of what was ailing her.

"Here's the information I first recorded from Verity," she told Lil. "I guess we can consider it our baseline."

Alice replayed what she had saved the other day, when she had first brought Verity here.

The mix of neuro-nan Verity had on board was truly awesome. Her brain was far from normal; in fact, Alice was pretty sure that the removal of the matrices, and the sustaining nan they continued to send into Verity's cells, would be a bad shock to her entire system. But the life of everyone on board was at stake. It was a terrible dilemma. The nan was completely intertwined with every cell, and had probably been an integral part of each developmental stage of her growth. Alice wondered if any provision had been made for its removal or cessation at some point and thought not, and cursed those who had done this to Verity.

"Okay, Lil, got that?"

Lil nodded.

"Okay. Now here's where I isolated the Memphis nan."

The first time, it had taken quite a while to isolate it from the models made from the biosamples she had taken from Verity. The infinitesimally small crystals were constantly attempting to create links and grow. They were successful . . . Alice had run some numbers, which flashed before her again . . . on average, they were successful 52 percent of the time.

"If you run these numbers out," said Alice, "a critical mass will be reached sometime tomorrow. And she's infecting everyone. See—the Memphis nan is so successful because the matrices create a friendly environment for it. The docking sites it uses are also being used by the Memphis nan—see how the Memphis nan has disguised itself with that outer ring? It mimics the outer ring of the Cincinnati nan, to which the matrices are very receptive. And within *that*—well, you can see that the Nawlins Plague is a real tight fit. Do you know which one the plague is, Lil?"

Lil flashed a brief, startling look at Alice—startling because Alice couldn't quite place it. "Yes," she said. "I know. I can see that Verity is like Typhoid Mary. She's the linchpin of the whole group here."

"Apparently these people are all exquisitely sensitive to one another," said Alice. She sighed. Probably someone smarter than her could figure out a way to fight the Memphis nan from within. Obliterate one of the docking sites, perhaps. The problem was that she did not have the expertise to run the possible outcomes. And even if she could, she would still have no idea how changes she made might correspond to mental or emotional states. It would be completely hit or miss, most likely miss.

"Okay." The screen flickered. Alice slapped the console with the palm of her hand. "Damn. Get back on—okay. Here we are real-time."

She moved her baseline to the left, put a progress report from yesterday in the middle, and ran Verity's present state on the right. It flickered on the screen, then came into focus. Still, Alice squinted.

"I must be tired. Is there some kind of extra cell in there?" She enlarged the video, upset. Had Verity picked up something else in Angelville? She watched for a moment.

Yesterday's screen showed that the Nawlins Plague had been surrounded by the Memphis information. The Memphis nan had overtaken the plague. It had been vanishing from Verity. She was being healed of the Nawlins Plague.

"Well," said Lil, her voice shaking, "looks as if Clean Mind came up with a cure for the plague. And they thought it couldn't be done. What a genius."

Alice glanced at Lil. Her voice had a strange note in it. Were those tears in her eyes? Maybe she was going to go off the deep end too.

"That would jibe with the loss of color vision, wouldn't it? It seems to me that all these people go nuts over the color blue. But take a look here, Lil. That was yesterday. *This* is what's happening now." She pointed to the screen on the right. "The plague seems to be . . . *regrowing.* See those hexagonal tubes? They're growing that lattice structure. It attracts the Memphis information . . . look—it sucks the Memphis nan away from the plague cells and ties it up. Neutralizes it. Don't you think?"

Alice propped her elbows on the console and rested her chin on her hands. She frowned. "But . . . so what? It's still hopeless. There's so much going on. How can I possibly invent a cure?"

"No—look," said Lil, her voice excited. "The plague is surging back. I think that's good, in this case. People say that the plague gives people hope. A reason to live. The things Verity lacks right now. Just ask Peabody." Her voice had an odd, ironic cast, as if she barely believed it herself.

A tentative piano chord from Jack brought Alice back to the present. Nothing to do but test out Verity's crackpot theory. Why not?

"Okay boys," she said. "Ready."

Jack and Blaze, sitting outside in the sunlight, started the show.

> Now Stackerlee, he was a bad ole man
> And he wanted the world to know
> He toted a .32-20
> And a smokeless .44

Alice watched clinically, skeptically, as the old story of Stackerlee filled the air. Jack and Blaze made an effortless, haunting harmony of it and the breaks were a wonder too.

Verity's brain waves gradually assumed synchronicity with the music over the course of five minutes. To Alice's surprise, a slight smile appeared on Verity's face as she lay there with her eyes closed.

Alice switched to a different view. The Memphis crystals were being attacked—regularly, systematically, with each rhythmic surge of electricity in the brain. They were actually dissolved by the tubes, which were replicating, as if the new electrical environment in the brain induced by the music provided them with the right chemicals for growth and maybe some sort of enhanced intelligence. The tubes disassembled the crystals into harmless components, which swirled away.

She remembered that the Nawlins Plague had another symptom. Constant singing. Perhaps there was something which music did to the brain that superseded, and overwhelmed, every other influence, an effect that the creator of the Nawlins Plague had used to augment its power, a self-enhancing feedback loop.

The plague, quite possibly, could save them from nihilism.

"I'll be damned," Alice said, though neither she nor anyone else could hear it. "I'll bet it doesn't have to be the *blues*. I'll bet *any* music would work."

11

◇◇◇

Delta Blues

Thirty-five

○○○○○○○○○○○○○○○○○○

Mattie's Blues

I watched Mattie dive off the skiff again and again, admiring the neat way she went into the water without a splash. She ranged far, surfacing twenty feet or more from the skiff. Then she'd dive in a different direction.

It was about noon, and sweltering. I considered taking a dip myself but it was too hot to make the effort. It was hard for me to believe that people had voluntarily endured this heat and accomplished the task of building cities so far south. Maybe it was hotter now than it had been before.

I never saw anybody go for swimming like Mattie did. She swam early every morning and several times each evening after we stopped for the night. She always took a healthy snack of leftovers for that big catfish—pounds of food in a big bucket. Apparently he was tagging along—no surprise, considering the huge meals she provided.

Today, she'd wanted to stop at noon and swim and feed him and Lil vetoed it. Mattie threatened to go to Verity and after a minute Lil agreed that we could stop for half an hour or so. I'm not sure if it was because she didn't want Verity disturbed or because she thought Verity would agree to it anyway. Or maybe it was just because Mattie cursed and made such a stink whenever she was crossed. Verity got better for a while this morning but then was just as bad. Alice said it was to be expected but that she was pulling ahead. I didn't know how she could figure out what to expect. Jack and I took turns playing for her and when I did the blues just welled up in me and I forgot the time and put every ounce of myself into it and thanked Alma constantly. I was thrown into that world where Verity was, that world of hopelessness and death and senselessness, the world where the blues were born, and I organized it and it fell apart between each note in the silence and then I would organize it again, and then the whole thing linked together like a sheet of sound and my heart and being would soar and I could only hope the same thing was happening to her. After two hours or so Alice would make me go away and let Jack take a turn. She said she didn't want me to get too tired.

When Mattie wasn't being Sam Clemens, she was being Mattie. But that was less and less. It made me sad and angry, too. She was such a fascinating girl. Sometimes she sat in the dining room and made mandalas. She just drew them with a pencil at first, intricate, hypnotic things, and then Lil found some paints for her somewhere and she really went to town. She'd start off with something, some shape, in the center, it didn't seem to matter what. Or maybe it would just be a space. Then it would grow outward, a circle, in swirls and lines and connections. I asked her about them and she said, "It reminds me that there aren't any mistakes."

"What do you mean by that?" I asked. They were all different, and all quite lovely. I tacked them up around the boat.

"Because I might think of putting something—like this—" She squiggled a jagged shape about three layers out from the center and yeah, it did look ugly and off balance and the picture was ruined.

"I'm sorry," I said. "I didn't mean to bother you."

She laughed, an odd mix of the Twain and Mattie laughs. "You can't," she said. "That's the whole point. This just reminds me that I can *use* something that looks like a mistake"—she repeated the ugly shape all round the mandala—"make it into a part of it all. I think about how to restore the balance." To my amazement, she quickly added another symbol, three bars with a dot at the end of the middle bar, and when she was finished I saw what she meant. It was harmonious again.

"But that's boring," she said. "What would he call it? Trite." Then there was a snake, like the one in Memphis, and I shuddered, and then a soaring bird. Then she batted the piece of paper away. "I'm getting pretty dry," she said, and went for the whiskey.

"Do you think you should drink that?" I asked.

"I don't think it really does much to me," she said, slugging it back. "It's just a prop. You know. Keeps me in character. Like in that play about Oklahoma. It was pretty hard to stay in that character. Might have helped if I'd had some whiskey." She laughed at my look and said, "Really, it's like water. I think it's part of what's happened to me. You know, he drank *constantly,* like a *fish,* isn't that what they say? Morning, noon, and night. Didn't bother him. Doesn't bother me. Ask me anything about him, anything at all. I can't help it, anyway, can't stop it, and you can't make me."

I had her teach me the song she kept singing, "Oh, What a Beautiful Morning." It made a nice break from the blues.

Now, as I watched, she surfaced in the brownish water but stayed where she was for a while, treading water, which glimmered out around her thin arms. Then she turned with a satisfied look on her little face and climbed up on the skiff and yelled "Okay!" I pulled the skiff to the boat with the rope; she climbed the ladder and I followed.

When I got up to the deck the look of satisfaction had turned into a deep frown. "There's going to be trouble," she muttered to herself, and sighed.

"What kind of trouble?" I asked just to be sociable. Seemed to me we had nothing but trouble. A different sort might be interesting.

"You'll see," she said darkly. She pulled her white dress on over her still-wet white bathing suit and her brown skin was set off wonderfully by all that white. She would be quite beautiful when she grew up, I thought. Not that she seemed the sort to care. I think that Masa cared. I wondered what she was like, inside LA. Did she even have a body? Or think that she did?

Jack would be on his blues watch for another hour, singing and playing to Verity before it was my turn, so I followed Mattie's dripping path up to the pilothouse. It had a nice view and something interesting was always brewing.

Mattie climbed up on her stool and Twain scowled. "Well, Your Highness, are you ready to proceed?"

She just nodded, staring anxiously out the window. She gripped the brass rail tight. Twain rang his bells and bellowed his orders and the paddlewheel took life and we started to ponderously move.

"There's an island around the bend," Mattie said. I thought I heard trepidation in her voice, but also resolve.

"Island number seventy-three," said Twain testily. "I know that."

"Yes," she said. "We need to take the east channel around it."

"Absolutely not," said Twain. "It's too narrow."

"Not anymore," said Mattie. "And on the other side is a huge whirlpool. It measures more than a third of a mile across. We'd perish there. We'd whirl round and round forever. And beyond that, if you ever get out, are rapids. Too rough and sharp for the boat. A long, treacherous waterfall."

"You have a wonderful imagination when you put a full charge on it," said Twain. "That's absolutely first-rate nonsense."

"There's no time to argue about this, man," said Mattie, her voice trembling. We nosed around the bend. "There's the island now." It was small, probably about a mile away. I was starting to get a bit nervous. That was quite a scene that she'd described.

"I'll not get stuck again like we did at Angelville," said Twain.

"We won't get stuck!" said Mattie, her voice shrill. I knew she was utterly serious because she didn't even take the time to remind him that at Angelville he'd ignored her advice as well. "Turn," she repeated. *"Now."*

When he didn't respond, she continued, talking fast and low like she'd thought about it more than once.

"I'm trying to save you. And all of us. From yourself. From myself. From all of us, from all we think and from all we are. You are stubborn unto death, in the face of all evidence before you that you should change your ways. Have you ever heard of *hubris?"*

"I believe it's in my vocabulary," said Twain.

"That's your problem. Once you set on a course, as with that cursed Paige Typesetting Machine, you'd rather pour a fortune into it and bankrupt your family than admit that you were wrong. Always trying to get rich quick, the whole damned country trying to get rich quick with gold or rubies or machines or weapons or—or this *stuff* that's made you and I freaks. That's what we are! Samuel!"

"I thought *you* were Samuel," he remarked calmly, nudging the wheel a bit and taking a deep puff of his cigar.

"Samuel. Listen to me. We are both dreams. Both of us were dreamed by greedy fools the like of which the world has never seen before and if we don't wake up—if we can't wake up, you and I, and those like us, then the world will never get another goddamned *chance* to dream, do you hear what I'm saying? We have to pull together now! We have to put both of our sorry severed selves together and get this ship of fools to Norleans!" Angry tears stood in her eyes and she dashed them away. "You're not listening! WE HAVE BEEN DREAMED BY DREAMERS OF UNSPEAKABLE EVIL!" she shouted. "DREAMERS who are WORSE THAN GOD! I'm TELLING you! I'M TELLING YOU THIS BECAUSE I LOVE YOU!" She finished in a shouting thunder that made me fear for her lungs.

"There, there," he said, in a soothing tone of voice. "You get mighty stirred up for a little girl."

"That's right, that's right." She was fairly jumping up and down now. "Pretend you can't hear me. That's you all over. Ignore what's right in front of you—the truth!—for some fantasy that you prefer. Well, that's the human way. But I'll tell you the truth of it. Hold on to your hat for it's a very rough ride."

Her voice changed and she hiccuped as she spoke. She was hysterical. Her voice was hoarse. I wondered what I should do. I eyed the island uncomfortably as she shifted into high gear. The very cadence of her voice changed and I knew she was in deep water now, out of her head, somewhere else, quoting Mark Twain, the real one:

" '*Nothing* exists; all is a dream. God—man—the world—the sun, the moon, the wilderness of stars—a dream, all a dream; they have no existence. *Nothing exists save empty space—and you!* . . . Strange, indeed, that you should not have suspected that your universe and its contents were only dreams, visions, fiction! Strange, because they are so frankly and hysterically insane—like all dreams: a God who could make good children as easily as bad, yet preferred to make bad ones . . .' "

She paused, breathing hard, her eyes wild, her hair frizzed out round her head like the halo a lion might wear if lions could be angels. James was staring at her and nodding. I figured maybe all that stuff really meant something to him.

"And that's what SATAN would say if HE were here. And what I say—me, Mattie, is the same thing: *Wake up!* It's a dream! I know because it came upon me like one. But you can WAKE UP! And turn, man turn, or we'll all die, and it will be the death of ALL dreams! For all people everywhere! These fools *have* to get to New Orleans! Please! Listen to me! There's a vortex, a huge vortex, a waterfall—"

"Where *do* you get your information?" asked Twain, showing no sign of heeding her. "If I may be so bold as to ask."

"From a fish!" she retorted and while he was laughing she grabbed the wheel with both hands and wrenched it to the left.

They struggled for a moment, Mattie grunting and Twain more surprised than challenged, I suppose.

Then he raised an arm, caught her against her waist, and sent her flying. She landed with a hard thump on her back and gasped as the wind was knocked out of her.

I was astonished. It wasn't like him to do something like that. I ran over to her to help her up but she sprang up almost instantly and darted out through the door.

"Troublesome pipsqueak," muttered Twain. "Please convey to her my abject apologies, if you would. I don't know what came over me. But I can't have her grabbing at the wheel like that. A pilot can't allow it. It's dangerous."

I thought of her swims and I thought of Verity and of how she could learn things just by touch. Although what Mattie claimed sounded outlandish, I thought that it might be possible.

"She could be right," I said, my heart in my throat. Which one was right? The man who was only and who would always be, tragically, what he was designed to be, unless he could change, right here and now? Or the young girl, filled to overflowing with two lives, two powerful, raging, unmanageable lives, filled with conviction and courage . . .

"Could we stop, perhaps, and send a scout . . . ?"

"Do you *doubt* me?" he hollered.

"I only thought—"

The right channel was wide, smooth, and inviting. It bent round farther to the right and was lost to view. The left channel was narrow, a mere creek sluicing through the woods, overshadowed by trees.

"See for yourself," he said.

"I know how it looks, but let's—"

The door slammed open.

Mattie stood there, brown and hazel and gold and white, straight as a stick, a young girl burning with a sickness new to the world.

Braced in both her hands was a black, shiny gun. She held it steady and she held it on Twain.

"Move away," she told me, her voice steely. *"Move!"*

I stared at her for a second. Maybe two. I saw so clearly, as time hung still and the paddlewheel churned and the split in the way came closer, inexorably closer, John waving that rifle around, pointing it at my chest—

I moved.

The current was quickening and I could feel the boat careening toward the right channel.

"You!" she said, addressing Twain.

"What now?" asked Twain lightly, not taking his eyes from the river. "I'm sorry . . ."

"You'll be sorrier if you don't move away. I'll shoot you!"

That earned a glance. His cigar dropped from his mouth and rolled across the floor. "Why, you—" he said. He took two strides toward her and grabbed her wrist.

The boat began to swing round from the rear from the force of the current, twisting so it faced west.

"NO!" screamed Mattie in my general direction. "DON'T LET IT GO THAT WAY!"

I ran toward the wheel. It was almost too difficult for me to turn the boat; almost too late. We were forced toward the opposite, wide shore across a veritable lake of water, which pulled and twisted the boat in a bizarre braid of currents. I wrestled with the wheel while I heard shouts and grunts behind me. James sprang to assist and even his strength seemed diminished. "HELP!" I yelled into the voicetube and a single unmistakable shot reverberated in that small cabin.

I glanced aside to see Mattie sprawled flat on her back, the gun next to her on the floor. She scrambled to her feet and looked at Twain in horror.

"I didn't mean—*help* him!" she cried, and ran to the wheel, which came just to the top of her head, and pushed with James and me.

By pushing with all our might while she pulled on levers and set up a wild series of countermoves with the paddlewheel, we got the boat turned . . . a bit . . . a touch more . . . she leaned on the throttle, teeth clenched, eyes wild . . . yes!

The *Queen* shot into the cutoff and we cracked through branches at a frightfully fast speed. I heard cries from the passengers and the trees on the island to our right gave way to a low, treeless stretch of sand and rocks and I looked to the right.

A boat larger than ours, a rusted cargo barge of some sort, drifted slowly in a huge, inward-slanting arc. I thought I heard piteous cries as several people on the deck, tiny from where we were, raised their arms in entreaty. I caught a glimpse of the letters RN and saw rafts aswirl, some holding people who looked like they were sprawled out for a nap but who were probably dead, perhaps having leapt off and then struggling onto their raft again when they found they could not escape. I saw two bodies tangled in a huge snag of roots which slowly tumbled over and over, carrying its ghastly cargo. The great whirlpool was filled with logs and even the roof of a house and other, less recognizable debris, slowly and inexorably circling, drawing in everything which came near it, imprisoning it forever in its endless swirling energy beneath the blue, cloudless sky fringed by desolate forest.

I saw this scene of horror for only a minute before the trees closed in again, but it imprinted itself on my mind, good for a nightmare from which I still wake screaming.

Lil appeared at the door. "I heard a shot—"

Then she saw Twain and she gasped, bent over him. "He's dead," she said, after a moment, and looked up at both of us.

Then whatever she said was lost as a roar rose from beyond the forest at our right: the roar of water thundering through a narrow fast chute. Ahead the cathedral row of overarching trees ended abruptly and we shot down and out into a vast and horrifying scene.

We spun around with the force of the water cascading from the other side of the island. Rocks big as houses cut water to white ribbons, trees stuck between them like chaff in the teeth of a giant. The roiling, muddy water foamed and crashed not a hundred feet from our boat, which was helpless as a toy. A log shot out of the rapids as if from a cannon and sailed straight toward us, missing our prow by mere feet. I was shaking.

"He wouldn't listen to me," Mattie was saying. I think she'd been saying it for a long time. Her voice was unusually subdued. "He just wouldn't listen. I thought sure he was going to wake up soon. I *so* wanted him to wake up. I believe that it was just possible. But now he can't ever. I'm sorry. Thank you," she said to me, and then to James, and then she collapsed onto the floor.

Lil wanted to wrap Twain in a sheet and toss him over the side. She called this "burial at sea" and argued that it was honorable.

Mattie insisted that we stop and have a proper funeral and burial. She was crying the entire time, slow, distantlike tears that welled from her eyes as she stared, like she was seeing something far away.

Jack and I dug the grave on top of a lonely green bluff overlooking the river. From up there the river looked grand and amazingly huge, stretching off into the distance, snaking here and there as if crazed, shimmering gold and rose in the sunset.

Jack wanted to sing a blues song but Verity insisted on a hymn. Alice knew a gospel hymn and sang it a capella, her voice sure and deep and big as it dipped and soared over the river in fascinating, hypnotic ripples of pure beauty and yearning. If Mark Twain had a soul, Alice's voice conveyed it straight to heaven, with flourishes.

Mattie was shaking uncontrollably by the time it was over, and it was getting dark. Alice bundled her into a sweater and asked James to carry her. I was surprised when Mattie didn't object, but clung to James like a baby.

We walked single file down to the boat, which sat like some sort of dream, as Mattie had said, white on the black water, light fanning from the filigrees as if painted on the river by a brush dipped in moonlight. A ship of fools, dreamed by my country's past. Heading nowhere. I was almost sure of it. Heading nowhere.

Thirty-six

○○○○○○○○○○○○○○○○○○

Blues in the Night

Mattie woke with a start and it was the middle of the night with no moon and she was terribly alone. Alice had insisted on sleeping in the bed next to hers, but she was alone in the universe now. Twain was gone. He was the only one who understood her, and she had killed him.

She had known him for so short a time. Surely she could live without him. Surely she could.

But she didn't want to.

She slid out of bed without making a sound. The door creaked, so she just climbed out the window and walked toward the rear of the boat where the ladder was and sat down. Maybe in a few minutes she'd go in and see what Josh had to say.

She heard footsteps but recognized them and didn't turn. After a minute the Professor squatted next to her.

"I will ask you one last time," he said, sounding unhappy.

"No," said Mattie. She didn't look at him but stared out at the dark shore.

"I'm afraid that you will change your mind later and I won't be here."

"Why don't you come with us?" asked Mattie, in a tone that was curious rather than entreating.

"A boat is too confining," he said. "I've heard things about Nawlins. Whatever it is now, I don't think that I could help there. They wouldn't need me. I would be useless. Out there"—he waved his arm toward the dark shore—"I can help."

"That makes sense," said Mattie.

"Let me leave something for you, in case you change your mind." He settled onto the deck awkwardly and opened his case. "Hold out your hand."

Mattie hesitated for a moment, then shrugged and held out her hand. A drop of something fell on it and she pulled it back.

"Don't worry," he said. "I will do nothing without your permission. Let me see it now. Ah. Yellow. Then purple. Two steps. That is unusual."

Now she watched curiously as he put a few drops of yellow in one tiny bottle and purple in another. "Yellow. Just put the whole bottle on your hand. Wait thirty seconds. Then purple. Can you remember that?"

"If I can't remember that I'd be better off dead anyway."

He looked sad as he arranged the vials in a small leather holder which he took out of yet another compartment. He sealed the top and handed it to her. "This is in the Meme of the Most Holy Lord," he said. "Would you mind doing me a favor and rowing me over to where that old ferry road comes down to the river? It's right over there and the current is not strong here in the cove."

Mattie put the leather pouch in the pocket of her robe. "Not at all," she said. "Ready?"

"As rain."

"That's right as rain," she said.

Thirty-seven

○○○○○○○○○○○○○○○○○○

Changing Blues

Verity's gloves flickered back on sometime in the night. She woke to their light but this time the messages were different. Nothing about chores or any other mundane issue. And, thankfully, miraculously, not a single snake or eye.

Instead, she saw pictures of Norleans, the Norleans she had come to know through the fleeting visions in her mind. Cobblestone streets, small shops, wrought-iron balconies, flowers brilliant in the sun. A river wharf where sunlight danced on water, burnishing vast black freighters, was a mute unknowing witness to the trade of a country. The pictures though fluid were fixed as to content; alluring and comforting, enticing as though they released within the person experiencing them the chemicals of home and hope.

The music continued, playing through the voicetube from the pilot-house, Jack and Blaze keeping their own watches against the dark. Every once in a while that changed and she could even remember that Blaze had told her that Peabody had fixed things up so that he could play those records from Cincinnati.

Verity lay in bed, quietly enjoying the absence of the All-Seeing Eye, feeling strangely victorious though she really had nothing to do with vanquishing it. It had washed through her, a horrible disease, and Blaze and Alice and Jack and Peabody and that strange little man had created a cure. She wasn't sure if just one of those attempts had been the right one or if they all needed to be together. It didn't matter. It was good to be connected once again, to the others. The others were there. When

Mattie was Twain, she professed the belief that there were no others, that all was self, and that self was only a thought adrift in space. Twain thought that honesty; Verity knew it for madness. Even the woman with the bee tattoo knew it. She had made the Norleans Plague. And it had gone wrong, and she knew it, and she suffered.

That woman might well be dead by now. For the Norleans Plague had existed since before Verity was born. It had drained the bulk of the population from the land surrounding the Mississippi and its tributaries. But where had it taken them, and why?

Verity tried to envision the bee woman as she might be today but could not.

How long would this bright moment last? Would it last forever, or only for a few hours, or for a few minutes? Suddenly she realized that she and all of them were on the peak of a wave that would soon subside into the trough again. But maybe if they *remembered,* and kept *remembering,* the brightness would last, and last forever.

At least her hands were better. They no longer ached. They were cool. She wondered where Blaze was, and fell asleep.

Thirty-eight

○○○○○○○○○○○○○○○○○○○

Little Girl Blues

Alice started awake, and wondered why. Then she saw that Mattie's bed was empty and jumped up, pulling on her jeans and zipping them as she left the room.

The moon was gone, but the stars were so brilliant that they lit the river with a faint eerie glow. Alice stood still for a moment, hearing the familiar river rush and a sudden, unmistakable splash—

Verity! Or one of those other sick ones—

Alice sprinted toward the sound and saw a ripple in the water near the ladder. She took a flying dive and arrowed into the water, into the center of the ripple, and grabbed the body there, which began fighting, towed it to the surface, and began to stroke toward the boat, ignoring the blinding sheet of information this touch engendered, then realized it was not Verity. It was—

Mattie spluttered, "Let me go, goddamn it! I'm all right!" She pushed on Alice's arm with all her might and Alice released her. They faced each other, treading water, in the calm cove where they'd anchored.

"Can't a body take a swim?" complained Mattie.

"In the middle of the night?" asked Alice, still stunned by the force of Mattie's being, overwhelming even though diluted by water.

"Any time I please," retorted Mattie.

"I thought you were Verity or one of the others—"

"One of the poor plagued fools," said Mattie, her tone ironic. "One of the damned human race."

"Of which you are still a member. How about some coffee?" asked

Alice. She did not like Mattie out here in the water, or herself either. Who knew what kind of deadly creatures might be swimming round here? Snakes, alligators—

One of them brushed her leg and she screamed and flailed toward the ladder. Mattie's laughter followed her. "It's only Josh," she jeered.

"I don't care if it's my long-lost sister," panted Alice, and heaved herself out of the water. "I thought you said that wasn't his name, anyway."

"It's not," said Mattie. "But that's how you think of him." Mattie dove down for a moment and then resurfaced. "I'm finished," she said. "Let's go."

Mattie was trembling when Alice turned at the top of the ladder to pull her up, surprised at how light the child was, though she was almost five feet tall. Nothing but skin and bones. "You shouldn't be smoking those cigars," Alice said. "Or drinking whiskey either. You need to listen to me. I'm your doctor."

"You're fired then." But she didn't object as Alice nipped into an empty room and pulled a blanket from an empty bed, bundled it round the wet girl, and continued on toward the galley.

Thirty-nine

◇◇◇◇◇◇◇◇◇◇◇◇◇◇◇◇◇◇

Definitely K Street Blues

I was surprised to see Mattie come into the galley, soaking wet, followed by Alice. It was after midnight.

"Good. You have coffee," said Alice, and went straight over and poured two cups. She handed one to Mattie.

Some music was playing quietly. It came from an overhead speaker. This meant that Peabody was still awake too, in his little laboratory of wires.

Alice smiled at me. "Gospel music. Reminds me of when I was little. We use to go to a church in Southwest Washington." She hummed along as she sat Mattie in a chair. "Drink your coffee," she told Mattie. "Your lips are blue."

"That's ridiculous," said Mattie, but was obedient, for once.

"What happened to you two?" I asked.

"She tried to drown me," said Mattie, as Alice sat down.

"But she was too tough," said Alice. "Maybe you shouldn't drink coffee. You need your sleep."

"I don't need sleep but if I did this wouldn't keep me awake for a minute," said Mattie, and with both hands round the cup drank half of it at once. "We have to get under way in a few hours, anyway. I have to get you jokers down to *Nawlins*. But tomorrow will be an easy day. Anything would be easier than today." She sighed and sat back in her chair and in thirty seconds was asleep.

"What was she doing in the river?" asked Jack.

"Josh tells her the way to go," I said. It was pretty unusual for me to know something that everyone else didn't know.

"Oh, really?" said Jack, looking bemused. "Well, I've heard of stranger things. Unfortunately." He brightened. "Well, how about some poker?"

"Where do you keep the whiskey?" asked Alice.

"What are we going to bet?" I asked, as Jack got the whiskey from a nearby cupboard.

"Our stories," said Alice, and poured us all drinks.

"You've already heard mine," I said.

"I know," said Alice, shoving the cards toward Jack. "And mine is pretty dull. Cut."

"I'm not allowed to tell my story, so I can't lose," said Jack, grinning. But his eyes were bleak and serious. I saw he and Alice look at each other over the top of his cards.

"You're dying to tell me," she said. "You have to tell someone. Good for the soul and all that. After all, I think it's about the end of the road. Don't you?"

"What are you talking about?" asked Jack.

"Norleans isn't there," said Alice. "But you knew that."

I opened my ears and studied my cards, though I felt a slight shock. I kept my face neutral. This was poker, after all. The stakes were interesting, to say the least. I kept dead calm and still though my heart beat hard. If Norleans wasn't there, where the hell were we going?

Alice was right about Jack. It took a while for him to drink half the bottle, and finally he went down in flames. But he kept pretending to play and we pretended along with him, dealing cards and bidding hand after hand.

"You're in a pretty deep hole," said Alice at last. "I don't think you can get back out, at least not tonight. So what's your story?"

He stared at his cards. "I guess my story is really Elaine."

"How did you meet her?" asked Alice.

"At MIT," he said.

"What were you doing there?"

"Getting a doctorate in statistics. She was doing postdoc work in learning and memory. She got there by way of Harvard Medical School. Sequed into artificial medicine—nanicine. It was very hot stuff at the time and MIT was one of the hotbeds, along with UCLA Davis."

It was my deal. I wondered if Elaine was Lil. Alice cut the cards and I spun them round the table. Jack was sufficiently wound up now and continued on his own as he examined his hand.

"In essence, Elaine was at the heart of the development of nanotech plagues. But that came several years later. When I met her—" Here he looked puzzled, as if he'd tried to figure this out more than once. "—I suppose that her seriousness attracted me. Maybe I would have liked to be that serious, I don't know. That focussed. But I just don't have the personality for it. I have a sense of humor. It took me years to see that she just didn't." He twisted his face into a wry smile. "Such is love.

"She didn't go in for glamour—at least, not then. By the time we got to Washington, all that changed. But I'm getting ahead of myself. Two, please."

I gave him two more cards and gave myself one and Alice stood. He took another drink and I was pretty sure that Alice understood this next part but it was kind of new to me.

"Let me tell you what she was working on. The biochemical processes which cement events into memory involve discrete releases of certain neurotransmitters. If artificial analogs are there at the appropriate moment, they can augment this natural process. The war on aging and senility was on. Learning is like memory, except more active, more aggressive, changing the very structure of the brain. She taught me all this. I was pretty involved in complexity theory at that point, and we kind of synergized one another's progress. What does it take to effect a phase change in the brain? How does it happen naturally, in children, in adults? How could we do it artificially? I was only peripherally a part of their team, but it was pretty heady stuff."

He sighed deeply and slugged back the rest of his whiskey. "Full house," he said, and laid down his cards. Better than ours. He gathered up all the cards but kept on talking like some kind of plug had been pulled. I wondered how long ago this all was but I didn't dare stop him to find out.

"I wish to hell I'd realized a lot earlier that my taste for this fanatic might turn out to be my fatal flaw. I was a dedicated middle-of-the road guy, perfect for government service. She didn't want to marry, but she dated no one else and neither did I. So after a few years we got married. When the government recruited her, we went to Washington, right into the heart of the storm. Cut," he said, and shoved the cards at me, then dealt.

"The city was full of lobbyists and payola, all sharking around the heralded release of the memory nans, the learning nans. Oodles of money to be made. But of course the Defense Department was working on the fringes of things. There was an ugly world out there, a world of religious fanatics who would not hesitate to kill with any means at their command. The Defense Department wanted to develop defenses against them. They had a complicated nan spy net throughout the world. I guess Elaine kind of wanted me out of her hair—I found out why, later—and she put me on to them. I was perfect for them. They trained me. I was a smart and affable guy. My social skills were pretty good—after all, I was able to develop the semblance of a blazing love affair in the heart of an ice queen, and even got her to marry me. In the believable guise of a statistician, since I was one, I gained access to all kinds of information about the international progress of the Flower Cities. And passed it on to the good guys, I thought. All these individual projects were feeding into the development of the Flower Cities, but everybody had to make their nut up front because they were afraid that once the information got out everything would be free. So this created a hell of a lot of secrecy, the biggest informational bottleneck you'd ever want to see. This was after we started getting the signal, of course."

"The what?" I had to ask.

Jack asked, "Need any cards?"

I threw down a trey in hopes of expanding a pair of jacks I seemed to have grown attached to.

"I'll skip ahead," he said. "Just to get it over with. Where are those cigars?"

Alice knew exactly where they were and gave him matches too. She gave me a meaningful glance and I didn't ask any more questions. He was talking about the quasar, of course.

"By then we were living high on the hog. She'd gone glamorous on me and I didn't mind. At first she was actually coached, because they had her going to lots of parties and social events. But she got to like it pretty well. Damn, I remember that night in such detail! I can't—"

"You have to," said Alice. Her voice was absolutely neutral. I could tell that she meant that it was something he had to do for his own good.

He gave up pretending to play cards. He didn't look at us, but at someplace inside. He held on to the table with both hands as he talked like it might try to fly away. "We had a condo linked to a warren of private tunnels of course. Everyone did by then. It was the kind of place that gangstas would have loved to break into but they couldn't. The condo association had voted to accept advertisements projected no more than three inches to help with maintenance fees. That night there was one for a new Indonesian restaurant and I thought that Elaine and I could go sometime. I remember all this because I was nervous as hell. Sweating like a pig. I had stolen something from her lab. Well, after all, I was a spy. But I'd done it for myself. I thought. I kept hearing somebody behind me but every time I glanced back there was no one there. I wanted to run but I forced myself to walk. I remember that I was irritated because the scanner greeted me by name and I thought I'd suppressed that. I didn't see any reason for anyone who might be around to know my name." He gripped his glass tightly but did not drink.

"The elevator ride to the forty-third floor only took a few seconds. It had been years since Washington had gone vertical. I was glad because our view was just stunning. I helloed when I went inside and searched every room even though she was supposed to be at a party but the place was empty. I'd told her that I had to work that night and indeed I did. I went in my office and locked the door. That damned view! I'll always remember that too, I guess."

"Nice, eh?" asked Alice. She had a distant look in her eyes and was blinking a lot.

"We could see the Capitol, and the river, and all those lights. But down below there were neighborhoods of unimaginable terror. Elaine didn't think about them but I did. To her the people there were less than human. I sat down at my desk and took out my package. It was a slim black thing about three by four inches and it came open in the middle. I thought of a prayer book even though I hadn't been to church since I was a kid."

"What was it?" asked Alice.

"A prototype. Primitive compared to what was to come, but groundbreaking. On one side was a screen with ten choices. Inside were compartments filled with the raw materials with which to create psychoreactive molecules. There used to be drugs that could heal depression. Drugs that could eliminate the hallucinations of schizophrenics. Drugs that opened the neural pathways between the fore- and hindbrain, giving the sociopath the empathy which he or she formerly lacked. But those I held in my hand were infinitely more sophisticated. They built a succession of powerful images that played out on the user's eyelids, like dreams, only so fast that the victim—I thought of them as victims—couldn't possibly consciously remember what they had seen. But other components anchored the emotions thus generated into memory. These images were selected after virtual centuries of work with real humans by people like Elaine, and the statistical results had been created by people like me. What a team. Like electric shocks in reverse, the user could be led down a very precise emotional path. Beliefs could be precisely inculcated."

He got up and started to pace. Mattie opened her eyes sleepily and watched.

"I had in that little box Christianity, Hinduism, Buddhism, and Islam. I had Nihilism, Atheism, and Existentialism. Perhaps I inadvertently got a dose of that. I had Totalitarianism, Marxism, Nazism, Communism, Democracy. It seems so commonplace now, so primitive compared to what's happened since. But back then—I held the world in my hand and I knew it. The origins of the world we live in now. I was drenched in sweat. I had the roots of pornography, spiritual ecstasy, criminal behavior, statesmanship. I had idiocy, workaholism, sloth. Whatever was not in there specifically would come, and in much more sophisticated ways, and much more biochemically directly. I was amazed, terrified. I knew that it was happening, but having that in my hand, after laying careful plans for a month to get it—well, that made it real."

Jack ripped off the tie he always wore and flung it on the table. He loosened the top buttons of his shirt and leaned over the table, looking me in the eye. "By calling up a particular profile, I could cause the molecules in the gel to combine in a particular formation. At that point something like RNA would record it and pass through a membrane into a liquid which would then organize itself according to the directions. That was a failsafe feature—if the soup wasn't there, the stuff didn't travel any farther. Of course, that night it was there. In a matter of seconds, a vial of chemicals suspended in a liquid would become available in a tiny compartment on one side. A minuscule concentration could multiply quickly in the water supply. It could enter a building through the ventilation system. You could put it in the food of a schizophrenic friend and turn him into a crack scientist, able to see things in a coldly real way. Replication like this was strictly, absolutely forbidden by all sorts of laws and treaties. Limited nan, to produce products, had been used for a decade or two. This was not limited. And someone had been very careless with it, too. That's what amazed me. A little while later I wasn't quite so amazed."

He shoved back from the table and ran his hand across his head. *"That* was what I had been working on. That little box. Gathering information that went into it. I had to find out. That's why I took it. I had to know. I wasn't sure what I was going to do with it. There was no way I could destroy the information. It was there, out in the world. Forever. For good or for ill and that looked pretty much on the ill side to me."

He slumped back into his chair and continued in a low voice. "There had been a lot of meetings around that time that I had been excluded from. Except for Elaine, I wouldn't have known. Not that she told me, but certain routines of ours had been disrupted and I finally made it my business to find out why. I guess they thought Dr. Statistics a bit simpleminded. A bit too much of a champion of unwashed humanity. Elaine had heard me hold forth often enough. At that point, looking at what I'd gone to such excruciating trouble to pilfer, I was only surprised that they had allowed such as me to be that close to this project. Elaine had spoken from time to time about a possible separation, saying she thought it might be unfair of her to keep me from having relationships with others when she was so very caught up in work. Of course, this was no problem for me, because I understood that she had to work very hard and very long. So the matter was dropped and probably those who put her up to it threw up their hands in despair. Perhaps even now they were thinking of other ways to take me out of the picture. I was certain that they could not reveal them to Elaine for fear that she would tell me; too certain, I suppose. We are all so frighteningly malleable, as that little box in front of me could so quickly prove if put to use."

He stopped. Alice got up and poured him some coffee. He drank some. After a moment she asked gently, "What next, Jack?"

He bit his lip. "Well, I started playing with the thing. I pulled up the schematics of *IQ 250*. Although intelligence had a different paradigm by then, the old label was still used. In my slow, stupid way, I pondered. If this really worked, of course they had all taken a healthy dose of *IQ Infinity,* which no doubt lurked here somewhere. But then, I was certain that they had not. I doubted that they had enhanced themselves in any way."

"Why?" Mattie asked, though her eyes were still closed.

He glanced at her. "Well, for one thing, it was dangerous. It was the kind of thing they liked to test out on people far away. People who were enemies. However that was defined that particular day. It was far too rudimentary, too crude to risk using on oneself. That was my assessment. Plus, there was a chance of being found out by those who had commissioned the project."

"Who was that?" Alice asked.

"The Department of Defense. I probably knew more about that end of it than Elaine, though I'm sure it would have been difficult for her to credit me with that." He sighed. "I wondered, were there antidotes? Blocks? Perhaps that was simply the pad marked *Idiocy.* Why develop *Idiocy,* anyway? That certainly made no sense. Except as a weapon. What did it mean? Surely there were enough average people in the world that *Idiocy* could have been bypassed. Except, perhaps, to anticipate its development elsewhere. Or to render the war machines of other countries utterly impotent." He sat down again.

"My mind spun round as *Idiocy* commenced. I must have touched it." He gave us an anguished look. "There were no failsafes. They were all one-way streets. Just as you can't squeeze time back into a tiny, powerful dot, just as you can't unmake an omelet, so it was necessary to take the new brain-state and develop the means to lead it to a new state once *Idiocy* had been achieved. Just using *IQ 250* would not do the trick. I found this out later. But that night, in my gleaming power, I was shocked to hear a beep and see a blinking light at the top of the right-hand leaf. I was horrified. It told me that *Idiocy* had been completed and was in the door at the side.

"I was frantic. I felt like the sorcerer's apprentice. There had to be some way to undo it. Of course. These states were all made from the same grab bag of molecules. Maybe I could just activate the opposite— *IQ 250*. And did so, terrified, I suppose, that *Idiocy* would get loose and flow through the city. . . .

"At the moment that *IQ 250* appeared on the tiny screen, Elaine walked in the door." Jack's voice trembled, now, but he continued. "I was tremendously surprised because not only was she holding a gun, but there was a man with her. Some colleague I had met briefly at a party. They had obviously been drinking quite a lot. They all did, at those parties. There were more sophisticated ways to experience euphoria, of course, but the ritual of drinking had something to do with showing their solidarity with one another. Ancient human rites are hard to eradicate.

"She thanked me and told me that I'd performed exactly as I'd been expected to, although it took a damned long time. She waved me out of the way with the gun and I refused to move and the man took the gun from Elaine and got a little more aggressive.

"Elaine got scared and told him not to hurt me and he laughed. Then he saw that I'd activated it. He asked her to tell him what it said. She told him *IQ 250* and I tried to tell them that it wasn't, that it was *Idiocy,* but he hit me on the head with the gun and I fell down, holding my head, which was bleeding. I was seeing stars but I heard him telling Elaine that they should take it, why not? Something about how they didn't have to have it at the drop point for another half hour and that no one would know.

"Elaine objected at first but then they both grabbed at it and I think I tried to grab it or something and he hit me again and this time it knocked me out.

"When I came to I don't think much time had passed. The book was gone and I heard them laughing outside the door. I pushed it open a bit.

"Elaine was sprawled on the couch, smiling. I saw him through the window dividing the kitchen from the living room. He had the water on and was just staring at it. I don't want to talk anymore. I'm tired."

Alice got up and started to massage his shoulders. "I think you're almost done now," she said. "You might as well finish. It won't take long, will it?"

"No," he said in a defeated voice, and tears stood in his eyes. He talked faster then. "Elaine turned to face me. She frowned and asked who I was. She tilted her head and the look in her eyes broke my heart. I wished that *IQ 250* had been in that gel. I would have stood there and cried like a baby had not that creep turned from the faucet and picked up the gun from the counter. He could still do that. It doesn't take a nanotech engineer to do that. An idiot can do that. He fired it. He missed me." Jack was sobbing now, his face in his hands. "He hit Elaine, instead. Her head jerked to one side. I knew she was dead. I ran into the room and grabbed the book from the coffee table, and ran down the hall. Even stupid, the man knew to pursue me, but the elevator wouldn't work for him. Oh, Elaine," he sighed and shook his head. "So very long ago. Eons. So much has happened since then."

"You joined the International Underground," said Alice. "What did they call themselves then?"

Jack laughed and wiped his face with a napkin. "It was so secret that we didn't even know what it was called."

"And that's where you met Lil."

"That's right, Doctor Nosy," said Lil. She was standing in the doorway. "Are you happy now? Come to bed, Jack. You're going to feel really bad in the morning. Oh, but what do you know, it *is* morning."

I felt pretty bad myself. But I was glad that Lil wasn't Elaine. And it was a bad day altogether. Not because of the whiskey, but that didn't help.

As I got up to go to bed, I noticed that Alice's glass was still full.

Forty

○○○○○○○○○○○○○○○○○○○

Lost Future Blues

The next morning everyone gathered on the decks to watch, in dread and amazement, Baton Rouge. Or what once had been Baton Rouge.

Blaze scooted some wooden chaises next to the railing and helped Verity settle in one. "Can you see?" he asked, and she nodded. She seemed better, but it was hard to tell.

But there was no doubt that this was Baton Rouge, the Gateway to New Orleans. Half-drowned as it was, there were signs all over, ads and billboards and directions and invitations.

The western bank of the Mississippi had vanished, receded. In its place was a new waterscape, tiny islands scattered to vision's end. They were completely covered with vegetation. Around them, tall trees grew right out of the water.

They slowed to pick up rafters every few minutes. Most of them were disoriented and frightened, afraid of drifting off into the bayou and never reaching Norleans. Just about every raft carried one or two dead people, or some had been buried along the way. The past few nights the refugees had slept five and six to a room, and out on the decks.

Time seemed to stand still as the *Queen* chugged past the unbelievably huge port, ten—*twenty*—times as big as Cincinnati's, lined with empty slips and silent, rusting cranes. Once it must have been full of clanking, clanging life. Now it was just spooky.

The blues the boat played echoed off the flat steel and concrete of various wharves and came back to them across the stretch of water. Blaze decided that Peabody must have spent the night rigging the boat somehow so that it was like a giant speaker. Peabody didn't seem to need much sleep. Blaze's own eyes burned from staying up till dawn with Jack and Alice. Jack's tragic story had opened a new place of darkness within him. It was terribly sad. How many other millions, billions of stories like that were there?

Anticipation had the rafters on edge. They milled around on the decks, talking in excited bursts. Their eagerness to reach Norleans took the form of a mild, flashing buzz at first—flashing, truly, because their hands had begun to flash with small pictures again.

Blaze watched as, one after another, rafters approached Verity and thanked her for getting them out of Cincinnati. He realized that something had changed during the night. Some kind of barrier had broken, like a fever.

Relief filled Blaze. He knew that a lot of what had been ailing Verity had to do with feeling bad that she had freed them, and given them the plague, because of all their subsequent trials. There was something, too, about them not living forever anymore—but being able to be *themselves* again. A wrenching decision, he imagined, if you had to decide which path to take. He couldn't fathom having to make it for someone else, as Verity had for them.

Not everyone was pleased—one man cursed Verity, and Blaze just barely kept from punching him. Instead he suggested that Norleans was still a long swim and the man skulked away. Another man came and told Verity that he was a changed person for having been in Cincinnati so long and having lived all those emotions. He said that one plain life wasn't long enough to even begin to understand what emotion and meaning were all about.

But all that ceased as their surroundings increased in strangeness. The passengers quieted as Baton Rouge's old downtown came into view.

The Flowers atop the buildings were dead husks. Discolored streaks ran down the sides of the buildings; many of them had crumpled like those in Memphis, but their construction was different. The Memphis skyscrapers had been glasslike, metallic, hard-surfaced; tilted and racked by flood and earthquake. These buildings were more like rotting vegetables. A stench hung over the river.

Lil joined Blaze and Verity at the railing, looking forward anxiously. Verity smiled up at her but it looked like it took a lot of energy. Blaze took Verity's hand. It was cool, though it flashed now and then with little twinges of light. She glanced at him but he couldn't tell what she was thinking.

"What are we going to do when it isn't there?" Blaze asked Lil.

Lil turned her head. "What are you talking about?" she asked sharply.

"Norleans," Blaze said. "Alice says that it isn't there."

"How would she know?"

"Beats me," Blaze said.

"It's there," said Verity, and it was the first thing she'd said since Twain's funeral. "I *know* it's there."

"You've got the plague," Blaze told her.

"Yes," she said happily. "I do. But I mean—it's somewhere. Isn't it, Lil?"

Lil turned to look at Verity and her eyes were shocking; full of pain. Blaze saw all kinds of emotions on her face—disbelief, regret, anger, resignation. It was the strangest look he'd ever seen. Then Lil hurried away, almost running.

"Where is she going?" asked Verity dreamily, as if she hadn't heard what Lil said or seen the look on her face.

"I think she has something to discuss with Alice," Blaze said.

They watched the shore pass by, and seagulls screamed overhead. It was disquieting to see how big Baton Rouge was—*fifty* times bigger than Cincinnati?—but after forty-five minutes Blaze saw a sign that said Cinclare and realized that at one time there had been so much industry and commerce here that one city had blended into the next.

And everyone who lived here had died. Or had run away. Or set out for the Territory. Or drifted down the river to—

Where are we *going?* he wondered. He decided that it might be a good idea to make some alternate plans. No one else seemed to be thinking along those lines.

He remembered Cairo, the train, Shaker Hill. He thought of all the places they'd been and of all of them he liked the little towns along the Ohio, the farming villages with their windmills and old tech. Maybe Verity could get better there.

On the other hand . . . he considered the Territory, where Mattie had come from, where the land stretched bleak and strange for so very, very far. It might be interesting to travel out that way, if Verity would want to, if they could take everything they needed.

But then he thought about the things he'd learned from Peabody and the things he'd learned from Jack, and Alice, and everyone he'd met on this trip and he realized that he wanted to know more. More about what was happening, more about what had happened. He didn't know if there was anyplace in the world he could do that but maybe he could find out.

Well, maybe it wouldn't be too much longer before he'd have to decide what to do if Norleans really wasn't there. But then, of course, it might be too late. Maybe it was already too late.

Peabody was at the wheel and Alice was sitting next to Mattie on a cot in the pilothouse when Lil came in, looking dazed and tired.

Lil stared out the window at Baton Rouge, crossed her arms, and sighed. "You know," she said to Alice. "You knew all along."

"Knew what?" asked Alice. "Not to mention I've only been on the boat a week or so."

"About Norleans."

"What about it?" asked Alice, trying to contain the exasperation that trying to have a conversation with Lil evoked.

"About what happened after the flood."

"Well," said Alice, "so what if I do? And it's just the best information that I have, which isn't saying much. And it's old information. More like a rumor. I don't even know *when* it was supposedly destroyed. Thirty years ago? Forty? I wasn't even around here that long ago. I think the people at Madge's Landing said there was a hurricane, but I haven't been the least bit curious. Maybe it's all been built back up, Lil, eh? Calm down. I didn't think you had the plague."

"I just don't know what they'll all *do* if it's not there," said Lil. Alice noted that Lil's hands were trembling, very slightly. Her voice rose high. "What are we going to do? *What has everyone with the plague been doing all these years? Where have they gone when they saw it wasn't there?*"

Alice looked at her keenly. "Me saying it's there or it isn't there isn't going to change what we'll find when we get there. If it's not there then we'll just have to decide what to do about it, right?" She paused. "If I didn't know you better I'd say that you were having a hysterical attack."

Lil grasped the back of a chair and took deep, deliberate gulps of air. "The closer we get, the more real it seems. From far away, I could dream . . . that maybe Norleans was really still there, just enclosed in a Zone. I could believe that maybe they were able to build it back up, and that all the people with the plague had made it there, and that they were all getting ready for some—some amazing *rejuvenation*. I thought—well, just now I thought that maybe you knew something I didn't. I mean—I haven't been sure. I've only *hoped . . .*"

"Gracious, Lil," said Alice, "how could I know more about *anything* than *you?* Why, whatever you think you know supersedes any rumors I've heard by *magnitudes.* So get hold of yourself. If you think it's there, why, I'm sure it's there."

"I don't really know," said Lil, calming. "Sorry. I just—after all this way—I got a little . . . flustered. It has to be *somewhere.* I just have to believe it. If it isn't—"

"Sure," said Alice. "Want me to see if I can find you something for those shakes?"

"What can we do?" asked Lil, in a whisper. "It will be a complete uproar. Chaos. They're expecting Norleans. They've been expecting it for so long. So *deeply.* These people and . . . everyone else . . ."

"You have too, haven't you?"

"Not like them."

"Maybe they're more sensible than you think."

"Who knows," said Lil. She rubbed her arms briskly, as if she was cold, though it was sweltering. She laughed, once. She held out her hands and stared at them. Then she clenched them and shook her head. "Sometimes—well, realizing something horrible, something awful. Can be. Very hard. Even if you knew it. Even if you knew it all along."

"Are you talking about having fooled yourself?" asked Alice.

"Something like that, I guess," said Lil.

The two woman looked at each other.

"These cigars aren't half-bad," said Peabody from the wheel. "Anybody want one?"

"Me," said Mattie.

"Look, Mattie, I want you to rest today," said Alice. "No cigars, understand? No whiskey. Peabody can pilot the boat, can't he? You said it's just a simple stretch."

"He doesn't know how to deal with whirlpools and cuts and all," she said, but her voice shook like that of a frustrated child and she was drenched in sweat.

"That's true," said Peabody. "But this part of the river is pretty tame, isn't it? I mean, it was dredged out years ago."

"You can see it's jumped its banks," said Mattie through chattering teeth.

"Well, I'd know better than to steer smack dab through the streets of a city," said Peabody.

"I want to take her into New Orleans," whispered Mattie fiercely. "That's what *he* would have wanted."

"I want to do some tests on you down in the room," said Alice, frowning at Mattie. She brushed the girl's hair back from her forehead.

"*No* tests!" said Mattie. "I *told* you. I'm *fine!*"

"You're a very sick girl," said Alice.

"I'm *not* a girl!" she said. " 'And you are not you—you have no body, no blood, no bones—' "

"Oh, Mattie," breathed Alice, and there were tears in her eyes as she picked the girl up with some difficulty and said, "I'm going to try a cold bath." She carried her out the door and Lil was alone with Peabody.

Lil paced in the small cabin. "We just have rumors. That's all anyone has. That's why it took me so long to risk this trip—"

Peabody just smiled broadly around his cigar. "People are funny, aren't they?"

"You've got the plague too," she said resignedly.

"That's so," he said, and smiled some more.

"Well, what did they think about all this in Chicago? What do *you* think? You know more than you're saying. That's about all that I know about you."

"I reserve the right to remain inscrutable," said Peabody.

"I guess it's all a big joke to you," said Lil, and left the pilothouse, slamming the door behind her.

"Hardly," said Peabody. But there was no one left to hear him.

Verity lay soaked in sweat, though the sun wasn't even out. The air was heavy; it seemed as if her lungs couldn't extract enough oxygen from it. There was no breeze, and magnificent frigate birds hovered overhead, looping round again and again, diving for fish in the still afternoon, their backslanting wings vulturelike against the gray sky.

There was an air of restless anticipation on the boat. People stood talking to one another about what they would do when they got to Norleans, how they would feel, how wonderful it would be. The few children ran back and forth on the decks screaming.

The *Queen* churned on and on, past the desolate wasted unending city, on a course of a slow, broad loop that hugged the line of buildings.

Verity napped now and then on her chaise. Blaze kept bringing her drinks and food but she didn't eat anything; she felt sick. For long moments she felt like she was sinking into the blackness but then it would lift. She was irritated and confused and uncomfortable. Mattie was right. Identity—thinking of yourself as one person or another—was all just a fiction.

But the thought of getting to Norleans—finally!—could lift her from those thoughts. Even though she knew that urge was just some sort of combination of chemicals in her mind. And that was the most irritating thing of all. Even now, she was still being manipulated. Maybe it was silly to want to control all this, to think that she could. Maybe she could ask Alice to think about it some more—

But maybe that was all being human ever was and ever would be. Chemicals in the brain. Hormones that made one believe in the existence of a soul.

Somehow, though, the sum was more than the parts. Except when the blackness came. Then it was easy to believe that everyone was just reacting, not deciding, and that humans were a sort of fluff that would soon blow away, leaving the coast clear for whatever would come next.

A far cry from Mother Ann's eternity, for which she and so many others had lived and died.

Even her loose cotton dress was too much weight to bear. Too hot. Her dress stuck to her and every time she moved rivulets of sweat rolled down her face. Gulls shrilled round the boat, their harsh cries echoing from the close gray sky. Tremendous live oaks growing through the dead corridor's pavements were dwarfed by the seemingly endless procession of deserted buildings. It was as if a poison was on the land. There were not even bands of children, not a single sign of humans. Verity thought she saw odd phosphorescent glimmers now and then deep in the heart of the thatch of rotting buildings, like seeing a single slash of sunlight on a cornstalk several rows into the field, but decided it was probably her imagination.

Shortly after noon, Lil returned to the deck. Even she had made a concession to the weather. She had abandoned her glitter dress and shoes, and was wearing white shorts, a red strapless halter, and over that a navy blue short-sleeved shirt, unbuttoned, that flapped in a sudden, teasing breeze. Her hair, instead of flowing long and loose, was braided back tightly from her face in narrow rows, and she'd wound the ends of the braids into some knot pinned atop her head. Her face looked different, thus revealed—sharper, younger.

"How are you doing, Verity?" she asked. She leaned against the railing, gazing forward like everyone.

"It's the end of a long trip," said Verity. "I don't know. I feel tired. Kind of worried. But this place—" She grimaced. "It might have been dreamed up by that thing in Memphis. Norleans will be *wonderful* after all this misery. Won't it?"

Lil's sigh was deep. She wiped sweat from her face with her shirttail. "I hope so," she said. "I hope so. I wish that breeze would come back." She pulled off her shirt, balled it up, and tossed it down behind her.

The elegant lines of Lil's face, seen from the side, woke something in Verity. That high cheekbone, determined chin, long neck, and narrow shoulder, undisguised by clothing or hair for the first time, were deeply, utterly familiar, burned into her—

Lil turned her head a bit, as if she felt Verity's gaze, and looked at her with questioning eyes. "What?"

Below Lil's neck, between her left shoulder and her spine, Verity saw a bee tattoo.

It might not be called a tattoo, strictly speaking. It glowed soft gold against—no, *within*—Lil's black skin.

Verity struggled to breathe. Her body was galvanized by a series of emotions that crescendoed into searing rage.

"Why?" Verity slowly rose from the chair, still unable to believe. It was some mistake, or some sisterhood, or a random accident. It couldn't have been *Lil.* Not Lil, herself, alone . . .

But she knew in her heart it was true.

"Why did you create the Norleans Plague, Lil?"

Lil's face was suffused with the strangest expression for a moment.

Her face was soft and open, as if the weight of years had vanished. She looked at Verity with eyes suddenly direct, filled with candor.

"It's that tattoo, isn't it?" Lil asked gently. "I'm sorry, I forgot. I included it in some of the visuals. It's been so long. So very, very long."

A great blue heron took flight from a nearby hummock. Thunder rumbled in the distance.

"I can't believe—" said Verity. "You've killed so many people. You killed my family at Shaker Hill. The plague did. And here we all are now, and what's going to happen? Where are we going? Why?"

"I'm sorry," said Lil. "I look very different now, don't I?"

"Your eyes are the same," said Verity. "The look in them. Except— sadder, I guess. Your face is different. It's more aged. Your skin is a bit darker, I guess. Jack told me that's easy to change. Your hair is a lot longer. But I feel like I should have known—all this time—"

"No one was meant to know," said Lil. "I've been careless today. Keeping the tattoo was an affectation, a foolish sentimental thing. It meant something to us, back in those days when we thought we were saving the world. We thought that the Flower Cities were a major leap in human evolution—but that they were being subverted because of the innate selfishness of humans, because of all sorts of subtle characteristics that might even be invisible to us."

Lil bowed her head. "And maybe—and maybe in coming in among the plagued like this, where the image of who I once was still exists, I *wanted* to be found out. It's been difficult—so difficult. Horrible to know what's happened to all our plans."

"What *were* your plans?" asked Verity.

She felt as if she were floating, seamless and nerveless, reactionless in a dream more strange than anything that had come before. I should be angry, she thought, but the affront was so vast, so all-encompassing, that she was just numb.

"Norleans was a free city," said Lil. "Free of government control, that is. It was a safe haven from all of the madness of the world at that time. A place of life and hope. One woman practically owned the whole place. She created a community of learning. The water was rising, even then, but slowly, so it was rather beautiful, with canals instead of streets. A lot of people in the scientific and technical communities gathered there. It was like a pilgrimage. Anyone who wished to could stay—the whole, deep, fascinating culture was still there, voodoo and all—but our activities weren't proscribed by any government, local or otherwise. A lot of cities had by then proclaimed their independence from the United States. We did too. Our philosophy was simple—we wanted to spread information. And we wanted to have an interdisciplinary situation. We wanted as many people as possible to know as much as possible about the reality of what was happening. We wanted cross-pollination of ideas. It was the secrecy of governments that brought us to our knees, the ingrained tribalism and nationalism and just the basics of human nature that brought us down. At the turn of the millennium, around 2000, the human population had a thin veneer of people who really understood technology, who understood what was happening, how things worked, how it had all come about. But it was almost as if there was a direct conspiracy to keep people from going through the intrinsic basic human developmental tasks of learning not only the language of the written word but the language of mathematics, the language of computers, the grammar by which our very minds work. And that got worse with nanotechnology, that selfishness, that us-and-them. It all happened so *fast,* before I was born, of course. It was as if a whirlwind seized a bewildered world, a whirlwind of human making, all of it slanted toward exactly the wrong ends. The development of reliable educational nan was one of the challenges we gave ourselves.

"The international organization of which I became a part infiltrated all of the Flower Cities in the world to try and find out what was happening. I gave Peabody a hard time, the other day, but to tell you the truth, back then Chicago was a model city. Most of them weren't.

"We wanted to get people down to Norleans as quickly as possible. Give them a taste of freedom. Give them the opportunity to become educated, in one of the many fabulous ways that were becoming possible. Give them choices. Give them the opportunity to participate in the rebirth of the world."

"Did you know about the signal?" asked Verity.

Lil looked surprised. "Well, we probably knew as much as anyone. But that information was the tightest. Even when it was starting to bathe the Earth, if there were people or organizations that knew more about it, they weren't talking. I think that most everyone who knew anything was silenced, early on, or became part of an elite. Of course, *we* didn't last long—maybe five years. In the early days we maintained the magrail system to get people to the city, but it was blown up time and time again, and we thought, Well, the river will always be there. They sure can't stop this river. That was years and years ago. Years and years. The Norleans Plague is extremely simple, made of a few very strong images to which practically everyone in North America responds. And it meant a lot more to me. I loved the idea of people rafting out of slavery—slavery to nanotech, to Flower Cities gone awry, or even to ignorance of all that might be possible—to the freedom of New Orleans. The golden color was an inescapable by-product we thought might serve as a sort of bonding device, at one point, but what you call the plague was unfinished when it was released."

Lil continued talking after a moment of silence. She seemed to be talking to herself as much as to Verity. "There was still a lot more testing to do but we learned that the National Guard, or what passed for it at that stage of the game, had been sent to take out New Orleans. They were closing in on us, fast. We were not popular with what was left of the government. We didn't have weapons, we had no way to defend ourselves. Most of the scientists were complete pacifists.

"Anyway, a group of radicals—radical even for us—left with an imperfect prototype of my information 'plague,' as these multi-medium distribution information packets had come to be called. MDI was the name at the Defense Department because they could be disseminated through the air or through the water. This particular MDI became known as the Norleans Plague.

"Anyway, those radicals thought we were too slow; too cautious. We followed them, of course. About ten of us left, including Jack and me. We were able to find only two of the radicals. We learned soon enough that they had been successful in the dissemination process.

"One of our committees had developed a plan to grow a floating city. It was to be like a country—completely independent. We were going to move New Orleans there—or, rather, re-create certain aspects of the city, floating in the Caribbean, and then inhabit it. So I included visions of what I imagined it would be like. But of course, they didn't have time to start the floating city."

"Why not?" asked Verity.

"Jack and I heard that after we left the military drowned the city. Drowned it, with no warning. Destroyed the levees. It was a massive, sudden flood surge. All our friends and colleagues died, most likely. It was a massacre. They picked their time cleverly. I think that they might have been waiting several years for the optimum conditions. A hurricane was building and everybody was preoccupied with preparing for it. Right in the middle of the flood surge, the hurricane hit. So it must have been . . . bedlam. Complete bedlam. After that, there was a complete blackout. We couldn't get within a hundred miles of the city, nor could any couriers or spies. There were massive Zones. Maybe they were seeded by the National Guard. And they were controlled by someone who most definitely didn't want information to be free."

"What are Zones?" asked Verity.

Lil said, "Everything was fragmented after the Third Wave. The Third Wave created the Zones. They're places where nanotech surged and kind of made everything uniform, as if it was one entity.

"Zones are terrifying. You can enter a Zone without knowing it, since everything looks the same. But it's been replaced. A Zone can be anything, theoretically. It can embody a single belief, it can embody no beliefs, it can be as devoid of consciousness as a plant, even though the beings look like people and go through all the motions—at least it seems that way if you don't look too hard. We've heard that there are Zones scattered all through the South and the East. They seem to be self-limiting. Not like Cincinnati at all, which was informed by intelligence."

Lil's eyes were anguished as she looked at Verity. "I was heartbroken. I fell into the deepest depression that you can imagine. At that point, what I had participated in was so unspeakable that I didn't think of myself as worthy to have a part in another such enterprise, if there ever was one."

"So there might really be a floating city?" asked Verity.

Lil shook her head. "I doubt it. Jack thinks so. He's heard rumors that another faction had been building it all along. I think that's a fairy tale. A chimera. They weren't far enough along in their plans. And the people who knew how to do it must have all drowned. Alice hasn't heard of it, and she's been living much closer to the Gulf than us."

"What happened after you left New Orleans?" asked Verity.

"We settled in Kentucky. I isolated myself completely. I guess I was kind of nuts. The mountains reminded me of my childhood. I was just protecting myself. I thought I had good reason. Jack went out fairly often, to various cities, or what remained of them. He stayed plugged into whatever network survived. He still believes in it."

She laughed, sadly. "Maybe there's more to that than I think, but back then, and even now, I thought that everything was in complete tatters, and that whatever he was doing must be ridiculous; meaningless. I didn't even want to know what was happening, what he did, when he was out. I was too . . . stupid, I guess, to try and alleviate the way I felt about everything with any sort of easy fix. I thought that I needed to suffer. I was inordinately afraid of finding myself in a Zone, and in my night-mares our little house in the hills was surrounded by Zones and it prac-tically took dynamite to pry me out.

"Then Jack heard about the liberation of Cincinnati. Not any details, just that a lot of people were setting out down the river. For some rea-son that really excited me. Cincinnati was tight as a tick, completely iso-lated and self-referential. If it broke, maybe that was significant. I was reluctant but Jack convinced me that we needed to go, to find out what was happening. And we had to hurry! If we hadn't met you on the gam-bling island, we would have tried for further downstream. It was just like the old days for him, I guess. Almost like a party, a celebration of life, and we'd had so little of that excitement over the years. And once I was on the boat, my old feelings and ways of dealing with things kicked in. I thought maybe I could matter again. I could try and help some of my victims. Find atonement, in a way. Another stupidity."

Jack slipped next to Lil and put his arm around her. "Why don't you tell her the whole story?"

Lil shrugged. "What for? It's kind of too much for one day. Doesn't make any difference, anyway."

"Might as well get it off your shoulders," said Jack. "Maybe I'll tell her."

Lil was silent.

"Lil stole the World Genome Project," Jack said.

"What do you mean?" asked Verity. "What *is* it?"

Jack said, "It was a library of the genome of every species living from around 2000 on, until so many of them were wiped out. Plants and animals. Lil got a lot of good references from working on the Chameleon Project, and that's how she got a job at the NIH."

"Oh, Jack, I'm not very proud of the Chameleon Project," said Lil.

"You should be. It was groundbreaking." He smiled at Verity. "It's how we met. Very romantic, actually. It was a project to imbue anything or anyone with characteristics that you, the consumer, would find attractive. Whether it was a political candidate or toilet paper. The beginning of using metapheromones, actually. My assignment was to steal the specs for the Defense Department."

"Of course," said Lil, "I knew what he was up to immediately. I caught him lurking in the network and asked him over. He came to the office—a fly-by-night company on Dupont Circle. Of course I was really working for the underground. Even my company didn't know that. I thought Jack was cute, in a serious kind of way."

"Cute!" said Jack. "What a word."

"Well, you were," she said. "You weren't very good at what you were doing. Not yet. Not only were you completely transparent, but I could see your heart wasn't in it."

"She arranged for some misinformation about the Chameleon Project to fall into my hands," said Jack. "No wonder I didn't get a promotion."

Lil continued, "Anyway, the underground heard a year or two later that Jack had stolen an important government prototype, and wanted to deal."

Verity remembered dimly that Blaze had told her something about Jack—some prototype, and his wife being killed. She didn't interrupt.

Lil said, "They sent me to evaluate him and what he had, since I'd had that previous contact with him, even though it had been brief and I hadn't seen him since. He was a wreck. But he was definitely sincere. I recruited him on the spot."

"Yeah," said Jack, grinning. "I'll say she did. Even though I was so transparent."

"Oh, shut up," said Lil.

Jack turned serious. "I would have died without her. It was that simple. I just wanted to hand over what I had to someone who could put it to good use and check out. But she convinced me that there was an alternative. She showed me that there might be a light at the end of the tunnel. Something to work toward. Some way to get through this horrible crisis that humanity was going through."

Lil sighed. "I don't know if I was doing you any favors, after all."

"It's not over yet, Lil."

She shook her head. "I think that you heard wrong, Jack. When they drowned New Orleans, things just weren't far enough along to continue with the floating plan."

"We'll see," he said.

"We can't go back," she said.

"There's not much to go back to," he said. "It's time to go forward. I thought we'd gone over this enough times—"

"You're right Jack," she said. "It's just hard to go ahead into—nothing. It has been an *interesting* trip, though."

"More fun than sitting at home," said Jack.

"What about the genome?" asked Verity.

Lil ducked her head and frowned. Then she jerked it upright and looked ahead again. "I almost went straight, there, at the NIH. Those people were doing incredible work. They were the most dedicated people in the world."

"And you were one of them," said Jack, obviously proud.

"I played a very minor part," said Lil. "Of course, with such a big project, everyone did. And the thing is, information was *free* there. For the first time ever, it seemed to me. No secrecy. Everyone had access to what everyone else was doing. No backbiting. We were all working together under a terrific, world-ending deadline. Species were disappearing at such a fast rate that it was, simply, frightening. The very biomass was being depleted."

"It seems all right now," said Verity. "There are birds, fish, insects, plants . . ."

"Ah, you can't tell," said Lil. "Not from here. It does seem richer locally, as if the world might be slowly recovering. But it might not be able to. Not soon enough for us, anyway, or, rather, our descendants. It takes eons to build up from nothing, which is what parts of the ocean are like, and much of the continents."

"So . . . how did you steal it?" asked Verity.

"It's not that I really stole it," said Lil. "It belongs to everyone. But I'm keeping it."

"Where?"

Jack took Lil's hands. He kissed them. "Here," he said. He ran his hands up her arms. "Here," he said. "And here." He gathered her into a close embrace and kissed her, hard, for a long moment. He let go, and they were both breathing hard. "When I kiss her, I feel like I'm kissing the universe. And when I—"

"That's *enough,* Jack Hamilton," said Lil, her cheeks faintly red. "I'm sure she gets the picture." She turned to Verity. "Washington surged. It doesn't happen overnight, necessarily. It just seems like it in the end, because after a certain critical mass is reached it goes a lot faster. Actually, it started across the river, in a storage room at the Pentagon. Of course, they kept the surge a secret as long as they could, like maybe it would go away, or maybe they'd think of a way to stop it in time. But it was one of those things without an antidote. There were plenty of things like that. But our organization knew. We tried to get the city evacuated but two very good people were killed for trying to bring to the public's attention that they were Zone fodder. Then we heard that they were hoping that it wouldn't cross the river—but they forgot to blow up the bridges. Anyway, the Potomac is not a very wide river. With any kind of wind it would have jumped. At that point people started realizing what was happening and there was general panic. It was the middle of the night. I know that no one went back to NIH because when I went back it was completely deserted."

"We were just one step ahead of it," said Jack. "But Lil insisted on going to NIH and downloading the library. I was sure it would kill her."

"It would have," said Lil. "It still could. But it's locked in. None of it can get loose into the rest of me. Unless . . ." She paused, then continued. "It's kind of like artificial blood, maybe that's the best analogy. It circulates in me, it stays alive. The information constantly updates itself, keeps itself from degrading."

"Why didn't anyone else do it?" asked Verity.

"Maybe someone did. And maybe in other parts of the world the information is still there, still intact. But if so I don't know about it. See, it was what I was planning to do all along. I'd prepared my body for it. It's why I got that NIH job. To get that information *everywhere.* Even though we all cooperated amongst ourselves, there was still the government mind-set that the information just belonged to *our* government, *our* country. But the project was never finished. It might never have been. It was so intoxicating to stay there, and learn *more* and *more* and *more.*"

"So the World Genome was in New Orleans, right?" asked Verity.

Lil shook her head. "Unfortunately, no. The NIH system was incredibly complex, and one of the things we were working on was reproducing it in New Orleans so the information could be decompressed. I did leave samples in various places as backups but I'm sure that they were lost in the flood."

Verity touched Lil's bee tattoo with her finger almost reverently. Her anger had vanished. "I've seen this so often," she said. "It's so strange that it's *you*. . . ."

Lil looked at the people milling around on the deck, in seeming euphoria. Song rang out here and there, mostly blues that they'd been learning since Memphis. Her face was pensive.

"Lil," said Jack in a warning voice, looking at her closely, "don't get started, now."

"I should apologize to all of them," said Lil in a low, desperate voice. "All of them and everyone who's ever gotten the plague. I'm sure a lot of them are dead, aren't you, Jack? *Aren't* you?" Her voice was angry; bitter.

"There's the possibility that a lot of them got to Norleans, Lil," said Jack. "In time. It really *could* be there. *Trust* me, Lil. I've always trusted you."

"You have," she said, taking his hand. She sighed. "I really have to face what's happened, Jack. It's about time. I've been hiding for too long. Maybe a personal reckoning is the most that I can hope for now, although it seems pretty trivial in the face of all this misery. All my life, I've thought that maybe we—the human race—were going to break through to the next level. To some kind of *openness,* the next level of evolution. I know there is one. That's the way natural systems work. For good or for ill, I've been part of pushing things through, even though it seems that we've fallen backwards into the dark ages instead."

She turned and looked at Jack. "But Norleans probably is gone. That's what I think. I guess this was my penance, to come down here too, where I sent so many people. To their death, I suppose. There's nothing out there but wilderness—the bayou, the Gulf, uninhabited islands, and a whole lot of snakes. Have you noticed what's happened in the past half hour, Verity? Where's the shore? The land is completely drowned now. It's like a lake here, part of the Gulf. All that beauty, all that hope! All those clear-sighted people and our vision—gone. No target for the plagued. For all these years. I knew it, in my heart, of course. That's what upset me so."

She dropped into a chair and said to Verity, while staring out at the strange, ruined shore, "I worked, you know, on several antidotes. Jack took them round here and there, on trips that took months, but the plague that I made—" Her laugh was sardonic. "The plague that *I* made is quite a survivor, I'm afraid. It takes the new stuff in and gets that much stronger, that much less vulnerable. I had hope, once we landed in Cairo, that there *was* a completely resistant population. I had to hope. I knew that most likely once the Cincinnatians got off the boat their strain of the plague would overcome any sort of vaccine the Caironians had, and that they too would be rushing downriver to—die. Hope is a funny thing. As unrealistic as any dream that Twain might have had. Maybe he was right. Maybe it *is* all a dream—scientific method and all. All part of a strange, dark dream, and if we ever woke from it there would be nothing. Nothing."

She put her face in her hands. Her thin shoulders shook with sobs.

Verity hunkered down and pushed Lil's hands away; held Lil's face between her hands as Jack stood helplessly by. Lil's eyes were full of agony.

"It's not true," Verity said. "I've been to nothing and I've come back. We—humans—are *something*. For good or for bad—which are ideas *we* made up—we really *do* exist."

"I'm so sorry," Lil whispered. "I'm just so sorry."

"I know," said Verity. "I am too. For all that I've done. I gave the people in Cincinnati the plague. I think that was part of what I've been feeling lately. But you were trying to do good."

"That doesn't matter," said Lil.

Verity had nothing with which to comfort Lil, because she knew that what she said was true. It wasn't your intentions that mattered. It was the result.

12

◇◇◇

Crescent City

Forty-one

○○○○○○○○○○○○○○○○○○

To Miss New Orleans

Alice perched on a stool at the front of the pilothouse, leaning forward to get the best view of the river. The weather was sultry beyond belief. She wished it would rain. But even that wouldn't really take the edge off the heat. When it rained, instead of just being hot, you were hot and wet.

While Mattie slept, directly due to a sedative Alice had slipped her, and about which she felt no guilt, Peabody stood at the wheel with nothing much to do. Alice realized that she'd been so busy tending sick people that she'd never really had time to talk to Peabody. But clearly he was holding everything together in his quiet way. She sensed that he had some kind of overview that everyone else lacked.

Now that Verity was better and the general panic of the suicides and sickness was subsiding, Alice had time to turn her attention to Mattie. She was waiting for her synthesizer room to come up with some sort of cure for Mattie; she'd taken some samples for it to work on. Except that it kept stopping, and she had to start the evolution again.

She also now had time to notice that they were going nowhere, and that it seemed too late to jump ship. Not that she could have, not without dragging Mattie away with her and she doubted she had the strength.

As Peabody steered he brought up some map and punched through twenty or so before pausing.

"That's interesting," said Alice, looking over his shoulder. "Why didn't Twain and Mattie use them?"

"They're not much good except right about here," said Peabody. "This area has been pretty stable. You can see that it was quite developed and this was a major corridor of trade. So naturally it's been pretty well fortified in addition to all the work done on it in previous centuries. Lots of concrete work down below. In fact there was an entire multimillion-dollar channel dredged over a hundred years ago just to protect New Orleans. Flooded out all the farmers, but New Orleans didn't care. We just have to stick close to that line of submerged buildings."

The decks were full. Everyone on the boat had turned out, and no wonder considering how stifling the rooms were. Alice idly pressed a green patch glowing at her right elbow. Linked hypertext of all kinds of articles were available, it said. Quantum Functional Parameters. Photonic Devices Index. Submillimeter Wave Adjustment. Organometallic Components.

"This is nice," Alice said.

"Oh, it's a very nice boat," said Peabody. "A bit warped, is all. Considering that it emanates from such a mad port, it's been a wonderful boat."

"Do you think that Norleans is there?" asked Alice.

Peabody shook his head. "Nah. Hasn't been there for decades. First they let the river loose on it, and then there were the earthquake floods. It was always below sea level." He waved his arm to the west. "See how the river is spreading out here? That's swamp, to the west-southwest. New Orleans is under water. And the Mississippi has washed out over the delta. Lake Pontchartrain isn't separate anymore."

"You've known this all along."

"More or less."

"And you said nothing."

"No. I've said nothing."

"Why is that, I wonder?"

"Oh, because I've got the plague," he said, with a slight smile. "Go, go, go!"

"Right," Alice said. "Whatever you've got, it hasn't interfered with your thought processes much."

He shook his head. "I beg to differ, dear Doctor. Before the plague, I cared for nothing. I cared for nothing that was going on out in the wide world beyond my happy home in my happy city, though I knew full well which way the wind was blowing. Now I care. I care about getting to Norleans."

"Which is drowned."

"One of them," said Peabody, "is drowned."

"Ah," said Alice thoughtfully. "How do you know?"

"You are trying to put me on the spot," said Peabody, but didn't look uncomfortable.

"I do enjoy that sort of thing," said Alice.

"Well, if it amuses you to know," said Peabody, "not all the satellites are dead. Some of them weren't knocked out completely. And occasionally those who know how and are diligent can pick up information. There are chaos-based algorithms that enable one to pinpoint possible times. Which are quite rare."

"Is that all?" asked Alice.

"That's all I want to talk about," said Peabody.

Alice pushed a few more buttons and stared absently at the information received. "You know," she said, "when I was in medical school there were rumors that a new kind of human had appeared. They were all born in pretty much the same month. Roughly, nine months after the first electromagnetic shock wave that knocked out radio. I thought it was pretty mysterious how quickly that rumor vanished."

Peabody looked at Alice sharply, then shrugged. "Must have been nothing to it."

"Maybe not," said Alice. "Well, then, that's that." She continued looking at her screen. "I'm not sure how up-to-date this is, but the delta is big and confusing. A million channels. No clear way through. We could easily die there. Run aground in a blind channel."

Peabody nodded. "That's what I'm afraid of." He sighed. He looked over at Mattie. He sighed again. "Don't tell her."

"How long, do you think?"

He looked at his map. "Well, if my estimate is correct, we'll be in the vicinity in about another two hours. Right around sundown. We could stop here, if you'd rather, and go on in the morning. . . ."

Alice said, "No, I think that the timing is just perfect."

She left and strolled down to the galley through such a crowd that she honestly wondered where they had all been hiding themselves. A lot of rafters had come on board. But they weren't very hungry, apparently— the galley was empty.

Something cold, she thought. Iced tea and lemonade would be nice. Iced tea, lemonade, and a few soothing chemicals. Perhaps even a slight bonus of euphoria. Why not. They deserved at least a little euphoria. Perhaps they ought to stay euphoric for the next week or so. Worse things had been done to them.

She rolled up her sleeves and got to work.

Mattie woke yelling bloody murder.

She sprang from the cot and ran to the window, climbed up on her stool. "Where are we?" she demanded, glaring at the river. "What's this? I can't believe I fell asleep. We're only about five miles from Norleans."

"That's true," said Peabody.

"And you were just going to let me sleep!"

"I was just getting ready to wake you," said Peabody. "My watch is supposed to last another ten minutes. Right?"

"I suppose," she said grumpily.

"I'll bring you some supper," said Peabody.

"I'm not hungry," she said. "But . . . I need to go swimming."

"No, you don't," Peabody said gently. "Not now, anyway."

"I'm the pilot, and I say when we stop the boat, cub," she retorted. "And we stop here."

She jangled bells and pulled levels and the mighty churning came to a gradual halt. She gave the order to throw out the drag, grinned at Peabody, and yanked her shift over her head. In her bathing suit, she was a slim brown girl with long, fragile-looking limbs and tiny, new breasts. She walked straight and proud as royalty out of the pilothouse. Peabody heard grumbles and complaints arising down below—"Hey, we're almost at Norleans!" and the like—and noticed Alice passing out drinks on the hurricane deck.

Peabody slid open a little door in the pilot's console and took out a bottle of very nice whiskey he'd found in Cairo. Tonight he felt the need of something strong.

"Here's to you, my dear," he said quietly, as Blaze's "Mississippi Blues" played, and a dancing, singing, shouting party evolved throughout the boat. "Here's to you. And to the signal. If only you'd waited." The whiskey was almost effervescent, from Scotland if you believed the label, and he sipped it slowly.

Mattie was back in twenty minutes dripping and quiet. She sat on her stool and stared out at the water.

"Well?" asked Peabody.

"You were right," she said. "I didn't need to go swimming until tomorrow. But then—" She looked at him with resignation in her eyes, and fear. And courage and resolve as well. "How much farther do you think we have to go?" she asked.

"You weren't asleep."

"Not really."

"I'm not sure," he admitted.

"Well, I'll just have to hold out that long," she said. She started to shiver again. "What's this called, anyway? The ague?" She grabbed the blanket from the cot.

"Doesn't Alice know?"

"She has some fancy name for it," said Mattie. "She says I'll die if I don't take her medicine."

"Take it, then," urged Peabody. He held her thin shoulders gently. "Please, my dear, take it."

"Her stuff won't work anyway," she said. "And if it did, if she removed Twain before we got out of here, we'd all die."

"No we wouldn't," said Peabody. "That's utterly ridiculous."

"Don't lie to me," said Mattie. "I can't stand it." She stared out the window. "It's he who *feels* the river. It's he who translates what I know into a way to use the currents, to feel our way through the cuts, to keep from flying up onto the banks, and bashing the brains out of the boat, or letting the river take us down the wrong channel because the wheel wasn't twitched at just the right second."

She paused a long moment before speaking again, in a quiet, certain voice.

"The life of the world is at stake. Is it not? The true life of the world. The life I felt—out there in Elysia—" Her voice became that of a girl again, a young girl with her whole life—hard, but real—in front of her.

Peabody looked out the window. On his face was a pained, thoughtful expression.

"I know that it's true," she said. "Don't try thinking up some kind of fancy blather. I've listened to what all of you know—Jack, Lil, you, Blaze, Verity. Even James. Especially James. And Lil—she doesn't know, but I *felt* what she has inside of her." She looked down at her hands. "I don't know what it is, really, but it's like an explosion of light when I touch her. And then pictures of plants, animals, people—oh, it doesn't die down for a good ten minutes. And just look at all those nuts from Cincinnati, down there—shining! But they're like children. So—" She turned to Peabody, and looked him directly in the eye. Her gaze was deep and steady. "What makes it so necessary that this trip be completed, for someone like you, or Lil? Why are you so hell-bent on getting down this river? *You* know a lot more than you're saying, too! It has something to do with that signal. And it has something to do with figuring out a way to keep what's happened to me from happening to other people, people with no way out. It has to do with whether humans will control nanotech, or whether nanotech will control them. And this is the last stand, this golden city place where all the scientists have gone. Lil told me about the scientists. I'm young, but I'm not stupid, and I'm a lot less ignorant than I was just a few weeks ago, thanks to the Bee from St. Louis. So tell me—is it so important that this boat get to Nawlins, wherever or whatever it is? I think I deserve a straight answer."

"You're right," said Peabody in a low voice. "It's very important. But not important enough for you to sacrifice your life. Nothing would be that important. It would be better for us to all die."

"Now *that's* what I call ridiculous," Mattie said, lifting her chin slightly. "For one thing, I won't die. And furthermore, unless Alice's stuff works, and I don't think it will, I don't really *have* a choice. Do I?"

Peabody looked distressed. "Mattie—"

"Let me put this to you another way, Peabody. If I were to forsake Twain and live on as Mattie, there would be no one to bring us through and I'd die anyway, wouldn't I? It's just pure common sense. It's nothing glorious. It's just the path I have to take. One of those old-time Christians Twain had so much fun with and hated so blackly when he got old might think of it in that way, as a sacrifice or something. A way to get into heaven. I don't. Life in Elysia was hard. There was no way around it. I guess it made me hard, too, but it gave me clearer sight than all these hoo-hoos on the boat. I'd say it made me strong, that's all. You do what you have to do, Peabody."

She looked him straight in the eye. "If I do this, I might still live. But you know what, Peabody? I'd rather die doing this, being here, than live to be a hundred in Elysia. I'm not just a girl. I'm an old man. I've traveled round the world, many times. I love technology. I invested in it. I ruined my life for it. But it's the future. And it's us, now. What do you want, man—to go back to being a microbe? To go back to where Satan—or God, who is identical, I've found—cracks his whip and we all cringe? To go back to being slaves to fairy tales and rumors and the political and economic whims of bad people?"

Her voice, still strong, rose. "No—this is me, and I am this. It's glorious. That's all. And what's out there, anyway?" She swept her arm in a gesture that indicated the universe. "That's us too. And *that* is what will get me. My comet. It's coming for me even now."

"There's another way," said Peabody, a desperate note in his voice. "We *might* get through on luck."

"On luck?" asked Mattie. "How many thousands of little hummocks block our way to the Gulf, do you think? For years it was a full-time dredging job to keep the mouth of the Mississippi open to the Gulf. Sam Clemens remembers that! But that channel is wrecked and I don't believe there've been any dredgers at work recently. This is the bayou. Land and water mixed together. Swamp. Even with Twain and Josh, we might not find a way out the other side. With them, we have a slight chance."

"Mattie, please change your mind."

But she said, "That's enough. I think we've covered all the important points."

Then she was all Twain. She assumed his dignity with a slightly changed face and subtle gestures that exuded powerful authority. "Get my white suit, cub. Make sure it's pressed. We're heading into New Orleans this evening and I want to look spiffy at the club. And you've neglected to ready my cigar."

"Sorry, sir," said Peabody, his face sad. "It won't happen again." The tone of his voice was one of admiration and respect, as to an equal.

"We're a team, then?" she asked. Her voice was strong but he saw her blink.

"Guaranteed," he said.

"I'll be counting on you," she said. "Now go."

Verity turned and walked away from the door, where she had been listening.

She didn't have to tell them what she'd come to say. They already knew.

The boat churned down the river again, chopping at the water as they rounded a broad bend golden in the sunset. People were dancing to the blues, crying and singing, hollering about freedom and happiness and how the world was one.

Verity saw it first, she thought, since no one else seemed to notice. Alice was walking round looking extremely distressed. She stopped next to Verity and said, "I tried. God knows I tried. But I don't think it's going to work." She sighed heavily and twisted her hands together. "It just didn't come out right. I just saw the final evolution readouts. It's completely null. It evolved into . . ."

"Lemonade," said Verity. "Perfectly delicious lemonade. I'm getting to be quite fond of it. Thank you."

"Oh," said Alice, slumping down onto a bench, "you just don't understand. It was supposed to *do* something. It was supposed to *help*. And there's nothing—nothing for Mattie, either. That's the worst part."

Verity felt Alice's defeat. They stood high on the boat, just below the pilothouse, and she looked upward. She knew Mattie was at the wheel, though she couldn't see her through the slanted glass. She could feel the girl's resolve and courage through the very lineaments of the boat. She allowed herself to be infused by it. She lifted her chin. She wondered where Lil was, where Blaze was.

The water was like a lake rather than a river. The waves sent forward by the boat were a series of glimmering curves stretching into the distance.

And straight ahead it was, it had to be: New Orleans.

Only the tops of the buildings were visible, crowned by vital, powerful, amazingly detailed, and staggeringly vast Flowers. Verity thought her heart would break, remembering Cincinnati and all that had happened there. There had been beauty as well as terror, and so much hope.

She had to think of the world as a place of beauty and hope, she realized, for her child as much as for herself. For no matter what Mattie said about the damned human race, that was the latter-day Twain speaking, the one who saw American Imperialism, life, and religion, as dark; deluded; lies. Yet Mattie still held true to some force within herself. Verity understood what Mattie had to do now and she feared for her.

"Oh, God," moaned Alice. "This is it."

For it was certain that they were here at last, at the apex of their overwhelming desire. And that desire would not be satisfied. The voices of the passengers grew loud as Alice saw it—what everyone saw. The terrible visage of a drowned city.

"It can't just be that the water's risen," Alice said in wonder. "I think the quakes must have hit hard here too."

Some of the buildings tilted crazily, and a story or two of mirrors sent forth blinding flashes. But above them—oh, it was weird, unearthly, and Alice had seen many things on the edge of imagination's possibilities. She had seen several living Flower Cities in her day, but it was much more strange to see one that should be dead seemingly alive, living past its planned function, as if it had crossed some impossible threshold.

Mattie turned east to avoid a bridge that peeked through the surface of the water. She steered straight through the center of town, up a broad boulevard lined with sagging, drowned towers. Perhaps half of the building's height was above water. Their reflections, and that of the massive Flowers growing at the apex of each building, shimmered on the still water. Alice looked over the side, down into the canyons of the drowned city, where a green fur of algae clothed the buildings, and saw other Flowers, swaying dreamily with the currents below.

Huge fish, ten feet long and more, swam through open windows beneath them. A great flock of white cranes wheeled against the evening sky, where the clouds were dispersing to reveal a luminous virginal blue. There were no Bees. They needed humans to live.

But then Mattie brought the boat to a slow drift as people hailed them from ahead, from the unglassed windows of one of the towers. Several hundred of the rafters from Cincinnati, who'd left before them, ragged and delirious, were camping in one of the buildings. They were ferried aboard with johnboats, greeted with laughter and tears, and the boat rode even lower in the water. They gasped out stories of strange lights in the sky, a rescue program they thought they'd activated, monsters in the deep, and the short-circuited history of Norleans with which they'd finally been able to relieve their ungloved maddened receptors. Norleans, they babbled, Norleans was still ahead.

But no one knew exactly where.

After, amid the singing and confusion, the *Queen* drifted over a place where the buildings had been too low to break the surface of the water.

"It's the French Quarter," said Lil, tears on her face. "Look, Jack. Remember? Can you see, down there. The church steeple! That's where we lived, behind the church . . . oh, Jack. There's no one. No one." Jack hugged her to him as she sobbed.

Next to Alice, Verity smiled. And her skin began to glow.

The golden glow had subsided, in the past few weeks, under the onslaught of the All-Seeing Eye. But now, tiny pictures began to dance down Verity's arms, upon her neck, her back, her legs—every place unconcealed by her thin dress was alight with pictures. Some of them had color and all were perfectly, minutely resolved, sharp and precise.

Alice was struck dumb, seeing these pictures wash across Verity's body, while Verity seemed not to notice, intent instead on Norleans. Alice, looking around, saw that all the plagued people were similarly affected.

Lil stepped next to her, whispered, "This is it, Doc. I think my heart is going to pound out of my chest." Tears filled her eyes, and one spilled slowly down her cheek. "This is where it all happened. Such a long time ago. Being here at last—what will it do to them? I'm so *afraid.*"

Blaze pushed through the crowd and stood next to Verity. He looked tremendously excited, and held a guitar. He opened his mouth to speak, then closed it. He stared at Verity and then exclaimed with wonder in his voice, "Verity, that's"—he traced the motion of a face down her arm— "that's *Russ,* I guess. He looked a little different to you—oh—oh, Sare! Sare—" He choked a bit. He pushed Verity's sweat-soaked hair back from her forehead, and kissed her. "What's going on?" he whispered hoarsely. He put his arm around her shoulders; shook his head. "Every time I turn around, you are more and more strange. Oh, Ver."

And then a cascade of deep, intense memories overwhelmed Verity— memories of home, of love, of deep full days. Each generated a flood of images, and as she looked at her arms, herself amazed, she saw pictures she did not recognize. Jostled by people pressing next to her she saw that they too were covered with pictures and on the face of the woman next to her flashed a picture which looked a lot like John, as he used to be. . . .

The setting sun intensified and the people became utterly still, their skin awash with pictures—pictures traded, floating through the still, windless air, metapheromones transferred among themselves, symbolized by the part of the brain that did such things, transmitted by specialized molecules generated by their genetically modified bodies in ways much more sophisticated than the ancient pheromonal systems of humans previous to the first nanotech wave.

It was a new language, and they were stuttering in it, evolving the grammar, glowing with meaning, overflowing with information, with memory, which each ached to share.

And then a song began faintly; strengthened. It started somewhere, as a thought, which was soon echoed by all of them. Probably, during that interval, there were a thousand other thoughts and impulses which were not magnified, which did not oscillate among them. The age-old, slow meme of style was sharpened; had attained lightning speed.

It was one of the blues songs they had been hearing lately, poignant and sweet and filled with longing, branched with haunting, delicious harmonies which spontaneously arose. A certain amount of singers chose each part, some of them switching, switching again, until a natural four-part division balanced; full and magnificent as it swelled through the evening air as though it were the precise expression of the haunting wilderness that it infused, something about being born by the river and that a change is going to come. Blaze's guitar accompanied them; it rang out clear and strong over the system Peabody had rigged. After that Blaze sang song after song, and Verity noticed that he had a different guitar, not his red one, and he'd sing one line over Peabody's system and everyone sang along, but it was like they knew it and he was only reminding them and sometimes one of them would sing one line and he'd know that song right off and play that too.

And the images on their bodies changed to those of Flower Cities, and within Verity Rose emerged and gave forth her eternal cycled life in points of light, suffusing Verity past tears and far into some new and freer realm of truth, one she had not known existed, which loosened her chest and helped her sing more clearly, and then the pictures became those of a ship, rising into space, and finally there were no more pictures but only singing, slow sweet dancing, tears and laughter, and the will to go past—*past!*—the promised land, and into the unknown future.

They slowly sailed through a vast waterswept garden of brilliant purple Iris, glowing white Hyacinth, and Lilies of every imaginable shape and hue. Each Flower was a city block across, or larger. Orchids hung in a huge sweeping arc overhead, anchored in the crown of a building still living, still drawing life from its roots. It was like Home—Cincinnati. But it was not. It was new, and drowned, and past, all in one swift hour. And now there was truly, only Downriver, the Territory, a Nawlins of the mind and of the soul.

The rafters cast fear from them in great and glorious dance. Verity's gift, her Shaker Gift of dance, returned, but this time it came toward her from everyone around her, and the dance changed, changed, with each new heightening of music, with a new step, a new gesture, which they all incorporated as if it were a great mandala of motion in which there were no mistakes but only eternal motion, part of a pattern annealing and annealing again, through contraction and expansion and the music was all blues, all intense, all yearning, and maybe even all-powerful as the sun set gloriously red and pink and golden across the lake and the treed marshes around them.

Then—

There was a pause, a silence, a slight shift among the singers, the dancers, the image-bearers learning their new language.

They were washed clean of color and of song and of motion, and stood silent. The paddlewheel was the only sound, and the splash of its waves, in the twilight.

A new picture appeared among the Cincinnatians, generated from those Mattie had stopped to pick up, the people who had been camping in the ruined tower of downtown New Orleans. Everyone knew where it came from. And they all knew what it was.

Norleans. The real one.

A glorious white city, complexly structured, tinged golden with sunlight and blue where it caught the vast ocean's reflection, glowed from hands and faces, an insistent tattoo eliciting tears and joy.

Heaven, thought Verity, in the wondrous haze of revelation, too weak to resist the overwhelming pull, the beauty of this future place, this jewel awaiting them . . . farther. Farther on. Even more wonderful, more fabulous, than the Norleans first promised, back in those first golden days when song filled them with such fervor.

Their minds were filled with glory.

The dance resumed, more slowly now, and their songs were low and fervent, rich with harmonies and yearning.

With the pictures and whatever chemicals of hope the ragged band had absorbed from the still-Flowered buildings, the plague was reinforced, renewed, strengthened, though it had never left them. But now it was boosted to new heights.

They were ready to go on. Norleans, the *real* Norleans, was still ahead.

Only Verity was able to wonder, *What if it is ruined too?* Then dance and song overwhelmed her, and washed doubt away on a flood of overwhelming promise.

For the present.

"Well, Doc," said Lil in the midst of it all, *"something* happened." She was silent for a long moment, and her shoulders lifted. "At least they didn't die," she whispered.

Then they were past the city. Gradually, they quieted. All that was left was the wild beauty of the place, and the many-beckoning channels of the delta fingering off in the distance, each a molten golden river in the blazing setting sun, soon replaced by stars.

Fear swept in with night, after the remaining rafters abandoned their crafts and boarded the boat until Verity worried that there might be too many of them to hold.

They paused on the brink of a maze with many paths and only a few exits.

The mysterious, unmapped Mississippi River Delta.

Forty-two

○○○○○○○○○○○○○○○○○

Blues

That evening on the *American Queen* as we drifted through the remnants of Norleans is something I'll never forget. I became a part of the rafters that night, in a way, because of Alma's guitar. I don't believe in miracles anymore, but finding it again was like a miracle. One of the folks we picked up, a man who'd been in the Cairo riots, had it on his raft.

I saw it, the neck sticking out of the wigwam, as he climbed up the ladder from the johnboat, just as I stuck out my hand to help him over the side.

When I saw the guitar I yanked that guy aboard so fast he sprawled onto the deck behind me, saying "Hey!" I didn't even stop to ask him about it. I figured instantly that he'd fished it out of the water around Memphis, right after we ran into the paddlewheel.

I dove from the *Queen,* stroking hard for that raft before it was lost again. I finally caught up with it, dragged myself onto the raft, crawled across it, grabbed Alma's guitar, and hugged it to myself. I think I even spoke to it a minute or two, like it was a person.

Then I tried one chord. And then another. And after that came the flood.

I played and played, out there as we drifted into New Orleans, and it was still in tune, and all that had happened to me welled up and changed to blues. I sang Verity's blues, Lil's blues, Jack's blues, Twain's blues, and Mattie's blues too. They were all stories of pain and loss and I gave them rhythm and form. I just knew I could have healed Verity in a snap, if I'd had Alma's guitar. I was oblivious to everything else. After a while a woman grabbed my arm, surprising me. I hadn't even noticed her rowing toward the raft. She made me get into a johnboat and rowed me back to the *American Queen.*

In the middle of all the dancing and singing there was Verity, swarming with pictures of light. And Alma's guitar knew just what to say; it filled me too with pictures, musical pictures, sweeping me toward the end of my own journey from anger and disillusionment, from having no identity, to something just beginning to take shape, giving me, truly, life beyond death. I was the servant of the blues, thanks to Alma's potion, and they surged through me, and set all the wreckage of my heart and mind to rights, gave me a new vision, so wide and free. That night was the grandest party you could ever imagine.

But then it was over and the fear set in.

You could hardly get around on the boat, it was so crowded. Alice and Lil set up all kinds of routines for rationing food and even for using the bathroom. Jack had a crew yank all the seats out of the auditorium and we were using them for fuel, because whatever George had done in Memphis had messed up the way the boat processed power from stuff in the water.

Peabody seemed to think Norleans was out there somewhere. We had no choice but to believe him. Lil seemed kind of driven by that belief, and the demented rafters we'd picked up in Norleans, who'd been there for several weeks, babbled about some kind of directions they'd tried to follow to let somebody know they wanted to be picked up. The plagued ones probably would have mutinied and driven the boat on without us had we even tried to go back. They'd not been satisfied with drowned old Norleans; it didn't have the stuff they needed to be healed and they were all the more frantic. I figured that if we paddled all the way to Africa they'd jump off, kiss the ground, and call it Norleans. Lil, who was thinner than matchsticks by now, said that there was supposed to have been some kind of antidote administered once they got to the *real* Norleans.

After we'd been trying to get through the swamp for four days or so, everybody was on edge. Even the blues didn't seem to help.

The endless bayous were beautiful, but primal and fear-making. The air smelled of water and decaying trees. Some of the hummocks had palms on them, and brilliant strange flowers, orange and red and yellow, growing on vines with leaves as big as Mattie, and unearthly plants I'd never imagined in my wildest dreams. The channels reminded me of a spiderweb, going every which way, most too narrow to accommodate the *Queen.*

The air was thick with birds and those weird, haunted cypress trees were everywhere, draped with old-man's-beards, I called them, pale green and deathlike in the still, wet air. The *Queen* snagged them when Mattie piloted us through tight channels. The air seemed greenish, like it was twilight, because the sun was filtered through so many leaves. The water was the color of clear dark tea and so still that it reflected us, and birds, and the trees that grew out of it perfect as a mirror.

Peabody said that the mouth of the Mississippi—actually, the last hundred miles or so of the river—had been engineered to keep the water from flowing into the Atchafalaya River Basin, south and west of New Orleans. "They called them Water Control Structures," he said, and pointed out one on an old chart, just north of the old Louisiana border. But they'd done that over a hundred years ago. Without maintenance, and particularly after the earthquake and years of typical Mississippi rampages, they all eventually failed, and the levees washed out.

Mattie went slow; so slow that sometimes I wanted to scream. The turtles outpaced us. The water didn't seem to have any current at all. All the channels looked the same. We might have been going in circles.

Mangrove trees lined every island, rising out of the water on their thin leglike roots as if they were birds poised for flight. White ibises paced the shallows, with their queer curved beaks. It was glorious to see flocks of wood storks take flight. You could hear their wings beating, and they were completely white when folded. But when their wings spread out you could see that the ends of them were black and it was a beautiful surprise. Some of the birds, like the great blue herons, acted like pets. They stood on the deck and swallowed fish heads whole; you could see them stuck in their long snaky necks. I saw the most beautiful flower I'd ever seen: a delicate yellow orchid, about a foot from my face, cascading in graceful arcs from a cypress branch as we glided past.

Alice passed out something she called good old-fashioned bug dope several times a day; she'd brought a supply of it from Madge's Landing. We needed it. Alice looked grim and haggard. She kept trying to evolve something for Mattie, that's what she called it, but the boat didn't seem to be able to do that kind of thing either. James fiddled with it but said that 99 percent of the interfaces had deteriorated beyond use, and the other one percent was not enough through which to do anything of any value.

In spite of the ghostly gloom, there was a feeling of excitement among the rafters but I expect that was just Alice's medicine. I had my share of it, even though she said it did nothing, her shoulders slumped. I guess she felt pretty useless. But I drank it and it made me happy, even if it was some sort of illusion, or "placebo effect" like she called it. Why not? Our lives might end pretty soon. Might as well enjoy the last days.

I thought through plans for swamp island living. I saw a village of swampers once, or thought I did, through the binoculars—a few old shacks and docks. But it was probably deserted. Maybe it wouldn't be so bad—if there was fresh water. It was getting brackish fast. But there were fish and birds and who knows what all to eat there on those low islands. You could rig a sail to a raft and get around that way, with poles and wind.

James was wildly angry. At Mattie, and at the rest of us for allowing her to continue. But we had no choice; there was no cure despite Alice's endless attempts. I think Mattie reminded him of Masa, and of how she just slipped away from him at the end. He no longer accepted things as they were, as he had on the train. He wanted desperately to change what was happening to Mattie. He sampled her and he said that the Twain information she'd received was forcing her body to change too swiftly for the effects to be properly assimilated. It was a learning program for adults, not for children, and its presence in her body triggered changes only the brain architecture of a thoroughly initiated adult student could sustain.

When Mattie wasn't piloting she was lying on her little cot, spouting Twain, delirious, while the boat was anchored. James actually started the boat once while she was sleeping and ran it into a sandbar, despite having sampled the water beforehand. It didn't move, and gave him no clues. We spent hours slogging in the water getting the boat free. Of course all of us itched to help but I watched Mattie careful, every move she made, and I would have made different ones often enough and those moves would have wrecked us. I guess everyone realized it.

There was no way we could get through that place without Mattie being Twain and only she could feel what Josh had to say. We all tried it but it was no use. To us he was just a huge cold fish who disdainfully let us touch him. We were completely, absolutely helpless. Maybe he just liked her, and would only release the information to her. That made sense if he was some sort of spy fish, like Alice said, ready to imprint on the first person with receptors who touched him for a certain length of time. Who knows. I wondered where Mattie got her receptors, and Lil said that she'd inherited them from her Hopi grandmother, a famous lawyer. I felt so terribly normal, even with Alma's blues, among all these strange people.

Mattie swam every hour or so, running her hands along Josh's sides, her eyes staring wide and strange. I went with her, in the johnboat, and held a big gaff to fend off snakes. Once a cottonmouth swam straight for her, white mouth wide, but even then Mattie didn't seem scared, only determined and bent on one thing: getting us through. I smacked it hard and it sank into the river. Sometimes snakes dropped from trees onto the boat; that was good for a commotion. Alligators slid into the water when we approached with hardly a splash. They looked like logs when they were in the water floating just below the surface except that logs don't have eyes. Once I saw a huge golden cat, standing stock-still in shady jungle, watching us.

I watched James pretty carefully. He made himself useful on the boat, took care of people. He mentioned one time that he knew how to make more of himself and that was kind of strange. That was not something that I could do. Peabody said beings like James were the Fourth Wave, and that it was just beginning. I wasn't sure what he meant, but he sounded pretty sure about it. How did James learn things, how did he know things? I was sure that if I asked he would explain it to me in great detail. Maybe someday I'd be able to understand his answers.

Lil watched Mattie as sorrowfully as anyone else. In her I saw Esu, the Trickster, the figure at the crossroads. All her life she'd been at the edges and the center at the same time, doing what she could to make things right. I could see that Lil felt pretty bad about the plague. But she'd pull through. She had to. She had the life of the world running through her body. She carried the code of the world within her very self, the way black music had once sent coded messages through society. There were people who had done lots worse things than Lil with lots less cause, I guessed. And it wasn't really her fault, the plague. It was just another one of the silly, stupid things that happened to humans. It got out of her control.

I wasn't quite sure what sort of crossroads we were at, but I could feel that current pulling both ways. Out of the delta, with its confused passages, emerging onto the open sea toward something that nobody wanted to talk about. Or we might sink in the shoals and be food for Josh and his kind. Not just us on the boat, but everyone in the world. Whoever was left. I understood Shaker Hill now, and Russ. A few people had lived and died there with dignity and hope and purpose. What more could you ask for?

It seemed that a lot of people had asked for more. And a lot hadn't, but got it anyway.

All kinds of thoughts were running through my mind. One afternoon I tried to tell Verity about them.

We were sitting in her room and I had been playing the guitar for at least an hour. I set it aside, to rest my hands, and sat back in my chair.

"You seem different," Verity said. Her tone was thoughtful: it was not bad that I was different, or good.

"I am."

She got up and started walking around the room, stopping at the dresser where I had put a vase of profusely blooming yellow flowers, branches of a low tree that grew on the hummocks.

"These smell nice," she said, wistfully. She turned and looked at me. "It's all gone," she said. "The past. And everyone. Except you. And you're right—heaven is gone too. All those years, thinking about heaven, about Mother Ann—" She shrugged.

"Verity, heaven is the body." I jumped up, excited now. "We were always in our *minds,* at Shaker Hill. Don't you see? Thinking. Learning and living that distant, abstract philosophy, denying everything we felt within ourselves as if it was bad. But it's *not* bad. Heaven is in our bodies."

She looked at me warily.

"In *dance.*"

"I've always danced," she said. *"We* always danced, us Shakers. Didn't we? In a trance. I felt like I was getting messages—messages from Mother Ann. And I never remembered the dances—all of *you* danced with me, and learned every new dance, and wrote them down." She laughed bitterly. "But there was no Mother Ann. The dances weren't coming from anywhere."

"Sure they were! Even though the Shakers tried so hard to separate body and mind, even they couldn't do it. That was *spirit,* that movement. You *know* it, Verity."

"I suppose I do," she said, and I could tell she was remembering something from Cincinnati, when she was Queen, something she didn't want to talk about.

"That's what the blues is," I continued eagerly. "It came from the music of African dance, and for Africans dance was the union of the spirit and the body, the crossroads of . . . eternity and temporality, spirit and matter. That's what makes what's happening *here* sacred. *Now! This* is where everything important is happening. Not in some distant impossible heaven! This is all there is—and it's *enough,* Verity! *Believe* me! It took me a long time to figure this out. I know how you feel."

The words tumbled out and I didn't know if they were mine or Alma's. It didn't matter. *You are the horse. The blues is the rider.* I had been ridden, hard. And that ride—that possession of me by the blues— had restored my life. Verity knew what that was like too, I was sure, even though she couldn't talk about it.

"It's like," I said, a thought striking me, "it's like nan, inside our bodies. Nan—it was a thought. But that thought, that *idea,* has changed our bodies—rearranged the very matter of ourselves, and the world. Nan patterns matter with thought, with molecular control. It's been out of control—*our* control, though. It's a balancing act, like dance. We need to find out where we've been so we can maybe decide where we want to go. We have to understand matter, we have to understand that we're made of matter, we *are* matter. It's up to us to make that a *good* thing, whatever good means to us. Freedom, maybe, whatever that is. Ecstasy. A new kind of divinity, a divinity of song and dance and music and rhythm. A divinity of *us."*

There I was nattering along just as if I *was* all thought, when really I couldn't stand it anymore, suddenly, to be so apart from Verity. Her . . . the way her collarbones met, making that hollow. Her breasts, beneath her thin shirt, and her long, slender legs, brown from the sun as they'd never been before. Her eyes, filled with so much pain and knowledge and something *else,* called me—

I grabbed her. But that's too rough a word. I *embraced* her, and held her close, and then I was kissing her at last, hard and deep, all my feelings, all my new *life,* flowing through me. She was holding me so tight it hurt, and moaning, kind of, deep in her throat, and then we were at each other, like we'd never been allowed before. In two minutes our clothes were scattered across the floor, and we were on the bed. Our lovemaking was fierce. All our waiting, all those long years of everlasting *no* changing to explosive *Yes! Now!* was a thing of joy—

Then I stopped, stricken—

"What?" she whispered. Her hand, run lightly down my back, sent a shiver through me.

"The baby—"

She laughed, her rounded bare belly against mine. It felt so *good.*

"It's all right. Alice told me it would be all right."

"Why would Alice—?"

"I asked," she said. In the silence I heard her heart beating hard. "I missed you. I need you. I—"

"Love you," I finished with her, shouting, and we laughed, and cried, and did what the blues told us to do, long after night fell, and then we slept, cradled by the bayou, released by the dance we did into our very selves.

Forty-three

○○○○○○○○○○○○○○○○○○○

True Grit Blues

Their third day out from New Orleans, Mattie stomped around her room, swearing. The boat was not moving. They were waiting for her to return to the pilothouse and continue down the channel, which pressed in upon them on both sides so the hammock trees brushed the boat. "Where are those goddamned cigars!" she yelled to no one in particular, for she was alone. She slammed her wardrobe door and stood still, shivering.

A bird flying past the window caught her eye, and she paused.

The sun filtered through rustling palm fronds stained the very air a vital, life-filled green. Mattie took one step toward the window, then another, freed for a moment from Twain's constant, exhausting vigilance. The morning breeze blew sweet-smelling orange flowers onto the deck, the petals drifting past the window like some exotic rain. Entranced, she went to the sill, put both her hands on it, and stared.

So beautiful.

She turned at a sound. James stood in the open doorway.

"I brought you a drink," he said. He held a glass of pink-tinged liquid toward her.

She blinked, and swallowed. Her chin went up. "What's in it, simulacrum?" she asked, walking over and yanking open the top drawer of her dresser. "It's a mighty strange color. Wouldn't be something Alice cooked up, would it? Now, where in the dad-gum world did I hide them this time?" She slammed the top drawer and opened the next, and pitched wrinkled clothing on the floor. "It's irritating as hell. The boat isn't making cigars anymore. Not even bad ones. I bet Alice had something to do with it. I'm running dreadful low."

He didn't say anything. She turned and looked at him, leaving the drawer open.

"You didn't say what's in that muck. You can't lie to me, simulacrum, can you?"

"My name is James," he said, holding the glass out to her.

She smiled. "You'll always be simulacrum to me. Why do you want to force that slosh on me, anyway?"

"I can't stand to see you die," he said flatly. "Does that seem so strange to you? Why *won't* you drink it? Tell me why, at least."

"Why?" she asked, as if surprised. "Remember what we talked about, that night with the Professor? About free will? About vision? About dreams?"

"This has nothing to do with all that," he said savagely.

"It has everything to do with that. Now, where—ah! Salvation!"

She fished a dented cigar from a drawer, cut off the end with an expert twist of the penknife she pulled from the pocket of her white suit and flipped open, and tossed the tobacco nub carelessly on the floor. James pulled out a match and lit it almost as if he could not help himself and it took two tries.

She puffed, thin cheeks drawn in, and briefly closed her eyes. When she opened them and spoke it was in Twain's rough voice. Her words were quiet yet sonorous, deliberate and thoughtful, intense; steeped in belief.

"There is a place beyond. I can feel it. A place beyond the imperialism that created the slavery and exploitation which has plagued humankind. A place where people—our loved ones—live forever. As *themselves,* not brainless angel folk with frivolous wings. Themselves, with all their infuriating, beautiful, heartbreaking twists. A place where the heaven *we* had, Livy and I and the girls—the love, the harmony, the freedom from material cares—*truly exists!* And I can take humanity there. *I can take them there.* And no one else can."

"That's Twain talking," said James, in an angry voice.

Mattie stared at him for a minute. She put the cigar in an ashtray, rubbed her eyes with the back of her hands. She looked with reddened eyes at James, and said, in her own voice, gently, "No, simulacrum, it's me. It's me. And I mean it. I believe it." She stepped next to him, reached up, touched his face. "You were a slave, weren't you? In a way?"

He blinked a few times, his blue eyes staring, but without offense. "I guess you could have said so, in the beginning. That's why I was created. More like a servant, I suppose, and a willing one. But Blaze freed me. He forced freedom on me. It's taken me a long time to figure out what that means to me. It took me a long time just to learn how to *think.*"

He was quiet for a minute. "I'm glad that Blaze took me off the train, Mattie. I was terrified when he did it. And I'm glad that I met you. Because you know what? I've just been intelligence without a soul, without vision. All the makings are here. I can change. I can learn. But on the train, it was the same as being in the dome. Finished, complete, self-referential. Just because *I*—a *James*—never existed in the old LA doesn't mean that I can't learn to be myself now. I can invent myself. I can invent myself in a way that the people who created me, who created what led to me, never could."

Mattie grinned. "That's right, James." Then her grin faded. "You know what I think? You're like something out of my grandpa's prayer book. You were *created.* Not *born* like the rest of us. You're from another realm, beyond us, but . . . maybe you're human, too. Not that I believe that, mind you. Not for a second. But if it was true you'd be kind of like Jesus, you know? Dream, vision . . . whatever you want to call it it's all *purpose,* James. Remember that. We're just creatures of chance. We've been created out of matter. God didn't make us. Not the kind of God a lot of folks believe in, anyway. That doesn't make sense. Twain knew that. That means it's up to *us* to give purpose to chance. We have to take responsibility for what happens. For what we can make happen. *That's what I'm doing.* It's a choice I've made. Out of my own free will."

"That's just *it,* Mattie," said James. "You don't have a choice."

"I do," she said firmly. "I'm *making* all this mean something. It's my responsibility."

"That's what *I* want to do," James said, slowly. "Make it all mean something."

"Good for you, then," she said. "Maybe you'll be more than a fake man yet."

"Mattie, I'm *not . . .*" He fell silent.

"You're unique," said Mattie quietly. "A unique creature. But you still don't know who or what you are. You're part of what I'm saving, James. All that we still don't know, but might someday."

He went down on his knees before her, so that she was looking straight into his face. His hands were on her shoulders, solid and strong, reminding her of her father. "Please, Mattie. Please take it. I don't want to be saved. Not like that. It's not fair. You're the best one here."

She shook her head. "You're wrong. I'm no better and no worse than any of them. I'm just an ordinary human. And you're—" She stopped.

"I'll never be human," he said. "Not like the rest of you, not really. And I don't want to be."

"You *don't?*"

He burst out laughing and jumped up. "Good lord, no!" He was laughing then harder and harder and she was laughing with him, harder and harder, and they hugged each other at the same moment. He spun her around, so that her feet left the floor, so fast that for a moment she was a little girl again and her father was doing it, making her dizzy, and she shrieked with delight. She closed her eyes, and laughed, and laughed, and laughed—and she suddenly it all changed over—

"You're *crying*," she said.

"So are you," he pointed out. "Oh, Mattie."

James staggered to a stop and set her gently down, his face most definitely sad.

"I'm sorry, James," she said quietly. She wiped her eyes on a T-shirt straggling from the drawer. "I've got to get back to the pilothouse."

By the next day, Mattie was all Twain, raving at times about a comet that was coming to get her, allowing no one to take the wheel as they inched through the frightfully shallow flats ("I could pilot this boat across a field of heavy dew!" she'd yell); steering with such confidence that no one dared speak to her to break her concentration.

James kept harping at Alice all the time. "You need to give her the medicine," he whispered, as they stood outside the pilothouse door.

"She doesn't want it," said Alice wearily. "And it wouldn't work anyway. If I thought it was worth a damn, I'd pour it down her throat myself."

"It's all we have. She's not sane," said James. "So she shouldn't have a choice."

"Who says I'm not sane, simulacrum?" came Mattie's voice from inside the pilothouse. "I'm miles more sane than you!" Sometimes she was strong and hearty as anything and then they all had hope that she'd last until they got to—wherever they were going.

"Just be quiet," whispered Alice. "Already she's afraid to eat or drink anything."

"Aren't there other ways to get it into her?" he whispered back.

"I'd like to see you try, fake man," Mattie yelled back.

He scowled, a look that he had mastered with ease, probably because he saw so much of it around him.

Mattie struck a pose and lit into one of her Twain routines—" 'There is something curious about this—curious and unaccountable. There must be two Americas: one that sets the captive free, and one that takes a once-captive's new freedom away from him and picks a quarrel with him with nothing to found it on; then kills him to get his land.' "

She took a deep breath and continued in her own voice, but just as loud: "And that's what it's all *about,* fake man. We have to *end* that once and for all! And I'm telling you—you're a fugitive. They're going to be after you! They're going to want to take you back! Dismantle you! Once you're not doing them any good anymore! Once they can't make *money* off of you! All this nanotechnology stuff—it's struggling to be *freeee!* Look at all these rafters—will they be *slaves* to nanotechnology? Or will they be *free?* Who's going to be the boss?" She let go of the wheel and flung her arms wide; raised her voice and bellowed roughly in Twain's voice to the tune of "The Battle Hymn of the Republic":

> In a sordid slime harmonious, Greed was born in yonder ditch,
> With a longing in his bosom—and for other's goods an itch—
> As Christ died to make men holy, let men die to make us rich—
> Our god is marching on—

"One of those little ditties Livy didn't want me to publish, bless her soul," Mattie said, staggering as she retook the wheel. "But that's our history! The history of the country. The history of the world. Men sending other men to war for their own profit. Will it be different now? Can we *make it new?* Can humanity truly *change?* Oh, it's up to you fake man, it's up to you. You were created, not born! You are the *new holiness of the universe!"*

James turned away, his face wretched, as Mattie continued to emote, and laugh, and scream, and pilot with a delicate touch and a determined, desperate face, engaged in a constant, exhausting struggle.

One morning piercing screams came from the pilothouse. Blaze, Alice, and Verity were there in an instant, along with everyone else in earshot.

James was trying to hold Mattie down but it was clearly not possible. From somewhere she found the strength to slither like an eel, bite like an alligator, and kick like a mule. She smacked the glass from his hand and it smashed against the doorframe.

"I don't want it, simulacrum, understand?" she said, panting, as she struggled to her feet. "There's more to being human than *you* know."

He stared at her, his face savage. "Well, I'm *learning,* Mattie. I'm *learning,* aren't I?"

She gave him a long, measuring look. "Seems you are, James," she said.

Amazingly, she hugged him. Even more amazingly, he burst into great, deep sobs while she comforted him.

For a moment, she was Mattie, through and through.

Blaze pounded on the wall of the pilothouse with his fist. "Let's take this boat back to Cincinnati," he shouted. "No—let's take it to *Cairo,* and put her on the train to LA. *Somewhere* there's a cure!"

Peabody just shook his head sorrowfully. "We'll be lucky if this boat lasts another week."

"And Mattie?" Blaze yelled. "How long is *she* going to last?"

Alice, her face filled with grief, started to say something, then just turned away and went to Mattie.

"It's not your choice," they all heard Mattie say, and her voice was clearly Mattie's not Twain's. "It's mine."

"All the sounds of the earth are like music," sang Mattie, her voice thin and high and quite pretty as she swayed back and forth on her stool in front of the wheel. Her white dress gleamed in the sunset, and the rays of the waning sun beat through the open window with the power of an enraged beast.

> The breeze is so busy it don't miss a tree
> And an old weeping willow is laughing at me—

She straightened and gasped, just a little, staring at something. She was so thin that her arms looked like sticks. It was beyond fear of a cure; she lacked all appetite. Her hair floated outward from her head in the late afternoon like a golden-brown lion's mane.

Peabody and Alice looked at each other.

"Sir, it's getting dark," said Peabody. "At least have something to eat. Isn't it time to stop?"

"I'll tell you when it's time to stop, cub," she said. But her voice did not have its customary sternness.

The grip of the swamp had loosened gradually during the day, and finally there was more water than land. They were at the center of an irregular circle of low, flat islands covered with scrub. The shallow water glowed with twilight—brilliant, translucent green, like a fine gem—and it was hard to tell where the water stopped and the sky began. The day had been crushingly hot, but a sudden cooling breeze washed through the pilothouse and the boat turned on its own and picked up speed.

"Is that a current?" asked Peabody, jumping to his feet.

"Of course," said Mattie, but she sounded weak with relief. She was quiet for a minute, as if trying to master her voice. "It's the main channel. Just where Josh felt it. The open sea is only a few knots past that far island." She was quiet for another moment, as she peered through the window. The sky had deepened overhead to an intense, deep blue, with a few stars visible. Her words came quick and sharp. "Tell me, cub, what's that bright light up there in the sky? Is it Halley's Comet?" She had reached into her pocket; now her hand paused. Her voice held a deep thrum of excitement.

"Absolutely not, sir!" said Peabody, with alarm. He stood next to Mattie and peered out the window. The lemon sky still glowing on the horizon brightened, as twilight tinged it blue on evening's turning verge, and it was not the sun, and it was not a star.

Peabody said, "It's . . . quite powerful . . . but it must be just a satellite."

"You lie," she whispered, and collapsed into his arms, and hung there limp.

A small leather pouch fell from her hand and two vials of colored liquid bounced from it. The purple one smashed open and whatever was in it soaked into the floor.

Mattie from Elysia died as the *American Queen* drifted into the Gulf of Mexico, free of the delta swamps.

It was night. The path of the moon on the water led outward, toward infinity. It was like the Territory: vast, free, all promise and hope.

The crossroads were behind them. Mattie had brought them through.

No one really cared, though. Not just then. The price had been too high.

Forty-four

○○○○○○○○○○○○○○○○○○

Sad-Hearted Blues

After Mattie died I thought I'd cry forever but it passes. It passes but there's nothing left to feel.

I couldn't think of Mattie being in heaven, and that made everything worse. I understood then why people invented it in the first place.

Josh hung around the boat for another day. I was watching the morning he turned back, a huge shadowy swirl just beneath the surface, and headed back the way we came. I wondered if he knew.

James was definitely in mourning. This was the second death he'd experienced in his life. We tried to comfort him the best we could. I was surprised at how quickly he seemed to be changing. He seemed more and more like a natural person. I had a feeling that, had he fallen in among the fish, he would now be swimming with abandon.

Once we were free of the delta, we followed a series of huge towers across the Gulf of Mexico. For some reason, Peabody knew to do this. I kept asking him how he knew and he said that it wasn't a secret. When we got to one, the next was just barely visible in the binocs and we headed toward it. I suggested that he might try getting the Norleans radio station Verity said she'd heard once, and he said that we didn't have a radio stone for Norleans, though he'd looked for one in Cairo. And besides, he said, all his systems were down now.

The waves were six, eight feet high at times, the water more shades of blue and green than you could possibly imagine. We pitched unendurably and I was often sick. The days were still hot and sticky, with white puffy clouds overhead shadowing patches of the sea in the mornings. In the afternoons, the sky always darkened on the horizon, and black clouds rushed toward us and lashed the boat with wind and rain while lightning played the water too close for comfort. Flying fish zipped the bow and landed on the lower decks, and porpoises curved sleekly alongside with their strangely merry smiles.

We caught what rain we could in big tarps and pots. I felt tremendously anxious about the water situation. We couldn't last long without it, and Lil and Alice were setting up some sort of recycling system. Any automatic systems on the boat were pretty well shot, and probably all the salt completely did things in. I could tell that they were getting worried too.

The plaguers, mostly, were not. They had faith. Faith doesn't necessarily have much to do with reality. Some of them kept talking about how we had to go to the towers and activate a signal that would call a rescue boat from Norleans. When I asked Lil about it her face went sad and she said yes, the towers had been part of the plan. You would think that being right about something might cheer her up, but it didn't. Peabody just said that he had his compass, which adjusted for the magnetic changes, and that was all he needed.

We didn't even talk about what would happen when we ran out of wood. The gingerbread might be good for a hundred miles. After that we had a lot of furniture.

Despite everything, a new excitement was in me because of Verity, kind of a low, happy hum of contentment that caught me in odd moments, even when I was thinking of Mattie. Mattie wouldn't have minded. It was what she'd wanted—for us to have the chance to live and grow. To give us the chance to do something as important as she had done.

What changes I'd been through since leaving Cincinnati! Then, I could barely remember my name, and when I could, I was confused and bitter. Now, I felt like I could do anything, learn anything, be anything.

I saw Alice poking at Peabody's screen up in the pilothouse and I started spending a lot of time there. Turns out that there were lessons on all kinds of things—magnetism, chemistry, physics, math. They started out easy and then got hard and I liked them. I could always go back to the last one if I got lost. It took up the time. It took up a lot of time, actually, because the boat was stopping continually and each time it did I had to start over again. There were odd, interesting asides, like how the changes in the magnetic field had affected the behavior of animals, especially migratory birds. A lot had changed since radio had been ruined.

The sky at night was vast and dazzling with stars, rivers of pure light. I felt again like I'd felt on the train—the magnificence of it, but this time with no barrier between it and me. I felt I could almost reach out and touch those stars, they looked that close. And the night wind was cool and balmy. I found the tutorial about the stars and read all about the birth of the universe and how it all expanded and contracted and, poof, there was the end of everything. Maybe. Or maybe it would go on forever. It was almost like God the way they talked about it, those people who found out so much about time and space. It just might do, as a replacement for that kind of awe. And I found a pretty interesting one about a moon colony and then one about something called the signal. It wouldn't give me any information.

Peabody was cool as a cucumber despite all our troubles. He chugged on day and night, letting me take the wheel to spell him. I could almost see why Mattie would have found it hard to give up, even if she hadn't been Twain—I felt like the king of the world up there, steering that big boat beneath the stars.

On the second night Peabody told me about the signal, after I pestered him about it.

"The signal is from space," he said. "From intelligent beings. Or some form of intelligence—who knows if they could even be described as beings? For instance, the signal could *be* them."

"Why do you know about them?" I asked. Far below, gleaming phosphorescence glimmered in the water, so it looked as if we sailed through a sea of stars.

He hesitated for a moment and I thought he was going to say something, but stopped. The look on his face was pensive. It was the look he always got if he mentioned his wife. Finally he said (and I got the feeling he started to say something else then stopped), "I know about them because I had a deep curiosity about them. I spent my life learning things that would help me know more, trying to get to the heart of the matter.

"At first they thought it was a quasar. SETI—the search for extraterrestrial intelligence—insisted that it was not, all along. But the source didn't matter, on one level, because they had practical issues to deal with. If communications interruptions continued at the same rate, then we'd have complete washout within a decade. Period. Plus all kinds of terrorist nan had been developed that could deal a death blow to fiber-optic cable anyway. They couldn't have the world in a panic about aliens—they had work to do to insure that a semblance of civilization continued, or that at least some humans who would have access to knowledge would survive. The cities of the modern world grew because of commerce, but this would be a return to the self-contained medieval model, depending on the outside world as little as possible."

"So the signal is some sort of weapon?" I asked.

"That's not clear either," said Peabody. "What's happened here could just be some sort of side effect of what they're doing. They could be completely unaware of us and what's happening here. Of course it's human nature to think that we're at the center of everything. But it's not true. I do know that study ships were sent off—nanotech lightships with colonizing capabilities. But they knew that they couldn't communicate with us once they left, despite the complicated protocols they'd developed to try and get round, or through, the problem. I'd say they're gone for good."

It was pretty hard to digest all that Peabody had to say. We had been living on a farm in the middle of nowhere believing in angels. I felt like I was bursting through levels and levels and that maybe there were an infinite number of them and that was a nice thought, because it made me feel so alive. I didn't need heaven anymore. All this was more wonderful than any heaven could possibly be. But all this about the signal had happened before I was born and to hear Peabody talk it really made no difference. It appeared to me that he'd kind of given up, there in Chicago, but that now he was coming back to life. I asked him how he happened to come across our boat and he said it was a happy accident. The more I listened to him, the less I thought that was true. All kinds of organizations were prowling round the country, each with their own network. I wondered who Peabody really was, and what else he knew.

One morning the boat was involved in its usual heaving gyrations and James lost his balance and fell against Peabody.

"I'm sorry," he said, grasping Peabody's arms and staggering to his feet. Then he looked at his hands and back at Peabody, his expression incredulous. For a moment I hung on that expression; it was so full, so far beyond anything I'd yet seen on his face.

Then he said, "Who . . . *what* . . . are you? I seem to remember . . . there's something in the dome . . ."

Peabody sighed. I'd never seen him look so uncertain. "I'm not sure," he said, his eyes sad and oddly hungry. "I'm just not sure. I'm going to Norleans to find out. I hope I can find out there. I truly do," he said.

"What was in the dome?" I asked James.

James frowned. "It's kind of like a myth. That's the nearest I can come to the flavor of it. It was one of the places we could go. Something about a rain that changed humans. A rain with seeds that came from another galaxy."

"Go on," said Peabody eagerly. "Go on!"

James looked at Peabody oddly. "It's a myth, that's all. A story people make up to explain things. That's all I know, from the dome."

Peabody nodded to himself. "Makes sense," he murmured. "Makes sense." And he would speak no more of it. He said he'd told me all he knew, which was more than most people knew, because anyone who knew about the signal, early on, had apparently disappeared. Except for those who dared speak of it only in coded terms.

Like a myth. Like the blues.

I had to be satisfied with that, but I wasn't. But I'd have to wait. Apparently Peabody had been waiting for quite a long time.

The universe, apparently, was even stranger than I'd imagined.

Forty-five

○○○○○○○○○○○○○○○○○○○

New Orleans Blues

The *Queen* was rimed with salt. There had been no rain for three days, and water supplies were low. They were in an endless blue desert, broken occasionally by high metal towers. The water was so rough that they could not venture very close to the towers, and eventually they left them behind. Peabody said they were in the Caribbean, based on the chart where he marked off their progress as best he could. Tension was high.

But on the morning of the fifth day, Peabody announced, with rare excitement in his voice, that they were nearing New Orleans.

They were all in the pilothouse—Blaze, Verity, Alice, Jack and Lil, Verity, and James. The *Queen* wallowed in the waves. The paddlewheel was often out of the water. The constant beating had loosened everything and the creaking was getting on everyone's nerves. They all strained their eyes, but there was nothing to be seen. There was no land in sight. Certainly not a city.

"Are you sure, Peabody?" asked Jack.

"No," he said, raising his binoculars.

They must have been only about three miles away when Verity saw it—or, rather, *realized* that it was there. She was thunderstruck, because it was huge. A huge, hidden *thing* floating in a tropical sea.

It was blue and green, which was why it was so hard to see. But no . . . it shimmered, reflective, like a mirage. . . .

"That's *it!*" whispered Lil. She gripped the sill and leaned forward through the open window. "It's . . . it's like a dream, isn't it, Jack? It's so beautiful. Like a jewel in the sea. I really didn't think . . . Oh, my God. I guess they didn't die." She blinked away tears. "Maybe all those rafters lived after all. Somehow."

"Maybe," said Jack, very gently. He briefly traced Lil's tattoo with a finger, then pulled her tight against his side.

"Who do you think is in there?" asked Alice nervously.

"Aliens," said Peabody mischievously.

"Oh, I hope not," said Lil fervently, and Peabody laughed.

Verity, standing next to them, reflected that *she* was probably as alien as someone from outer space.

And her child? She put one hand on her belly and watched the vast floating city before them assume contours, shadowy at first then sharp and clear. No telling about her child. She felt fear, anticipation, and hope.

Blaze shook her arm and pointed. Off to the west, a regatta of white sails skimmed the blue-green sea.

Lil thrust binoculars at Verity. "I'm shaking so much I can't hold them. What do you see?"

As the boat poised at the top of a crest before thumping downward with the usual jarring smash, Verity gasped. "Islands," she said. "Beautiful golden islands at the foot of each . . . tower. . . . Each island is *huge.*"

"Those are the breakwaters," said Jack. "They just float on the surface too, like the city. Although I'm sure there's a certain amount of interesting subsurface architecture. The underwater environments were to be used to simulate space travel." His voice held wonder. "Just the way they planned. But I don't know about any towers. Let me look." Verity handed him the binoculars. "It appears to be much more of a fortress than we thought it would be, Lil."

"They probably have their reasons," she said.

"Think they'll be glad to see us?" asked Blaze. No one answered.

They labored closer. Their progress seemed excruciatingly slow. Below, on the pitching decks, the Cincinnatians stood in a great mob. They were not even singing.

Lil said, "I can't stand it. Go faster, Peabody!"

Peabody laughed. "I'm going as fast as we can without tearing this tub apart. You don't want to swim, do you?"

Now they were close enough for Verity to make things out better. The city assumed a focus. It rose to a central peak, somewhat like a tent, formed of fanciful towers, multilevel terraces. Verity had an impression of a floating forest.

"It seems a lot bigger than Cincinnati," Verity said.

"It grows," Lil answered. "It grows to accommodate a growing population." Hope shone in her face, and Verity knew that Lil hoped it had grown so large in order to accommodate victims of her plague.

They came abreast of one of the islands. Turquoise water shimmered in vast lagoons formed by stony enclosures around each island. Two women pulled a fish-filled net into a boat in the middle of the lagoon, while others picnicked on a golden beach where coconut palms cast a hatchwork of shadows on the sand. Small colorful boats rested on the beach. One by one people noticed them and soon everyone was waving with both arms.

"They grow all kinds of things in the lagoons, algae and fish and sea vegetables," said Jack. He looked slightly dazed. "It's amazing. They did it. They really did it."

Peabody followed a string of buoys between two of the islands, which sloped upward rather steeply on their seaward side, then descended in a more gentle incline on the city side. As they passed the crest Verity looked back. "Are those orchards?" she asked. "And fields of . . . soybeans?" The city sides of the islands were evidently farms.

Lil nodded, apparently too overcome to speak.

Verity wondered if the city was anchored, or floated willy-nilly, or was powered here and there for reasons beyond her ken.

"Look!" she said, handing the binoculars to Lil. "People!"

And there they were, leaning from long, curved ledges, waving and cheering, apparently, though all they heard on the boat was the slap of waves and the constant chug of the paddlewheel.

Huge letters appeared along the side of the city, as ornate as the calligraphy with which was written the name of the *American Queen*:

WELCOME TO NEW ORLEANS, THE CRESCENT CITY

Lil said, "I guess we made it." Tears shone on her face, and she hugged Jack. "You were right, Jack."

"As always," said Jack, but his voice shook just a bit and he let out a deep breath.

The vast, stubby towers holding New Orleans dwarfed the *Queen* as the city's shadow eclipsed them. They were of clear, thick material that reduced whatever was inside to colorful blurs. The water was luminous where the towers vanished beneath the sea's surface, and Verity saw heavy steel cables thick as tree trunks vanishing downward.

The sound of the paddlewheel echoed along with the sound of their own voices. The rafters filled the air with an excited hum. Then one of the towers glowed phosphorescent green and Peabody looked round at them, shrugged, steered the boat toward it.

As they approached it seemed as if part of it just dissolved, revealing glowing light within.

"Sure you want to go?" asked Peabody, and Lil said, "Stop *teasing* us!" and Peabody laughed. The *Queen* rode the waves closer. The light inside grew as they approached.

They passed through the opening.

After they were inside the door grew smaller behind them. The inside was luminous, and it seemed as if there were no edges. There was just the smell of salt, the sound of water, and the nearly invisible shell of their enclosure. The water was not completely calm, but the waves were muted.

Shouts echoed through the enclosure. Ahead was a wharf with slips filled with all manner of seacraft. A group stood on the wharf holding curious instruments: tubas, trombones, and trumpets. At a signal, they struck up a tune that filled the harbor place.

After a moment, Blaze gasped with laughter. A hysterical edge to his voice, he said to Jack, "Is that what I think it is?"

"Absolutely," said Jack, laughing so hard he doubled over. He wiped tears from his eyes. He burst into laughter again. "Do You Know What It Means To Miss New Orleans—" and they shouted out the words together, tunelessly, as if drunk. Above the wharf, on a balcony, a huge crowd had gathered. They waved and yelled, almost drowning out the band.

Peabody piloted the *Queen,* battered and limping from the long journey, into one of the slips. Behind them a wall shot up and the water calmed and people stood there on the edge of the wharf waiting for them to put down the gangplank.

Those in the pilothouse heard shouted exchanges about why there was no gangplank.

The small party in the pilothouse stood in a circle and looked at each other for a moment, dazed. It seemed impossible. They had arrived.

Peabody pulled a half-empty bottle of whiskey and smudged glasses from a cupboard, and poured them all a sip.

"To Mattie," he said.

The whiskey burned Verity's throat and brought tears to her eyes. She looked round the pilothouse, which had seen so much. The wheel was burnished from months of use. Mattie's stool was still there, next to the wheel. Peabody's piloting clutter lay on the shelf below the window.

A vast roar arose as a team of people hurried down an incline carrying a makeshift gangplank. The boat trembled with the impact of trampling feet and cacophonous cheering.

As of one accord they all began to laugh and cry and hug each other and Verity knew, suddenly, that one part of her life was over.

And that another part was about to begin.

The balcony on which Verity sat was so high she felt as if she were flying. She liked that feeling. At times she rather hoped that she might become a Bee again someday, if only to experience that joy.

The day was exhilarating and bright. The sea was blue as far as the eye could see; sparkling and infinite. The sky was blue as well, without a cloud, and gulls wheeled round the various towers and plazas and streets which fell away, far below. In all this light it seemed that it would be impossible for the darkness to catch up with her, ever. She could begin to feel strong in this place, once again.

She was sitting around a table with a crowd of people. Lil sat on one side of her and Blaze on the other. Jack and Alice were there as well, and James.

Mattie was not.

The world became dark and sound receded. Verity sighed. Blaze heard her and reached for her hand. They looked at each other and she knew he knew what she was thinking.

"So much gone," he said.

Various officials from the city, which, she had learned, thought of itself as a non-country, a concept she was trying to grasp, were feasting them, after settling them in spacious, comfortable quarters.

Peabody stood to one side of the balcony, speaking earnestly to a small group. Peabody had seemed at home immediately. He expressed concern about hurricanes, but was told that Norleans had weathered even a Category Five storm, which interested him tremendously. He wanted to know every detail about the city, from its inception to the present day. He was not wasting a minute.

The rafters had been dispersed throughout the city, paired with hosts who took them into their homes. But first they were taken to a clinic where the Norleans Plague was at last neutralized. For each group of plaguers who reached New Orleans, a cure had been grown by the tremendously advanced AI at the heart of the city. Now the terraces overflowed with Cincinnatians, each inevitably surrounded by a crowd of curious Norleaners.

Jack and Lil were beginning to catch up with what had happened so long ago. They now knew that the floating city had been privately financed and masterminded by the same woman who had gathered the scientific community to New Orleans. Nurturing the vision fostered by the city of her birth, she had tried to keep her project as secret as possible, knowing that New Orleans was under siege. Wary of sabotage, she used New Orleans almost as a decoy, and set up detailed evacuation plans that were executed at the last minute. Lil and Verity had learned, to their vast relief, that for years boats were kept in New Orleans to ferry rafters here. Even now they responded once or twice a year to signals from the towers, though many were false. Evidently, a rescue boat had passed them going the other way, having received the signal, long delayed by atmospheric conditions, from the rafters who first reached Norleans.

"Look," said Jack, and nudged Lil. "Over there. Isn't that Marie?" They had an appointment to meet with her the next day, if they felt up to it. They both remembered meeting her at a long-ago opulent party in the French Quarter, and hearing rumors of her voodoo rituals on the shores of Lake Pontchartrain, quite different from the original rituals. Neither had dreamed she was so powerful.

On a terrace a step down from theirs, a tall black woman with flowing hair stood, surrounded by a crowd. Perhaps feeling Jack's gaze, she lifted her eyes, smiled broadly, and waved at them.

An older woman came and dropped into the chair next to Verity. Her hair was white and Verity thought of delphiniums when she looked into the woman's eyes.

"I think I recognize you," Verity said.

The woman nodded. "We met way upriver. On the Ohio. When we passed over Rising Sun. That's where I'm from."

"Yes, I remember," said Verity. The trip coalesced for her suddenly, now, when it seemed to be ending—the quiet wonder of the wakening souls, then their wild rampages. Their growing memories, melded into a play; their injuries in the bombing. And then, at last, the pictures which blossomed in New Orleans, which grew daily in complexity and depth, as they learned how to use their new language.

"I want to thank you," the woman said to Verity.

"For what?" asked Verity.

"For getting us out of Cincinnati," said the woman. She reached over and touched Verity's arm and the back of her hand had a tiny, bright picture of a child on it. "I had some angry moments, thinking about what happened, about how we left Cincinnati. We didn't have a choice. You chose for us. There was a glory about Cincinnati. A fearfulness, and a glory. Maybe you can't have one without the other. But I wanted the future when I went in there and I got it full strength. Now, here, it seems like we're back to square one. And yet—I have a feeling that this is the future too. The Cincinnati future didn't work out quite right. It was kind of like a little backwater, where mosquitoes grow. Oh, what am I trying to say? Stagnant.

"I'll probably never remember half of what happened during the Cincinnati years of my life. It was like being tumbled round in one of those rock-smoothing machines. Now time is slower, and it keeps on moving straight, and I'm *me* and I know it. There. Does that make sense to you?"

"Yes," said Verity. "Yes, it does."

"Well, I hope it does," said the woman, and patted Verity's arm. Then she left.

Lil lifted her glass of champagne. "Here's to the future," she said. "Whatever it might hold."

"Could be just about anything," said Jack, his dark face somber.

"Seems like we've been through something close to that already," said Blaze, and they all laughed, and drank to something—perhaps the future and whatever it might hold, or perhaps just one another, while white gulls wheeled overhead and a steady sea wind blew strong to the west.

The next afternoon Alice stood next to James, who stared out over Norleans, down its green-terraced splendor to the open sea. Being wonderstruck was common, Alice had noticed, to all of those from the *Queen,* including herself. The glorious architecture of the terraced city grown from seawater was filled with astonishing versions of humankind, who used all kinds of nan enhancements without suffering apparent ill. It was a place of mastery and harmony. And though they had just arrived, Alice had caught hints of the greater purpose of Norleans, as well, a purpose that infused the city with a fervor she'd never before experienced. But she felt removed from it. She knew where her happiness lay.

"The Professor would say that this place was balanced," said James, looking at the rainbow pattern on his hand, meaningful only to him. "These people have free will. They can *choose. . . .*"

His voice broke, and Alice knew that he was thinking about Mattie. She put an arm around him and held him tight and after a stiff moment he relaxed into her embrace.

"It's the city she saw," he whispered. "She talked to me about it. 'The place where our loved ones live forever,' she said. But it's awful to be here without her. *She* could have lived forever here, too."

"I know," murmured Alice, trying to comfort James as her own heartache sharpened. "I know."

"The thing is," James continued, "she succeeded. She knew what she wanted to do and she did it. And she gave me a great gift. She gave me the gift of myself. I think that here I can truly grow and learn. And give. Whatever gifts *I* have to give. I don't know what they are yet."

Alice patted him on the back. Scientists had swarmed all over James when they learned what he was but after the initial frenzy she fended them off for him, since he seemed incapable of doing so. She saw that he was overwhelmed, not only because of Mattie, but because of the importance accorded him. He needed time to assimilate the fact that others indeed found him vitally important, time to balance that with his own embryonic but growing sense of self. Alice felt that James was in need of a physician as much as any of her patients had been, though he suffered no physical ailments. Growing a soul was hard work. It would take time and patience. And a good deal of privacy, she suspected.

The sea breeze freshened, sweeping away the doldrums of the afternoon. The festivities behind them, the hypnotic beat of the music, became louder. The sun drew near the sea and subtle lights appeared along the wall where she and James stood. On the terraces, to drumbeats, gypsy colors swirled as those from China, Poland, Russia, Korea—names which now had as little meaning as the United States of America—manifested their own ancient forms of dance, adapted to the music occurring now, and waves of change swept through them like wind playing across a vast field of grass. These people seemed to live to dance, able to meld celebration with their utterly serious purpose. They would party all night. At least, they had last night.

Alice sighed. Parties bored her. And in spite of the beauty and shared joy, they didn't need her here.

She thought of Madge's Landing, there on the banks of the slow, wide Mississippi. In the midst of all this brightness, this openness to the sky and sea, she yearned for the river mists, the sky glimpsed through towering live oaks, her neighbors, and her home. She had strolled through the acres of gardens and parks that flowed like flower-filled veldts through the terraces, but they felt foreign and unsatisfying. She wondered if there was a way to return, now that her duties were almost over. She had managed to save some rafters. She had probably helped Verity, at least in some fashion, though she certainly could not claim to have healed her. She had only been able to verify that healing was taking place, which was more than enough for her. She knew that the loss of Mattie would always haunt her. If only she'd had the time to turn her attention to Mattie sooner. If only she'd had the expertise, the tools . . . if only Mattie hadn't been so stubborn.

Well, she had been stubborn, and fixed on some vision that seemed, in the end, to give her a deeper satisfaction than most people would ever know.

But now only James still needed her. Still, his need was great. It would hold her until he was ready to fly, to live on his own terms in this bright place, unique in all the world, where the new was brewing with heady urgency.

She linked her arm through his. "Come on, James, let's take a stroll and then go back to that little restaurant on St. Anne Street for dinner. Shall we?" The previous night he had talked, in the candle-filled courtyard, of Masa, and Mattie, and then of the pain and wonder of having been brought into existence from seeming nothingness.

"I'd like that," he said.

They slipped through the crowd and, as evening grew, descended to the quaint and quiet streets below.

Forty-six

○○○○○○○○○○○○○○○○○○

Blue Skies

The morning shower passed over in minutes, leaving the cobblestones on Royal Street glimmering, and Verity stepped out from beneath a sheltering awning. Seagulls wheeled above, crying, and the streets began to fill with people.

The sun was much more powerful here than in Ohio, instantly hot in the morning. It burnished everything to golden radiance as Verity turned up Bienville, shielding her eyes with her free hand every few minutes as she glanced upward. After a few minutes she checked the address glowing on the back of her hand.

Mattie, in a sling on her chest, was asleep, and heavy for her two months. Verity hoped she would sleep for a while. Her own eyes were heavy from awakening for the previous night's feedings.

The distinctive architecture of the French Quarter glistened in the morning sun. Slices of red brick, stone, and colorful shutters ranged up the narrow street. Verity passed the Shop of the Golden Man and smiled; the seeds for lovely learning toys were there, and manifested in his shop-window. Already Mattie enjoyed one or two of his creations: mobiles to help the focussing of her eyes, and things to touch and roll around.

The fragrance of beignets baking wafted down the street from some unseen source. Her stomach growled. One beignet, made with spirulina-based flour, could supply her protein needs for one day, and was more delicious than she could have imagined. Blaze was quite taken with lobsters and had one practically every night, each time in a different restaurant, if Mattie allowed them the luxury. Lobsters and crabs thrived in the large farming ponds surrounding Norleans; all manner of plants and animals grew in the nitrogen-rich seawater that exploded with life after being pumped from the depths; the city depended on the heat-exchange technology which had, in fact, been essential to its growth.

Later in the day the streets would be thick with music and troupes of dancers, dancers evolving thought and language through motion. Even the scientists danced here, *especially* the scientists, indistinguishable from the throngs of incredibly varied pilgrims from all over the world who had made it to Norleans, refugees from and progenitors of nan alike, the strangely changed survivors. And, Verity had learned, the completely human, yet more-than-human denizens who, like Peabody, had arrived here drawn by a golden tide of thought and yearning, coupled with what hard information they could glean about themselves, their earth-altering past, and the future that information promised.

Verity found herself looking forward to her afternoon's session with the debriefer assigned her. The woman, an African who chose to manifest an ancient tribal tattoo over much of her body, worked with Verity on a shaded, breezy patio on the west side, a short train and elevator hop from the French Quarter, where Blaze and Verity lived. Every Cincinnatian spent several hours a day in these sessions, in which layers of their hidden history were brought to light and consciousness. Many Cincinnatians were in a position, because of the knowledge they had before Cincinnati was converted, to add substantially to the mosaic of what was known about the three waves of nanotechnology. The Cincinnati dialect of what Lil had called an emergent mind was now a part of the city's international grammar, a form of visual communication taken up with enthusiasm by the citizens of New Orleans.

As Peabody had mentioned, the world was on the verge of a Fourth Wave. The tremendous undercurrent of excitement threading through every moment of every day, in the faces and mien of all Verity met, had to do with the feeling that *this* time would be different.

In her brief time here, she had not had time to learn more about what the Widder Jones had alluded to, the lightships sent out, the reasons why radio had ceased to be dependable, though that information was open and free. It had been pretty absorbing to give birth and care for Mattie. But soon, when she felt that she and Rose were balanced enough, she would move to new realms of endeavor and knowledge.

In Norleans, that was gloriously possible.

She walked a few more steps, turned back, checked her hand. That was the address—a row of French doors open to the street, flanked by pots of red geraniums.

She stepped through a green-painted doorframe scratched and battered as if by decades of neglect into darkness and paused as her eyes adjusted.

The room smelled of spilled beer and cigarette smoke. Her nose wrinkled. She put her hand over Mattie's head as if to shield her, though the toxins could not actually harm her, and hurried past the pool table. A vagrant ray of sunlight illuminated a mosaic of liquor bottles behind the bar, where a single man sat drinking. He paid her no attention.

It was possible, if one so wished, to do nothing except party here in Norleans. It was all information.

She was through the room quickly enough and started up the stairs on the other side. Her feet clanged on the open metal stringers. At the landing, she stopped in front of a narrow, open window to catch her breath and adjust Mattie.

In that instant, the precise juxtaposition of balconies against the street scene below, the terraced lines falling to the sea, the rhythm of windows and rooflines and doors, snapped into some larger template and deepened, as if she were falling back into herself, through layer after layer of memory.

Recognition dawned.

She gazed out over an utterly familiar quadrant of Norleans. Utterly familiar, though she had never been here before.

Except in vision.

The river trip unreeled within her—the pain, the uncertainty, the sorrow. She looked at her hand again. It had flashed when she rose before dawn with a message from Lil to meet her here. . . .

She hurried to the upper landing on the clanging stairs and pushed through the green swinging door at the top.

Lil jumped up from a chair when Verity emerged. "I've been waiting," she said. She embraced Verity and Mattie in a single hug.

Behind Lil was a small, high-ceilinged café where, beneath the collection of small, exquisite European paintings arranged on the vivid red walls, people drank coffee and read news manifested by their tables, if they wished. Zydeco music, a fusion of blues and Cajun, played softly. A woman reading a magazine behind the coffee bar looked up and smiled at Verity. The scuffed marble floor was faintly golden.

Verity stared over Lil's shoulder, taking it all in. Lil pulled back and smiled crookedly at Verity.

"Welcome—home?" Lil whispered. Her eyes were questioning, oddly yearning. "This is one thing that went according to plan."

"I remember . . ." stammered Verity, then stopped, beyond words. The vision of the Norleans Plague met her—now, here, in this precise moment and place—and merged with the memory deep inside her, bringing it into the light of the present.

Mattie woke and waved her arms. Lil took Mattie, bounced her a few times, and laid the baby on her own shoulder. "Come on," she said, gesturing with her head. "Our breakfast is getting cold."

Lil led Verity between tables toward a sun-drenched balcony where mugs of coffee steamed beside a plate of beignets on a wrought-iron table.

Potted palms rustled in the salty morning breeze as Verity approached the open French doors. In front of her, Lil's bee tattoo glowed golden below Lil's short-cropped hair.

She touched the bee with one finger, lightly. Lil turned her head, a questioning look on her face.

"Thank you for bringing me here," Verity said.

"In spite of it all?" Lil asked, her eyes startled; hungry.

"In spite of it all," said Verity firmly. She reached up and held Lil's face between her hands, tried to pour her own certainty into Lil's brown eyes. "In spite of it all."

Lil bit her lip and blinked. She let out a deep breath. Her face relaxed. Verity realized it was the first time she had ever seen Lil look this way. Maybe it was the way she had looked before everything had happened, when she was a child in the mountains, and her parents were still alive— peaceful; radiant.

"Thank you, Verity," she said quietly, after a minute. "That means everything to me."

The glimpse of blue ocean expanded in front of Verity, then seemed to explode and flood her being with joy as she stepped through the doorway into the light of a glorious new morning.

Epilogue
○○○○○○○○○○○○○○○○○○○○

This is the territory for me, New Orleans. It's a territory of the mind.

Verity had her baby. A girl with dark eyes and golden brown skin. Her name is Mattie. I think she's the smartest baby in the world, never mind that she's the only baby I've ever known. Verity and I have a fine apartment, all sunlight and books and ways to learn that aren't as strong as the interstices, though methods like that are available. Verity has been studying Flower City theory, and helping add to the information they have here about Cincinnati. She knows a lot about Cincinnati; so many things that she still spends several hours a week being debriefed, as they call it.

The music here is stunning; extraordinary. I play often and I'm always learning. I'm filled with, overwhelmed by, transformational patterns of sound. Everyone here is. It's a powerful, moving force that's opening up the world.

There's a whole section of Crescent City that is just like old New Orleans, and that's where people come to listen to me. Well, that's one way to do it, anyway. I'm studying the works of a composer named Duke Ellington. He wrote short songs, operas, indigos, and long, intricate pieces called rhapsodies. Right now I like the rhapsodies the best, their rising energy; their subtle beauty. I think it's possible that he was the greatest musical genius that ever lived.

But that's not all I do. New Orleans is a community of scientists, from all around the world, harvested from the wrecks of the Flower Cities, from the intelligence communities Jack and Lil came from. There are a lot of unique people here, and more coming every day. Some of them, including Jack, are going out to study some of the Zones pretty soon. Strange discoveries abound. I have so much to learn before I can even begin to understand the Signal, and how lightships work, and just the basic things Peabody seems to have grown up knowing. For instance, that light in the sky that Mattie saw just before she died: it wasn't a satellite. But it's so complicated that it will be a long time before any of us understand it.

I've died and gone through hell and come back to life. And now I see that there's so much more to it than I ever imagined there was, at Shaker Hill. And also, sadly, less, in some ways. But that's the way it is. There, I believed in God, in Mother Ann. Nanotechnology was evil; like the devil, perhaps, even though we Shakers were not inclined toward personifying evil in that way.

But because of nanotechnology there has been a revolution within me. Mattie, as Twain, helped me see that this revolution is not new, and not unique to me. The idea that all was not wrought by God but by forces humans were just beginning to be able to see caused an uproar during the age when Mark Twain lived. Because of Darwin, honest thinkers had to face those facts, and the effects of this new raw thinking, untouched by God and angels, smashed through society like a cannonball. The idea that humans should take control of things on a very deep level because there's no one else to do it, no Godlike being to offend or please, is somehow hard for humans to grasp. But I've had to try. I had no choice. That simple realization has changed me, from the inside out.

Nan can help me learn; it can do things to my brain. Nanotechnology can be enslaving, and it can also be liberating. I'm considering my choices very carefully now. It's the first time I've had the opportunity to do that.

I'm human. That's as divine as I ever want to be. It's enough. Being human means that I can learn all the things that those before me learned, and find ways to understand what we are, and what we may become, in this sea of complexity we call life.